THE

CRYSTAL SINGER
TRILOGY

THE CRYSTAL SINGER TRILOGY

Crystal Singer

Killashandra

Crystal Line

ANNE McCAFFREY

A DEL REY® BOOK

BALLANTINE BOOKS • NEW YORK

A Del Rey® Book
Published by Ballantine Books

This work was originally published as three separate volumes by Ballantine Books as *Crystal Singer* in 1982, *Killashandra* in 1985, and *Crystal Line* in 1992.

Library of Congress Catalog Card Number: 95-090940

ISBN: 0-345-40292-8

Text design by Alexander J. Klapwald
Cover design by Michelle T. Gengaro
Front cover: left and right illustrations: © Michael Whelan,
center illustration: © Rowena Morrill

Manufactured in the United States of America

First Edition: January 1996

10 9 8 7 6 5 4 3 2 1

Contents

Crystal Singer

To Kate and Alec and their children

Author's Note

Crystal Singer is based on four stories originally published in Roger El-wood's *Continuum* series. *Crystal Singer* is considerably expanded from these stories, thanks to the technical assistance of Ron Massey, Langshot Stables, Surrey. His long explanations and careful notes permitted me to venture daringly where no man had gone before.

Chapter 1

Killashandra listened as the words dropped with leaden fatality into her frozen belly. She stared at the maestro's famous profile as his lips opened and shut around the words that meant the death of all her hopes and ambitions and rendered ten years of hard work and study a waste.

The maestro finally turned to face her. The genuine regret in his expressive eyes made him look older. The heavy singer's muscles in his jaw relaxed sorrowfully into jowls.

One day, Killashandra might remember those details. Just then, she was too crushed by overwhelming defeat to be aware of more than her terrible personal failure.

"But . . . but . . . how *could* you?"

"How could I what?" the maestro asked in surprise.

"How *could* you lead me on?"

"Lead you on? But, my dear girl, I didn't."

"You did! You said—you said all I needed was hard work. Haven't I worked hard enough?"

"Of course you have worked hard." Valdi was affronted. "My students must apply themselves. It takes years of hard work to develop the voice, to learn even a segment of the outworld repertoire that must be performed."

"I've repertoire! I've worked hard and now—*now* you tell me I've no voice?"

Maestro Valdi sighed heavily, a mannerism that had always irritated Killashandra and was now insupportable. She opened her mouth to protest, but he raised a restraining hand. The habit of four years made her pause.

"You haven't the voice to be a *top-rank* singer, my dear Killashandra, but that does not preclude any of the many other responsible and fulfilling . . ."

"I won't be second rank. I want—I *wanted*"—and she had the satisfaction of seeing him wince at the bitterness in her voice—"to be a top-rank concert singer. You said I had—"

He held up his hand again. "You have the gift of perfect pitch, your musicality is faultless, your memory superb, your dramatic potential can't be criticized. But there is that burr in your voice which becomes intolerable

5

in the higher register. While I *thought* it could be trained out, modified—"
he shrugged his helplessness. He eyed her sternly. "Today's audition with
completely impartial judges proved conclusively that the flaw is inherent
in the voice. This moment is cruel for you and not particularly pleasant for
me." He gave her another stern look, reacting to the rebellion in her stance.
"I make few errors in judgment as to voice. I honestly thought I could help
you. I cannot, and it would be doubly cruel of me to encourage you further
as a soloist. No. You had best strengthen another facet of your potential."

"And what, in your judgment, would that be?"

He had the grace to blink at her caustic words, then looked her
squarely in the eye. "You don't have the patience to teach, but you could
do very well in one of the theater arts where your sympathy with the problems of a singer would stand you in good stead. No? You are a trained synthesizer? Hmmmm. Too bad, your musical education would be a real asset
there." He paused. "Well, then, I'd recommend you leave the theater arts
entirely. With your sense of pitch, you could be a crystal tuner or an air-
craft and shuttle dispatcher or—"

"Thank you, maestro," she said, more from force of habit than any
real gratitude. She gave him the half bow his rank required and withdrew.

Slamming the panel shut behind her, Killashandra stalked down the
corridor, blinded by the tears she'd been too proud to shed in the maestro's
presence. Though she half wanted and half feared meeting a fellow student who would question her tears and commiserate with her disaster, she
was inordinately relieved to reach her study cubicle without having encountered anyone. There she gave herself up to her misery, bawling into
hysteria, past choking, until she was too spent to do more than gasp for
breath.

If her body protested the emotional excess, her mind reveled in it. For
she had been abused, misused, misguided, misdirected—and who knows
how many of her peers had been secretly laughing at her dreams of glorious triumphs on the concert and opera stage? Killashandra had a generous
portion of the conceit and ego required for her chosen profession, with no
leavening of humility; she'd felt success and stardom were only a matter of
time. Now she cringed at the vivid memory of her self-assertiveness and
arrogance. She had approached the morning's audition with such confidence, the requisite commendations to continue as a solo aspirant a foregone conclusion. She remembered the faces of the examiners, so pleasantly
composed; one man nodding absent-mindedly to the pulse of the test arias
and lieder. She'd been scrupulous in tempi; they'd marked her high on
that. How could they have looked so—so impressed? So encouraging?

How could they record such verdicts against her?

"The voice is unsuited to the dynamics of opera. Unpleasant burr too
audible." "A good instrument for singing with orchestra and chorus where
grating overtone will not be noticeable." "Strong choral leader quality: student should be positively dissuaded from solo work."

Unfair! Unfair! How could she be allowed to come so far, be permitted to delude herself, only to be dashed down in the penultimate trial? And to be offered, as a sop, choral leadership! How degradingly ignominious!

From her excruciating memories wriggled up the faces of her brothers and sisters, taunting her for what they called "shrieking at the top of her lungs." Teasing her for the hours she spent on finger exercises and attempting to "understand" the harmonics of odd off-world music. Her parents had surrendered to Killashandra's choice of profession because it was, at the outset, financed by Fuerte's planetary educational system; second, it might accrue to their own standing in the community; and third, she had the encouragement of her early vocal and instrumental teachers. Them! Was it the ineptitude of one of those clods to which she owed the flaw in her voice? Killashandra rolled in an agony of self-pity.

What was it Valdi had had the temerity to suggest? An allied art? A synthesizer? Bah! Spending her life in mental institutions catering to flawed minds because she had a flawed voice? Or mending flawed crystals to keep interplanetary travel or someone's power plant flowing smoothly?

Then she realized her despondency was merely self-pity and sat upright, staring at herself in the mirror on the far wall, the mirror that had reflected all those long hours of study and self-perfection. Self-deception!

In an instant, Killashandra shook herself free of such wallowing self-indulgence. She looked around the study, a slice of a room dominated by the Vidifax, with its full address keyboard that interfaced with the Music Record Center, providing access to a galaxy's musical output. She glanced over the repros of training performances—she'd always had a lead role—and she knew that she would do best to forget the whole damned thing! If she couldn't be at the top, to hell with theater arts! She'd be top in whatever she did or die in the attempt.

She stood. There was nothing for her now in a room that three hours before had been the focal point of every waking minute and all her energies. Whatever personal items remained in the drawers or on the shelves, the merit awards on the wall, the signed holograms of singers she'd hoped to emulate or excel, no longer concerned her or belonged to her.

She reached for her cloak, ripped off the student badge, and flung the garment across one shoulder. As she wheeled around, she saw a note tacked on the door.

Party at Roare's to celebrate!

She snorted. They'd all know. Let them chortle over her downfall. She'd not play the bravely smiling, courageous-under-adversity role tonight. Or ever.

Exit Killashandra, quietly, stage center, she thought as she ran down the long shallow flight of steps to the mall in front of the Culture Center. Again, she experienced both satisfaction and regret that no one witnessed her departure.

Actually, she couldn't have asked for a more dramatic exit. Tonight, they'd wonder what had happened. Maybe someone would know. She knew that Valdi would never disclose their interview; he disliked failures, especially his own, so they'd never hear about it from him. As for the verdict of the examiners, at least the exact wording handed her would be computer sealed. But someone would know that Killashandra Ree had failed her vocal finals and the grounds for failure.

Meanwhile she would have effectively disappeared. They could speculate all they wanted—nothing would stop them from that—and they'd remember her when she rose to prominence in another field. Then they'd marvel that nothing so minor as failure could suppress her excellence.

Such reflections consoled Killashandra all the way to her lodgings. Subsidized students rated dwellings—no more the depressing bohemian semifilth and overcrowding of ancient times—but her room was hardly palatial. When she failed to reregister at the Music Center, her landlady would be notified and the room locked to her. Subsistence living was abhorrent to Killashandra; it smacked of an inability to achieve. But she'd take the initiative on that, too, and leave the room now. And all the memories it held. Besides, it would spoil the mystery of her disappearance if she were to be discovered in her digs. So, with a brief nod to the landlady, who always checked comings and goings, Killashandra climbed the stairs to her floor, keyed open her room, and looked around. There was really nothing to take but clothing.

Despite that assessment, Killashandra packed the lute that she had handcrafted to satisfy that requirement of her profession. She might not care to play the thing, but she couldn't bear to abandon it. She packed it among the clothes in her carisak, which she looped over her back. She closed the door panel, skipped down the stairs, nodded to the landlady exactly as she always did, and left quietly.

Having fulfilled the dramatic requirement of her new role, she hadn't any idea what to do with herself. She slipped from walk-on to the fastbelt of the pedestrian way, heading into the center of the city. She ought to register with a work bureau; she ought to apply for subsistence. She ought to do many things, but suddenly Killashandra discovered that "ought to" no longer ruled her. No more tedious commitments to schedule—rehearsals, lessons, studies. She was free, utterly and completely free! With a lifetime ahead of her that ought to be filled. Ought to? With what?

The walkway was whipping her rapidly into the busier sections of the city. Pedestrian directions flashed at cross-points: mercantile triangle purple crossed with social services' circle orange; green check manufactory and dormitory blue hatching, medical green-red stripes and then airport arrow red and spaceport star-spangled blue. Killashandra, paralyzed by indecision, toyed with the variety of things she ought to do, and was carried past the crosspoints that would take her where she ought to go.

Ought to, again, she thought, and stayed on the speedway. Half of Killashandra was amused that she, once so certain of her goal, could now be so irresolute. At that moment it did not occur to her that she was suffering an intense, traumatic shock or that she was reacting to that shock—first, in a somewhat immature fashion by her abrupt withdrawal from the center; second, in a more mature manner, as she divorced herself from the indulgence of self-pity and began a positive search for an alternate life.

She could not know that at that very moment Esmond Valdi was concerned, realizing that the girl would be reacting in some fashion to the demise of her ambition. Had she known, she might have thought more kindly of him, though he hadn't pursued her beyond her study nor done more than call the Personnel Section to report his concern. He'd come to the reassuring conclusion that she had sought refuge with a fellow student, probably having a good cry. Knowing her dedication to music, he'd incorrectly assumed that she'd continue in the study of music, accepting a choral leadership in due time. That's where he wanted her, and it simply did not occur to Valdi that Killashandra would discard ten years of her life in a second.

Chapter 2

Killashandra was halfway to the spaceport before she consciously decided that that was where she ought to go—"ought" this time not in an obligatory but in an investigative sense. Fuerte held nothing but distressing memories for her. She'd leave the planet and erase the painful associations. Good thing she had taken the lute. She had sufficient credentials to be taken on as a casual entertainer on some liner at the best or as a ship attendant at the worst. She might as well travel about a bit to see what else she *ought* to do with her life.

As the speedway slowed to curve into the spaceport terminal, Killashandra was aware of externals—people and things—for the first time since she'd left Maestro Valdi's studio. She had never been to the spaceport before and had never been on any of the welcoming committees for off-planet stellars. Just then, a shuttle launched from its bay, powerful engines making the port building tremble. There was, however, a very disconcerting whine of which she was almost subliminally aware, sensing it from the mastoid bone right down to her heel. She shook her head. The whine intensified—it had to be coming from the shuttle—until she was forced to clamp her hands over her ears. The sonics abated, and she forgot the incident as she wandered around the immense, domed reception hall of the port facility. Vidifax were ranked across the inner segment, each labeled with the name of a particular freight or passenger service, each with its own screen plate. Faraway places with strange sounding names—a fragment from an ancient song obtruded and was instantly suppressed. No more music.

She paused at a portal to watch a shuttle off-loading cargo, the loading attendants using pneumatic pallets to shift odd-sized packages that did not fit the automatic cargo-handling ramp. A supercargo was scurrying about, portentously examining strip codes, juggling weight units, and arguing with the stevedores. Killashandra snorted. She'd soon have more than such trivia to occupy her energies. Suddenly, she caught the scent of appetizing odors.

She realized she was hungry! Hungry? When her whole *life* had been shattered? How banal! But the odors made her mouth water. Well, her credit ought to be good for a meal, but she'd better check her balance rather than be embarrassed at the restaurant. At a public outlet, she inserted her digital wristunit and applied her right thumb to the print plate. She was agreeably surprised to note that a credit had been added that very day—a student credit, she read. Her last. That the total represented a bonus did not please her. A bonus to solemnize the fact that she could never be a soloist?

She walked quickly to the nearest restaurant, observing only that it was not the economy service. The old, dutiful Killashandra would have backed out hastily. The new Killashandra entered imperiously. So early in the day, the dining rooms were not crowded, so she chose a booth on the upper level for its unobstructed view of the flow of shuttles and small spacecraft. She had never realized how much traffic passed through the spaceport of her not very important planet, though she vaguely knew that Fuerte was a transfer point. The vidifax menu was long and varied, and she was tempted several times to indulge in the exotic foods temptingly described therein. But she settled for a casserole, purportedly composed of off-world fish, unusual but not too highly spiced for a student's untutored palate. An off-world wine included in the selection pleased her so much that she ordered a second carafe just as dusk closed in.

She thought, at first, that it was the unfamiliar wine that made her nerves jangle so. But the discomfort increased so rapidly that she sensed it couldn't be just the effect of alcohol. Rubbing her neck and frowning, she looked around for the source of irritation. Finally, the appearance of a descending shuttle's retroblasts made her realize that her discomfort must be the result of a sonic disturbance, though how it could penetrate the shielded restaurant she didn't know. She covered her ears, pressing as hard as she could to ease that piercing pain. Suddenly, it ceased.

"I tell you, that shuttle's drive is about to explode. Now connect me to the control supervisor," a baritone voice cried in the ensuing silence.

Startled, Killashandra looked around.

"How do I know? I know!" At the screen of the restaurant's service console, a tall man was demanding: "Put me through to the control tower. Is everyone up there deaf? So you *want* a shuttle explosion the next time that one is used? Didn't you hear it?"

"I heard it," Killashandra said, rushing over to plant herself in the view of the console.

"You heard it?" The spaceport official seemed genuinely surprised.

"I certainly did. All but cracked my skull. My ears still hurt. What was it?" she asked the tall man, who had an air of command about him, frustrated though he was by officious stupidity. He carried his overlean body with an arrogance that suited the fine fabric of his clothes—obviously of off-world design and cloth.

"She heard it too, man. Now, get the control tower."

"Really, sir . . ."

"Don't be a complete subbie," Killashandra snapped.

That she was obviously a Fuertan like himself disturbed the official more than the insult. Then the stranger, ripping off an oath as colorful as it was descriptive of idiocy, flipped open a card case drawn from his belt. Whatever identification he showed made the official's eyes bulge.

"I'm sorry, sir. I didn't realize, sir."

Killashandra watched as the man pressed out a code, then his image dissolved into a view of the control tower. The off-worlder stepped squarely before the screen, and Killashandra politely moved back.

"Control? The shuttle that just landed can't be permitted to take off; it's resonating so badly half the crystals in the drive must be overheating. Didn't anyone up there hear the beat frequency? It's broadcasting secondary sonics. No, this is not a drunk and not a threat. This is a fact. Is your entire control staff tone deaf? Don't you take efficiency readings for your shuttles? Can't you tell from the ejection velocity monitor? What does a drive check cost in comparison to a new port facility? Is this shuttlestop world too poor to employ a crystal tuner or a stoker?

"Well, now that's a more reasonable attitude," said the stranger after a moment. "As to my credentials, I'm Carrik of the Heptite Guild, Ballybran. Yes, that's what I said. I could hear the secondary sonics right through the walls, so I damn well know there's overheating. I'm glad the uneven drive thrust has registered on your monitors, so get that shuttle decoked and re-turned." Another pause. "Thanks, but I've paid my bill already. No, that's all right. Yes . . ." and Killashandra observed that the gratitude irritated Carrik. "Oh, as you will." He glanced at Killashandra. "Make that for two," he added, grinning at her as he turned from the console. "After all, you heard it as well." He cupped his hand under Killashandra's elbow and steered her toward a secluded booth.

"I've a bottle of wine over there," she said, half protesting, half laughing at his peremptory escort.

"You'll have better shortly. I'm Carrik and you're . . . ?"

"Killashandra Ree."

He smiled, gray eyes lighting briefly with surprise. "That's a lovely name."

"Oh, come now. You can do better than that?"

He laughed, absently blotting the sweat on his forehead and upper lip as he slid into his place.

"I can and I will, but it *is* a lovely name. A musical one."

She winced.

"What did I say wrong?"

"Nothing. Nothing."

He glanced at her skeptically just as a chilled bottle slid from the service panel.

Carrik peered at the label. "A '72—well, that's astonishing." He flipped the menu vidifax. "I wonder if they stock Forellan biscuits and Aldebaran paste?—Oh, they do! Well, I might revise my opinion of Fuerte."

"Really, I only just finished—"

"On the contrary, my dear Killashandra Ree, you've only just begun."

"Oh?" Any of Killashandra's associates would have modified his attitude instantly at that tone in her voice.

"Yes," Carrik continued blithely, a sparkling challenge in his eyes, "for this is a night for feasting and frolicking—on the management, as it were. Having just saved the port from being leveled, my wish, and yours, is their command. They'll be even more grateful when they take the drive down and see the cracks in the transducer crystals. Off the true by a hundred vibes at least."

Her half-formed intention of making a dignified exit died, and she stared at Carrik. It would take a highly trained ear to catch so small a variation in pitch.

"Off a hundred vibes? What do you mean? Are you a musician?"

Carrik stared at her as if she ought to know who or what he was. He looked around to see where the attendant had gone and then, leaning indolently back in the seat, smiled at her enigmatically.

"Yes, I'm a kind of musician. Are you?"

"Not anymore." Killashandra replied in her most caustic tone. Her desire to leave returned immediately. She had managed very briefly to forget why she was at a spaceport. Now he had reminded her, and she wanted no more such reminders.

As she began to rise, his hand, fingers gripping firmly the flesh of her arm, held her in her seat. Just then, an official bustled into the restaurant, his eyes searching for Carrik. His countenance simulated relief and delight as he hurried to the table. Carrik smiled at Killashandra, daring her to contest his restraint in front of the witness. Despite her inclination, Killashandra realized she couldn't start a scene. Besides, she had no real grounds yet for charging personal-liberty infringement. Carrik, fully aware of her dilemma, had the audacity to offer her a toast as he took the traditional sample sip of the wine.

"Yes, sir, the '72. A very good choice. Surely, you'll . . ."

The serving panel opened on a slightly smoking dish of biscuits and a platter of a reddish-brown substance.

"But, of course, Forellan biscuits and Aldebaran paste. Served with warmed biscuits, I see. Your caterers do know their trade," Carrik remarked with feigned surprise.

"We may be small at Fuerte in comparison to other ports you've seen," the official began obsequiously.

"Yes, yes, thank you." Carrik brusquely waved the man away.

Killashandra stared after the fellow, wondering that he hadn't claimed insult for such a careless dismissal.

"How do you get away with such behavior?"

Carrik smiled. "Try the wine, Killashandra." His smile suggested that the evening would be long, and a prelude to a more intimate association.

"Who are you?" she demanded, angry now.

"I'm Carrik of the Heptite Guild," he repeated cryptically.

"And that gives you the right to infringe on my personal freedom?"

"It does if you heard that crystal whine."

"And how do you figure that?"

"Your opinion of the wine, Killashandra Ree? Surely your throat must be dry, and I imagine you've a skull ache from that subsonic torture, which would account for your shrewish temper."

Actually, she did have a pain at the base of her neck. He was right, too, about the dryness of her throat—and about her shrewish temper. But he had modified his criticism by stroking her hand.

"I must apologize for my bad manners," he began with no display of genuine remorse but with a charming smile. "Those shuttle drive-harmonics can be unnerving. It brings out the worst in us."

She nodded agreement as she sipped the wine. It was a fine vintage. She looked up with delight and pleasure. He patted her arm and gestured her to drink up.

"Who are you, Carrik of the Heptite Guild, that port authorities listen and control towers order exorbitant delicacies in gratitude?"

"You really don't know?"

"I wouldn't ask if I did!"

"Where have you been all your life that you've never heard of the Heptite Guild?"

"I've been a music student on Fuerte," she replied, spitting out the words.

"You wouldn't, by any chance, have *perfect* pitch?" The question, unexpected and too casually put forth, caught her halfway into a foul temper.

"Yes, I do, but I don't—"

"What fantastic luck!" His face, which was not unattractive, became radiant. "I shall have to tip the agent who ticketed me here! Why, our meeting is unbelievable luck—"

"Luck? If you knew why I'm here—"

"I don't care *why*. You are here, and so am I." He took her hands and seemed to devour her face with his eyes, grinning with such intense joy she found herself smiling back with embarrassment.

"Oh, luck indeed, my dear girl. Fate. Destiny. Karma. Lequoal. Fidalkoram. Whatever you care to name the coincidence of our life lines, I should order magnums of this fine wine for that lousy shuttle pilot for endangering this port terminal, in general, and us, in particular."

"I don't understand what you're ranting about, Carrik of Heptite," Killashandra said, but she was not impervious to his compliments or the charm he exuded. She knew that her self-assurance tended to put off men, but here a well-traveled off-worlder, a man of obvious rank and position, was inexplicably taken with her.

"You don't?" He teased her for the banality of her protest, and she closed her mouth on the rest of her rebuff. "Seriously," he went on, stroking the palms of her hands with his fingers as if to soothe the anger from her, "have you never heard of crystal singers?"

"Crystal singers? No. Crystal tuners, yes."

He dismissed the mention of tuners with a contemptuous flick of his fingers. "Imagine singing a note, a pure, clear middle C, and hearing it answered across an entire mountain range?"

She stared at him.

"Go up a third or down; it makes no difference. Sing out and hear the harmony return to you. A whole mountainside pitched to a C and another sheer wall of pink quartz echoing back in a dominant. Night brings out the minors, like an ache in your chest, the most beautiful pain in the world because the music of the crystal is in your bones, in your blood—"

"You're mad!" Killashandra dug her fingers into his hands to shut off his words. They conjured too many painful associations. She had to forget all that. "I hate music. I hate anything to do with music."

He regarded her with disbelief for a moment, but then, with an unexpected tenderness and concern reflected in his expression, he moved an arm around her shoulders and, despite her initial resistance, drew himself against her.

"My dear girl, what happened to you today?"

A moment before, she would have swallowed glass shards rather than confide in anyone. But the warmth in his voice, his solicitude, were so timely and unexpected that the whole of her personal disaster came tumbling out. He listened to every word, occasionally squeezing her hand in sympathy. But at the end of the recital, she was amazed to see the fullness in his eyes as tears threatened to embarrass her.

"My dear Killashandra, what can I say? There's no possible consolation for such a personal catastrophe as that! And there you were"—his eyes shone with what Killashandra chose to interpret as admiration—"having a bottle of wine as coolly as a queen. Or"—and he leaned over her, grinning maliciously—"were you just gathering enough courage to step under a shuttle?" He kept hold of her hand which, at his outrageous suggestion, she tried to free. "No, I can see that suicide was furthest from *your* mind." She subsided at the implicit compliment. "Although"—and his expression altered thoughtfully—"you might inadvertently have succeeded if that shuttle had been allowed to take off again. If I hadn't been here to stop it—" He flashed her his charmingly reprehensible smile.

"You're full of yourself, aren't you?" Her accusation was said in jest, for she found his autocratic manner an irresistible contrast to anyone of her previous acquaintance.

He grinned unrepentantly and nodded toward the remains of their exotic snack. "Not without justification, dear girl. But look, you're free of commitments right now, aren't you?" She hesitantly nodded. "Or is there someone you've been seeing?" He asked that question almost savagely, as if he'd eliminate any rival.

Later, Killashandra might remember how adroitly Carrik had handled her, preying on her unsettled state of mind, on her essential feminin-

ity, but that tinge of jealousy was highly complimentary, and the eagerness
in his eyes, in his hands, was not feigned.

"No one to matter or miss me."

Carrik looked so skeptical that she reminded him that she'd devoted
all her energies to singing.

"Surely not all?" He mocked her dedication.

"No one to matter," she repeated firmly.

"Then I will make an honest invitation to you: I'm an off-worlder on
holiday. I don't have to be back to the Guild till—well"—and he gave a
nonchalant shrug—"when I wish. I've all the credits I need. Help me spend
them. It'll purge you of the music college."

She looked squarely at him, for their acquaintanceship was so brief
and hectic that she simply hadn't had time to consider him a possible companion. Nor did she quite trust him. She was both attracted to and repelled
by his domineering, high-handed manner, and yet he represented a challenge to her. He was certainly the exact opposite of the young men she had
thus far encountered on Fuerte.

"We don't have to stay on this mudball, either."

"Then why did you come?"

He laughed. "I'm told I haven't been on Fuerte before. I can't say
that it lives up to its name, or maybe you'll live up to the name for it?
Oh come now, Killashandra," he said when she bridled. "Surely you've
been flirted with before? Or have music students changed so much since
my day?"

"You studied music?"

An odd shadow flickered through his eyes. "Probably. I don't rightly
remember. Another time, another life perhaps." Then his charming smile
deepened, and a warmth entered his expression that she found rather unsettling. "Tell me, what's on this planet that's fun to do?"

Killashandra considered for a moment and then blinked. "You know,
I haven't an earthly?"

"Then we'll find out together."

What with the wine, his adept cajolery, and her own recklessness,
Killashandra could not withstand the temptation. She ought to do many
things, she knew, but "ought" had been exiled someplace during the second bottle of that classic vintage. After spending the rest of the night nestled in Carrik's arms in the most expensive accommodation of the
spaceport hostelry, Killashandra decided she would suspend duty for a
few days and be kind to the charming visitor.

The vidifax printout chattered as it popped out dozens of cards on
the resorts of Fuerte, more than she had ever suspected. She had never water skied, so Carrik decided they'd both try that. He ordered a private
skimmer to be ready within the hour. As he sang cheerily at the top of a
good, rich bass voice, floundering about in the elegant sunken bathtub of
the suite, Killashandra recalled some vestige of self-preserving shrewdness
and tapped out a few discreet inquiries on the console.

1234/AZ . . .

CRYSTAL SINGER . . . A COLLOQUIAL GALACTIC EUPHEMISM REFER-
RING TO MEMBERS OF THE HEPTITE GUILD, BALLYBRAN, WHO MINE CRYS-
TAL RANGES UNIQUE TO THAT PLANET. REF: BALLYBRAN, REGULUS
SYSTEM, A-S-F/128/4. ALSO CRYSTAL MINING, CRYSTAL TECHNOLOGY,
'BLACK QUARTZ' COMMUNICATIONS. WARNING: UNAUTHORIZED LAND-
ING ON BALLYBRAN INTERDICTED BY FEDERATED SENTIENT PLANETS,
SECTION 907, CODE 4, PARAGRAPHS 78-90.

The landing prohibition surprised Killashandra. She tried to recall
details from her obligatory secondary school course on FSP Rights and Responsibilities. The 900 Section had to do with life forms, she thought, and
the Code 4 suggested considerable danger.

She tapped out the section, code, and paragraphs and was awarded
a request for *Need to Know?* As she couldn't think of one at the moment,
she went to the planetary reference, and the display rippled across the
screen.

BALLYBRAN: FIFTH PLANET OF THE SUN, SCORIA, REGULUS SECTOR:
THREE SATELLITES; AUTHORIZED LANDING POINT, FIRST MOON,
SHANKILL; STANDARD LIFE-SUPPORT BASE, COMMERCIAL AND TRAN-
SIENT ACCOMMODATIONS. NO UNAUTHORIZED PLANETARY LANDINGS:
SECTION 907, CODE 4, PARAGRAPHS 78–90. SOLE AUTHORITY: HEPTITE
GUILD, MOON BASE, SHANKILL.

Then she followed dense lines of data on the spectral analysis of Scoria and its satellites, Ballybran being the only one that rated considerable
print-out, which Killashandra could, in part, interpret. Ballybran had a
gravity slightly lower than galactic norm for human adaptability, a breath-
able atmosphere, more oceans than land mass, tidal complications caused
by three moons, as well as an exotic meteorology stimulated by sunspot activity on the primary.

PRINCIPAL INDUSTRIES: (1) BALLYBRAN CRYSTALS (2) THERAPEUTIC
WATERS.

1) BALLYBRAN LIVING CRYSTAL VARIES IN DENSITY, COLOR, AND
LONGEVITY AND IS UNIQUE TO THE PLANET. VITAL TO THE PRO-
DUCTION OF CONTROL ELEMENTS IN LASERS; AS A MATERIAL FOR
INTEGRATED-CIRCUIT SUBSTRATES (OF THE LADDER HIERARCHY); POSI-
TRONIC ROBOTICS; AS TRANSDUCERS FOR ELECTROMAGNETIC RADI-
ATION (FUNDAMENTALS OF 20 KHZ AND 500 KHZ WITH AUDIO
SECONDARIES AND HARMONICS IN THE LOWER FREQUENCIES) AND HEAT
TRANSDUCERS; AS OPTHERIAN SOUND RELAYS AND MUSICAL INSTRU-
MENTS; BLUE TETRAHEDRONS ARE A CRUCIAL PART IN TACHYON DRIVE
SYSTEMS.

"BLACK" QUARTZ, A PHENOMENON LIMITED TO BALLYBRAN, IS THE

CRITICAL ELEMENT OF INSTANTANEOUS INTERSTELLAR COMMUNICA-
TION, HAVING THE ABILITY TO FOLD SPACE, OVER ANY DISTANCE, SO
THAT MAGNETICALLY, ELECTRICALLY, AND, AS FAR AS IS KNOWN, OPTI-
CALLY, THERE IS NO EFFECTIVE SEPARATION BETWEEN TWO COUPLED
RESONATING SEGMENTS REGARDLESS OF THE ACTUAL DISTANCE BE-
TWEEN THEM.

TIMING ACCURACY OVER A DISTANCE OF 500 LIGHT-YEARS HAS PRO-
DUCED CONSISTENT ACCURACY OF 1×10^{-6} OF THE CESIUM ATOM TIME
STANDARD.

BLACK QUARTZ IS CAPABLE OF ACHIEVING SIMULTANEOUS SYNCHRO-
NIZATION WITH TWO OTHER SEGMENTS AND SO PROVIDES A RING-LINK
BACKUP SYSTEM. FOR EXAMPLE, WITH SIX QUARTZ SEGMENTS, A TO F, A IS
LINKED TO C, D, & E; B IS LINKED TO C, E, & F . . .

That was more than she ever wanted to know about black quartz
communications, Killashandra thought as diagrams and computations
scrolled across the screen, so she pressed on to more interesting data. She
slowed the display when she noticed the heading "Membership" and reversed to the start of that entry.

CURRENT MEMBERSHIP OF THE HEPTITE GUILD ON BALLYBRAN IS
4425, INCLUDING INACTIVE MEMBERS, BUT THE NUMBER FLUCTUATES
CONSIDERABLY DUE TO OCCUPATIONAL HAZARDS. THE ANCILLARY
STAFF AND TECHNICIANS ARE LISTED CURRENTLY AT 20,007. ASPIRANTS
TO THE GUILD ARE ADVISED THAT THE PROFESSION IS HIGHLY DANGER-
OUS, AND THE HEPTITE GUILD IS REQUIRED BY FEDERATION LAW TO
DISCLOSE FULL PARTICULARS OF ALL DANGERS INVOLVED BEFORE CON-
TRACTING NEW MEMBERS.

Four thousand four hundred and twenty-five seemed an absurdly
small roster for a galaxy-wide Guild that supplied essential elements to so
many industries. Most galaxy-wide guilds ran to the hundreds of millions.
What were those ancillary staff and technicians? The notation of "full particulars of dangers involved" didn't dissuade Killashandra at all. Danger
was relative.

THE CUTTING OF BALLYBRAN CRYSTAL IS A HIGHLY SKILLED AND
PHYSICALLY SELECTIVE CRAFT, WHICH, AMONG ITS OTHER EXACTING
DISCIPLINES, REQUIRES THAT PRACTITIONERS HAVE PERFECT AND AB-
SOLUTE PITCH BOTH IN PERCEPTION AND REPRODUCTION OF THE TONAL
QUALITY AND TIMBRE TO BE FOUND ONLY IN TYPE IV THROUGH VIII
BIPEDAL HUMANOIDS—ORIGIN: SOL III.

CRYSTAL CUTTERS MUST BE MEMBERS OF THE HEPTITE GUILD, WHICH
TRAINS, EQUIPS, AND SUPPLIES GUILD MEDICAL SERVICES FOR WHICH
THE GUILD EXACTS A 30 PERCENT TITHE FROM ALL ACTIVE MEMBERS.

Killashandra whistled softly—30 percent was quite a whack. Yet Carrik seemed to have no lack of credit, so 70 percent of his earnings as a Cutter must be very respectable.

Thinking of Carrik, she tapped out a query. Anyone could pose as a member of a Guild; chancers often produced exquisitely forged documentation and talked a very good line of their assumed profession, but a computer check could not be forged. She got affirmation that Carrik was indeed a member in good standing of the Heptite Guild, currently on leave of absence. A hologram of Carrik, taken when he used his credit plate for spaceflight to Fuerte five days before, flowed across the viewplate.

Well, the man was undeniably who he said he was and doing what he said he was doing. His being a card-tuned Guild member was a safeguard for her so she could relax in his offer of an "honest" invitation to share his holiday. He would not leave her to pay the charges if he decided to skip off-world precipitously.

She smiled to herself, suddenly feeling sensuous. Carrik thought himself lucky, did he? Well, so did she. The last vestige of "ought" was the fleeting thought that she "ought to" register herself with the Fuertan Central Computer as a transient, but since she was by no means obligated to do so as long as she didn't require subsistence, she did nothing.

As she was beginning to enjoy her new found freedom, several of her classmates began to experience twinges of anxiety about Killashandra. Everyone realized that Killashandra must have been terribly upset by the examiners' verdict. Though some felt she deserved the lesson, for her overbearing conceit, the kinder of heart were disquieted about her disappearance. So was Maestro Esmond Valdi.

They probably would not have recognized the Killashandra who was sluicing about on water skis on the southern seas of the Western Hemisphere or swathed in elegant gowns, escorted by a tall, distinguished-looking man to whom even the most supercilious hoteliers deferred.

It was a glorious feeling to have unlimited funds. Carrik encouraged Killashandra to spend, and practice permitted her to suspend what few scruples remained from years of eking necessities out of student allotments. She did have the grace to protest his extravagance, at least at the outset.

"Not to worry, pet. I've credit to spend," Carrik reassured her. "I made a killing in dominant thirds in the Blue Range about the time some idiot revolutionists blew half a planet's communications out of existence." He paused; his eyes narrowed as he recalled something not quite pleasant. "I was lucky on shape, too. It's not enough, you see, to catch the resonances on what you're cutting. You've got to hope you remember which shape to cut, and that's where you're made or broken as a crystal singer. You've *got* to remember what's high on the market or remember something like that revolution on Hardesty." He pounded the table in emphasis, pleased with that particular memory. "I did remember that all right when it mattered."

"I don't understand."

He gave her a quick look. "Not to worry, pet." His standard phrase of evasion. "Come, give me a kiss and get the crystal out of my blood."

There was nothing crystalline about his lovemaking or the enjoyment he derived from her body, so Killashandra elected to forget how often he avoided answering her questions about crystal singing. At first, she felt that since the man was on holiday, he probably wouldn't want to talk about his work. Then she sensed that he resented her questions as if they were distasteful to him and that he wanted, above all, to forget crystal singing, which did not forward her plan. But Carrik was not a malleable adolescent, imploring her grace and favor. So she helped him forget crystal singing, which he was patently able to do until the night he awakened her with his groans.

"Carrik, what's the matter? Those shellfish from dinner? Shall I get the medic?"

"No, no!" He twisted about frantically and took her hand from the communit. "Don't leave me. This'll pass."

She held him in her arms as he cried out, clenching his teeth against some internal agony. Sweat oozed from his pores, yet he refused to let her summon help. The spasms racked him for almost an hour before they passed, leaving him spent and weak. Somehow, in that hour, she realized how much he had come to mean to her, how much fun he was, how much she had missed by denying herself any intimate relationships before. After he had slept and rested, she asked what had possessed him.

"Crystal, my girl, crystal." His sullen manner and the haggard expression on his face made her drop the subject.

By the afternoon he was almost himself. But some of his spontaneity was gone. He went through the motions of enjoying himself, of encouraging her to more daring exercises on the waterskis while he only splashed about in the shallows. They were finishing a leisurely meal at a seaside restaurant when he finally mentioned that he must return to work.

"I can't say so soon?" Killashandra remarked with a light laugh. "But isn't the decision rather sudden?"

He gave her an odd smile. "Yes, but most of my decisions are, aren't they? Like showing you another side of fusty, fogey Fuerte."

"And now our idyll is over?" She tried to sound nonchalant, but an edge crept into her tone.

"I must return to Ballybran. Ha! That sounds like one of those fisherfolk songs, doesn't it?" He hummed a banal tune, the melody so predictable that she could join in firm harmony.

"We do make beautiful music together," he said, his eyes mocking her. "I suppose you'll return to your studies now."

"Studies? For what? Lead soprano in a chorus of annotated, orchestrated grunts and groans by Fififidipidi of the planet Grnch?"

"You could tune crystals. They obviously need a competent tuner at Fuerte spaceport."

She made a rude noise and looked at him expectantly. He smiled back, turning his head politely, awaiting a verbal answer.

"Or," she drawled, watching him obliquely, "I could apply to the Heptite Guild as a crystal singer."

His expression went blank. "You don't want to be a crystal singer."

The vehemence in his voice startled her for a moment.

"How do you know what I want?" She flared up in spite of herself, in spite of a gnawing uncertainty about his feelings for her. She might be the ideal partner for lolling about a sandy beach, but as a constant companion in a dangerous profession—that was different.

He smiled sadly. "You don't want to be a crystal singer."

"Oh, fardles with that 'highly dangerous' nonsense."

"It is true."

"If I've perfect pitch, I can apply."

"You don't know what you're letting yourself in for," he said in a toneless voice, his expression at once wary and forbidding. "Singing crystal is a terrible, lonely life. You can't always find someone to sing with you; the tones don't always strike the right vibes for the crystal faces you find. Of course, you can make terrific cuts singing duo." He seemed to vacillate.

"How do you find out?" She made her tone ingenuous.

He gave an amused snort. "The hard way, of course. But you don't want to be a crystal singer." An almost frightening sadness tinged his voice. "Once you sing crystal, you don't stop. That's why I'm telling you, don't even think about it."

"So . . . you've told me not to think about it."

He caught her hand and gazed steadily into her eyes. "You've never been in a mach storm in the Milekeys." His voice was rough with remembered anxiety. "They blow up out of nowhere and crash down on you like all hell let loose. That's what that phrase on Retrieval means, 'the Guild maintains its own.' A mach storm can reduce a man to a vegetable in one sonic crescendo."

"There are other—perhaps less violent—ways of reducing a man to a vegetable," she said, thinking of the spaceport official of the supercargo worrying over drone-pod weights—of teachers apathetically reviewing the scales of novice students. "Surely there are instruments that warn you of approaching storms in a Crystal Range."

He nodded absently, his gaze fixed above her head. "You get to cutting crystal and you're halfway through. You know the pitches will be changed once the storm has passed and you're losing your safety margin by the minute, but that last crystal might mean you'd get off-world . . ."

"You don't get off-world with every trip to the Ranges?"

He shook his head, frowning irritably at her interruption. "You don't always clear the costs of the trip or past damages, or you might not have cut the right shape or tone. Sometimes the tone is more important than the shape, you know."

"And you have to remember what'll be needed, don't you?" If she had perfect pitch, and she knew she had an excellent memory, crystal singing seemed an ideal profession for her.

"You have to *remember* the news," he said, oddly emphasizing the verb.

Killashandra was contemptuous of the problem. Memory was only a matter of habit, of training, of mnemonic phrases that easily triggered vital information. She had plenty of practice in memorization.

"Is there any chance that I could accompany you back to Ballybran and apply—"

His hand had a vise grip on hers; even his breath seemed to halt for a moment. His eyes swept hers with an intense search. "You asked. Remember that!"

"Well, if my company—"

"Kiss me and don't say anything you'll regret," he said, abruptly pulling her into his arms and covering her mouth so completely she couldn't have spoken.

The second convulsion caught him so soon after the climax of their lovemaking that she thought, guiltily, that overstimulation was the cause. This time, the spasms were more severe, and he dropped into a fevered, exhausted sleep when they finally eased. He looked old and drawn when he woke fourteen hours later. And he moved like an advanced geriatric case.

"I've got to get back to Ballybran, Killa." His voice quavered, and he had lost his proud confidence.

"For treatment?"

He hesitated and then nodded. "Recharging, actually. Get the spaceport on the communit and book us."

"Us?"

"You may accompany me," he said with grave courtesy, though she was piqued at the phrasing of an invitation that was more plea than permission. "I don't care how often we have to reroute. Get us there as fast as possible."

She reached the spaceport and routeing, and after what seemed an age and considerable ineptitude on the part of the ticket clerk, they were passengers confirmed on a shuttle flight leaving Fuerte in four hours, with a four-hour satellite delay before the first liner in their direction.

He had an assortment of personal things to pack, but Killashandra was for just walking out and leaving everything.

"You can't get such goods on Ballybran, Killa," Carrik told her as he slowly began to fold the gaudy grallie-fiber shirts. The stimulus of confirmed passage had given him a surge of energy. But Killashandra had been rather unnerved by the transformation of a charming, vital man into a quivering invalid. "Sometimes, even something as inconsequential as a shirt helps you remember so much."

She was touched by the sentiment and his smile and vowed to be patient with his illness.

"There are hazards to every profession. And the hazards to crystal singing—"

"It depends what you're willing to consider a hazard," Killashandra replied soothingly. She was glad for the filmy, luminous wraparounds, which were a far cry from the coarse, durable student issue. Any hazard seemed a fair price for bouts of such high living and spending. And only 4,425 in the Guild. She was confident she'd make it to the top there.

"Do you have any comprehension of what you'd be giving up, Killashandra?" His voice had a guilty edge.

She looked at his lined, aging face and experienced a twinge of honest apprehension. Anyone would look appalling after the convulsions that had wracked Carrik. She didn't much care for his philosophical mood and hoped that he wouldn't be so dreary all the way to Ballybran. Was that what he meant? A man on vacation often had a different personality than when working at his profession?

"What have I to look forward to on Fuerte?" she asked with a shrug of her shoulders. She wouldn't necessarily have to team up with Carrik when she got to Ballybran. "I'd rather take a chance, no matter what it entails, in preference to dragging about forever on Fuerte!"

He stroked her palm with his thumb, and for the first time his caress didn't send thrills up her spine. But then he was scarcely in a condition to make love, and his gesture reflected it.

"You've only seen the glamorous side of crystal singing—"

"You've told me the dangers, Carrik, as you're supposed to. The decision is mine, and I'm holding you to your offer."

He gripped her hand tightly, and the pleasure in his eyes reassured her more thoroughly than any glib protestation.

"It's also one of the smallest Guilds in the galaxy," she went on, freeing her hand to finish packing the remaining garments. "I prefer those odds."

He raised his eyebrows, giving her a sardonic look more like his former self. "A two-cell in a one-cell pond?"

"If you please, I won't be a second-rate anything."

"A dead hero in preference to a live coward?" He was taunting her now.

"If you prefer. There! That's all our clothing. We'd better skim back to the spaceport. I've got to check with planetary regulations if I'm going offworld. I might even have some credit due me."

She took the skimmer controls, as Carrik was content to doze in the passenger seat. The rest did him some good, or he was mindful of his public image. Either way, Killashandra's doubts of his reliability as a partner faded as he ordered the port officials about imperiously, badgering the routeing agent to be certain that the man hadn't overlooked a more direct flight or a more advantageous connection.

Killashandra left him to make final arrangements and began to clear her records with the Fuerte Central Computer. The moment she placed her wrist-unit and thumb in place, the console began to chatter wildly, flashing red light. She was startled. She had only programmed a credit check, keyed in the fact that she was going off-world, and asked what immunization she might require for the systems they were to encounter, but the supervisor leaped down the ramp from his console, two port officials converged on her, and the exits of the reception hall flashed red and hold-locks were engaged, to the consternation of passersby. Killashandra, too stunned to react, instead stared blankly at the men who had each seized an arm.

"Killashandra Ree?" the supervisor asked, still panting from his exertions.

"Yes?"

"You are to be detained."

"Why?" Now she was angry. She had committed no crime, infringed no one's liberties. Failure to register change of status was not an offense so long as she had not used planetary resources without sufficient credit.

"Please come with us," the port officials said in chorus.

"Why?"

"Ahh, hmmmm," the supervisor mumbled as both officers turned to him. "There's a hold out for you."

"I've done nothing wrong."

"Here, what's going on?" Carrik was once more completely himself as he pushed through to place a protecting arm around Killashandra. "This young lady is under my protection."

At this announcement, the supervisor and officials exchanged stern and determined stares.

"This young lady is under the protection of her planet of origin," the supervisor announced. "There is some doubt as to her mental stability."

"Why? Because she accepted an honest invitation from a visitor? Do you know who I am?"

The supervisor flushed. "Indeed I do, sir," and though the man spoke more respectfully, he left no doubt that his immediate aim was to extract Killashandra from Carrik's patronage.

"Well, then, accept my assurances that Miss Ree is in excellent health, mental and physical." Carrik gestured for them to admire Killashandra's tanned and trim figure.

The supervisor was adamant. "If you'll *both* please come this way." His officers straightened resolutely.

As there was nothing for it but to comply, Carrik reminded this unexpected escort that they had booked shuttle flights due to lift off in one hour. He had every intention of keeping that schedule—and with Killashandra Ree. Rather than give rise to further speculation about her mental state, Killashandra remained uncharacteristically quiet.

"I suspect," she whispered to Carrik after they were shown into a small office, "that the music school may have thought me suicidal." She giggled, then attempted to mask the noise behind her hand when the supervisor glanced up at her nervously. "I just walked out of the center and disappeared. I saw no one who knew me on the way here. So they did miss me! Well, that's gratifying." She was inordinately pleased, but Carrik plainly did not agree. Well, she had only to reassure the authorities, and she was certain she could. "I think their reaction is rather complimentary, actually. And I'm going to make a dramatic exit from Fuerte, after all."

Carrik awarded her a look of pure disgust and folded his arms solidly across his chest, his expression fading to one of boredom. He kept his eyes fixed on the screen, which was scrolling through the departure information.

Killashandra half expected to see her father, though she found it difficult to imagine him bestirring himself on her behalf. But she did not expect Maestro Esmond Valdi to enter the small office, acting the outraged mentor, nor was she prepared for the attack he immediately launched on Carrik.

"You! You! I know what you are! A silicate spider paralyzing its prey, a crystal cuckoo pushing the promising fledglings from their nests."

As stunned as everyone else, Killashandra stared at the usually dignified and imperturbable maestro and wondered what role he thought he was playing. He had to be acting. His dialogue was so—so extravagant. "Silicate spider!" "Crystal cuckoo!" If nothing else, his analogies were incorrect and uncalled for.

"Play on the emotions of an innocent young girl. Shower her with unaccustomed luxuries and pervert her until she's spoiled as a decent contributing citizen. Until she's so besotted, she has been brainwashed to enter that den of addled mentalities and shattered nerves!"

Carrik made no attempt to divert the flow of vituperation or to counter the accusations. He stood, head up, smiling tolerantly down at the jerky motions of Valdi.

"What lies has he been feeding you about crystal singing? What glamorous tales has he used to lure you there?" Valdi whirled toward Killashandra, his stocky figure trembling with outrage.

"I asked to go."

Valdi's wild expression hardened into disbelief at her calm answer.

"You *asked* to go?"

"Yes. *He* didn't ask *me*." She caught Carrik's smile.

"You heard her, Valdi," Carrik said, then glanced at the officials witnessing the admission.

The maestro's shoulders sagged. "So, he's done his recruiting with a master's skill." His tone registered resignation, he even managed to effect a slight break in his voice.

"I don't think so," Killashandra said.

Maestro Valdi inhaled deeply, obviously to support one last attempt to dissuade the misguided girl. "Did he tell you about ... the mach storms?"

She nodded, hiding her amusement at his theatricality.

"The storms that scramble the brain and reduce the mind to a vegetable existence?"

She nodded dutifully.

"Did he fill your mind with garbage about mountains returning symphonies of sound? Crystalline choruses? Valleys that echo arpeggios?" His body rippled upward in an effort to express the desired effect of ridicule.

"No," she replied in a bored tone. "Nor did he feed me pap that all I needed was hard work and time."

Esmond Valdi, maestro, drew himself up, more than ever in an exaggeration of a classical operatic pose.

"Did he also tell you that once you start cutting crystal, you can never stop? And that staying too long away from Ballybran produces disastrous convulsions?"

"I know that."

"Do you also *know*"—Valdi rocked back on his heels—"that something in the water of Ballybran, in its very soil, in those crystals, affects your mind? That you don't *re-mem-ber*?" He separated the verb carefully into syllables.

"That could be a distinct advantage," Killashandra replied, staring back at the little man until he broke eye contact.

She was the first of the three to feel a peculiar itch behind her ears in the mastoid bone; an itch that rapidly became a wrenching nauseating pain. She grabbed Carrik by the arm just as the subsonic noise touched him and as Esmond Valdi lifted protecting hands to his ears.

"The fools!" Carrik cried as panic contorted his features. He threw aside the door panel, running as fast as he could for the control-tower entrance. Killashandra scurried after him.

Carrik vaulted the decorative barrier and landed in a restricted area, where he was deterred by a hastily engaged force curtain. "Stop it! Stop it!" he screamed, rocking in anguish and clawing at the curtain, oblivious to the sparks flying from his fingers.

Though the pain was no less bearable for Killashandra, she had presence of mind enough to bang on the nearest communit, to strike the fire buttons, press the battery of emergency signals. "The shuttle coming in—something's wrong—it's dangerous!" she yelled at the top of her operatically trained lungs. She was barely conscious of the panic in the vast reception hall resulting from her all too audible warning.

The possibility of a stampede by a hysterical mob was evident to those in the control tower, where someone, in reflex action, slapped on the abort signal to warn off all in-transit craft. Moments later, while the communit demanded an explanation from Killashandra or from anyone who could make himself heard over the bedlam in the reception area, a nova blossomed in the sky and rained molten fragments on the spaceport below. The control tower was unable to contain the destruction within the grappling field, and soon parts of the shuttle were scattered over several kilometers of the Port Authority and the heavily populated business district.

Apart from bruises, lacerations, and a broken arm, there were only two serious casualties. A technician on the tarmac was killed, and Carrik would have been better off dead. The final sonic blast knocked him unconscious, and he never did fully recover his senses. After subspace consultation with Heptite Guild medics, it was decided to return him to Ballybran for treatment and care.

"He won't recover," the medic told Killashandra, whereupon Maestro Valdi instantly assumed the role of her comforter. His manner provided Killashandra with a fine counterirritant to her shock over Carrik's condition.

She chose to disbelieve the medic's verdict. Surely, Carrik could be restored to mental health once he was returned to Ballybran. He had been away from crystal too long; he was weakened by the seizures. There'd been no mach storm to scramble his mind. She'd escort him back to Ballybran. She owed him that in any reckoning for showing her how to live fully.

She took a good look at the posturing Valdi and thanked her luck that Carrik had been there to awaken her senses. How could she have believed that such an artificial life as found in the theater was suitable for her? Just look at Valdi! Present him with a situation, hand him the cue, and he was "on," in the appropriate role. None existed for these circumstances, so Valdi was endeavoring to come up with a suitable one.

"What will you do now, Killashandra?" he asked somberly, obviously settling for Dignified Elder Gentleman Consoling the Bereaved Innocent.

"I'll go with him to Ballybran, of course."

Valdi nodded solemnly. "I mean, after you return."

"I don't intend to return."

Valdi stared at her, dropping out of character, and then gestured theatrically as the air-cushion stretcher to which Carrik was strapped drifted past them to the shuttle gate.

"After that?" Valdi cried, full of dramatic plight.

"That won't happen to me," she said confidently.

"But it could! You, too, could be reduced to a thing with no mind and no memories."

"I think," Killashandra said slowly, regarding the posturing little man with thinly veiled contempt, "that everyone's brains get scrambled one way or another."

"You'll rue this day—" Valdi began, raising his left arm in a classical gesture of rejection, fingers gracefully spread.

"That is, if I *remember* it!" she said. Her mocking laughter cut him off midscene.

Still laughing, Killashandra made her exit, stage center, through the shuttle gate.

Chapter 3

Captain Andurs alerted Killashandra when the ship emerged from hyperspace and Ballybran was fully visible.

"Good view," he told her, pointing to the two inner moons, positioned at 10 and 5, but Killashandra only had eyes for the mysterious planet.

She had heard enough to expect just about anything from her first glimpse. Consequently she experienced an initial disappointment—until she caught sight of the first crystal flare: a piercing stab of light as the sun's rays reflected from an open crystal on one of the three visible continents. Cloud cover swirled across most of the ocean area, occluded two subcontinents in the Southern Hemisphere, but where the sun shone, occasional pinpoints of blinding light were visible—light that was all color, yet white and clear.

"How can they stand the intensity down there?" she demanded, squinting to reduce the keen glare.

"According to what I hear, you don't notice it on the surface."

"According to what I hear" had prefaced most of Captain Andurs's statements about Ballybran, a sour comment on the restriction against his landing on one of the richest planets in the galaxy.

From fellow passengers and garrulous crew members, Killashandra had gleaned additional information about crystal singers and Ballybran, a lot of which she discounted since most merely paraphrased Maestro Valdi's comments. Andurs, despite his limited first-hand knowledge, had proved to be the most informative. He had been on the space run from Regulus to Ballybran for nine standard years and was always listening, so he had heard more than anyone else—certainly more than she had been able to extract from the cryptic vidifax of the three ships she had traveled on during the voyage. There was something mysterious about Ballybran and the Heptite Guild and its members—a mystery that she deduced from what *wasn't* said about those three subjects. Individuals had privacy; so did certain aspects of any interstellar mercantile company, and one understood that references to certain planetary resources were understated or omitted. But the lack of routinely available printout on Ballybran, the Guild, and its select members doubled her suspicions.

Conversely, she had been tremendously impressed by the Guild's tacit power: high-rank medicorps men had awaited Carrik at the three intermediary ports. She herself had been accorded the most deferential treatment. She'd had very little to do other than check the life-support cradle that carried Carrik. The cradle was programmed for IV feedings, therapy, bathing, and the necessary drugs. The apparatus was checked by technicians at each port. Nothing, apparently, was too good for a Heptite Guild member. Or his escort. She'd had open credit in the ships' stores, was a member of the captain's private mess on all three ships. Except for the fact that she was left strictly alone, she thoroughly enjoyed the excitement of her first interstellar journey.

Possibly because the trip was nearly over, she had received most of her information from Andurs the previous night as he judiciously nursed a Sarvonian brandy through the evening.

"I hear it often enough to begin to believe it's possible . . . but they say crystal gets into your blood."

"That'd kill you," Killashandra replied though Carrik had used the same phrase.

"I can't tell whether they mean that the credits are so good," Andurs continued, ignoring her comment. "Crystal singers really whoop it up—big spenders, fun people—until the shakes start. Funny about that, too, because crystal singers are supposed to heal faster than other humans, and they're not supposed to be as susceptible to the planetary goolies and fevers that catch you no matter what immunization you've got. And they stay younger." That capability annoyed Andurs. "I asked one of 'em about that. He was drunk at the time, and he said it's just part of singing crystal."

"Then there'd be a lot of people willing to sing crystal . . ."

"Yeah, but you also risk the shakes or . . ." Andurs jerked his thumb over his shoulder to indicate Carrik in his cabin, "I'd rather grow old."

"That doesn't happen often, does it?" Killashandra asked, startled. She'd had the impression that Carrik's collapse was unusual.

"He's the first I've seen that bad," Andurs admitted. "Oh, they get the fevers, sometimes bad enough to be packed out in freezebags but not—" and he touched his forehead with one finger. "Not my business, but how did he get that way?"

His question, though an obvious one, startled Killashandra because no one else throughout the journey had asked, as if they were afraid of the answer.

"He was fine until we got to Fuerte Spaceport. Then a shuttle came in with a badly resonating drive. It exploded, and he got caught in the sonic backlash."

"Good of you to escort him back."

"I owed him that." Killashandra meant it. "You said the Guild maintains offices on the moon? Is that where you apply for membership as well?"

He looked at her in amazement. "Oh, you don't want to be a singer."

"Why not?"

Andurs leaned toward her, staring hard into her eyes. "You weren't forced to come with him, were you? I mean, *he* didn't do anything to you?"

Killashandra didn't know whether to laugh or become angry. "I don't know where you come from, Captain Andurs, but on Fuerte privacy is respected."

"I didn't mean to imply that it wasn't . . ." Andurs responded hastily, raising his hand to fend off her outrage.

"Do I look as if I've been conditioned?"

"No, actually you don't. It's just that you strike me as a sensible woman, and crystal singing isn't sensible. Oh, I know. I've heard all the fardling rumors, but that's spaceflot because all the singers I've seen—and I've seen a lot in nine years on this run—never bother anyone. They keep to themselves, really. But there is something very peculiar indeed about Ballybran and crystal singing. I do know"—and he glanced over his shoulder, a needless caution since they were alone in the lounge—"that not every one who applies and gets accepted makes it as a singer. Whoever goes down to that planet"—he pointed toward the floor—"stays there. Only singers leave. And *they* always return."

"How many people apply for entry into the Guild?" Killashandra was remembering the 20,007 technicians as well as the 4,425 singers, and she wondered what the gross was if the net was so small.

"I can't answer that precisely." Andurs seemed perplexed as he scratched his head. "Never thought about it. Oh, I get a few applicants almost every trip. Think we've got eight, possibly nine on this flight. You get to know who's commercial traveling, and who's hoping." Andurs grinned at her. "We do have four Guild-vouched passages besides yours. That means these people have been screened at a Guild center somewhere. You know that tall, thin, black-haired fellow?"

Killashandra nodded, remembering the man who had boarded the ship at the last transfer point. He'd stared at her inquisitively, and once she had found him standing outside her cabin, a strange wild look on his face.

"He's come on his own. I wouldn't say he'd be accepted."

"Oh?"

Andurs twirled his brandy glass for a long moment before he answered. "Yeah, I don't think he's the type they want."

"What is the type they want?"

"I don't really know," Andurs replied after a moment, "but he's not it. The Guild will pay your way back to the nearest transfer point," he added as if this would be sufficient compensation for rejection. "I'll let you know when we emerge, Killa. Ballybran's one of the more interesting planets to see a moon's eye view of—especially if there's a storm in progress."

Killashandra remained at the view screen until Ballybran was eclipsed by the bulk of its largest moon, Shankill. If you've seen one moon installation, you've seen them all, she thought as she watched the domes and blackened landing pits swivel past. Her attention was briefly arrested by the sight of a second vessel swinging up over the horizon, a shuttle craft from the size of it, small enough to make no work of the landing. She thought she caught a flash of the Heptite Guild dodecahedron on the nose, but the shuttle moved into shadow too quickly for her to check.

Whatever reception she had subconsciously hoped for was vastly different from the one she received from Lanzecki, the Resident Master of the Heptite Guild. He was standing at the portal when the ship opened its airlock: a dour man, with a swarthy complexion and a squat figure, clothed in dull colors. The only things bright and active about him were his wide-set piercing brown eyes, which moved incessantly, seeming to catch more in one darting glance than they ought.

He gestured to the two men accompanying him who were dun garbed as well. They silently entered the ship and paced down the corridor, Killashandra in the lead. She had never felt more superfluous. In Carrik's stateroom, Lanzecki used that moment's hesitation to press the panel plate open. He glanced once at the still figure on the carrier, his face expressionless. He motioned the others to enter and take the carrier.

"Thank you, Killashandra Ree. You have an open ticket to whatever destination you desire and a credit of one thousand galactic units." He proffered two vouchers, each emblazoned with the Heptite Guild dodecahedron black-quartz crystal. He accorded her a deferential bow, and then, as the men guided Carrik past, he followed them down the corridor.

For a moment, Killashandra stared at the departing trio, the two metallic voucher slips clinging with static attraction to her fingers. "Guild Master? Lanzecki? Sir? Wait . . ." The stately progress continued without pause. "Of all the ungrateful—"

"I'd not call them ungrateful," said Captain Andurs, who had approached from the other end of the corridor. He craned his head to glance at the vouchers. "Not at all."

"I didn't expect praise," Killashandra exclaimed, though that indeed was what she had expected. "Just a word or two."

"You've got the important ones," Andurs reminded her with a wry smile. "One thousand. They're an odd lot at best," he went on as the Guildsmen turned toward the accordioned portal maw. "Like I said, there's all kinds of spaceflot about that Guild. I see strange things banging this old can from system to system, and I pretend not to see half of them." Suddenly, he slid his arm about her shoulders. "Now that the dead meat's gone, how about you and me—"

"Not now," Killashandra irritably pushed his arm away. "I want a word with that Guild Master first." She strode rapidly down the corridor toward the portal.

She never saw Carrik again, though he was listed among the inactive membership for a good many years. Not that she glanced at the lists, active or inactive, very often once the thrill of seeing her own name inscribed had passed.

She came to a halt at the opaque force screen of the debarkation arch, which blinked readiness to receive her credentials and reason for business on Shankill. She ignored it, watching in frustration as the Guild Master's figure disappeared through one of the five irised exits from the small lobby beyond the arch. She raced back to her cabin to jam her belongings into the carisak. By the time she had returned to debarkation, much to her disgust, she had to join the queue of passengers. As she waited, fighting her impatience, Captain Andurs emerged from the ship's forward section and made for the secondary gate by the debarkation arch. He caught a glimpse of her and turned back, a quizzical smile on his face.

"Going through with it, Killa?" he asked. He slid a hand up her arm to grip her elbow. Andurs's eyes had the sort of intensity she had begun to associate with desire, a pleasing response considering her abrupt manner with him earlier.

"Why not? I've been given no reason to stop and a very good one to try."

Andurs grinned. "Well, you'll find the process takes time. I'll be in the transients' hostel for at least five days." He made a grimace of resigned distaste and shrugged. "I'll be seeing you," he added with a half note of questioning, though his smile was inviting.

It irked Killashandra to see him jauntily present his wrist to the plate on the smaller arc and watch the entrance dilate immediately. When she finally submitted her wrist to the identity plate at debarkation control, she had become somewhat resigned to delay.

She was asked for her reason to land on Shankill.

"I wish to apply for membership in the Heptite Guild. I have perfect pitch," she added.

The display requested her credit rating, and Killashandra disdainfully slipped in the Guild voucher. It was instantly accepted, and the substantial credit balance displayed. The unit purred, clicked, and then, as a fax sheet rolled from the print slot, the arch dilated to permit access to the Shankill Moon Base. She was advised to read and conform to all rules and regulations of the Shankill Authority, which were included in the printout as were directions to transient accommodations, catering facilities, and the public areas of the installation.

She passed through the arch and into the lobby with the five exits. The third iris swirled open, and Killashandra, taking the hint, proceeded down that corridor to the hostel. She was surprised to emerge into a large open area, high-ceilinged and lined with holograms of trees lightly stirring in an absent breeze. A glow radiating from the plasglassed skylight simulated sunlight. She wondered, as she crossed the floor to the reception area, if the mock light also followed Ballybran's rotational period.

Her second surprise was to find a human attendant behind the reception counter. "Killashandra Ree?" he asked politely, unsmiling.

She suppressed a desire to ask "Who else?" and nodded.

"You will not have had time to read the rules and regulations pertaining to Shankill Moon Base, therefore, it is my duty to request that you do so immediately upon settling in your accommodation. Failure to comply will result in restriction of personal liberty to prevent endangering the lives of others through ignorance. Please synch your digital to Ballybran's rotation with which all base times are synchronized. If you do not understand anything in the instructions, I am at your service to explain. Place your wrist unit on the plate. Thank you."

More accustomed to the monotone of machine-issued instructions, Killashandra could only stare at the man, wondering if he was some sort of android, though she'd never heard of such lifelike replicas of humans. Then he smiled slightly and tapped the plate.

"Been on a moon base before?" the man asked in a tone remarkably informal after his mechanical speech.

"No," she said as she placed her wrist to the plate and her thumb in the depression.

"This is my tenth. I'm an apprentice in satellite security. We get to do the routine work, you see. Not that anything's ever gone wrong here"—he pointed his forefinger firmly toward the floor to indicate the entire base—"though there's always a first time. Like our training programmer says, there's always a first time, and we're supposed to make sure that first times don't occur. That's why you'll find human specialists like me on moon bases. People get so used to machines and displays and automatic cautionary signs that they don't sink in"—he tapped his forehead—"and that's how accidents can happen."

"Seems like good psychology," Killashandra agreed absently, for she was noting with pleasure the winking green credit balance. A key poked above the flush counter. The man handed it to her.

"My name's Ford. You'll read that your room has its own life-support system that comes on-line automatically in case of failure of the base system. Only, by Brennan's left ear, don't get caught in a hostel room during a leak-out or a break—that's a sure way to go berk."

Killashandra wanted to tell him that his psychology had a flaw if this was how he was supposed to reassure her. But she refrained, smiled, and promised she'd read the instructions. Then she glanced about her.

"Your key's tuned to your room. It'll find you your way back from any point in the base," Ford said jovially. "Just go through that door," he added, leaning across his counter and pointing to the left.

Killashandra felt the tug of the key in that direction, and giving Ford another smile, she set off.

The key plate of the door frame was glowing in welcome as she approached her assigned room. She inserted the key, and the door panel retracted with a *whoosh*. As she walked in, she could see why Ford didn't recommend a protracted stay on the premises; the compact room would give anyone claustrophobia. All the bodily comforts compacted into a space 3½ meters long, 2 meters wide, and 3 high. A three-drawer captain's bed occupied most of the space. Above it was shelving, from the base of which projected the angled audiovisual unit, obviously usable only to the occupant of the bed. Any esthetics of space or decor had been waived in considerations of safety and survival. To be sure, one wasn't compelled to remain in this room. In fact, from the authority's viewpoint, it was probably advisable that the room be occupied only for sleep.

Killashandra flipped the carisak to the foot of the bed and plopped down on it, noticing for the first time the row of labeled switches and buttons along the wall and the wall slots from which, according to the labels, table, reading lamp, and an individual catering unit would emerge. She grimaced. Everything at fingertip control. She wondered if Ford's presence was to reassure the transients that they were indeed human rather than extensions of some computer. Ford certainly exhibited humanity.

Sighing, she dutifully pulled the rules and regulations to her. She had promised. Besides, forewarning herself seemed wise even if, as Ford had averred, nothing had ever happened on Shankill Station.

According to the fax sheet, he was correct. The Shankill Moon Base had been functioning safely for 334 years, Standard Galactic. The original installation had been considerably expanded when Federated Sentient Planets restricted habitation of Ballybran because of the planet's dangers.

Killashandra had to reread that part twice. So the planet itself was dangerous, though obviously that danger had been overcome since people were now working and living on the surface.

The following paragraphs blithely changed subject and began enumerating safety hazards, regulations, and individual responsibilities. Killashandra dutifully read on, hearing an echo of Ford's warning: "There's always a first time." As a transient, her main responsibilities were first to seek the red-striped areas of whatever corridor or public place she inhabited on hearing either rapid hoots (oxygen leak) or sharp short whistles (penetration) or intermittent siren (internal fire or emergency) and then to stay out of everyone's way. Sustained hoots, whistles, or siren indicated the end of the emergency. If she was in her quarters, she was to lie on the bed—not that there was anywhere else in the room to be comfortable during enforced incarceration. In all crises, helmeted personnel were authorized to command unhelmeted individuals to any task required to end the emergency.

She turned the sheet over and studied the map of the base, which, comparing the total with the part she had already seen, must be immense. Some units were composed of nine sprawling levels, most subsurface; each one could be sealed for all had back-up life-support systems. The largest areas were cargo and maintenance facilities, the Guild and administration. Diagrams of the two smaller bases on the moons, Shilmore and Shanganagh, decorated the bottom of the sheet. These were both meteorological stations, and Shanganagh seemed to be completely automated.

Meteorology seemed to be the preoccupation of Ballybran, Killashandra thought—was that the danger on the planet? Its weather? Carrik had mentioned the incredible mach storms. That the winds of Ballybran were ferocious enough to merit such a nickname was frightening enough.

She scanned the map again, noting the proximity of the Guild Complex to the transients' quarters. Two tunnels/corridors/avenues—whatever—over and the small unit between was the debarkation facility. She grinned at the convenient juxtaposition. Could it be completely fortuitous? Could she just walk over and present herself as an aspirant?

She suddenly experienced an unexpected diffidence and studied her digital. She was well within the normal working hours of most commercial establishments. She had read the important safety regulations, and she would certainly look for the red-striped area in any corridor and public place she entered. With a twitch of her shoulders, she strengthened her resolve and pressed the wall stud to activate the speech-recognition system.

"Request details for applying to Heptite Guild for membership."

The display rippled on.

APPLICATION FOR CONSIDERATION OF MEMBERSHIP IN HEPTITE GUILD REQUIRES PHYSICAL FITNESS TEST SG-1, PSYCHOLOGICAL PROFILE SG-1, EDUCATION LEVEL 3 PREFERRED BUT EXCEPTIONS CONSIDERED, PERFECT AND ABSOLUTE PITCH BOTH IN PERCEPTION AND REPRODUCTION OF THE TONAL QUALITY AND TIMBRE TO BE FOUND ONLY IN TYPE IV THROUGH VIII BIPEDAL HUMANOID, ORIGIN SOL III. MUTANTS NEED NOT APPLY.

APPLICATION MADE ONLY THROUGH HEPTITE GUILD OFFICES: SHANKILL MOON BASE, MAIN RECEPTION FACILITY.

FEDERATED SENTIENT PLANETS REQUIRE FULL DISCLOSURE OF ALL DANGERS INHERENT IN PROFESSION TO PROSPECTIVE CANDIDATES ONCE PHYSICAL, PSYCHOLOGICAL, AND APTITUDE TESTS HAVE BEEN PASSED TO THE SATISFACTION OF THE GUILD EXAMINING BOARD.

BALLYBRAN IS AN INTERDICTED WORLD, SECTION 907, CODE 4, PARAGRAPHS 78–90. FOR DETAILS, CONSULT HEPTITE GUILD.

"Well," Killashandra murmured, "information received by dribs and drabs. Heptite Guild, please."

The screen resolved around a woman's face.

"Heptite Guild, Shankill Moon Base. May I assist you?"

"Killashandra Ree," she managed, mindful of courtesy, for she hadn't expected a personal answer. "I'd like to know if your member, Carrik, is all right?"

"He made the journey safely to the surface."

"I mean, will he recover?"

"That is possible but not predictable."

The woman's face was composed and obviously expectant.

"How do I get to be a Guild member?" Her query was blurted out. "I did tap data retrieval."

The woman smiled politely. "I am permitted to release additional information to interested persons. Your room designation?" Killashandra gave her the information. "You will have access to the relevant data until 0800 tomorrow. If you desire the preliminary examinations, you may present yourself to the Guild during normal working hours."

The image faded, which was just as well because Killashandra was consumed with curiosity as to what more of Ballybran's mysteries would be revealed by the promised additional data. Not all, she was certain.

The display began with a historical summary of the planet. Furious, she was about to cancel the program when it occurred to her that the wise performer studied the role and the composer, to understand his intent, before any audition. If the Guild had released this data to her, they would also know if she had availed herself of the courtesy. Joining the Heptite Guild might not depend alone on perfect pitch, good physical condition, and the right psychological adjustment—or why were there so few members?

She settled herself to study the material, though the preliminary paragraphs on "man's ever-pressing need for material resources in his search of the galaxies" reminded her depressingly of secondary school's orientation propaganda. She didn't have to wade through much of that but got quickly to the section on Spican quartz.

In a routine explore and evaluate search, Scoria's planets were probed. Ballybran, the only one with suitable atmosphere and gravity, gave happy evidence of crystal and quartz formations in its inverted ranges. A team was dispatched, Barry Milekey of Trace its leader. The initial findings of the geologists indicated a planet of immense potential, and samples were rushed back to Sector Research Division. The E and E of Ballybran had lucked out. The first crystal sample to be analyzed properly, a blue porphyry type, proved, due to peculiarities of its composition, a marvelous optical storage device, allowing computers virtually instantaneous access to improbably large volumes of data stored in matrixes of exceptionally small dimensions. The crystal's fine-grain synapse structure enabled even a smallish (1 cm^3) segment to serve as a gigaword memory.

However, it was Milekey's discovery of the so-called black quartz—under normal conditions neither black nor quartz—that led to the complete revolution of interstellar communications. Owing to its thermal characteristics, Black Ballybran is a pigmented rock crystal, translucent in natural light.

Under certain types of magnetic stress, Black Ballybran, for lack of any better description, absorbs all light and seems to become *matte* black. Milekey had observed this phenomenon when he chipped the first lump from the black crystal face.

Again by accident, while being examined by the crystallographers, the substance's true properties were discovered. If two identical segments of black quartz were subjected to synchronized magnetic induction, a two-way communication link was established between the crystal segments. When investigators increased the distance between the samples, it was discovered that, unlike other electromagnetic phenomena, black quartz eliminated the time lag.

Concurrent with the laboratory discoveries and proposed applications of the new crystals came the first of several problems to be solved in the mining of this rich source. The first E and E team had only gathered up loose chips of the various types of crystal, or such larger chunks as had already been fractured from the mother lode. In attempts to cut with ordinary carbon-10 blades, the crystal had shattered. Laser cutters were tried, but they shattered, melted, or damaged the crystal.

The habit of one of the crystallographers of singing as he worked led to an unexpected solution. The man noticed that some crystal faces would resonate to his voice, and he suggested the use of a subsonic cutter. Though not completely successful, experiments along this line finally produced the sophisticated audio pickup that resonated, amplified, and reduced the required note to set the subsonic diamond blade.

Once the problem of wresting unblemished crystals from the face was solved, Ballybran was opened to private miners. During the next spate of storms, those miners who heeded the warnings promptly and reached the sheltered valley sustained no injury. The imprudent were discovered in the storm's wake, dead or mad. Storm winds blowing across the resonant Crystal Range coaxed enough sonics from the sensitive rock to shatter unprotected minds.

Keenly aware of the unexplained deaths of the nine miners, everyone became conscious of previously ignored physical discomforts. The meditechs began filing reports of disorientation, hypo- and hyperthermic spells, erratic sense perceptions, muscular spasm and weakness. No one in the several base camps escaped the minor ailments. Most symptoms passed, but some victims found one sense or another—in most cases hearing—to be affected. The medical team was hastily augmented, and everyone was put through exhaustive tests. At first, crystal was suspected of inducing the symptoms. However, those handling the crystal off-planet appeared unharmed by contact, while meteorologists and support technicians who never touched the stuff on Ballybran, were also affected. Crystal was absolved. The planet's ecology then became the prime target for intensive examination, and this area of investigation proved positive. The spore producing the symptoms was soon isolated, and the planet Ballybran was placed on Code 4 as a preventive measure.

Killashandra turned off the display to ponder that. Anything below Code 15 was a stern prohibition against landing. Ballybran's spore produced complicated reactions—sometimes fatal—in the human body. Yet the culprit had been isolated, but the planet was *still* on a Code 4!

Evasion! Killashandra thought, irritated. She started the display again, but the text now cited the formation of the Heptite Guild. She halted it.

What was it Andurs had said? "Only singers leave the planet." Obviously, the handicapped remained on Ballybran. Twenty-thousand-odd staff and technicians as opposed to singers. Killashandra snorted. Those were better odds, actually, than the ones against achieving stellar rank in the performing arts. She rather liked that. Yes, but what happened if you weren't one of the one-in-five? What sort of technical workers were employed?

She queried the vidifax.

"Technicians: Ballybran crystal workers, tuners, artificers of crystal drive components and interstellar resonating units, meditechs, programmers, mechanics, therapists, agronomists, caterers . . ." the list continued down to menial functions.

So, once committed to Ballybran, only singers left. Well, she'd be a singer. Killashandra pushed aside the console and, knitting her fingers behind her head, leaned back on the narrow bolster.

What contributed to that subtle difference between singer and support staff? Particularly if perfect pitch was a prerequisite to leaving the planet. If infrasonic cutters were used to extract the crystal from the rock face, sheer strength wasn't the second requisite. Attitude? Aptitude?

The spore disease? Killashandra drew the console back to her and tapped out a recall.

"This area of investigation proved positive, and the spore producing the illness was isolated . . ."

"Isolated," Killashandra muttered under her breath. "Isolated but not negated, or cured, and the planet Code 4."

So it had to be immunity to the spore itself that determined who sang crystal?

Nothing ventured, nothing gained, she thought, and tapped out a query on the spore. She chuckled as the display announced a restricted subject. Only so much information then was vouchsafed the candidate. Fair enough. Privacy was as much the right of a Guild as an individual, and the FSP required full disclosure before a candidate took the final irrevocable plunge.

She pushed back the console and swung off the bed. Pausing just long enough to brush her hair and check the fall of her tunic, she slid aside the door panel. It closed quietly behind her.

When she reached the ramp connecting levels, she studied the wall map mounted there. She was two levels below and to one side of the Guild, and there was but one access to that part of the base. She hurried up the ramp with an aggressive stride. It felt good to walk about. After confinement for nine days in shuttles and spaceships, even a moon base seemed spacious. The amenities of Shankill reflected its use as a commercial as well as resident scientific facility. Considerable thought and care had been taken to approximate planetary surroundings, to make residents and transients forget the hostile conditions outside. Holograms on the out-side of the rampway depicted a pleasant mountain scene that, Killashan-dra was sure, would change in lighting to coincide with the base's diurnal pattern. It was close to midday "outside," but she ignored the faint com-plaints from her stomach.

Through a lock, past the red-hatched area she had promised herself to seek out, the corridor widened into a broad foyer. Set around the wall were holograms of trees and flowers, nodding and dipping among the banked bright-leaved shrubs. She thought the decorator had mixed the flora of several planets in the display, but with holograms that scarcely caused botanical problems. Besides, the effect was colorful.

The catering facility below her was set out on several levels, the first one a wide corridor between two beverage areas, one with a human atten-dant. She bore left, entering another short corridor that bridged the cater-ing and Guild areas.

Though it crossed her mind that the Guild offices were closed for midday meals, she was surprised to gain instant admission to the reception area. There, she stopped in wonder.

Moon base or not, the twelve-sided hall was immense, the ceiling at least 5, possibly 6 meters high. An immense crystal artform, multicolored and faintly luminous, hung from the center of the arches that supported the ceiling. A curved console was the only furnishing in the open chamber, but Killashandra noted the lights of display niches set at random levels on the sidewalls.

"Well," she uttered in soft amazement, then heard the chandelier chime in response. It was not, as she'd initially thought, a lighting fixture. It also seemed to incorporate a variety of crystal forms and colors: some masterpieces of crystal artifice. Surely a waste. Suddenly she realized the mass was slowly rotating, its luminous ends sending motes of light about the room, changing patterns as it turned and always accompanied by the soft, almost subliminal chiming.

If the noise didn't twist you, thought Killashandra, the light would mesmerize. She declined the subtle hypnosis and began to prowl about the enormous reception hall. The first niche held a fan of minute shards of a pale-pink crystal, the sort probably utilized as computer chips or transduc-ers. She wondered how sharp their edges might be. The next display pro-vided magnification to show crystalline threads of various hues and diameters. Surely, one didn't "cut" those. Perhaps the yellowish crystal fractured into such strands.

The porcupine of a crystal drive unit dominated the next showcase, but the largest area was devoted to the black crystal, which, indeed, was neither black nor, apparently, a crystal. When she moved on to the next wall of the dodecahedron and squinted through one of the eyeholes, she saw another piece, very definitely black in the special lighting.

Suddenly, the chandelier chimed, and, startled, Killashandra turned to find the tall, thin, nervous man from the spaceship standing at the en-

trance. He had cleared his throat noisily, and the chandelier was responding to the harsh sound. He now looked as if he were going to dash from the
hall in terror.

"Yes?" she asked, forestalling his flight. She might as well find out
what was haunting him.

"No mean to break privacy," he blurted out in a hoarse whisper. He
obviously had encountered the peculiar reaction of the chandelier before.
"But the man with you on the ship? He was a singer?"

"Yes."

"What happened to him? That spore get him?"

"No," Killashandra replied. The poor man's eyes threatened to pop
out of his head he was so worried. "He was caught in the sonic backlash
when a shuttle blew up. Sensory overload."

The relief brightened his face, and he mopped at his forehead and
cheeks with a film.

"They tell you only so much and not enough. So when I saw him—"

"You want to become a crystal singer?"

He gulped, his larynx cartilage bobbing up and down in his
nervousness.

"Are you a singer?" There was awe in his voice. "I thought you must
be from the way the captain was treating you." He wasn't so certain of that
now, obviously.

"No, I'm not."

His attitude changed instantly as he straightened up and thrust his
shoulders back.

"Well, I'm going to be," he stated firmly, and the chandelier echoed
him. He glanced nervously above and seemed to draw his head protectively into his shoulders.

"If that's what you want," Killashandra said equably, and then
strode past him. She'd seen all of the hall she wanted and could do with
some food.

"You mean, you won't try to argue me out of it?" he asked, following her.

"Why should I?"

"Everyone else does."

"I'm not everyone else."

"It's supposed to be very dangerous."

"I'm not worried."

"Are you going to apply, too?"

She stopped and turned on him so swiftly that he nearly walked
into her.

"You're invading my privacy—"

"Oh, no, no." He fended off such an accusation with raised arms and
a startled expression. "But why else would you be in the Heptite Hall?"

"To buy crystal."

"You're not a buyer—"

"You're invading my privacy!" She stalked off as fast as she could, half tempted to press the close button on the panel that separated the linking corridor with the catering foyer.

"I just wanted to talk . . ." His voice followed her but he at least had remained behind.

The energy generated by her irritation carried her past the bar area to a T-junction of aisles leading to business stalls and cubicles, some closed by privacy screens. Broadleafed plants lined a short flight of steps into the dining area. Service slots and bright-orange menu panels were positioned against the walls, and she was making her way to the nearest when she heard herself called.

"Over here, Killashandra Ree," Captain Andurs rose from a group of spacemen to beckon her. "C'mon. Join us."

Well, he'd at least be protection against that imbecile if he followed her, so she waved back and stepped up to scan the menufax. She was overwhelmed by the selections scrolling on display. When she spotted the seafood casserole she'd eaten that momentous evening at Fuerte, she ordered it.

"Brew's good, too," Andurs said, coming to assist her. He deftly punched a sequence, paused and tapped again. "Goes down better with some of these."

She was about to protest his abruptness, all too familiar with the vagaries of overprogrammed and stubborn student hall catering units, when the service panel slid open to reveal all three orders. Efficiency was a pleasure.

"Here, have a sip of the brew and see if you like it," Andurs suggested, offering her the liter glass. "No sense making unnecessary trips. Spoils conversations. See, I told you it was good. It's not processed: allowed to age normally, and that means a good brew. They know how here." Then he dialed up not only a liter glass for her but a large beaker as well. "I'd stick to the brews here or your own planet's ferment or distillations if they stock 'em—and I'd be surprised if they didn't. You could really turn off on some drinks if you have the wrong metabolism, you know."

"I appreciate the advice," she said as they made their way back to the others.

"Do you?" Andurs sounded cynical. "We've been rescheduled. We'll be on our way tomorrow, 1000 base time. Rush cargo. Bound for Regulus Exchange. You can use that Guild voucher and cross the Milky Way if you've a mind to."

"I've a mind to stay here and see how it goes."

"Done any checking?" he asked, lowering his voice, for they were nearly to the table now.

"Enough."

"No matter what prints out, it wouldn't be enough or all the truth." Andurs' tone was dourly repressive.

"By FSP law, they have to make full disclosure of the dangers."

Andurs snorted, but they had reached the table by then and he was disinclined to continue that discussion.

She had only just been introduced to the flight engineer, whom she hadn't met during the journey, when she noticed tension on the faces of the supercargo and the second officer. Curious, she glanced over her shoulder to see what caused their dislike and then half turned in her chair to get a clear look.

Two men and a woman stood there observing the seated diners. It was not their rough, stained garments, the scarred boots, or unkempt hair that caught Killashandra's eye—though these were unusual enough in a society that respected cleanliness—but the trio's imperious bearing, a sort of lofty disdain that excluded everyone else, and the brilliance of their eyes. The tableau, briefly held during the trio's survey, broke up as the three moved purposefully toward a corner table where, as Killashandra followed their progress, two other similarly attired people sat.

"And who do they think they are?" Killashandra asked, as annoyed by their manner as the second officer and supercargo. Even as she spoke, she knew the answer, for she had seen that hauteur, that inner luminosity before—in Carrik. "Singers, are they?"

"Yes," said the super flatly.

"Are they always like that?"

"Wasn't your friend Carrik?" Andurs countered.

"Not exactly like that."

"Then he was most unusual," the super replied in a daunting tone. "They're at their worst just in from the Ranges—as those are. Lucky for us, Andurs, there are two Monasterian ships in. They'll ship out on those."

Andurs nodded curtly and then, as if to make certain Killashandra did not continue the sore subject of singers, began a volley of questions about supplies and cargo waybills. Taking the hint, she applied herself to her food but did cast surreptitious glances toward the fascinating group of singers. Killashandra was all the more surprised that they seemed not to have much to say to each other, though the trio had deliberately sought out the pair. Nor did they leave their table longer than it took one of them to dial and collect several wine beakers at a time. They paid no attention to others in the now-crowded dining area.

Since there was considerable traffic, greeting of friends, and good-natured teasing from table to table, Killashandra could make some discreet evaluations. A good relationship seemed to exist between base residents—Guild members or not—and transients. She recognized the various professions and skills by the distinctive uniform colors and hatchings of calling and rate. The travelers were garbed in whatever suited their fancies, the styles and fashions of two or three dozen cultures and disciplines. Ship personnel always wore the space-dark uniforms, sober counterpoint to the riot of civilian dress. Several life-supported aliens appeared briefly in the

main foyer but they quickly retired to the catering level that accommodated their exotic requirements.

Having leisurely finished their meal, the supercargo and engineer excused themselves, claiming duties before liftoff. Andurs waved them a
genial go-ahead and then turned to Killashandra.

"D'you see what would happen if you become a singer?"

"What?" she asked guilelessly.

Andurs flicked his fingers impatiently at the aloof quintet. "You'd be
alone. Wherever you went."

"I wasn't alone with Carrik. He was very good company."

"For a specific reason, I've no doubt, and don't spout Privacy at me."

Killashandra laughed at his sour reply. "The reason was mutual, my
friend. And I still don't see why the crystal singers are at fault."

" 'And who do they think they are?' " he mimicked in a fair imitation
of her instinctive reaction to the singers.

"Well, I also didn't notice anyone making them welcome the way
everyone else—"

"Nor will you. Disagreeable bastards, that's what they are. And they
always act that superior."

"Carrik—" she began, remembering how much fun he had been.

"He might have been halfway gone by the time you met him. They
change—and not for the better."

"They would have to, wouldn't they?" she said, somewhat abruptly,
for Andurs's irrational insistence on generalities annoyed her. "The fax
said they take rigorous physical, psychological, and aptitude tests. Only
the best are taken, so they would be above the ploddies you have to put up
with everywhere else in the galaxy."

"You don't understand. They are *very* different!" Andurs was becoming agitated in his effort to explain.

"I'll never understand if you won't be specific."

"Well, I can." Andurs almost leaped at her offer. "The singer in the
brown tunic—how old would you say he is? And don't stare at them too
hard. They can be offensive if irritated. Especially when they're just off the
Ranges like that set."

Killashandra had noticed the brown-clad man; he was the tallest
one and exuded some of the same magnetic quality that had distinguished
Carrik.

"I'd say about second half of his third decade, perhaps beginning of
his fourth."

"I'm in my fourth and have been making this run for nine years standard. I know he's been a singer for at least nine decades because his name's
appeared on the passenger lists for my ship for that long."

Killashandra glanced discreetly over at the subject in question. It was
hard to believe the man was well over his first hundred years. Modern science delayed the worst ravages of physical degeneration but—

"So eternal youth is your gripe?"

"No, not mine. Frankly I wouldn't want to have more than ten or twelve decades. It's not just that singers look young longer, though that does get at some, it's—it's other differences . . ."

"Psychological? Professional? Physical? Or financial?"

"Look, the point is, there are differences that the rest of us note, sense, feel, and resent in singers!" Andurs was vehement now, pounding one fist into the other palm to emphasize his points. "Whatever it is separates you forever from the rest of mankind. Is that what you want?"

Killashandra gave the question due consideration before she looked Andurs in the eye and said, "Yes. Crystal singers are a rigidly selected, highly trained professional minority. And I want to be a member of that sort of group. I've had some training in that direction already," she added with a sour smile.

"Then your bringing Carrik back . . ." Andurs's nostrils flared with suspicion, and he leaned away from her.

"Was what I owed the man," she added hastily, for she didn't like that expression to appear so soon, and for no cause, on Andurs's face. She honestly had been motivated by regret for Carrik's condition. "Who knows? I may not pass the requirements. It harms no one for me to try, does it?" She gave Andurs a sweet, somewhat tremulous smile. "I was not motivated toward any goal when I encountered Carrik, you see—"

"Then ship out with me—or on any of the other ships. This"— Andurs's forefinger pointed at the floor—"is a dead end."

Killashandra sneaked one more look at the crystal singers—proud, aloof, and curiously radiant. She contrived a thoughtful frown for Andurs's benefit, but the group, remote and inaccessible, were indeed people apart, clearly marked by a subtle difference that set them above humans otherwise no less physically attractive or intelligent. This distinction would cause singers to be singled out no matter where they were. Forever, Killashandra thought, as Stellar performers when basking in the applause of adoring audiences. Since she was deprived of the one, she would try for this.

"There is something about them . . ." she said aloud with a diffident lift of her shoulders and a wry smile. "You know, you're right about the brew—" and she turned a more winning smile at Andurs.

"I'll get more."

She spent a pleasant evening with the captain, though she was glad that it was just an evening, for his limitations soon became apparent. Carrik had had many revelations for her. But when Andurs left for his ship at date change, it was only with expressions of regret and additional urgings for her to be on board. Though he was only going as far as Regulus Exchange, Killashandra could pick up a ship bound anywhere in the galaxy with her Guild voucher.

She thanked him, affecting more drowsiness than she felt, and left him with the notion that she had been swayed by his persuasions and person.

She didn't learn until much later that his ship, the *Rag Blue Swan Delta*, had delayed departure until peremptorily forced to leave by an aggravated landing officer. By that time she was already in the Guild block of the base.

Chapter 4

Arriving punctually at the beginning of business hours, Killashandra was not the only one so prompt. Some of the dozen or so milling about the large reception area were quite obviously buyers, peering at the displays and jotting entries on their wrist units. The tall, thin young man was there. He looked startled to see Killashandra and swerved away from her. Just as Killashandra noted two men and a woman emerge from a panel in the far side of the dodecahedron, someone stamped in from the base entrance. Killashandra glimpsed a set, hard, angry face and the close-cropped hair of a space worker as the bone-thin figure of a female swept past her.

The chandelier responded to the vibrations of her passage and picked up the tone of her voice. From the resonance of the chiming artform, Killashandra knew the woman was making demands. What surprised Killashandra more was that the Guild woman did not pay any attention, her head remaining bent over the module. The angry space worker repeated her question, sharp enough now for Killashandra to hear that the woman was demanding to be taken immediately for testing as a Guild candidate.

Suddenly, one of the Guildsmen, excusing himself from his conversation with a buyer, touched the programmer on her arm, directing her gaze to the now irate space worker. Another angry spate of words jarred the crystal drops, although the Guild programmer seemed not the least disturbed either by her discourtesy or the space worker's ire. In the next moment, the panel at the back of the room opened again, and the space worker moved toward it, her head set at an aggressive angle, her stride jarring her slender frame. The panel closed behind her.

A sigh attracted Killashandra's attention, and she turned to find a young man standing beside her. He would have deserved a second look anywhere, for he possessed close-curled red hair, a recessive trait rarer now than the true blond. He had evidently watched the interchange between the space worker and the Guild programmer as if he had anticipated such a confrontation. His sigh had been one of relief.

"She made it," he murmured under his breath, and then, noticing Killashandra, smiled at her. His unusually light-green eyes twinkled in mischief. The antipathy Killashandra had instinctively felt for the space worker was replaced by an instant affinity to the young man. "She's been in a snit, that one, the whole journey here. Thought she'd go through the debarkation arch like a projectile when it started laying on the formality. And after all that . . ." He spread his hands wide to express his astonishment at her ease.

"There's more to it than going through a doorway," Killashandra said.

"Don't I just know it, but there was no telling Carigana. For starters, she was annoyed that I got to do the prelim at Yarro on Beta VI. As if it were a personal affront to her that she had to come all the way here." He stepped closer to Killashandra as a knot of people, buyers from their varied manner of dress, entered. "Have you taken the plunge yet?" And then he held up his hand, grinning so winningly when Killashandra stiffened at such a flagrant breach of privacy that she couldn't, after all, take offense. "I'm from Scartine, you know, and I keep forgetting manners. Besides, you don't look like a buyer"—his comment was complimentary for he gestured with good-humored contempt at the finery of most of the other occupants of the hall—"and transients would never venture further than the catering area, so you must be interested in crystal singing . . ." He raised his eyebrows as well as the tone of his voice in question.

It would have taken a far more punctilious person than Killashandra to depress his ingenuous manner, but she answered with the briefest of smiles and a nod.

"Well, because I've been through the prelim, I've only to report my presence, but if I were you, though I'm not, and it's certainly not my wish to invade your privacy, I'd give Carigana a chance to get organized before I followed her in." Then he cocked his head, grinning with a sparkle at odds with his guilelessness. "Unless you're hanging back with second thoughts."

"I've thoughts but none of them seconds," Killashandra said. "You did the prelim at Yarro?"

"Yes, you know the tests."

"SG-1's, I hear."

He shrugged diffidently. "Medigear feels the same for all levels, and if you're adjusted, the psych is nothing. Aptitude's aptitude and a fast one, but you look like you've done tertiary studies, so what's to knot your hair over?" His expression was sharp as his eyes flicked to the wall through which Carigana had passed. "If you've got hair!"

"Those tests—they're not complicated, or painful, or anything? . . ." The tall nervous young man had sidled up to them without either noticing his approach.

Killashandra frowned slightly with displeasure, but the other young man grinned encouragingly.

"No sweat, no stress, no strength exerted, man. A breeze," and he planed his hand in a smooth gesture indicating ease. "All I got to do now is go up to the panel, knock on the door, and I'm in." He snapped the shoulder strap of his carisak.

"You've been given the full disclosure?" the dark-haired man asked.

"Not yet." The red-head grinned again. "That's the next step and only done here."

"Shillawn Agus Vartry," the other said formally, raising his right hand, fingers spread in the galactic gesture that indicated cooperation without weapon.

"Rimbol C-hen-stal-az" was the red-head's rejoinder.

Killashandra wasn't in the mood to be drawn into further conversation about applying for Guild membership, not with this Shillawn swallowing and stammering his way to a decision. She accorded Rimbol a smile and the salute as she backed away courteously before veering toward the module with more assurance than she felt. Once there, she spread her fingers wide where the movement would catch the woman's eye.

"I'd like to apply for membership to the Heptite Guild," she said when the woman raised her head. Killashandra had meant to say she wanted to become a crystal singer, but the words had shifted in her mind and mouth with uncharacteristic discretion. Perhaps Carigana's very bad example had tempered her approach.

The programmer inclined her head in acknowledgment of the request, her fingers flashing across the terminal keys. "If you will proceed through that entrance." She motioned toward the opening panel in the wall.

Killashandra could just imagine how anticlimactic that mild phrase must have been for the storming Carigana. She smiled to herself as the panel closed behind her without so much as a sigh. Exit Killashandra Ree softly and with no fanfare.

She found herself in a short corridor, with a series of color-coded and design-patched doors on either side, and made for one that opened quietly. Just as she entered the room from one door, a man with an odd crook to one shoulder entered from another. He gave her such a quick searching look that she felt certain he had had to greet Carigana.

"You agree to submit to SG-1 examinations of physical, psychological, and aptitudinal readiness? Please state your name, planet of origin, and whatever rank you hold. This information is being processed under the Federated Sentient Planets' conditions regarding admission into the Heptite Guild of Ballybran." He ran through the speech in two breaths, staring expectantly at her while her mind caught up with his rote comments.

"Yes, I Killashandra Ree of Fuerte, agree to the examinations. Rank, tertiary student in performing arts, released."

"This way, please, Killashandra Ree." She followed him into an anteroom, the usual examination facility. The panel on one door blazed red, and Killashandra supposed that Carigana was within, being subjected to the same tests she was about to undergo.

She was shown to the next cubicle, which held the couch and hood that were standard physical diagnostic equipment for her species. Without a word, she settled herself on the couch as comfortably as possible, inured since childhood to the procedures, to the slightly claustrophobic sensation as the upper half of the diagnostic unit swung down over her. She didn't mind the almost comforting pressure of the torso unit or the tight grip across one thigh and the hard weight on her left shin, but she never could get used to the constricting headpiece and the pressures against eyes, temple, and jaw. But cerebral and retinal scanning were painless, and one never felt the acupuncture that deadened the leg for the blood, bone marrow, and tissue samples. The other pressures for organ readings, muscle tone, heat and cold tolerances, sound sensitivity, were as nothing to the final pain-threshold jolt. She had heard about but never before experienced the pain-threshold gamut—and hoped never to have to do so again.

Just as she was about to scream from the stimuli applied to her nerve centers the apparatus abruptly retracted. As her nervous system tingled with the aftereffect, she did groan and massaged the back of her neck to ease muscles that had tensed in that split second of measurable agony.

"Take this restorative now, please," the meditech said, entering the room. He gave her a glass of carbonated green liquid. "Set you right. And if you'll just sit here," he added as a comfortable padded chair rolled to the center of the room while the medigear slid to the left. "When you are recovered, press the button on the right chair arm, and the psychological test will begin. A verbal address system is used. Responses are, of course, recorded, but I'm sure you're familiar with the procedures by now."

The drink did clear the last miasma of the threshold test from her senses, making her feel incredibly alert. All the better preparation for psychological testing.

Killashandra had always had mixed feelings about that sort of evaluation—so much might depend on one's frame of mind at that particular hour, day, and year. She experienced her usual halfhearted desire to give all the wrong answers, but this was coupled with the keen awareness of self-competition. Too much depended on the exams. She had no need to play any of the games she might have risked at other levels and times. She could not, however, comprehend the purpose of some questions that had never been asked during any other evaluation session. Of course, she'd never applied to the Heptite Guild before, so their criteria were bound to be different. Nor had she undergone a computerized verbal address psych test before, which was generally conducted face to face with a human examiner.

Toward the last few moments of the session, the speed of questioning increased to the point where she was actually sweating to produce answers to the displayed questions in an effort to keep up the pace.

She could still feel her heart racing when the Guild man returned, this time bearing a tray with steaming food packs.

"Your aptitude tests will be presented after you've eaten and rested. You may request entertainment from the fax or sleep." At his words, a contour couch appeared from a storage area. "When you are ready, inform the computer and the final examination will begin."

Killashandra was ravenous and found the nutritious meal delicious. She sipped the hot beverage slowly and asked for soothing Optherian "balances" to clear her mind of the tensions caused by the last portion of the psych tests.

In her previous evaluation sessions, the manner of the human attendants had often indicated the level of her performance—and she was accustomed to scoring high. But the Guild tech had been so impersonal, she couldn't guess how she was doing.

After she'd finished her meal, she elected to continue and signaled her readiness. Whereupon she was tested for pitch, the severest evaluation of that faculty she'd ever endured, including estimates of vibrational errors and unnerving subliminal noises below 50 and above 18,000 cycles. That recorded, the testing moved on to deceptively complex hand-eye coordinations that again left her drenched with sweat. She was run through a series of depth-perception exams and spatial relationships. The latter had always been one of her strong points, but by the time the session was over, she was wrung out with fatigue and was shaking.

Maybe it was wishful thinking on her part, but when the meditech returned, she fancied something of respect in his glance.

"Killashandra Ree, since you have completed the first day's examinations up to standard, you are now the guest of the Guild. We have taken the liberty of transferring your personal effects to more comfortable quarters in the Guild block. If you will follow me . . ."

Ordinarily, such an action, taken without her consent, would have constituted an invasion of privacy, but her energies were too depleted for her to summon up a protest. She was led deeper into the Guild block, down three levels from the main and the only entrance, or exit, to the rest of Shankill Base. Her easy penetration of the hallowed precinct amused rather than alarmed her. There was really no need for her to be isolated from the rest of the base population after what were very standard examinations. Except for the pain-threshold test, she had nothing to warn any other prospective applicant about. Unsuccessful applicants would be more dangerous to the Guild because of their disappointment. What happened to them, she wondered? What, for instance, had become of the angry Carigana? She'd be glad to be out of that one's vicinity in the event of her failure. And where were Rimbol and that irritating, twitchy young man, that Shillawn something?

How far into the Guild did she have to go to get this free room and board, she wondered, fatigue irritating her. She desired nothing more than to stretch out and sleep. She felt as drained as she had the night of the final student concert. How long ago was that now? In terms of distance or time? She had no patience with her own conundrums. How much farther now?

The Guild man had paused at a door, which slid open.

"If you'll put your print on file, you will find your belongings within.

At the end of this corridor is a common lounge, although you will also find catering facilities in your room. Tomorrow you will be summoned for the final phase."

A bleep from the man's wrist unit curtailed any questions she might have asked; for he acknowledged the reminder, inclined his head politely to her and retraced his steps.

She placed her thumb in the depression for the print lock and entered her new accommodation. It was not only larger—spacious in comparison to the hostel room—it was also more luxuriously appointed. A chair was drawn up to a small table, already set with a beaker of brew from the catering panel, which was lit. Killashandra gratefully sampled the drink, noting that the menufax was set to fish selections. She wondered just how much information the Guild had already had programmed about her since she had given her name, planet of origin, and rank. Deliberately, she spun the display to other proteins and ordered what was described as a hearty casserole of assorted legumes and a light wine.

She had just finished her meal when the door announced a visitor. She hesitated a long moment, unable to imagine who would be calling; then the door added that the visitor's name was Rimbol, who required a word with her. She pressed the door release.

Rimbol leaned in, grinning. "C'mon out for a bit. Just for a drink. It's free." Then he winked. "Neither Carigana nor Shillawn are present. Just some others who've already passed their prelims. C'mon."

The amusement in his wheedling voice was the deciding factor. Killashandra knew herself well enough to realize that even if she tried to sleep, she'd only play back the tests and become so depressed over omissions and commissions that she'd never achieve a true rest. A few drinks and a bit of relaxation in Rimbol's infectious company would do her much more good, especially if both Carigana and that nervous Shillawn were absent.

She was a bit taken aback, however, when 'just some others' numbered twenty-nine. Rimbol, sensing her surprise, grinned and gestured at the catering area.

"A brew's what you need. This is Killashandra," he announced in a slightly raised voice to the room in general. Her presence was acknowledged by slight nods or smiles or a brief hand gesture. A certain degree of informal companionship was already enjoyed by the others. The group, involved in some sort of four-player card game, didn't even look up as she and Rimbol collected their drinks.

"You make thirty, you know," Rimbol said as he guided her to a seat on the one unoccupied lounger. "Shillawn and Carigana thirty-two, and there's supposed to be one more going through prelim today. If that's a pass, it means we'll all go down to Ballybran tomorrow."

"That is, if no one gets scared after disclosure," said a girl who wandered over to join them. "I'm Jezerey, late of Salonika in the Antares group."

"I didn't think they canceled after disclosure," Rimbol said, frowning in surprise.

"You may well be right, but I do know that thirty is the smallest group they'll train," Jezerey went on, settling herself on the couch with a long sigh. "I've been waiting seven weeks standard." She sounded disgusted. "But Borton"—and she gestured toward the card players—"has been here nine. He'd just missed a class. Nothing will make him decline. I'm not so sure about one or two of the others—and we've got a few to spare. Rimbol says that nothing would unpersuade that Carigana, and from the look on her face when old Crookback brought her in, I'm as glad she decided she didn't like us either and stayed in her room. Space workers are odd lots, but she's—she's—"

"She's just intense," Rimbol noted when Jezerey faltered. "I don't think she trusts space stations any more than spaceships. She was tranked to her brows on the trip here. Shillawn"—and Rimbol favored Killashandra with a wry expression—"was knackered out of his bones, so *I* invaded Privacy and put a knockout in his brew. Got him to bed."

"Why would someone like him want to be a crystal singer?" Killashandra asked.

"Why do any of us?" Rimbol answered, amused.

"All right, why would you?" Killashandra fired the question right back at him.

"Wasn't allowed to continue as an instrumentalist. Not enough openings on my mudball for a string player. Crystal singing's the next best thing."

Killashandra nodded, looking to Jezerey.

"Curiously enough," the girl said with a bemused expression, "I was redundant in my profession, too. Limb-replacement therapist. And the Dear knows there're enough accidents on Salonika." She wrinkled her nose and then caught the puzzled expressions of Rimbol and Killashandra. "Mining world, asteroid belts around us and the next planet out. Next to mining, you might say replacement was our biggest industry."

"Space workers aren't apt to be redundant, either," Killashandra commented, looking at Rimbol.

"Carigana wasn't. Psyched out when her safety cable snapped—I get the impression she was deep-spaced a long time before they found her. She didn't say"—and Rimbol emphasized the last word—"but she's probably unstable for such employment."

Jezerey nodded sympathetically.

"Shillawn?" Killashandra asked.

"Told me he was a chemotech," Rimbol replied. "His project was finished up, and he was given an assignment he didn't like. Underground. He's a touch claustro! I think that's what makes him so nervous."

"And we all have perfect pitch," Killashandra said more to herself than the others because the phrases Maestro Valdi had spat accusingly, particularly the one about a "silicate spider," came appropriately to mind. She dismissed the niggling suspicion as invalid.

An explosive curse burst from one of the card players, and his earnest request for arbitration from any and all in the room interrupted their private conversation.

Although Killashandra took no part in the intense discussion that followed, she deemed it good sense to lend her presence to a group with whom she might be spending considerable time. She also saw them as a group with no other common factor—aside from the invisible prerequisite of perfect pitch—than age. All seemed to be within their third decade; most apparently just finished with tertiary education; no two from the same system or planet.

Killashandra remained on the fringes of the good-humored but volatile game discussion until she had finished another glass of the very good brew. Then she quietly retired, wondering as she prepared for sleep just how thirty-plus people from so many different planets had all heard of the crystal singers.

She had just finished her morning meal when a soft, deep chime brought her attention to the screen. She was requested to go to the lounge room.

"You sneaked away nice and early," a cheerful tenor said behind her. She turned to find Rimbol approaching, the awkward figure of Shillawn just behind him. "Missed the fun, you did."

"Who won the argument?" she asked after a courteous nod to Shillawn.

"No one and everyone. It was the arguing that was fun!" The red-headed lad grinned.

They had reached the lounge by then, and from the other corridors the rest of the successful filed, some re-forming the groups she'd noticed the previous evening. Only Carigana seemed apart; she sat on the back of one of the loungers glowering at everyone. Something about the angry girl was familiar to Killashandra, but she couldn't place what.

Just then, from the fourth entrance, limped a tall woman holding the left side of her long gown slightly away from her thigh. Her gaze swiftly scanned the room, counting, Killashandra thought, and made her own tally. Thirty-three. Out of what gross number of applicants, she wondered again, over the nine weeks Jezerey had said Borton had waited?

"I am Borella Seal," the woman announced in the clear, rich voice of a trained contralto. Killashandra regarded her with closer interest. "I am a miner of crystal, a crystal singer. Since I am recovering from an injury sustained in the Ranges, I have been asked to disclose to you the dangers of this profession." She pulled aside the long gown and revealed wounds so ugly and vividly contused that several people recoiled. As if this was the very reaction she had wanted, Borella smiled slightly. "I will expose the wound again for a specific purpose other than arousing nausea or sympathy. Take a good look now."

Shillawn's elbow nudged Killashandra, and she was about to give him a severe reprimand for such a private insult when she realized he was drawing her attention to Carigana. The girl was the only one who approached Borella Seal and bent for the close inspection of the long gashes scoring the upper leg.

"They appear to be healing properly, though you ought to have had them bonded. How'd you get 'em?" Carigana was clinically impersonal.

"Two days ago, I slipped on crystal shale and fell fifteen meters down an old worked face."

"*Two* days?" Anger colored Carigana's voice. "I don't believe you. I've seen enough lacerations to know ones as deep as these don't heal that much in two days. Why the color of the bruising and the state of the tissue already healed show you were injured weeks ago."

"Two days. Singers heal quickly."

"Not that quick." Carigana would have said more, but Borella Seal gestured dismissal and turned to the others.

"By order of the Federated Sentient Planets, full disclosure of the dangers peculiar to and inherent in this profession must be revealed to all applicants who have satisfactorily completed the initial examinations." She accorded them a slight nod of approval. "However, as is also permissible by FSP law, professional—problems—may be protected by erasure. Those to whom this practice is unacceptable may withdraw."

"How much is erased?" Carigana asked.

"Precisely one hour and twenty minutes, replaced by a recollection of oversleeping and a leisurely breakfast."

"On record?"

"If requested, the Guild supplies the information that a minor but inadmissible physical defect has been discovered. Few question the Heptite Guild." For some reason Killashandra thought that fact amused Borella. Carigana's frown had deepened. "Any objectors?" Borella asked, looking straight at the space worker.

When no other voice was raised, she asked them to file before the screen she then activated, giving their name and stating their willingness to comply with erasure. The process didn't take long, but Killashandra felt that she had taken an irrevocable step as her acceptance was officially and indisputably recorded.

Borella then led them down a short hall to a door, Carigana the first to follow. Her gasp and half halt as she passed the entrance forewarned the others but in no way prepared anyone for the display in that short corridor. On either side were bodies in clear fluid—all but one glinted as if coated with a silicon. The planes of the faces looked rock hard; limbs, fingers, and toes were extended as if solidified, and not by the rigor of death. The crystalline sheen couldn't be some trick of the light, Killashandra thought, for her own skin showed no change. What roiled her stomach were the facial expressions: three looked as if death had overtaken them in a state of insanity; two appeared mildly surprised, and the sixth angry, her hands raised toward some object she had been trying to grasp. The last was the most grisly: a charred body forever in the position of a runner, consumed by a conflagration that had melted flesh from bone.

"This is what happens to the unprotected on Ballybran. It could also happen to you, though every effort is made to reduce such risks to a minimum. If you wish to retire now, you are completely at liberty to do so."

"External danger does not constitute a Code 4 classification," Carigana said, her tone accusatory.

"No, it doesn't. But these are representative of two of the dangers of Ballybran which the Heptite Guild is required by Federated Sentient Planets to reveal to you."

"Is that the worst that can happen?" Carigana asked scornfully.

"Isn't being dead enough?" someone asked from the group.

"Dead's dead—crystal, char, or carrion," Carigana replied, shrugging her shoulders, her tone so subtly offensive that Killashandra was not the only one who frowned with irritation.

"Yes, but it is the manner of dying that can be the worst," said Borella in such a thoughtful way that she had everyone's attention. She accorded them the slightest smile. "Follow me."

The grim corridor opened on to a small semicircular lecture hall. Borella proceeded to a small raised platform, gesturing for the group to take the seats, which would have accommodated three times their number. As she turned to face them, a large hologram lit behind her, a view of the Scorian system, homing quickly on Ballybran and its three moons. The planet and its satellites moved with sufficient velocity to demonstrate the peculiar Passover of the moons, when all three briefly synchronized orbits—a synchronization that evidently took place over different parts of the parent world.

"The crystallization displayed in the corridor is the most prevalent danger on Ballybran. It occurs when the spore symbiont, a carbon silicate occurring in an unorthodox environment peculiar to Ballybran, does not form a proper bridge between our own carbon-based biological system and the silicon-based ecology of this planet. Such a bridge is essential for working on Ballybran. If the human host adapts properly to the spore symbiont, and I assure you it is not the other way round, the human experiences a significant improvement in visual acuity, tactile perceptions, nerve conduction, and cellular adaptation. The first adaptations are of immense importance to those who become miners of crystal, the crystal singers. Yes, Carigana?"

"What part of the body does the symbiont invade? Is it crystalline or biological?"

"Neither, and the symbiont invades cellular nuclei in successful adaptations—"

"What happens to the unsuccessful ones?"

"I shall discuss that shortly if you will be patient. As part of the cell nucleus, the symbiont affects the DNA/RNA pattern of the body, extending the lifespan considerably. The rumor that crystal singers are immortal is exaggerated, but functional longevity is definitely increased by fifty or more *decades* beyond actuarial norms. The adaptation provides an immunization to ordinary biological disease, enormously increasing the recuperative ability. Broken bones and wounds such as mine are, I warn you, part of the daily work of a crystal singer. Tolerance to extremes of heat and cold are also increased."

And pain, no doubt, Killashandra thought, remembering not only the test but Borella's lack of discomfort with her deep wounds.

Behind the singer, the holograms were now views of Ballybran's rugged terrain, quickly replaced by a time-lapse overview from one of the moons, so that the planet's twelve continents were visible in seconds.

"On the negative side, once acclimated to Ballybran and adapted to the symbiont, the singer is irreversibly sterile. The genetic code is altered by the intrusion of the symbiont into the nuclei, and those parts of the DNA spiral dealing with heredity and propagation are chemically altered, increasing personal survival traits as opposed to racial survival—a chemical alteration of instinct, if you will."

Carigana gave a pleased sound like a feline expression of enjoyment.

"The other, and basically the most important negative factor, is that a singer cannot remain too long away from Ballybran's peculiar ecology. The symbiont must recharge itself from its native place. *Its* death means the death of the host—a rather unpleasant one, for death from extreme old age occurs within a period inversely related to the host's elapsed lifespan."

"How long can a singer stay away from Ballybran without ill effect?" Killashandra asked, thinking of Carrik and his reluctance to return.

"Depending on the strength of the initial adaptation, and that varies, for periods of up to four hundred days. A singer is not required to be absent for longer than two hundred days on assignment off-planet. Two hundred and fifty days is suitable for leisure. Sufficient, I assure you, for most purposes."

Killashandra, seated behind the space worker, saw Carigana draw breath for another question, but Borella had changed the hologram to show a human writhing in the grip of a shaking fever, all too reminiscent of the hypothermia that had affected Carrik. The man was seized by massive convulsions. As the focus tightened first to his hands, then his chest and face, he aged from an athletic person in his third, possibly fourth decade, to a wrinkled and dehydrated, hairless, shrunken corpse in the time it took viewers to gasp.

"He was one of the first singers to make a successful symbiotic adaptation. He died, regrettably, at Weasust while setting up the black quartz relay station for that sector of the FSP. It was the first time a singer had been absent for a prolonged period but that particular danger had not yet been recognized."

"Did you know him?" Shillawn asked with a perception that surprised Killashandra, for she had wondered the same thing.

"Yes, I did. He trained me in the field," Borella replied, dispassionately.

Killashandra made some mental calculations and regarded the flawless complexion and erect figure of their mentor with surprise.

"Is that Milekey man still alive?" Carigana asked.

"No. He died during a major fault in the Range which bears his name."

"I thought this symbiont kept you from broken bones and wounds?"

"The symbiont provides increased recuperative ability but cannot replace a severed head on a body whose wounds have resulted in complete blood loss. For less drastic injuries—" and she pulled the gown aside from her left leg.

Rimbol's soft whistle of astonishment summed up Killashandra's amazement, too. They had all seen the purple bruising and lacerations: now the contusions were faintly yellow splotches, and the wounds were visibly closing.

"What about those for whom the symbiont doesn't work?" asked the undaunted Carigana.

"The main purpose of the intensive physical examination was to evaluate rejection and blood factors, tissue health, and chromosome patterns against those of the known successful adaptations." A graph appeared on the screen, the line indicating success rising triumphantly over the past three decades where it had hovered in minor peaks over a span of three hundred or more years. "Your tests indicate no undesirable factors evaluated against records now dating back over three hundred twenty-seven standard years. You all have as good a chance as possible of achieving complete acceptance by the symbiont—"

"The odds are five to one against."

Killashandra wondered if Carigana gave even the time of day in that same hostile tone.

"No longer," Borella replied, and a light appeared on the upward swing of the graph line. "It's now better than one out of three. There are still factors not yet computed which cause only partial adaptation. I am compelled by FSP law to emphasize that."

"And then?"

"That person obviously becomes one of the 20,007 technicians," Shillawn said.

"I asked *her*." Carigana gave Shillawn a scathing glance.

"The young man is, however, right."

"And technicians never leave Ballybran." Carigana's glance slid from Borella to Shillawn, and it was obvious what her assessment of Shillawn's chances were.

"Not without severe risk of further impairment. The facilities on Ballybran, however, are as complete as—"

"Except you can't ever leave."

"As you are not yet there," Borella continued imperturbably, though Killashandra had the notion the Singer enjoyed sparring with the space worker, "the problem is academic and can remain so." She turned to the others. "As I was about to point out, the odds have been reduced to three out of five. And improving constantly. The last class produced thirty-three Singers from thirty-five candidates.

"Besides the problem of symbiont adaptation required for existence on Ballybran, there is an additional danger, of the more conventional type." She went on less briskly, allowing her comments on the odds to be absorbed. "Ballybran's weather." The screen erupted into scenes of seas lashed into titanic waves, landscapes where ground cover had been pulped. "Each of the three moons contains weather stations, and sixteen permanent satellites scan the surface constantly.

"Scoria, our primary, has a high incidence of sun-spot activity." A view of the sun in eclipse supported that statement as flares leaped dramatically from behind the eclipsing moon's disk. A second occluded view showed the primary's dark blotches. "This high activity, plus the frequent conjunction of the moons' orbits, a triple conjunction being the most dangerous obviously, ensure that Ballybran has interesting weather."

A bark of laughter for such understatement briefly interrupted Borella, but her patient smile suggested that the reaction was expected. Then the screen showed a breathtaking conjunction of the moons' orbits.

"When the meteorological situation becomes unstable, even in terms of Ballybran's norms, the planet is subjected to storms which have rated the euphemism, mach storm. As the Crystal Ranges of Ballybran extend downward rather than up,"—the screen obediently provided a view from a surface vehicle traversing the down ranges at speed—"one might assume that one need only descend far enough below the planet's surface to avoid the full brunt of wind and weather. A fatal assumption. The Ranges constitute the worst danger." The view changed to a rapid series of photographs of people, their expressions ranging from passive imbecility to wild-eyed violence. "The winds of the mach storm stroke the crystal to such sonic violence that a human, even one perfectly adapted to his symbiont, can be driven insane by sound.

"The vehicles provided by the Guild for singers' use have every known warning device, although the most effective one is lodged in the bodies of the Singers themselves; the symbiont, which is more sensitive to the meteorological changes than any instrument man can create. Sometimes the human element overcomes the keen senses of the symbiont, and a singer is impervious to warnings.

"Such injury is the main reason for the tithe levied by the Guild on all active members. You may be certain of the best possible care should such an accident befall you."

"You said the symbiont increased recuperative ability for structural damage," the irrepressible Carigana began.

"A broken mind is scarcely a physiological problem. Within its scope, the symbiont is a powerful protector. It is not in itself sentient, so though it could restore damaged brain tissue, it cannot affect what man chooses to designate 'soul'."

Somehow Borella's tone managed to convey the notion that Carigana might not possess that commodity. Killashandra was not the only one to catch that nuance, which apparently eluded its intended target.

"How was the symbiont first discovered?" Killashandra asked, determined that Carigana was not going to dominate the session.

"By the first prospector, Milekey. He made a successful adaptation with the spore, considering the transition illness to be only some irritating infection."

"He wasn't the only one on that mission, according to the fax," Shillawn said.

"No, he wasn't, though the deaths of the other members of his geology team were not at first linked to Ballybran. Milekey made several excursions into the Ranges to examine crystal faces and cut new types for evaluation. He also helped develop the first effective cutter. His personal tapes indicate that he felt a strong compulsion to return to Ballybran frequently, but, at the time, it was thought that this was merely due to his interest in the crystal and the increasing uses to which it could be put. He also did not connect his ability to avoid the storms to the presence of the symbiont.

"This aspect was discovered when the transition disease struck cutter after cutter, leaving crystalized bodies similar to those in the hall."

"There's one that was charred," Rimbol said, swallowing against nausea.

"And that is the third danger of Ballybran. Fortunately not as prevalent these days since common sense and education in the use of equipment decrease the probability. The Crystal Ranges can build up localized high-voltage and sonic charges near which ordinary communits do not operate properly, nor do other types of electrical equipment, some of which are necessary to the operation of sleds and conveniences. Fireballs can occur. And, despite all the precautions, a singer can be volatilized. It is a danger we must mention."

"You say that those who do not make a good adaptation to the symbiont specialize in technical work—but what constitutes a poor adaptation?" Jezerey asked, leaning forward, elbows on her knees.

"Some impairment of one or more of the normal physical senses. But this is often coupled with an extension to the other senses not impaired."

"What senses?" Shillawn asked, his thin throat muscles working as if he had trouble getting the words out.

"Generally hearing is impaired." Borella gave a slight smile. "That's considered a blessing. No shielding has ever been invented to silence the full fury of a mach storm. Often eyesight increases into the ultraviolet or infrared spectra, with an ability in some to sense magnetic fields. Increased tactile sensitivity has enabled artistically inclined guildsmen to produce some of the most treasured art of modern times. There is, however, no way of predicting what form the impairment will take, nor what compensation will be effected."

"Have you pretty pictures of the victims?"

"The handicaps are rarely visible, Carigana."

"The handicap plus sterility plus immolation on a storm-lashed planet in exchange for a greatly increased lifespan? That constitutes the Code 4?"

"It does. You have thus been duly informed of the risks and the permanent alteration to your chemistry and physical abilities. Any further pertinent questions?"

"Yes. If you say there are more singers these days, how does that affect individual profit with so many cutting in the Ranges?" asked Carigana.

"It doesn't," Borella replied, "not with the expanding galactic need for the communications link provided only by black quartz from Ballybran; not when singers are capable, quick and cautious; not when there are people, like yourself, motivated to succeed in joining our select band."

Attuned as her ear was to nuances in vocal tone, Killashandra did not quite perceive how Borella could deliver such a scathing reprimand with no variation in the pitch or timbre of her voice. Yet a sudden flush of humiliation colored Carigana's space-tan skin.

"How often are there injuries like yours?" a girl asked from the back of the theater.

"Frequently," Borella replied with cheerful unconcern. "But I'll be back in the Ranges"—Killashandra caught the note of longing, for it was the first time emotion had shown in the Singer's contained voice—"in a day or two."

"Singing crystal is worth such risks, then?" Killashandra heard herself ask.

Borella's eyes sought hers and held them as a slow smile crossed her lips.

"Yes, singing crystal is worth any risk." The force of that quiet statement caused a silence. "I shall leave you to discuss the matter among yourselves. When you have made your decision, just follow me." She moved toward the door at the side of the platform. It opened and closed with a soft *whoosh* behind her.

Killashandra looked over at Shillawn and Rimbol, noticed that the others were seeking emotional support from their nearest neighbors. Carigana, deep in a sullen mood, was pointedly ignored. Killashandra rose to her feet with an energy that attracted all eyes.

"I made up my mind before I ever arrived," she said. "And I don't scare easily, anyhow!"

She strode down the steps toward the exit, hearing the movement of others behind her, though she didn't turn her head. A curious elation, tinged with apprehension and a certain fearfulness, seized her as she passed the portal. Then it was too late.

Killashandra wasn't sure what she had expected to find on the other side of the door panel. She half thought Borella might be present to see how many had not been deterred. Instead, she was surprised to find uniformed members of the FSP Civil Service, their faces and attitudes as grave as if they were at a disintegration or interment. The senior officer motioned her to follow the first person in line, a male who, in turn, gestured Killashandra toward another of the cubicles that seemed to infest all levels of the moon base. Behind her, she heard the surprised intake of breath of whichever candidate had directly followed her.

A slab table and two chairs occupied the small room. She moved toward one seat, but the officer's gesture stopped her.

"Bontel Aba Gray, Rank 10, FSP Civil Service, Shankill Moon Base, Ballybran, date 23/4/3308: applicant will present identity to the outlet, stating aloud name, rank, and planet of origin."

Only after Killashandra had disgustedly complied with the formality was she allowed to seat herself opposite Bontel Gray.

"Is it true that you have received physical, psychological, and aptitude tests under the auspices of the Heptite Guild?"

"Yes."

"You have been informed of the hazards involved in the Code 4 classification of the planet Ballybran?"

"Yes." She wondered how Carigana was accepting the additional aggravation. That is, if Carigana had passed through the door.

Gray then questioned her in depth on Borella's lecture. Each of Killashandra's answers was recorded—but for *whose* protection, Killashandra wondered. She was reaching her aggravation point when he stopped.

"Do you swear, aver, and affirm that you are here of your own free will, without let or hindrance, conditioning or bribery, by any person or persons connected with the Heptite Guild?"

"I certainly do so swear, aver, and affirm."

He glanced at the ident slot, which suddenly glowed green. Placing both hands on the table as if wearied by this duty, Gray pushed himself to his feet. "The formalities are now concluded," he said with a tight smile. "May you sing well and profitably."

The man remained standing as she rose and left. She had the impression, a sideways glance, that he unfastened his tunic collar, his expression sliding into regret as he watched her leave.

Borella was in the main hall, her eyes focused on each cubicle door as it opened and a recruit appeared. Killashandra noticed that just the faintest hint of satisfaction appeared on the woman's face as her entire "class" reassembled.

"A shuttle waits," she said, once more leading the way.

"When do we get this spore business done?" Carigana asked, striding ahead of two others to reach Borella.

"On Ballybran. We did, at one point, use an artificial exposure, but the effects were no less successful than the natural process. Generally, infection occurs within ten days of reaching the surface," she added before Carigana could inquire. "The adaptation process can vary—from no more than mildly uncomfortable all the way to dangerously febrile. You will all be monitored, naturally."

"But haven't you discovered which physical types are more apt to react severely?" Carigana seemed annoyed.

"No," Borella replied mildly.

Further questions from Carigana were forestalled by their arrival at the shuttle lock. Nor were they the only passengers—in fact, the applicants were apparently the least important, a fact that obviously caused Carigana to seethe. Borella casually motioned them all to seating in the rear of the vessel and slipped in beside a striking man whose garb of violently colored, loosely sewn patches suggested he might be a singer returned from holiday.

"Much of a catch?" His drawled question caught Killashandra's ear as she passed. It was almost as much of an insult as the expression in his eyes as he observed the recruits filing to seats.

"The usual," Borella replied. "One can never tell at this stage, you know."

The tone of Borella's voice made Killashandra stare over her shoulder at the woman. The depth and resonance was gone, replaced by a sharper, shrewish, yet smug note. So the impressing and impressive detachment of the successful singer, condescending to interpret the hazards of her profession to the eager but uninformed, was a role played very well by Borella. Killashandra shook her head against that assumption. The terrible lacerations on Borella's leg had been no sham.

"Crystal cuckoo?" "Silicate spider?" Had Maestro Valdi some measure of truth in his accusations?

Well, too late now—having sworn, averred, and affirmed, every opportunity to renege was behind her. Killashandra fixed her seat buckle for the weightless disengagement of the shuttle from moonlock.

Chapter 5

The journey was not long, and it was smooth, allowing Killashandra time for reflection. Was the shuttlecraft pilot a failed singer recruit? How poor an adaptation still allowed rank and status within the Guild structure? She suppressed the nagging fear of failure by remembering the graph, indicating the recent upswing of the incidence of success in symbiosis. She distracted her grim thoughts by cataloging the other candidates, determining in advance to stay well away from Carigana, as if the irascible woman would welcome a friendly overture. Rimbol, on the other hand, reminded her pleasantly of one of the tenors at her Music Center, a lad who had always accepted the fact that his physical and vocal gifts would keep him a secondary singer and player. At one point, Killashandra had despised the boy for that acceptance: now she wished she had bothered to explore how he had achieved that mental attitude, one she might be forced to adopt. She wondered if the tenor might not have done better, attempting to become a crystal singer. Why had so little been said at the Music Center about this alternative application of perfect and absolute pitch? Maestro Valdi must have known, but his only suggestion had been to tune crystal, not sing it.

She wished for the distraction of views of nearing Ballybran, but the passenger section had no port, and the viewscreen set over the forward bulwark remained opaque. She felt the entry into the atmosphere. The familiar shuddering shook all the passengers, and Killashandra felt the drag nausea and disorientation and the impression of exterior sound. She tried to recall the screen printout of the planet. The image that was brightest in her memory was of the conjunction of the three moons, not the continental masses of Ballybran and the disposition of the Crystal Ranges.

Concentrate, concentrate, she told herself fiercely in an effort to overcome entry side effects. She had memorized complicated music scores, which obediently rolled past her mind, but not the geography of her new home.

At this point, she could feel the retro blasts as the shuttle began to slow. Gravity increased, shoving her flesh against her bones, face, chest, abdomen, thighs—more a comforting pressure, like a heal suit. The shuttle continued to maneuver and decelerate.

The final portion of any journey always seems the longest, Killashandra thought as she grew impatient for the shuttle vibration to cease, signaling arrival. Suddenly, she realized that her journey had begun a long time before, with her passive trip on the walkway to the Fuertan space facility. Or had it begun the moment she had heard Maestro Valdi confirm the auditors' judgment of her career potential?

Forward motion ceased, and she felt the pressure pop in her ears as the entry was unsealed. She inhaled deeply, welcoming the fresher air of the planet.

"D'you think that's wise?" Shillawn asked from across the aisle. He had his hand over his nose.

"Whyever not? I've been on spacecraft and stations for too long not to appreciate fresh, planet-made air."

"He means, about the symbiont and its natural acquisition," Rimbol said, nudging her ribs with his elbow. He grinned with mischief.

Killashandra shrugged. "Now or later, we've got to get it over with. Me? I prefer to breathe deeply." And she did, as a singer would, from deep in her belly—her back muscles tightening, her diaphragm thickening until her throat, too, showed the distension of breath support.

"Singer?" Rimbol asked, his eyes widening.

Killashandra nodded, exhaling slowly.

"No openings for you, either." He made a sound of disgust. Killashandra did not bother to contradict him. "You'd think," Rimbol went on, "that with all the computer analysis and forecasting, they'd know up front instead of wasting your time. When I think of what—"

"We can leave now," Shillawn said, interrupting them with the peculiar tracheal gulp that characterized his speech.

"I wonder how many musicians make their way into this Guild by default," Killashandra muttered over her shoulder to Rimbol as they made their way out.

"Default? Or deliberately?" he asked, and prodded her to move forward when she faltered.

She had no time to think about "deliberately" then, for she had reached the disembarkation ramp and had her first glimpse of Ballybran's green-purple hills on one side and the uncompromising cubes of buildings on the other. Then she was inside the reception area where personal effects were being wafted up on a null-grav column.

"After recruits have collected their baggage, they will please follow the—ah—dark gray stripe." A voice issued from speaker grills. "Room assignments will be given at the reception lounge. You are now designated as Class 895 and will answer to any announcements prefaced by that number. Again, recruits now arriving by shuttle from Shankill Moon Base are designated Class 895. Proceed, Class 895, along the corridor marked with the dark gray stripe for room assignments."

"Couldn't care less, could he?" Rimbol said to Killashandra as he slung a battered carisak over one shoulder.

"There's the guide line." Killashandra pointed at the wall of the far lefthand corridor. "And Carigana's ahead by half a light-year." She watched as the girl's figure marched purposefully out of sight up the ascending rampway.

"Surprised?" Rimbol asked. "Hope we don't have to share accommodations."

Killashandra shot him a startled look. Even as a lowly student on Fuerte, she had had privacy. What sort of a world was his Yarro?

The other shuttle passengers had quickly dispersed, Borella and her companion taking the far right ramp, while the center two received the bulk of the arrivals.

"You'd think with all the color available in the galaxy, they'd find brighter markers," Shillawn remarked gloomily when he caught up with Rimbol and Killashandra.

"Distinctive, if not colorful," Killashandra remarked, reaching the ramp. "Though there's a quality about this gray . . ." and she passed her hand across the painted line. "Textured, too. Hatch pattern."

"Really?" Rimbol touched the stripe. "Strange."

Carigana had already disappeared around the first curve of the ramp, but the three were otherwise the vanguard of Class 895. How dull to be designated by a number, Killashandra thought, having considered herself out of classrooms forever a scant few weeks before. And if they were 895, and the Guild had been operating for 400 standard years, how many classes did that make a year? Just over two? And thirty-three in this one?

Now that the first excitement of landing on Ballybran had waned, Killashandra began to notice other details. The light, for instance, was subdued on the rampway but had a clarity she hadn't encountered before. Rimbol's sturdy boots and Shillawn's shoes made no sound on the thick springy material that carpeted the hallway, but her slippers produced a quiet shuffling. She felt the textured band again, curious.

They passed several levels, each color coded in one of the dull chromatics, and Killashandra assumed there must be some reason for the use of such drab shades. Suddenly, the ramp ended in a large room, obviously the reception lounge for recruits—but it also held comfortable seating units, an entertainment complex, and across one end, audiovisual booths.

A dun-garbed man of middle years with a sort of easily forgettable face rose from one of the seating units and walked toward them. "Class 895? Your adviser am I, Tukolom. With me you will remain until adaptation and training have ceased. To me your problems and complaints you will bring. All members of the Guild are we, but senior in rank to you am I, to be obeyed, though harsh or unjust am I not."

His smile, meant to be reassuring, Killashandra knew, barely lighted his eyes and did not rouse any friendliness in her, though she saw Shillawn return the grin.

"Small class though this be, your quarters are here. Kindly to leave what you have brought in any room of your choosing and join in food and drink. To begin the work tomorrow. To orient yourselves in this facility today."

He gestured to the left-hand corridor leading off the lounge where open doors left patches of light on the textured carpet.

"Is only to put thumb print in door lock to receive privacy."

Others had arrived as Tukolom spoke, and while Killashandra gestured to her companions to proceed to the private rooms, he began his little speech all over again to the next batch. Rimbol pointed at the first door on the left, closed and red lighted to indicate the occupant did not wish to be disturbed. Carigana!

With a snort, Killashandra marched down the hall, almost to its end, before she indicated to Rimbol and Shillawn which room she intended to take. She saw them move for the rooms on either side of her. She pressed her thumb into the plate, felt the vibration as the print was recorded, and then entered the room, the door panel sliding soundlessly behind her.

"This facility has been programmed to respond to any change in your life signals," announced a pleasant voice, rather more human than mechanical. "You may program the catering units and audiovisual units and change any furnishing not to your liking."

"My liking is for privacy," Killashandra said.

"Programmed," the voice dispassionately replied. "Should your physical health alter on the monitors, you will be informed."

"I'll probably inform you," Killashandra muttered under her breath, and was pleased to hear no reply. Just as well, she thought. She tossed her carisak to the bed. Some people preferred to have a voice responding to their idle remarks: she preferred the sanctity of quiet.

Her quarters were as good as the guest facility in the Shankill Base, nothing gaudy but certainly substantial: bed, table, chairs, writing surface, tri-d screen, the customary audiovisual terminals, a catering slot convenient to the table, a storage closet. The hygienic unit was larger than expected, and it included a deep bath. She flipped on the small fax dispenser and watched as all varieties of bathing lotions, salts, fragrances, and oils were named as available.

More than pleased, Killashandra dialed for a foaming fragrant bath, at 35° C, and the tub obediently began to fill itself.

You never feel completely clean, Killashandra thought, as she undressed, using the spray cabinets on ship and station. You really needed to soak in the hot water of a full-immersion bath.

She was drying off in warm air jets when Tukolom announced it was his pleasure to meet Class 895 in the lounge for the evening meal.

Tukolom's curious syntax appeared to function only in spontaneous remarks. It was totally absent from the flood of information he imparted to them during that meal. He also refused to be deflected from his set passages by questions or to be diverted by Carigana when she anticipated his points.

Since it was obvious to everyone except Carigana that it was useless to interrupt Tukolom and since the food presented a variety of hot and cold dishes, protein, vegetable and fruit, the Class 895 listened and ate.

Tukolom discoursed first on the sequence of events to befall them. He stated the symptoms common to the onset of the symbiotic illness, occurring between ten and thirty days after exposure, beginning with headache, general muscular soreness, irritability, blurred vision, and impaired hearing. Such symptoms were to be reported to him immediately and the person afflicted to return to the room assigned, where the progress of the adaptation could be monitored. Any discomfort would be alleviated without affecting the course of the symbiotic intrusion.

"When rape is inevitable, huh?" whispered the irrepressible Rimbol in Killashandra's ear.

Meanwhile, Class 895 would have orientation courses on the history and geography of Ballybran, instruction in the piloting of ground-effects craft, meteorology lectures, and survival techniques. The class would also be requested to perform duties within the Guild relevant to the preservation of cut crystal and restoration of facilities after any storm. Normal work hours and days were in effect, which would allow ample time for recreation. Members were encouraged to continue any hobbies or avocations that they had previously enjoyed. Once members had been cleared for use of surface vehicles, they might take whatever trips they wished as long as they filed and had had approved a flight plan with control center. Special clearance and a proficiency test were required for the use of water vessels.

As abruptly as he had started his lecture, Tukolom concluded. He looked expectantly around.

"Is this the main Guild installation?" Carigana asked, caught by surprise at the opening.

"The main training area, yes, this is. Situated on the largest continental mass which bears the largest of the productive Crystal Ranges, Milekey and Brerrerton. The facility is located on the Joslin plateau, sheltered by the Mansord upthrust on the north, the Joslin discontinuity on the south, to the west by the White Sea and the east by the Long Plain. Thus, the installation is generally sheltered from the worst of the mach storms by its felicitous situation."

Tukolom had perfect recall, Killashandra decided: a walking data retrieval unit. Rimbol must have reached a similar conclusion, for as her eyes slid past his, she saw amusement twinkling. Shillawn, however, continued to look impressed by the man's encyclopedic manner.

"How many other settlements are there?" Borton asked.

"Learning tomorrow's lesson today a good idea is not," Tukolom pronounced solemnly. He then neatly avoided further questions by leaving the lounge.

"Aurigans are impossible," Carigana announced, frowning blackly at the departing figure. "Always dogmatic, authoritarian. Could they find no one else suitable as a mentor?"

"He's perfect," Rimbol replied, cocking his head as he regarded Carigana. "He's got total recall. What more could you ask of a teacher?"

"I wonder . . ." began Shillawn, stammering slightly, "if he had it before he . . . got here."

"Didn't you hear that Borella woman?" demanded Carigana. "Most handicaps are sensory . . ."

"At least his syntax improves when he recalls."

"Every other human species in the galaxy, and some not so human," Carigana continued undeterred, "can manage interlingual except the Aurigan group. It's a delusion on their part. *Anyone* can learn interlingual properly." She was swinging one leg violently; all the while the corners of her mouth twitched with irritation, and her eyes blinked continually.

"Where are you from?" Rimbol asked guilelessly.

"Privacy." She snapped the qualification curtly.

"As you will, citizen," Rimbol replied, and turned his back on her.

That was also an insult but not an invasion of Privacy, so Carigana had to be content with glaring about her. Class 895 averted its eyes, and with a noise of disgust, Carigana took her leave. The space worker had had a dampening effect on the entire group because suddenly everyone began to talk. It was Rimbol who dialed the first drink, letting out a whoop.

"They've got Yarran beer! Hey, come try a real drink!" He exhorted all to join him and before long had everyone served, if not with the Yarran beer he touted, at least with some mild intoxicant. "We may never get off this planet again," he said to Killashandra as he joined her, "but they sure make it comfortably homelike."

"A restriction is only restricting because you know it exists," Killashandra said. " 'Nor iron bars a prison make,' " she added, dredging up an old quote unexpectedly.

"Prison? That's archaic," said Rimbol with a snort. "Tonight let's enjoy!"

Rimbol's exuberance was hard to resist, and Killashandra didn't care to. She wanted to abandon her skeptical mood, as much because she didn't want to echo Carigana as to purge her mind of its depressions. There had been some small truth in the space worker's complaints, but blunt though Killashandra knew herself to be, even she could have made points more tactfully. Of course, the girl was probably on a psych-twist, from what Rimbol had learned of her. How had she passed that part of the Guild preliminary exams? More importantly, if Carigana was so contemptuous of the Guild, why had she applied for admission?

Conversations swirled pleasantly all around her, and she began to listen. The recruits came from varied backgrounds and training disciplines, but each and every one of them, geared to succeed in highly skilled work, had been denied their goals at the last moment. Was it not highly coincidental that all of them had hit upon the Heptite Guild as an alternative career?

Killashandra found that conclusion invalid. There were hundreds of human planets, moon bases, and space facilities offering alternative employment to everyone, that is, except herself and Rimbol. In fact, the two musicians could probably have taken on temporary assignments in their original fields. A second objection was that thirty-three people were an infinitesimal factor among the vast multitudes who might not have jobs waiting for them in their immediate vicinities. Colonial quotas were always absorbing specialists, and one could always work a ship one-way to get to a better employment market. She found the reflections a tri-fle unsettling, yet how could such a subtle recruitment be accomplished? Certainly no probability curve could have anticipated her crossing Carrik's path in the Fuertan space port. His decision had been whimsical, and there could have been no way of knowing that her aimless wandering would take her to the space port. No, the coincidence factor was just too enormous.

She sat for a few moments longer, finishing the Yarran beer that Rimbol had talked her into trying. He was telling some involved joke to half a dozen listeners. By no means as shy with drink in him and lacking his stammer, Shillawn was talking earnestly to one of the girls. Jezerey was half asleep, though trying to keep her eyes open as Borton argued some point with the oldest recruit, a swarthy faced man from Amodeus VII. He had his second mate's deep space ticket as well as radiology qualifications. Maybe the Guild needed another shuttle pilot more than they needed crystal miners.

Killashandra wished she could gracefully retire. She did not intend making the same mistakes with this group that she had in the Music Center. Carigana had already provoked dislike by her unacceptable behavior, so Killashandra had a prime example she was not going to emulate. Then she caught Jezerey's eyes as the girl yawned broadly. Killashandra grinned and jerked her head in the direction of the rooms.

"You can talk all night if you want to," the girl said, rising, "but I'm going to bed, and so is Killashandra. See you in the morning." Then she added as the two reached the corridor, "Shards, was I glad of an excuse. G'night."

Killashandra repeated the salute and, once in her room, gratefully gave the verbal order to secure her privacy until morning.

A curious glow at the window attracted her attention, and she darkened the room light that had come on at her entrance. She caught her breath then at the sight of the two moons: golden Shankill, large and appearing far nearer than it actually was; just above it, hanging as if from a different radius altogether, the tiny, faintly green luminescence of Shilmore, the innermost and smallest moon. She was accustomed to night skies with several satellites, but somehow these were unusual. Though Killashandra had never been off Fuerte before she met Carrik, she had had every intention of traveling extensively throughout the galaxy, as a performing soloist of any rank would have done. Perhaps it was because she might be seeing only these moons for the rest of her life that they now had a special radiance for her. She sat on the edge of her bed, watching their graceful ascent until Shilmore had outrun her larger companion and disappeared beyond Killashandra's view.

Then she went to bed and slept.

The next morning, she and the other recruits learned the organization of the Guild Complex and were obliquely informed that the higher the level, the lower the status. They were introduced rapidly to the geology of Ballybran and made a beginning with its complex meteorology.

Trouble started about midafternoon as the students were viewing the details of the Charter of the Heptite Guild as a diversion after meta-maths. Rimbol muttered that the Guild was damned autocratic for a member of the Federated Planets. Shillawn, swallowing first, mumbled about data retrieval and briefing.

It took a few moments before the import of the section dealing with tithes, fee, and charges was fully understood. With a growing sense of indignation, Killashandra learned that from the moment she had been sworn in at the moon base as a recruit, the Guild could charge her for any and all services rendered, including a fee of transfer from the satellite to the planet.

"Do they charge, too, for the damn spores in the air we're breathing?" Carigana demanded, characteristically the first to find voice after the initial shock. For once, she had the total support of the others. With a fine display of vituperation, she vented her anger on Tukolom, the visible representative of the Guild that she vehemently declared had exploited the unsuspecting.

"Told you were," Tukolom replied, unexpectedly raising his voice to top hers. "Available to you was that data at Shankill. The Charter in the data is."

"How would we have known to ask?" Carigana retorted, her anger fueled by his answer. "This narding Guild keeps its secrets so well, you're not led to expect a straight answer to a direct question!"

"Thinking surely you would," Tukolom said, unruffled and with an irony that surprised Killashandra. "Maintenance charges only at cost are—"

"Nowhere else in the galaxy do students have to pay for subsistence—"

"Students you are not." Tukolom was firm. "Guild members are you!"

Not even Carigana could find a quick answer to that. She glared around her, her flashing eyes begging someone to have a rejoinder.

"Trapped us, haven't you?" She spat the words at the man. "Good and truly trapped. And we walked so obligingly into it." She flung herself down on the seating unit, her hands flopping uselessly about her thighs.

"Once trained, salary far above galactic average," Tukolom announced diplomatically into the silence. "Most indebtedness cleared by second year. Then—every wish satisfy. Order any thing from any place in galaxy." He tendered a thin smile of encouragement. "Guild credit good anywhere for anything."

"That's not much consolation for being stuck on this planet for the rest of your life," Carigana replied with a snarl.

Once she had absorbed the initial shock, Killashandra was willing to admit that the Guild method was fair. Its members must be furnished with private quarters, food, clothing, personal necessities, and medical care. Some of the specialists, the singers especially, had a further initial outlay for equipment. The cost of the flitter craft used by crystal singers in the Ranges was staggering; the sonic cutting gear that had to be tuned to the user was also expensive and a variety of other items whose purpose was not yet known to her were basic singer's tools.

Obviously, the best job to have on Ballybran was that of a crystal singer even if the Guild did "tithe" 30 percent of the crystal cut and brought in. She duly noted the phrase, *brought in*, and wondered if she could find a vocabulary section in the data bank that would define words in precisely the nuance meant on Ballybran. Interlingual was accurate enough, but every profession has terms that sound familiar, seem innocuous, and are dangerous to the incompletely initiated.

A wide variety of supporting skills put the singers into the Ranges, maintained the vehicles, buildings, space stations, research, medical facilities, and the administration of it all. Twenty thousand technicians, essential to keep the four thousand or so singers working, and this very elite group was somehow recruited from the galaxy.

The argument over entrapment, as Carigana vehemently insisted on calling it, continued long after Tukolom left. Killashandra noticed him as he gradually worked his way from the center of the explosion, almost encouraging Carigana to become the focus, then adroitly slipped down a corridor. He's pulled the fade-away act before, Killashandra thought. Perversely, she then became annoyed because she and her group were reacting predictably; it was one thing to have a stage director prescribe your moves on stage, quite another to be manipulated in one's living. She had thought to be free of overt management, so she experienced a surge of anger. To rant as Carigana was doing solved nothing except the immediate release of an energy and purpose that could be used to better advantage.

Ignoring Carigana's continuing harangue, Killashandra quietly moved to a small terminal and asked for a review of the Charter. After a few moment's study, she left the machine. There was no legal way in which one could relinquish membership in the Heptite Guild except by dying. Even in sickness, mental or physical, the Guild had complete protective authority over every member so sworn, averred, and affirmed. Now she appreciated the FSP officials and the elaborate rigmarole. On the other hand, she had been *told*; she could have withdrawn after full disclosure if she hadn't been so eager to flaunt Maestro Valdi and prove to Andurs that she'd be right as a crystal singer. The section on the Guild's responsibilities to the individual member was clear. Killashandra could see definite advantages, including the ones that had lured her to Ballybran. If she became a crystal singer . . . She preferred "singer" to the Guild's dull job description, "cutter."

"Ever the optimist, Killa?" Rimbol asked. He must have been standing behind her a while.

"Well, I prefer that role to hers." She inclined her head sharply in Carigana's direction. "She's beating her gums over ways to break a contract that we were warned was irrevocable."

"D'you suppose they count on our being obstinate by nature?"

"Obviously, they have psychologists among the membership." Killashandra laughed. "You want what you can't or shouldn't have or are denied. Human nature."

"Will we still be human after symbiosis?" Rimbol wondered aloud, cocking his head to one side, his eyes narrow with speculation.

"I can't say as I'd like Borella for an intimate friend," Killashandra began.

"Nor I." Rimbol's laugh was infectious.

"I did hear her come out with a very human, snide comment on the shuttle."

"About us?"

"In general. But I *liked* Carrik. He knew how to enjoy things, even silly things, and—"

Rimbol touched her arm, and the glint of his blue eyes reminded her of the look in Carrik's when they'd first met.

"Comparisons are invidious but . . . join me?"

Killashandra gave him a longer, speculative look. His gaiety and ingenuous appearance, his gregariousness, were carefully cultivated to counterbalance his unusual coloring. The expression on his face, the warmth of his eyes and smile, and the gentle stroking of his hand on her arm effected a distinct change in her attitude toward him.

"Guaranteed Privacy between members of equal rank." His voice was teasing and she had no desire to resist his temptation.

With Carigana's strident voice in their ears, they slipped down the corridor to her room and enjoyed complete Privacy.

The next morning Tukolom marshaled Class 895, some of whom were decidedly the worse for a night's drinking.

"Borton, Jezerey, also Falanog, qualified are you already on surface and shuttle craft. To take your pilot cards to Flight Control on first level. Follow gray stripe down, turn right twice, Guild Member Danin see. All others of this class with me are coming."

Tukolom led without turning to discover if he was being followed, but the class, sullen or just resigned, obeyed. Shillawn stepped in behind Killashandra and Rimbol.

"I figured it out," he said with his characteristic gulp. His anxiety to please was so intense that Killashandra asked him what he had figured out. "How much it will all cost until we start earning credits. And . . . and what the lowest credit rating is. It's not too bad, really. Guild charges at cost and doesn't add a tariff for transport or special orders."

"Having done us to get us here, they're not out to do us further, huh?"

"Well"—and Shillawn had to shuffle awkwardly to keep a position where his words would be audible only to Rimbol and Killashandra—"it *is* fair."

Rimbol shrugged. "So, what is the lowest Guild wage? And how long will it take to pay off what we're racking up just by breathing?"

"Well"—Shillawn held up his jotter—"the lowest wage is for a caterer's assistant and that brings in three thousand five hundred credits plus Class three accommodations, clothing allowance and two hundred luxury units per standard year. We're charged at the base-level accommodations, shuttle passage was only fifteen cr, but any unusual item from catering—except two beakers of beverages up to Grade four—is charged against the individual's account. So, if you don't eat exotic, or drink heavy, you'd clear off the initial levies at a c.a.'s pay in"—Shillawn had to skip after them as he glanced down at his jotter and lost his stride—"in seven months, two weeks and five days' standard."

Rimbol caught Killashandra's eye, and she could see that the young Yarran was hard put to suppress his laughter.

"Why did you only consider the lowest-paid member, Shillawn?" she asked, managing to keep her voice level.

"Well, that was practical."

"You mean, you didn't compute any of the higher grades?"

"The highest-paid position is that of the Guild Master, and such information is not available."

"You did try?" Now it was Killashandra's turn to have to skip ahead or be overrun by Shillawn's long legs.

"I wanted to see just what areas are open to the average member . . ."

"How high could you retrieve data?"

"That's the good part," Shillawn beamed down at them. "The next rank after Guild Master is crystal cutter—singer, I mean. Only the credit varies too erratically, depending as it does on how much usable crystal a cutter brings in."

"If crystal singers are second, who's third in rank?"

"Chief of Research, Chief of Control, and Chief of Marketing. All on equal rating."

"Credit per year?"

"Their base pay is 300,000 pgy, plus living, entertainment, travel, and personal allowances 'to be determined'."

The base figure was sufficient to draw an appreciative whistle from Rimbol.

"And, of course, you're going to be Chief of Control, I expect," a new voice said and the three friends realized that Carigana had been listening.

Shillawn flushed at her sarcasm.

"And you'll be chief rant-and-raver," Rimbol said, unexpectedly acerbic, his blue eyes signaling dislike.

Carigana flipped her thumbnail at him and strode on, head high, shoulders and back stiffly straight.

"Any sympathy I had for that woman is fast giving place to total antipathy," Rimbol said, making an even more insulting gesture at the space worker's back.

With her head start on the rest of Class 895, Carigana was first to reach the ground-craft depot, but she had to wait until the flight officer checked in all thirty. They were taken to a large section inside a gigantic Hangar that housed three vehicles on simulation stands. The first was a skimmer, the general workcraft, which could be adapted for variations of atmosphere and gravity and could be driven by children. A single bar controlled forward, reverse, and side movement. The skimmer had no great speed but plowed its air cushion with equal efficiency over land, water, snow, mud, ice, sand, or rock. Its drive could be adapted to a variety of fuels and power sources.

The second stand simulated an airsled, not as clumsy as its name implied and capable of considerable speed and maneuverability. It was the long-haul craft, the crystal cutter's official vehicle, capable of delivering cargo and passengers to any point on Ballybran.

The third simulator was a satellite shuttle; it caused Rimbol's eyes to widen appreciatively, but Killashandra sincerely hoped she would not be asked to pilot it.

Though all were bored by waiting their turn, Killashandra had no trouble with the skimmer simulation. The sled was more complex, but she felt she acquitted herself fairly well, though she'd certainly want a lot more practice in the vehicle before flying any distance.

"You know who failed the skimmer test?" Rimbol asked, joining her as she emerged from the airsled.

"Shillawn?" But then she saw the gangly man still waiting on line.

"No. Carigana!"

"How could anyone not be able to fly a skimmer?"

"A skimmer needs a light hand." Rimbol's smile was malicious. "Carigana's used to a spacesuit. Ever noticed how she always turns her entire body around to face you? That's from wearing a servomech for so long. That's why her movements are so jerky—overcorrected. She overreacts, too. As we all know. Hey, we'd better scurry. Instructor Tukolom"—and Rimbol grinned at the title with which the flight officer had pointedly addressed their tutor—"says we're due back at the training lounge for the afternoon's entrancing lectures."

Carigana might well have been floating in deep space in a servomech suit for all the notice she gave to Tukolom's recitations on the care and packing of crystal cuttings. He informed Class 895 that they must pay strict attention to these procedures, as one of their first official tasks for their Guild would be to prepare crystal for export. As he spoke—he reminded them—crystal cutters were in the Ranges, making the most of the mild spring weather and the favorable aspects of the moons. When the cutters returned, Class 895 would be privileged to have its first experience with handling crystal, in all its infinite variety . . . and value.

The reverence with which Tukolom made the announcement showed Killashandra a new and unexpected facet of the humorless instructor. Did crystal affect even those who did not sing it? How long had Tukolom been a Guild member? Not that she really wanted to know. She was just intrigued by his uncharacteristic radiance when discussing, of *all* the dull subjects, the packing of crystal.

As soon as Tukolom released the class from the lecture, she murmured something about returning in a moment to Rimbol and slipped away to her room. She drew out the console and tapped the Flight Office, requesting the use of a skimmer for personal relaxation. The display spilled out a confirmation that she could use vehicle registry VZD7780 for two hours, confined to overland flight.

As she slipped from her room, she was relieved to see Rimbol's door open. He was still in the lounge, so she suppressed the vague disquiet she felt about sneaking off without him. Her first visit to the Crystal Ranges was better experienced as a solo. Besides, if Rimbol and Shillawn couldn't figure out how to obtain a clearance, they didn't deserve one.

The vast Hangar complex was eerily empty. A light breeze sighed through the vacant racks for singers' airsleds as Killashandra hurried to the skimmer section. An airsled engine revved unexpectedly and caused her to leap inches off the plascrete surface; then she saw the cluster of mechanics on the far side of the building, where lights exposed the sled's drive section.

Killashandra finally located the VZD rack and her assigned craft at the top of the skimmer section. The vehicle was sand-scraped, although the plasglas bubble was relatively unscathed. She climbed in, backed the skimmer carefully clear of the rack, and proceeded from the Hangar at a sedate pace.

"Pilot may fly only in area designated on master chart," a mechanical voice announced; to her left, an opaque square lit to display an overlay of the Joslin plateau, the Guild Complex out of which a small flashing dot, herself, was moving.

"Pilot complies."

"Weather alert must be obeyed by immediate return to Hangar. Weather holding clear and mild: no storm warning presently in effect." As she cleared the Hangar, she noticed three figures emerge from the ramp. She chuckled—she'd got her skimmer first.

She didn't want to be followed, so she pushed the control bar forward for maximum speed. The master chart cut off just at the fringe of the Milekey Range to the northeast but close enough for her to see exactly what she had mortgaged her life for. It was suddenly very necessary to Killashandra to stand on the edge of this possible future of hers; to be close to it; to make it more vivid than Tukolom's carefully recited lessons; to make her understand why Borella had smiled in longing.

The old skimmer didn't like being pushed to maximum speed and vibrated unpleasantly. None of the function dials were in the red, so Killashandra ignored the shaking, keeping on the northeasterly course. The Brerrerton Range would have been closer, almost directly south, but Milekey had been the range Carrik frequently mentioned, and her choice had been subconsciously affected by him. Well, the others were certain to head to the nearer range, which was fine by her.

Once she had bounced over the first hill, Killashandra saw the smudge of the Range, occasionally reflecting the westering sun. Beneath her, the dull gray-green shrub and ground cover of Ballybran passed without change. Dull exteriors so often hid treasures. Who could ever have thought Ballybran worth half credit? She recalled the model of the planet that Borella had shown them on Shankill. It was as if cosmic hands had taken the world and twisted it so that the softer interior material had been forced through the crust, forming the jagged ranges that bore crystal, and then capriciously the same hands had yanked the misshapen spheres out, the ridges falling inward.

The plain gave way to a series of deep gullies that in a wetter season, might have become streams. The first of the jagged upthrusts coincided with the edge of her chart, so she settled the skimmer on the largest promontory and got out.

To either side and before her, the planet's folds stretched, each cline peering through a gap or a few meters higher than the one before. Shading her eyes, she strained to see any evidence of the shining crystal that was the hidden and unique wealth of such an uninviting planet.

The silence was all but complete, the merest whisper of sound, not wind, and transmitted not through the atmosphere but through the rock under her feet. A strange sound to be experienced so, as if her heel were responding to a vibration to which her keen ears, expectant, were not attuned. Not precisely comprehending the urge to test the curious unsilence, Killashandra drew a deep breath and expelled it on a fine clear E.

The single note echoed back to her ears and through her heels, the resonance coursing to her nerve ends, leaving behind, as the sound died away, a pleasurable sensation that caressed her nervous system. She stood entranced but hesitated to repeat the experience, so she scanned the dirty, unpretentious mounds. Now she was willing to believe what Carrik had said and, equally, was credulous of the hazards attached. The two facets of singing crystal were linked: the good and bad, the difficult, the ecstatic.

She quickly discarded a notion to fly deeper into the Range. Common sense told her that any crystal in the immediate vicinity would long since have been removed. A more practical restraint was Killashandra's recognition that it would be easy to lose oneself beyond the curiously reassuring flatness of the plain and the sight of the White Sea. However, she did skim along the first ridges, always keeping the plain in sight and at the edge of her flight chart. The undulating hills fascinated her as the sharper, young thrusts and anticlines of Fuerte had not. Ballybran's ranges tempted, taunted, tantalized, hiding wealth produced by titanic forces boiling from the molten core of the planet: a wealth created by the technical needs of an ever-expanding galactic population and found on an ancient world with no other resources to commend it. That was ever the way of technology: to take the worthless and convert it into wealth.

Eventually, Killashandra turned the skimmer back toward the Guild Complex. She had renewed her determination to become a singer, which had been dampened somewhat by Tukolom and an instructional mode that subtly ignored the main objective of the recruits—becoming a crystal singer. She could understand why their initiation took the form it had—until the symbiosis occurred, no lasting assignments could be made, but other worthwhile skills and ranks could be examined. She sighed, wondering if she could sustain another defeat. Then she laughed, remembering how facilely she had shrugged off ten years' hard work when Carrik had dangled his lure. Yet, to be perfectly honest, he hadn't dangled: he'd argued against her taking such a step, argued vehemently.

What had she said to Rimbol about being denied making an object more desirable? And it was true that the maestro's histrionic condemnation of Carrik and crystal singers had done much to increase her desire. She had, of course, been so elated by her interlude with Carrik that the luxurious standard of living—and playing—to which he had introduced her had been a lure to one who had had no more than student credit. Carrik's fascinating personality had bemused her and given her the recklessness to throw off the restraints of a decade of unrewarded discipline.

Now that she had stood close to crystal source, felt that phenomenal vibration through bone and nerve, a call to the core of her that her involvement with music had never touched, she was strengthened in her purpose.

A lone figure was climbing about the skimmer racks when Killashandra returned. She noticed eight other empty slots as she parked her vehicle. The figure waved urgently for her to remain by her skimmer and quickly climbed up to her. Killashandra waited politely, but the man checked the registry of the skimmer first, then ran his hands along the sides, frowning. He began a tactile examination of the canopy without so much as glancing at her in the seat. He muttered as he made notations on his jotter. The display alarmed him, and for the first time he noticed her, opening the canopy.

"You weren't out long. Has something happened to one of the others? Nine of you went out!"

"No, nothing's wrong."

Relieved, he gave a pull to the visored cap he wore.

"Only have so many skimmers, and I shouldn't ought to've given out nine to recruits, but no one else requested."

Killashandra stepped from the skimmer, and the Hangar man was instantly inside, running fingers over the control surface, the steering rod, as if her mere physical presence might have caused damage.

"I'm not careless with equipment," she said, but he gave no indication he had heard.

"You're Killashandra?" He finished his inspection and looked around at her as he closed the canopy.

"Yes."

He grunted and made another entry on his jotter, watching the display.

"Do you always inspect each vehicle as it's used?" she asked, trying to be pleasant.

He made no comment. Was it because of her lowly rank as a recruit? A sudden resentment flared past the serenity she had achieved in the range. She touched his arm and repeated her question.

"Always. My job. Some of you lot are damned careless and give me more work than necessary. Don't mind doing my proper job, but unnecessary work is not on. Just not on."

A loud whine from the service bays startled Killashandra, but the Hangar man didn't flinch. It was then that she realized the man was deaf. A second ear-piercing whine erupted, and she winced, but it elicited no reaction from the man. Deafness must be a blessing in his occupation.

Giving the returned skimmer one last sweep of his hand, the Hangar man began to climb to check another vehicle, unconscious of Killashandra's presence. She stared after him. Had his job, his dedication to the preservation of his skimmers, supplanted interest in people? If she received deafness from the symbiont, would she detach herself from people so completely?

She made her way down to the Hangar floor, startled each time the engine being repaired blasted out its unbaffled noise. She might have renounced music as a career, but never to hear it again? She shuddered convulsively.

She had been so positive on Fuerte that hers was to be a brilliant career as a solo performer, maybe she'd better not be so bloody certain of becoming a crystal singer and explore the alternatives within the Guild.

Suddenly, she didn't want to return to the recruits' lounge, nor did she wish to hear the accounts of the other eight who had skimmed away from the Guild Complex. She wanted to be private. Getting out by herself, to the edge of the range, had been beneficial, the encounter with the Hangar man an instructive countertheme.

She walked quickly from the Hangar, caught by the stiff breeze and bending into it. The eastern sky was darkening; glancing over her shoulder, she saw banks of western clouds tinged purple by the setting sun. She paused, savoring the display, and then hurried on. She didn't wish to be sighted by the returning skimmers. Finally past the long side of the Complex, she struck out up a low hill, her boots scuffling in the dirt. A warm spicy smell rose when she trod on the low ground cover. She listened to the rising wind, not merely with her ears but with her entire body, planting her boot heels firmly in the soil, hoping to experience again that coil of body-felt sound. The wind bore the taint of brine and chill but no sound as it eddied past her and away east.

There the sky was dark now, and the first faint stars were appearing. She must study the astronomy of Ballybran. Strange that this had not been mentioned in the lectures on meteorology; or was it a deliberate exclusion since the knowledge would have no immediate bearing on the recruits' training?

Shanganagh, the middle moon, rose, honey-colored, in the northeast. She seemed almost to creep out, much as Killashandra was doing, to be away from the more powerful personality of Shankill and the erratic infringements of Shilmore. Killashandra grinned—if Rimbol were symbolized by Shankill, that would make Shillawn, Shilmore. Shanganagh was the odd one out, avoiding the other two until inexorable forces pulled her between their paths at Passover.

Shanganagh paled to silver, rising higher and lighting Killashandra's way until she reached the crest of a rolling hill and realized that she could walk all night, possibly getting lost, to no purpose. Student pranks had been tolerated, in their place, on Fuerte in the Music Center, but it would be quite another matter here where an old deaf Hangar man cared more for his vehicles than the people who used them.

She turned and surveyed the crouching hulk of the Guild, its upper stories lit by the rising moon, the remainder sharp black thrusts of shadow. She sat down on the hillside, twisting her buttocks to find some comfort. She hadn't realized how huge the Complex was and what a small portion of it was above the surface. She had been told that the best quarters were deep underground. Killashandra picked up a handful of gravel and cast the bits in a thin arc, listening to the rattle as bush and leaf were struck.

The sense of isolation, of total solitude and utter privacy, pleased her as much as the odors on the wind and the roughness of the dirt in her hand. Always on Fuerte, there had been the knowledge that people were close by, people were seeing, if not intently observing her, impinging on her consciousness, infringing on her desire to be alone and private.

Suddenly, Killashandra could appreciate Carigana's fury. If the woman had been a space worker, she had enjoyed the same sense of privacy. She'd never needed to learn the subtle techniques of cutting oneself from contact. Well, if Killashandra understood something of Carigana's antisocial manner, she still had no wish to make friends with her. She spun off another handful of dirt.

It was comforting, too, to know that on Ballybran, at least, one could take a nighttime stroll in perfect safety—one of the few worlds in the Federated Sentient Planets where that was possible. She rose, dusted off her pants, and continued her walk around the great Guild installation.

She almost stumbled as she reached the front of the building, for a turf so dense that it felt like a woven fabric had been encouraged to grow there. The imposing entrance hall bore the shield of the Heptite Guild in a luminous crystal. The tall, narrow window facing south gave off no light on the first level, and most were dark on the upper stories. She wondered which ratings were so low as to live above ground. Caterers' assistants?

Killashandra was beginning to regret her whimsical night tour as she passed the long side of the building, the very long side. Ramps, up and down, pierced the flat wall at intervals, but she knew from Tukolom's lecture that these led into storage areas without access to the living quarters, so she trudged onward until she was back at the vast Hangar maw.

She was very weary when she finally reached the ramp to the class's quarters. All else was quiet, the lounge empty and dark. Though Rimbol's door light was green, she hurried past to her own. Tomorrow would be soon enough for companionship. She went to sleep, comforted by the irrevocable advantage of privacy available to a member of the Heptite Guild.

Killashandra wasn't as positive of that the next afternoon as she struggled to retain her balance in the gusts of wind and, more importantly, tried not to drop the precious crate of crystal. The recruits had been aroused by the computer at a false dawn they had to take on faith. The sky was a deep, sullen gray, with storm clouds that were sucked across the Complex so low they threatened to envelop the upper level. The recruits had been told to eat quickly but heartily and to report to the cargo officer on the Hangar floor. They were to be under her supervision until she released them. Wind precautions were already evident; the 12-meter-high screen across the Hangar maw was lowered only to admit approaching airsleds; evidently the device was to prevent workers' being sucked from the Hangar by fierce counterdraughts.

Cargo Officer Malaine took no chances that instructions would be misunderstood or unheard. She carried a bullhorn, but her orders were also displayed on screens positioned around the Hangar. If they had any doubts as they assisted the regular personnel in unloading, the recruits were to touch and/or otherwise get the attention of anyone in a green-checked uniform. Basic instructions remained on the screen; updates blinked orange on the green displays.

"Your main assignments will be to unload, very, very carefully, the cartons of cut crystals. One at a time. Don't be misled by the fact that the cartons have strong hand grips. The wind out there will shortly make you wish you had prehensile tails." Cargo Officer Malaine gave the recruits a smile. "You'll know when to put on your head gear," and she tapped a closefitting skull cap with its padded ears and eyescreen. "Now"—and she gestured to the plasglas wall of the ready-room facing the Hangar—"the sleds are coming in. Watch the procedure of the Hangar personnel. First, the crystal singer is checked, then the cargo is off-loaded. You will concentrate on off-loading. Your responsibility is to transfer the crystal cartons safely inside. Any carton that comes in is worth more than you are! No offense, recruits, just basic Guild economics. I also caution you that crystal singers just in off the Ranges are highly unpredictable. You're lucky. All in this group have been out a good while, so they'll probably have good cuttings. Don't drop a carton! You'll have the singer, me, and Guild Master Lanzecki on your neck—the singer being first and worst.

"Fair does not apply," Malaine said in a hard voice. "Those plasfoam boxes"—and she pointed at the line of Hangar personnel hurrying to the cargo bay, white cartons clutched firmly to their chests—"are what pay for this planet, its satellites, and everything on them. No one gets a credit till that cargo is safely in this building, weighed in, and graded—Okay, here's a new flight coming in. I'll count you off in threes. Line up and be ready to go when called. Just remember: the crystal is important! When the klaxon sounds—that means a sled is out of control! Duck but don't drop!"

She counted the recruits off, and Killashandra was teamed with Borton and a man she didn't know by name. The recruits formed loose trios in front of the window, watching the routine.

"Doesn't seem hard," the man commented to Borton. "Those cartons can't be heavy," and he gestured at a slim person walking rapidly carrying his burden.

"Maybe not now, Celee," Borton replied, "but when the wind picks up—"

"Well, we're both sturdy enough to give our teammate a hand if she needs one," Celee said, grinning with some condescension at Killashandra.

"I'm closer to the ground," she said, looking up at him with a warning glint in her eyes. "Center of gravity is lower and not so far to fall."

"You tell him, Killa." Borton nudged Celee and winked at her.

Suddenly Celee pointed urgently to the Hangar. The recruits saw a sled careen in, barely missing the vaulted roof, then plunge toward the ground, only to be pulled up at the last second, skid sideways, and barely miss a broadside against the interior wall. A klaxon had sounded, its clamor causing everyone to clap hands over his ears at the piercing noise. When the trio looked again, the airsled had slid to a stop, nose against the wall. To their surprise, the singer, orange overalls streaked with black, emerged unscathed from the front hatch, gave the sled an admonitory kick, gestured obscenely at the wind, and then stalked into the shelter of the cargo bay. Then she, Borton, and Celee were being beckoned out to the Hangar floor.

As Killashandra grabbed her first carton from a singer's ship, she clutched it firmly to her chest because it was light and could easily have been flipped from a casual grip by the strong wind gusting about the Hangar. She got to the cargo bay with a sigh of relief, only to be stunned by the sight of the crystal singer, who was slumped against a wall while snarling at the medic who was daubing at the blood running down the singer's left cheek. Until the last carton from his sled was unloaded, the crystal singer remained at his observation point.

"By the horny toes of a swamp bear," Celee remarked to Killashandra as they hurried back for more cartons, "that man knows every narding *one* of his cargo, and he sure to bones knows we're doing the unloading. And the bloody wind's rising. Watch it, Killashandra."

"Only two more in that ship," Borton yelled as he passed them on his way in. "They want to hoist it out of the way!"

Celee and Killashandra trotted faster, wary of the hoist now descending over the disabled ship. No sooner had they lifted the last two cartons from the sled than the hoist clanked tight on its top. At that instant, Killashandra glanced around her and counted five more sleds wheeling in, fortunately in more control. Seven unloaded vehicles were heading to the top of the sled storage racks.

As the Hangar became crowded, unloading took longer, and keeping upright during the passage between sled and cargo bay became increasingly more difficult. Killashandra saw three people flung against sleds, and one skidded against the outer wind baffle. An incoming sled was caught in a side gust and flipped onto its back. Killashandra shook her head against the loud keening that followed, unsure whether it was the sound of the gale or the injured singer's screaming. She forced her mind to the business of unloading and maintaining her balance.

She was wheeling back from the bay for yet another load when someone caught her by the hair. Startled, she looked up to see Cargo Officer Malaine, who jerked the helmet from Killashandra's belt and jammed it atop her head. Abashed at her lapse of memory, Killashandra hastily straightened the protective gear. Malaine gave her a grin and an encouraging thumbs up.

The relief from the wind's noise and the subsidence of air pressure in her ears was enormous. Killashandra, accustomed to full chorus and electronically augmented orchestral instruments, had not previously thought of "noise" as a hazard. But to be deaf on Ballybran might not be an intolerable prospect. She could still hear the gale's shrieks, but the cacophony was blessedly muffled, and the relief from the sound pressure gave her fresh energy. She needed it, for the physical strength of the gale hadn't abated at all.

In the course of her next wind-battered trip, a wholesale clearance of sleds took place behind her back. The emptied sleds were cleared, and the newer arrivals slipped into the vacant positions. Some relief from the wind could be had by darting from the wind shadow of one sled to that of the next. The danger lay in the gap, for there the gale would whip around to catch the unwary.

Why no one was killed, why so few ships were damaged inside the Hangar, and why not a single plasfoam container was dropped, Killashandra would never know. She was at one point certain, however, that she had probably bumped into most of the nine thousand Guild members stationed in the Joslin Plateau Headquarters. She later learned her assumption was faulty: anyone who could have, had carefully contrived to remain inside.

The cartons were not always heavy, though the weight was unevenly distributed, and the heavy end always ended up dragging at Killashandra's left arm. That side was certainly the sorest the next day. Only once did she come close to losing a container: she hefted it from the ship and nearly lost the whole to a gust of wind. After that, she learned to protect her burden with her body to the wind.

Aside from the intense struggle with the gale-force winds, two other observations were indelibly marked in her mind that day. A different side of crystal singers, their least glamorous, as they jumped from their sleds. Few looked as if they had washed in days: some had fresh wounds, and others showed evidence of old ones. When she had to enter a sled's cargo hold to get the last few cartons, she was aware of an overripe aroma exuding from the main compartment of the sled and was just as glad that there was a fierce supply of fresh air at her back.

Still the sleds hurled themselves in over the wind baffle and managed to land in the little space available: the gale was audible even through her ear mufflers, and the force of the wind smacked at the body as brutally as any physical fist.

"RECRUITS! RECRUITS! All recruits will regroup in the sorting area. All recruits to the sorting area!"

Dazed, Killashandra swung around to check the message on the display screens, and then someone linked arms with her, and they both cantered into the gale to reach the sorting area.

Once inside the building, Killashandra nearly fell, as much from exhaustion as from pushing her body against a wind no longer felt. She was handed from one person to another and then deposited on a seat. A heavy beaker was put into her hands, and the noise-abatement helmet was removed from her head. Nor was there much noise beyond weary sighs, an occasional noisy exhalation that was not quite a groan, or the sound of boots scraping against plascrete.

Killashandra managed to stop the trembling in her hands to take a judicious sip of the hot, clear broth. She sighed softly with relief. The restorative was richly tasty, and its warmth immediately crept to her cold extremities, which Killashandra had not recognized as being wind sore. The lower part of her face, her jaw and chin, which had been exposed to the scouring wind, were also stiff and painful. Taking another sip, she raised her eyes above the cup and noticed the row opposite her: noticed and recognized the faces of Rimbol and Borton, and farther down, Celee. Half a dozen had black eyes, torn or scratched cheeks. Four recruits looked as if they'd been dragged face down over gravel. When she touched her own skin, she realized she, too, had suffered unfelt abrasions, for her numb fingers were pricked with dots of blood.

A loud hiss of indrawn breath made her look to the left. A medic was daubing Jezerey's face. Another medic was working down the row toward Rimbol, Celee, and Borton.

"Any damage?" Killashandra, despite her exhausted stupor, recognized the voice as that of Guild Master Lanzecki's.

Surprised, she turned to find him standing in an open door, his black-garbed figure stark against the white of piled crystal cartons.

"Superficial, sir," one of the medics said after a respectful nod in the Guild Master's direction.

"Class 895 has been of invaluable assistance today," Lanzecki said, his eyes taking in every one of the thirty-three. "I, your Guild Master, thank you. So does Cargo Officer Malaine. No one else will." There wasn't even a trace of a smile on the man's face to suggest he was being humorously ironic. "Order what you will for your evening meal: it will not be debited from your account. Tomorrow you will report to this sorting area where you will learn what you can from the crystals brought in today. You are dismissed."

He withdraws, Killashandra thought. *He fades from the scene. How unusual. But then, he's not a singer. So no sweeping entrances like Carrik or the three singers at Shankill, nor exits like Borella's.* She took another sip of her broth, needing its sustenance to get her weary body up the ramp for that good free meal. Come to remember, the last good free meal she'd had had also been indirectly charged to the Guild. She was, as it happened, one of the last of the recruits to leave the sorting area. A door opened somewhere behind her.

"How many not yet in, Malaine?" she heard Lanzecki ask.

"Five more just hit the Hangar floor, one literally. And Flight says there are two more possible light-sights."

"That makes twenty-two unaccounted—"

"If we could only get singers to register cuts, we'd have some way of tracking the missing and retrieve at least the cargo . . ."

The door swooshed tight, and the last of the sentence was inaudible. The exchange, the tone of it, worried her.

"Retrieve the cargo." Was that the concern of Malaine and Lanzecki? The *cargo*? Malaine certainly had stressed the cargo's being more valuable than the recruits handling it. But surely the crystal singers themselves were valuable, too. Sleds could be replaced—another debit to clear off one's Guild account—but surely singers were a valuable commodity in their own peculiar way.

Killashandra's mind simply could not cope with such anomalies. She made it to the top of the ramp. She had to put one hand on the door frame to steady herself as she thumbed her door open. A moan of weariness escaped her lips. Rimbol's door whisked open.

"You all right, Killa?" Rimbol's face was flecked with fine lines and tiny beads of fresh blood. He wore only a towel.

"Barely."

"The herbal bath does wonders. And eat."

"I will. It's on the management, after all." She couldn't move her painful face to smile.

After a long soak absorbed the worst fatigue from her muscles she did force herself to eat.

An insistent burp from the computer roused her the next morning. She peered into the dark beyond her bed and only then realized that the windows were shuttered and the gale still furious outside.

The digital told her that it was 0830 and her belly that it was empty. As she started to throw back the thermal covering, every muscle in her body announced its unreadiness for such activity. Cursing under her breath, Killashandra struggled up on one elbow. No sooner had she put her fingers on the catering dial than a small beaker with an effervescent pale-yellow liquid appeared in the slot.

"The medication is a muscle relaxant combined with a mild analgesic to relieve symptoms of muscular discomfort. This condition is transitory."

Killashandra cursed fluently at what she felt was the computer's embarrassingly well timed invasion of Privacy, but she drained the medicine, grimacing at its oversweet taste. In a few moments, she began to feel less stiff. She took a quick shower, alternating hot and cold, for unaccountably her skin still prickled from yesterday's severe buffeting. As she was eating a high-protein breakfast, she hoped that time would be allowed for meals today. She doubted that the rows of crystal containers could all be sorted and repacked in one day. And such a job oughtn't need the pace of yesterday.

Sorting took four days of labor as intense as fighting the storm wind, though presenting less physical danger. The recruits, each working with a qualified sorter, learned a great deal about how not to cut crystal and pack it and which forms were currently profitable. These were in the majority, and most of the experienced sorters directed a constant flow of abuse at singers who had cut quantities of the commodity then most overstocked.

"We've got three ruddy storage rooms of these," muttered Enthor, with whom Killashandra was sorting. "It's blues what we need and want. And blacks, of course. No, no, wrong side. You've got to learn," he said, grabbing the carton Killashandra had just lifted to the sorting table. "First, present the singer's ident code." He turned the box so that the strip, ineradicably etched on the side, would register. "Didn't have that little bit of help and there'd be war unloading, with cartons getting mixed up every which way and murder going on."

Once the ident number went up on the display, the carton was unpacked and each crystal form carefully put on the scale, which computed color, size, weight, form, and perfection. Some crystals Enthor immediately placed on the moving belts, which shunted them to the appropriate level for shipment or storage. Others he himself cocooned in the plastic webbing with meticulous care.

The sorting process seemed boringly simple. Sometimes it was not easy to retrieve the small crystals that had been thrust at any angle into the protective foam. Killashandra almost missed a small blue octagon before Enthor grabbed the carton she was about to assign to replacement.

"Lucky for you," the sorter said darkly, glancing about him, brows wrinkled over his eyes, "that the singer who cut this wasn't watching. I've seen them try to kill a person for negligence."

"For this?" Killashandra held up the octagon, which couldn't have been more than 8 centimeters in length.

"For that. It's unflawed." Enthor's quick movement had placed the crystal on the scale and checked its perfection. "Listen!" He set the piece carefully between her thumb and forefinger and flicked it lightly.

Even above the rustling and stamping and low-voiced instructions, Killashandra heard the delicate, pure sound of the crystal. The note seemed to catch in her throat and travel down her bones to her heels.

"It's not easy to cut small, and right now this piece's worth a couple of hundred credits."

Killashandra was properly awed and far more painstaking, risking her fingers to search a plasfoam carton that seemed heavier than empty. Enthor scolded her for that, slapping her gloves across her cheek before he tugged one of his off and showed her fingers laced by faint white scars.

"Crystal does it. Even through gloves and with symbiosis. Yours would fester. I'd get docked for being careless."

"Docked?"

"Loss of work time due to inadequate safety measures is considered deductible. You, too, despite your being a recruit."

"We get paid for this?"

"Certainly." Enthor was indignant at her ignorance. "And you got danger money for unloading yesterday. Didn't you know?"

Killashandra stared at him in surprise.

"Just like all new recruits." Enthor chuckled amiably at her discomfort. "Not got over the shock, huh? Get a beaker of juice this morning? Thought so. Everyone does who's worked in a gale. Does the trick. And no charge for it, either." He chuckled again at her. "All medical treatment's free, you know."

"But you said you got docked—"

"For stupidity in not taking safety precautions." He wiggled his fingers, now encased in their tough skin-tight gloves, at her. "No, don't take that carton. I will. Get the next. Fugastri just came in. We don't want him breathing down your neck. He's a devil, but he's never faulted me!"

"You're being extremely helpful—"

"You're helping me, and we're both being paid by the same source, this crystal. You might as well know *this* job properly," and Enthor's tone implied that she might not have as good an instructor in any other sector. "You might end up here as a sorter, and we sorters like to have a good time. What'd you say your name was?"

"Killashandra."

"Oh, the person who brought Carrik back?" Enthor's tone was neither pleased nor approving: he just identified her.

Obscurely, Killashandra felt better: she wasn't just an identity lost in the Guild's memory banks. People besides Class 895 had heard of her.

"Did you know Carrik?"

"I know them all, m'dear. And wish I didn't.—However, it's not a bad life." He gave another of his friendly chuckles. "A fair day's wage for a fair day's work and then the best possible domestic conditions." His grin turned to a knowing leer, and he gave her a nudge. "Yes, you might remember my name while you can, for you won't if you become a singer. Enthor, I am, level 4, accommodation 895. That ought to be easy for you to remember, as it's your class number."

"What was yours?" Quickly, Killashandra sought a way to turn the conversation away from his offer.

"Class number? 502," he said. "Nothing wrong with my memory."

"And you're not deaf."

"Couldn't sort crystal if I were!"

"Then what did the symbiont do to you?" She blurted it out before she realized she might be invading his privacy.

"Eyes, m'dear. Eyes." He turned and, for the first time, faced her directly. He blinked once, and she gasped. A protective lens retracted at his blink. She saw how huge his irises were, obscuring the original shade of the pupil. He blinked again, and some reddish substance covered the entire eyeball. "That's why I'm a sorter and why I know which crystals are flawless at a glance. I'm one of the best sorters they've ever had. Lanzecki keeps remarking on my ability. Ah, you'll shortly see what I mean . . ."

Another sorter, a disgruntled look on his face, was walking toward them with a carton and escorted by an angry singer.

"Your opinion on these blues?" The singer, his face still bearing the ravages of a long period in the Ranges, curtly took the container from the sorter and thrust it at Enthor. Then the singer, with the rudeness that Killashandra was beginning to observe was the mark of a profession rather than a personality, blocked the view of the sorter whose judgment he had questioned.

Enthor carefully deposited the carton on his work space and extracted the crystals, one by one, holding them up to his supersensitive eyes for inspection, laying them down in a precise row. There were seven green-blue pyramids, each broader in the base by 2 or 3 centimeters.

"No flaws perceived. A fine shear edge and good point," Enthor rendered his opinion in a flat tone markedly different from his conversational style with Killashandra. With an almost finicky precision, he wiped and polished a tiny crystal hammer and tapped each pyramid delicately. The fourth one was a half note, instead of a whole, above the third, and thus a scale was not achieved.

"Market them in trios and save the imperfect one for a show piece. I recommend that you check your cutter for worn gaskets or fittings. You're too good a singer to make such an obvious mistake. Probably the oncoming storm put you off the note."

The attempt at diplomacy did not mollify the singer, whose eyes bulged as he gathered himself to bellow. Enthor appeared not to notice, but the other sorter had stepped backward hastily.

"Lanzecki!"

The angry shout produced more than the swift arrival of Lanzecki. A hush fell over the sorting room, and the singer seemed unaware of it, his savage glance resting on Enthor, who blithely tapped figures into his terminal.

Killashandra felt a hand on her shoulder and stepped obediently aside to allow Lanzecki to take her place by Enthor. As if aware of the Guild Master's presence, Enthor again tapped the crystals, the soft tones falling into respectful silence.

Lanzecki was not listening: he was watching the dials on the scales. One eyebrow twitched as the half tone sounded and the corresponding digits appeared on the display.

"Not a large problem, Uyad," Lanzecki said, turning calmly to the flushed singer. "You've been cutting that face long enough to fill in half tones. I'd suggest you store this set and fill it to octave. Always a good price for pyramids in scale."

"Lanzecki . . . I've *got* to get off-planet this time. I have got to get away! I won't survive another trip to the Ranges . . . not until I've had time off this bloody planet!"

"This is but one carton, one set, Uyad-vuic-Holm. Your cargo has been very good according to the input here," for Lanzecki had made use of the terminal even as Uyad's manner changed from ire to entreaty. "Yes, I think it'll be sufficient to take you off-planet for a decent interval. Come, I'll supervise the sort myself."

Simultaneously, several things happened: working noises recommenced in the room; Lanzecki was guiding the distressed singer to another sorting slide, his manner encouraging rather than condescending, which Killashandra could not help but admire in the Guild Master; the other sorter had returned to his position. Enthor swiftly packed the offending pyramids, marked their container, and dealt it to a little-used slide above his head, then, seeing her bemused, gave her a friendly dig in the ribs.

"An even pace makes light of the biggest load. Another box, m'dear."

Even pace or not, they didn't seem to be making much of an impression on the mound of containers waiting to be sorted. What made a repetitive day interesting was the tremendous input of information Enthor divulged on crystal, grading, sound, and disposition. When he noticed she was taking a keen interest in the valuations, he chided her.

"Don't sweat your head remembering prices, m'dear. Change every day. Value's computed by the Marketing Office before we start sorting, but tomorrow, values might be totally different. One aspect of crystal's enough for me to cope with: I leave the merchandising to others. Ah, now here's beauty in rose quartz! Just look at the shading, the cut. Dooth's work, or I miss my guess," and Enthor peered at the carton, blinking his eyes for a lens change. "I don't. I'd know his cut among the whole roster's."

"Why?" Killashandra leaned closer to inspect the octagon. It was beautiful, a deep pale pink with a purple tinge, but she couldn't understand Enthor's enthusiasm.

The sorter took a deep breath as if to explain and then exhaled sharply.

"Ah, but if you *knew*, you'd have my rating, wouldn't you?" He blinked again and regarded her with a shrewd narrowing of his eyes.

"Not necessarily," she replied. "*I'd* prefer to sing crystal . . ."

Enthor looked from her to the rose octagon. "Yes, perhaps *you* would at that. However, I recognize Dooth's cut when I see it. When—if—you cut crystal, you will know crystal that is so fine, so rare."

With both hands, he laid the heavy jewel on the scale plate, running two fingers over his lips as he watched the configurations change and settle.

"I thought you said there was a surplus of rose crystal . . ."

"Not of this weight, color, or octagonal," he said, his fingers tapping out a sequence. "I happen to have heard"—and Enthor lowered his voice—"that someone very highly placed in the Federated Planets is looking for large pieces this hue." He lifted the octagon to the coating rack where the deep pink was swiftly cocooned from sight with plastic webbing, and at a touch of his finger on the terminal, an identifying code was stippled along the hardening surface.

At the close of the first day of sorting, Killashandra felt as tired as she had after unloading in the gale. She said as much as Shillawn and Rimbol joined her in a weary trudge to their lounge.

"We're getting paid for our efforts," Shillawn said by way of cheering them.

"Yesterday we got a danger bonus as well," Killashandra said, not to be outdone.

"Making use of the data banks, are you?" Rimbol asked, grinning at her with some malice. Killashandra hadn't admitted to him that she'd taken a skimmer out the evening before the storm, but he'd known.

"Told we were. Available to us is the data." Killashandra so aptly mimicked Tukolom's ponderous tones that she had the other two laughing. "I'm going for a shower. See you in the lounge later?"

Rimbol nodded, and so did Shillawn.

In the catering slot by her bed was another beaker of the lemon liquid. She drank it and had her shower, by the end of which she felt sufficiently revived to enjoy a quiet evening at dice with Rimbol and Shillawn.

Though no more peevish crystal cutters added excitement to the sorting routine during the next three days, Killashandra did have an unusual slice of luck. Halfway through the second day, Lanzecki and the handsome woman Killashandra guessed must be the chief marketing officer walked swiftly into the sorting room and marched right up to Enthor.

"Gorren's conscious. Muttering about black crystal. Have any of his cartons been released to you yet?"

"By my bones, no!" Enthor was shocked and amazed. Shocked, he later confided to Killashandra, that Gorren's cuttings had been stored separately and amazed because he hadn't known that Gorren had returned. He'd half expected to hear, Enthor continued solemnly, that Gorren had been one of the singers trapped in the Ranges by the storm. Gorren's black crystals were always entrusted to Enthor for evaluation.

A work force was hastily assembled in the sorting room, checking the labels of the many boxes still waiting evaluation. The group that had unloaded Gorren's ship—his had been the one to overturn—were identified and summoned. Fortunately, the handlers were regular Hangar personnel, and since they had known the cartons were Gorren's and valuable, they had placed them on a top layer, fifth stack, with buffering layers on either side.

Reverently, the eleven valuable cartons were handed down. Since it had been impressed constantly on Killashandra that very little could damage these specially constructed boxes or their contents, and she'd seen some of these same men indifferently lobbing cartons through the air to one another, she reflected that the presence of Lanzecki and Chief Marketing Officer Heglana had a salutary effect.

She was more surprised to see the two officials each take up a carton and was delighted when Enthor, his expression severe, pressed one firmly into her body, waiting until she had grasped the handles tightly.

Killashandra was elated by Enthor's confidence in her and walked the short distance back to the sorting room with the black crystal crammed against her breasts. Unaccountably, she was trembling with tension when she deposited her burden safely beside the others.

Later, she remembered that Enthor had moved with his normal dispatch to unpack: it was probably just because so many important people were watching and she herself caught their suppressed excitement that Enthor appeared to be dawdling. Tension can be transferred, and the sorting room was certainly crackling despite the hush. Those at nearby sorting tables had managed to be in positions to observe the unpacking, while those not directly in the Guild Master's view had suspended work completely, watching.

As Enthor lifted the first black crystal from its protecting foam, a sigh rippled through the watchers.

"Flipped right over, didn't he?" Heglana remarked, and made a clicking sound in her throat. Lanzecki nodded, his eyes on Enthor's hands.

The second black was larger, and to Killashandra's surprise, Enthor did not place it safely apart from the first but against the first where it seemed to fit securely. She felt a tingle at the very base of her head that spread upward across her skull. She shook her head, and the sensation dissipated. Not for long. A third, the largest crystal, fit against the second, a fourth and a fifth. The tingle in her head became a tightening of the scalp. Or was it her head bones pressing outward against her skin, stretching it?

"Five matched crystals. Gorren hadn't imagined it." Lanzecki's voice was level, but Killashandra sensed his satisfaction with such a cut. "Quality?"

"High, Lanzecki," Enthor replied calmly. "Not his best cut, but I dare say the flaws, minute as they are, will not impair the function if the units are not too far separated."

"Five is a respectable link," Heglana said, "for an interplanetary network."

"Where are the flaws? In the king crystal?"

"No, Lanzecki"—Enthor's fingers caressed the largest of the five as if reassuring it—"in the first and fifth of the cut." He gestured to either side. "Marginal." He deftly transferred the interlocking quintet to the scales and ordered his sequence. The display rested at a figure that would have made Killashandra exclaim aloud had she not been in such company.

Whoever Gorren was, he had just made a fortune. She mentally deducted the requisite 30 percent tithe. So Gorren had a small fortune, and there were ten more cartons to unpack.

Enthor removed the contents of three containers while Lanzecki and Heglana observed. Killashandra was somewhat disappointed by these, though the two watching nodded in satisfaction. The smaller units were not as impressive, though one set contained twelve interlocking pieces, the "king" crystal no longer than her hand at octave stretch and no thicker than her finger.

"He may be down to the base of this cutting," Lanzecki said as the fourth container was emptied. "Proceed, Enthor, but transfer the total to my office for immediate display, will you?" With an inclination of his head to Enthor, he and Heglana swiftly left the sorting room.

A universal sigh ran about the room and activity picked up on all the other tables.

"I don't think we've come to the prize yet, Killashandra," Enthor said, frowning. "The hairs on the crest of m'neckio . . ."

"The what?" Killashandra stared at him, for he was describing exactly her sensation.

Enthor shot her a surprised glance. "Scalp itch? Spasm at the back of your head?"

"Am I coming down with symbiont fever?"

"How long have you been here?"

"Five days."

He shook his head. "No! No! Too soon for fever." He narrowed his eyes again, turning his head to one side as he squinted at her. Then he pointed to the seven remaining containers.

"Pick the next one."

"Me?"

"Why not? You might as well get used to handling"—he paused, scrubbed at his close cropped hair—"crystal. Myself, I don't agree with Master Lanzecki. I don't think Gorren has come to the end of the black face he's been cutting. Gorren's clever. Just enough substantial stuff to get off-planet, and slivers now and then. That way he's got Lanzecki in a bind and a route off-planet any time he chooses. Pick a carton, girl."

Startled by the command, Killashandra reached for the nearest box, hesitated, and drawn by a curious compulsion, settled her hands on its neighbor. She picked it up and would have given it over to Enthor, but he gestured for her to place it on the table, its ident facing the scanner.

"So open it!"

"Me? Black crystal?"

"You chose it, didn't you? You must learn to handle it."

"If I should drop—"

"You won't. Your hands are very strong for a girl's, fingers short and supple. You won't drop things you want to hold."

Tension, like a frigid extra skin about her torso, crept down her thighs. She had felt this way, standing in the wings before an entrance in the Music Center, so she took three deep breaths, clearing her lungs and diaphragm as she would if she were about to sing a long musical phrase.

Indeed, when her questing fingers closed on the large soapy-soft object in the center of the plasfoam, she exhaled a long, low "ah" of surprise.

"NO!" Enthor turned to her in outrage. "No, no," and he darted forward, clapping his hand to her mouth. "Never sing around raw crystal! Especially"—and his tone was intense with anger—"near black crystal!" He was so agitated that he blinked his lens on and off, and the red of his unprotected eyes effectively cowed Killashandra. Enthor looked about him in a frenzied survey to see if anyone at the nearer tables had heard her. "Never!"

She didn't dare tell him at that juncture that the black crystal had vibrated in her hands at her spontaneous note and her finger bones had echoed the response of other segments still unpacked.

With an effort, Enthor regained his composure, but his nostrils flared, and his lips worked as he struggled for calm.

"Never sing or whistle or hum around raw crystal no matter what the color. I can only hope you haven't inhibited the magnetic induction of a whole ring linkage with that ill-advised—ah—exclamation. I'll say it was an exclamation if I should be asked." He let out one more unaspirated breath and then nodded for her to take out the crystal.

Killashandra closed her eyes as she freed the heavy block. Enthor was not going to like this if she had indeed blurred raw crystal. Told she had been and at some length and with considerable emphasis by Tukolom all about the subtle and delicate process by which segments of the black quartz crystal were subjected to synchronized magnetic induction, which resulted in the instantaneous resonance between segments as far apart as five hundred light years. The resonance provided the most effective and accurate communications network known in the galaxy. That she might have inadvertently damaged the thick block she now exposed to Enthor's startled gaze weighed heavily in her mind.

With an intake of breath for which she might have returned him his caution on sound, Enthor reverently took the dodecahedron from her.

"How many more are with it?" he asked in an uneven voice.

Killashandra already knew how many there should be. Twelve, and there were. She retrieved them from their webbing, handing them carefully to Enthor, though they were not as massive or tall as the king crystal. They fit as snugly to the central block as they had lived with it until Gorren had cut the crystals from the quartz face.

"Well!" Enthor regarded the matched set on the scale.

"Are—are they all right?" Killashandra finally found a contrite voice for the urgent question.

Enthor's little hammer evoked a clear tone that rippled from her ear bones to her heels, like an absolving benison. Even without Enthor's verbal reassurance, she knew the crystal had forgiven her.

"Luck, m'dear. You seem to have used the note on which they were cut. Fortunate for me."

Killashandra leaned against the sorting table to balance her shaky self.

"A set like this will provide a multiple linkage with thirty or forty other systems. Magnificent!" By this time, Enthor was examining the thirteen crystals with his augmented vision. "He cut just under the flaw," he murmured, more to himself, then remembered the presence of Killashandra. "As one would expect Gorren to do."

Brusquely but with precise movements, he put the crystals on the scale. Killashandra allowed herself an unaspirated sigh at the size of the huge fortune in credits Gorren had just acquired.

"Magnificent!" Enthor said. Then he gave a chuckle, his glance back at Killashandra sly. "Only Lanzecki will have the devil's own time persuading Gorren to cut anything for the next two galactic years. There's not that much black being cut. Being found. Still in all, that's Lanzecki's problem, not mine. Not yours. Bring another carton, m'dear. You've the knack of picking them, it seems."

"Luck," Killashandra said, regarding the remaining boxes, none of which seemed to draw her as that other had done.

She would rather have been wrong but the rest of Gorren's cut was unexciting. The small clusters, absolutely flawless, would be quite sufficient for the larger public entertainment units that provided realistic sensual effects, Enthor told her.

That night, most of the recruits insisted on her telling them about the black crystal, and Lanzecki and the chief marketing officer, for they had been unable to hear much and not permitted to stare. She obliged them, including a slightly exaggerated version of Enthor's dressing down that she felt would be salutary. Besides, the telling relieved the tension she still felt at how close she had come to buggering up enough credit to ransom a planet.

"What could they do to you if you had?" Shillawn asked, swallowing nervously as if he envisioned himself muffing it in a similar instance.

"I don't know."

"Something bizarre, I'm sure," Borton said. "Those singers don't spare anyone if their cuttings are mishandled. I was lucky enough to be the sorter who did Uyad's cut." Borton grinned. "I hid in the storage behind enough cartons, so I didn't get much of the back blast."

"So that's where you were," Jezerey asked, teasing.

"Bloody well told. I'm not here to bucket someone else's bilge."

Conversation continued about the variety of cuts and sizes and colors of the crystals from the Brerrerton and Milekey Ranges. Killashandra added nothing else, considering it more discreet to remain silent. When she could do so without attracting attention, she rose and went to her room. She wanted to think and recall the sensation of handling that massive black crystal. It hadn't been really black, not black at all, nor clear the way the rose or indeed any of the other crystals had been. She had accepted the designation at the time, for surely Enthor knew his crystals, and certainly the black quartz was different.

She tapped data retrieval for all information on black quartz crystal and specimens thereof. The data included black crystal in segmented units, none quite like the dodecahedron. Another display showed an octagon in its luminous, unchanged state, then the same form shading gradually to a matte black as it responded to thermal changes artificially induced. The data began to take up the lecture Tukolom had given, and she switched it off, lying back and recalling the sensation of her first contact with black crystal.

The next day, recovery teams brought in the cargo from sleds that had not reached the safety of the Guild Complex, and depression settled over the sorting room when the cartons, dinged, scarred, and discolored, were deposited on sorting tables. The mood was partially lightened when two containers disgorged some good triple and quadruple black crystal.

"What happens to them?" Killashandra asked Enthor in a low voice.

"To what?"

"The crystal of the singer who didn't make it."

"Guild." Enthor's terse reply seemed to imply that this was only fair.

"But doesn't a Guild member have the right to dispose of the . . . things of which he dies possessed?"

Enthor paused before opening the carton before him.

"I suppose so," he finally answered. "Problem is most singers outlive their families by hundreds of years; they tend to get very greedy; don't make many friends off-world and are unlikely to remember them if they have. I suppose some do. Not many."

Halfway through the next day, the backlog of crystal cartons having been substantially reduced, the recruits were assigned to help the Hangar crew clean and resupply the singers' sleds, for the storm was blowing itself out. There was some disgruntlement, but the Hangar officer hadn't the look of someone to antagonize. It seemed to Killashandra that discretion was necessary.

"I'm not going to clean out someone else's filth for the nardy day's credits that gives," Carigana said. "No one ever cleaned up for me in space, and I'm not doing it on the ground. Pack of vermin, that's all they are, for all their airs and arrogance." She glared at the others, daring them to follow her example. Her contempt as she walked off was palpable.

Remembering the state of some of the sleds, Killashandra would have been sorely tempted to follow—if anyone other than Carigana had set the example.

"We do get paid. And it's better than twiddling your fingers!" Shillawn caught at Killashandra's arm as if he had divined her thoughts.

"Doesn't matter to me," the Hangar officer went on, forgetting Carigana the instant she was out of sight, "but there is a bonus for every rank finished. The first eight are already done. Singers can make life intolerable for those who don't assist them. This storm is nearly blown out, and there'll be singers frothing to get into the Ranges. Met'll give 'em clearance by midday tomorrow. Get on with it. Get 'em cleaned and stocked and the singers out where they belong."

He resumed his seat at the control console, peering out at the vast orderly ranks of airsleds where the regular suppliers were already at work. He frowned as his gaze rested briefly on the undecided recruits; the grimace deepened as he saw a damaged sled being hoisted for repair.

"There must be some way the Guild handles dossers like Carigana," Borton said, squinting after the space worker. "She can't get away with it!"

"We don't have to clean up after a bunch of shitty singers," said Jezerey, her eyes flashing her personal rebellion. "I remember some of those sleds. Faugh!" and she pinched her nose shut with two fingers.

"I want a closer look at some of the equipment inside the sleds," Rimbol said, turning on his heel toward the sled racks.

"Closer smell, too?" asked Jezerey.

"You get used to any stinks in time," Rimbol said, waving off that argument. " 'Sides, it keeps my mind off other things."

"Those sleds will keep your mind off many things," Jezerey snapped back.

They were all silent a moment, knowing exactly what Rimbol meant. They were near the earliest day of onset of the symbiotic fever.

"We do get paid. And the Hangar officer mentioned a bonus . . ." Shillawn let his sentence fall off, swallowing nervously.

"Hey, you, there. You recruits. I could use some help."

A supplier, by the shade of his uniform, leaned out of an upper level. Jezerey continued to grumble, but she followed the others toward the array of cleaning equipment.

Not since Killashandra had left her family's small tree farm on Fuerte had she had to muck out on this scale. By the fifth sled, as Rimbol had suggested, she had become inured to the various stenches. It was also, as he had said, worth the chance to examine a crystal singer's airsled firsthand: at its worst and, after proper restoration, at its best.

The sled's control console took up the bow section, complete with pilot safety couch. Built into the couch's armrests were an assortment of manual override buttons. Alongside the main hatch were the empty brackets for the crystal cutter; the instruments were serviced after each trip to the Ranges. The main compartment was the singer's in-range living accommodations, adequate if compact. A thick webbing separated the forward sections from cargo storage and the drive section.

Her supplier, to give the ancient man his proper title, was so deaf that Killashandra had to shake him violently to get his attention. However, once she had asked a question (for his lipreading was good), she received an encyclopedic answer and a history of the particular sled and its singer. The fellow might be elderly, but he worked so swiftly that Killashandra was hard-pressed to do her share in the same time.

The supplier, for he admitted no name to Killashandra's polite inquiry, seemed to have a passion for orderly, gleaming, well-stocked vehicles. Killashandra wondered at his dedication since the order he cherished would so soon deteriorate to slime and shit.

"One can always get at crystal," the old man said. He invariably pointed out the five hatches: the one into the main compartment, the bottom through the drive area, and the two on either side and the top of the storage compartment. "Strongest part of the sled as well. On purpose, of course, since it's crystal is important. If a singer gets injured, or worse"—and he paused reverently—"especially if a singer's injured, the crystal can be salvaged, and he isn't out of credit. Singers get very incensed, they do, if they're done on crystal, you know. Maybe you will. You be a recruit, don't you? So this is all new to you. Might be the only time you see a sled. Then again, it might not—no, safety net is always fastened." He did the catches himself, a mild reproof to her quickness in stowing the empty crystal containers. "Can't have these, full or empty, bouncing about in flight or in a storm."

He consulted his wrist unit, peering around at the hatch to confirm the sled number.

"Oh, yes, special orders for this one. Never eats animal protein. Prefers nonacid beverages." He beckoned to Killashandra to follow him to Stores. He took her past the sections from which they had been restocking, and into a blandly pink section. She rather hoped the food wasn't the same color. It'd be enough to put her off eating entirely.

The sled's catering unit did not allow much diversity, but the supplier assured her that the quality was always the best that was obtainable even if the singers sometimes didn't realize what they were eating in the frenzy of their work.

Frenzy, Killashandra decided, was an inadequate description of the state in which most sleds had been left, though the supplier reminded her time and again that the storm that had forced all the singers in had caused some of the internal spillage.

After another wearying day, she had helped clean and stock ten sleds, three more, her supplier noted, than he would have been able to do himself.

Technically, the next day was a rest day, but the Hangar officer told the recruits that any who cared to continue would get double credit.

Shillawn shoved his hand up first; Rimbol, grimacing at Killashandra, followed with his; and she, perforce, volunteered as well. The Hangar officer, however, was surprised when all present signaled their willingness. He grunted and then went back into his office.

"Why did we volunteer?" asked Jezerey, shaking her head.

"Thoughts of double credits to be earned, staving off the pangs and uncertainties of debt!" Rimbol rolled his eyes. "My supplier had a thing about debt."

"Mine did, too," Killashandra replied.

"At this rate"—and Borton pulled across his shoulders at aching muscles—"we'll be ahead of the Guild even before we get the fever."

"They'll charge us for time off then without due cause," said Jezerey sourly.

"No," Shillawn corrected her. "All medical treatment is free."

"Except you don't get paid for work you can't do."

"May you never stand outside during a full Passover," said Rimbol, intoning his blessing in a fruity voice.

"I don't think I've worked this hard since I was a kid on my father's fishing trawler," Borton continued. "And fishing on Argma is done in the ooooold-fashioned way."

"Which is why you studied spaceflight?" asked Killashandra.

"Too right."

"Well, you're slaving again," said Jezerey, fatigue making her sullen.

"But we're Guild members," Rimbol mocked her.

"Reducing our initial debt," Shillawn added with a sigh of relief.

"All green and go!"

At Rimbol's quip, they reached the top of the ramp and the lounge. Rimbol made drinking motions to Killashandra, smiling wistfully.

"Not until I'm clean, really clean!"

"Me, too," Jezerey said, her whole body giving way to a shudder.

They all made for their private quarters. Carigana's redlit door caught Killashandra's gaze as she passed it.

"Don't worry about her, Killa. She's trapped by more than just the Guild," Rimbol said, taking her elbow to move her on.

"I'm not sorry for her," Killashandra replied, obscurely annoyed by herself and Rimbol's remark.

"No one's ever sorry about anything here," Shillawn commented almost sadly. "No one thanks anyone. No one has good manners at all."

This was very true, Killashandra thought as she wallowed in steaming-hot, scented water, scouring the stench of the day's labors from body and breath.

The matter of debt stuck in her mind, and the old supplier's obsession with it. She pulled the console before her as she lay languidly on her bed after her bath.

Suppliers earned more than caterer's assistants. And bonuses for speedy completion of their duty. She tapped for her own account and discovered that her labors were covering her living expenses and eating away at the shuttle fare. If she got double time for the next day and perhaps a speed bonus, she'd be clear of debt. It was only then that she remembered the two Guild vouchers. If she submitted them, she might even be able to pay for whatever equipment her postsymbiosis rank required. A soothing thought. To be one step ahead of the Guild. Was that what prompted the supplier?

Out of curiosity, she asked for a roster of the Guild in rank order. It began with Lanzecki, Guild Master, then the chiefs of Control, Marketing, and Research, and the names of active singers followed. That information wasn't in the form Killashandra wanted. She thought a moment and then asked for enlistment order. Barry Milekey was the first member of the Guild. The names, with the planet of origin, rolled past on the display. They must all be dead, she thought, and wondered that no such notation was made. Once a crystal singer, always a crystal singer? No, some of these must have been support personnel. *If* Borella's statistics were to be believed since the rate of adaptability to the symbiont spore had been low in the early days of the Guild. What did surprise her was that nearly every planet of the Federated Sentient Planets inhabited by her life form was represented on the Guild roster. Several planets had more than a fair share, but they were heavily populated worlds. There were even two Fuertans. That was an eye opener. What the listing did not show was when they had joined the Guild. The names must be listed in order of membership, for it was certainly not alphabetical. Borella's name flashed by, then Malaine's and Carrik's. She wondered if Enthor's had passed already but, on cue, his appeared. He originated from Hyperion, one of the first planets settled in Alpha Proxima in the Great Surge of exploration and evaluation that forced the organization of the Federated Sentient Planets. Was he younger than Borella, Malaine, or Carrik? Or had he joined as an older man? And the supplier, who wouldn't admit to a name—when had he joined? She shuddered. Sorter aptly fitted Enthor's skill, whereas supplier was a glamorous title for a job that could have been done mechanically and wasn't. Cutter, applied to a crystal singer, certainly didn't imply the rank the designation commanded.

She flipped off the console. Computers hadn't changed all that much since their invention; one still had to know what question to ask even the most sophisticated system. The Guild's tremendous data banks, using Ballybran crystals with their naturally structured synapselike formation, stored data nonvolatilely for indefinite retention, but Killashandra was far more adept at finding obscure composers and performers than galactic conundrums.

Later, she joined the others in the lounge for a few drinks, wondering if Shillawn had fathomed any startling interpretations from his time with the data banks. He was far too involved in figuring out a mechanical means of cleansing the sleds, and Killashandra was glad when Rimbol tapped her arm and winked.

"I think I'm too tired for much, Killa," he said as they reached his room, "but I'd like my arms around something warm, friendly, and in my decade."

Killashandra grinned at him. "My sentiments entirely. Can your account stand a Yarran beer?"

"And one for you, too," he replied, deliberately misinterpreting her.

They slept soundly and in harmony as if, indeed, the company kept was mutually beneficial. When the computer woke them, they ate heartily, without much conversation but still in accord, and then reported to the Hangar officer. As they were the first to arrive, the man looked with some anxiety back up the ramp.

"They'll be along," Rimbol told him.

"I've got sleds that must be ready by midday. You two start with these. Other numbers will come up on the display boards when I find out which flaming singers will lift their asses out of the racks today."

Killashandra and Rimbol hurried off, hoping to be out of his range if the other volunteers didn't arrive. They had cleaned and stocked eight sleds by midday. Numbers had disappeared periodically from the display, so Killashandra and Rimbol knew that other recruits had gone to work.

Almost at the stroke of 1200 hours, raised voices, echoing in the vastness of the Hangar, warned Killashandra and Rimbol of the influx.

"I don't like the tone of that," she said, giving a final swipe to the cutter brackets on the sled they had just readied.

"Sound of angry mob in the distance," Rimbol said, and pulling her arm, urged her into the stock rooms and behind a half-empty section where they had a view of the rack beyond them as well as the Hangar entrance.

Bangs, curses, metallic slammings, and the thud of plastic resounded. Drive motors started, too fast for such an enclosed space, Rimbol told Killashandra. She plugged her fingers in her ears. Rimbol grimaced at one particularly loud screech and followed her example. The exodus didn't take long, but Killashandra was wide-eyed at the piloting and wondered that the singers didn't collide with such antics. As abruptly as the commotion had started, it ended. The final sled had veered off to the Brerrerton Ranges.

"We did eight sleds?" Rimbol asked Killashandra. "That's enough at double time. Let's go. I've had enough!"

When they reached the lounge, it was empty. Carigana's door was red-lit and closed. Rimbol still held Killashandra's hand. Now he pulled her toward him, and she swayed against his lean body.

"I'm not tired now. Are you?"

Killashandra was not. Rimbol had a way about him, for all his ingenuousness and deceivingly innocent appearance, that was charmingly irresistible. She knew that he counted on his appeal, but as he didn't disappoint and gave no evidence of possessiveness, she complied willingly. He was like his Yarran beer, cool, with a good mouth and a pleasant aftertaste: satisfying without filling.

They joined the others as they straggled back to the lounge, consoling themselves for their scraped and solution-withered fingers with thoughts of the double credits accruing to their accounts.

"You know what the Guild can do, though?" Shillawn began, seating himself opposite Rimbol and Killashandra. He swallowed and then sipped at his own drink in quick gulps.

"Guild do what?" Borton and Jezerey asked, joining the others.

"About dossers like her." Shillawn nodded his head in Carigana's direction.

"What?" Jezerey asked, sliding into a lounger, her eyes bright with anticipation.

"Well, they can reduce her rations."

Jezerey didn't think much of that discipline.

"And other amenities can be discontinued at random."

"Such as?" Jezerey realized that Shillawn's face was contorted more by amusement than the effort to speak.

"Well, such as cold water instead of hot: the same with food. You know, the cold hot and the hot cold. Then the computer takes to making noises and shuffling the sleeping unit. Other furniture collapses when least expected, and, of course, the door doesn't always respond to your print. And," Shillawn was warming to the delighted response of his audience— "and since you have to print in for any meals, and it wouldn't be accepted"—he spread both arms wide and smirked again—"all sorts of insidious, uncomfortable, miserable things can happen."

"How in the name of any holy did you get the computer to tell you that?" Killashandra demanded. Her request was seconded by the others.

"Didn't ask the computer," Shillawn admitted, casting his eyes away from them. "I asked the supplier I worked with yesterday."

Rimbol burst out laughing, slapping his thighs. "The best computer is still the human brain."

"That's about all my supplier has left that's human," Shillawn said in a disgusted tone of voice.

"And that's happening to Carigana?" Jezerey asked, her expression hopeful.

"Not yet, but it could if she keeps up. Meanwhile, she's two days in debt for bed and biscuits, and we're four ahead."

"Yet Guild rules state—" Borton began.

"Sure"—and Rimbol chortled again—"but they haven't deprived someone of shelter or sustenance, just made them bloody hard to acquire or uncomfortable."

"I dread the thought of a future as a stockist or a supplier," Jezerey said, echoing the unspoken anxiety in everyone, judging by the gloom that settled over the quintet.

"Think positively," Shillawn suggested with a slight stammer that impeded the advice.

"Well, we ought to know fairly soon," Rimbol said. "We've been here eight days now."

"Almost nine." Shillawn's correction was automatic.

"Tomorrow?" Jezerey's voice held a tinge of horror.

"Could be much longer than ten days if I remember what Borella said about the incubation period," Shillawn reassured her in a mock cheerful tone.

"That's enough, friend," Killashandra said firmly, and drained her beaker. "Let us eat, drink, and be merry—"

"For tomorrow we die?" Rimbol's eyebrows shot upward.

"I don't intend to die," Killashandra replied, and ordered a double beaker of Yarran beer for herself and Rimbol.

They had quite a few refills before they went to bed together. As Killashandra woke in her own room, she assumed they'd ended up there, but Rimbol was gone. The light was far too brilliant for her eyes, and she dimmed the plasglas on the unshuttered windows. After the storm and its attendant hard labor, it was pleasant to look out on the hills. She scoffed at herself for missing "a view." The rain must have encouraged growth, for vivid reddish-purple blooms tinged the slopes, and the gray-green vegetation was brighter. Doubtless she would grow to love the seasonal changes of Ballybran. Until she'd gone with Carrik to see the sights of Fuerte, she hadn't quite appreciated natural scenery, too accustomed to the holograms used in performances.

Carigana was the first person she saw as she entered the lounge. Killashandra hoped the day would improve from that point. The space worker had an ability to ignore people, so that Killashandra was not obliged to acknowledge her presence. The woman's obstinancy annoyed her. No one had forced her to apply to the Heptite Guild.

The recruits were laggard, and by the time all had assembled, Tukolom was clearly impatient.

"Much to be done is this day," he said. "Basic lessons delayed have been—"

"Well, it will be a relief to sit and relax," someone said from the center of the group.

"Relax is not thinking, and thought must earnest be," Tukolom replied, his eyes trying to find the irreverent. "Geography today's study is. All of Ballybran. When adjusted you are, another continent may you be sent to."

Carigana's exaggerated sigh of resignation was echoed by others, though Tukolom stared only at her for such a public display of insolence. Carigana's vocabulary of monosyllables punctuated Tukolom's fluid explanations throughout the morning until someone hissed at her to stop it.

Whoever had organized the lecture material had had a sense of humor, and though Killashandra wagered with herself that Tukolom could not have been aware of the amusing portions of his rote discourse, she, and others, waited for these leavening phrases. The humor often emphasized the more important aspects of the lessons. Tukolom might be reciting what he had patiently learned or switching mental frames in an eidetic review, but he had also learned to pace his delivery. Knowing the strain of uninterrupted speaking, Killashandra was also impressed by his endurance.

"I wouldn't mind farming in North Ballinteer," Rimbol confided in her as they ate lunch during the midday break. "Nice productive life, snow sports in the winter . . ."

Killashandra stared at him. "Farmer?"

"Sure, why not? That'd be meters ahead of being a supplier! Or a sorter. Out in the open . . ."

"In mach storms?"

"You heard your geography lesson. The produce areas are 'carefully situated at the edge of the general storm belts or can be shielded at need'." Rimbol imitated Tukolom's voice and delivery well, and Killashandra had to laugh.

That was when she saw a group moving together with a menacing deliberation, closing off one corner and its lone occupant. Noting her preoccupation, Rimbol swiveled and cursed under his breath.

"I knew it." He swung out of his chair.

"Why bother, Rimbol? She deserves it."

"She can't help being the way she is. And I thought you were so big on Privacy on your world. On mine, we don't permit those odds."

Killashandra had to accede to the merit of that reply and joined him.

"What do I care about that?" Carigana's strident voice rose above the discreet murmur addressed to her by the group's leader. "And why should you? Any of you? They're only biding their time until we get sick. Nothing matters until then, not all your cooperation or attention or good manners or volunteering"—and her scorn intensified—"to clean up messes in sleds. Not me! I had a pleasant day—What?" She snapped her head about to the questioner. "Debit?" She tossed her head back and laughed raucously. "They can take it out of my hide—later. Right now, I can get anything I want from stores. If you had any intelligence, you'd do the same thing and forget that stuffed mudhead—"

"You helped unload crystal . . ." Killashandra heard Jezerey's voice.

"Sure I did. I wanted to see this crystal, just like everyone else . . . Only "—and her tone taunted them—"I also got wise. They'll work you at every mean, disagreeable, dirty grind they've got until the spore gets you. Nothing will matter after that except what you're good for."

"And what do you expect to be good for?" Jezerey demanded.

"Crystal singer, like everyone else!" Carigana's expression mocked them for the ambition. "One thing sure. I won't be sorting or supplying or mucking in mud or . . . You play along like good cooperative contributing citizens. I'll do what I choose while I still have eyes and ears and a mind that functions properly."

She rose quickly, pushing herself through the unsympathetic crowd, then pounded down the corridor to her room. The red light flashed on.

"You said something about Privacy?" Killashandra couldn't refrain from asking Rimbol as they turned desultorily away from the silent group.

"She does prove the exception," he replied, unruffled.

"What did she mean about a mind that functions properly?" Jezerey asked, joining them. She was no longer as confident as she had been when confronting Carigana.

"I told you not to worry about it, Jez," Borton said, coming behind her. "Carigana's got space rot, anyhow. And I told you that the first time I saw her."

"She's right about one thing," Shillawn added, almost unable to pronounce the 'th'. "Nothing really does matter until the symbiont spore works."

"I wish she hadn't said 'sick'," and Jezerey emphasized her distaste with a shudder. "That's one thing they haven't shown us . . . the medical facilities . . ."

"You saw Borella's scar," Shillawn said.

"True, but she's got full adaptation, hasn't she?"

"Anyone got headache, bellyache, chills, fever?" Rimbol asked with brightly false curiosity.

"Not time yet." Jezerey pouted.

"Soon. Soon." Rimbol's tone became sepulchral. Then he waved his hand in a silencing gesture and jerked his thumb to indicate Tukolom's return. He gave a heavy sigh and then grinned because he inadvertently echoed Carigana. "I'd rather pass time doing *something* . . ."

That was the unanimous mood as the recruits turned to their instructor. The ordeal of symbiotic adaptation was no longer an explanation delivered in a remote and antiseptic hall on a moon base: it was imminent and palpable. The spore was in the air they breathed, the food they ate, possibly in the contact of everyone they'd worked with over the past ten days.

Ten days, was it? Killashandra thought. *Who would be first?* She looked about her, shrugged, and forced her mind to follow Tukolom's words.

Who would be first? The question was in everyone's eyes the following morning when the recruits, with the exception of the obdurate Carigana, assembled for the morning meal. They sought each other's company for reassurance as well as curiosity. It was a bright clear day, the colors of the hills mellower, deeper, and no one raised any objection when Tukolom announced that they would visit the succession houses on the Joslin plateau where delicacies were grown.

When they arrived in the Hangar for transport, they witnessed the return of a heavy-duty wrecker, a twisted knot of sled dangling from its hoist. The only portion of the airsled that resembled the original shape was the storage area, though the under and right hatch were buckled.

"Do they plan all this?" Rimbol quietly asked Killashandra in a troubled voice.

"The recovered sled? Perhaps. But the storm—C'mon now, Rimbol. Besides, what function would such a display serve? We're stuck here, and we'll be singers . . . or whatever." Killashandra spoke severely, as much to reassure herself as Rimbol.

He grunted as if he had divined her anxiety; then jauntily he swung up the ramp to their transport vehicle without another glance at the wreck.

They sat together, but neither spoke on the trip, although Killashandra began several times to point out beautiful clusters of flowering shrubs with vivid, often clashing, shades of red and pink. The gray had completely disappeared from the ground cover, and its rich deep green was now tinged with brown. Rimbol was remote, in thought, and she felt that fancies about flora would be an invasion of his privacy.

The moist humidity and lush aromas of the huge hothouses reminded Killashandra of Fuerte's tropical area, and Carrik. The agronomist demonstrated the baffles that deflected the mach winds from the plasroofs as well as the hydroponics system that could be continued without human assistance. He also lectured on the variety and diversity of fruits, vegetables, grasses, lichens, fungi and exotics available to the Guild caterers. When he went on to explain that research was a part of the Agronomy Department, improving on nature wherever possible in sweetness, texture, or size, he led them outside the controlled-climate units.

"We must also improve on nature's whimsy," he added just as the recruits noticed the work crews and the damage to the next building.

Killashandra exchanged glances with Rimbol, who was grinning. They both shrugged and joined the agronomists in finishing the storm repairs.

"At least, it's only finishing," Rimbol muttered as he pressed a trigger on a screw gun. "What do they do when they haven't got three decades of recruits to fill up work gangs?"

"Probably draft suppliers and sorters and anyone else unoccupied. At least, here everyone takes a turn," she added, noticing that both Tukolom and the chief agronomist were heaving plastic as willingly as Borton and Jezerey.

"There, now, you can let go, Killa." He stood back to survey the panel they had just secured. "That ought to hold . . . until another boulder gets casually bounced off the corner."

Shielding her eyes from the glare of the sun to her left, Killashandra peered northerly, toward the Crystal Ranges.

"Don't even think about it," Rimbol said, taking her hand down and turning her. He gathered up his tools. "I wonder what's in store for us tomorrow?"

He had no banter on the return trip, nor had anyone else. Killashandra wished she'd thought to ask the agronomist about the ground-cover plants and shrubs. And amused herself by wondering if he bothered with such common varieties.

Tension put an effective damper on recruit spirits that evening, a damper unrelieved even by some moderate drinking. Rimbol, who had been the class wit, was not disposed to resume that mantle.

"Are you all right?" Killashandra asked him as he stared into his half-empty beer.

"Me?" He raised his eyebrows in affected surprise at her question. "Sure. I'm tired. No more than the accumulation of more hard work in the past . . . few days than I've had to do in years. Student living softens the muscles."

He patted her arm, grinning reassuringly, and finished his beer, politely ending that subject. When she returned with a refill of her own beaker, he was gone. *Well*, she thought sadly, *he has as much right to Privacy as I, and neither of us is good company tonight.*

Sleep did not come easily that night for Killashandra. She doubted she was alone in her insomnia, though that was no consolation. Her mind continually reviewed the symptoms Borella had described for the onset of the adaptation. Fever? Would she recognize one, for she'd never had a severe systemic illness. Nausea? Well, she had had bad food now and again or drunk too much. Diarrhea? She'd experienced that from overeating the first sweet yellow melons as a girl. The thought of being completely helpless, weak in the thrall of an alien invasion—yes, that was an appropriate description of the process—was abhorrent to Killashandra. Cold swept across her body, the chill of fear and tension.

It had all seemed so easy to contemplate on Shankill: symbiosis with an alien spore would enrich her innate abilities, endow her with miraculous recuperative powers, a much increased lifespan, the credit to travel luxuriously, the prestige of being a member of a truly elite Guild. The attractive parts of a felicitous outcome of her adaptation to the spore had, until this dark and lengthy night, far outweighed the unemphasized alternatives. Deafness? She wouldn't have sung professionally anyhow, not after what the judges had said about her voice, but the choice not to sing had to be hers, not because she couldn't hear herself. To be a sorter, like Enthor, with his augmented vision? Could she endure that? She'd bloody have to, wouldn't she? Yet Enthor seemed content, even jealous of his ability to value crystal.

Had she not desired to be highly placed? To be first sorter of the exclusive Heptite Guild qualified. How long would it take to become first sorter? With lives as long as those the inhabitants of Ballybran could lead?

How long would it have taken her to become a singer of stellar rank, much less solo performer anywhere, had her voice passed the jury? The thoughts mocked her, and Killashandra twisted into yet another position in which to find sleep.

She was well and truly caught and had no one to blame but herself. Caught? What was it the older singer had asked Borella on the shuttle? "How was the catch?" No, "Much of a catch?" "The usual," Borella had replied. "One can never tell at this time."

Catch? Fools like herself, warned by Carrik and Maestro Valdi, not to mention the FSP officials, were the catch, those who would trade solid reality for illusion—the illusion of being wealthy and powerful, feared, and set apart by the tremendous burden that came with crystal singing.

And no guarantee that one would become a singer! Carigana had been right. Nothing would matter until adaptation, for none of the lectures and work had been specifically oriented toward the role of the singer: nothing had been explained about the art of cutting crystal from the face, or how to tune a cutter, or where in the Ranges to go.

Tossing, Killashandra recalled the contorted features of Uyad, arguing for credit to take him off-planet: the stained singers stumbling from their sleds across the wind-battered Hangar—and the condition of those sleds that gave an all-too-brutal picture of the conditions that singers endured to cut enough crystal to get off the planet.

Yet Borella's voice had held longing when she spoke of returning to the Crystal Ranges . . . as if she couldn't wait.

Would singing crystal be analogous to having the lead role in a top-rank interstellar company?

Killashandra flailed her arms, shaking her head from side to side. Anything was better than being classed as an anonymous chorus leader. Wasn't it?

She rearranged her limbs and body into the classic position for meditation, concentrated on breathing deeply and pushing back all extraneous and insidious conjectures.

Her head was heavy the next morning, and her eyes felt scratchy in their sockets. She'd no idea how long she had slept finally, but the brightness of the morning was an affront to her mental attitude; with a groan, she darkened the window. She was in no mood to admire hillsides.

Nor was anyone else in a much better state, ordering their breakfasts quietly and eating alone. Nonetheless, Killashandra was disgusted not to have noticed the absences. Especially Rimbol's. Later, in a wallow of private guilt, she rationalized that she had been groggy with lack of sleep and certainly not as observant as usual. People were straggling into the lounge. It was Shillawn, stammering badly, who first noticed.

"Killashandra, have you seen Rimbol yet? Or Mistra?" Mistra was the slender dark girl with whom Shillawn had been pairing.

"Overslept?" was her immediate irritated reaction.

"Who can sleep through the waking buzz? He's not in his room. It's—too empty."

"Empty?"

"His gear. He had things when he came. Nothing's there now."

Killashandra half ran to Rimbol's room. It was, as Shillawn had said, very empty, without the hint of a recent occupation, antiseptically clean.

"Where is Rimbol, former occupant of this room?" Killashandra asked.

"Infirmary," a detached voice said after a negligible pause.

"Condition?"

"Satisfactory."

"Mistra?" Shillawn managed to ask.

"Infirmary."

"Condition?"

"Satisfactory."

"Hey, look, you two"—and Borton diverted the attention of the group waiting in the corridor—"Carigana's gone, too."

The forbidding red light on that door was off.

Shillawn gulped, glanced apologetically at Killashandra. Carigana's condition, too, was satisfactory.

"I wonder if dying is considered satisfactory," Killashandra said, seething with frustration.

"Negative," replied the computer.

"So we get whisked away in the night and never seen again?" Jezerey asked, clinging to Borton's hand, her eyes dark and scared.

"Distress being noted by sensitive monitors, proper treatment immediately initiated," Tukolom said. He had arrived without being noticed. "All proceeds properly." He accorded them an almost paternal smile that faded quickly to an intense scrutiny of the faces before him. Apparently satisfied, he beckoned them to follow him to the lounge.

"He makes me feel as if I ought to have come down sick, too," Jezerey murmured so that just Killashandra and Borton heard.

"I wish the hell I had," Killashandra assured her. She tried not to imagine Rimbol, tossing feverishly, or convulsed.

"Today concerns weather," Tukolom announced portentously and frowned at the groans from his audience.

Killashandra hid her face and gripped her fingers into fists until her nails dug painfully into her palms. And he has to pick today to talk about weather.

Some of what he said on the subject of meteorology as that science applied to Ballybran and its moons penetrated her depression. In spite of herself, she learned of all the safety devices, warnings, visual evidences of imminent turbulence, and the storm duties of Guild members—*all* available personnel were marshaled to unload singers' airsleds, not just unclassified recruits.

Tukolom then guided his meek students to the met section of the Guild control rooms, and there they were able to watch other people watching satellite pictures, moon relays, and the printout of the diverse

and sensitive instrumentation recording temperatures, suspended particles, wind speed and direction from the sensor network on the planet.

Killashandra didn't think much of herself as a met worker. The
swirling clouds mesmerized her, and she found it difficult to remember
which moon view she was supposed to observe. The computer translated
the data into forecasts, constantly updated, compared, overseen by both
human and machine. Another sort of symbiosis. One she didn't particularly care to achieve.

Tukolom shepherded them down to the Hangar again, to accompany
a maintenance crew to one of the nearby sensor units. They were filing
aboard the transport when Jezerey went into a spasm, dropping to the
plascrete, her face flushed. She moaned as a convulsion seized her.

Borton was on his knees beside her, but two strangers appeared as if
teleported, inserted her into a padded cocoon, and bore her off.

"Entirely normal are such manifestations of the adaptation,"
Tukolom said, peering into Borton's face as the man stared anxiously after
his friend. "Delay these technicians longer we may not."

"They don't bloody care," Borton said in a savage tone, bouncing into
the hard seat next to Killashandra. "She was a package to them. They're
glad to see us get sick."

"I'd rather come down than watch others," Killashandra replied, softening her voice out of compassion for his distress. She already missed Rimbol's irreverent comments and his sustaining good humor. Borton had
been paired with Jezerey all during their long wait on Shankill.

"Not knowing 'when' gets to you."

Borton stared out at the hills passing under the transport, immersed
in his concern, and she did not invade his privacy.

Jezerey's collapse cast a further pall over the remaining travel.
Shillawn, sitting across the aisle from Killashandra, swallowed with such
rhythmic nervousness that she couldn't look in his direction. The habit had
always irritated her; now it was a major aggravation. She looked in the
other direction past Borton, to the swiftly changing view. The colors of the
brush, the stunted trees, even the glancing lights the sun struck from exposed rock formations formed a delightful visual display. Though she had
always been acutely aware of stage motion, rhythm, and flow, Killashandra had not had much opportunity to view the natural state. The surface of
this rugged, unkempt, ancient planet emphasized the artificiality of the
performing arts world and its continual emphasis on the "newest" form of
expression. She had once considered the performing arts the be-all and
end-all of ambition. Ballybran, in its eternal struggle for survival against
gigantic natural forces, appealed to another instinct in her.

The recruits examined the weather station, its sensors fully extended
and the thick trunk of the unit completely extruded from the installation into which it retreated like a burrowing animal during "inclement
weather." Their guide's phrase occasioned wry laughter. He even smiled

at their response. Ballybraners had struck Killashandra as a humorless crew, and she wondered if the fever would wrest her sense of the ridiculous from her. Rimbol wouldn't be the same person without his funning.

Tukolom then announced that they would assist the technician by applying to the weather station a protective film against gale-flung particles. The recruits had first to scrape off the previous application, not an arduous job since the gale had removed most of the substance, which was not a jelly, a lubricant or a true paint.

Killashandra found the scraping and painting soothing occupations, for she had to concentrate on keeping her brush strokes even. Overlapping was better than skimping. She could see where the alloy of the arm she worked on had been scored in thin lines that argued other workers had not been as conscientious. Concentration kept her from disturbing reflections such as Rimbol's being "satisfactory" and Jezerey's convulsions.

Borton demonstrated his anxieties by being loud in complaint on the return journey, nagging at Tukolom for more details than the "satisfactory" prognosis. Although Killashandra sympathized with the former shuttle pilot's concern for his friend, his harangues began to irritate. She was sorely tempted to tell him to turn it off, but the scraping and painting had tired her, and she couldn't summon the energy to speak.

When the transport settled back at the Hangar, she made sure she was the last to descend. She wanted nothing more than a hot bath and quiet.

Nor was she refreshed at all by the bathing. She dialed for a Yarran beer and for information on Rimbol. He was continuing "satisfactory," and the beer tasted off. A different batch, she thought, not up to the standard of the Guild at all. But she sipped it, watching the dying day color her hillside with rapid shifts into the deepest purples and browns of shadow. She left the half-finished beer and stretched out on her bed, wondering if the fatigue she felt was cumulative or the onset of the symbiotic fever. Her pulse was normal, and she was not flushed. She pulled the thermal cover over her, turned on her side, and fell asleep wondering what would be found for the remainder of the recruits to do on the morrow.

The waking buzz brought her bolt upright in the bed.

"Lower that narding noise!" she cried, hands to her ears to muffle the incredible din.

Then she stared about her in surprise. The walls of her quarters were no longer a neutral shade but sparkled with many in the all-too-brilliant morning sun. She turned up the window opacity to cut the blinding glare. She felt extraordinarily rested, clearer of mind than she had since the morning she realized she didn't owe Fuerte or the Music Center any further allegiance. As she made for the toilet, the carpeting under her bare feet felt strangely harsh. She was aware of the subtle odors in the facility, acrid, pungent, overlaid by the scent she used. She couldn't remember spilling the container last night. The water as she washed her face and hands had a softness to it she had not previously noticed.

When she shrugged into her coverall, its texture was oddly coarse on her hands. She scrubbed them together and then decided that perhaps there'd been something abrasive in the paint she had used the day before. But her feet hadn't painted anything!

Noise struck her the moment the door panel opened. She flinched, reluctant to enter the corridor, which she was startled to find empty. The commotion was coming from the lounge. She could identify every voice, separating one conversation from another by turning her head. Then she noticed the guide stripe at the far end of the corridor, a stripe that was no longer dull gray but a vivid bluish purple.

She stepped back into her room and closed the panel, unable to comprehend the immense personal alteration that had apparently transformed her overnight.

"Am I satisfactory?" she cried out, a wild exultation seizing her. She threw her arms about her shoulders. "Is MY condition satisfactory?"

A tap on her door panel answered her.

"Come in."

Tukolom stood there with two Guild medics. That did not surprise her. The expression on Tukolom's face did. The mentor drew back in astonishment, expressions of incredulity, dismay, and indignation replacing his customary diffidence. It struck Killashandra as peculiar that this man, who had undoubtedly witnessed the transformation of thousands of recruits, should appear displeased at hers.

"You will be conducted to the Infirmary to complete the symbiosis." Tukolom took refuge in a rote formula. His hand left his side just enough to indicate that she should leave with the medics.

Thoroughly amused at his reaction and quite delighted with herself, Killashandra stepped forward eagerly, then turned with the intention of picking up the lute. Now that she knew she'd have her hearing the rest of her life, she wanted the instrument.

"Your possessions to you will be later brought. Go!" Tukolom's anger and frustration were not covert. His face was suffused with red.

There was not the least physical or philosophical resemblance between Tukolom and Maestro Valdi, yet at the moment Killashandra was reminded of her former teacher. She turned her back on Tukolom and followed her guides to the ramp. Just as she emerged from the corridor, she heard Tukolom peremptorily calling for attention. Glancing back over her shoulder, she saw that every head was turned in his direction. Once again, she had made a major exit without an audience.

Chapter 6

It was bad enough to be whisked away as if she'd committed a crime, but the meditechs kept asking if she felt faint or hot or cold, as if she was negligent when she denied any physical discomfort. Therefore, she could scarcely admit to a sense of vitality she had never previously experienced, to the fact that everything about her, even their plain green tunics, had taken on a new luster, that her fingers twitched to touch, her ears vibrated to minute sounds. Most of all, she wanted to shout her exultation in octaves previously impossible for the human voice.

The extreme anticlimax came when the chief meditech, a graceful woman with dark hair braided into an elaborate crown, wanted Killashandra to submit to the physical scanner.

"I don't need a scanner. I have never felt so well!!"

"The symbiont can be devious, my dear Killashandra, and only the scanner can tell us that. Do please lie down. You know it doesn't take long, and we really need an accurate picture of your present physical well-being."

Killashandra stifled her sudden wish to scream and submitted. She was in such euphoria that the claustrophobic feel of the helmet didn't bother her, nor did the pain-threshold nerve jab do more than make her giggle.

"Well, Killashandra Ree," Antona said, absently smoothing a strand into her coronet, "you are the lucky one." Her smile as she assisted Killashandra to her feet was the warmest the young woman had seen from a full Guild member. "We'll just make certain this progress has no setbacks. Come with me and I'll show you your room."

"I'm all right? I thought there'd be some fever."

"There may be fever in your future," Antona said, smiling encouragingly as she guided Killashandra down a wide hall.

Killashandra hesitated, wrinkling her nose against the odors that assailed her now: dank sweat, urine, feces, vomit, and as palpable as the other stenches, fear.

"Yes," Antona said, observing her pause, "I expect it'll take time for you to become accustomed to augmented olfactory senses. Fortunately, that's not been one of my adaptations. I can still smell, would have to in my profession, but odors don't overwhelm me. I've put you at the back, away from the others, Killashandra. You can program the air conditioner to mask all this."

Noises, too, assaulted Killashandra. Despite thick sound-deadening walls, she recognized one voice.

"Rimbol!" She twisted to the right and was opening the door before Antona could stop her.

The young Scartine, his back arched in a convulsion, was being held to the bed by two strong meditechs. A third was administering a spray to Rimbol's chest. In the two days since she had seen him, he had lost weight, turned an odd shade of soft yellow, and his face was contorted by the frenzy that gripped his body.

"Not all have an easy time," Antona said, taking her by the arm.

"Easy time!" Killashandra resisted Antona's attempt to draw her from the room. "The fax said satisfactory. Is *this* condition considered satisfactory?"

Antona regarded Killashandra. "Yes, in one respect, his condition is satisfactory—he's maintaining his own integrity with the symbiont. A massive change is occurring physically: an instinctive rejection on his part, a mutation on the symbiont's. The computer prognosis gives Rimbol an excellent chance of making a satisfactory adjustment."

"But . . ." Killashandra couldn't drag her eyes from Rimbol's writhing body. "Will I go like that, too?"

Antona ducked her head, hiding her expression, an evasion that irritated Killashandra.

"I don't think that you will, Killashandra, so don't fret. The results of the latest scan must be analyzed, but my initial reading indicates a smooth adaptation. You'll be the first to know otherwise. Scant consolation, perhaps, but you *would* barge in here."

Killashandra ignored the rebuke. "Have you computed how long he'll be like that?"

"Yes, another day should see him over the worst of the penetration."

"And Jezerey?"

Antona looked blankly at Killashandra. "Oh, the girl who collapsed in the Hangar yesterday? She's fine—I amend that." Antona smiled conciliatorily. "She is suffering from a predictable bout of hyperthermia at the moment and is as comfortable as we can make her."

"Satisfactory, in fact?" Killashandra was consumed by bitterness for that misleading category but allowed Antona to lead her out of Rimbol's room.

"Satisfactory in our terms and experience, yes. There are degrees, you must understand, of severity with which the symbiont affects the host and with which the host rejects the symbiont." Antona shrugged. "If we knew all the ramifications and deviations, it would be simple to recruit only those candidates with the requisite chromosomes. It isn't that simple, though our continuous research gets closer and closer to defining exact parameters." She gave Killashandra another of her warm smiles. "We're much better at selection than we used to be."

"How long have you been here?"

"Long enough to know how lucky you are. And to hope that you'll continue so fortunate. I work generally with self-treating patients, since I find the helpless depress me. Here we are."

Antona opened a door at the end of the corridor and started to retrace her steps. Killashandra caught her arm.

"But Rimbol? I could see him?"

Another expressive shrug. "If you wish. Your belongings will be along shortly. Go settle in," she said more kindly. "Program the air conditioner and rest. There's nothing more to be done now. I'll inform you of the analysis as soon as I have the results."

"Or I'll inform you," Killashandra said with wry humor.

"Don't dwell on the possibility," Antona advised her.

Killashandra didn't. The room, the third she'd had in as many weeks, was designed for ease in dealing with patients, though all paraphernalia was absent. The lingering odors of illness seeped in from the hall, and the room seemed to generate antiseptic maskers. It took Killashandra nearly an hour to find a pleasant counterodor with which to refresh her room. In the process, she learned how to intercept fax updates on the conditions of the other patients. Never having been ill or had occasion to visit a sick friend, she didn't have much idea of what the printout meant, but as the patients were designated by room number, she could isolate Rimbol's. His monitor showed more activity than the person in the next room, but she couldn't bring herself to find out who his neighbor was.

That evening, Antona visited her room, head at a jaunty angle, the warm smile on her face.

"The prognosis is excellent. There'll be no fever. We are keeping you on a few days just to be on the safe side. An easy transition is not always a safe one." A chime wiped the smile from her face. "Ah, another patient. Excuse me."

As soon as the door closed, Killashandra turned on the medical display. At the bottom, a winking green line warned of a new admission. That was how Killashandra came to see Borton being wheeled into the facility. The following day, Shillawn was admitted. The fax continued to display "satisfactory" after everyone's condition. She supposed she agreed, having become fascinated with the life-signal graphs until the one on Rimbol's neighbor unexpectedly registered nothing at all.

Killashandra ran down the hall. The door of the room was open, and half a dozen technicians could be seen bent over the bed. Antona wasn't among them, but Killashandra caught a glimpse of Carigana's wide-eyed face.

Whirling, she stormed into the chief medic's office. Antona was hunching over an elaborate console, her hands graceful even in rapid motion on the keys.

"Why did Carigana die?" Killashandra demanded.

Without looking up from the shifting lights of the display, Antona spoke. "You have privileges in this Guild, Killashandra Ree, but not one gives you the right to disturb a chief of any rank. Nor me at this time. I want to know why she died more than you possibly could!"

Rightly abashed, Killashandra left the office. She hurried back to her room, averting her eyes as she passed the open door to Carigana's. She was ashamed of herself, for she didn't genuinely care that Carigana was dead, only that she had died. The space worker had really been an irritant, Killashandra thought candidly. Death had been a concept dealt with dramatically in the Music Center, but Carigana was Killashandra's first contact with that reality. Death could also happen to her, to Rimbol, and she would be very upset if he died. Even if Shillawn died.

How long Killashandra sat watching the life-signs' graphs, trying to ignore the discontinued one, she did not know. A courteous rap on the door was immediately followed by Antona's entrance, and her weary expression told Killashandra that quite a few hours must have passed. Antona leaned against the door frame, expelling a long sigh.

"To answer your question—"

"I apologize for my behavior—"

"We don't know why Carigana died," Antona went on, inclining her head to accept the apology. "I have a private theory with no fact to support it. An intuition, if you will, that the desire to be acceptable, to surrender to the symbiont is as necessary to the process of adjustment as the physical stamina, which Carigana had, and those chromosomes which we have established as most liable to produce a favorable adaptation. You did want to become a crystal singer very much, didn't you?"

"Yes, but so do the others."

"Do they? Do they really?" Antona's tone was curiously wistful.

Killashandra hesitated, only too aware of the inception of her own desire to become a crystal singer. If Antona's theory held any merit, Killashandra should also be dead, certainly not so blatantly healthy.

"Carigana didn't like anything. She questioned everything," Killashandra said, drawn to give Antona what comfort she could. "She didn't have to become a crystal singer."

"No, she could have stayed in space." Antona smiled thinly, pushed herself away from the wall, and then saw the graphs on the display. "So that's how you knew. Well"—and she tapped the active graph in the left-hand corner—"that's your friend, Rimbol. He's more than just satisfactory now. The others are proceeding nicely. You can pack your things. I've no medical reason to keep you here longer. You'll be far better off learning the techniques of staying alive in your profession, my dear, than sitting death-watch here. Officially, you're Lanzecki's problem now. Someone's coming for you."

"I'm not going to get sick?"

"Not you. You've had what's known as a Milekey Transition. Practically no physical discomfort and the maximum adjustment. I wish you luck, Killashandra Ree. You'll need it." Antona was not smiling. Just then, the door opened wider. "Trag?" The chief meditech was surprised, but her affability returned, that moment of severity so brief that Killashandra wondered if she had imagined it. "I shall undoubtedly be seeing you again, Killashandra."

She slipped out of the room as an unsmiling man of medium build entered. His first look at her was intent, but she'd survived the scrutiny of too many conductors to be daunted.

"I don't have much to pack," she said, unsmiling. She slid off the bed and swiftly gathered her belongings. He saw the lute before she picked it up, and something flickered across his face. Had he once played one?

She stood before him, carisak over her shoulder, aware that her heart was thumping. She glanced at the screen, her eyes going to Rimbol's graph. How much longer before he was released? She nodded to Trag and followed him from the room.

Killashandra was soon to learn that Trag was reticent by nature, but as they made their way down the Infirmary corridors, she was relieved to be conducted in silence. Too much had happened to her too fast. She realized now that she had feared her own life-signs would suddenly appear on the medical display. The sudden reprieve from that worry and her promotion out of the Infirmary dazed her. She did not appreciate until later that Trag, chief assistant to the Guild Master in charge of training crystal singers, did not normally escort them.

As the lift panel closed on the Infirmary level, Trag took her right hand and fastened a thin metal band around her wrist.

"You must wear this to identify you until you've been in the Ranges."

"Identify me?" The band fitted without hindering wrist movement, but the alloy felt oddly harsh on her skin. The sensation disappeared in seconds, so that Killashandra wondered if she had imagined the roughness.

"Identify you to your colleagues. And admit you to singer privacies."

Some inflection in his voice made the blood run hot to her cheeks but his expression was diffident. At that point, the lift panels opened.

"And it permits you to enter the singer levels. There are three. This is the main one with all the general facilities." She stepped with him into the vast, vaulted, subtly lit lobby. She felt nerves that had been strung taut in the Infirmary begin to relax in moments. Massive pillars separated the level into sections and hallways. "The lift shaft," Trag continued, "is the center of these levels of the complex. Catering, large-screen viewing, private dining, and assembly rooms are immediately about the shaft. Individual apartments are arranged in color quadrants, with additional smaller lifts to all other levels at convenient points on the outer arc. Your rooms are in the blue quadrant. This way." He turned to the left and she followed.

"Are these my permanent quarters?" she asked, thinking how many she had had since meeting Carrik.

"With the Guild, yes."

Once again, she caught the odd inflection in his voice. She supposed it must have something to do with her being out of the Infirmary before any of the others of her class. She was curiously disjointed. She had experienced that phenomenon before, at the Music Center, on days when no one could remember lines or entrances or sing in correct tempi. One simply got through such times as best one could. And on this, certainly a momentous one in *her* life, acquiescence was difficult to achieve.

She nearly ran into Trag, who had halted before a door on the right-hand side of the hall. She was belatedly aware that they had passed recesses at intervals.

"This apartment is assigned to you." Trag pointed to the lock plate.

Killashandra pressed her thumb to the sensitized area. The panel slid back.

"Use what is left of the morning to settle in and initiate your personal program. Use whatever code you wish: personal data is always voice coded. At 1400 hours, Concera will escort you to the cutter technician. He'll have no excuse not to outfit you quickly."

Killashandra noted the cryptic remark and wondered if everyone would address her comments she couldn't understand yet apparently ought to. As she mused on what "ought to" had accomplished for her, Trag was striding back down the hall.

She closed the panel, flicked on the privacy light, and surveyed her permanent Guild quarters. Size might denote rank here as on other worlds. The main room here was twice the size of her ample recruit accommodation. To one side was a sleeping chamber that was apparently all bed. A door on one wall was open to a mirrored dressing area that, in turn, led into a hygiene unit with a sunken tank sprouting an unusual number of taps and dials. On the other side of the main room was a storage closet larger than her student room on Fuerte and a compact dining and self-catering area.

"Yarran beer, please." She spoke more to make noise in the sterile and ringingly quiet place. The catering slot opened to present a beaker of the distinctive ruddy beer.

She took the drink to the main room, sipping as she frowned at the utilitarian furnishings. Laying her lute carefully on a chair, she let her carisak slip off her shoulder and onto the floor, seized by an urge to throw her possessions around the stark apartment, just to make it look lived in.

Here she was, Killashandra Ree, installed in spacious grandeur, achieving status as a crystal singer, that fearsome and awful being, a silicate spider, a crystal cuckoo with a luxurious nest. This very afternoon, she was to be tuned to a cutter that would permit her to slice Ballybran crystal, earn stunning totals of galactic credits, and she would cheerfully have traded the whole mess for the sound of a friendly voice.

"Not that I'm certain I have a friend anywhere," she said.

"Recording?"

The impersonal voice, neither tenor nor contralto, startled her. The full beaker of beer trembled in her hand.

"Personal program." That was what Trag had meant. She was to record those facts of her life that she wished to remember in those future times when singing crystal would have scrambled her memory circuits.

"Recording?"

"Yes, record and store to voice print only."

As she gave such facts as her date and place of birth, the names of her parents, grandparents, sisters, and brothers, the extent and scope of her education, she stalked about the main room, trying to find exactly the right spot in which to display her lute.

"On being awarded a grant, I entered the Music Center." She paused to laugh. How soon did one begin to forget what one wished to forget?

"Right now!"

"Recording?"

"End of recording. Store." And that was that. She knew she could reconsider, but she didn't want to remember those ten years. She could now wipe them out. She would. As far as she would be ever after, henceforth, and forevermore concerned, nothing of moment happened after the grant award until she encountered Carrik. Those ten years of unremitting labor and dedication to ambition had never occurred to Killashandra Ree, Cutter in the Heptite Guild.

To celebrate her emancipation from an inglorious past, Killashandra dialed another beer. The digital indicated an hour remained before Concera was to take her to the appointment. She ordered what was described as a hearty, nourishing soup of assorted legumes. She checked her credit, something she must not forget to do regularly, and found herself still in the black. If she were to enter the rest of the Guild voucher and her open ticket, she would have quite a healthy balance. To be consumed by the equipment of a crystal singer. She'd keep those credits free.

That reminded her of Shillawn, and of other credit-debit discussions. She keyed the Guild's commissary, ordered additional furnishings, rugs of the Ghni weavers, and by 1400, when Concera touched her door chime, Killashandra had wall-screens that mixed the most unlikely elements from an ice-world to the raving flora of the voracious Eobaron planets. Startling, but a complete change from sterility.

Concera, a woman of medium height and slender build, glided into the main room, exclaimed at the sight of the wall-screens, and looked questioningly at Killashandra.

"Oh, aren't you clever? I would never have thought of combining different worlds! Do come right along. *He* has such a temper at the best of times, but without his skill, we, the singers I mean, would be in a terrible way. He *is* a superior craftsman, which is why one humors his odd temper. This way."

Concera covered quite a bit of ground with her gliding gait, and Killashandra had to stretch her legs to keep pace.

"You'll get to know where everything is very soon. It's nice to be by oneself, I feel, instead of in a pack, but then different people have different tastes," and Concera peered sideways at Killashandra to see if she agreed. "Of course, we come from all over the galaxy, so one is bound to find someone compatible. This is the eighth level where most of the technical work is done—naturally the cutters are made here, as they are the most technical of all. Here we are."

Concera paused at the open entrance and, with what seemed unexpected courtesy, pushed Killashandra ahead of her into a small office with a counter across the back third and a door leading into a workshop. Her entry must have triggered an alarm in the workroom, for a man, his sun-reddened face set in sour lines, appeared in the doorway.

"You're this Killashandra?" he demanded. He beckoned to her and then saw Concera following. "You? I told you you'd have to wait, Concera. There's no point, no point at all, in making you a handle for three fingers. You'll only outgrow it, and there's all that work could be put to better use."

"I thought it might be a challenge for you—"

"I've all the challenges I need, Concera." He replied with such vehemence that when he returned his stare to Killashandra, she wondered if his disagreement with the woman would spill over on to her. "Let me see your hands."

Killashandra held them, palm up, over the counter. He raised his eyebrows as he felt with strong impersonal fingers across the palm, spread her fingers to see the lack of webbing from constant practice, the hard muscle along the flat of the hand and thumb pad.

"Used your hands right, you have." He shot another glance at Concera.

It was only then that Killashandra noticed that the first two fingers on Concera's left hand had been sheared off. The stumps were pinkish white, healed flesh but oddly shaped. It occurred to Killashandra in a rush that made her stomach queasy that the two missing digits were regenerating.

"If you stay, you be quiet. If you go, you won't be tempted. This'll take two–three hours."

Concera elected to leave, which had no positive effect on the morose technician. Killashandra had naively assumed that tuning a cutter would be a simple matter, but it was a tedious process, taking several days. She had to read aloud for a voice print from boring printout on the history and development of the cutting devices. She learned more than she needed to know—some of the more complicated mechanisms proved unreliable in extremes of weather; a once-popular model was blamed for the high-voltage discharge which had carbonized the corpse Killashandra saw on Shankill. The most effective and reliable cutter, refined from Barry Milekey's crude original, required that the user have perfect pitch. It was a piezoelectric device that converted the crystal singer's vocal note and rhythm into high-frequency shock waves on an infrasonic carrier. The cutting edge of the shock wave was pitched by the singer to the dominant tone of the "struck" crystal face.

Once set to a voice pattern, the infrasonic device could not be altered. Manufacture of such cutters was restricted to the Guild and safeguarded yet again by computer assembly, the program coding known only by the Guild Master and his executive assistant.

As Concera had mentioned, the technician was a temperamental man. When Killashandra was reading aloud, he was complaining about various grievances with the Guild and its members. Concera and her request for a three-fingered handle was currently his favorite gripe—"Concera is cack-handed, anyway, and always splitting her grips." Another was that he ought to have had another three weeks fishing before returning to work. The fish had just started to bite, and would she now sing an octave in C.

She sang quite a few octaves in various keys and decided that there were worse audiences than apparently receptive audition judges. She hadn't used her voice since the day she met Carrik; she was sore in the gut from supporting tone and aware the sound was harsh.

When Concera glided into the room, Killashandra was overwhelmingly relieved.

"Back tomorrow, same time. I'll do casts of your good ten fingers." And the man sent an arch glance at Concera.

Concera hurried Killashandra out of the workshop and the office.

"He does like his little jokes," she said, leading the way down one corridor and left at the next. "I only wanted a *little* favor so I could go back into the Ranges without wasting so much time." She entered a room labeled "Training," sighing as she closed the door and flicked on the privacy light. "Still"—and she gave Killashandra a bright smile, her eyes sliding from a direct contact—"we have your training to take in hand." She waved Killashandra to one of the half-dozen chairs in the room facing a large hologram projector. She picked up a remote control unit from a shelf, darkening the room and activating the projector. The outsized lettering of the Guild's rules, regulations, and precepts hovered before them. "You may have had a Milekey Transition, but there's no easy way to get over this."

"Tukolom—"

"Tukolom handles only basic information, suitable for anyone joining the Guild in any capacity." Concera's voice had a note of rancor. "Now you must specialize and repeat and repeat." Concera sighed. "We all have to," she added, her voice expressing patient resignation. "If it's any consolation to you, I'd be doing this by myself and I've always found it much easier to *explain* than memorize." Her voice lightened. "You'll hear even the oldest singers muttering regs and restricts any night in the Commons Hall. Of course, you'll never appreciate this drill until it's *vital*! When you reach that point, you won't remember how you know what you do. Because that's when you really *know* nothing else."

Despite Concera's persuasive tone, Killashandra found the reasoning specious. Having no choice in study program or teacher, Killashandra set herself to memorize regulations about working claims, claiming faces, interference with claims, reparations and retributions, fines and a clutter of other rules for which she could see no need since they were obvious to anyone with any sense.

When she returned to the privacy of her quarters and the anomalies of her wall-screens, she checked with the Infirmary and was told that Rimbol was weak but had retained all his senses. Shillawn, Borton, and Jezerey were satisfactory, in the proper use of that word. Killashandra also managed to extract from data retrieval the fact that injured singers like Concera and Borella undertook the role of preceptor because of the bonus involved. That explained the spiteful remarks and ambivalent poses.

The next morning, when Concera drilled her on her understanding of each section of the previous day's subjects, Killashandra had the notion that Concera silently recited paragraph and section just one step ahead of her pupil.

The afternoon was spent uncomfortably, in the workshop of the Fisherman, where casts were made of her hands. The Fisher maundered on about having to make hundreds of casts during a singer's lifetime. He told her she wasn't to complain to him about blisters from hand grips, an affliction that he alleged was really caused by a muscling up that wasn't *any* fault of his.

Killashandra spent that evening redecorating her room.

She had a morning drill with Concera, spent a half hour with the Fisher, who grumbled incessantly about a bad morning's fishing, the inferiority of the plastic he had to work with, and the privileges of rank. Killashandra decided that if she were to ruffle at every cryptic remark tossed her way, she'd be in a state of constant agitation. The remainder of the afternoon, Concera reviewed her on crystal shapes, tones, and the combinations that were marketable at the moment: black crystals in any form always having the highest value. Killashandra was to review the catalog, commit to memory which shape was used for what end product, the range in price, and the parameters of value variation in each color. She was taken through the research departments, which sought new uses for Ballybran crystal. There she noticed several people with the eye-adjustment of Enthor.

In the days that followed, she was given instruction in the sled-simulator, "flying" against mach storm winds. By the end of the first lesson, she was as battered, sweaty, and trembling as if the flight had been genuine.

"You'll have to do better than that," the instructor commented unsympathetically as she reeled out of the simulator. "Take a half hour in the tank and come back this afternoon."

"Tank?"

"Yeah, the tank. The radiant fluid. Left-hand taps. Go on! I'll expect you back at 1500."

Killashandra muttered the terse instructions all the way back to her rooms, shedding her clothes as she made her way to the tank. She turned on the left-hand taps, and a viscous liquid oozed out. She got the temperature she wanted and dubiously lowered herself into the tank. In minutes, tension and stress left her muscles, and she lay, buoyed by the radiant bath, until the stuff cooled. That afternoon, her instructor grudgingly admitted that she had improved.

A few days later, half a morning through a solo training flight across the White Sea where thermal patterns made good practice, every visual warning device on the controls turned red, and a variety of sirens, claxons, bells, and nerve-tinglers was activated. Killashandra immediately veered northeast to the Guild Complex and was relieved when half the monitors desisted. The rest blared or blinked until she had landed the sled on its rack and turned off the power. When she complained to her instructor about the warning overload, he gave her a long, scathing look.

"You can't be warned too often about the approach of turbulence," he said. "You singers might be as deaf as some of us no matter how we rig cautions. While you remember advice, remember this: a mach storm won't give you a second chance. We do our fardling best to insure that you have at least one. Now change your gear for cargo handling. A blow's on the way!"

He strode off, waving to attract attention from a cluster of Hangar personnel.

The storm was not rated Severe and only the southeast section of the continent had been alerted. Forty singers had logged out in that general area, and thirty-nine straggled in. The flight and Hangar officers were conferring together as Killashandra passed them.

"Keborgen's missing. He'll get himself killed!"

"He's been bragging he was out for black. *If* he managed to remember where the claim is . . ."

Killashandra had no excuse to linger near the two at that point, but when the other ships had been cleared and racked, she stayed on after the rest of the unloaders had been dismissed.

The wind was not strong enough at the Complex to require the erection of the baffles, so Killashandra stationed herself where she could watch the southern quadrant. She also kept an eye on the two officers and saw them abandon their watch with a shrug of shoulders and shakes of the head.

If Keborgen had actually cut black crystal, she would've liked to have unloaded it. She wasn't needed on the sorting floor. She consoled herself with the knowledge that she had racked up some danger credit already, and wasn't much in the red for decorating her room and days of uncredited instruction. Being a recruit had had advantages.

She was crossing the Hangar to return to her quarters when she heard the sound, or rather felt it, like a thread dragged across exposed nerve ends. She wasn't yet accustomed to her improved vision, so she shook her head and blinked, expecting to clear the spot on the right retina.

It stayed in position in the lower right-hand quadrant, dipping and swaying. Not a shadow in her own eye but a sled, obviously on course for the Complex. She was wondering if she should inform anyone when wrecker personnel began to scramble for the heavy hoist sled. In the hustle, no one noticed that Killashandra had joined the team.

The wrecker didn't have far to go for the sled plowed into the hills forty klicks from the Complex. The comtech could get no response from the sled's pilot.

"Bloody fool waited too long," the flight officer said, nervously slapping his fingers against his thigh. "Warned him when he went out, not to wait too long. But they never listen." He repeated variations of those sentiments, becoming more agitated as the wrecker neared the sled and the damage was visible.

The wrecker pilot set his craft down four long strides from the singer's sled.

"You others get the crystal," the flight officer shouted as he plunged toward the crumbled bow of the sled, which was half buried in loose dirt.

As Killashandra obeyed his order, she glanced back on the sled's path. She could see, in the distance, two other slide marks before the crashing sled had bounced to a stop.

The storage compartment had withstood impact. Killashandra watched with interest as the three men released the nearest hatch. As soon as they emerged with cartons, she darted in. Then she heard the moans of the injured crystal singer and the drone of curses from the flight officer and medic attending him.

The moment she touched the nearest carton, she forgot the injured man, for a shock, mild but definite, ran along her bones from hand to heel to head. She gripped the carrier firmly, but the sensation dissipated.

"Move along. Gotta get that guy back to the Infirmary," she was told by returning crewmen.

She picked the carton up, minding her steps, ignoring the exhortation of the crewmen who passed her. She crouched by the carton as the cocoon of the injured singer was deftly angled into the wrecker.

During the short trip back to the complex, she wondered why there was such a fuss. Surely the symbiont would repair the man's injuries, given the time to do so. She supposed that the symbiont relieved pain. Borella hadn't appeared uncomfortable with her awful thigh wound, and Concera, given to complaints, had said nothing about pain in her regenerating fingers.

As soon as the wrecker landed, the singer was hurried to waiting meditechs. Hugging the carton that she devoutly hoped contained black crystal, Killashandra walked straight through the storage area into the sorting room. She had no problem finding Enthor, for the man almost bumped into her.

"Enthor," she said, planting herself and pushing the carton at him, "I think this has black crystal."

"Black crystal?" Enthor was startled; he blinked and peered frowningly at her. "Oh, it's you. You?" His lensed eyes widened in surprise. "You? What are you doing here?" He half turned in the direction of the Infirmary and then up to the recruits' level. "No one's been cutting black crystal—"

"Keborgen might have been. He crashed. This is from his sled." She gave the carton an urgent shove against his chest. "The flight officer said he had been out to cut blacks."

Out of habit, Enthor took hold of the carton, quite unable to assimilate either her explanation or her sudden appearance. Killashandra was impatient with Enthor's hesitation. She did not want to admit to the contact shock she had felt in Keborgen's sled. Deftly, she propelled Enthor at his table, and though still perplexed, he presented the ident to the scan. His hands hovered briefly but dropped away as he twisted toward Killashandra.

"Go on," she said, annoyed by his dithering. "Look at them."

"I know what they are. How did you?" Enthor's indecision was gone, and he stared, almost accusingly, into her eyes.

"I felt them. Open it. What did Keborgen cut?"

His unearthly eyes still on hers, Enthor opened the box and lifted out a crystal. Killashandra caught her breath at the sight of the dull, irregular 15 centimeter segment. Consciously, she had to make her lungs expel air as Enthor reverently unpacked two additional pieces that fit against the first.

"He cut well," Enthor said, scrutinizing the trio keenly. "He cut very well. Just missing flaw. That would account for the shapes."

"He has cut his last," the deep voice of the Guild Master said.

Startled, Killashandra whirled and realized that Lanzecki must have arrived moments before. He nodded to her and then beckoned to someone in the storage area.

"Bring the rest of Keborgen's cut."

"Is there more black in it?" Enthor asked Killashandra as he felt carefully about in the plaspacking.

Killashandra was vibrantly aware of Lanzecki's intense gaze.

"In that box or the cargo?"

"Either," Lanzecki said, his eyes flickering at her attempt to temporize.

"Not in the box," she said even as she ran her hand along the plasfoam side. She swallowed nervously, glancing sideways at Lanzecki's imposing figure. His clothing, which she had once thought dull, glinted in a richness of thread and subtle design very much in keeping with his rank. She swallowed a second time as he gave a brief nod of his head and the six cartons from Keborgen's sled were deposited on Enthor's table.

"Any more black crystal?" Enthor asked.

She swallowed a third time, remembered that the habit had irritated her in Shillawn, and ran her hands over the cartons. She frowned, for a curious prickle rippled across her palms.

"Nothing like the first one," she said, puzzled.

Enthor raised his eyebrows, and she could only have imagined his eyes twinkling. He opened a box at random and removed, carefully, a handful of cloudy slivers, displaying them to Lanzecki and Killashandra. The other boxes held similar slivers.

"Did he cut the triad first or last?" Lanzecki spoke softly as he picked up a finger-long splinter, examining its irregularities.

"He didn't say?" Enthor ventured quietly.

Lanzecki's sigh and the brief movement of his head answered that question.

"I thought the precious symbiont healed—" Killashandra blurted out before she knew she was going to speak.

Lanzecki's eyes halted her outburst.

"The symbiont has few limitations: deliberate and constant abuse is one. The age of its host is another. Add the third factor—Keborgen stayed too long in the Ranges despite storm warnings." He turned back to look at the three pieces of black crystal on the weighplate and at the credit valuation blinking on the display.

If Keborgen was dead, who inherited the credit? She jumped as Lanzecki spoke again.

"So, Killashandra Ree, you are sensitive to the blacks, and you have enjoyed a Milekey Transition."

Killashandra could not avoid the Guild Master's disconcerting appraisal. He seemed neither as remote nor detached as he had the day she had arrived at Shankill with Carrik. His eyes, especially, were intensely alive. A nearly imperceptible upward movement of his lips brought her restless gaze to his mouth. Wide, well-shaped lips evidently reflected his thoughts more than eye, face, or body. Did she amuse him? No, probably not. The Guild Master was not known for his humor; he was held in great respect and some awe by men and women who were awed by little and respected nothing but credit. She felt her shoulders and back stiffen in automatic reaction to the flick of amusement.

"Thank you, Killashandra Ree, for your prompt discovery of that triad," Lanzecki said with a slight inclination of his head that reinforced his gratitude. Then he turned and was gone, as quickly as he had arrived.

Exhaling, Killashandra leaned against Enthor's table.

"Always good to know black when it's near you." Enthor paused as he gingerly unpacked shards. He blinked his eyes to focus on the weight display. "Trouble is finding it in the first place."

"What's the second place?" she asked impudently.

Enthor blinked his lens into place and gave her a shrewd look. "Remembering where the first place was!"

She left him, walking back through Sorting to Storage and out onto the Hangar deck, the shortest way back to an arc lift down to her quarters. Hangar personnel were busy dismantling Keborgen's wreck. She grimaced. So a damaged ship was repaired as long and as often as necessary during its owner's lifetime—and then stripped. Had Carrik's sled been dismembered?

She halted at a sudden notion, wheeled and stared out at the hills in the direction of Keborgen's erratic last flight. She half ran to the Hangar Ready Room for a look at the met printout, continuously displayed and updated by the minute.

"That storm to the southeast? It's dissipating?"

The weather officer glanced up, a frown on his face. Forestalling rejection, Killashandra held up her wristband. He immediately tapped out a replay of the satellite recording, which showed the formation of the storm and its turbulent progress along the coast of the main continent and the Milekey Ranges. The gale had blown up quickly and, as unpredictably as most Ballybran storms, caressed one large sector of the Range and then roiled seaward across the edge of the Long Plain where warm air had met its colder mass.

"I was on the wrecker which brought Keborgen in, but I must have dropped my wrist unit there. Can I use a skimmer?"

The met officer shrugged. "For all of me you can have a skimmer. No weather to speak of in our zone. Check with Flight."

Flight thought her cack-handed to have dropped equipment and assigned her a battered vehicle. She paused long enough to note that the recovery pattern of the wrecker was still displayed on the emergency screen. Once she left the office, she made notes on her wrist unit.

She unracked the skimmer and left the Hangar at a sedate pace entirely consistent with a routine errand, then flew to the crash site. She was increasingly possessed by the thought that Keborgen, trying to outrun the storm, surely must have come back to the Complex by the most direct route. Though Concera had maundered on and on about how careful singers were to protect their claims by using devious routes to and from, Keborgen might just as easily have flown straight in the hope of reaching safety. His sled had come in well behind the others from the same area.

Given that possibility, she could establish from data retrieval the exact second when the storm warning had been broadcast, compute the maximum speed of his sled, the direction of flight at the time of his crash, and deduce in what general area he had cut black crystal. She might even do a probability computation on the length of time Keborgen had delayed at his claim by the span of time it had taken the other thirty-nine singers to return.

She hovered the skimmer over the crash site. The sharp mounds were beginning to soften as a brisk breeze shifted the soil. Skewing the skimmer, she located the next skid mark and two more before she spotted the raw scrape across the bare rock of a higher slope. She landed to examine the marks closely. The scar was deeper on the north side, as if the sled had been deflected by the contact. She stood in the mark and took bearings through her wrist unit. Then she returned to the skimmer and quartered the sector, looking for any other evidence of Keborgen's faltering, bumping last flight.

Shadows and sunset made it inadvisable for her to continue her search. Killashandra checked her bearings and then returned to the Complex.

Chapter 7

Killashandra leaned back from the terminal in her room, noted that the time display marked an early-morning hour. She was tired, her eyes hot with fatigue, and she was ravenous. But she had every bit of data she could extract from the Guild's banks that might be useful in narrowing her search for Keborgen's black-crystal claim. She keyed the program into the privacy of her personal record, then stood and walked stiffly, arching against the ache in her back, to the catering unit where she dialed for a hot soup. Though she had stored the data, she couldn't stop thinking about her plan. And all the obstacles to its implementation.

Keborgen was dead. His claims, wherever they had been, were now open according to the vast paragraphs on "Claims, the making and marking thereof, penalties for misappropriation, fines and restrictions," and all subparagraphs. However, the claim first had to be found. As Enthor had said, that was the first problem. Killashandra might have theories about its location, but she had neither sled to get there and look nor cutter to take crystal from the "open" face. Her research revealed that Keborgen had worked the claim for at least four decades and analysis proved that twelve black-crystal cuttings had come from the same face, the next to last one some nine years previously. The second problem, as Enthor had so pithily stated, was remembering.

To relieve the tedium of drill, Killashandra had asked Concera how singers found their way back to claims after an absence, especially if memory was so unreliable.

"Oh," Concera had replied airily, "I always remember to tell my sled what landmarks to look for. Sleds have voice print recorders so they're dead safe." She hesitated, looking in an unfocused way that was habitual with her. "Of course, storms do sometimes alter landmarks, so it's wiser to record contour levels and valleys or gorges, things that aren't as apt to be rearranged by a *bad* blow. Then, too," she continued in a brighter voice, "when you've cut at a particular face a few times, *it* resonates. So if you can recall even the general direction and get there, finding the exact spot is much easier."

"It isn't so much singing crystal then, as being sung to by crystal," Killashandra had noted.

"Oh, yes, very well put," Concera said with the false cheerfulness of someone who hadn't understood.

Killashandra finished the soup and wearily shuffled to the bedroom, shedding her coverall. She wasn't unsatisfied with the information she'd accumulated. She could narrow the search to older claim markings in the geographical area dictated by the top speed of Keborgen's elderly sled, the time the storm warning was issued, and the registered storm wind speed.

She fretted about one point. Keborgen's sled recorder. She had seen the sled being dismantled, but would the Guild technicians have rescued the record for the data that might be retrieved? She wasn't certain if anyone had ever broken a voice code. It hadn't been so much as whispered that it was possible. Though the rules did not state the Guild was able to take such an action, a terrible breach of privacy under FSP rights, the Charter didn't specifically deny the Guild that right, either, once the member was dead. On the other hand, Trag had said that private personal records were irretrievable.

The darkness and absolute silence of her bedroom compounded her sudden doubt. The Guild could and occasionally did exhibit a certain ruthlessness. For sanity's sake, she had better decide here and now whether or not the Guild adhered faithfully to its stated and endlessly cited principles. She took a sudden comfort in the very length of the Charter. Its voluminous paragraphs and sections obviously reflected contingencies and emergencies that had been dealt with over four hundred years of usage and abuse.

With a sigh, Killashandra turned over. Avoiding restrictions and defying laws were completely in the human condition. As the Guild prohibited, it also protected or the bloody planet would have been abandoned to the spores and crystal.

She woke later in the morning to the insistent buzz of her terminal. She was informed that her cutter was now ready and she was to collect it and report to training room 47. Groggy from insufficient sleep, Killashandra took a quick shower and ate a good meal. She found herself directing glances to the computer console, almost as if she expected last night's data to spring from the cover and expose itself.

Computers had to deal with fact, and she had one advantage that wouldn't compute: a sensitivity to black crystal—Keborgen's black crystal. Computers did not volunteer information, either, but she had few doubts that with the news of Keborgen's death, the opening of his rich claim would be widely known. Only 39 singers had come in from that same storm. She couldn't know how many other singers had returned from leave and were available to search. She knew that the odds against her finding the claim were good on the one hand and unlikely on the other. The delivery of her cutter she took as propitious.

She was waiting for the lift when she heard her name called in an incredulous shout.

"Killashandra! I'm recovered. I'm a singer, too."

Herself astonished, she turned to find Rimbol striding toward her.

"Rimbol!" She returned his enthusiastic embrace, acutely aware that she hadn't given him any thought at all in several days.

"I was told you'd got through the transition satisfactorily, but no one else's seen you! Are you all right?" Rimbol held her from him, his green eyes searching her face and figure. "Was it just the fever, or did you come see me at one point?"

"I did at several points," she replied with perfect truth and instinctive diplomacy. "Then I was told that I was interfering with your recovery. Who else is through?"

Rimbol's expression changed to sorrow. "Carigana didn't make it. Shillawn is deaf and has been assigned to research. Mistra, Borton, Jezerey, bless the pair; in total twenty-nine made it. Celee, the spacer, made only a tolerable adjustment, but he's got all his senses, so he's been shunted to shuttle piloting. I don't think that goes against his grain, anyway."

"And Shillawn? Does he mind?" Killashandra knew her voice was sharp, and Rimbol's face clouded until she hugged him. He was going to have to learn not to care so much about people now. "I really think Shillawn will be happier in research than cutting. Celee was already a pilot, so he's lost nothing . . . Antona told me Carigana wouldn't surrender to the spore."

Rimbol frowned, his body stiffening so that she released him.

"She rebelled against everything, Rimbol. Didn't you ask Antona?"

"No." Rimbol ducked his head, a silly grin on his face. "I was afraid to while others were going through transition."

"Now it's all over. And you're installed on singer level." She saw the wristband and showed him hers. "Where're you bound for now?"

"To be fitted with my cutter." His green eyes brightened with enthusiasm.

"Then we can go together. I'm to collect mine."

They had entered the lift, and Rimbol half turned in surprise.

"Collect it?"

"They did tell you how long you've been ill, didn't they?" Killashandra knew her quick question was to give herself time. Rimbol's eyes mirrored surprise and then perplexity. "Oh, I lucked out. I had what Antona calls a Milekey Transition, so they pushed me out of the Infirmary to make room for someone else and put me into training to keep me out of mischief. Here we are, and don't mind the technician's manner. He hates to be kept from his fishing."

They had come to the cutter office and found Jezerey, Mistra, and two others.

"Killashandra! You made it!"

Killashandra thought there was a note of unwelcome surprise in Jezerey's voice. The girl looked gaunt and had lost her prettiness.

"Quiet out here," the Fisher said, his voice cutting through Killashandra's attempt at reply. He had a cutter in his hand, patently new.

"You. Killashandra," and he beckoned her brusquely to the counter as the others stepped back.

Killashandra was uncomfortably aware of the attention focused on her as she accepted the device. Then she curled her fingers around the power grip, the right hand on the guide, and forgot embarrassment in the thrill of being one step closer to the Crystal Ranges. She gave a little gasp as she saw that her name had been incised in neat letters on the plas housing that covered the infrasonic blade.

"Bring that back to be serviced after every trip, d'you hear? Otherwise, don't fault me when it doesn't cut proper. Understand?"

Killashandra would have thanked him, but he had turned to the others, beckoning to Borton. Cutter in hand, Killashandra turned and saw the indignation in Jezerey's eyes, the hurt, surprise, and betrayal in Rimbol's.

"Antona tossed me out of the Infirmary," she said, more to Rimbol than the others, but they all seemed to accuse her. "So the Guild put me to work."

Holding her head high, she gave them all a polite smile and left the office.

As she marched down the hall to the lift shafts, she was perversely angry with herself, with their ignorance, and with the Guild for thrusting her ahead of the others. She remembered similar scenes in the Music Center when she had achieved a role or an instrumental solo after unremitting practice and knew that the majority of her peers had favored another. Then she had been responsible. Now, though she had done nothing, consciously, to provoke her fellow recruits, she was being faulted because she'd had a bit of luck, just as she'd been blamed at the Music Center for hard work. What was the use!

"Watch that fardling cutter!" A savage tone interrupted her mortified self-pity, and someone shoved her to the right with unnecessary force. "I said, watch it!"

The man backed hastily away from her, for Killashandra had instinctively raised the cutter at the aggressive voice. Her confusion was further complicated by the knowledge that she had been careless and now was acting the fool. To be brought to task did not improve her temper.

"It's not on."

"It's bloody dangerous, on or off. Haven't you had the proper guidance with that?" The tall man glaring at her was Borella's companion from the shuttle.

"Then complain to Borella! She instructed us."

"Borella?" The singer stared at her with a perplexed frown. "What has she to do with you?"

"I was one of her recent 'catch,' I believe was her word."

His frown increased as his eyes flicked over her, pausing at the wristband.

"Just received your cutter, my dear?" He smiled now with supercil-

ious condescension. "I'll forget any charge of discourtesy." With a slight
bow and a sardonic grin, he strode on to the workshop.

She stared after the man, aware again of the strange magnetism of the
crystal singer. She'd been furious with him, and yet her anger had been
partially fed by his diffidence and her wish to impress him. Had Carrik
once been like that, too? And she too green to know?

She continued to the lift and entered. The encounter with the singer
had restored some perspective to her. Whatever else, she was a crystal
singer: more of one than the rest of her class by a physical anomaly and a
time factor that were no connivance of hers.

As she entered training room 47, she received another surprise. Trag
was there, leaning against a heavy plastic table, arms folded across his
chest, obviously awaiting her.

"I'm not late?" she asked, and experienced a second jolt of confusion,
for the tones of her question seemed to echo sourly in the room. Then she
saw the unmistakable plasfoam cartons on the table behind Trag. "Oh,
how curious?"

"Soured crystal," he said, his deeper voice resounding as hers had.
Then he extended his hand for her cutter.

She released it to him, somewhat reluctantly since it was so recent an
acquisition. He inspected every part of the device, even unsheathing the
infrasonic blade, which he gave the keenest scrutiny. He moved to her left
side, proffering the cutter and watching as she took it by the grips. He
checked her hand position and nodded.

"You are familiar with the controls?" he asked, although he must
have known that the Fisher had carefully explained them. "And the
process of tuning?" She nodded again, impatient with the catechism.

Now with a disregard for its contents that made her catch her breath,
he dumped onto the plastic table a crystal carton. Trag grinned.

"This is soured crystal. Sent to us from some of the nearer systems
which never bother to employ tuners. These will teach you how to learn
that weapon you carry."

For one horrified second, Killashandra wondered if Trag had been a
witness to her encounter with the other singer. She glanced down at the
device which, she realized, could be used as a weapon.

From the carton, Trag took five octagons of rose crystal. With a hammer similar to the one Enthor had used, he tapped each in turn. The third
crystal was sour, off significantly.

"Now the five must be retuned to match. I suggest you sing them a
full note below this"—and he tapped the faulty octagon—"and shave the
top of this until it rings pure against the infrasonic cutter." He placed the
soured crystal in an adjustable standing vise. He tightened the braces and
tugged to be sure the crystal was secure. "When this sings properly, you
merely recut the others in scale."

"How did it go sour?"

"Bracket flaw. Common enough in rose quartz."

"Dominant or minor?"

"Minor will be acceptable."

He nodded at her control grip, and she turned on the cutter, remembering to brace her body against the power that would surge through the handle. Trag tapped the sour crystal with his hammer, and she sang the minor note below, twirling the tuner with her thumb until the sound of the cutter matched her pitch.

The crystal screamed as she laid the blade against it. It took every ounce of self-control she had not to pull away.

"Slice it evenly," Trag commanded, his abrupt order steadying her.

The rose scream blended into a purer tone as the infrasonic cutter completed its surgery. Trag signaled her to turn off the cutter, ignoring her trembling hold. He tapped the crystal, and it sang a pure A minor. He tapped the crystal next in line. A major.

"Go to the G minor," he said, fastening the second octagon in place.

Killashandra found it took an effort to erase the echo of the major note from her mind. Turning on the cutter, setting the tuner to G minor, this time she was ready for the power surge and the cry of crystal. It was not as shrill, but the rose octagon seemed to resist the change in note as she drew the blade across it. Trag tapped the recut G minor and nodded approval, setting the third in the vise.

When Killashandra had recut the five, she felt drained and, in a bizarre fashion, elated. She had actually cut crystal. She leaned against the table, watching Trag repack them and make appropriate notations on the carton. Then he reached for a second container. Bracket rub again, and Trag made a few derogatory comments on technicians who did not recognize that proper bracketing prolonged the life of crystal.

"How would beginners like me learn if someone didn't make such mistakes?" she asked. "You surely don't use fresh crystal from the Ranges."

"Those octagons were relatively new. They ought not need tuning yet. I object to carelessness in any form."

Killashandra rather thought he would and determined to give him no cause to complain about her.

She recut the contents of nine boxes, twelve sets of crystal, blue, yellow, and rose. She had earnestly hoped that one of the boxes might reveal black crystal, and as the last box was unpacked to expose two squat blue dodecahedrons, one with a vertical split, she asked if black never had to be recut.

"Not within my service," Trag said, glancing at her keenly. "That is partly because the segments are separated and partly because their installation is handled by technicians of impeccable training and standard. Black does not suffer from bracket erosion or mishandling. Black crystal is too valuable." He put the damaged blue into the brace, split side exposed. "This will require a slightly different technique with your blade. If you slice off the damaged portion entirely, you will have destroyed the symmetry of the form. Therefore, the entire piece must be reshaped, scaled down in the dodecahedron. Ordinarily, one goes from major to minor, minor to major down the scale. This time, you must drop at least a sixth to achieve a pure note. As blues are nearly as common as rose, error presents no great loss. Relax. Proceed."

Killashandra had felt unequal to such an exercise, but Trag's inference that she could err with impunity stiffened her resolve. She heard the sixth below the moment she tapped the blue, set her cutter, and was slicing before he had time to step out of her way. She made the next two cuts without hesitation, listening to the change of pitch in the crystal. Curtly, she nodded for him to turn the dodecahedron in the vise and did three more passes. Only when she had completed the recutting did she turn off her device. Then she stared challengingly at Trag. Blandly, he placed the second crystal in the grips, tapped it and then the recut dodecahedron. They were in tune with each other.

"That is sufficient for one day, Trag."

At the unexpected voice behind her, Killashandra whirled, the cutter again rising in automatic defense, as Lanzecki finished speaking. With the slightest movement of his lips, he eyed the blade turned broadside to him. Instantly, she lowered it and her eyes, embarrassed and agitated by her reaction, and utterly wearied by the morning's intense concentration.

"I'd always heard that Fuerte was a pacific planet," Lanzecki said. "Nevertheless, you take to cutting well, Killashandra Ree."

"Does that mean I can get into the Ranges soon?"

She heard Trag's snort at her presumption, but Lanzecki did not reflect his chief assistant's attitude. The brown eyes held hers. Meeting that appraising stare, she wondered why Lanzecki was not a crystal singer: he seemed much more, so much more than Carrik or Borella or any of the other crystal singers she had met or seen.

"Soon enough not to jeopardize a promising career. Soon enough. Meanwhile, practice makes perfect. This exercise"—and Lanzecki gestured to the boxes of tuned crystal—"is but one of several in which you must excel before you challenge the Ranges."

He was gone in one of those fluid movements that was swift enough to make Killashandra wonder if Lanzecki had actually made his visit. Yet his brief appearance was undeniable by the effect he had on her and Trag.

The assistant Guild Master was regarding her with covert interest.

"Take a radiant bath when you reach your quarters," Trag said. "You are scheduled for sled simulator practice this afternoon." He turned away in dismissal.

The training pattern held until the next rest day, though she wished the two elements could have been reversed, with the sled simulation in the morning when her reflexes were fresher and the cutting in the afternoon so she could collapse. There proved to be a reason for that apparently irrational schedule. As she would invariably be flying the sled after she had cut crystal, she must learn to judge blunted reactions.

The radiant baths, the viscous liquid a gentle pressure on her tired body, its thick whirling like the most delicate of massages, did freshen after a morning's intense cutting drill. She checked with the computer and discovered that she was being paid a tuner's wage for her morning work but charged for the flight officer's instruction in the afternoon.

After six days of such an exhausting routine, she looked forward to a day of relaxation. A low-pressure ridge was moving in from the White Sea, so rest day might be cloudy with rain. She had begun to develop the Ballybraners' preoccupation with meteorology, encouraged by Trag's invariable questions about weather conditions at the start of each training session.

Her flight instructor also pressed heavily on weatherwise acumen. His insistence made more sense than Trag's since a good deal of her simulation drill involved coping with turbulence of varying degrees and types. She began to distinguish among the tonal differences of the warning equipment with which the simulator was equipped. Sound could tell her as clearly as the met display the kind and scope of the gale her practice flights trained her to survive.

Privately, Killashandra decided the warnings were an overkill situation; after being banged at, rung out, and buzzed, your mind would turn off most of the noise. The nerve tingler, last of the series of cautionary devices, couldn't be ignored.

Meanwhile, her practice performance developed from merely adequate to perfect automatic reaction as she simulated flights over every sector of Ballybran, land, sea, and arctic ice. She learned to identify, within seconds of their being displayed on her plan board, the major air and sea currents everywhere on the planet.

As she practiced, so she learned confidence in her vehicle. The sled was highly maneuverable with VTOL capabilities and a variety of assists to the basic crystalline drive, which had been highly refined for Ballybran's unusual conditions.

Killashandra had had only glimpses of the other members of Class 895. Rimbol had waved cheerfully at her from a distance, and she saw Jezerey scooting across the Hangar floor once, but Killashandra wouldn't count on her tolerance unless the girl's temper had markedly improved since the last time they'd met. Jezerey might be more amenable now that she and the others were in full training.

She saw Borton first as she wandered into the Commons Hall of the singers' level. It was an evening when most of the Guild's full members could relax. No storms were expected despite the low-pressure ridge, and Passover—the ominous conjunction of the three moons that produced the fiercest storms—was nine weeks away. Borton didn't see Killashandra, for he and the others in the lounge with him were on the far side. Augmented vision had advantages: see first; plan ahead.

She ordered Yarran beer, a beaker for herself and a pitcher for the group. She was annoyed with herself for anticipating a need for subtle bribery, but an offer made in good faith was unlikely to be refused. Especially of Yarran beer.

Borton saw her coming when she was about twenty meters away. His expression was of mild surprise, and he beckoned to her, speaking to someone hidden from view by the high back of the seating unit. A stir, exclamations, and Rimbol emerged, meeting her with a wide grin. The sense of relief she felt caused the pitcher to wobble.

"Don't waste a drop of good Yarran," he admonished, rescuing it. "Not everyone's down. Some are flaked out in radiant tanks. Shillawn has been transferred to the North Helton continent. That's where they do most of the pure research. Would you believe it, Killa? He doesn't stammer anymore."

"No!"

"Antona said the symbiosis must have corrected the fault in his palate." Rimbol was being determinedly affable, Killashandra thought as she took a place on the wide seating unit. Jezerey, seated in a corner of the unit, acknowledged Killashandra's arrival with a tight smile, Mistra nodded, and Celee and two other men whose names she couldn't call to mind greeted her. All of them looked tired.

"Well, I can't really say I'm sorry Shillawn didn't make it as a singer because he certainly won't be wasted in research," Killashandra said, raising her beaker in a circular toast to him.

"You mean, you haven't cut crystal yet?" Jezerey asked, a strident note in her voice as she pointed to the wristband evident as Killashandra made her toast.

"Me? Bloody no!" The disgust and frustration in her tone made Rimbol laugh, head thrown back.

"I told you she hadn't got that far," he said to Jezerey. "She only collected the cutter the day we met her."

Killashandra overtly eased the band on her wrist, aware now that it constituted her passport to friendship as well as to singer levels.

"Furthermore, Jezerey," she went on, letting resentment sharpen her words, "I'll be spending weeks more tuning crystal and simulating gale flights before I'm so much as allowed to put my nose past skimmer chart range. And by then there'll be Passover storms!"

"Oh, yes." Jezerey's attitude brightened, and her smile was complacent. "We'll all be storm bound then."

Killashandra was sensitive to the perceptible change of the atmosphere around her and decided to secure the advantage.

"I may be a little ahead of you in training—you do know that injured singers take it on only for the bonuses? Good. Well, once you've got those wretched cutters, you'll know what 'tired' means. Cut in the morning, then they send you on simulator flights, and when you're not doing either of those, it's drill; regs, rules, claims, fines—" Groans rose from her listeners. "Ah, I see you're getting the drills."

"So what other jollies are we to get?" Rimbol asked, his eyes sparkling with an almost malicious delight.

Most of those present were interested in any details she'd give concerning the retuning of crystal. She explained as best she could, truthfully if not fully, for she said nothing about Lanzecki's flattering appearances, her empathy with black crystal, and the rapid progress she seemed to be making in cutting difficult forms. She found it took an effort to be discreet, for she had never practiced tact in the Music Center. She'd be spending the rest of a very long life with these people, had nearly lost their friendship once through circumstances beyond her control, and she wasn't knowingly going to jeopardize it again.

Sufficient beer and other intoxicants were consumed by the recruits to make it a convivial evening. Killashandra found herself ready to be on old terms with Rimbol, and many of the tensions that had built over the past few weeks were dissolved in that most harmonious of activities.

When they woke, rested, they continued, although Killashandra was a trifle surprised to find that they had ended up in Rimbol's quarters. Location made little difference, as the apartments were in every respect similar. He had done little to furbish his rooms and solicited Killashandra's assistance. In this way, they passed agreeable hours and virtuously ended with a game reviewing rules and regulations from the clue of a phrase. In the glow of utter relaxation, Killashandra came very close to mentioning Keborgen's black crystal to Rimbol, rationalizing her evasion later by her desire not to burden her friend with unnecessary detail.

The next week, she suggested to Concera that she join the others in their classes rather than hold Concera up. The singer's two fingers were complete except for nails.

"You're not holding me up," Concera replied, her eyes sliding past Killashandra's, her mouth pursing with angry frustration. "Those others evidently have priority over a singer of my long standing. Besides, I only accepted you as a favor, I much prefer single teaching to group learning. Now let's go on to claims and counterclaims."

"I know those paragraphs sideways, frontwise, and backward."

"Then let's start in the middle of one," Concera said with unexpected levity.

As Killashandra really could rehearse claims and counterclaims as well as she boasted, she could also let her mind deal with her biggest problems: how to get her sled, how to get Lanzecki's attention and obtain clearance to cut crystal rather than chant about it. With the prodigious Passover storms looming only nine weeks off, she had to speed up. Research in the data banks about post-Passover problems indicated that it would be weeks before a new singer would be permitted to claim hunt in Ranges made more dangerous than ever by the ravages of Passover. Keborgen's claim could be so altered that her sensitivity to his black crystal might be nulli-fied. Mach storms could damage or substantially alter an exposed crystal face, flawing deep into the vein and rendering it useless. She *had* to get out soon.

Lanzecki had been in the habit, over the preceding two weeks, of ap-pearing as if teleported, generally when Killashandra was retuning crystal under Trag's scrutiny. Once Lanzecki had sat in the observer's seat of the sled simulator while she flew a particularly hazardous course. Instead of making her nervous, his presence had made her fly with heightened per-ception. Lanzecki also roamed through the Commons in the evenings, stopping for a word with this or that group, sorter, or technician. Now, when she very much wished him to materialize, he wasn't anywhere to be seen.

The fourth day, she casually asked Concera if she'd encountered the Guild Master and was told that Trag would know better where to find him. Trag was not the easiest person to question or converse with at all except in the handling of cutter or about incisions into crystal. Gathering all her self-assurance, Killashandra resorted to stratagem on the sixth day.

Trag had her shaving cones: she had ruined three the day before and quite expected to spend the morning's lesson avoiding future failures. Af-ter she had made a cut, she would look behind her. The fourth time, Trag frowned.

"Your attention span has been longer. What's the matter?"

"I keep thinking the Guild Master will appear. He does, you know, when I least expect it."

"He's on Shankill. Attend to your business."

She did, with less enthusiasm than ever, deeply grateful that the mor-row was a rest day. She had half promised to spend that evening and the next day with Rimbol: half promised because her urgency to reach the Ranges was in no way shared by the young Scartine. Trag released her at the end of the gruelingly precise session, his impassive face giving her no indication that she had learned to cut cones properly, though she felt in every muscle of her aching hands that she had achieved some proficiency.

She considered a radiant bath before the afternoon's flight practice. Instead, she put in a call for Rimbol: his company would be a soothing an-odyne for her increasing frustration. Waiting for his answer, she had a quick hot shower. She paced her apartment, wondering where in hell's planets Rimbol had got to. Her mealtime was nearly gone, and she hadn't eaten. She ordered a quick meal from the catering unit, bolting the hot food, adding a seared mouth to her catalog of grievances before she went to the Hangar level.

She was now one of many using the sled simulator so she had to be on time. She knew the flight was only an hour long, but this one, a compli-cated wind and night problem that kept her preternaturally alert and made her wish she'd taken the radiant bath instead of the shower, seemed end-less. She was very pleased to avoid several crashes and emerge unscathed from the simulator. She waved impudently at the flight training officer in his booth above the sled and passed the next student, Jezerey, on her way.

"He's either crash happy or he hates me," Killashandra commented to Jezerey.

"Him? He's crazy. He killed me three times yesterday."

"Kill or cure?"

"That's the Guild's motto, isn't it?" Jezerey replied sourly.

Killashandra watched the girl enter the simulator, wondering. She hadn't been killed yet. She thought of going to the ready room and watching Jezerey's flight. No one else was in the ready room, so she dialed a carbohydrate drink to give her blood sugar level a boost. She was watching Jezerey take off when she became conscious of someone in the doorway. She turned and saw the Guild Master.

"I understand you've been looking for me," he said to compound her astonishment.

"You're on Shankill. Trag told me so this morning."

"I was. I am here now. You have finished your afternoon's exercises?"

"I think they've about finished me."

He stood aside to indicate she should precede him.

"The severity of the drills may seem excessive, but the reality of a mach storm is far more violent than anything we can simulate in the trainers," he said, moving toward the lift while touching her elbow to guide her. "We must prepare you for the very worst that can occur. A mach storm won't give you a second chance. We try to insure that you have at least one."

"I seem to hear that axiom a lot."

"Remember it."

Killashandra expected the lift to plummet to the singers' level. Instead, it rose and, tired as she was, she swayed uncertainly. Lanzecki steadied her, hand cupped under her elbow.

"The next bad storm is Passover, isn't it?" She was making conversation because Lanzecki's touch had sent ripples along her arm. His appearance in the ready room had already unnerved her. She glanced sideways at him as unobtrusively as possible, but his face was in profile. His lips were relaxed, giving no hint of his thoughts.

"Yes, eight weeks from now is your first Passover."

The lift stopped, and the panels retracted. Killashandra stepped with him out into the small reception area. No sooner had he turned to the right than the third door opened. The large room they entered was an office, with one wall covered by a complex data retrieval system. Printout charts hung neatly from the adjacent wall. Before it, a formidable console printed out fax sheets that neatly folded into a bin. Several comfortable chairs occupied the center of the room, one centered at the nine screens that displayed the meteorology transmissions from the planet's main weather installations and the three moons.

"Yes, eight weeks away," Killashandra said, taking a deep breath, "and if I don't get out to the Ranges before it comes, it will be weeks, according to every report I've scanned—"

Lanzecki's laugh interrupted her.

"Sit." He pushed two chairs together and pointed a commanding finger to one.

Amazed that the Master of the Heptite Guild laughed and infuriated because she had not been able to state her case, she dropped without much grace into the appointed chair, her self-confidence pricked and drained. Presently, she heard the familiar clink of beakers. She looked up as he handed one to her.

"I like Yarran beer myself, having originated on that planet. I'm obliged to the Scartine for reminding me of it."

Killashandra masked her confusion by drinking deeply. Lanzecki knew a great deal about Class 895. He raised his glass to her.

"Yes, we must get you out to the Ranges. If anyone can find Keborgen's claim, it's likely to be you."

Feeling the beaker slip through fingers made nerveless by shock, she was grateful when he took the glass and put it on the table he swung before her.

"Conceit in a singer—voice or crystal—can be a virtue, Killashandra Ree. Do not let such single-mindedness blind you to the fact that others can reach the same conclusions from the same data."

"I don't. That's why I've got to get out into the Ranges as soon as possible." Then she frowned. "How did *you* know? No one followed me that night. Only you and Enthor knew I'd reacted to Keborgen's crystals."

Lanzecki gave her a long look that she decided must be pity, and she dropped her gaze, jamming her fingers together. She wanted to pound him or stamp her feet violently or indulge in some release from the humiliation she was experiencing.

Lanzecki, sitting opposite her, began to unlock her fingers one by one.

"You played the pianoforte as well as the lute," he said, his fingertips gently examining the thick muscle on the heel of her hand, the lack of webbing between her fingers, their flexible joints and callused tips. If this hadn't been her Guild Master, Killashandra would have enjoyed the semicaress. "Didn't you?"

She mumbled an affirmative, unable to remain quite silent. She was relieved, taking a deeply needed breath as he leaned back and took up his drink, sipping it slowly.

"No one did follow you. And only Enthor and I knew of your sensitivity to Keborgen's black crystal. Very few people know the significance of a Milekey Transition beyond the fact that you somehow escaped the discomforts they had to endure. What they will never appreciate is the totality of the symbiotic adjustment."

"Is that why Antona wished me luck?"

Lanzecki smiled as he nodded.

"Does that have something to do with my identifying black crystal so easily? Did Keborgen have a Milekey, too?"

"Yes, to both questions."

"That totality didn't save his life, did it?"

"Not that time," he said mildly, ignoring her angry, impudent question. Lanzecki voice-cued a display screen, and the guild's chronological roster appeared. Keborgen's name was in the early third. "As I told you that evening, the symbiont ages too, and is then limited in the help it can give an ancient and abused body."

"Why Keborgen must have been two hundred years old! He didn't look it!" Killashandra was aghast. She'd had only one glimpse of the injured crystal singer's face, but she never would have credited twenty decades to his age. Suddenly, the pressure of hundreds of years of life seemed as depressing to Killashandra as her inability to get into the Ranges.

"Happily, one doesn't realize the passage of time in our profession until some event displays a forcible comparison."

"You had a Milekey Transition." She shot her guess at him as if it were undeniable.

He nodded affirmation.

"But you don't sing crystal?"

"I have."

"Then . . . why . . ." and she gestured around the office and then at him.

"Guild Masters are chosen early and trained rigorously in all aspects of the operation."

"Keborgen was . . . but he sang crystal. And you have, too." She sprang to her feet, unable to assimilate the impact of Lanzecki's quiet words. "You don't mean . . . I have to train to be . . . You're raving!"

"No, you are raving," Lanzecki replied, a slight smile playing on his face as he gestured her to her seat and pointed at her beer. "Steady your nerves. My only purpose in having a private talk with you is to reassure you that you will go out into the Ranges as soon as I can arrange a shepherd for you."

"Shepherd?"

Killashandra was generally quick enough of wit to absorb the unexpected without floundering, but Lanzecki's singular interest in her, his awareness of intentions that she had kept utterly private, and his disclosures of the past few minutes had left her bewildered.

"Oh? Concera neglected to mention this facet of training."

"Yes, a shepherd, Killashandra Ree, a seasoned singer who will permit you to accompany him or her to a worked face, probably the least valuable of his claims, to demonstrate in practice what, to that point, has been theory."

"I've had theory up to my eyeballs."

"Above and behind them is better, my dear, which is where your brain is located, where theory must become reflex. On such reflexive knowledge may lie your survival. A successful crystal singer must have transcended the need for the *conscious* performance of his art."

"I've an eidetic memory. I can recite—"

"If you couldn't, you wouldn't be here." Lanzecki's tone reminded Killashandra of her companion's rank and the importance of the matter under consideration. He took a sip of his beer. "How often has Concera told you these past few weeks that an eidetic memory is generally associated with perfect pitch? And how often that memory distortion is one of the cruel facets of crystal singing? Sensory overload, as you ought to know, is altogether too frequent an occurrence in the Ranges. I am not concerned with your ability to remember: I am concerned with how much memory distortion you will suffer. To prevent distortion, you have been subjected to weeks of drill and will continue to be. I am also vitally concerned in a recruit who has made a Milekey Transition, retunes crystal well enough that Trag cannot fault her, who drives a sled so cleverly that the flight officer has given her patterns *he* wouldn't dare fly, and a person who had the wit to try to outsmart as old a hand at claim-hiding as Keborgen."

Lanzecki's compliments, though delivered as dry fact, disconcerted Killashandra more than any other of the afternoon's disclosures. She concentrated on the fact that Lanzecki actually wanted her to go after Keborgen's claim.

"Do you know where I should look?"

Lanzecki smiled, altering the uncompromising planes of his craggy face. He crossed one arm on his chest, supporting the elbow of the other, sipping at his beer.

"You've been doing the probability programming. Why don't you retrieve the data you've been accumulating?"

"How do you know what I've been doing? I thought my private voice code was unbreakable!"

"So it is." The sardonic look on Lanzecki's face reproved her for doubting. "But your use of data retrieval for weather, sled performance, and the time you have recently spent programming was notable. In a general way, what recruits or newly convalesced singers do is unregarded. However, when the person in question is not only sensitive to black crystal but signs out a skimmer to track the crash of a sled known to have transported black crystal, a quiet surveillance and a performance check are justified. Don't you agree? My dear girl, you are a very slow drinker. Finish it up and call up your program on Keborgen." He stood and indicated that she was to sit at the big console. "I'll get more beer for us and something to munch." He sauntered off to the catering unit.

Killashandra quickly took her place at the console, voice-coding the program. Though she might have doubted before now, Lanzecki's reproof reassured her. Nor did she doubt that he wanted more black crystal from Keborgen's claim, and if she offered the Guild the best chance of retrieving the loss, he would support her.

"Did you know Keborgen?" she asked, then realized that this must sound a stupid query to his Guild Master.

"As well as any man or woman here did."

"Part of my theory"—and Killashandra spoke quickly, tapping for the parameters she had stored on sled speed, warning time, and storm winds' velocity based on Keborgen's crash line—"is that Keborgen flew out direct."

Lanzecki put a fresh beaker on the ledge of the console, a tray of steaming morsels beside it, and smiled indulgently at her.

"No consideration, even his own safety, would have weighed more with Keborgen than protecting that claim."

"If that was what was expected of him, mightn't he once, in his desperate situation, choose the straight course?"

Lanzecki considered this, leaning against the console edge.

"Remember, he'd left escape to the last minute, judging by his arrival," Killashandra added earnestly. "The sled was not malfunctioning: the medical report postulated that he was suffering from sensory overload. But when he set out, he would have known from the met that the storm would be short. He would have known that everyone else would have cleared out of the Ranges so a direct route wouldn't be observed. And he hadn't cut that claim in nine years. Would that be important?"

"Not especially. Not for someone who had sung as long as Keborgen." Lanzecki tapped his forehead significantly and then looked down at the display where her parameters overlaid the chart of the area. "The others are searching west of your proposed site."

"Others?" Killashandra felt her mouth go dry.

"It's a valuable claim, my dear Killashandra; of course, I have to permit search. Don't be overly anxious," he added, resting one hand lightly on her shoulder. "They've never sung black."

"Does being sensitive to it give an advantage?"

"In your case, quite likely. You were the first other person to touch the crystal after Keborgen cut it. That seems to key a perceptive person to the face. *Seems*, I emphasize, not does. Much of what we should like to know about cutting crystal is locked within paranoid brains; silence is their defense against detection and their eventual destruction. However, one day, we shall know how to defend them against themselves." He was standing behind her now, cupping her shoulders with his hands. The contact was distracting to Killashandra, though she fancied he meant to be reassuring. Or supportive, because his next words were pessimistic. "Your greatest disadvantage, my dear Killashandra, is that you are a total novice when it comes to finding or cutting crystal. Where"—and his blunt forefinger pointed to the rough triangle on the map—"would your projected flight place his claim?"

"Here!" Killashandra pointed without hesitation to the spot, equidistant from the northern tip of the triangle and the sides defined.

He gave her shoulders a brief squeeze and moved off, walking slowly across the thick carpeting, hands behind his back. He tilted his head up, as if the blank ceiling might give him back a clue to the tortured reasoning of a dying crystal singer.

"Part of the Milekey Transition is a weather affinity. A spore always knows storm, though its human host may choose to trust instrumentation rather than instinct. Keborgen was old, he'd begun to distrust everything, including his sled. He would have been inclined to rely on his affinity rather than the warning devices." Lanzecki's bland expression cautioned her against such ignorance. "As I told you, the symbiosis loses its capabilities as the host ages. What you haven't accounted for in your program is Keborgen's desperate need to get off-planet during Passover—and he hadn't quite enough credit to do so. A cut of black crystal, any size, would have insured it. Those shards would have been sufficient. My opinion is that, having cleared them, he found he had a flawless cut. He ignored both the sled's warnings and his symbiont and finished the cut. He lost time."

He paused behind Killashandra again, put both hands on her shoulders, leaning slightly against her as he peered at the overlay.

"I think you're nearer right on the position than the others, Killashandra Ree." His chuckle was vibrant, and the sound seemed to travel through his fingers and down her shoulders. "A fresh viewpoint, unsullied as yet by the devious exigencies of decades spent outwitting everyone, including self." Then, releasing her when she did not wish him to, he continued in a completely different tone of voice. "Did Carrik interest you in the Guild?"

"No." She swung the console chair about and caught a very curious and unreadable movement of Lanzecki's mouth. His face and eyes were expressionless, but he was waiting for her to elaborate. "No, he told me the last thing I wanted to be was a crystal singer. He wasn't the only one to warn me off."

Lanzecki raised his eyebrows.

"Everyone I knew on Fuerte was against my leaving with a crystal singer in spite of the fact that he had saved many lives there." She was bitter about that, more bitter than she had supposed. While she knew it had not been Maestro Valdi's fault, if he hadn't initiated the hold on her, Carrik and she would have been well away from Fuerte and that shuttle crash; Carrik might still be well. But would she have become a singer?

"Despite all that is rumored about crystal singers, Killashandra, we have our human moments."

She stared at Lanzecki, wondering if he meant Carrik's saving lives or warning her against singing.

"Now," and Lanzecki walked to the console and touched a key. Suddenly, the triangle of F42NW down to F43NW in which Killashandra hoped to search was magnified on the big display across the room. "Yes, there's plenty of Range totally unmarked."

At that magnification, Killashandra could also discern five paint splashes. Within the five-klick circle centering on the paint splash, the tumbled gorges and hills were under claim. A singer could renounce his claim by listing the geographical coordinates, but Concera had told Killashandra that such an occurrence was rare.

"You could search an entire ravine and still miss the hoard inside the face," Lanzecki said, staring at the target area. "Or come a cropper with the claim's rightful owner." He reversed the magnification, and slowly the area was reduced until it faded into the rocky wrinkles surrounding the bay.

"Monday you will go out. Moksoon is not willing. He never is. But he's trying to get off-planet; with a decent cut and the bonus for shepherding, he could make it this time.

"Killashandra?"

"Yes, I go out on Monday. Moksoon is not willing but for the bonus—"

"Killashandra, you will find the black crystal!" Lanzecki's eyes took on an uncanny intensity, reinforcing his message and the strength of his conviction that Killashandra Ree was an agent he could command.

"Only if I'm bloody lucky." She laughed, recovering her equilibrium as she gestured to the vast area she'd have to comb.

Lanzecki's eyes did not leave hers. She was reminded of an ancient piece of drama history: a man had hypnotized a girl, a musical idiot, into vocal performances without peer. She couldn't recall the name, but to think of Lanzecki, Resident Master of one of the most prestigious Guilds in the Federated Sentient Planets, attempting to . . . ah . . . Svengali her into locating the nardy precious black crystal was ludicrous. Only she couldn't suggest that to Lanzecki, not when he was regarding her in so disconcerting a fashion.

Suddenly, he threw up his head and started to laugh. He abandoned his whole body to the exercise, his chest caving in, his ribs arching, his hands spread on his thighs as he bent forward. If anyone had told her five minutes before that Guild Master Lanzecki was capable of humor at all, she'd have thought them mad. He collapsed into a seating unit, his head lolling against its back as he roared.

His laughter had an oddly infectious quality, and she grinned in response. Then laughed, too, to see the Guild Master so reduced in dignity by mirth.

"Killashandra . . ." He gasped her name as the laughter subsided. "I do apologize, but the look on your face . . . I've thrown the reputation of the entire Guild into jeopardy, have I not?" He wiped moisture from the corners of his eyes and straightened up. "I haven't laughed in a very long time."

A wistful quality in that last remark made Killashandra change her reply.

"They used to say at Fuerte that I'd have been a good comic singer if I hadn't been so hipped on leads."

"I find nothing comic about you, Killashandra," he said, his eyes sparkling as he held out his hand.

"Dramatic?"

"Unexpected."

He took the hand she had unconsciously extended, caressing the palm with the ball of his thumb before turning her hand over and dropping a kiss in it.

She caught her breath at the spread of sensation from her palm through her body to the nipples on her breasts. She wanted to snatch her hand from his but saw the tender smile on his lips as he raised his head. Lanzecki had his eyes and face under control; his mouth betrayed him.

The pressure he exerted on her hand to draw her to him was as inexorable as it was gently and deftly done. With her across his thighs, her body against his, and her head in the crook of his arm, he brought her hand again to his mouth, and she closed her eyes at the sensuality of that delicate kiss. Her hand was placed palm down against warm skin, and she felt him stroke her hair, letting one curl wrap round his finger before he dropped his hand to her breast, lightly and with skill.

"Killashandra Ree?" His low whisper asked a question that had nothing to do with her name but everything that pertained to who she was.

"Lanzecki!"

His mouth covered hers in so light a caress that she was at first unaware of being kissed. It was so with the rest of her first experience with the Guild Master, a loving and sharing that paled into insignificance any other encounter.

Chapter 8

When she gradually awakened the next morning, she found his fingers lightly clasping her upturned hand. Her slight movement of surprise caused his fingers to tighten, then caress. Opening her eyes, she turned her head toward him, to meet his eyes, sleepily narrow. They were lying, she on her back, he on his stomach, stretched out, the only point of contact the two hands, yet Killashandra felt that her every muscle and nerve was in tune to him and his to her. She blinked and sighed. Lanzecki smiled, his lips relaxed and full. His smile deepened, as if he knew of her fascination with his mouth. He rolled to his back, still holding her right hand, now pulling it up to kiss the palm. She closed her eyes against the incredible sensation the lightest touch of his lips created within her.

Then she noticed the fine white lines across his bare arm and chest, parallel in some places, criss-crossed in others.

"I believe I mentioned that I sang crystal," he said.

"Cut crystal would be nearer the truth from the look of you," she said, raising her upper body to see the rest of his well-muscled torso. Then she frowned. "How do you know so accurately what I'm thinking? No one mentioned a telepathic adaptation to the spore."

"There is none, darling. I have merely become adept at reading expressions and body language over the decades."

"Is that why you're Guild Master instead of singer?" She had heard, and savored, the endearment.

"There must be a Guild Master."

"Trag would never make it."

"Now who is telepathic?"

"Well, you'd better watch your mouth."

"My mouth said nothing about Trag's future."

"It didn't have to. So, are recruits deliberately selected?"

His mouth gave nothing away to her. "Where did you get that idea, Killashandra Ree?" His eyes were laughing, denying her remembrance of Borella's conversation to the other singer on the shuttle from Shankill.

"The notion had occurred to me from the pounds of prevention FSP applies to keep people from joining the Guild."

"The FSP"—and Lanzecki's mouth drew into a thinner line—"is also the largest purchaser of crystal. Especially black crystal." He rolled back to her, his eyes on her mouth. "This is my rest day, too. I earnestly desire to relax in your good company." He was indeed as earnest as she could have wished and exceedingly obliging. While they paused to eat, she asked him how they had moved from his office suite to his apartment on the singer level.

"Private lift." He gave a careless shrug of his cicatriced shoulders as he sought morsels of food in the rich spicy sauce. "One of my perquisites."

"Is *that* how you do your appearing act?"

Lanzecki grinned at her, delighted in an unexpectedly boyish way— *that* put her guiltily in mind of Rimbol—that he had disconcerted her.

"I often have need to 'appear' unexpectedly."

"Why?"

"In your case?" His smile altered slightly, his lips taking a bitter twist. "Serendipity. I liked your misplaced loyalty to Carrik. I wished you well away from the Scoria system. Once you passed the entrance requirements, you became my responsibility."

"Isn't everyone in the Guild?"

"More or less. But you, Killashandra Ree, had a Milekey Transition."

"You do this every time? . . ." She was piqued by his candor and gestured with all the contempt of an outraged opera heroine around the bedroom.

"Of course not," he said with a burst of laughter. He caught her hand and kissed her palm with the usual effect, despite her indignation. "This is not one of my perks, darling. It is a privilege you have granted me. I did— and have no doubts on that score for the duration of your memory—want to know you before you went into the Ranges."

"Before?" She caught that subtle emphasis.

He made an untidy pile of their dishes and shoved them into the disposal slot.

"Before singing crystal has stung your blood."

He turned back, and she could see the sadness in the droop of his mouth.

"But you've sung crystal?"

He put both hands on her shoulders, looking down at her. There was no expression in his eyes; the planes of his face were still, the line of his mouth uncompromising.

"Do you mean that after I have sung, I won't be any good? Or any more good to you?" She flung the options at him.

Instead of repudiating either, he caught her resisting body up in his arms, laughing as he swung her around and around, tight against him.

"My darling, I shall make love to you until tomorrow morning when I shall . . . shepherd . . . you to your sled and to Moksoon. You shall endeavor your best, once Moksoon has demonstrated the cutter's art on an actual face, to find Keborgen's claim. When you return from your first trip"—and he gave an enigmatic laugh—"I shall still be Guild Master. But you"—and here he kissed her—"will be truly a crystal singer."

He did not let her speak then; nor did they return to the subject of their occupations.

The following morning, Lanzecki was completely the Guild Master when she met him and the petulant Moksoon in the flight officer's ready room. She had been out in the Hangar checking *her* sled, putting her cutter in its brackets with a loving snap, aware of the acrid, chemical tang of new plastic and metal from the run-in of the drive.

Moksoon was not Killashandra's notion of a shepherd for her first trip into the dangerous Milekeys. That he was as dubious about her was unmistakable in the sidelong glances he gave her. A slightly built man who had probably always had a wizened appearance to his face, he looked old, odd enough in a crystal singer. He also looked thoroughly annoyed, for the maintenance officer was suavely explaining why it had taken so long to repair his sled. Since Lanzecki had explained to her that Moksoon's most important qualification as her guide was that he was known to be cutting in the Bay area, Killashandra knew that the delay had been contrived.

"Remember, of course, Moksoon, that the bonus alone sees you safely off-planet," Lanzecki said, deftly entering the conversation. "This is Killashandra Ree. Master recorder on! Moksoon, this will be on continuous replay in your cabin. You are shepherding Killashandra Ree in accordance with Section 53, Paragraphs one through five. She is cognizant of the fact that she is entitled to nothing that she may cut under your direction at your claim. She is entitled to stay with you two working days when she will depart to seek a claim of her own. She will never make any attempt to return to your claim under Section 49, Paragraphs 7, 9, and 14. Killashandra Ree, do you . . ." And Killashandra found herself repeating, affirming, avowing, under the strict penalties imposed by the Heptite Guild that she would obey the strictures of the two sections and the paragraphs cited. Moksoon was also required to repeat his willingness, which was forced, above and beyond the bonus offered, to instruct her in the cutting of crystal for the two-day period as allowed by Guild rules and regulations.

Moksoon's repetition was so marred by lapses into silence and prompts from Lanzecki and the flight officer that Killashandra had half a mind to revoke her contract. Lanzecki caught her eye, and her rebellion ended.

The official recording made, replicas were patched into the communications units of both sleds. The flight officer escorted Moksoon to his vehicle, slightly canted to the left and battered in spite of fresh paint that attempted to blend the most recent repairs into the older dings. Lanzecki strode beside Killashandra to her brand new sled.

"Use the replay whenever he falters. Your switch is rigged to activate his."

"Are you sure that Moksoon is the right—"

"For your purpose, Killashandra, the only one." Lanzecki's tone allowed no argument. "Just don't trust him about anything. He's cut crystal too long and sung too long alone."

"Then why—" Now Killashandra was totally exasperated.

Lanzecki cupped her elbow and half lifted her into her sled.

"His hands will automatically do what you need to see. Watch how he cuts, what he does, not what he says. Heed your inner warnings. Watch your Met report as often as you think of it. Fortunately, you'll think of it often enough the first trip out. Passover's in seven weeks. Storms *can* blow up days before the actual conjunction. Yes, I know you know all this, but it bears repeating. He's in and belted. No time now. Follow him. The charts of the Bay area have been put on instant review. Be sure to pack crystal as soon as you have cut, Killashandra!"

He had smoothly engineered her departure, Killashandra thought, giving her no time for regrets and none for personal farewell. Yesterday, she reminded herself, he had been Lanzecki the man. Today he was Guild Master. Fair enough.

Moksoon took off just as she switched on her sled's drive. His craft canted even in the air, a distinctive silhouette, like that of a person with one shoulder higher than the other. Despite her severe doubts about Moksoon, Killashandra experienced a rush of elation as she drifted her sled from the Hangar. She was going to cut crystal at last. At last? She was first out of Class 895. She thought of Rimbol and grimaced. She ought at least to have left a call for him, explaining her absence. Then she remembered that she had placed a call to him that hadn't been answered. That could suffice!

Bollux, but that fool Moksoon was running like a scared mushman! She increased the speed of her sled, closing to a proper following distance. In a peculiar change of direction, Moksoon now headed due north and dropped to a lower altitude, skimming the first folds of the Milekey Range. As she was above him, she caught his second, easterly shift, and then he disappeared over a high fold. She decelerated to a near hover, scanning both ends of the drop as she approached it. He was hovering on the north end of the fault. She caught the merest glint of sunlight on the orange of his sled, then flew on to the next ravine as if she hadn't spotted him and mimicked his tactics until he showed at the southern edge, just as she'd expected.

"Twithead's forgotten I'm supposed to follow him," she said, and slapped on the replay. The one in his sled would project its message. She sighed deeply, resigned to a long and difficult day, but suddenly his sled popped up into sight, and Moksoon made no immediate attempt to evade her.

She checked his new heading, south at four, which was an honest direction for Moksoon's eventual destination. She wondered how long she could trust the reinforcement of the replay. A direct flight would get them to the Bay area in two hours at the reasonable speed Moksoon was maintaining. She might not know where he was leading her, but she had the advantage over him in a new sled capable of speed and maneuverability.

Even on a direct course, Moksoon was an erratic flyer. There shouldn't have been thermals or violent air currents at his level, but his sled bounced and lolled. Was he trying to make her air sick following?

Why had Lanzecki chosen this man? Because of his faulty memory? Because, once Moksoon had achieved his desired trip off-planet, he would not, in the fashion of crystal singers of long service, remember that he had shepherded one Killashandra Ree into the Bay's Range. Well, that was logical of Lanzecki, provided she could also find Keborgen's claim. Before the others who were looking for it. Patently, Lanzecki was backing her.

"Once a singer has cut a certain face, she only needs to be in its general area and she'll feel the pull of the sound," Concera had said. "Your augmented vision will assist in distinguishing the color of crystal beneath storm film, base rock, and flaw. Catch the sun at the right angle and crystal cuttings are blindingly clear."

Phrases and advice flooded through Killashandra's mind, but as she looked down at the undulating folds of the Milekey Ranges, she entertained serious doubts that she would ever find anything in such a homogeneous land. Kilometers in all directions flowed in similar patterns of fold, ridge, valley, gorge.

A sudden stab of piercing light made her clutch the yoke of the sled to steady herself. She peered down and saw an orange slice of sled top, half hidden by an overhang and deep in the ravine, only its luminescent paint and her altitude disclosing it. On the highest of the surrounding ridges was the splash of paint indicating a claim.

That crystal flash, as unlikely as everything else that had been happening to her recently, confirmed that some of the other improbables might also be true on Ballybran.

Fardles! Where had Moksoon got to? During her brief inattention, the old singer's orange sled had slipped from view. She speeded up and caught a glimpse of the orange stern winding through a deep ravine. Without changing altitude, she matched pace with his cautious forward movement, her viewscreen on magnify. Since she had his sled well in view, she did not reactivate the tape. He might just as easily slam into one of the odd stone buttresses that lined the canyon if she startled him.

She checked the heading; Moksoon had gone north by 11. Suddenly, he oozed up and over a ridge, down into a deeper, shadowed valley. She dove, noting quickly that the deep went south. Unless he flipped over the intervening fold, Moksoon would have to follow the southerly course. That gorge continued in its erratic fashion stubbornly south by 4. She couldn't see Moksoon in the shadows, but there was no place else he could be.

The long winding of the gorge ended in a blockade of debris, the erosion of a higher anticline. There was no sign of Moksoon. He had to be in the gorge, hiding in shadow. Then she saw the faded claim blaze on a ridge. Even in Ballybran's climate, the stuff was supposed to take decades to deteriorate so much. A released claim always had the piss-green countermark—not that she'd seen any of those during her pursuit of Moksoon.

Cautiously, she guided her sled down the rock slide and into the gorge. In some places, the sides nearly met; in others, she had a view of Ranges folding beyond. Something glinted in the little sunlight that penetrated. She increased the magnification and was surprised to see a thin stream meandering the base of the gorge. There had been no lake at the blocked point, so she assumed that the little stream went underground in its search for an outlet to the Bay.

She was beginning to feel anxious when an oxbend revealed a wider valley; the orange sled was parked on the right, on a shadowed ledge that would have been invisible from all except a direct search of this particular canyon.

She keyed the replay and turned up the volume so that Lanzecki's voice was echoing off the rock walls as Moksoon slipped and slid toward her, the crystal cutter held safely above his head.

"Claim jumper! Claim jumper!" he shrieked, stumbling to the ledge on which she had rested her sled. He turned on the cutter, held it well in front of him, as he approached her sled door.

"In accordance with Section 53, Paragraphs 1 through 5 . . ." the replay roared.

"Lanzecki? He's with you?" Moksoon glanced wildly around and above him, searching for another sled.

"Playback," Killashandra yelled through Lanzecki's amplified words. "I'm *not* claim jumping. You're *shepherding* me. You get a *bonus*." She used her voice training to shoot her message through the pauses in the recording.

"That's me!" Moksoon pointed accusingly at her sled from which his own hesitant voice emanated.

"Yes, you made the tape this morning. You *promised* to *shepherd* me for the *bonus*."

"Bonus!" Moksoon lowered the cutter, though Killashandra adroitly maneuvered herself farther from its point.

"Yes, *bonus*, according to Section 53, Paragraphs 1 through 5. Remember?"

"Yes, I do." Moksoon didn't sound all that certain. "That's you speaking now."

"Yes, promising to abide by Section 49, Paragraphs 7, 9, and 14. I'm to stay with you two days only, to watch an expert cut crystal. Lanzecki recommended you so highly. One of the best."

"That Lanzecki! All he wants is cut crystal." Moksoon snorted in sulky condemnation.

"This time you'll have a bonus to get you off-world."

The cutter point down now, the fingers of the tired old man so slack on the grip, Killashandra hoped he wouldn't drop it. She'd been told often enough how easily the wretchedly expensive things damaged.

"I gotta get off Ballybran. I gotta. That's why I said I'd shepherd."

Head bent, Moksoon was talking to himself now, ignoring the replayed affirmations.

Suddenly, he swung the tip of his cutter up and advanced towards her menacingly. Killashandra scooted back as far as she could on the ledge.

"How do I know you won't pop right back in here when I'm off-world and cut my claim?"

"I couldn't find the bloody place again," she said, exploding, discretion no advantage in dealing with the fanatic. "I haven't a clue where I am. I had to keep my eyes on you, zipping here and dropping there. Have you forgotten how to pilot a sled? You sure have forgotten a perfectly valid agreement you made only five hours ago!"

Moksoon, his eyes little slits of suspicion, lowered the cutter fractionally. "You know where you are."

"South at four is all I bloody know, and for all the twists and turns in this ruddy gorge, we could be north at ten. What in damnation does it matter? Show me how to cut crystal and I'll leave in an hour."

"You can't cut crystal in an hour. Not properly." Moksoon was scathingly contemptuous. "You don't know the first thing about cutting crystal."

"You're quite right. I don't. And you'll get a huge bonus for showing me. Show me, Moksoon."

With a combination of cajolery, outrageous flattery, constant repetition of words like "bonus," "Lanzecki expects," "off-world," and "brilliant Cutter," she pacified Moksoon. She suggested that he eat something before showing her how to cut and let him think she was fooled into offering from her own supplies. For a slight man, he had a very hearty appetite.

Well fed, rested, and having filled her with what she knew must be a lot of nonsense about angles of the sun, dawn, and sunset excursions down dark ravines to hear crystal wake or go to sleep, Moksoon showed no inclination to pick up his cutter and get on with his end of the bargain. She was trying to think of a tactful way of suggesting it when he suddenly jumped to his feet, throwing both arms up to greet a shaft of sunlight that had angled down the ravine to strike their side just beyond the bow of his sled.

A peculiar tone vibrated through the rock on which Killashandra was sitting. Moksoon grabbed up his cutter and scrambled, emitting a joyous cackle that turned into a fine, clear ringing A sharp below middle C. Moksoon sang in the tenor ranges.

And part of the ravine answered!

By the time she had reached him, he was already slicing at the pink quartz face his sled had obscured. Why the old—

Then she heard crystal crying. For all his other failings, Moksoon had an astonishing lung capacity for so old a man. He held the accurate note even after his pitched cutter was excising a pentagon from the uneven extrusion of quartz, which flashed from different facets as the sunlight shifted. The dissonance that began as he got deeper into the face was an agony so basic that it shook Killashandra to her teeth. It was much worse than retuning crystal. She froze at the unexpected pain, instinctively letting loose with a cry of masking sound. The agony turned into two notes, pure and clear.

"Sing on!" Moksoon cried. "Hold that note!" He reset his infrasonic cutter and made a second slice, cropped it, sang again, tuned the cutter, and dug the blade in six neat slashes downward. His thin body shook, but his hands were amazingly steady as he cut and cut until he reached the edge. With an exultant note, he jumped to a new position and made the bottom cut for the four matched crystals. "My beauties. My beauties!" he crooned and, laying the cutter carefully down, dashed off to his sled, reemerging seconds later with a carton. He was still crooning as he packed the pieces. There was a curious ambivalence in his motions, of haste and reluctance, for his fingers caressed the sides of the octagons as he put them away.

Killashandra hadn't moved, as stunned by the experience of crystal as she was by his agile performance. When she did sigh to release her tensions, he gave an inarticulate shout and reached for his cutter. He might have sliced her arm off, but he tripped over the carton, giving her a head start as she raced back to his sled, stumbled into it, and hit the replay button before she slid the door closed. It caught the tip of the cutter.

And Lanzecki had suggested she go with this raving maniac? Lanzecki's voice rolled out, reverberated back, and made a section of the rock face above the sled resonate.

"I'm sorry, Killashandra Ree," Moksoon said, a truly repentant note in his voice. "Don't break my cutter. Don't close that door."

"How can I trust you, Moksoon? You've nearly killed me twice today."

"I forget. I forget." Moksoon's tone was a sob. "Just remind me when I'm cutting. It's crystal makes me forget. It sings, and I forget."

Killashandra closed her eyes and tried to catch her breath. The man was so pitiful.

"I'll show you how to cut. Truly I will."

Moksoon's recorded voice was duly affirming his willingness to shepherd her, Section 53. She could break his cutter with one more centimeter of leverage on the door. Her own voice dinned into her ears, affirming and averring to abide by section and paragraph.

"You'd better be able to show me something about cutting crystal that I couldn't learn at the Complex."

"I'll show you. I'll show you how to find song in the cliffs. I'll show you how to find crystal. Any fool can cut it. You've got to find it first. Just don't close that door!"

"How do I keep you from trying to kill me?"

"Just talk to me. Keep that replay on. Just talk to me as I'm cutting. Give me back my cutter!"

"I'm talking to you, Moksoon, and I'm opening the door. I haven't damaged the cutter." The first thing he did when she eased up the pressure was examine the tip. "Now, Moksoon, show me how to find song in the cliffs."

"This way, this way." He scrabbled to the outcropping. "See . . ." and his finger traced the faultline, barely discernible. "And here." Now a glint of crystal shone clearly through the covering dirt. He rubbed at it, and sunlight sparkled from the crystal. "Mostly sunlight tells you where, but you gotta *see*. Look and see! Crystal lies in planes, this way, that way, sometimes the way the fold goes, sometimes at right angles. You sure you can't find your way back here?" He shot her a nervous glance.

"Positive!"

"Rose always drops south. Depend on it." He ran his finger tips lightly down the precipice. "I hadn't seen this before. Why didn't I see this before?"

"You didn't look, did you, Moksoon?"

He ignored her. At first, Killashandra thought a breeze had sprung up, highly unlikely though that was in this deep gorge. Then she heard the faint echo and realized that Moksoon was humming. He had one ear to the rock wall.

"Ah, here. I can cut here!"

He did so. This time, the crystal cry was expected and not as searing an experience. She also kept herself in Moksoon's view, especially when he had completed his cuts. She got a carton for him, carried it back and stored it, all the time talking or making him talk to her. He did know how to cut crystal. He did know how to find it. The gorge was layered in southerly strips of rose quartz. Moksoon could probably cut his claim for the rest of his Guild life.

When the sun dropped beyond the eastern lip of the gorge, he abruptly stopped work and said he was hungry. Killashandra fed him and listened as he rambled on about flaw lines and cuts and intruders, by which he meant noncrystal rock that generally shattered the crystal vein.

Since she recalled Enthor's poor opinion of rose quartz, she asked Moksoon if he cut other colors. It was an unwise question, for Moksoon had a tantrum, announcing that he'd cut rose quartz all his working life, which was far longer than she'd drawn breath, or her parents, or her grandparents for that matter, and she was to mind her own business. He stalked off to his sled.

Taking the precaution of locking her door panel, she made herself comfortable. She wasn't sure that she could endure, or survive, another day with the paranoid Moksoon. She didn't doubt for a moment that the uneasy rapport she had finally achieved would fade overnight in his crystallized brain pan.

In the cool darkness of the gorge, where night made the rocks crack and tzing, she thought of Lanzecki. He had wished to know her, he said, before she sang crystal. Now that phrase had both an overtone of benediction and a decided implication of curse. Would just one trip to the Crystal

Ranges alter her so much? Or had their nights and day together occurred to form some bond between them? If so, Lanzecki was going to be very busy over the next few weeks, cementing links between Jezerey, Rimbol— and then Killashandra's sense of humor overruled vile whimsies. Lanzecki might be devious but not that damned devious!

Besides, none of the others had made Milekey Transitions or appeared sensitive to black crystal. It was a concatenation of circumstances. And he had said that he liked her company. He, Lanzecki, liked her company. But Lanzecki the Guild Master had sent her out with crazed Moksoon.

Killashandra set her waking buzz for sunrise so that she'd be out of the gorge before Moksoon woke.

Chapter 9

She woke to darkness and a curious pinging. Cautiously, she put her head out the sled door, checking first in Moksoon's direction. Not a sign of life there. She looked upward, between the steep walls of the gorge, to a lightening sky. After her hide-and-seek with Moksoon the day before, she appreciated the navigational hazards of semidark. She also didn't wish to be around when the old crystal singer roused.

She checked that all her lockers were closed and secure, an automatic action learned during her simulated-flight instruction. Fortunately, she had made "dark" landings and takeoffs in imaginary shallow canyons and deep valleys, though she wished she'd paid more attention to the terrain just beyond Moksoon's claim. She couldn't risk retracing yesterday's circuit to the avalanche.

She strapped into her seat, turned the drive to minimum power, easing up half a meter by the vertical and out ten horizontal, then activated the top scanner to be sure of her clearances.

The sky was light enough for her purposes but not as yet touched with the rising sun. She lifted slowly, carefully, her eyes on the scanner to be sure she didn't bounce off an unexpected outcropping.

Abruptly, she was above the gorge and hovered, quickly switching the scan to under-hull and magnify. Her departure had not aroused Moksoon. With luck, he would have forgotten that she'd been there until he received his bonus. And how *she* had worked for that!

The notion that one day she might be as Moksoon now was crossed her mind, but that, she firmly assured herself, was a long time in the future. She'd make it as future as possible.

She proceeded with fair haste to the F42NW–43NW where five old paint splashes made an irregular pattern on Lanzecki's aerial map. The sun was rising, an awesome sight at any time, but as it gilded the western folds and heights of the Milekey Range, it was truly magnificent. She settled the sled on a flattened, eroded syncline to enjoy the spectacle of morning breaking as she ate breakfast. It was a lovely clear morning, the light breeze tainted with sea, for the Bay was not far. She checked meteorology, which indicated that the clear, dry weather was confirmed for the next six hours.

She would come in over F42NW at altitude and proceed to F43NW, just to get an overall picture. If her hunch was right, and Lanzecki's privileged information had only confirmed it, one of those five claims had to be Keborgen's black crystal.

From height, the area looked desolate—valleys and ravines, blind canyons, few with water, and not so much as a glint of crystal shine in the morning sun. Furthermore, one of the painted claim marks was newer than the others. The sun reflected off the mark. Had one of the other singers actually found Keborgen's claim? She reminded herself sternly that none of the others had come this far north. One new claim mark among five. But Lanzecki's original aerial scan had displayed five old marks.

Killashandra caught her breath. Keborgen had not been to this claim in nine years. Because he couldn't remember where it was? He had garnered useful shards and splinters and a triad, worth a fortune of credit. Might he not have used up his margin of time between storm warning and escape to repaint his claim so he could find it more easily after the storm?

Killashandra searched her mind about claims and claim-jumping. Nothing prevented her from checking the circumscribed area. Lifting or cutting crystal was the felony.

She reduced her altitude and swept round the claim in a circle roughly five klicks in diameter from the brightly painted ridge mark. She could see no other sled, though she hovered over several shadowed ledges and overhanging cliffs to be sure. She also noted no spark or glint of sun-struck crystal. After the initial survey, she landed on the ridge. The paint was new, only scored here and there by the last storm. She could see edges of the old where the new had been applied in haste. Then she found the paint container, wedged in some rocks where it had been thrown or wind-swept. She hefted it, smiling in exultation. Yes, Keborgen didn't want to forget *this* claim. He'd wasted time to preserve it.

She looked out across the ridges and nearest gullies and wondered where. From this vantage point, she could see the five klicks in every direction.

Since Keborgen had obviously cleared the crystal shards from his site, there'd be none to indicate where he'd worked. But he would have had to hide his sled from aerial observation, as Moksoon had done.

So Killashandra spent the rest of the morning flying search patterns over the circle. She found five locations; two partial hides in the south on 7 quadrant, an undercut in west 10, a very narrow blind valley in 4, and two shadowed gorges in north 2. On her master chart, she noted each location by some distinguishing contour or rock and the angle at which she had been flying to discern it.

She had no further support from the weather, for a drizzle began midafternoon. There'd be no sunset flashes to lead her, no sun-warmed crystal to speak. She saw no advantage in sitting on the claim ridge, either. There were other singers looking for Keborgen's claim. No sense being so visible.

"Eena, meena, pitsa teena," she chanted, pointing at one site on each syllable. "Avoo bumbarina, isha gosha, bumbarosha, nineteen hundred and one!"

"One" was the west 4 undercut.

As she approached from the south, she noticed that the ridge was curiously slanted. Since it was protected on all sides by higher folds, the erosion had not been caused by wind. She landed the sled as well as she could on uneven ground beside the overhang. She would inspect first. As she pulled on wet-weather gear, she noticed that debris had showered on either side of the ledge, which was, in fact, just the right length for a sled.

Much heartened, she went out and prowled around. The rock falls were of long residence, well chinked with grit and dirt. The ledge was solid, but at one end heterogeneous rocks had been tamped in for critical reinforcement. A little scrape of orange paint along the inside wall was her final reassurance. A sled had parked there. She parked hers with a sense of accomplishment.

She was not so happy after she had climbed to the highest point above the blind valley. She stared about her in the mizzling gloom. The valley was in the form of a blunted crescent, any part of which was an easy hike from the undercut. Crystal singers exerted themselves only to cut crystal, not heft it any distance. Keborgen's claim had to be somewhere in the valley.

She slithered down the rocky side, adding more rubble to what was scattered about. When she returned to her sled, she checked the met report. Cloud cover ending midday, unless the cold front moving up from the southern pole picked up speed. She'd probably have a clear afternoon and sun on the southern tip of the valley. Rain or not, she told herself, she'd be out at first light. Keborgen had made two obvious mistakes: fresh claim and old sled paint.

Keborgen's cutting eluded her the entire damp gray morning as she searched the crescent for any signs of cutting, rubbed her hands and fingers raw scraping at stone. The valley's walls varied in height, on the longer curve up to 10 meters, sloping down to a dip almost directly across from the undercut. From the bottom of the valley, she couldn't see any signs, even accounting for the fact that Keborgen had taken crystal rubble with him.

She clambered back to her sled for something to eat, totally discouraged. She might just as well have braved Moksoon another day for all she had accomplished on her own.

A sudden gleam of light attracted her attention to the window. Clouds were scuttering across the sky to the north, and she saw patches of bright sky. As she left her sled, a light breeze blew directly into her face. Suddenly, sunlight shafted from the clouds, blinding after almost two days of dismal gray.

With sun, she might just be lucky enough to catch crystal flash—if she was turned in the right direction at the exact moment. Keborgen's cut could not have built much dirt cover after the short storm.

The sun was more west than east. She'd have a better chance if she was facing the west. She scrambled up the valley side to the ridge, turning to her right, and stopped. With the sun shining, she could discern what the rain had hidden the day before, a clear if uneven and winding path of packed dirt, suitable for an agile pair of feet. The path had been worn by a long-legged man, and as she eagerly followed it, she occasionally had to hop or stretch. She was so much occupied with her footing that she would have tripped into the fault if she had not first noticed the tamped-down flat space 2 meters from the edge. Just where someone could leave crystal cartons. It could have been excitement at first, but Killashandra felt a prickling along her legs. Then she heard the soft sighing, more noise than so light a breeze should make. It was as if someone distant were humming softly, and the sound floated to her on the breeze. Only this sound emanated ahead of her.

Trembling, she took the last two steps and looked down into a trench, a V shape, slanting down toward the valley floor, some 10 meters below the lowest arm of the V. Muddy water oozed off the V point. Water had collected in a too obviously geometric puddle halfway down the uneven side. Uneven because Keborgen had left foot rests for easy access to the heart of his claim. As she descended, she could feel black crystal surrounding her. When she reached the bottom, she knelt by the symmetrical pool, a fingertip deep, and felt its sides. Smooth. Her fingers tingled.

Rising, she looked around. Roughly 6 meters long, carefully cut to maintain that rough, natural look, the V opened to a width of 4 meters on the ravine side. Reverently now, she took a waste-cloth and brushed mud away. The dull shine of cold black crystal was revealed. Using the cloth, she mopped away the water. Keborgen's triad had been cut true, but to themselves, not to the angle of the vein, leaving this little wedge to accumulate water. No, this little piece was flawed, storm damage, more than likely. She caressed it, feeling the roughness of the flaw. Then she began excitedly to clean the ledge, to find out where the flaw stopped, where was the good black crystal. Ah, here, at the side, just where Keborgen had stopped cutting when the storm arrived.

How big, how deep, how wide was this crystal vein? This treasure store? Killashandra's elation overwhelmed her initial caution; laughing, she scrubbed at first this spot in the opposite wall, then along the slanty arms of the V, mopping the disguising grit and mud from the crystal and giggling softly to herself. Her titter echoed back to her, and she began to laugh, the louder sound reverberating.

She was surrounded by crystal. It was singing to her! She slid to the floor, oblivious of the mud, stroking the crystal face on either side of her, trying not to giggle, trying to *realize*, get it through her dazed brain, that she, Killashandra Ree, had actually found Keborgen's black crystal claim. And it was hers, section and paragraph.

Killashandra was unaware of the passage of time. She must have spent hours looking around the claim, seeing where Keborgen had cleared flawed crystal from the outside. He had undoubtedly expected to return once the storm had blown out. He was cutting from a shelf a meter above the higher arm of the V. He was an astute cutter, for he hadn't ravaged crystal but worked for flawless cuts, the triads, and quartets, the larger groupings that would command the highest price from the greedy FSP who were eager to set up the crystal links between all inhabited planets. Keborgen had kept a natural-fault look to his claim, allowing the foot of the V to gather mud and dirt that wind and water would spill naturally across the lower part. By comparison, Moksoon was a very lazy cutter, but then he had only rose quartz.

The crystal around her began to crackle and tzing, soft reassuring noises. As if, Killashandra thought fancifully, it had accepted the transfer of ownership. Enchanted, she listened to the soft sounds, waiting almost breathless for the next series until she also became aware of chill, that she sat in true dark, not shadow.

Reluctantly and still bemused by the crystalline chorus, she hoisted herself from the claim, retracing the rough path to her sled.

Relative sanity returned to her in the clean newness of her vehicle. She sat down and made a drawing of the claim, testing her recall of the dimensions, jotting down her assumptions on Keborgen's work routine.

She'd get an early start in the morning, she thought, looking at her cutter. She'd have several clear days now.

"I'll have several clear days?" The certainty of her thought on that score astonished her. She snapped on the met forecast. Tomorrow would be fair, with a likelihood of several more to come.

What had Lanzecki said about a weather affinity in the Milekey Transition? That she could trust her symbiont? Distrust of the mechanical had brought about Keborgen's belated start to safety. Ah, but if he'd stopped to repaint his claim mark, he *had* listened to some warning.

Killashandra hugged her arms tightly to her. In theory, the symbiotic spore was now part of her cellular construction, certainly no part of her conscious mind nor a restless visitor in her body. At least until she called upon its healing powers. Or resisted its need to return to Ballybran.

She made a voice-coded note on the recorder about her instinctive knowledge of the weather. She could keep a check on that.

She remembered to eat before she lay down, for the excitements of the day had fatigued her. She set her buzz alarm for twenty minutes before sunrise. Breakfasted, and refreshed by her sleep, she was on the summit path as the sun's first rays found their way over the top of the far range, cutter slung over her shoulder, carton swinging from her free hand.

She left the carton where Keborgen had left his—how long would echoes of the dead accompany her in this site?—and stepped down into the claim. Sun had not yet reached even the higher point of the V. It would be easier to cut now, she thought, before the crystal started its morning song. She wiped clean the protuberance she meant to cut, roughly 50 centimeters long by 25 centimeters high and varying between 10 and 15 centimeters wide. She had to follow the ridges left by Keborgen's last cuts. Why ever didn't he just make straight lines? Flaws? She ran her hands across the surface, as if apologizing for what she was about to do. The crystal whispered under her touch.

Enough of this, she told herself severely. She imagined that both Trag and Lanzecki were watching, then struck the shelf with the tone wedge. Sound poured over her like a tsunami. Every bone and joint reverberated the note. Her skull seemed to part at its seams, her blood pulsed like a metronome in time with the vibrations. Echoes were thrown back to her from the other side of the claim and, oddly soured, from the crescent valley.

"Cut! You're supposed to tune your cutter to the note and cut!" Killashandra shouted at herself, and the echo shouted back.

Nothing as devastating as this had occurred when Moksoon had sung for note. Was it because she was sensitive to the black, not pink, nor attuned to his claim? He had also not been standing in the center of his claim but on granite. Nor was this experience like the scream of retuned crystal: there was no agony, no resentment in that glorious resonance, overpowering as it was.

She did not have to strike the crystal again. The A was locked in her head and ears. She hesitated just once more as she steadied the infrasonic blade to make the first incision. As well, for only an unconscious resolve, an obstinacy that she had never had to invoke, kept her cutting. Sound enveloped her, an A in chords and octaves, a ringing that made every nerve end in her body vibrate in a state that wasn't painful, was oddly pleasurable but curiously distracting. She felt the blade sound darken and pulled it out. She made the second vertical cut just before Keborgen's mark. This block would be shorter than the others and narrower. It couldn't be helped. She gritted her teeth against the coursing shock as blade met crystal and sound met nerve. Her hands seemed to respond to the endless hours of drill under Trag's direction, but she didn't consciously tell herself to stop the second vertical cut. Some practiced connection between hand and eye stopped her. She let that instinct assist her in making the horizontal slice that would sever the crystal from the vein. Its cry was not as fierce.

Carefully, she put the cutter down, awed by the thread-thin separation she had caused. With hands still shaking from the effort of guiding the cutter, she tipped the rectangle out and held it up. Sun caught and darkened the oblong, showing to her wondering eyes the slight deviation from a true angle. She couldn't have cared less and wept with joy as the song of sun-warmed black crystal, now truly matte black in response to heat, seeped through her skin to intoxicate her senses.

How long she stood in awed thrall, holding the rectangle into the sun like an ancient priestess, she would never know. A cloud, one of the few that day, briefly obscured the light and broke the song. Killashandra was conscious then of the ache in her shoulders from holding weight aloft and a numbness in fingers, feet, and legs. She was strangely unwilling to release the crystal. "Pack crystal as soon as you have cut." The echo of Lanzecki's advice came to her. Moksoon, too, had packed as soon as he had cut. She remembered how reluctant the crazed old singer had seemed to release the rose into the carton. Now she appreciated both advice and example.

Only when she had snuggled the crystal block into its plastic cocoon did she realize her debilitation. She leaned, drained of strength, against the crystal wall and sank slowly to the floor, marginally aware of the murmuring crystal against which she rested.

"This will never do," she told herself, ignoring the faint, chimed echo of her voice. She took a food packet from her thigh pouch and mechanically chewed and drank. The terrible lethargy began to ease.

She glanced at the sky and realized that the sun was dropping to the west. She must have spent half a good clear day admiring her handiwork.

"Ridiculous!"

The scoffing "d" sound spat back at her.

"I wouldn't mock if I were you, my friend," she told the claim as she eyed the cuts for the second block. She'd want to get this one squarer or she'd end up with a suspiciously symmetrical puddle as Keborgen had done.

She didn't need to tap for pitch: the A was seared into her mind. She turned on and adjusted the cutter, nerving herself for the crystalline response. She was almost overset by the pure, unprotesting note given back. Immensely relieved, she made the two vertical cuts, watching to keep the cutter blade straight. She made the third, horizontal slice and cursed herself for unconsciously following the pattern of her first, uneven cut. Sensation palpably oozed off the cut black, but this time she knew crystal tricks and quickly buried it beside its mate in the carton.

The third crystal ought to have been the easiest. She made the first cut deftly, pleased with her expertise. But the vertical incision to sever the rectangle from the face went off the true pitch. She halted, peered in at the grayish, pale-brown mass, touched it and felt, not tactilely, but through the nerves in her fingertips that she was cutting on flaw. If she moved a half centimeter out . . . The block would not match the other two but the crystal cried clear. She turned it over and over in her hands, her back carefully to the sun, inspecting the block for any other sign of flaw. This was, she told herself sternly, an excuse to caress it with fingers that delighted in the smooth, soapy texture, the whisper of sound, the sensations that reached her nerves as delicate as . . . as Lanzecki's kiss in her palm?

Killashandra chuckled, her laughter tinkling back from all sides. Lanzecki, or recollections of him, would seem to constitute an anchor in this exotic arena of sound and sensation. Would he appreciate that role? And when, or if, she returned to Lanzecki's arms, would she remember crystal in them?

Thoughts of him effectively blotted the lure of the third rectangle that she packed away. She was then aware of a coolness, a light breeze, where before the air had been warm and still. Looking westward, she realized that she had once more been crystal-tricked. The day was almost over, and she'd only three black crystals to show for sixteen hours' work—or mental aberration. There was a whole side to be cut.

Obviously there was much about the cutting of crystal that could not be explained, programmed, or theorized. It had to be experienced. She hadn't acquired enough tips or tricks or insights from watching Moksoon. She had learned a good deal from observing Keborgen's cutting. Intuition suggested that she would never learn all there was to the cutting of crystal. That ought to make a long life as a singer more eventful. If she could just handle the frustration of losing hours in contemplation of her handiwork!

The three crystals were quiescent in their packing case, but her hands lingered on it as she fixed the stowage webbing. She assembled a large hot meal for herself and a beaker of Yarran beer. Taking food and drink outside, she strode to the dip and seated herself on a convenient boulder.

She watched the sun set on her claim and the moons rise. The cooling crystal cried across the blind valley that separated them.

"You had your way—" and Killashandra stopped her mocking sentence as her first word was echoed back from the newly exposed crystal. "You who—" And the vowel came back to her, in harmony. Amused by the phenomenon, she pitched a second "you who" a third lower and heard it chime in with the faint reverberations of the first. She laughed at her whimsy. Crystal laughed back. And the first stirrings of the night breeze as great Shankill moon rose brought counter harmonies to her solo.

She sang. She sang to the crystal; the wind learned the tune, though gradually the crystal chorus died as the last sun warmth left it, and only the wind softly repeated her lyric line.

Shilmore rose and the night air brought a chill that roused her from a trance of the kind that Maestro Valdi must have meant. He was right, she thought. Crystal song could be addictive and was utterly exhausting. She staggered back to the sled. Without shedding her coverall, Killashandra drew the thermal sheet over her as she turned her shoulder into the mattress. And slept.

A faint sound roused her. Not the buzzer, for she hadn't remembered to set an alarm. Groggily, she raised her head, staring in accusation at the console, but there was no warning light and certainly no buzz. However, *something* had awakened her.

Outside the sled, the sun was shining. She pushed herself off the bed and dialed a strong stimulant. The time display read midmorning. She'd missed five hours of cutting light! She'd a cramp in one shoulder, and her knees ached. The heat of the drink flowed through her, dispersing the sluggishness of her mind and easing her muscles. She drank as quickly as she could, dialed a second cup, shoved protein bars into her coverall pockets. Unbracketing her cutter, she slung it across her back, got another carton, a handlight, and was on her way to the claim ten minutes after waking. The sound that woke her had been the crack of raw black crystal feeling the touch of sun.

First she had to clear splinters that had fallen from the end of her cut, the result of the night's chill and the morning's sun. Stolidly, she set her mind and collected the small pieces, dropping them into the packing case. With the handlight, she could now see where another flaw crazed the crystal quartz on the hillside. Using the inner edge of the previous day's shelf, however, she could make an interlocking group, four medium—or five smaller—rectangles. She'd cut these now, let the chill crack off flaw. A little expeditious trimming on the ravine side and the temperature would remove the blemishes. Tomorrow she'd have a rare day's cutting.

Killashandra set her nerves for the first incision of the infrasonic cutter and was relieved to endure less shock. Relieved and dismayed. Was the claim admitting her right to it by lack of protest? Or did one day attune her body to the resonance? She had half wished to experience that pleasurable, nerve-caressing distraction, as if a highly skilled lover were inside her body.

She did not remember, due to those reflections no doubt, to pack away as soon as she'd turned off the blade. She did remember to shield the rectangle from the sun as she stroked it, totally in rapport with her creation. She admired the clever angle she had contrived to make an old cut—

And suddenly realized that she had been communing with the violated crystal. She resolutely packed it away, and the next four were stowed as soon as she laid the cutter down. She had to teach herself the automatic sequence. "Habit," Concera had endlessly and rightly said, "is all that saves a singer."

Killashandra set herself to clearing the ravine face, but the sun's reflection off the quartz pained her eyes. She'd wasted too much time in sleep and in crystal thrall.

She woke in the night suddenly, an odd apprehension driving sleep from her mind. Uneasily, she checked the stored cartons, wondering if something had caused them to resonate. Outside the night was clear, the moons had set, and the Range was deep asleep. She glanced at the console and the storm alarms. She cursed under her breath. She hadn't had a met reading. The printout showed clouds moving in from the White Sea, some turbulence, but at an altitude that might reach the dominant easterly air current and dissipate. A pattern to watch, to be sure.

She slept uneasily until the first crack of light. Apprehensively she dialed a met printout. The picture wasn't alarming, though cloud cover had increased in depth and speed. A high-pressure area was coming south, but no storm warning was issued for the Bay area. If a storm were making, she'd've had a satellite warning by now.

The continual awareness of something out of kilter made cutting easier. She completed a cut of four large five-sided blacks, had stored all the debris, when the pressure of her subjective anxiety became too intense to continue. Operating on an intuition too powerful to be refused, she slung the cutter over her shoulder, grabbed a carton in each hand, and started back to the sled. Halfway there she heard the hooter and nearly tripped for looking up at the still-cloudless sky above her.

She tapped out an update for the weather. The hooter was only the first warner: a watch-the-weather-picture caution. Everything inside her head was far more alarmed than the Guild's signal. The Met displayed a brewing turbulence that could flow either north or south, depending on the low pressure ridge.

She stared at the display, not at all reassured. She did her own calculations. If the very worst occurred, the storm could boil across the tip of the main continent and run across her position in four or five hours, building speed at a tremendous rate once it acquired the impetus of the advancing ridge.

"I thought you were supposed to warn us!" she shouted at the other silent storm-alerts. The hooter had automatically ceased blaring when she had programmed the weather picture. "Four, five hours. That doesn't give me time to cut anything more. Just sit here and stew until you lot wake up to the danger. Isn't anyone analyzing the met patterns? Why all this rigmarole about distant early warnings and weather sensors if they don't bloody work?"

As she vented her tension in a one-sided tirade, she was also rigging her ship for storm-running. The four precious cartons of black crystal were securely webbed in front of the mocking empties. She changed her coverall and realized from the grime on her wrists and ankles that she hadn't bathed since coming to the Ranges. She wanted to reappear at the Complex looking presentable. A quick wash was refreshing, and she ate a light meal as she did some computations of deviation courses that would disguise the direction from which she came and confuse other singers called in by the storm. She had just completed what would be a most elaborate break-out when the first of the dead-earnest storm warnings came on.

"About bloody time! I came to that conclusion an hour ago."

Airborne, she skimmed ridge and hollow, heading north at 11 for half an hour. She turned on a western leg for twenty minutes and was starting a southern track when she flipped over a gorge that looked familiar. A blur of orange in the shadows brought to mind Moksoon and his wretched pink crystals. The storm readings were insistent now. She made another pass up the gorge and saw Moksoon bent over his outcrop, two cartons beside him. He ought to have been heading out, not calmly cutting as if he had all day and a mach storm wasn't bowling down.

She came in as quietly as she could, but the grating of her sled runners on the loose rock at the valley bottom warned Moksoon. He charged down the slope, cutter held aggressively. She slapped on the playback, turned up the volume, but he was caterwauling so loudly about Section 49 that he couldn't have heard it.

The wind however had picked up and made it difficult for him to swing and keep his balance, though Killashandra doubted that the infrasonic blade would do her sled much harm. Break his cutter.

"Storm, you addled pink tenor!" She roared out the open window.

Despite the wind scream, she could hear the hooter-buzzer-bell systems of his sled.

"Mach storm on the way. You've got to leave!"

"Leave?" Panic replaced wrath on Moksoon's face. He now heard her ship's klaxons as well as his own. "I can't leave!" The wind was tearing the sound from his mouth, but Killashandra could read his lips. "I've struck a pure vein. I've—" He clamped his mouth shut with caution and had to lean into a particularly strong gust to keep from being knocked over. "I've got to cut just one more. Just one more." He raced up the slope to his site.

Unbelievingly, Killashandra watched him raise his cutter, to tune it in the teeth of a gale. Cursing, Killashandra grabbed up her handlight. Not as sturdy a weapon as she'd've liked, considering the probable denseness of Moksoon's skull, but used with the necessary force in the right spot, it ought to suffice.

As she left her sled, she experienced a taste of what it would be like to be caught in a mach storm in the Crystal Ranges. Sound, waves of dissonance and harmony, streamed through her head. She covered her ears, but the sound maintained contact through the rock under her feet. The keening wails masked her slithering approach, and Moksoon was too preoccupied with cutting to see anything but the octagon he was excising. Just as she had braced herself to slug him, he laid the cutter down but caught a glimpse of her descending hand and flung himself to the side. She grabbed up his cutter and pelted for his sled, nearer than hers. He'd follow her for that cutter, she was positive. She bounced into his sled, plastered herself against the wall, the brackets digging into her shoulders, wincing against the shrill obligato of Moksoon's unheeded warning devices.

He was wilier than she'd credited him. Suddenly, a strong hand grabbed her left ankle and hauled her leg sideways, a rock coming down to crush her kneecap. But for the fact she still held his cutter, she would have been crippled. She brought the cutter handle up, deflecting the rock, bruising Moksoon's fingers. She pivoted on her captured foot and delivered a second blow to the old man's jaw. He hovered a moment until she thought she'd have to club him again, but it was the wind that supported him, then let him crumple.

Automatically, Killashandra bracketed his cutter. She tapped for a weather printout, which silenced three of the mind-boggling alarms. Glancing to the rear of the sled, she saw that Moksoon had not bothered to web his packed cartons. She did so, ignoring the filth and discarded food that littered the living section. Then she remembered that there were several cartons by his claim.

Luckily, she hadn't any rocky height to negotiate from Moksoon's sled to his claim or she wouldn't have made it back with the heavy cartons. Moksoon showed no signs of reviving. She lugged him into the sled, then deposited him on the couch. He didn't so much as groan. He was alive, though she was revolted by the grease on his neck as she felt for a pulse.

It was then she realized her dilemma. Two ships and one conscious pilot. She tried to rouse Moksoon, but he was completely oblivious, and she couldn't find the medaid kit that contained stimulant sprays.

The alarms attained a new height of distress, and she recognized that time was running out. She couldn't transport all of Moksoon's cargo to her sled. She had four cartons more precious than all of his. There *must* be something in Guild rules about rescue and salvage. She'd got two vouchers for escorting Carrik, so she decided the wind had gotten her wits. She made a battered dash to her own sled, slung her cutter over her shoulder and grabbed two cartons. The warnings in Moksoon's sled had climbed several deafening decibels toward the supersonic, but there was no way she could diminish them until she had taken off.

She staggered back to her sled, which was bouncing now from the gusting wind. She wondered if she could secure her craft, somehow keep it from being flung about the gorge, and decided against wasting the time.

She grabbed her remaining cartons and was glad of the weight to anchor her feet to the ground. She was gasping for breath as she finally closed the door of Moksoon's sled. He still lolled on the couch. She webbed her four cartons and secured her cutter among his empties. She strapped Moksoon tightly to the couch and then took her place at the console.

All sleds had similar control panels, though Moksoon's was much the worse for wear.

Moksoon's claim was a dangerously enclosed area from which to ascend into a wild storm. She fought to keep the vertical, fought again to increase the horizontal to clear the ridge top, then let the wind take the sled, hauling as hard as she could on the yoke toward the west.

The mach-tuned dissonances were worse in the air, and she made a grab for Moksoon's buffer helmet. It was stiff, dusty, and too small, but it blocked the worst of the wind-shriek. She'd not got it on a moment too soon, for the sled behaved like a crazed beast, plunging and diving wildly then sliding sideways. Killashandra learned appreciation of the simulation drills sooner than she would have liked.

It was as well she'd strapped Moksoon down, for he regained consciousness before they'd quite cleared the Milekeys and started raving about pain. She felt quite enough jabbing at her nerve ends through the ear pads.

Moksoon regained unconsciousness after throwing his head against the duralloy wall, so the last hour into the Guild Complex gave her sufficient quiet to ease her own aggravated nerves.

She had reason to be proud as she brought Moksoon's canting sled up over the wind baffles at the Complex and landed it conveniently close to the racks. She signaled for medics, and as she pointed them toward Moksoon, one of the Hangar personnel grabbed her arm and gestured urgently toward the Hangar office. The information that Lanzecki awaited her was reinforced by that message on the green display, blinking imperatively.

Cargo personnel had opened the sled's storage, and now Killashandra moved to collect her precious cutter and to point out the four cartons which held her blacks.

"Enthor!" she roared at the handlers. "Take these immediately to Enthor!"

Despite their obliging grins and nods, she wasn't sure they understood her urgency. She followed them, but halfway there, someone matched pace with her, tugging angrily at her arm.

"Report to Lanzecki," the Hangar officer yelled, pushing her away from Storage. The look in his eyes was not reassuring. "You might at least have saved the *new* sled!"

She jerked her arm free and, leaving the man astonished at her impudence, ran after her cartons. She saw the first handler just plop his burden down on the stack. She grabbed it and roared at the others to follow her into Sorting.

"Killashandra? Is it you?" a familiar voice asked. Without checking her determined forward march, she saw Rimbol following her, one of her cartons held carefully against his body.

Two absurdities impinged on her thoughts as she rushed into Sorting: Rimbol was unaware of the fortune of black crystal he carried, and he had trouble identifying her.

"Yes, it's me. What's the matter?"

"You haven't looked in a mirror lately, have you?" was Rimbol's reply. He seemed amused as well as surprised. "Don't scowl. You're terrifying, you—you crystal, you!"

"Be careful of that carton," she said, more commanding than she should be of a friend, and Rimbol's welcoming smile faded. "Sorry, Rimbol. I had one helluva time getting in. That bollux Moksoon wouldn't believe a storm was coming and him having trouble standing straight against the gusts."

"You brought another singer out of the Ranges?" Rimbol's eyes widened with incredulity, but whatever he had been about to add was cut off as Killashandra spied Enthor and called his name.

"Yes?" Enthor's query was surprised. He blinked at her uncertainly.

"I'm Killashandra Ree," she said, trying to keep the irritation out of her voice. She couldn't have changed that much since she'd last seen Enthor. "I've black crystal!"

"Black?"

"Yes, yes. Black! Here!"

"And how were so you fortunate as to find that which eludes so many?" an implacable voice demanded.

Killashandra was setting her carton down on Enthor's table, but the cold, ominous tone paralyzed her. Her throat went dry and her mind numb because no consideration was excuse enough for her to have ignored the Guild Master's summons, to make him seek her out.

"Well, it doesn't surprise *me* that you have," Enthor said, taking the box from her.

Lanzecki's eyes never left hers as he advanced. She let the sorting table support her shaking body and clutched its edge with nerveless fingers. Regulations and restrictions that could be levied against a disobedient member by the Guild Master sprang to her mind far more vividly than the elusive ones about rescue and salvage. His lips were set in a thin, hard line. The slight flare of his nostrils and the quick lift of his chest under the subtle gleam of his shirt confirmed that he had appeared through effort, not magic.

"You could improve on your acute angles," Enthor was saying as he unpacked her triad. "However, the credit is good." Enthor blinked before he peered approvingly at Killashandra. He noticed her immobility, looked around, not unsurprised to see the Guild Master, and back to Killashandra, aware now of the reason for her tension.

"Which is as well for Killashandra Ree," Lanzecki said with deep sarcasm, "since she has not returned in her new sled."

"Moksoon is all right?" Killashandra asked, anything to be able to speak in the face of Lanzecki's fury.

"His head will heal, and he will doubtless cut more rose quartz!"

That Lanzecki's tone was not derisory did not signify. Killashandra understood what was implied. Nor could she break from his piercing stare.

"I couldn't very well *leave* him," she said, the solace of indignation replacing fear. After all, Lanzecki had arranged for Moksoon to shepherd her.

"Why not? He would have shown no compunction in leaving you had the circumstances been reversed."

"But . . . but he was cutting. All the storm warnings were on in his sled. He wouldn't listen. He tried to slice me with his cutter. I had to knock him out before he . . ."

"You could be subject to claim-jumping, Section 49, Paragraph 14," Lanzecki went on irreconcilably.

"What about the section dealing with rescue and salvage?"

Lanzecki's eyelids dropped slightly, but it was Enthor who answered her in a startled voice.

"There are none, my dear. Salvage is always done by the Guild, not a singer. I would have thought you'd been taught to know what exactly *is* in rules and regs. Ah, now these . . . these are very good indeed. Two a trifle on the thin side."

Enthor had unpacked the quintet. For the first time, Lanzecki's attention was diverted. He shifted his body slightly so that he could see the weighplate. He lifted one eyebrow in surprise, but his lips did not soften with appeasement.

"You may come out of this affair better than you deserve to, Killashandra Ree," Lanzecki said. His eyes still glinted with anger. "Unless, of course, you left behind your cutter."

"I could carry that, and these," she retorted, stung more by his amusement than his anger.

"Let us hope then that Moksoon can be persuaded not to charge you with claim-jumping since you preserved his wreck of a ship, his skin, and his crystal. Gratitude is dependent on memory, Killashandra Ree, a function of the mind that deteriorates on Ballybran. Learn that lesson now!"

Lanzecki swept away from Enthor's table and walked down the long room to the farthest exit, thus emphasizing that he had come on discipline.

Chapter 10

Killashandra stayed with Enthor while he tallied her four cartons, though she was hardly aware of what the old Sorter was saying to her. She kept glancing toward the far door where Lanzecki had made his dramatic exit, aware of the surreptitious looks in her direction from other Sorters, aware of an emotion more intense than hatred, emptier than fear.

"Now *that'll* buy you your two sleds." Enthor's words penetrated her self-absorption.

"What?"

"Those black crystals brought you a total of twenty-three thousand credits."

"How much?" Killashandra stared incredulously at the displayed figures, blinking green. "But a sled only costs eight thousand."

"There's the tithe, my dear. Thirty percent does eat a hole in the total. Actually, you have to pay for two sleds, the one you lost and the replacement. Still, 16,100 clear does help."

"Yes, it does." Killashandra tried to sound grateful.

Enthor patted her arm. "You'd best take a good long radiant bath, m'dear. Always helps. And eat." Then he began to package her beautiful black crystal.

She turned away, unexpectedly feeling the separation from her first experience of crystal. The weight of the cutter made her sag as she slung it to her back. She would take it to be checked in the morning. She estimated she had just enough strength left to get her body back to her quarters and into the radiant bath. She took the nearest door out of the Sorting room, aware marginally that people were still rushing cartons in to Storage, that the howl of the wind was loud at this level even inside the Complex. She should be grateful! She was too weary to laugh or snort at her inappropriate choice of word. She got into the lift and its descent, though smooth, made her sink toward the floor. She was able to prevent complete collapse only by hanging on to the support rail.

She wobbled to her room, oblivious to the gaze of those in the Commons. As she walked, the drag of the cutter pulled her to the right, and once she caromed numbly from a doorway.

When she finally raised her hand to her own doorplate, she realized that she still wore the ident wristband. She wouldn't need that anymore, but she hadn't the strength to remove it. As she passed a chair, she dropped her right shoulder, and the cutter slid onto the cushioning. She continued to the tankroom where she stared in dazed surprise at the filling tank. Did her entry into the room trigger the thing? No, it was almost full. Someone must have programmed it. Enthor? Rimbol? Her mind refused to work. She tore at her coverall, then her sweatliner, pulling her boots off with the legs of her coverall, and crawled up the three steps to the platform around the tank. She slid gratefully—that word again—into the viscous liquid, right up to her throat, her weight supported by the radiant fluid. Fatigue and the ache of crystal drained from her body and nerves. In that suspension, she remained, her mind withdrawn, her body buoyed.

Sometime later, the room announced a visitor, and she roused sufficiently to deny entrance. She didn't want to see Rimbol. But the intrusion and the necessity of making a decision aroused her from her passivity. The fluid had provided the necessary anodyne, and she was acutely aware of hunger. She had pulled herself from the tank, the radiant liquid dripping from her body, and was reaching for a wrap when a hand extended the garment to her.

Lanzecki stood there.

"I will not be denied twice!" he said, "though I will allow you couldn't know that it was I at your door."

Surprised at his presence, Killashandra wavered on the edge of the tank, and he immediately held out a steadying hand.

"You can fill tanks and open doors?"

"One can be programmed, and the other was not locked."

"It is now?"

"It is," he said smoothly; his mouth, she quickly noticed, was amused. "But that can be changed."

For a picosecond, she wanted to call his bluff. Then she remembered that he had said she might be luckier than she deserved as Enthor tallied her cut. He had implied she had enough credit not only to buy a new sled but pay off what she already owed the Guild. Lanzecki had remembered the vouchers she still held. With those, she would have just enough. What mattered was that Lanzecki had remembered that margin at a time when he was rightfully infuriated by her disregard of her Guild Master's summons.

"I'm much too tired to change anything." She gathered the toweling about her and extended her hand to him, palm up, summoning a weary smile.

He looked from her smile to her palm, and his lips curved upward. Now he took a step forward. Placing both hands on her slender waist, he swung her down from the tank platform. She expected to be set on her feet. Instead, Lanzecki carried her into the lounge. The spicy aroma of a freshly cooked meal was heady, and she exclaimed with pleasure at the steaming dishes on the table.

"I expected you might be hungry."

Killashandra laughed as Lanzecki deposited her in the chair, and she gestured with the overblown gentility of an opera heroine for him to assume the other seat.

Not that evening or ever did Lanzecki ask her if she had found Keborgen's black crystal, though he had occasions later to refer to her claim. Neither did he ask her any details of her first trip to the Milekey Ranges. Nor was she disposed to volunteer any comment. Except one.

Having teased her adroitly, Lanzecki finally gave her the caress she had been anticipating so long, and the sensation was almost unbearable.

"Crystal touches that way, too," she said when she could talk.

"I know," he murmured, his voice oddly rough, and as if to forestall her reply, he began to kiss her in a fashion that excluded opportunity.

She awoke alone, as she had expected, and much later than she had planned, for the time was late evening. She yawned prodigiously, stretched, and wondered if another radiant bath would further her restoration. Then her belly rumbled, and she decided food was the more immediate concern. No sooner had she dialed for a hot drink than a message was displayed on her screen for her to contact the Guild Master when convenient.

She did so promptly before she considered convenience, expedience, or opportunity.

Her reply was cleared immediately, and her screen produced a visual contact with the Guild Master. He was surrounded by printout sheets and looked tired.

"Have you rested?" Lanzecki asked. Belatedly, Killashandra activated her own screen. "Yes, you look considerably improved."

"Improved?"

A slight smile tugged at his lips. "From the stress and fatigue of your dramatic return." Then his expression changed, and Lanzecki became Guild Master. "Will you please come to my office to discuss an extraplanetary assignment?"

"Will," not "would," Killashandra thought, sensitive to key words.

"I'll be there as soon as I've eaten and gotten dressed." He nodded and broke contact.

As she sipped the last of the drink, she took a long look at herself in the mirrors of the tankroom. She'd never been vain about her appearance. She had good strong face bones, wide cheeks, a high forehead, and thick, well-arched eyebrows, which she had not narrowed, as the natural emphasis made a good stage effect. Her jaw was strong, and she was losing the jowl muscles formed by singing. She slapped at the sides of her chin. No flab. Whatever produced the gaunt aspect of her face was reflected in her body. She noticed how prominent her collarbones were. If her appearance was now an improvement, according to Lanzecki, whatever had she looked like the previous day? Right now, she wouldn't have needed face paint to play Space Hag or Warp Widow.

She found something loose and filmy to wear, with ends that tied about her neck and wrists and a long full skirt. She stood back from the mirrors and did a half turn, startled by her full-length reflection. Something had changed. Just what she couldn't puzzle out; she had to see the Guild Master.

She was almost to the lift shaft when a group emerged from the Commons.

"Killashandra?"

"Rimbol?" Killashandra mocked his surprised query with a light laugh. "You ought to know me!"

Rimbol gave her an odd grin that relaxed into his usual ingenuous smile. Jezerey, Mistra, and Borton were with him.

"Well, you're more like yourself this evening than you were yesterday," Rimbol replied. He scratched his head in embarrassment, grinning ruefully at the others. "I didn't believe Concera when she kept saying singing crystal makes a big change, but now I do."

"I don't think I've changed," Killashandra replied stiffly, annoyed that Rimbol and, by their expressions, the others could perceive what eluded her.

Rimbol laughed. "Well, you've used your mirror"—and he indicated her careful grooming—"but you haven't *seen*."

"No, I haven't."

Rimbol made a grimace of apology for her sharp tone.

"Singers are notorious for their irritability," Jezerey said with an uncordial look.

"Oh, pack that in, Jez," Rimbol said. "Killa *is* just in off the Ranges. Is it as bad as it's made out, Killa?" He couched that question in a quiet tone.

"I would have been fine if I hadn't had to deal with Moksoon."

"Or the Guild Master." Rimbol was sympathetic.

"Oh, you stayed on?" Killashandra decided to brazen through that episode. "He was quite right, of course. And I pass on that hard-learned lesson. Save your own sled and skin in the Ranges. Will you be around later, Rimbol? I've got to see Lanzecki now." She allowed her voice to drop, expressing dread and looking for sympathy in their expressions. "I'd like to join you later if you're in the lounge."

"Good luck!" Rimbol said, and he meant it. The others waved encouragingly as she entered the lift.

She had much to think about during the short drop, and none of it about her interview with Lanzecki. How could she have changed so much in the past few days just by cutting crystal? Jezerey had never been overly friendly, but she had never been antagonistic. She was annoyed with herself, too, for that offhanded reassurance to Rimbol. "I would have been fine without Moksoon." Yet how could she possibly have explained the experience that had annealed her, confirmed her as a crystal singer? Maybe, alone with Rimbol, she would try to explain, forewarn him that once past the curious unpainful agony of the initial cut, there was an elevation to a totally bizarre ecstasy that could only be savored briefly or it overwhelmed mind, nerve, and senses.

She sighed, standing before the door to the Guild Master's office. In the second between the announcement of her presence and the panel's smooth retraction, she remembered how hard Concera had tried to explain some facets of crystal singing. She recalled the odd harsh tone in which Lanzecki had admitted knowledge of the tactile feel of crystal.

"Killashandra Ree." Lanzecki's voice came from the corner of his large office, and she saw him bent over a spotlighted work surface, layers of printout in front of him. He did not look up from his research until she reached him. "Did you have enough to eat?" he asked with more than ordinary courtesy and a close scrutiny of her face.

"I had a high-protein and glucose cereal—" she began because, as soon as he mentioned eating, she felt hungry again.

"Hmmm. A bowl was all you had time for, I'm sure. You've slept sixteen hours, so you've missed considerable nourishment already."

"I did eat in the Ranges. Really I did," she protested as he took her hand and led her to the catering console.

"You've still wit enough to feed yourself, but you can't know how immensely important it is to replenish reserves at this point."

"I won't be able to eat all that." She was appalled at the number and variety of dishes he was dialing.

"I get peckish myself, you know," he said, grinning.

"What happens that I need to eat myself gross?" she asked, but she helped him clear the catering slot of its first deposit, sniffing appreciatively at the enticing mixture of aromas from the platters.

"You'll never see a plump singer," he assured her. "In your particular case, the symbiont is only just settled into cell tissue. A Milekey Transition may be easier on the host, but the spore still requires time to multiply, differentiate, and become systemically absorbed. Here, start with this soup. Weather and other considerations compelled me to direct you into the Ranges prematurely as far as the process of your adaptation is concerned." He gave her a sardonic glance. "You may one day be grateful that you had only two days on your claim."

"Actually three. I didn't spend two with that twithead Moksoon. He's utterly paranoid!"

"He's alive," Lanzecki replied succinctly, with sufficient undertone to make the statement both accusation and indictment. "Three days! In ordinary training, you would not have gone out into the Ranges until the others were also prepared."

"They won't make it out before the Passover storms now." Killashandra was dismayed. If she had had to wait that long . . .

"Precisely. You were trained, eager and clever enough to precipitate the event."

"And you wanted that black crystal."

"So, my darling, did you."

The caterer chimed urgently to remind them to clear the slot for additional selections. Lanzecki slapped a hold on the remainder of the programmed order.

"Even with your help, I'll never eat all this," Killashandra said after they had filled the small table and three more dishes remained in the slot.

"Listen to me while you eat. The symbiont will be attenuated after intense cutting. I could see that in your face. Don't talk. Eat! I had to be sure you ate last night, once the radiant fluid had eased your nerves. Your metabolism must be efficient. I would have thought you'd have been awakened by hunger a good four hours ago."

"I was eating when I got your message."

He grinned as he inserted a steaming, seeded appetizer into his mouth. He licked his fingers as he chewed, then said, "My message was programmed the moment your caterer was used." He stuffed another piece of appetizer into her mouth. "Don't talk. Eat."

Whatever it was he fed her was exceedingly tasty. She speared another.

"Now, several unexpected elements are in display. One"—and he ate a spoonful of small brilliant green spheres—"you brought in five medium black crystals for which we have received an urgent request." He waved his empty spoon at the printout layers on his desk. "Two, you have no sled, nor can Manufacturing produce a replacement before the Passover storms. Which, by the way, were heralded by that unpredicted blow in the Bay area. Short, hard, but destructive. Even though conjunction occurs over the seas north and east of this continent, Passover is going to be particularly nasty, as it coincides with spring solstice. Weather is generally cyclical on Ballybran, and the pattern which has been emerging coincides with '63 . . . 2863GY, that is—eat, don't gawk. Surely you have wandered through data retrieval, Killashandra, and discovered how long I've been a member. Fuerte cannot have eradicated human curiosity, or you wouldn't be here."

She swallowed as the significance of his qualifying the century occurred to her.

"But not how long you've been Guild Master."

He chuckled at her quick reply, passing a dish of stewed orange-and-green milsi stalks to her. "Excellent for trace minerals. The Passover turbulence will be phenomenal even in terms of Ballybran's meteorological history. Which, I might add, goes back further than I do. Don't choke now!" he rose to give her a deft thump between her shoulder blades. "Even the Infirmary level will shake. You, so recently exposed to crystal for the first time, will be severely affected by the stress. I can, as Guild Master, order you off Ballybran," and his face fell into harsh immobile lines, impersonal and implacable. But his mouth softened when he saw her determined expression. "However, I would prefer that you cooperate. The five blacks you brought in are currently, if you'll forgive the pun, being tuned and should be ready for shipment. I would *like* to assign you to take them to the Trundimoux system and install them."

"This duty will provide me with the margin of credit for my future foolishness?"

Lanzecki chuckled appreciatively.

"Think about the assignment while you eat some fried steakbean."

"It is, then, a suggestion?" she asked around a large mouthful of tasty legume.

"It is—now—a suggestion." His face, mouth, and tone were bland. "The storms will soon be hammering the Ranges and forcing singers in. Others would undertake the assignment happily, especially those who haven't cut enough crystal to get off-world at Passover."

"I thought Passover was an incredible spectacle."

"It is. Raw natural forces at their most destructive." A lift to his shoulders suggested that it was a spectacle to which he was inured and yet . . .

"Do *you* leave during Passover?"

He gave her a keen glance, his dark eyes reflecting the spotlights over his work desk.

"The Guild Master is always accessible during Passover." He offered her some lemon-yellow cubes. "A sharpish cheese, but it complements the steakbean."

"Hmmm. Yes, it does."

"Help yourself." He rose and took the next dishes from the catering slot, which had been maintaining them at the appropriate heat. "Will you have something to drink?"

"Yarran beer, please." She had a sudden craving for the taste of hops.

"Good choice. I'll join you."

She glanced at him, arrested by some slight alteration of tone, but his back was to her.

"Rimbol's from Scartine, isn't he?" Lanzecki asked, returning with a pitcher and two beakers. He poured with a proper respect for the head of foam. "He should cut well in the darker shades. Perhaps black, if he can find a vein."

"How could you tell?"

"A question of resonance, also of the degree of adaptation. Jezerey will do lighter blues, pinks, paler greens. Borton will also tend to cut well in the darker. I hope they team up."

"Do you know who will cut what?"

"I am not in a position to imply anything, merely venture an informed guess. After all, the Guild has been operating for over four hundred years galactic, all that time collecting and collating information on its members. It would show a scandalous want of probity not to attempt more than merely a determination of probability of adjustment to Ballybran spore symbiosis."

"You sound like Borella's come-all-ye pitch," Killashandra replied.

Lanzecki's lips twitched in an amusement that was echoed by the sparkle in his brilliant eyes. "I do believe I'm quoting—but whom, I've forgotten. How about some pepper fruit? Goes with the beer. I've ordered some ices to clear the palate. A very old and civilized course but not one taken with beer." As he passed her the plate, the tangy scent of the long, thin furry fingers did tempt her to try one. "As I was saying, by the time candidates are through the Shankill checkpoint, as many variables as can be resolved have been." He began to pile empty plates and dishes into one untidy stack, and she realized that while he had sampled everything, she had eaten far more. Yet she didn't feel uncomfortably full. "You ought to have been shown the probability graph," he said, frowning as he rose. He tossed the discards deftly into the waste chute before pausing yet again at the catering slot.

"We were." She nibbled at another pepper fruit while wondering why his face showed no trace of aging. He wasn't singing crystal anymore, but that was the ostensible reason for the specious youthfulness. "We were told nothing about individual capabilities or forecasts."

"Why should you be? That would create all sorts of unnecessary problems." He set two dishes of varicolor sherbets, two wine glasses, and a frosty bottle on the table.

"I couldn't eat another thing."

"No? Try a spoonful of the green. Very settling to the stomach and clears the mouth." He seated himself and poured the wine. "The one critical point is still adaptation. The psychological attitude, Antona feels, rather than the physical. That space worker, Carigana, should not have died." Lanzecki's expression was one of impersonal regret. "We can generally gauge the severity of transition and are prepared for contingencies."

Killashandra thought of the smooth disappearances of Rimbol and Mistra during the night, of meditechs collecting Jezerey before she had fallen to the plascrete. She also recalled her indignation over "condition satisfactory."

"How do you like the wine?"

"Does it have to be *so* mechanical?"

"The wine?"

"The whole process."

"Every care is taken, my dear Killashandra," and Lanzecki's tone reminded her incontrovertibly that he was Guild Master and that the procedure she wished to protest was probably of his institution.

"The wine's fine."

"I thought you'd appreciate it." His response was as dry as the wine. "Not much is left to chance in recruiting. Tukolom may be a prosy bore, but he has a curious sensitivity to illness which makes him especially effective in his role as tutor."

"Then it was known that I—"

"You were not predicted." He used the slightest pause between each word for emphasis, and raising his glass to her, took a sip.

"And . . ." It was not coquetry in Killashandra that caused her to prompt him but the strongest feeling that he had been about to add a rider to that surprise comment.

"And certainly not a Milekey, nor resonant to black crystal. Perhaps"—and his quick reply did, she was positive, mask thoughts unspoken—"we should initiate handling crystal with recruits as soon as possible. But"—and he shrugged—"we can't program convenient storms which require all-member participation."

"Rimbol said you couldn't have planned that storm."

"Perceptive of him. How did those ices go down?"

"They went." She was surprised to find dish, bottle, and wine glasses empty.

"Fine. Than we can start on more."

"More?" But already a pungent spicy odor emanating from the caterer had sharpened her appetite. "I'll bloat."

"Very unlikely. Had you gone out with your class, this is exactly what would have been served on your return from the Ranges. Yarran beer, since you have cultivated a taste for it, would be appropriate to wash down the spicefish." He dialed for more. "Beer has also, for millennia, had another normal effect on the alimentary system."

His comment, delivered in a slightly pompous tone, made her laugh. So she ate the spicefish, drank the beer, responded to certain natural effects of it, and, at one point, realized that Lanzecki had coaxed, diverted, and bullied her into continuously consuming food for nearly three hours. By then, her satiation was such that when Lanzecki casually repeated his suggestion that she install the black crystal, she agreed to consider it.

"Is *that* why you've stuffed and drunken me?" she demanded, sitting erect to feign indignation.

"Not entirely. I have given you sufficient food to restore your symbiont and enough drink to relax you." He smiled away her defective grammar and any accusation of coercion. "I do not wish you to endure Passover's mach storms. You might be ten levels underground, buffered by plascrete a meter thick, but the resonances cannot be"—he paused, averted his face, searching for the precise word—"escaped." He turned back to her, and his eyes, dark and subtly pained, held hers, his petition heightened by the uncharacteristic difficulty in expressing his concern.

"Do you ever . . . escape?"

The delicate bond of perception between them lasted some time, and then, leaning across the table, he kissed her question away.

He escorted her back to her quarters, made certain she was comfortable in the bedroom, and suggested that in the morning she take her cutter down to be checked and stored, that if she was interested in weather history, she could review other phenomenal Passover storms in the met control the next day at eleven and see something of Storm Control tactics.

The next morning, she reflected during her shower and notably hearty breakfast on Lanzecki's extraordinary attentions to her, sensual as well as Guild. She could see why Lanzecki, as Guild Master, would exploit her eagerness to get into the Ranges and secure Keborgen's priceless claim. She'd succeeded. Now, in an inexplicable reverse, Lanzecki wanted her off-planet. Well, she could decide this morning when she watched the weather history, whether that was the man or the Guild Master talking. She rather hoped it was the former, for she did like Lanzecki the man and admired the Guild Master more than any man she had so far encountered.

What had he meant when he said she was unpredicted? Had that been flattery? The Guild Master indulging a whimsy? Not *after* he had assisted her in getting out into the Ranges; not *after* she had successfully cut black crystal? Especially, not after Lanzecki had very forcefully defined to her in the Sorting Room the difference between the man and the Guild Master.

She winced at the memory. She had deserved that reprimand. She could also accept his solicitousness for her health and well-being. He wanted more black crystal—if that was his motive. All right, Killashandra Ree, she told herself firmly, no section or paragraph of the Charter of the Heptite Guild requires the Master to explain himself to a member. Her ten years at Fuerte Music Center had taught Killashandra that no one ever does a favor without expecting a return. Lanzecki had also underscored self-preservation and self-interest with every object lesson that was presented.

She didn't really want to leave Ballybran, though it was probably true that she could use the credit margin of an off-world assignment. She looked up the payment scale; the credit offered was substantial. Perhaps it would be better to take the assignment. But that would mean leaving Lanzecki, too. She stared grimly at her reflection in the mirror as she dressed. Departing for that reason might also be wise. Only she'd better mend her fences with Rimbol.

Grateful that she would not have the additional expense of replacing the cutter or facing the Fisher with that request, she brought the device up to Engineering and Training. As she entered the small outer office, she saw two familiar figures.

"I'm not going to be caught here again during Passover," Borella was saying to the singer Killashandra remembered from the shuttle.

"Doing your bit again on recruits, Borella?" the man asked, negligently shoving his cutter across the counter and ignoring the technician's sour exclamation.

"Recruits?" Borella stared blankly.

"Remember, dear"—and the man's voice rippled with mockery—"occasionally, you pass the time briefing the young hopefuls at Shankill station."

"Of course, I remember," Borella said irritably. "I can do better than that this time, Olin," she went on smugly. "I cut greens in octave groups. Five of them. Enough for an Optherian organ. Small one, of course, but you know that *that* addiction will last a while."

"I'm rather well off, too, as it happens." Olin spoke over her last sentence.

Borella murmured something reassuring to him as she handed over her cutter to the technician, but showed a shade more concern for the device. Then she linked her arm through Olin's. As they turned to leave, Killashandra nodded politely to Borella, but the woman, giving Killashandra's cutter a hard stare, walked past with no more sign of recognition than tightening her clasp on Olin's forearm.

"Of course, there are those unfortunate enough to have to stay here." Her drawl insinuated that Killashandra would be of that number. "Have you seen Lanzecki lately, Olin?" she asked as they left the room.

For a moment, Killashandra was stunned by the double insult, though *how* Borella would have known where the Guild Master spent his time was unclear. She resisted the insane urge to demand satisfaction from Borella.

"Are you turning that cutter in or wearing it?" A sour voice broke through her resentment.

"Turning it in." She handed the cutter to the Fisher carefully, wishing she didn't have to encounter him as well.

"Killashandra Ree? Right?" He wasn't looking at her but inspecting the cutter. "You can't have used this much," and he peered suspiciously at handle and blade casing. "Where'd you damage it?"

"I didn't. I'm turning it in."

The Fisher was more daunting than Borella and her rudeness.

"You could have left it in your sled, you know," he said, his tone not quite so acerbic now that he had assured himself that one of his newest cutters had not been misused. "No one else can use it, you know," he added, obviously making allowance for her ignorance.

She was not about to admit to anyone that she had lost the sled.

"I'm going off-planet for Passover," she said and belatedly realized that he had no such option.

"Go while you can, when you can," he said gruffly but not unkindly. Then he turned and disappeared into his workroom.

As she made her way back to the lift, Killashandra supposed she ought to be relieved that someone remembered her. Possibly the Fisher was able to associate her with a device he had so recently crafted. Or perhaps it was common knowledge through the Guild that Lanzecki had berated a new singer.

She shouldn't let the encounter with Borella rankle her. The woman had inadvertently confirmed Lanzecki's advice. Furthermore, if Moksoon could not remember Killashandra from moment to moment, how could she fault Borella? How long did it take for a singer's memory to disintegrate? Killashandra must learn to overcome habits and values acquired on Fuerte in the Music Center. There one sought to put people under obligation so they could be called in as support for this role or that rehearsal room, to form a trio or quartet, throw a party on limited credit, all the myriad arrangements that require cooperation, good will, and . . . memory of favors past. As Lanzecki had pointed out, "Gratitude depends on memory." The corollary being "memory lasts a finite time with a singer." The

only common bond for crystal singers was the Guild Charter and its regulations, rules, and restrictions—and the desire to get off Ballybran whenever one could afford that privilege.

Carigana shouldn't have died? Now why did that come to mind,
Killashandra wondered as she stepped out of the lift at Meteorology. According to the ceiling-border message panel, the viewing was already in
progress in the theater. As she hesitated, another lift, this one full of
people, opened its door, and she accompanied the group to their mutual
destination.

The theater was semidark and crowded, people standing along the
walls when all seating was occupied. On the wide-angle screen, cloud patterns formed and reformed with incredible speed. At one point, Killashandra saw Rimbol's face illumined; beside him were Borton and Jezerey. She
recognized other members of Class 895 and the weather man who had
taken them to the sensor station. The turbulence of the storm was not audible. Instead a commentator droned on about pressure, mach-wind velocities, damage, rain fall, snow, sleet, dust density, and previous Passover
tempests while a print display under the screen kept pace with his mono-
logue. Killashandra managed to find space against the far wall and looked
over the engrossed audience for Lanzecki's face. She hoped he hadn't
made his offer of the off-planet trip to anyone else. If he was being mag-
nanimous, surely he would also give her first refusal.

Then she became caught up in the storm visuals, thinking at first they
must have been accelerated—until she compared wind velocities and decibel readings. She was aghast at the fury of the storm.

"The major Passover storm of 2898," voice and print informed viewers, "while not as severe or as damaging as that of 2863, also formed in
the northeast, during spring solstice, and when Shilmore was over the
Great Ocean in advance of Shanganagh and Shankill. The inauspicious opposition of the two nearest planets will emphasize the violence of this
year's storm. Seeding, improved emulsions, and the new wave disruptor
off the coasts of Buland and Hoyland should prevent the tsunami drive
across the ocean which caused such widespread havoc on the South Dur-
ian continent."

The screen switched frequently from satellite pictures to planetary
weather stations where the wind shifts were marked by waves of debris
flung in vertical sheets. Killashandra fell into that mesmerized state that
can befuddle the mind, and for one hideous second she almost heard
windshriek. A particularly frenzied cross-current of detritus shattered the
trance by inducing motion nausea. She hastily left the theater, looking for a
toilet. The moment she reached the soundproof stability of the quiet corridor, her nausea waned, only to be replaced by the gnawing of severe
hunger.

"I had breakfast," she said through clenched teeth. "I had plenty of
breakfast."

She entered a lift, wondering just how long the postrange appetite remained critical. She punched for the infirmary level and swung into the same anteroom she had entered barely four weeks before.

No one was on duty.

"Is anyone here?" she demanded acidly.

"Yes," the verbal address system responded.

"I don't want you. I'd like to see—"

"Killashandra Ree?" Antona walked through the right-hand door panel, an expression of surprise on her face. "You can't have been injured?" The chief medic took a small diagnostic unit from her thigh pocket and advanced toward Killashandra.

"No, but I'm starving of the hunger."

Antona laughed, slipping the instrument back into her pocket. "Oh, I do apologize, Killashandra. It's not the least bit funny! For you." She tried to compose her face into a more severe expression. "But you put it aptly. You're 'starving of the hunger' for several reasons. While the others were convalescing from the fever, we could administer nutritional assists. You had no fever, and then you were sent out to cut. The appalling hunger, you realize, is quite normal. No, I see you don't, and you look hungry. I'm just about to have a morning snack. The lounge will be deserted, as everyone's peering at last year's storms. Join me? I can think of nothing more boring than to be compelled to eat mountains and gulp them down in solitary confinement. You did remember, of course"—and by this time Antona had guided her back to the lift and, at their destination, down the length of the lounge to a catering area as she talked—"that the symbiont takes twenty weeks to establish itself thoroughly. We have never managed to find out the average spore intake per diem since so much depends on the individual's metabolism. Now, let's see . . ." Antona pressed menu review. "You don't mind if I order for you? I know exactly how to reduce that hunger and restore the symbiont." Antona waited for Killashandra's agreement and then toured the catering area, dialing several selections at each post before signaling Killashandra to take a tray and start collecting the items delivered.

Food enough for the entire final year student complement of the Music Center presently covered two large tables, and Killashandra ravenously started to eat.

"If it's any encouragement, your appetite will slack off, especially after the symbiont has prepared for Passover." She smiled at Killashandra's groan. "Don't worry. You'll have no appetite at all during the height of Passover—the spore buries itself in crevices." Antona smiled. "In the Life lab, we have rock crabs and burrow worms over four hundred years old." Antona's grin became wry. "I don't suppose that aspect of Ballybran's ecology figured in your orientation. There isn't much life on this mudball, but what there is lives in symbiotic relation to the spore. That's how it keeps itself alive, by increasing the survival mechanisms of whatever host it finds. It behooves us, the new dominant life form, to study the indigenous."

As she ate, Killashandra found Antona's ramblings more interesting than Tukolom's lectures. It did cross her mind that Antona might just be indulging in the luxury of a captive audience. Antona was not lazy with fork and spoon, so her "morning snack" must have answered a real need if not as urgent as Killashandra's.

"I keep trying"—and Antona emphasized that word—"to correlate some factor, or factors, which would once and for all allow us to recruit without anxiety." She paused and looked with unfocused eyes to one corner of the dining area. "I mean, I knew what I was to do before I came here, but if I had made the complete adjustment, I'd've been required to sing crystal." Antona made a grimace of dislike, then smiled radiantly. "The prospect of having all the time in the world to delve into a life form and carry through a research program was such a gift—"

"You didn't want to be a crystal singer?"

"Shards and shades, girl, of course not. There's more to life here than that."

"I had the impression that crystal singing was the function of this planet."

"Oh, it is," and Antona's agreement rippled with laughter. "But the crystal singers could scarcely function without support personnel. More of us than you, you know. Takes five and three-quarters support staff to keep a singer in the Ranges. Furthermore, the Guild doesn't have the time or the facilities to train up members in every skill needed. There are plenty of people from the Federated Sentient Planets quite willing to risk adaptation and the possibility of having to sing crystal to come here in other capacities."

"I'm a little confused . . ."

"I shouldn't wonder, Killashandra. You do come from Fuerte, and that conservative government had off notions about self-determination. I did wonder how you came to be recruited, though you are one of our nicer surprises." Antona patted Killashandra's arm reassuringly. "The Fuertans we've had in previous decades also made good hosts." Suddenly, Antona frowned, eying Killashandra speculatively. "I really must run your scans again. I've developed five separate evaluation tests, two at the primary level, which, if I say so myself"—and Antona smiled modestly—"have increased the probability figures by thirty-five percent."

"I didn't think the Guild was permitted active recruiting," Killashandra said, doggedly returning to that blithe comment.

Antona looked startled. "Oh, nothing *active*. Certainly less blatant than service programs. The FSP definitely frowns on any sort of conditioning or coercion due to the specific adaptation, you see. That's a direct contradiction of the freedom of movement in the FSP Charter. Of course, when FSP recruits, no one dares complain but it's common knowledge what Service people do." She emitted a sort of giggle. "Freedom of movement, indeed. Most good citizens of the FSP never leave or want to leave their home worlds, but they have to be *able* to do so according to FSP, and that forces us to use the Shankill clearing point."

"Don't you mind being restricted to this planet?"

"Why should I?" Antona did not appear to be resigned.

"Singers seem very keen to get off Ballybran," Killashandra said, but her mind was chaotic, remembering Carigana's intransigence, the farce of the Shankill Moon Recruitment, Rimbol's passing his "preliminaries," Carigana and her "trap," the way Killashandra found herself reacting to the suspicion that Antona had confirmed.

"Singers *should* leave Ballybran whenever possible," she said, completely sincere and much at her ease. "It's a tense, demanding profession, and one should be able to . . . escape . . . from one's work to completely different surroundings."

"Escape." That was the verb Lanzecki had used. "Do you escape *your* work, Antona?"

"Me? Of course. My work is in the Infirmary and the labs. I have the whole planet to roam and the moons if I wish a change of view."

"Even at Passover?"

Antona chuckled indulgently at Killashandra's jibe. "Well, everyone holes up during Passover. Or gets off the planet if possible." She leaned over to touch Killashandra's arm. "For your own sake, I wish you hadn't cut so near to Passover, but you can be sure I'll help you all I can."

"Why should I need help?" Killashandra had no trouble affecting innocent surprise. "I've only cut once."

"The most dangerous cut of them all. I'm really surprised that Lanzecki permitted it. He's *so* careful about his new singers. I *had* to pass you over to training, my dear. No point at all in keeping you with sick people. But this Passover is the most inconvenient one, and it *will* be ages before the weather settles and damage can be cleared. I suppose Lanzecki wanted to get as much crystal cut as possible when he could. Of course, repair won't concern you as a singer. You'll be sent out as soon as possible to check your claims for storm alteration."

"What will happen because I have cut crystal once?"

"Oh, dear." Antona inhaled deeply and then exhaled on a short, exasperated breath. "I will blather on. Very well, then, I'd have to tell you soon, anyhow. It's only I don't like to alarm people unnecessarily."

"You have unless you come to the point."

"You've been told that storms in the Crystal Ranges are lethal because the winds whip resonance out of the mountains that produce sensory overload. During Passover, the entire place, right down to its core, I sometimes feel, quivers—a noise, a vibration, multiple sonics are formed and transmitted which cannot be"—Antona gave another shrug of helplessness—"escaped. We'll sedate you, and you can be harnessed safely in a radiant tub in the Infirmary, which has special shielding. Every possible care will be taken."

"I see."

"No, you'll hear. That's worse. Now eat. Actually, at your stage, a surfeit of food is the best cushion I could prescribe. Think of the sedation as hibernation; the food is protection."

Killashandra applied herself to the untouched dishes, while Antona silently and slowly finished her last portion.

"Do the others go through this, too?" Killashandra flicked her hand at the array of plates.

"Oh, we all start eating quantities now."

"Will the others have to be sedated and—"

"They'll be uncomfortable, but so will anyone with hearing—and quite a number who are in other respects clinically deaf hear storm resonance. We provide maskers. The white noise relieves the temporary tinnitus caused by turbulence. We really do try to help."

"I'm sure you do."

"Small comfort, you may think, but all things are relative. Just read the early history of the Guild and the members' comments. Oh, dear, I don't want to be caught here." Antona's hasty rising caused Killashandra to look around. People were streaming in from the lifts. "I'll just slip out the back. You finish your meal!" She pointed imperatively at the remaining dishes and then retreated into a dimmer area of the Commons.

Killashandra finished the milsi stalks and regarded the final dish of nut-covered cubes. People were lining up at the catering areas, the first serving themselves with generous trays. So she wasn't the only hungry one.

"*Here* she is!" Rimbol's delighted cry startled her. She twisted in the chair and saw the Scartine. Mistra, Jezerey, Borton, and Celee were close behind him. "I told you I saw her at the storm scan. You get hungry or something?" His eyes bright with mischief, Rimbol began to count the empty plates.

"You must have cut a lot of crystal to afford all that," Jezerey commented. Her eyes were unfriendly.

"Antona's orders. I didn't have a convalescence like you lot, so I'm eating for two now."

"Yes, but you got out into the Ranges, and we're stuck here!" Jezerey was almost savage. Borton shook her arm.

"Cut that, Jez. Killa didn't do it to spite you, you know." Borton looked across to Killa, his eyes entreating.

"Yes, you did get out into the Ranges," Mistra said in her soft voice, "and I'd very much appreciate it, Killashandra, if you'd tell us what actually does happen when you cut. I've got the awfullest notion that they don't tell us all, for all they do tell."

"Here, get rid of the debris"—Rimbol was shoveling dishes and plates together—"and someone order beer and things. Then Killashandra can divulge trade secrets."

Killashandra was not in a confessional mood, but the mute appeal in Mistra's brown eyes, the wary concern in Rimbol's, and Borton's stiff, blank expression could not be denied by a classmate, no matter what doctrine of self-preservation Lanzecki was preaching. Jezerey would find her own level; that was certain. Rimbol, Mistra, and Borton were a different matter.

Celee returned then with pitchers and beakers. "Look, since singing isn't my trade, why don't I just shuttle food for you?" he asked goodnaturedly. He winked at Killashandra to emphasize his indifference to the outcome of his adaptation.

Orders were given him, and as he left, complaining that his back would be broken, the others settled at the table and looked expectantly at Killashandra.

"Most of what happens is explained," Killashandra began, not knowing precisely how to describe the phenomenon.

"Theory is one thing. Where does it differ from practice?" Mistra asked gently.

"She doesn't say much but she gets to the point," Rimbol noted while raising his eyes in comic dismay.

Killashandra smiled gratefully at Mistra.

"Those storm simulation flights—the real thing can be worse. I didn't cut squarely for all the practice I had retuning soured crystal. I suppose your hands get stronger, but don't be surprised if your first block has a reptilian outline." She was rewarded with a chuckle from Rimbol, who clowned with an exaggerated wiggle of his torso. "You know you've got to be shepherded into the Ranges by some experienced singer? Well, keep one fact perfectly clear: he or she is liable to forget from moment to moment that you are legally supposed to be with him. Mine damned near sliced my leg off. Just keep the tape playing on repeat so he can't forget it. Talk to him all the time, keep yourself in his sight, especially after he's just cut crystal . . ."

"Yes, yes, we've been told that. But when you find crystal . . ." Jezerey interrupted abruptly.

Killashandra looked at her coolly. "When" the girl said. "It's if, not when—"

"But you found crystal. Black crystal," Jezerey began indignantly.

"Shut up, Jez." Borton pressed his fingers warningly into her shoulder, but she shrugged off his hold.

"The unexpected starts when you cut your own crystal. You tap for the note on the face and then tune the cutter and then . . ." Killashandra was back in the fault, the first black segment, uneven cut line and all, weighing in her palms, dazzling her with its slow change in sunlight from transparency to the black matte of the thermally responsive crystal, losing herself in the memory of that shimmering resonance, feeling the incredible music in her blood and bones . . .

An insistent tugging on her sleeve finally broke her trance.

"Killa, are you all right? Shall I get Antona? Killa?" Rimbol's urgent and anxious questions brought her to dazed awareness of her present position. "You've been away for—"

"Six minutes, four seconds," Borton added, tipping his wrist to see the display.

"What?"

"What? she says"—Rimbol turned to the others with a teasing manner—"when she's been visiting her claim on the sly. Look, friends, no visible means of contact and yet our fair lady— Does it truly take that kind of a hold on you, Killa?" He dropped his antic pose and touched her gently on the arm, his face concerned.

"Well, I didn't think it could get me sitting here with my friends, but this advice I will freely give you, having just demonstrated. Cut, and pack! If you don't, you may stand there like I just was and commune with your crystal until the storm breaks over you."

"Communing with crystal!" Jezerey was impatient, skeptical.

"Well, it might not happen to you." Killashandra tried to speak mildly, but Jezerey aggravated her. "Got your sled yet?" she asked Rimbol.

"Yes . . ." Rimbol said.

"But we're not allowed to use them," Jezerey finished, glaring at Killashandra.

"Which might be just as well, considering your performance on the simulator," Borton said.

"So crystal singing is really addictive? How fast is the habit formed?" Rimbol was off in a seriocomic vein to lighten the tension that was developing. "Can it be broken? Is it profitable?"

"Yes, fast, no, and yes," Killashandra responded. "Don't let me inhibit your enjoyment of your meal." She rose quickly, keeping Rimbol from rising by a restraining hand on his shoulder. "See you tonight here?"

She hardly waited for his answer, for she had seen a figure entering the Commons at the far end, moving with Lanzecki's unmistakable stride. She walked to intercept him.

He was Guild Master, she realized, as he scanned the faces in the lounge. He barely paused as she reached him.

"I'd like that assignment."

"I thought you would."

No more than that and they had passed each other, he for the catering area and she for the lifts.

Chapter 11

It was a relief to be back in her quarters. Somehow the absurdity of the bizarre, triatmospheric wall-screen restored to her a sense of the absurd. Her attempt to verbalize her experience of crystal cutting to her friends and its aftermath disturbed her. How could memory, even of such an ecstatic moment, dominate mind and body so? She had broken that first communion with the crystal block by packing it. Or had she? And whom could she ask? Was addiction why it was so easy for a singer to lose the data retrieval function of the mind?

Had she hesitated over Lanzecki's offer because she actually didn't want to be far from the Ranges? She remembered then the longing in Borella's voice to return to the Ranges when her wound had healed. On the other hand, Borella could now not wait to get off the planet.

The ambivalence, Killashandra decided, could be explained. Oddly enough, it was analogous to having the starring role in a large company. The applause could be the crystal singing in your hand, fresh from the vein, stimulating, ecstatic. The same emotional high every time you cut, until body and mind were exhausted by the clamor, the concentration. The thrall of crystal confounded by the urgent need of rest and relief.

She had seated herself by the computer keyboard, motivated to record some of her reflections. The automatic time display winked the change of hour. Even thinking about crystal took enormous hunks of time. She'd been back in her room more than two hours.

Briskly sitting upright, she keyed for the original entry she had made and listened dispassionately to her voice rehearsing the few facts she had entered. Then she tapped the record tab.

"I found an abandoned black crystal vein and cut with success. The trick with crystal is to pack it away before the song gets to you in the sun. I lost my sled trying to save old Moksoon. A waste of a good sled. Lanzecki is generous, and I shall be installing the five interlocking segments I cut in the Trundimoux system. That way I avoid Passover storms which are expected to be unusually violent."

She played back the terse synopsis of her last two weeks. Would the bones of experience remind her of the degree and emotional heights at some later time? She sniggered at her own pretentiousness. Well, she never had considered herself any sort of a playwright.

As she leaned back in the console chair, she became aware of rumbling in her belly.

"Not again!"

To deny the stimulus of hunger, she determinedly dialed a furniture catalog though she had nothing to put on tables or shelves since she had hung her lute on the wall. She thought of playing the instrument which she hadn't done in a long time, but the E string broke the moment she turned the pin. Very carefully, she replaced the lute. Then, clenching her teeth, she made for the caterer in angry strides to assuage her unacceptable appetite.

She was dialing vigorously when the communit buzzed.

"Lanzecki here."

"Are you linked to my catering dial?"

"It is not coincidence. Guild Masters are allowed to eat when their daily duties permit. May I join you?"

"Yes, of course." She sounded as genuinely welcoming as she could after her facetious greeting.

Lanzecki was, she supposed, as much a victim to pre-Passover appetite as anyone else. Nor did she suppose him to be exploiting her by conveniently dispatching her off-world. Or . . . taking the cup of protein broth she had dialed as Lanzecki's call came through, she went to the console and checked with Marketing. The display confirmed that the Trundimoux order for a five-piece communications system utilizing black-crystal components had been received five days before. The order was priority rated by the FSP sector chief. She returned to the caterer and dialed enticing food for a tired, hungry man.

And it was Lanzecki the man who entered her apartments as she was vainly trying to squeeze plates, platters, and pitchers onto the limited surface of her table. She really ought to have got in more furniture.

"I started," she said, waving at her soup. "I didn't think you'd mind." She handed him a steaming cup.

"Nor do I." As he smiled, the tension lines around his eyes and mouth eased.

"I had a morning snack with Antona after hunger overcame me during the storm scan," she said as he seated himself, stretching out his legs.

"She undoubtedly reassured you that we're all eating heartily at this moment."

"She ate a lot, too."

Lanzecki laughed. "Don't worry. You'll have no appetite during Passover."

"But I won't be here."

"The instinct operates independently of your physical whereabouts. Especially, I regret to inform you, when your transition was so recent."

"So long as I'm not gorging like this while I'm installing the crystals." Some planets, particularly new ones like the Trundimoux system with limited food supplies, might consider a hearty appetite unbecoming.

"No, more likely you'll be sleeping it all off." He finished his soup and seemed more interested in picking out his next item. "Tomorrow, Trag will instruct you in installation procedures. We had a secondary communication from the Trundimoux giving us the disposition of the five units. I understand that the kindly call them Trundies; the informed style them the Moux."

"The what?" Killashandra demanded on a laugh, for she couldn't see herself using either nickname.

"Two crystals will be installed on mobile mining stations. Trundimoux has three asteroid belts. That's how they can afford black crystal." Lanzecki snorted. "They've fortunes in ore whirling about, waiting to be grappled. The third unit is to be on the one habitable planet and one each on the large satellites of the gas and the ice planets. Trundimoux mining operations have been seriously hampered by lack of real-time communications, so they mortgaged half a belt and, I expect, will discharge that indebtedness in short order. Originally, the system was exploited merely for the asteroid ores, with several multi-hulks hauling the metal to the nearest manufacturing system—Balisdel, I think it is. The Balisdelians got greedy, Trundimoux miners rebelled, settled the better planet and one of the outer moons. In less than seventy-five years, they're a going concern."

"With money enough for black-crystal communications."

"They'd already a linkage with Balisdel and two other systems, but this will be their own internal link. Yarran beer?" Lanzecki rose to dial the order.

Killashandra laughed. "Who drank Yarran beer before Rimbol got here? Besides you."

"The discovery was by no means original with me, either. Yarran beer is as close to addictive as anything can be for us."

There was a heaviness about Lanzecki this evening, Killashandra thought. It wasn't fatigue, for he moved as easily as ever for a man of his build.

"I'd forgotten how pleasant the taste is," he went on, returning with a pitcher and two beakers.

"Is this Passover going to be that bad?" she asked.

Lanzecki took a long draught of the beer before he answered, but his eyes were twinkling, and his mouth fell into an easier line.

"We always plan for the worst and generally are not disappointed. The challenge thus presented by each new Passover configuration is irresistible, forces that are changeless and changing, as unpredictable as such natural phenomena are."

Killashandra was startled by his unexpected philosophizing and wondered if she had been wrong about his mood.

"You actually enjoy this!"

"Hmmm. No—'enjoy' is not the appropriate word. Stimulated, I think, would be more accurate." He was teasing her. His lips told her that. Teasing, but something more, something deeper, the element that caused the heaviness about him. "Stop thinking and eat. I've ordered up a particular delicacy which I hope you'll enjoy, too. Catering goes to great pains at this time of Ballybran's cycle, and we must respond."

Tonight, his appetite equaled hers as they sampled the marvels of taste and texture that had been conjured from the cuisines of all the elegant and exotic worlds in the Federation. Lanzecki knew a great deal about food and promised her that one day he would personally prepare a meal for her from raw produce to finished dish.

"When eating is not a necessity, as it is now, but can be enjoyed," and his eyes twinkled at the repetition of that word "in complete *leisure*."

"We're not at leisure now?"

"Not completely. As soon as I have satisfied my symbiotic self, I must meet with the storm technicians again."

She suppressed an irrational disappointment that their dinner was not a prelude to another loving night.

"Thank you, dear heart," he said.

"Thank me? For what?"

"For being . . . aware."

She stared at Lanzecki for a long moment.

"You're certain telepathy is not in the symbiotic . . ."

"Absolutely not!" Lanzecki's assurance was solemn, but she wasn't sure about his mouth.

Killashandra rapidly catalogued some of her responses to him and sighed.

"Well, I am sorry you're not staying!"

Lanzecki laughed as he reached for her hand and kissed it lightly. Not light enough so that she didn't respond to his touch.

"I have never intended to invade your privacy, Killashandra, by watching the shift and flow of your thoughts and emotions. I enjoy them. I enjoy you. Now"—and he rose purposefully—"if it were anything but storm tactics . . ." He kissed her palm again and then strode swiftly from the room.

She let her hand fall back to her lap, Lanzecki's graceful compliment echoing through her mind. Quite one of the nicest she had ever been paid.

Oddly enough, that he had been invading a Fuertan's treasured privacy, once her most defended possession, did not distress Killashandra. If Lanzecki continued to "enjoy" what he saw. She took a long swallow of beer. How much she had changed since that aimless, aching ride on the pedestrian way to Fuerte's spaceport! How much of the change was due to her "symbiotic self"? That, too, had been an invasion of privacy to which she had, before officialdom of the FSP, agreed.

Now that she had held crystal, vibrant in the palm of her hand, light and sound coruscating off the sun-warmed quartz, she felt no regrets for loss of privacy, no regrets for an invasion that had been entrance into a new dimension of experience.

She laughed softly at her whimsy. She finished the beer. She was sleepy and satiated, and tomorrow would be a wearying day. She hoped that Trag did not get reports from Enthor on the raggedness of her first cuttings.

The next morning, after a sturdy breakfast, she reported to Trag in the cutting room. Other members of Class 895 were already busy under the supervision of Concera and another Guild member. Killashandra greeted Concera and smiled at the others.

Trag jerked his head to a side door, and she followed him. She experienced a double shock, for there on the work table amid installation brackets and pads were five black crystals. And she didn't respond to their presence at all!

"Don't worry!" Trag picked up the nearest one and tossed it negligently at her.

She opened her mouth to scald him with an oath when the object reached her hands and she knew it wasn't black crystal.

"Don't you ever frighten me that way again!" Fury was acid in her belly and throat.

"Surely you didn't think we'd risk the black in practice." Trag had enjoyed startling her.

"I'm too new at this game to know what is risked," she replied, getting her anger under control. She hefted the block in her hand, wanting more than anything else to loft it right back at Trag.

"Easy now, Killashandra," he said, raising a protective hand. "You knew it wasn't black crystal the moment you walked into the room!"

The coolness in Trag's voice reminded her that he was a senior Guild member.

"I've had enough surprises in the Ranges without having to encounter them here, too, Trag." As she controlled panic and rage, she also reminded herself that Trag had always been impersonal! Her relations with Lanzecki were clouding other judgments.

"Coping with the unexpected must become automatic for a singer. Some people never learn how." Trag's eyes shifted slightly to indicate the room behind them. "You proved just now that your instinct for the blacks is reliable. Now"—and he reached out to take the block from her hand—"let us to the purpose for which these were simulated." He put the block among its mates.

Only then did she realize that the five mock crystals had been cast in the image of those she had cut, wiggles, improper angles and size.

"This substance has the same tensile strength and expansion ratio as black crystal but no other of its properties. You must learn today to install crystal properly in its bracketing with enough pressure to secure it against vibration but not enough to interfere with intermolecular flow." He showed her a printed diagram. "This will be the order and the configuration of the Trundimoux link." He tapped the corresponding block as he pointed out its position, repeating what Lanzecki had rattled through.

"Number one and two, the smallest, will be on mining stations, number three on the gas planet satellite, number four on the ice planet satellite, and number five, the largest crystal, will be installed on the habitable planet. You and you alone will handle the crystals."

"Is that Guild policy?" How much more did she have to learn about this complex profession.

"Among other considerations, no one in the Trundimoux system is technically capable." Trag's voice was heavy with disapproval.

Killashandra wondered if he considered them "Trundies" or "Moux."

"I would have thought Marketing would handle installation."

"Generally." His stiff tone warned her off further questions.

"Well, I don't suppose I'd've been saddled with the job if I hadn't lost my sled and if Passover weren't so near."

She got no visible reaction from her rueful comment.

"Remember that," Trag advised, and added with an unexpected wryness, "if you can."

Installing crystal in padded clamps was not as simple as it had sounded, but then, as Killashandra was learning, nothing in the Heptite Guild was as simple as it sounded. Nevertheless, by evening, with arm, neck, and back muscles tense and hands that trembled from the effort of small, strong movements, eyes hot from concentration on surface tension readings, she believed she understood the process.

She was philosophical when Trag said they would repeat the day's exercise on the morrow, for she knew she must be motion perfect during the actual installations. Guild members had a reputation to maintain, and she would be up to Trag's standard of performance even if this was the only installation she ever made. Since her notion tallied with Trag's, she was undaunted by his perfectionism.

Lanzecki joined her again for her evening "gorge," but he excused himself as soon as he'd finished. She didn't mind so much that night because she was very tired.

By mealtime the following day, she had secured Trag's grudging approval for a deft, quick, and competent installation within a time limit he had arbitrarily set.

"Why not take more time?" she'd asked reasonably. "Installing a link between people ought to be an occasion."

"You won't *have* time," Trag said. "You'll be on an inbound gravity deflection course. There'll be no *time* to spare."

He gave her no chance to query his emphasis on time. With a curt nod, he left the room. Maybe Lanzecki would be in an expansive mood. If, she qualified to herself, he joined her for dinner.

Dinner? She was starving for her midday meal. As she passed through the main training room, Rimbol had just finished making a diagonal cut under Concera's tutelage.

"Are you eating soon?" she asked Rimbol and the older singer.

"I'm always eating!" Rimbol's reply was half groan, half belch, and Concera laughed.

"Finish the last cut," Concera told him.

"Go save us a table." Rimbol shooed her off, then turned his attention to his cutting.

Killashandra went directly to the Commons and found the dining area well occupied, tables stacked with a variety of dishes that bore witness to the problem of symbiotic instinct. She was about to order something to sustain her during the search for a free table when a large group vacated one of the booths. She ordered hastily, dialing for beer in a pitcher and beaker and setting them about the table to prevent occupation. She had retrieved her first order and was already eating as Rimbol, Concera, and two others of Class 895 joined her.

The meal became a convivial occasion, and all made suggestions of this or that favored delicacy they'd discovered during what Concera styled "the hunger."

"It's so good to have new members," she said in a giddy voice, waving her beaker of beer, "to remind us of things we've forgotten. I can't think, of course, who it was the last time, but Yarran beer is so satisfying."

Rimbol rose, bowed to the entire table. "Be upstanding all. Let us toast to the brewers of Yarran beer. May they always be remembered—by somebody!"

As the company hastily stood, the table was knocked askew, and before the toast could be made, the surface had to be mopped and more beer dialed.

Killashandra was suffused by a sense of camaraderie that she had often observed in the Music Center but had never been part of. She supposed it was Rimbol's special gift that, given half a chance, he could make an occasion of any gathering. She said little, smiled much, and ate with a heartier appetite for such good company.

As she sat facing the dispensing area, she found herself identifying high-ranking Guild members as well as singers obviously just in from the Ranges, some of whom were gaunt, nervous, and confused by the throng of diners. Others, despite the same noise-pollution discomfiture, appeared in very good spirits. The nervous ones hadn't cut enough crystal to get off-planet, Killashandra thought, and the relaxed ones had. Certainly, when Borella entered with Olin and another pair of singers, they were a vivacious group. Obstreperously so, Killashandra thought, for they would whisper among themselves, then burst into laughter as they looked with mock surreptitiousness at silent diners.

Though Rimbol was joking with Concera and Celee, he had noticed Borella's table.

"D'you know?" he said in an undertone to Killashandra, "she doesn't remember any of us."

"I know. She has been out in the Ranges since we were recruited."

Killashandra knew she wasn't excusing Borella, and she didn't need to explain to Rimbol.

"I know, I know, but that was only a few months ago." Rimbol's blue eyes were clouded with worry. "Do we lose our memories that quickly?"

"Borella's sung a long time, Rimbol." Killashandra could not reassure herself, either. "Have you started your personal file? Good. That's the way to remember what's important."

"I wonder what she considers important." Rimbol looked at Borella with narrowed eyes.

"Getting off this planet during Passover!" Even to herself, Killashandra sounded sharp. Rimbol threw her a startled look, and then he laughed. "I only know because I heard her talking to that tall fellow, Olin." Killashandra added in an easier manner. "Say, have you been in contact with Shillawn at all?"

"Sure have. In fact, we're meeting here tomorrow. Join us?"

Killashandra met Rimbol's mildly challenging stare.

"If I'm free. I'm scheduled to take some crystals to the Trundimoux system. Evidently, having cut crystal, I'd be particularly susceptible to Passover, so they're whipping me off the planet."

"Once I thought I'd have no trouble keeping up with you, Killa." Rimbol's expression was rueful.

"What d'you mean by that?" Killashandra was aware of a flurry of unexpected feelings: anxiety, surprise, irritation, and a sense of loss. She didn't want to lose her friendship with Rimbol. She put her hand on his arm. "We're friends, remember. Class 895."

"*If* we remember."

"What is the matter with you, Rimbol? I've been having such a good time." Killashandra gestured at the others laughing and chatting, and the evidences of a hearty meal. "I haven't had a chance to see much of anyone because of that wretched Milekey Transition and being shepherded out by that sonic-shorted Moksoon—"

"Not to mention finding black crystal."

She took a deep breath against her seething reaction to Rimbol's implicit accusation.

"When"—she began slowly and in a taut voice—"you have been in the Ranges looking for crystal, then you will know what I cannot possibly explain to you now." She rose, the tenuous sensation of comradeship abruptly severed. "Give my regards to Shillawn if you'd be so good as to remember."

She excused herself and stalked past a startled Concera, who tried to protest Killashandra's exit.

"Let her go, Concera. She has matters of great importance to attend."

Striding quickly into the main aisle, Killashandra nearly ran into Trag just entering the dining area.

"Killashandra? Don't you ever watch the call display?" Trag pointed to the moving line above the catering area, and she saw her name flashing. Trag took her arm and hurried her toward the lifts. "The Trundimoux ship is at Shankill. We've been holding the shuttle for you."

"The Trundimoux ship? Leave?" Killashandra glanced back at the table she had so hurriedly left. Only Concera was looking in her direction. She gave Killashandra a little wave for reassurance.

"They made time around their last sun and are here ahead of schedule and cannot hold at slow much longer or they'll lose momentum."

"I'll only need a few things . . ."

Trag shook his head impatiently and pushed her into a waiting lift.

"A carisak is being prepared for you on the Base. Anything else you require, your accommodations and expenses are to be met by the Trundimoux. There's no time to lose now!"

Killashandra's protests waned. Her initial confusion turned quickly to resentment. Not only was she leaving without a chance to vindicate herself in Rimbol's opinion, she wasn't to see Lanzecki either. Or perhaps he had planned so hasty a departure to prevent her from embarrassing him? Soured as she was by Rimbol's accusations, it was easy to include Lanzecki.

That Milekey Transition might have appeared to be a blessing, but that bit of "luck" had alienated her from the few friends she had ever made and left her vulnerable to speculations and subtly accused of harsh and indefensible suspicions.

"We were not expecting the Trundimoux to arrive so soon," Trag said, "but that may be fortuitous with Passover not long away." He thrust a sheaf of printout at her as she was puzzling that cryptic remark. "Antona said you were to read this. Medical advice on symbiotic adjustment and replenishment, so examine it carefully. The crystals are already on board the shuttle and locked in the supercargo's security hold. This is your Guild identification"—he offered her a slim folder like the one Carrik had carried—"and the Guild band," which he clasped around her right wrist. "With these, you have access to planetary governing organizations, including the Session of the Federated Sentient Planets. Though they're a boring lot, and I cannot see this assignment leading to a meeting, it's wise to be prepared for all contingencies."

Access to the Session of the Federated Sentient Planets? Killashandra did not think Trag would joke about such a privilege. The stimulation of such prestige and surprise lifted her depression.

They had reached the Hangar level, and Trag's hand under her arm propelled her forward at a good pace toward the waiting shuttle. At the ramp, the boarding officer was gesturing them urgently to hurry. Trag increased his pace, and every inch of Killashandra wanted to resist as she glanced around the immense Hangar area for one glimpse of Lanzecki.

"C'mon! C'mon!" the boarding officer exhorted. "Stragglers can be left for tomorrow's shuttle!"

"Quiet!" Trag turned Killashandra just as she put her foot on the ramp. "The Guild Master has considerable confidence in your abilities. I do not think it is misplaced. Lanzecki wishes you a good voyage and a safe return! Remember!"

With that, Trag whirled, leaving Killashandra staring after him, his last words echoing in her mind.

"I canNOT close the ramp if you are standing on it," the boarding officer exclaimed petulantly.

Obedient in her confusion, Killashandra hastened into the shuttle. The ramp retracted, and the shuttle's door slid with a ponderous whoosh and hiss across the aperture.

"Don't just stand there. Get a seat." The boarding officer gave Killashandra a little push toward the rear of the shuttle craft.

She strapped herself into a seat without thinking, holding her identification folder and Antona's instructions with both hands resting on her thighs. She let her body relax to the motion of the shuttle as it lifted on air cushions and glided from the Hangar. Having no viewport, she endured what seemed hours before she felt the power surge as the crystal drive was engaged. She was thrust back into the cushioning of her seat as the shuttle took off. The pressure was welcome as a source of minor discomfort. She wished that the gravity drag pushing flesh and muscles against resisting bone might squeeze unwelcome thoughts from her head.

Then the shuttle was free of Ballybran's pull, and the relief of weightlessness was accompanied by the return of common sense to Killashandra's tumultuous thoughts. She had built into a personal tragedy two totally unrelated incidents: Rimbol's curiously aggressive attitude during an otherwise convivial occasion when she had felt particularly relaxed, and Lanzecki's apparent dismissal. She'd muddled these about with her tendency to dramatize and a subconscious guilt about her easy transition, the Keborgen incident, Lanzecki's unexpected friendship, her first overcharged trip into the Ranges, and pre-Passover sensitivity.

So. Deep breath and rationalize. Rimbol was also feeling pre-Passover sensitivity. Not only had Trag personally escorted her to the shuttle, but he had given her three different messages: the Guild Master had confidence in her. So, unexpectedly, had Trag, whom Killashandra knew to be harder to please than any other instructor she had ever studied with. And Lanzecki wished her a good voyage and a safe return.

Killashandra smiled to herself and began to relax. With the unstated import as reassurance, she ceased to regard the precipitous departure as more than coincidence. Still, she'd been on the handy end of coincidence rather much recently. From the moment the sorters recruited her class to help with crystal and Enthor had chosen her; her sensitivity to black crystal; a Milekey Transition that, according to Antona, no one could predict. Chance had been on Killashandra's side when she'd gone with the rescue team to Keborgen. True, an application of deduction and fact had helped her determine Keborgen's flight path. Her premature introduction to the Ranges had occurred at Lanzecki's direction, governed by the Guild's necessity to keep Keborgen's claim operative. She might not have found it, might have been deterred by the fresh claimer paint. She wondered about the effect of Passover storms on paint.

Then she remembered Antona's message, and shoving the Guild ident into a hip pocket, she unfolded the print sheet.

Antona had researched the foods available in the Trundimoux system and listed the best for Killashandra's needs. The list was ominously short. Antona reminded the new singer that her hunger would slacken but that she might also encounter considerable drowsiness as Passover point was reached. This effect most frequently occurred when symbiont and host were adjusting. Antona advised her to complete the installations as quickly as possible and gave her a mild stimulant to overcome lethargy. Antona ended by advising Killashandra not to return to Ballybran's surface until Passover was completed, and the farther away from the system she stayed, the better.

The message, typed by voice-printer, sounded like Antona in a cheerful way, and Killashandra was extremely grateful for the thoughtfulness that prompted it. Her uncertainties allayed, she mentally reviewed the installation procedures in which Trag had drilled her. Both he and Lanzecki had confidence in her. So be it.

The retrodrive and the swaying, dropping motion of the shuttle indicated it was maneuvering at the base docks. She felt the impact as the maneuver was successful.

"Clumsy!" a familiar voice commented several rows up from Killashandra.

"No doubt, one of your recruits showing off," the drawling voice of Olin replied.

She must really have been in a daze when she boarded the shuttle, Killashandra thought, if she hadn't noticed Borella and her companion. Killashandra had just unstrapped when she was surprised to hear her own name in Borella's unmistakably scornful voice.

"Killashandra Ree? Now how should I know whether she's on board or not. I don't know her."

The calculated indifference to what must have been a courteous query infuriated Killashandra. No wonder crystal singers had such bad reputations.

She made her way to the shuttle door, coming to an abrupt halt as her augmented vision was assaulted by the garishly uniformed pair standing to one side of the dock port. On the chests of each man, emblazoned in vivid, iridescent, and unharmonious colors, was a stylized symbol, a planet, two moons ringed by three whirling asteroid belts. The movement, Killashandra decided as she closed her eyes for a moment, must be due to the men's normal breathing and some special quality of the material.

"I'm Killashandra Ree," she said politely, but she could almost understand Borella's curt arrogance. To the more sensitive eyes of an altered human, the Trundimoux uniform was visually unbearable.

"Star Captain Francu of the Trundimoux Navy, at your service, Guild Member Ree." A stiff gesture introduced his companion. "Senior Lieutenant Engineer Tallaf."

By narrowing her eyes, Killashandra could filter out the appalling color and appreciate that these were very attractive men, lean as most spacers were, and equally obvious, uncomfortable. Nervous?

The shuttle pilot, his casual coverall a complete contrast to the Trundimoux officers', emerged from the lock.

"You're from the Trundy ship? Cargo's unloaded on the lower deck."

Killashandra noted Captain Francu's wince at the nickname and thought that the lieutenant was amused.

"Senior Lieutenant Supercargo Pendel is attending to that matter, Captain . . ."

"Senior Captain Amon, Francu. Pendel has been thoroughly briefed on the crystal?"

Francu stiffened.

"Where's your ship docked?" Amon continued, looking at his wrist unit.

"Our cruiser"—and Francu emphasized the type of vessel in such a pompous tone that Killashandra had a presentiment that her voyage companions might be very dull—"is in hyperbolic."

"Oh, your system did get the 78 then." Amon replied with such genial condescension that Killashandra nearly laughed aloud. The two officers exchanged startled glances. "Well, you'd hardly have got here so fast in any of your old 59s. Quite a compliment to you, Killa, for them to send their newest."

To her knowledge, Killashandra had never met Amon, but she didn't miss the slight wink that accompanied the abbreviated form of her name.

"I don't think the compliment is to me, Amon"—and she smiled understandingly at the officers—"but rather to the black crystals."

"You Trundies are lucky to get the quintet," Amon went on; he, too, had caught Francu's disapproval of the nickname.

"After all, there is an FSP priority for the Trundimoux system," Killashandra interjected diplomatically. Amon might be getting some pleasure out of antagonizing Francu, but she was the one who had to travel with the man.

"True," Amon replied, and smiled affably. "Now, Killa, there are a few details . . ." and he began to shepherd her toward the Guild exit.

"Captain Amon, we were assured that there would be no delays as soon as the Guild—" Francu's wrist unit blurted a noise. "Yes? They are? Secured? We'll be in the cutter—"

"Not until Killashandra has cleared Shankill authority, Captain. If you'll just wait at—which port is your cutter at?"

"Level 4, port 18." Francu yielded the information with a look compounded of anger and apprehension. "We *are* hyperbolic."

"This won't take long."

Amon hustled her through the Guild door, and she smiled back reassuringly at the startled officers.

"What's all this nonsense about?" she demanded, breaking Amon's grip as the panel slid behind them. "If they're on hyperbolic, we've only so much time to catch up with their cruiser."

"Over here!" He grabbed her hand again and pulled her into a side room. The odors of food that assailed her aroused an instant appetite. She groaned.

"Eat!" Amon exhorted her. "You've got to cram as much as you can into your belly." He shoved some pepper fingers into her mouth. "You won't get a chance to eat while that cruiser is on interplanetary drive. Those 78s don't carry luxuries like catering devices, and the mess will be closed while they build speed. You'd starve. I got the ship to fix up a necessaries kit for you. I know the Trundies have females on board, but it isn't right for a singer to wear their uniforms. Your eyes'd bleed. There're lenses in this kit to filter the color intensities to the bearable level." Amon rattled through the inventory as he checked the items in the small bag. "Not much variety in clothing but good quality. I'll put in some of this food, too. We really have to hop if they're on hyperbolic. Bells and bollux, they must be separating some expensive rocks in their asteroid belts if they could buy a 78." He whistled. "I saw the length of the drone string they brought. However, if they traded with the Guild, I know who came out best. Here, try these nut meats. Heard you liked Yarran beer. Have a gulp to wash the meats down. Good. Now, another word of advice. Play crystal singer to the hilt with those belt knockers. That captain's a bad print, and I've seen enough to know. Eat! I can't hold you up much longer." He was covering the remaining uneaten dishes and stowing them in the kit. His wrist unit bleeped. "Yes? Yes, I know. Mere formalities? Fardles, she was starving to death, shafthead. It is rising Passover and you know cruisers. We'll be off in a pico." Amon slung her kit bag over her shoulder, thrust a bowl of small crispy fried squares in one hand, took up another dish and her beer in the other. "You can eat as we go, but Francu's cutting up stiff with Authority about the delay. Bells and bollux! Did anyone remember to warn you about the sleepies?" Amon was guiding her down the corridor to the peripheral lifts.

"Antona mentioned them. I've instructions and a stimulant."

"I put a strip of pink tablets in your stuff. Bollux! And you've only just been in the Ranges. It just isn't fair on you, you know."

"Trag trained me on installations."

"*Trag?* Oh, Lanzecki's shadow," and Amon appeared impressed. "It's not so much what you have to do as where and with what. The Trundies being a prime example of Problem. Here we go. Take a deep breath, girl, and you're on stage as Heptite Guild Member from now on. Good luck!"

Amon whipped the dish from her hand as she faced the door panel, motioned for her to wipe her mouth, and then the door slid apart.

Killashandra blinked as the raucous colors on the stiffly attentive escort of six men half blinded her. The haste with which she was then propelled into the cutter was indicative of the tension she sensed in the atmosphere. She barely had time to mumble thanks to Amon before the cutter airlock closed. Killashandra nearly fell over the crystal container, cross-tied in the center of the narrow aisle. She noticed the familiar Heptite dodecahedron and the rather astonishing large Trundimoux symbol. Even the stamp radiated offensive color. The captain indicated the seat she should take, and the lieutenant tested her seat webbing.

Rather to her surprise, the captain took the control seat, Tallaf sitting second in the traditional left-hand place. The release formalities were completed with Shankill Authority, and the lock coupling to the cutter was released.

Francu was a competent driver, but Killashandra had the distinct notion that cruiser captains rarely lifted lowly cutters from moon bases. Or was this a Trundie tradition? She must NOT fall into the habit of their nickname.

The cutter was equipped with external video cameras, so Killashandra rather enjoyed the spectacular views of Ballybran, little Shilmore, and the dazzling array of small and large merchant craft attached to the locks of the base or in synchronous orbit. Probably everyone was getting in for what crystal was available before Passover. She wondered if Andurs's ship was in a berth. As the cutter wended its way through the orbiting traffic, she didn't see *Rag Delta Blue Swan*.

The cruiser became visible early in the short trip. It was planet lit on its long axis, which made it seem larger. She had half expected it to be decorated in wild patterns, but the hull was the usual space orange. The drones tethered to it were much patched and dented. As the cutter was matching speed for contact, she could not judge the cruiser's forward motion, but it had that inevitable, inexorable, *military* look—"I am going in this direction, and nothing is stopping me." Which, Killashandra mused, was fair enough since the vessel was traveling on a hyperbolic trajectory utilizing the gravitational pull of whatever suns or planets that deflected it.

The captain made a clean insertion into the cruiser's dock, and a moment later the airlock bumped gently against the hull. The crewmen jumped to their feet. The captain, with Tallaf a half step behind, stopped abruptly at Killashandra's seat. Hastily, she unbuckled her webbing, realizing that she was holding up the landing drill.

With a hiss, the hatch swung open, and an incredibly high pitched whine pierced her skull. The noise stopped as quickly as it had started. Outside, two rows of stiffly attentive men formed an aisle from the cutter to a larger hatch. There, more officers, including two whose outlines were female, awaited her.

A snap and scuff behind her, and from the corner of her eye, Killashandra saw crewmen lifting the crystal container. She felt another twinge of apprehension about this assignment. Even if getting off-planet during Passover was vital to her, was this fuss and formality the right environment?

She took a deep breath and moved forward, head high, and stepped on to the cruiser's deck with the dignity of a reigning queen of ancient times.

The two female subordinate officers, Tic and Tac, for she never could get them to repeat their proper names above a mumble, escorted her to quarters, which made her student's cubicle at the Music Center seem spacious. However, she told herself firmly as she was shown the ingenious disposition of the tiny cabin's conveniences, that Ballybran had given her delusions of grandeur. The cramped accommodation would deflate her sense of self-importance to a manageable level. Tic and Tac demonstrated how the bunk could be converted to a table, where the jug of water—one per cabin—was stored, the panel behind which the tri-d was located and the ship's library code; they reminded her five times about water rationing. A toilet facility was cleverly tucked away but easily located by the chemical odor.

The hum of crystal through the deck plates gave Killashandra a chance to suggest that they must have flight duties. She wanted to place the lenses in her aching eyes to tone down the revolting color around her. Also, in the close confines of the room, the odors of her unfinished meal were apparent to her, if not to them, and she wasn't about to share. The few mouthfuls she'd been able to bolt on Shankill had only sharpened her appetite.

Tic and Tac did respond to another ear-piercing sound, promising to return to satisfy her smallest wish, once full drive had been established.

Closing the cabin door with one hand and kicking down the bunk were simultaneously possible in her new accommodations. As Killashandra stoked her symbiont's craving, she read the instructions on the lenses, pausing long enough in her eating to slip them over her irises. The demonic shades of the cabin settled into a bland wash. Ballybran had looked so dull to her at first! She finished the food Amon had packed, then tried to calculate how long it would be before her next meal.

She felt the drive taking hold, but the crystals were well tuned and caused her no twinges. She could do nothing more at this stage of the cruiser's journey, so she made herself as comfortable as possible on the narrow bunk and fell asleep.

Another ear-shattering whine brought her bolt upright on the bunk and very wide awake. Would there be any way for her to block that dreadful noise in her quarters?

"Journey speed achieved. Cruising drill is effective as of—now! All officers to the mess. Will Guild Member Killashandra Ree do us the honor of joining the assembly?"

She would also have to do something about receiving such ship-wide announcements.

"Guild Member Ree? Are you in hearing?"

"Yes, yes, of course," the Guild Member replied, hastily depressing the toggle so quaintly placed at eye level by her bunk. "Honored to join the officers' mess."

She emptied the carisak on the bed, sorted through the tunics and caftans, found the "sleepy" pills Amon had mentioned, and secured them in the arm pocket of her coverall. Then she changed into the more elaborately decorated caftan and was wondering where the officers' mess would be located on a 78 when a brief rap on her door was followed by its being opened by Tic or Tac.

"Privacy, sub, privacy. Never open my door until I have acknowledged."

"Aye, aye, ma'am, sorry, ma'am, I mean—" The girl had recoiled at Killashandra's severity.

"Isn't there a Privacy light on this cabin?" Killashandra could not contemplate easy access to her quarters with any equanimity either as a Fuertan or a Guild Member.

"No light, ma'am. This is an official vessel." The subordinate officer regarded her with anxious trepidation.

"Yes, of the Trundimoux system. But I am of the Heptite Guild and expect the courtesy of Privacy wherever I am."

"I'll pass the word, ma'am. None of us will forget."

Killashandra did not doubt that, but she must contrive the same respect from the officers. Francu would be no threat, but Tallaf . . . As Killashandra followed Tic to the officers' mess, she decided that she would retrieve a deck plan from the library as soon as she had the opportunity. The cruiser was obviously being refitted to Trundimoux requirements en route, for work parties were busy at various corridors and levels, all pausing to inspect her as she passed.

The officers' mess might have been a pleasant room but was poorly furnished, its walls hung with diagrams and hard copy, suggesting that it served a dual purpose. Francu formally introduced her to the numerous officers, some of whom immediately excused themselves to take up their watch duties. Those who remained were served a tiny cup of an inferior wine that the captain enjoined them to take to the mess table.

In Killashandra's estimation, the occasion rapidly deteriorated into a very bad comic opera in which no one had studied lines or recognized cues. Francu and his executive officer would never have advanced past preliminary auditions. The other flight deck officers seemed to take turns asking her conventionally stupid questions to which, piqued, she gave outrageous and contradictory answers. Only Tallaf, seated at the other end of the table, appeared to have a sense of humor. The supercargo, also placed at an inconvenient distance from her, was the only extraplanetarian. Since he seemed as bored as she was, she made a note to cultivate him as soon as possible.

The food served was dreadful, although from the appetites of the younger officers, it was evidently a feast. Killashandra could find nothing on the table that matched the items on Antona's list and, with great difficulty, chewed and swallowed the unappealing stodge.

Dinner ended with everyone's jumping to their feet and dedicating themselves to the further ambitions of Trundimoux system, against all natural obstacles and phenomena.

Killashandra managed to keep her expression composed during this unexpected outburst, especially when she realized that the younger subs were emotionally involved in their statement. When Killashandra considered that the system had managed to purchase a 78 as well as five black crystals, there might be some merit to unswerving dedication. The Guild inspired its members, too, but toward selfish rather than selfless aims. Well, the Trundimoux system's results were very good, but it was from the Guild that they made their most prestigious purchases.

The table was cleared efficiently by the mess crew, and Killashandra watched them, there being nothing else to do. She could think of nothing to say in the silence and dreaded the prospect of more evenings like this.

"Would you care for a drink, Guild Member?" the supercargo asked as he appeared at her side.

"Why, yes, a Yarran beer would top off that meal," she said with considerable irony, for beer would more likely bring the stodge back up.

To her utter amazement, the super gave her a bright smile.

"*You*"—and his emphasis implied that she should have been the last person in the galaxy to have such tastes—"like Yarran beer?"

"Yes, it's my favorite beverage. Have you heard of it?"

"Of course, I've heard of it," and the man's good-humored chuckle included those standing nearby. "I'm Yarran. Pendel's the name, ma'am. You shall have a beaker from my own keg!" He signaled to one of the mess crew, mimed the careful pouring of beer into a beaker, and held up two fingers.

"Guild Member," the captain said, stepping in, "we have wines—"

"Actually, Captain Francu, the Heptite Guild is partial to Yarran beer," she said, knowing that she was irritating the man, yet unable to resist. "If I'm not depriving you, super—"

"Depriving me?" Lieutenant Supercargo Pendel was enormously amused by the suggestion. Nor did Killashandra miss his quick glance at Francu or Francu's displeasure. "Not at all. My pleasure, I assure you. I keep telling 'em how satisfying a good Yarran brew is, far and above the ordinary since Terran malt and hops adapted well to our soil, but to each his own, I always say."

The beakers were served, and Francu's disapproval grew as Killashandra sipped with overt delight, though the beer was slightly flat, and she wondered how long it had been in Pendel's keg. Perhaps the Guild brewmasters excelled Yarra's own.

Pendel chattered away to her about different brews from different planets. Killashandra was relieved to find at least one traveled person among the Trundie belt-knockers. As long as they could stay on the subject of food and drink, Killashandra could give Pendel the impression of being widely-traveled herself.

"Do you remember much about Yarra?" he asked, as he signaled for another round of beer.

The phrasing of that question startled Killashandra, though she wasn't certain why, since Pendel's manner posed no threat.

"Of all the planets I have visited, it has the best brew and the most affable population. I wonder if the two are related? Have you been long away?"

"Too long and not long enough," the Yarran replied, his jolly face lengthening into sadness. He sighed heavily, taking the fresh beaker and sipping at it slowly. How the man could become homesick on one glass of flat beer, Killashandra wasn't certain. "However, it was of my choosing, and we Yarrans make the best of everything, and everything of the best."

Unexpectedly the harsh buzzer that announced watch changes penetrated the room. Killashandra took that opportunity to excuse herself from the mess.

Tac, for she'd seen Tic go off with the duty crew, guided Killashandra through the maze of companionways to her cell. As she slipped out of her caftan, she wondered how she was going to endure six days of this. And how was she going to replenish her symbiont on the *gundge* that was served? She was thinking that flat Yarran beer had a more soporific effect than the proper stuff as she fell asleep.

The next morning, it abruptly occurred to her that if Pendel had Yarran beer in his private supplies, he might have other delicacies, so she asked Tic, then on duty, to lead her to the supercargo's office.

She felt crystal as she passed a sealed and barred hatch, grinning over the useless precautions. For who could steal crystal in space? Or were the Trundies afraid of crystal's ensnaring the unwary? She experienced a start of amazement as Tic, after merely rapping on the panel, pulled it aside and entered. Presumably, Yarrans did not object to casual invasions of their privacy. Pendel was on his feet and full of genial welcomes in a cabin only slightly larger than hers. All three had to stand in close proximity to fit beside the bunk table. There were, however, a basket of fruit and a half-finished beaker of Yarran beer on the shelf.

"How may I serve you?" Pendel asked, smiling at Tic as he waved her out and closed the panel behind her.

Killashandra explained, giving him the list of Antona's suggested diet.

"Ah, I can supply you with these and more. What they choose to eat"—and he waved his hand in the general direction of the control section amidships—"is well enough if one is not used to better. But you, Guild Member—"

"Killashandra, please . . ."

"Yes? Well, thank you, Killashandra. You have been accustomed to the very best that the galaxy has to offer—"

"So long as my immediate dietary requirements are met"—and Killashandra pointed to Antona's list—"I will have no complaint." She could not help eyeing the fruit basket wistfully.

"Haven't you eaten yet this morning?" Appalled, Pendel deposited the basket in her hands, turning past her to haul back the panel and roaring at Tic, standing on guard. "Breakfast, immediately, and none of the glop." He glanced at the list. "Rations twenty-three and forty-eight and a second issue of fruit."

Consternation at having to relay such an order warred with fear in Tic's face.

"Go on, girl. Go on. I've given the order!" Pendel assured her.

"And I have seconded it!" Killashandra added firmly. Then she bit into a red fruit to ease the gnawing in her belly.

Pendel slid the panel closed and smiled with anticipatory glee. "Of course, we'll have Chasurt down in a pico . . ." The super rubbed his hands together. "Those rations are his. He's the medic," Pendel grimaced as he added, "with far more experience in space-freeze and laser burn. The rations contain just what your list specifies, high in trace minerals, potassium, calcium and such like."

The food and the medic arrived at the same time. But for Pendel's smooth intervention, Killashandra's breakfast would have been confiscated from Tic's nerveless hands by the irate Chasurt.

"Who gave orders to release *my* rations?" Chasurt, a stolidly built, blank-faced man of the late middle decades, reminded Killashandra of Maestro Valdi in his outraged indignation.

"I did!" said Pendel and Killashandra in chorus. Pendel took the tray from Tic's shaking hands and smoothly transferred it to Killashandra, who, moving herself and Chasurt's rations to the farthest corner of the cabin, left Pendel to impede Chasurt's effort at retrieval.

Eating with a speed not entirely generated by hunger, Killashandra consumed the hot cereal and nutmeat compound. Pendel was trying to get Chasurt to examine Antona's list, and Chasurt was demanding to know what he was to do if a real emergency were to occur, one in which sick people would need the rations that this—this—obviously healthy woman was devouring. The medic did not approve of Killashandra's haste. That Pendel had the right to order such rations seemed to infuriate Chasurt even more, and by the time Killashandra had finished the second dish, she felt obliged to interfere.

"Lieutenant Chasurt—"

"Captain! Guild Member," and, puce with the added insult, the man pointed to the rank emblem at his neck.

"All right, Captain," Killashandra accorded him an apologetic inclination of her head, "Pendel is acting on my behalf, obeying my instructions, which were firmly impressed on me by Chief Medical Research Officer Antona of the Heptite Guild Ballybran. It was understood by my Guild Master and myself that my requirements would be met on this voyage. If I am physically unfit to complete the installations, all your efforts will have been an expensive waste, and your system still incommunicado. I am given to understand that the journey to your system is not a long one, so I cannot think that my modest dietary needs will seriously deplete the resources of a newly commissioned 78. Will they?"

Chasurt's face had reflected several emotions as she spoke, and Killashandra, though not as adept as Lanzecki in reading body language, received the impression that Chasurt would have preferred the system to lose the interplanetary link. But that was an irrational premise, and she decided that Chasurt must be one of those officious people who must constantly be deferred to and flattered. She remembered Amon's advice and realized its merit with this sort of personality.

"Not wishing to remind you, Captain Chasurt, that in the Federated Sentient Planets' hierarchy, as a Guild Member traveling on Heptite Guild business, I outrank everyone on this ship, including Captain Francu, I will suggest that you check your data retrieval under Crystal Singers and be thus reassured in your dealings with me on this journey. Now, just pass me the fruit."

Chasurt had intercepted that basket, delivered during Killashandra's reply.

"Trace minerals are especially important for us," she said, smoothly reaching out to take the basket. She had to secure it with a bit of a jerk. Chasurt was livid. Killashandra nodded pleasantly at Tic and dismissed her before closing the panel on Chasurt's fury.

Pendel raised his Yarran beer in salute to Killashandra as he leaned against the wall.

"We'll have the captain next, you know."

"You seem to manage them rather well," Killashandra said between bites of the tangy redfruit.

"They can't get rid of me." Pendel chuckled, pressing the side of his nose and winking at her. "I'm employed by the Mining Consortium, not the Trundie Council. The MC is still keying the priorities. Oh, they're not bad sorts for parochial chaps with metal on the mind. They'll change. They'll change now for sure." Pendel swept his beaker from her to the sealed cabin where the crystal was secured.

"Do I have the suspicion that not all concerned wish to change?"

Pendel gave a laugh. "And when has that been news?"

A peculiar squawk was emitted by the communit, and Pendel winked at Killashandra.

"Captain here, super. What's this about special rations being issued without consultation?"

"Captain Francu"—Pendel's tone was a drawl, just short of insult—"I believe the orders read that Guild Member Ree's requirements are to be met by the—"

"They told me she didn't require anything special."

"Guild Member Ree doesn't require anything *special*, but as I've been telling you, the mess served on this ship isn't universally nourishing or satisfying. Chasurt has more than enough in stores. I should know. *I* buy for him."

There wasn't an audible click at the end of the exchange, but the captain's complaint had been dismissed. Killashandra regarded Pendel with more respect.

"Hard worker, that Francu. Runs a tight ship. Never lost a person. Just the sort of man to trust the newest ship to." Pendel rubbed the side of his nose, his broad grin implying all the negative facets of Captain Francu that he did not voice.

"I appreciate your cooperation and support, Pendel, almost as much as the beer. One more favor, if it's possible. Do I have to listen to all the ship's business?" Another harsh buzz punctuated her request.

"Just leave it with me, Killashandra," Pendel said comfortably. "I'll send round some handy rations for you in the meantime." He gestured apologetically at the plates and chips piled on the printouts on his desk, and she took the hint. She also took the second bowl of fruit, winking at Pendel as she left.

The man contrived well and shortly after Tic led her back to her dinky cabin, the unnerving sounds of command were muted.

Tic arrived, tapping politely and waiting for Killashandra's acknowledgment, with parcels of plain plastic in both hands. One was a variety of the special rations, the other an array of food. Tic kept her eyes averted from that luxury, but Killashandra perceived that any generosity from her would be ill advised. She thanked Tic and dismissed her until evening mess. Killashandra knew that she had to put in at least one appearance a day and sighed at the thought of such boredom. While she munched on Chasurt's prized packages, she occupied herself by studying the deck plan of the 78. Even as she watched, certain sections were updated and changed for purposes that escaped her. Was this to be a cargo ship, a passenger liner, or a training vessel? Its specifications meant nothing to her, but the length of the numericals was impressive.

She was duly escorted to the officers' mess, Chasurt and Francu mercifully absent, so she chatted with Tallaf, an agreeable enough young man without his captain's presence to inhibit him, though when he got flustered, his neck had the tendency to puff out. He admitted to being planetbred, educated for his duties as executive in theoretics rather than the practical. Most of the other officers and crew members were space or station born. His tone was a shade wistful, as if he regretted the difference between himself and his shipmates.

"I understand that your system has been isolated due to poor communications," Killashandra said conversationally.

Tallaf looked anxiously around him.

"I also understand that a step forward is not generally popular."

Tallaf regarded her with awe.

"Oh, come now, Tallaf," Killashandra said in a teasing voice, "that's been obvious to me since I boarded. I assure you, it's not an unusual phenomenon."

"Crystal singers get to go everywhere, don't they?" An ingenuous envy flickered across his face.

"Not necessarily. This is an unusual assignment for an unusual world and unusual circumstances." Tallaf preened a little at the implied compliment to his system. "Quite an achievement for an emergent political unit"—Killashandra was a little awed by her own eloquence—"to purchase a 78 and black crystals."

She watched Tallaf keenly as she spoke and decided that the young engineer was evidently *for* instant interstellar communications. She wondered briefly how the split of support went—spacers against planetaries or parochials against galactics. She sighed, wishing someone had given her more data on the Trundies. Perhaps there just wasn't much in the galactography.

Pendel arrived, smiling pleasantly to the small groups of officers standing around. It was then that Killashandra realized that she and Tallaf had formed a solitary pair. She smiled more graciously at Tallaf for his fortitude as a crewman appeared from the galley with two beakers of Yarran ale. Tallaf drifted away discreetly, and Killashandra toasted Pendel, whose jolly self evidently masked considerable prestige.

Pendel chuckled. "Good boy, that Tallaf."

"He's *for* crystal?"

"Oh, yes, indeed. That's why he's exec this trip. His first." Pendel's affable smile was truly in place as he glanced around the messroom. Killashandra was certain he knew exactly who should be there and who wasn't. "Not bad at all for a shakedown crew." Killashandra wondered what the deficiencies were. "A man looks for certain goals at certain times of his life," and his eyes caught hers over the rim of the Yarran beer glass. "Adventure brought me to this system two and a half decades ago. My timing was right. They urgently needed an experienced supercargo. They were being done out of their sockets on cargo rates." Pendel's tone was laden with remembered indignation. Then he smiled. "Can't do business properly without proper communication."

"Which is why crystal and this 78 are so important!" She tilted her glass toward him as if Pendel had single-handedly accomplished all. "You Yarrans are known for your perspicacity. Quite a few from your system have become crystal singers . . ." She was subtly aware of Pendel's reaction. "Oh, come now, Pendel," she continued smoothly, for if she couldn't have this man's support, she might well be left in Chasurt's hands, and that wouldn't suit. "Surely you don't believe the spaceflot about crystal singers?" She contrived a very amused gurgle of laughter.

"Of course not," and Pendel shrugged negligently, though his smile was not quite as assured.

"Especially now you've met and talked with me and discovered a crystal singer is as human as anyone on board this ship. Or"—and Killashandra glanced about the messroom and its subdued occupants—"perhaps a bit more so."

Pendel surveyed his fellow officers and grimaced.

"At least I can appreciate a proper brew," Killashandra continued, inwardly suppressing both apprehension and amusement. Pendel was nowhere near as cosmopolitan as he liked to appear, though in contrast to the other Trundies, he was tolerably informed about the galaxy. Somehow Killashandra must contrive to keep a friendly distance from him. "I do give them credit," and she glanced around her with an air of compliment.

"So evidently does the Heptite Guild." Pendel had recovered his basic optimism. "But none of us expected a crystal singer would install the things."

"The Federated Sentient Planets have their own schedule of priorities. Ours not to reason why." Killashandra couldn't remember where that line came from, but it seemed to apply.

Fortunately, the steaming platters and trays of their evening meal arrived, and Killashandra noted that only she and Pendel were served the one appetizing selection.

Without the repressive presence of Captain Francu and Chasurt, Killashandra managed to draw into conversation most of the older officers. Though the youngsters were far too shy to speak, she could sense that they were listening very closely and storing every word exchanged. The subs were still malleable, and if she could influence them favorably and maintain Pendel's good will by judicious flattery, she'd have done more than she'd been contracted to do. And the Trundies would need more crystal.

That night, as she stretched out on the appallingly hard bunk, she reviewed her extravagant performance of that evening. "Crystalline cuckoo" and "silicate spider," Maestro Valdi had called crystal singers. She thought she knew why now: the survival instincts of the symbiont. And judging from Pendel's subconscious reaction to her, she knew why the symbiont remained a trade secret. There were, she decided, more invidious threats than giving space and survival to a species that paid good value with the rent.

Chapter 12

Killashandra made good use of her next five days, having Tic or Tac lead her on exercise walks about the cruiser, dropping hints about the exacting nature of her work and how she had to keep fit. The silicate spider preparing its web for a Passover sleep. She had a few uncomplimentary thoughts about the Guild, mainly Lanzecki, for sending her among the uninformed without a hint that the Trundimoux were so parochial.

She did a great deal of listening to the subordinates when they relaxed enough to talk in her presence and to the general conversations, mostly good-natured slagging among work teams. She learned a great deal about the short and awesome history of the Trundimoux system and stopped referring to them as Trundies in the privacy of her thoughts.

As it had Pendel, the system had attracted many restless and adventurous people, a percentage of them either physically or temperamentally unsuited to the hazards. The survivors bred quickly and hugely, and natural selection again discarded the weaknesses and the weaker, some of whom could usefully work in the relative safety of the larger mining units. The second generation, who survived the rigors of knocking likely chunks of the suburanic metals out of orbit and jockeying their payloads into long drone strings, those hardy souls perpetuated their genes and became yet another variant of human. This system was, in its own way, as unique as Ballybran's, its entrance requirements as stringent and its workers as rigorously trained.

One night while juggling those elements in her mind—the dangers of space as opposed to the physical tests on Shankill—Killashandra waxed philosophical. The galaxy was not merely physical satellites circling flaming primaries but overlapping and intertwining metaphysical ones. She was currently the bridge between two such star systems and two totally opposite mental attitudes. She'd use the charm of one to survive in the other.

The Trundimoux had already developed some strong traditions, the evening's solemn dedication of the officers to their system's survival, the worship of water, a callousness toward death, a curious distrust of outsystem manufactured equipment. This, Killashandra thought, was why they were so assiduously altering the 78's interior. Then, after she'd seen some tri-di's of the mining stations and the space-built edifices themselves, she understood. In a spatial sense, the Trundimoux were adapting constantly to the needs of their hostile environment. In another, they were refusing to admit that any other system, hers included, had something worthwhile to offer them that couldn't be improved on.

Killashandra listened, too, to subtler opinions on the wisdom of instant interstellar communications. Some were skeptical that the crystals would work, due, it was claimed, to some peculiarity of the Trundimoux system that was designed to keep them isolated. Others thought it a shocking waste of time, effort, and precious metal-credit. The division of thought split age groups, first- and second-generation representatives, and even contracted extraplanetaries on local assignment.

Meanwhile, the cruiser was fast closing with its home system on its hyperbolic trajectory. Killashandra's appetite had leveled off, a relief to herself as well as to Pendel's dwindling supply of her requirements. Passover was occurring over Ballybran, and conjunction was as imminent as her first installation. She judiciously kept the stimulant tabs on her person.

The change in the crystal drive tone heralded her first unexpected nap. Tic's insistent tapping on her door panel roused her.

"Captain Francu's compliments, Killashandra Ree, and would you follow me to the bridge?"

Tic was suddenly very formal, not so much as a shy answering smile to Killashandra's acknowledgment. She followed the sub, much refreshed by her sleep, but she felt for the stimutabs in her sash pocket.

The bridge, a misnamed cavern midship, was busy and full. Tic found the captain among those circled about the dimension tank, caught his attention, presented Killashandra, and retreated.

"If you will observe the tank, Guild Member," the captain began at his most overbearing.

"I would if I could," Killashandra said, and smiling sweetly, inserted her hip between two male bodies and with a deft twist pushed the men sideways so that she occupied their previous vantage point. She left one officer between her and Francu, consoling the startled man with a soothing glance. "Ah, yes, fascinating." She *was* fascinated, though she wanted to give the distinct impression that this was scarcely the first time she had been on a bridge or gazed at a dimension tank. The cruiser was a very tiny blip, coasting inward, past the orbit of the outermost planet, toward the primary. Blinking lights indicated major mining stations in the asteroid belts; two tiny solid lights, the two moon bases. The bright planet, fourth from the primary, exuded a supercilious superiority despite being the last to be settled in the hard-working system.

"We are coasting now, Guild Member, if you haven't noticed the change of the drive—"

"A crystal singer is unusually sensitive to crystal drive, Captain—an occupational skill."

Francu set his jaw, unused to being interrupted for any reason.

"We are traveling on a hyperbolic course that will intersect the orbit of the two mining stations, which have deviated from their courses to meet us—"

"Sometimes progress can be awkward—"

Francu glared at her. "The moon bases provide no problem on their relative planes, though Terris will require a longer shuttle flight—"

"You will have a far more difficult maneuver in catching up with your planet, won't you?" and Killashandra pointed.

"Not at all," and it was Francu's turn to be scornful. "Merely a question of braking, using the planetary attraction, pick up the sun's gravitic pull marginally, deflect away and on to our next destination."

"How very clever of you." Killashandra winced inwardly, wondering why the man's simplest explanation evoked the worst side of her nature.

"You must realize, Guild Member, how tight the schedule is. I was informed that mounting the crystal takes no more than six minutes. We shall need every spare second available to get you to and away from these installation points—particularly at the planet. You do understand the spatial considerations?"

"It has always seemed essentially simple when expertly and efficiently handled, Captain Francu. I'm sure there'll be no problem." Six minutes. That gave her quite a safety margin, or had Trag in mind the lethargy that would soon overcome her? She gazed at the dimensional tank, smiling diffidently. Problem was, if she took less than six minutes installing at one point, it still wouldn't affect her arrival at the next one. "Thank you, Captain. May I have updated printout as we near each installation point?"

"Certainly. You will be given eighteen minutes' warning before each shuttle run."

"As much as that?" Again, Killashandra was reacting to Francu's grating manner.

"Ah, yes, I have to take the crystal from the super's locked room."

"Really, Captain, no one will steal it in Trundimoux space and, until all the elements are installed, they are quite harmless. The container can be webbed in at the shuttle lock for easier access now and give you that much more time to spare."

Captain Francu's anxiety about crystal itself warred with his time factors. He accorded her a stiff bow and turned resolutely back to contemplation of his dimensional tank.

"Close to first objective and give me a deviation check."

"How long before the first objective, Captain?"

"Five hours, six minutes, and thirty-six seconds, Guild Member."

Killashandra moved away from the tank, her place quickly taken by those she had ousted. She nodded to Tic, and the subbie, with an air of intense relief, hurried to guide her away from the bridge.

She would have liked to stay and watch the cruiser angle toward the first mining station, a delicate and tedious affair since four dimensions—

five, really, if one considered the captain's obsession with the time factor—
were involved.

Six minutes in which to cement or change the attitudes of an entire
system, six minutes five times gave her exactly one-half hour prime time.
Killashandra smiled to herself. The Trundimoux system had traditions already. She'd add to them an extrastellar treat. She'd alter Francu's plan
merely to slip in and slip out to a significant occasion that should be one of
the greatest rejoicing for the Trundimoux—they could talk with each other:
surely a moment for ceremony rather than secrecy. Six minutes wasn't
much time. She would see to it that it was enough, and a whole new mass
of rumor about crystal singers would circulate.

Trundimoux clothing was wildly colored, and bits of metal were woven into the fabric to refract whatever light was available. Even the life-
support units blazed with color, shocking oranges and vibrant pinks.
Offensive as such hues were to Killashandra, they served a purpose for the
Trundimoux space-bred population.

While the cruiser jockeyed toward its first destination, the mining station named Copper, she created her costume. Black for the crystal she
would carry: black and flowing to stand out against the gaudy Trundimoux in their tight-fitting garb. She wished for some of the cosmetics she
had abandoned in her student cubicle at Fuerte, but she was tall enough to
stand out, in black, her hair loose to her shoulder blades, unusual enough
in a society of space-goers with shaved or clipped hair.

Six minutes! That time bothered her even though she had mounted
the mock crystals in far less. Then she remembered. *Crystal* was what she
would be handling. She could get lost in touching crystal. She might, at
that, be grateful to Francu and his neat slots of time. She could count on
him to break a crystal trance. But she mustn't fall into one. *That* would
spoil the image she wished to create.

She worried about that problem until Tallaf arrived to escort her.

"Cutter's ready and waiting, ma'am," he said, alertly poised and very
formal.

"And the crystal?"

Tallaf cleared his throat; his eyes avoided hers, although she rather
thought that the young man was amused.

"Supercargo Pendel has conveyed the container to the lock, awaiting
your arrival. All webbed and secure."

Indeed the carton was, with a double row of alert guards standing as
far from the crystal as they could in the confines of the lock. The sides and
bottom of the carton were webbed securely to the deck, but the top had
been unsealed. One of the guards carried a seal-gun on his belt.

Killashandra strode forward, remembering to keep her full skirts
clear of her toes.

"Open it," she said to no one in particular. There was a brief hesitation, then Pendel performed that office, winking at her surreptitiously.

To her intense relief, the five crystals had been cocooned before shipment. She did not need to handle raw crystal until she reached the actual installation point. She picked up the small package, feeling the mild shock with a double sense of relief. Crystal knew she was there and responded but bided its time. And this was real crystal. She'd had a sudden horrid thought that, in a crazy set of errors, the mock shafts had been sent instead.

She held the package straight-armed before her as she walked to the cutter's entrance. No sooner was she seated than everyone seemed to move at double speed, webbing her in, taking their own places as the hatch was sealed. She was forced back into her cushions by the acceleration away from the cruiser.

"Are we running behind time, Tallaf?" she asked.

"No, ma'am, precisely *on* time."

"How far from the station lock to the communications room?"

"Exactly five minutes and twenty seconds."

"In free-fall?" Free-fall in this gown would be ridiculous. She wished she'd thought of that aspect before.

Tallaf looked surprised.

"All but the very small detector units have gravity, ma'am."

The cutter fired retrorockets, again pushing her into the cushions.

"I thought we were on time."

"We are, ma'am, but we're correcting to match velocities."

A second spate of jockeying occurred, but the actual docking was no more than a cousinly kiss. The deck crew was again working double time, and infected by their pace, she rose and entered the first of the mining stations. The five minutes and twenty seconds of travel time within Copper was spent twisting down corridors and jumping over security frames. She prided herself on managing all the awkward bits without stumbling or losing her balance, the cocoon of crystal held before her so that all could see. And many people were gathered at intersections wanting a glimpse of the momentous occasion.

It is a shame, Killashandra thought as she was ushered into the communications nerve center of the Copper Station, that this was not the linkage point. Nothing really exciting would happen here or on the other stations until the final shaft was fitted and their bonding would produce the instantaneous link.

Still, she was conscious of stares, hostile and thoughtful, as she was directed to the installation point. It was on the raised outer level of the huge room, an excellent vantage.

Killashandra mounted the shallow steps, her quick glance checking the brackets to be sure they were correct, and then turned to the center of the area. She stripped the plastic from the cocoon and held up the dull, muddy shaft. She heard the gasps as the assembled saw for the first time what they had mortgaged their system to buy. Even as she heard their mumble, the crystal warmed in her hands, turning the matte black which gave it its name. It vibrated against her hands, and before she could fall in trance, she whirled and laid the crystal in its place. The pressure arms moved silkily at her light touch. She brought the upper brackets to bear and, one finger on the still darkening crystal, increased the pressure on each side carefully. The crystal began to resonate along her finger, making her throat ache. She fought the desire to caress the crystal and made her hands complete the installation. As if burned, she snatched her hands back from the beautiful crystal mass. She took the small hammer and tapped the mounted crystal. Its pure note sang through the room's sudden hush.

Head high, she strode from the chamber, Tallaf running to get ahead of her, to lead her back to the cutter through the station's twists and turns.

Each step took her farther from the crystal, and she twisted with the pain of that separation. Another small matter no one had explained to her before: that it would be so difficult to leave crystal she had herself cut.

The brief ride to the cruiser did ease that pain. And so did the lethargy that slowly overcame her. It couldn't, she decided, be fatigue from that little bit of dramatization. It must be the sleepies that she'd been warned about. Conjunction was very near. Fortunately, she managed to stay awake until she reached her quarters.

"Tic, if I am disturbed for any reason whatsoever before the next station, I'll dismember the person! Understood? And pass that on to Pendel just to make sure."

"Yes, ma'am." Tic was trustworthy, and Pendel had authority.

Killashandra slid sideways onto the hard bunk, pulled the thin cover over her, and slept.

It seemed no time at all before a thumping and Tac's anxious voice called her politely but insistently.

"I'm coming. The next station has been reached?" She swallowed the stimulant, forced her eyes wide in an attempt to appear alert as she opened the door.

Tallaf was there with a tray of food, which she imperiously waved away.

"You'll need some refreshment, Killashandra," the young officer said, concern overcoming his previous formality.

"Are we at the next station?"

"I thought you'd need something to eat first."

She reached for the Yarran beer, trying not to exhibit the revulsion she felt at the smell of what once would have been a tempting meal. Even the beer tasted wrong.

"I'll just take this in my room," she said, closing the door panel and wondering if the nausea was due to the pill, the beer, her symbiont, or nerves. She made illicit use of drinking water and splattered her face. The effect was salutary. Without a qualm, she poured the Yarran beer down the waste disposal. Pendel would never know.

Tallaf rapped at her door panel again. This time, Killashandra was alert; the stimulant had taken effect. She swept forward, secure in the false energy and aware that more of the cruiser's crew were in evidence as she made her way to the lock.

Pendel was unlashing the top of the crystal carton, stepping back to give her space to extract the next crystal. Holding it at arm's length in front of her, Killashandra was congratulating herself on her smooth routine when she tripped getting over the cutter's hatch. She'd best raise the skirt a trifle in front before the first moon installation. However, no one had noticed her slight gracelessness, and she settled down for the ride.

Station Iron was larger than Station Copper but as haphazardly contrived as far as companionways, hatches, and corridors were concerned.

"This is more than five minutes twenty seconds, Tallaf," she said in a stern voice of complaint, wondering how long the stimutab lasted.

"Just in here, now."

Communications obviously rated more unfragmented space than any other of the stations' functions. And the larger station was reflected in the larger crowd that crammed into the area. Killashandra stripped the cocoon from the black crystal, held it up for all to see, and deposited it deftly in its position before it could woo her from her duties. Or maybe the stimulant helped counteract crystal's effect. Nonetheless, Killashandra still experienced the pain of leaving behind her forever the shaft of darkening crystal.

The stimulant kept her functioning on the slightly longer swing to catch up with the cruiser. She graciously accepted Pendel's offer of Yarran beer but, once alone, poured it down the drain. She squandered a day's water ration to quench her thirst and reached her bunk before sleep again overtook her.

It was harder for her to wake up when Tic roused her at the first moon. One stimulant kept her awake on the outbound trip, a second got her through the installation, but Tallaf had to wake her to disembark at the cruiser. Pendel insisted she eat something, though she could barely keep her eyes open. She did have soup and some succulent fruit since her mouth was dry and her skin felt parched. She ached for the crystal she had consigned forever to an airless moon.

Three stimulants roused her sufficiently for the fourth installation, and she had to sneak one into her mouth as she set the crystal in its brackets. She was doing her high priestess routine by reflex, only peripherally aware of the blur of faces that followed her every movement and the thrilled sigh as the crystal's pure note sounded in the communications room.

One thing she could say for the Trundimoux, when they found an efficient structure, they kept repeating it. All the communications rooms were of the same design. Blind, she could have found her way to the crystal mounting. Walking back, she kept tripping on the skirt hem she'd not had time to alter. Then Tallaf put one arm under hers. She concentrated on smiling serenely at the assembled until she had reached the cutter. She collapsed with relief into her seat.

"You're all right, Killashandra?" Tallaf was asking.

"Just tired. You've no idea how difficult it is to surrender crystal you've cut yourself. They cry when you leave them. Let me sleep."

But for that chance remark to Tallaf, Killashandra might have been forced to endure the ministrations of Chasurt, for her alternate periods of intense vivacity and somnolence had not gone unremarked. Nor were the opponents of the crystal communications purchase impressed by small unscintillating blocks received in exchange for massive drone loads of high-quality metals.

The moment he had seen Killashandra safely to her cabin, Tallaf had a word with Pendel. Pendel spoke quickly to others, and Chasurt was summoned to deal with a minor epidemic of food poisoning, investigate two other illnesses that required lengthy tests, and then was required to consult, at ordinary space-message exchange pauses, on a serious space-burn casualty.

Killashandra was roused for the longer shuttle flight to the planet's surface for the final installation. The extended sleep had been beneficial, and although she ran nervous fingers over the short length of stimulant tabs remaining, Killashandra thought she could defer their use. She accepted the fruit and glucose drink Pendel offered her, though she would dearly have loved water, even the stale recycled water the cruiser supplied.

She felt equal to this final scene until she saw the crystal container. Abruptly, she realized that this largest piece would be the hardest to surrender. She didn't dare have it on her lap all during the journey to the planet's surface.

"Bring the container on board. The king crystal will be safer that way," she said, curtly gesturing. She entered the shuttle before anyone could countermand her instruction.

Pendel and Tallaf hastily motioned the guard to comply, and the container was already aboard the shuttle, webbed tight, before Captain Francu arrived. He stopped abruptly, stared with rage and shock at the carton, then at Killashandra who smiled pleasantly at him.

"You carried the other crystals, Guild Member—"

"Ah, but this is a longer journey, captain, and unless that crystal is *safely* installed in your main communications room, all the others are useless and this voyage of your cruiser an exercise in futility."

"Captain, the time factors—" Tallaf stepped forward, his expression one of cautious concern.

Francu set his jaw, edged past the crystal to the stern of the cutter. She could hear the crack of metal tabs as he webbed himself in. She supposed that she was lucky that, in his current frame of mind, Francu wasn't the pilot.

The shuttle disengaged itself from the cruiser, seemed to hang suspended as the cruiser moved obliquely away from it. Actually, before the view ports were closed, Killashandra realized that the shuttle had done all the moving: the cruiser was inexorably set in its direction, and nothing would deter it.

She had meant to stay awake, but the scream and heat of entry into the planet's atmosphere roused her from another irresistible snooze. She stared about, momentarily startled by the unfamiliar surroundings. Hastily, she swallowed two stimutabs, smiling serenely around as if she had only been conserving her energy.

The shuttle had been brought to a complete halt before the medicine took effect, and she debated taking a third as the hatch was being opened.

A landing platform appeared at once, and from her seat, she could see the vast crowd assembled on both sides of a wide aisle leading to the huge communications building with its roof clusters of dish antennas, tilted like caps to the sky, caps raised to salute their own obsolescence.

"The crystal, Guild Member!" Francu's acid voice reminded her, too, of this final surrender.

She flipped open the carton and removed the king crystal, took a deep breath, and walked down the landing ramp, holding the crystal before her. She always played best to a full house, she reminded herself. The other installations were only rehearsals for this one.

The fresh air of the planet was naturally scented and crisp. She breathed in deeply and would not be hurried in this ceremonial walk.

Francu appeared at one side, Tallaf at her other, both muttering about walking faster.

"It's so good to breathe uncontaminated air. My lungs have been stifled. I must breathe."

"You must walk faster," Francu said, a smile jiggling his cheeks as he responded nervously to the presence of a large crowd of people in an open space greater than his huge new cruiser.

"If you can, Killashandra. We've a time boggle," said Tallaf, his voice anxious.

"They're all here to see the crystal," Killashandra noted, but she lengthened her stride, holding the cocoon above her head, hearing the surprised wave of exclamations, seeing the nearest drawing back. Was the crowd here to see crystal succeed, she wondered, or fail? This was not a receptive audience! She'd faced enough to sense the animosity and fear.

She strode on to the building's entrance, slightly outdistancing the two spacemen.

"We will have to hurry this, Guild Member," a man said, taking her arm as she passed the doorway.

"Yes, we will, or we can't be responsible for your safety."

She heard heavy metal doors thud shut behind her and a muffled noise emanating from outside and becoming louder.

"I've been given to understand that this project is not universally favored, gentlemen. But one message sent and received will disperse that . . ." and she indicated the crowd which had pressed in about the building.

"This way, Guild Member."

They were all almost running now, and she was annoyed that the urgency of the situation was going to ruin her performance. Ridiculous! How absurd to be put in such a position! Especially when she was possessed of an overwhelming desire to go to sleep again. She shoved the crystal into the crook of one arm—there was no one to impress with her theatrics in this hurry—and managed to stuff two more tabs into her mouth.

Then she was whirled into the main chamber of the immense building, where nervous technicians were more interested in the outward-facing security scanners than the printouts and displays common to their business.

"Do hurry with this one, Killashandra," Tallaf urged as she took the last few steps to the raised level and the empty niche where the king crystal would be mounted.

She stripped the plastic away with nervous fingers and suddenly found serenity and surcease as the bared crystal caressed her skin.

"Hurry!" Francu exhorted her. "If that thing won't give us a message from Copper—"

Killashandra withered him with a glance, but her dislike of him broke the tenuous enchantment she had been hoping to enjoy. Now she heard the noise of the crowd, the increasing pitch of its excitement and frustration. She dare not delay the mounting. Nor did she want to relinquish her black crystal to this system of ignorant savages, this society of metal-mongerers, this—

The black crystal was mounted, turning matte black as it responded to the heat of the room.

"Hurry!" "Has something gone wrong?" "It won't work!"

"Of course, crystal will sing," said Killashandra, raising the little hammer and striking the king block.

The rich full A of the king crystal rang through the large room, silencing the irreverent babble. Killashandra was transfixed. The A became the louder note of the five-crystal chord, the two F and two E crystals singing back to her through the king. The human voice cannot produce chords. With the pitch of the A dominant in her head, that was the note that burst from Killashandra as the shock of establishing the link between the five crystals enveloped her. Sound like a shock wave, herself the sound and the sounding board, vision over vision, a fire in her bones, thunder in her veins, a heart-contracting experience of pain and pleasure so intense and so total that every nerve in her body and every convolution of her brain echoed. The chord held Killashandra in a thrall more absolute than her first experience of crystal. Sustaining the note despite the agony of the physical mechanics of breath, Killashandra was simultaneously in the communications rooms of the two mining stations and the two moons. She splintered in sound from one crystal block to the next, apart and indissoluble, a fragment of the first message sent and instantly received and forever divorced from it.

"Copper to home. Copper to home base!" She knew the message, for it passed through her as well as the crystal. She heard the exultant reply and the incredulous response to its simultaneity. She had cut the crystals for this purpose, she had borne them to their various sites, and she had condemned them to sing for others. No one had told her they would cause her to sing through them in a space-crossing chord!

"Killashandra?" Someone touched her, and she cried out. Flesh upon flesh broke her awesome communion with the crystal link. She fell to her knees, too bereft to cry, too stunned to resist.

"Killashandra!" Someone raised her to her feet.

She could feel crystal power singing behind her through the king block, but she was forever excluded from its thrall.

"Get her back to the shuttle."

"Is it *safe*?"

"Of course, it's safe. The link works! The whole system knows that now!"

"Through this door, lieutenant. You'll have to detour. The crowd is blocking your way to the shuttle."

"We don't have time to detour."

"We'll break through the crowd. Carry her first. That'll make them give way!"

"They can't be afraid of a woman!"

"She's not a woman. She's a crystal singer!"

Killashandra was aware of being carried through a dense crowd. She heard a rapid clattering, and loud but jubilant cries and, somewhere in the section of her brain that recorded impressions, she correlated sound and cheers with applause. So many people in such proximity was an unexpected torture.

"Get me out of here," she whispered hoarsely, clutching the man who carried her with desperate hands.

He said nothing but quickened his pace, his breathing ragged with effort. He could barely disentangle himself from her when a second man came to his assistance.

"This delay may abort the whole intercept."

"Captain, we'd no idea how feelings ran here. No warning that there'd be such a crowd. We're almost there now."

"If we've lost the window—"

"We'll have a frigate standing by ready to catch up—"

"Do shut up and let me sleep. Stop joggling me so."

"Sleep?" The indignation in Francu's voice roused her briefly from her torpor. "Sleep she wants when—"

"Just settle yourself in this seat, Killashandra. I'll do the webbing."

"Drink. Need a drink. Anything. Water."

"Not now. Not now."

"Yes, now! I thirst."

"Captain, you fly. Here's water, Killashandra."

She drank deeply, aware that the substance was water, real water, crisp, clear, cool water, used only this once, for her consumption. Some of it spilled when she was jolted about, and she protested the loss, licking it from her hands. She was shoved away from the water by a tremendous force and pleaded to be given more to drink.

She was soothed, and then finally the weight was lifted, and she was given as much as she wanted to drink.

"Are you all right now, Killashandra?" She rather thought it was Tallaf asking.

"Yes. Now all I need is sleep. Just let me sleep until I wake."

Chapter 13

Waking up was a gradual and remarkably languorous process. Killashandra felt that she was unfolding in sections, starting with her mind, which sent out sleepy messages to her extremities that movement was possible again. She went through a long series of stretchings and yawnings, interspersed with rather wild and vivid flashes. At first, she thought them pico-dreams but then realized that all were from one viewpoint: hers! And she was overwhelmed by faces and applause and light flashing from the blackening crystal. An orgasmic sensation in her loins completed her unfolding and brought her to sharp consciousness and regret. Those half dreams had been lovely echoes of the linkage with black crystal.

Crystal! She sat up in bed and nearly caught her head on the bedside shelf. She was on the wretched cruiser! She glanced at her wrist unit, confirming it with the cabin time display.

"Three days! I've been asleep three days!" Antona had warned her.

Killashandra lay back, easing shoulder and tightening back muscles. She must have slept all three days in one position to have such cramps.

A soft scratching at her door panel caught her attention.

"Yes?"

"Are you awake, Guild Member?"

There were several answers she would have given if she hadn't recognized Chasurt's voice.

"You may enter."

"Are you awake?"

"I certainly wouldn't be answering you in my sleep. Come in!" As the door panel slid open, she added, "And would you ask Pendel if he can supply me with something decent to eat?"

"I will ascertain if food is advisable," the man said, holding in her direction a diagnostic tool similar to Antona's.

"Not the stodge that's served in the cruiser's mess but liquid and fruit—"

"If you'll just be cooperative—"

"I am!" Killashandra felt that attitude rapidly changing. "This sort of sleep phase is perfectly normal—"

"We haven't been able to contact Ballybran for specific instructions—"

"For what?"

"Proper treatment of your prolonged coma—"

"I wasn't *in* a coma. Did you not check the printout in your own medical library? I want something to drink. And eat."

"I am the cruiser's meditech—"

"Who has never met a crystal singer before and knows nothing of *my* occupational hazards." Killashandra had pulled on the nearest piece of clothing, her Guild coverall. Now she swung herself off the bunk and lurched past Chasurt, who made a vain attempt to grab her. "Pendel!" Killashandra started down the corridor. She surprised herself that she could maneuver so readily after the exhaustion that had overtaken her. The symbiont might take, but it also gave.

"Guild Member!" Chasurt was in pursuit, but she had the head start and longer legs.

She turned again, into the super's corridor, and saw Tic at Pendel's door, and then his head was visible.

"Pendel? I'm perishing for a glass of Yarran beer! Please say you have some fruit left? And possibly a cup of that excellent soup you served me some time a hundred years ago?"

By the time she reached his door, Pendel handed her a half-empty glass of Yarran beer for one hand and a fruit for the other. She squeezed past him and Tic, leaving them to block Chasurt.

"There you are, Killashandra," Pendel said, standing across the doorway so that Chasurt could not barge in. Tic moved staunchly in front of Killashandra as the second line of defense. "More fruit within hand. Now, Chasurt, don't get yourself knotted. Come with me, and you can add whatever nutrients and restoratives you feel are required to the soup I'm getting Killashandra. Put those stupid sprays back into your pockets. Crystal singers don't ordinarily require any medication. Don't you know anything beyond space-freeze and laser burn?"

Pendel hurried Chasurt away, signaling Tic to close the door and stand guard. Killashandra had finished the beer and started on the fruit. She closed her eyes with relief as juice and pulp soothed her parched mouth. She ate slowly, an instinct imposed on her by the symbiont, which knew very well what it required after fasting. With distaste, she remembered the mad hungers of pre-Passover and was grateful that the affliction had waned.

"Ma'am? . . ."

Killashandra only heard the soft whisper because there was no other sound in the cabin but her chewing.

"Tic?" It was the first time the girl had addressed her.

"Ma'am—thank you for the crystal!" Tic blurted her words. "Comofficer let me speak with my mother on Copper. Right away. No waiting. No worrying that something's gone wrong and I wouldn't hear . . . Comoff says with crystals I can call Copper any time I want!" Tic's eyes were round and liquid.

"I'm happy for you, Tic. I'm happy for you." Killashandra thought that response a little graceless on her part, but Tic's awed response embarrassed her.

The panel was suddenly whipped aside, and Tic tried not to fall into Killashandra's lap as Captain Francu, radiating fury, stood in the opening.

"My medic tells me that you have refused his assistance." The cubicle was too small for his oppressive manner.

"I do not need his assistance. I am a crystal singer—"

"While you are on board my vessel, you are under my orders—"

Killashandra rose, pushing Tic into the seat she had vacated, facing the captain with a wrath far more profound than his. From her thigh pouch, she produced the Guild ident and shoved it at the captain.

"Even you must recognize this authority!"

Pendel arrived at that moment, carrying a laden tray.

"Federated Sentient Planet Sessions authority!" Pendel gasped as he read, and the tray wavered in his grasp. "I've only seen one other."

"You are clearly suffering from aberrant behavior following a period of deprivation—" the captain began.

"Nonsense. Hand me that tray, Pendel. Thank you."

"Guild Member, attend me!"

"I am, but I'm also eating, as my body needs sustenance after my long rest."

"You were in coma—"

"I was doing what all crystal singers do, resting after a difficult and exhausting assignment. And that is all I wish to say until I've eaten."

"You are mentally affected, shoving an FSP authority at me to obtain food." Captain Francu was sputtering now.

"That authority will be invoked as soon as I find out the nearest transfer station—"

"You are to remain on this cruiser until the Five Systems' Satellite—"

"I will remain on this cruiser only as long as it takes me to call up a shuttle or cutter or gig from the next system. And my authority permits me to do so. Right?"

"Right," Pendel affirmed.

The captain glared at him and stared for a moment longer at Killashandra, speechless with suppressed anger. Then he turned on one heel and stamped down the corridor.

Tic was regarding Killashandra in white-faced perturbation.

"That's all right, now, girl," Pendel said to her soothingly. "You will, of course, discuss this with no one no matter how you are pressed. I don't think Captain Francu will care to remember the incident."

"How soon can I get off this ship? No offense to you and Tic, of course."

Pendel edged himself in front of his keyboard and tapped a code. It took longer than usual for the display to start rippling across the screen, and there were only four lines.

"I wouldn't suggest that one. Drone tanker and primitive food supplies." Pendel tapped again. The printout was denser. "Ah. We can arrange a transfer to a small but adequate changeover station for a Selkite direct to Scoria. Ordinarily, I wouldn't recommend Selkites for any reason, but you'd be the only passenger in their oxygen life-support section."

"Grand! I'll take it."

"Means another three days aboard us."

"I'll sleep a good deal of the time. Light meals when I need 'em."

"There's just one thing," and Pendel cleared his throat, ducking his head from her glance. "The Selkite reaches Ballybran just toward the end of the Passover storms. The original E.T.A. would land you well after they'd completed."

"Oh, you've been doing some retrieving, have you?' Killashandra grinned.

Pendel winked, laying his finger along his nose. "I did feel some objective information a wise precaution."

"So Chasurt decided the storms produced my mental aberrations?"

"Some such conclusion."

"No fool goes out in Passover storms. We leave the planet if at all possible. If not, sleep through it!"

"I had heard the rumor that crystal singers hibernated."

"Something of the sort."

"Well, well. Have another Yarran beer, Killashandra?"

Whatever caused Pendel such satisfaction, he preferred to keep to himself, but they enjoyed several glasses until drowsiness overcame her again. Pendel escorted her back to her cabin where Tac stood very much on duty. Small light meals were arranged, and Killashandra lay down to sleep, fervently blessing the forethought that had provided her with the FSP authority. And what had Francu intended to do with her if he had managed to overrule her? Give her to Chasurt to find out why crystal singers are different?

She wasn't well pleased to have to spend a few more days on the cruiser, but she could sleep and relax, now that the pressures of installation were behind her. And she had completed those well. Trag would be pleased with her. Even if some percentage of the Trundimoux were not. Pity about that!

Still, they'd given her a big hand. She'd knocked herself out to give them a new tradition. Her performance at the planet installation had turned an angry mob into a jubilant throng. Yes, she'd done well as a crystal singer.

Would she ever again be able to experience that incredible surge of contact as black crystal segments linked? That all-enveloping surge as if she were aligned with every black crystal in the galaxy?

She shuddered with the aching desire. She turned from that thought. There would be other such times; of that she was now certain. Meanwhile, once the storms of Ballybran were over, she could sing crystal.

Sing crystal? Sing?

Killashandra began to laugh, recalling herself as she strode into the planetary communications building, stage center with a near riot occurring around her. She, playing the high priestess, completing the ritual that linked the isolated elements of the Trundimoux! A solo performance if ever there was one. And she had played before an audience of an entire system. What an opening note she had struck with crystal! What an ovation! Echoes from distant satellites. She had done exactly as she had once boasted she'd do, had arrogantly proclaimed to her peers in Fuerte that she would do. She had been the first singer in this system and possibly the only crystal singer ever to appear in Trundimoux.

Killashandra laughed at the twisted irony of circumstance. She laughed and then cried because there was no one to know except herself that she had achieved an ambition.

Killashandra Ree was a singer, right enough. Truly a crystal singer!

Reprise

"What are you doing back now?" the lock attendant demanded as she entered. "Wough? What sort of transport were you on? You reek."

"Selkite," Killashandra said grimly. She had become used to her own fragrance within the Selkite's O-breather quarters.

"There's some ships no one will travel on. Pity you weren't warned." He was pinching his nostrils closed.

"I'll remember, I assure you."

She started for the Guild's transient quarters.

"Hey, there's no vacancies. Passover storms aren't over yet, you know."

"I know, but getting here was more important than waiting the storms out."

"Not if you had to travel Selkite. But there's plenty of space in the regular quarters," and the man thumbed the archway that she had entered so naively a few months before. "No travelers here yet. Doesn't make any difference with your credit where you stay, you know."

Killashandra thanked him and walked on through the blue-irised entrance toward the hostel, trying to remember the girl she'd been at that point and unable to credit how much had occurred since then. Including the simultaneous realization of two ambitions.

The aroma she exuded alerted Ford, still at his reception counter.

"But you're a singer. You oughtn't to be here." His nose wrinkled, and he shuddered, licking his lips. "Singers have their own quarters."

"Full up. Just give me a room and let me fumigate myself."

Killashandra advanced to the counter to put her wrist unit to the plate.

"No, no, that won't be necessary!" Ford handed her the key, his arm stretching out to keep as much distance from her as possible.

"I know I'm bad, but am I that bad?"

Ford tried to stammer an apology, but Killashandra let the key guide her to her quarters.

"I've given you the biggest we have." Ford's voice followed her through the hallway.

The room was down a level, and assuming that the lock attendant had been correct—that there were no visitors at that time—Killashandra began ripping off her stinking clothes. The key warmed at the appropriate room, and she shoved through the panel, shutting it and leaning against the door to shuck off her pants and footwear. She looked at the carisak and decided there was no point in fumigating those things. She stuffed everything into the disposal unit with a tremendous sense of relief.

The Shankill accommodation had only shower facilities but a decent array of herb and fragrance washes. She stood under the jets, as hot as the spray would come, then laved herself until her skin was raw. She stepped out of the shower enclosure, smelling her hands and her shoulders, bending to sniff her knees, and decided that she was possibly close to decontaminated.

It was only drying her hair that she realized she didn't have any fresh clothes to put on. She dialed the commissary and ordered the first coverall that appeared on the fax, then keyed for perfumes and ordered a large bottle of something spicy. She needed some spice in her life after the Selkite vessel. Well, Pendel had tried to warn her. Come to consider, even the Selkites were better than remaining in the vicinity of Francu or that bonehead Chasurt.

Then she remembered to take out her lenses and sighed with relief as color, decent soothing color, sprang up around the room.

She ordered a Yarran beer and wondered how Lanzecki had weathered Passover. Immured by herself in the Selkite ship, she had come to terms with lingering feelings of resentment for the Guild Master and wanted very much to continue in friendship with the man. Solitude was a great leveler: stinking solitude made one grateful for remembered favors and kindness. She owed Lanzecki more of those than accusations.

The beer was so good! She lifted her beaker in a toast to Pendel. She hoped that for every Francu she met, there would be at least one Pendel to be grateful for.

The door chime sounded. She wrapped a dry towel around her, wondering why her order was being delivered instead of sent by tube. She released the door lock and was about to slide the panel back when it was moved from without.

"What are you doing back here?" Lanzecki stepped into the room, looming angrily above her in the narrow confines. He closed the panel behind him and lobbed a parcel in the direction of the bed.

"What are you doing on Shankill?" She tried to tighten the towel above her breasts.

He brought both hands to his belt and stared at her, his eyes glittering, his face set in the most uncompromising lines, his mouth still.

"Shankill affords the most strategic point from which to assess the storm flows."

"Then you do escape from the storms," she said with intense relief.

"As I wanted you to escape them, but you're back here days early!" He swept an angry gesture with one arm as if he wanted to strike her.

232 ANNE McCaffrey

"Why not?" Killashandra had to stand her ground before him. "I'd finished the wretched installations. Were the storms as bad as predicted? I've heard nothing."

"You were scheduled to return on a comfortable passenger frigate seven days from now." He scrutinized her closely. "The damage could have been worse," he added grudgingly. She wasn't sure whether he referred to her or the storms.

"I took the Selkite freighter."

"I'm aware of that." His nostrils flared with distaste.

"I've tried to decontaminate. It was awful. Why wasn't I told about Selkites? No, I was, but I wouldn't listen because I couldn't stay one more moment on that fardling Trundie cruiser." The towel was coming loose as she remembered Francu. "Why didn't you at least warn me about the Trundies?"

Lanzecki shrugged. "We didn't have much on them, but you at least had no preconceptions or the residue of partial memories of other isolated systems to prejudice your actions."

"They may never deal with another crystal singer."

"They'll deal with the Guild." Lanzecki was smiling, his body relaxing, his eyes warming.

"More important, Lanzecki"—and she tried to step back, away from him until she'd aired her grievances—"why didn't you tell me about link-shock? I sang the king crystal, link and all, and they brought me to my knees."

"Link-shock's about the only thing that would." He put his warm hands on her shoulders and held her firmly, his eyes examining her face. "No one can describe link-shock. It's experienced on different levels by different personalities. To warn is to inhibit."

"I can certainly appreciate that!"

He chuckled at her sarcastic comment and began to draw her to him, his embrace as much of an apology as he was ever likely to give her.

"Some people feel nothing at all."

"I'm sorry for them." She was not sarcastic now.

"For you, Killashandra, to link a set of crystals you yourself cut binds you closer to black crystal." He spoke slowly, again with the hidden pain that she had once before heard in his voice. She let herself be drawn against his strong body, realizing how keenly she had missed him even as she had damned him, grateful now to give and receive comfort. "The Guild needs black-crystal singers."

"Is that why you've personally guided my career, Lanzecki?" She reached her hand to his lips, feeling them curve in amusement.

"My professional life is dedicated to the Guild, Killashandra. Never forget that. My personal life is another matter, entirely private." His lips moved sensuously across her fingers as he spoke.

"I like you, Lanzecki—damn your mouth." She bubbled with laughter and the joy of being with him again.

He took her hand and kissed the palm, the contact sending chills through her body.

"In the decades ahead of us, Killashandra, *try* to keep that in mind?"

Killashandra

This book is gratefully dedicated to
Ron and Chris Massey
of the Tidmarsh Stud, and their Arabian friends,
Ben, BC, Racqui, Linda and Winnie

Chapter 1

Winters on Ballybran were generally mild, so the fury of the first spring storms as they howled across the land was ever unexpected. This first one of the new season swept ferociously across the Milekey Ranges, bearing before its westward course the fleeing sleds of crystal singers like so much jetsam. Those laggard singers who had tarried too long at their claims were barely able to hold their bucking sleds on course as they bolted for the safety of the Heptite Guild Complex.

Inside the gigantic Hangar, its baffles raised against the mach winds, ordered confusion reigned. Crystal singers lurched from their sleds, half deafened by windscream, exhausted by their turbulent flights. The Hangar crew, apparently possessed of eyes in the backs of their heads, miraculously avoided injury as they concentrated on the primary task of moving incoming sleds off the Hangar floor and into storage racks, clearing the way for the erratic landings of the stream of incoming vehicles. The crash claxon pierced even storm howl as two sleds collided, one to dip over the baffle and land nose down on the plascrete while the other veered out of control like a flat rock skipping across water, coming to a crumpling halt against the far wall. A tractor zipped in to fasten grapples on the upside-down sled, removing it only seconds before another sled skimmed over the baffle.

That sled almost repeated the nose dive, pulling up at the last second and skidding across the Hangar floor to stop just inches away from the line of handlers carrying the precious cartons of crystal in to Sorting. Only a near miss, the incident was disregarded even by those who had barely escaped injury.

Killashandra Ree emerged from the sled, taking as a good omen the fact that her sled had skidded to a halt so close to the Sorting Sheds. She caught the arm of the next handler to pass her and firmly diverted him to her cargo door, which she flung open. She didn't have much crystal, so every speck she had cut was precious to her. If she didn't earn enough credit to get off-planet this time . . . Killashandra ground her teeth as she hurried her carton into the Sorting Shed.

As the man she had pressed into her service quite properly put her carton down at the Hangar end of a line of ranked containers, Killashandra's patience evaporated. "No, over here!" she shouted. "Not there! It'll take all day to be sorted. Here."

She waited until he had deposited her carton in the indicated row before adding her own. Then she strode back to her sled for a second load, commandeering two more unencumbered handlers on the way. Only after eight cartons were unloaded did she permit herself to pause briefly, coping with the multiple fatigues that assailed her. She had worked nonstop for two days, desperate to cut enough crystal to get off Ballybran. Crystal pulsed in her blood and bones, denying her rest in sleep, surcease by day, no matter how she tried to tire her body. Her only respite was immersion in the radiant fluid bath. But no one cut crystal from a bathcube! She had to get off-planet to ease the disturbing thrum.

For over a year and a half, ever since the Passover storms had shattered Keborgen's old claim, she had searched unremittingly for a workable site. Killashandra was realist enough to admit to herself that the probability of finding a new claim as important and valuable as Keborgen's black crystal was very low. Still, she had every right to expect to find some useful, and reasonably lucrative, crystal in Ballybran's Ranges. And, with each fruitless trip into the Ranges, the credit balance she had amassed from her original cutting of Keborgen's site and from the Trundimoux black crystal installation had eroded beneath the continuous charges the Heptite Guild exacted for even the most minor services rendered a crystal singer.

By fall, when everyone else she knew—Rimbol, Jezerey and Mistra—had managed to get off-planet, she had labored on, unable to make a worthwhile claim in any color. During the mild winter, she had doggedly hunted in the Ranges, returning to the Complex only long enough to replenish food packs and steep her crystal-weary body in the radiant fluid.

"You really ought to take a week or two up at Shanganagh Base," Lanzecki had said, intercepting her on one of her brief visits.

"What good would that really do?" she had replied, almost snarling at him in her frustration. "I'd still feel crystal and I'd have to look at Ballybran."

Lanzecki had given her a searching look. "You're in no mood to believe me," and he paused to be sure that he had her attention, "but you will find black crystal again, Killashandra. Meanwhile, the Guild has pressing needs in any shade you can find. Even the rose you so despise." A gleam shone in his black eyes and his voice turned lugubrious as he said, "I am certain that you will be distressed to learn that the Passover storms destroyed Moksoon's site, too."

Killashandra had stared at him a moment before her sense of the ridiculous got the better of her and she laughed. "I am inconsolable!"

"I thought you might be." His lips twitched with suppressed amusement. Then he reached down and pulled the plug on the radiant fluid. "You'll find more crystal, Killa."

It had been that calm and confident statement which had buoyed her flagging morale all during the next trip. Nor had it been entirely misplaced. The third week out, after disregarding two sites of rose and blue, she discovered white crystal but very nearly missed the vein entirely. If she had not been bolstering her spirits with a rousing aria, causing the pinnacle under her hand to resonate, she might have missed the shy white crystal. Consistent with her long run of bad luck, the white proved elusive, the vein first deteriorating in quality and then disappearing entirely from the face at one point, resurfacing half a mile away in fractured shards. It had taken her weeks to clear the fault, digging away half the ridge before she got to usable crystal. Only the fact that white crystal had such a variety of potentially lucrative uses kept her going.

Forewarned of the spring storm by her symbiotic adaptation to Ballybran's spore, Killashandra had cut at a frenzied pace until she was too hoarse to key the sonic cutter to the crystal. Only then had she stopped to rest. She had continued to cut until the first of the winds began to stroke the dangerous crystal sound from the Ranges. Recklessly, she had taken the most direct route back to the Complex, counting on the fact that she'd be the last singer in from the Ranges to protect her claim.

She had almost cut her retreat too fine: the Hangar doors slammed shut against the shrieking storm as soon as her sled had cleared the baffles. She could expect a reprimand from the Flight Officer for her recklessness. And probably one from the Guild Master for ignoring the storm warnings.

She forced several deep breaths in and out of her lungs, dredging sufficient energy to complete the final step necessary to leave Ballybran. On the last breath, she grabbed the top carton and walked it into the Sorting Room, depositing it on Enthor's table just as the old Sorter turned toward the shed.

"Killashandra! You startled me." Enthor's eyes flicked from normal to the augmented vision that was his adaptation to Ballybran. He reached eagerly for the carton. "Did you find the black vein again?" His face fell into lines of disappointment as his fingers found no trace of the sensations typical of the priceless, elusive black crystal.

"No such luck." Killashandra's voice broke on weary disgust. "But I devoutly hope it's a respectable cut." She half sat on the table, needing its support to keep on her feet, as she watched Enthor unpack the crystal blocks from their plastic cocoons.

"Indeed!" Enthor's voice lilted with approval as he removed the first white crystal shaft and set it with appropriate reverence on his work table. "Indeed!" He subjected the crystal to the scrutiny of his augmented eyes. "Flawless. White can so often be muddy. If I am not mistaken—"

"That'll be the day," Killashandra muttered under her breath, her voice cracking.

"—Never about crystal." Enthor shot her a glance from under his brows, blinking to adjust his eyes to normal vision. Killashandra idly wondered what Enthor's eyes saw of human flesh and bone in the augmented mode. "I do believe, my dear Killa, that you've anticipated the market."

"I have?" Killashandra pulled herself erect. "With white crystal?"

Enthor lifted out more of the slender sparkling crystal shafts. "Yes, especially if you have matched groupings. These are a good start. What else did you cut?" As one, they retraced their steps to the storage, each collecting another carton.

"Forty-four—"

"Ranked in size?"

"Yes." Enthor's excitement triggered hope in Killashandra.

"Forty-four, from the half centimeter—"

"By the centimeter?"

"Half centimeter."

Enthor beamed on her with almost as much enthusiasm as if she had brought him more black crystal.

"Your instinct is remarkable, Killa, for you could not have known about the order from the Optherians."

"An organ group?"

Enthor gestured for Killashandra to help him display the white shafts on the workbench.

"Yes, indeed. An entire manual was fractured." Enthor awarded her another of his beams. "Where are the rest? Quickly. Get them. If there's so much as one with a cloud—"

Killashandra obeyed, stumbling against the swinging door. By the time the crystal was sparkling on the table, she was shuddering and had to cling to the bench to keep upright. It took a century for Enthor to evaluate her cut.

"Not a single cloudy crystal, Killashandra." Enthor patted her arm and, taking up his little hammer, cocked his ear to the pure sweet notes each delicate rap coaxed from the crystal.

"How much, Enthor? How much?" Killashandra was hanging onto the table, and consciousness, with difficulty.

"Not as much, I fear, as black." Enthor tapped figures into his terminal. He pulled at his lower lip as he waited for the altered display. "Still, 10,054 credits is not be sneezed at." He raised his eyebrows, anticipating a pleased response.

"Only ten thousand . . ." Her knees were collapsing, the muscles in her calves spasming painfully. She tightened her grip on the table's edge.

"Surely that's enough to take you off-planet."

"But not far enough or long enough away." Blackness was creeping across her sight. Killashandra released one hand from the table to rub her eyes.

"Would Optheria be far enough?" a dry, amused voice asked from behind her.

"Lanzecki . . ." she began, turning toward the Guild Master, but her turn became a spin, down into the darkness which would no longer be evaded.

"She's coming round, Lanzecki."

Killashandra heard the words. She could not understand their sense.

The sentence, and the voice, echoed in her mind as if spoken in a tunnel. At the softest repetition, comprehension returned.

The voice was Antona's, the Chief Medical Officer of the Heptite Guild.

Sensation returned then, but sensation was limited to feeling something under her chin and a restraint about her shoulders. The rest of her body was deprived of feeling. Killashandra twitched convulsively and felt the viscous resistance of radiant fluid. She was immersed—that explained the need for chin support and the shoulder restraint.

Opening her eyes, she was not surprised to find herself in the tank room of the Infirmary. Beyond her were several more such tanks, two occupied, judging by the heads visible above the rims.

"So, you've rejoined us, Killashandra!"

"How long have you been soaking me, Antona?"

Antona glanced at a display on the tank. "Thirty-two hours and nineteen rinses." Antona shook a warning finger at Killashandra. "Don't push yourself like this, Killa. You're stretching your symbiont's resources. Abuses like this now can cause degeneration problems later on. And it's later on you really need protection. Remember that!" A mirthless smile crossed Antona's classic features. "If you can. Well, at least put it in your memory banks when you get back to your room," she added, with a sigh for the vagaries of singer recall.

"When can I get up?" Killashandra began to writhe in the tank, testing her limbs and the general response of her body.

Antona shrugged, tapping out a code on the terminal of the tank. "Oh, anytime now. Pulse and pressure readout's strong. Head clear?"

"Yes."

Antona pressed a stud and the chin support and shoulder harness released Killashandra. She caught the side of the tank, and Antona handed her a long robe.

"Do I need to tell you to eat?"

Killashandra grinned wryly. "No. My stomach knows I'm awake and it's rumbling."

"You've lost nearly two kilos, you know. Can you remember when you last ate?" Antona's voice and eyes were sharp with annoyance. "No use asking, is it?"

"Not the least bit," Killashandra replied blithely as she climbed out of the tank, the radiant fluid sheeting off her body, leaving her skin smooth and soft. She pulled the robe on. Antona held up a hand to balance her down the five steps.

"How much crystal resonance do you experience now?" Antona poised her fingers above the tank's small terminal.

Killashandra listened attentively to the noise between her ears. "Only a faint trace!" Her breath escaped her lips in a sigh of relief.

"Lanzecki said that you cut enough to go off-world."

Killashandra frowned. "He said something else, too. But I forget what." Something important, though, Killashandra knew.

"He'll probably tell you again in good time. Get up to your quarters and get some food into you." Antona gave Killashandra's shoulder an admonitory squeeze before she turned away to check on the other patients.

As Killashandra made her way up from the Infirmary level, deep in the bowels of the Guild Complex, she puzzled over the memory lapse. She had been reassured that most singers had several decades of unimpaired recall before memory deteriorated, but no fast rule determined the onset. She had been lucky enough to have a Milekey Transition ending in full adaptation to Ballybran's spore, an adaptation that was necessary for those inhabiting the planet Ballybran. That kind of Transition held many benefits, not the least of which was avoiding the rigors of Transition Fever, and was purported to include a longer span of unimpaired memory. In this one instance, she could, perhaps, legitimately blame fatigue.

As the lift door opened on the deserted lobby of the main singer level, not a singer was in sight. The storm had blown itself out. She paused to glance through to the dining area and saw only one lone diner. Pulling the robe more tightly about her, she hurried down the corridor to the blue quadrant and her apartment.

The first thing she did was call up her credit balance, and felt the knot that had been tightening in her belly dissolve as the figures 12,790 rippled onto the screen. She regarded the total for a long moment, then tapped out the all-important query: how far away from Ballybran would that sum take her?

The names of four systems were displayed. Her stomach rumbled. She shifted irritably in her chair and asked for details of the amenities in each system. The replies were not exciting. In each system the Terran-type planets were purely industrial or agricultural, having, at best, only conservative leisure facilities. From comments she had overheard, Killashandra gathered that because of their proximity the locals had seen quite enough of their neighbors from Ballybran and tended to be either credit crunchers or rude to the point of dueling offense.

"The only thing that's good about any of them," Killashandra said with disgust, "is that I haven't been there yet."

Killashandra had thought to take her long-overdue holiday on Maxim, the pleasure planet in the Barderi system. From all she'd heard, it would be very easy to forget crystal resonance in the sophisticated amusement parks and houses of hedonistic Maxim. But she hadn't yet the credit to indulge that whimsy.

Exasperated, she rubbed her palms together, noticing that the thick calluses from cutter vibrations had been softened by her long immersion. The numerous small nicks and cuts that were a singer's occupational hazard had healed to thin white scars. Well, that function of her symbiont worked efficiently. And the white crystal would assure her some sort of an off-planet holiday.

White crystal! Enthor has said something about a fractured manual!

Optherian sense organs used white Ballybran crystals and she had cut forty-four from the half centimeter on up in half-centimeter gradients.

Lanzecki had asked her a question.

"Would Optheria be far enough?" The words, remembered in his deep voice, sprang to mind.

She grinned with tremendous relief at retrieving that question and turned to the viewscreen to punch up his code.

"—Killa?" Lanzecki's hands were poised over his own terminal, surprise manifested by his raised eyebrows. "You haven't used the catering unit." He frowned.

"Oh, programmed to monitor that, did you?" she replied with a genuine smile at that reminder of their amorous alliance before her first trip into the Ranges. On her return from the Trundimoux System, they had had only a few days together before Lanzecki was swamped with work and she had to venture back into the Ranges. Since then, she had returned to the Complex only to replenish supplies or wait out a storm. Their reunions had consequently been brief. It was reassuring to realize that he wished to know when she was back.

"It seemed the ideal way to make contact. After thirty-two hours in a tank, you should be ravenous. I'll just join you, if I may . . ." When she nodded assent, he typed a quick message on his console and pushed his chair back, smiling up at her. "I'm hungry, too."

As further reassurance of her unimpaired memory, Killashandra had no trouble remembering Lanzecki's tastes. She grinned as she ordered Yarran beer. Though her stomach gurgled impatiently, she'd had no desire for food in so long that she was as glad to be guided by Lanzecki's preferences.

She was just slipping a brilliantly striped robe over her head when her door chimed an entry request. "Enter!" she called. On the same voice cue, the catering slot disgorged her order. The aroma of the dishes aroused her already voracious appetite.

She wasted no time in taking the steaming platters from the dispenser, grinning a welcome at Lanzecki as he joined her.

"The Commissary has asked me to relay a few well-chosen words of complaint about the sudden fad for Yarran beer," he said, taking the pitcher and the beakers to the table. He seated himself before filling the two glasses. "To your restoration!" Lanzecki lifted his glass in toast, his expression obliquely chiding her for that necessity.

"Antona's already scolded me, but I had to cut enough marketable crystal to get off-planet this time."

"You've certainly succeeded with that white."

"Don't I remember you saying something about Optheria just as I passed out?"

Lanzecki took a swallow of the Yarran beer before he replied. "Quite likely." He served himself a generous helping of fried Malva beans.

"Don't the Optherians utilize white crystal in that multi-sense organ of theirs?"

"They do."

So Lanzecki chose to be uncommunicative. Well, she could be persistent. "Enthor said that an entire manual was fractured." Lanzecki nodded. She continued. "And you did ask me would Optheria be far enough?"

"I did?"

"You know you did." Killashandra hung on to her patience. "You never forget anything. And the impression I got from your cryptic comment was that someone, and the inference was me"—she pressed her thumb into her chest—"would have to go there. Am I correct?"

He regarded her steadily, his expression unreadable. "Not long ago you gave me to understand that you would not undertake another off-world assignment—"

"That was before I'd been stuck on this fardling planet—" She noticed the wicked gleam in his eyes. "So, I'm right. A crystal singer *does* have to make the installation!"

"It was a shocking incident," Lanzecki said diffidently as he served himself more Malva beans. "The performer who damaged the organ was killed by the flying shards. He was also the only person on the planet who could handle such a major repair. As is so often the case with such sensitive and expensive equipment, it is a matter of planetary urgency to repair the instrument. It's the largest on the planet and is essential to the observances of Optheria's prestigious Summer Festival. We are contracted to supply technicians as well as crystal." He paused for a mouthful of the crisp white beans. He was definitely baiting her, Killashandra knew. She held her tongue. "While the list of those qualified does include your name . . ."

"The catch can't be the crystal this time," she said as he purposefully let his sentence dangle unfinished. She watched his face for any reaction. "White crystal's active, reflecting sound . . ."

"—Among other things," Lanzecki added when she paused.

"If it isn't the crystal, what's the matter with the Optherians, then?"

"My dear Killashandra, the assignment has not yet been awarded."

"Awarded? I like the sound of that. Or do I? I wouldn't put it past you, Lanzecki, to sucker me into another job like that Trundimoux installation."

He caught the finger she was indignantly shaking at him, pulling her hand across the laden table to his lips. The familiar caress evoked familiar responses deep in her groin and she tried to use her irritation with his methods to neutralize its effect on her.

Just then a communit bleep startled her. With a fleeting expression of annoyance, Lanzecki lifted his wrist unit to acknowledge the summons.

A tinny version of Trag's bass voice issued from the device. "I was to inform you when the preliminary testing stations reported," the Administration Officer said.

"Any interesting applicants?"

Although Lanzecki sounded diffident, even slightly bored, the curious tension about his lips and eyes alerted Killashandra. She pretended to continue eating in a courteous disregard of the exchange, but she didn't lose a syllable of Trag's reply.

"Four agronomists, an endocrinologist from Theta, two xenobiologists, an atmospheric physicist, three former spacers"—Killashandra noted the slight widening of Lanzecki's eyes which she interpreted as satisfaction—"and the usual flotsam who have no recommendations from Testing."

"Thank you, Trag."

Lanzecki nodded his head at Killashandra to indicate the interruption was concluded and finished off the dish of fried Malva beans.

"So what is the glitch in the Optherian assignment? A lousy fee?"

"On the contrary, such an installation is set at twenty thousand credits."

"And I'd be off-world as well." Killashandra was quite impressed with the latitude such a credit balance would give her to forget crystal.

"You have not been awarded the contract, Killa. I appreciate your willingness to entertain the assignment but there are certain aspects which must be considered by the Guild as well as the individual. Don't commit yourself rashly." Lanzecki was being sincere. His eyes held hers steadily and a worried crease to his brows emphasized his warning. "It's a long haul to the Optherian system. You'd be gone from Ballybran nearly a full year . . ."

"All the better . . ."

"You say that now when you're full of crystal resonance. You can't have forgotten Carrik yet."

His reminder conjured flashing scenes of the first crystal singer she had met: Carrik laughing as they swam in Fuerte's seas, then Carrik wracked by withdrawal fever and finally the passive bulk of the man, shattered by sonic resonance.

"You will in time, I've no doubt, experience that phenomenon," Lanzecki said. "I've never known a singer who didn't try to push himself and his symbiont to their limits. A major disadvantage to the Optherian contract is that you would lose any resonance to your existing claims."

"As if I *had* a decent claim among the lot." Killashandra snorted in disgust. "Rose is no good to anyone and the blue petered out after two days' cutting. Even the white vein skips and jumps. I cut the best of the accessible vein. With the kind of luck I've been enjoying, the storm has probably made a total bollix of the site. I am not—not, I repeat—spending another three weeks in a spade and basket operation. Not for white. Why can't Research develop an efficient portable excavator?"

Lanzecki cocked his head slightly. "It is the firm opinion of Research that any *one* of the nine efficient, portable and durable," a significant pause, "excavators already field-tested ought to perform the task for which it was engineered . . . except in the hands of a crystal singer. It is the opinion of Research that the only two pieces of equipment that do not tax the mechanical aptitude of a singer are his cutter—though Fisherman does *not* concur—and his sled, and you have already heard section and paragraph from the Flight Engineer on that score. Haven't you?"

Killashandra regarded him stolidly for a few moments, then remembered to chew what was in her mouth.

"Overheard him," she said, with a malicious grin. "Don't try to distract me from this Optherian business."

"I'm not. I am bringing to your notice the several overt disadvantages to an assignment that involves a long absence from Ballybran for what might, in the long run, be inadequate compensation." His expression changed subtly. "I'd rather not be professionally at odds with you. It interferes with my private life."

His dark eyes caught hers. He reached for her hands, lips curved in the one-sided smile that she found so affecting. She no longer shared a table with her Guild Master but with Lanzecki the man. The alteration pleased her. On numerous occasions, during sleepless nights in the Milekey Ranges, she had fondly remembered their love-making. Now, seated opposite the charismatic Lanzecki, she found that her appetite for more than food had been completely restored.

Her smile answered his and together they rose from the little table and headed for the sleepingroom.

Chapter 2

Killashandra pushed herself back from the terminal and, balancing on the base of her spine, stretched arms and legs as far from her body as bone and tendon permitted. She had spent the morning immersed in the Optherian entry of the *Encyclopedia Galactica*.

Once she had got past the initial exploration and evaluation report to the release of the Ophiuchine planet for colonization, and the high-flown language of its charter—"to establish a colony of Mankind in complete harmony with the ecological balance of his adopted planet: to ensure the propagation thereon of the Species in its pure, unadulterated Form." She kept waiting for the fly to appear in the syrupy ointment of Optheria's honey pot.

Optheria was an old planet in geological terms. A near-circular orbit about an aging sun produced a temperate clime. There was little seasonal change since the axial "wobble" was negligible, and modest glaciers capped both poles. Optheria was inordinately proud of its self-sufficiency in a civilization where many planets were so deeply in debt to mercantile satellites that they were almost charged for the atmosphere that encapsulated them. Optherian imports were minimal . . . with the exception of tourists seeking to "enjoy the gentler pleasures of old Terra in a Totally Natural World."

Killashandra, reading with an eye to hidden significances, paused to consider the implications. Although her experience with planets had been limited to living on two—Fuerte, her planet of origin, and Ballybran—she knew enough of how worlds wagged to sense the iron idealism that probably supported the Optherian propaganda. She tapped a question and frowned at the negative answer: Optheria's Charter Signers were not proselytizers of a religious sect nor did Optheria recognize a federal church. As many worlds had been colonized for idealist forms of government, religiously or secularly oriented, as for purely commercial considerations. The guiding principle of foundation could not yet be considered the necessary criterion for a successful subculture. The variables involved were too numerous.

But the entry made it clear that Optheria was considered efficiently organized and, with its substantial positive galactic balance of payments, a creditably administered world. The entry concluded with a statement that Optheria was well worth a visit during its annual Summer Festival. She detected a certain hint of irony in that bland comment. While she would have

247

preferred to sample some of the exotic and sophisticated pleasures available to those with credit enough, she felt she could tolerate Optheria's "natural" pastimes in return for the sizable fee and a long vacation from Ballybran.

She considered Lanzecki's diffidence about the assignment. Could he be charged with favoritism if he gave her another choice off-world assignment? Who would remember that she had been away during the horrendous Passover Storms, much less where? She'd been peremptorily snatched away by Trag, shoved onto the moon shuttle, and without a shred of background data about the vagaries of the Trundimoux, delivered willy-nilly to a naval autocracy to cope with the exigencies of installing millions of credits' worth of black communication crystal for a bunch of skeptical spartan pioneers. The assignment had been no sinecure. As Trag was the only other person who had known of it, was he the objector? He very easily could be, as Administration Officer, yet Killashandra did not think that Trag could, or did, influence Guild Master Lanzecki.

A second wild notion followed quickly on the heels of that one. Were there any Optherians on the roster of the Heptite Guild to whom such a job might be assigned? . . . The Heptite Guild had no Optherian members.

From her ten years in the Music Department of Fuerte's Culture Center, Killashandra was familiar with the intricacies of Optherian sensory organ instruments. The encyclopedia enlarged the picture by stating that music was a planetwide mania on Optheria, with citizens competing on a planetary scale for opportunities to perform on the sensory organs. With that sort of environment, Killashandra thought it very odd indeed that Optheria produced no candidates with the perfect pitch that was the Heptite Guild's essential entry requirement. And, with competitions on a worldwide scale, there would be thousands disappointed. Killashandra smiled in sour sympathy. Surely some would look for off-world alternatives.

Her curiosity titillated, Killashandra checked other Guilds. Optherians did not go into the Space Services or into galactic mercantile enterprises, nor were embassies, consulates or legates of Optheria listed in the Diplomatic Registers. There she lucked out by discovering a qualifier: As the planet was nearly self-sufficient and no Optherians left their home world, there was no need for such services. All formal inquiries about Optheria had to be directed to the Office of External Trade and Commerce on Optheria.

Killashandra paused in perplexity. A planet so perfect, so beloved by its citizens that no one chose to leave its surface? She found that very hard to believe. She recalled the encyclopedia's entry on the planet, searching for the code on Naturalization. Yes, well, citizenship was readily available for those interested but could not be rescinded. She checked the Penal Code and discovered that, unlike many worlds, Optheria did not deport its criminal element: any recidivists were accommodated at a rehabilitation center.

Killashandra shivered. So even perfect Optheria had to resort to rehabilitation.

Having delved sufficiently into Optheria's history and background to satisfy her basic curiosity, she turned to research the procedure necessary to replace a fractured manual. The installation posed no overt problems as the bracketing was remarkably similar to that required by the black communications crystal. The tuning would be more complex because of the broad-frequency variable output of the Optherian organ. The instrument was similar to early Terran pipe organs, with four manuals and a terminal with hundreds of stops, but a performer on the Optherian organ read a score containing olfactory, neural, visual, and aural notes. The crystal manual was in permanent handshake with the multiplex demodulator, the synapse carrier encoder, and the transducer terminal networks. Or so the manual said; no schematic was included in the entry. Nor could she remember one from her days at the Fuerte Music Center.

Dedicated Optherian players spent lifetimes arranging music embellished and ornamented for reception by many senses. A skilled Optherian organist could be mass-psychologist and politician as well as musician, and the effect of any composition played on the fully augmented instruments had such far-reaching consequences that performances and practitioners were subject to Federal as well as artistic discipline.

Bearing that in mind, Killashandra wondered how the manual could have been fractured—let alone have killed the performer at the same time, especially as that person had also been the only one on the planet capable of repairing it. Was there perhaps a spot of rot on the Optherian apple of Eden? This assignment could be interesting.

Killashandra pulled her chair back to the console and asked for visual contact with the Travel Officer. Bajorn was a long, thin man, with a thin face and a thin nose with pinched nostrils. He had preternaturally long, thin fingers, too, but much was redeemed by the cheerful smile that broke across his narrow face, and his complete willingness to sort out the most difficult itinerary. He seemed to be on the most congenial terms with every transport or freight captain who had ever touched down at or veered close to the Shanganagh Moon Base.

"Is it difficult to get to the Optherian System, Bajorn?"

"Long old journey right now—out of season for the cruise ships on that route. Summer Festival won't be for another six months galactic. So, traveling now, you'd have to make four exchanges—Rappahoe, Kunjab, Melorica, and Bernard's World—all on freighters before getting passage on a proper liner."

"You're sure up to date."

Bajorn grinned, his thin lips almost touching his droopy ears. "Should be. You're the fifth inquiry I've had about that system. What's up? Didn't know the Optherians went in for the sort of kicks singers like."

"Who're the other four?"

"Well, there's no regulation against telling . . ." Bajorn paused discreetly, "and as they've all asked, no reason why you shouldn't be told. You," and he ticked names off on his fingers, "Borella Seal, Concera, Gobbain Tekla, and Rimbol."

"Indeed. Thank you, Bajorn, that's real considerate of you."

"That's what Rimbol said, too." Bajorn's face sagged mournfully. "I do try to satisfy the Guild's travel requirements, but it is so depressing when my efforts are criticized or belittled. I can't help it if singers lose their memories . . . and every shred of common courtesy."

"I'll program eternal courtesy to you on my personal tape, Bajorn."

"I'd appreciate it. Only do it now, would you, Killashandra, before you forget?"

Promising faithfully, Killashandra rang off. Lanzecki had said there was a list. Were there only five names? Borella Seal and Concera she knew and she wouldn't have minded doing them out of the assignment; Gobbain Tekla was a total stranger. Rimbol had been cutting successfully, and in the darker shades just as Lanzecki had predicted. Why would he want such an assignment? So, four people had been interested enough to check Travel. Were there more?

She asked for a list of unassigned singers in residence and it was depressingly long. After some names, including her own, the capital I—for inactive—flashed. Perhaps unwisely, she deleted those and still had thirty-seven possible rivals. She twirled idly about in the gimbaled chair, wondering exactly what criterion was vital for the Optherian assignment. Lanzecki hadn't mentioned such minor details in the little he had disclosed. From what she had already learned of the planet and the mechanics of installation, any competent singer could do the job. So what would weigh the balance in favor of one singer?

Killashandra reexamined the list of her known rivals: Borella and Concera had both been cutting a long time. Gobbain Tekla, when she found his position on the Main Roster, was a relative newcomer; Rimbol, like Killashandra, was a rank tyro. When she inquired, she discovered that each of the others had been a redundant or a failed musician. Perhaps that was the necessary requirement. It certainly made sense for the installer to have an instrumental background. She rephrased her question to apply to all thirty-seven available singers. Nineteen fit that category.

Lanzecki appeared reluctant to offer her the assignment but she oughtn't to fault him. She was acutely aware of past concessions from her Guild Master. She had no right to expect an interrupted flow of benefits simply because he chose to share his bed with her. Nor, she decided, would she jeopardize their relationship by referring to the assignment again. Lanzecki might well be doing her a favor by not recommending her. She must keep that aspect of the situation firmly in mind. She might not be thrilled to vacation on the four systems to which her available credit would take her, but that was another string in her deplorable luck. She would get a rest from crystal and that was the essential requirement.

Her reawakened appetite reminded her that it had been some hours since breakfast. During lunch, she'd decide where to take herself. When, refreshed and revitalized, she returned to her labors for the Heptite Guild, she'd find a fresh vein of black crystal and *then* she'd get to the planet Maxim.

Before she could plan her vacation in any detail, Antona rang her from the Infirmary. "Have you eaten, Killa?"

"Is that an invitation or a professional query? Because I just finished a very hearty lunch."

Antona sighed. "I should have liked your company for lunch. There's not much doing right now down here. Fortunately."

"If it's just the company you want while you eat . . ."

Antona smiled with genuine pleasure. "I do. I don't enjoy eating by myself *all* the time. Could you drop down here first? You're still listed as inactive and you'll want that status amended."

On her way down to the Infirmary level, Killashandra first worried then chided herself for fearing there was more to Antona's request than a simple record up-date. It might have nothing to do with her fitness to take on the Optherian job. Nor would it be discreet to imply that she knew such an assignment was available. On the other hand, Antona would know more about the amenities of the nearby worlds.

The medical formality took little time and then the two women proceeded to the catering section of the main singer's floor of the Guild Complex.

"It's so depressingly empty," Antona said in a subdued voice as she glanced about the dimly lit portions of the facility.

"I found it a lot more depressing when everyone else was celebrating a good haul," Killashandra said in a glum tone.

"Yes, yes, it would be, I suppose. Oh, fardles!" Antona quickly diverted Killashandra toward the shadowy side. "Borella, Concera, and that simp, Gobbain," she murmured as she made a hasty detour.

"You don't like them?" Killashandra was amused.

Antona shrugged. "One establishes a friendship by sharing events and opinions. They remember nothing and consequently have nothing to share. And less to talk about."

Without warning, Antona caught Killashandra by the arm, turning to face her. "Do yourself a sterling favor, Killa. Put everything you've experienced so far in your life, every detail you can recall from cutting expeditions, every conversation you've had, every joke you've heard, put everything"—when Killashandra affected surprise, Antona gave her arm a painful squeeze—"and yes, I do mean 'everything,' into your personal retrieval file. What you did, what you said, what you felt"—and Antona's fierce gaze challenged Privacy—"how you've loved. Then, when your mind is as blank as theirs, you can refresh your memory and have something with which to reestablish *you*!" Her expression became intensely sad. "Oh, Killa. Be different! Do as I ask! Now! Before it's too late!"

Then, her customary composure restored, she released the arm and seemed to draw the intensity back into her straight, slim body. "Because I assure you," she said as she took the last few steps into the catering area, "that once your brilliant wit and repartee become as banal and malicious as theirs," she jerked her thumb at the silent trio, "I'll seek other company at lunch. Now," she said, her fingers poised over the catering terminal, "what are you having?"

"Yarran beer." Killashandra said the first thing that came to mind, being slightly dazed by Antona's unexpected outburst.

Antona raised her eyebrows in mock surprise, then rapidly dialed their orders.

They were served quickly and took their trays to the nearest banquette. As Antona tackled her meal with good appetite, Killashandra sipped her beer, digesting Antona's remarkable advice. Till then, Killashandra had had no opportunity to appreciate the viewpoint of a colleague who would not lose her memory as an occupational hazard. Stubbornly, Killashandra preferred to forget certain scenes in her life. Like failure.

"Well, you don't have long to wait for a fresh supply of cluttered minds," Killashandra said at last, blotting the beer foam from her upper lip and deferring conversation on Antona's unsettling advice.

"A new class? How did that privileged information seep out? You are only just out of an Infirmary tank. Well, you won't be allowed to brief them if that's what you had in mind, Killa."

"Why not?"

Antona shrugged and daintily sampled her nicely browned casserole before replying. "You've no injury to display. That's an important part of the briefing, you see—the visible, undeniable proof of the rapid tissue regeneration enjoyed by residents of Ballybran."

"Irresistible!" Antona gave Killashandra a sharp glance. "Oh, no complaints from me, Antona. The Guild can be proud of its adroit recruiting program."

Antona fastened a searching glance on her face and put down her fork. "Killashandra Ree, the Heptite Guild is not permitted by the Federated Sentient Planets to 'recruit' free citizens for such a hazardous profession. Only volunteers—"

"Only volunteers insist on presenting themselves, and so many of these have exceedingly useful skills ..." She broke off, momentarily disconcerted by Antona's almost fierce glance.

"What concern is that of yours, Killashandra Ree? You have benefited immensely from the ... selection process."

"Despite my unexpected inclusion."

"A few odd ones slip through no matter how careful we are," Antona said all too sweetly, her eyes sparkling.

"Don't fret, Antona. It's not a subject that I would discuss with anyone else."

"Particularly Lanzecki."

"I'm not likely to get that sort of an opportunity," she said, wondering if Antona knew or suspected their relationship. Or if her advice to remember loves and emotions had merely been a general warning to include all experience. Would Killashandra want to remember, decades from now, that she and Lanzecki had briefly been lovers? "Advise me, Antona, on which of our nearer spatial neighbors I should plan a brief vacation?"

Antona grimaced. "You might just as well pick the name at random for all the difference there is among them. Their only advantage is that they are far enough away from Ballybran to give your nerves the rest they need."

Just then a cheerful voice hailed them.

"Killa! Antona! Am I glad to see someone else alive!" Rimbol exclaimed, hobbling out of the shadows. He grinned as he saw the pitcher of beer. "May I join you?"

"By all means," Antona said graciously.

"What *happened* to you?" Killashandra asked. Rimbol's cheek and forehead were literally decorated by newly healed scars.

"Mine was the sled that did a nose dive over the baffle."

"It did?"

"You didn't know it was me?" Rimbol's mouth twisted in mock chagrin. "The way Malaine carried on you'd've thought I'd placed half the incoming singers in jeopardy by that flip."

"Did you rearrange the sled as creatively as your face?"

Rimbol shook his head ruefully. "It broke its nose, mine was only bloody. At that it'll take longer to fix the sled than for my leg to heal. Say, Killa, have you heard about the Optherian contract?"

"For the fractured manual? That could pay for a lot of repairs."

"Oh, I don't want it," and he flicked his hand in dismissal.

"Why ever not?"

Rimbol took a long pull of his beer. "Well, I've got a claim that was cutting real well right now. Optheria's a long way away from here and I've been warned that I could lose the guiding resonance being gone so long."

"And because you remembered that I haven't cut anything worth packing—"

"No." Rimbol held up a hand, protesting Killashandra's accusation. "I mean, yes, I knew you've been unlucky lately—"

"Who do you think cut the white crystal to replace the fractured Optherian manual?"

"You did?" Rimbol's face brightened with relief. "Then you don't need to go either." He raised his beaker in a cheerful toast. "Where d'you plan to go off-world?"

"I hadn't exactly made up my mind . . ." Killashandra saw that Antona was busy serving up the last of her casserole.

"Why don't you try Maxim in the Barderi system." Rimbol leaned eagerly across the table to her. "I've heard it's something sensational. I'll get there sometime but I'd sure like to hear your opinion of it. I don't half believe the reports. I'd trust you."

"That's something to remember," Killashandra murmured, glancing sideways at Antona. Then, taking note of Rimbol's querying look, she asked smoothly, "What've you been cutting lately?"

"Greens," Rimbol replied with considerable satisfaction. He held up crossed fingers. "Now, if only the storm damage is minimal, and it could be because the vein's in a protected spot, I might even catch up with you on Maxim. You see . . ." and he proceeded to elaborate on his prospects.

As Rimbol rattled on in his amusing fashion, Killashandra wondered if crystal would dull the Scartine's infectious good-nature along with his memory. Would Antona give him the same urgent advice? Surely each of the newest crystal singers had some unique quality to be cherished and sustained throughout a lifetime. Antona's outburst had been sparked by a long frustration. To how many singers over her decades in the Guild had she tendered the same advice and found it ignored?

". . . So I came in with forty greens," Rimbol was saying with an air of achievement.

"That's damned good cutting!" Killashandra replied with suitable fervor.

"You have no trouble releasing crystal?" Antona asked.

"Well, I did the first time out," Rimbol admitted candidly, "but I remembered what you'd said, Killa, about packing as soon as you cut. I'll never forget the sight of you locked in crystal thrall, right here in a noisy crowded hall. A kindly and timely word of wisdom!"

"Oh, you'd have caught on soon enough," Killashandra said, feeling a trifle embarrassed by his gratitude.

"Some never do, you know," Antona remarked.

"What happens? Do they stand in statuesque paralysis until night comes? Or a loud storm?"

"The inability to release crystal is no joke, Rimbol."

Rimbol stared at Antona, his mobile face losing its amused expression. "You mean, they can be so enthralled, nothing breaks the spell?" Antona nodded slowly. "That could be fatal. Has it been?"

"There have been instances."

"Then I'm doubly indebted to you, Killa," Rimbol said, rising, "so this round's on me."

They finished that round, refreshed by food, drink, and conversation.

"Of the four, I think you'd prefer Rani in the Punjabi system," Antona told Killashandra in parting. "The food's better and the climate less severe. They have marvelous mineral hot springs, too. Not as efficacious as our radiant fluid but it'll help reduce crystal resonance. You need that. After just an hour in your company, the sound off you makes the hairs on my arm stand up. See?"

Killashandra exchanged glances with Rimbol, before they examined the proof on Antona's extended arm.

Antona laughed reassuringly, laying gentle fingers on Killashandra's forearm.

"A perfectly normal phenomenon for a singer who's been out in the Ranges steadily for over a year. Neither of you would be affected but, as I don't sing crystal, I am. Get used to it. That's what identifies a singer anywhere in the Galaxy. But the Rani hot springs will diminish the effect considerably. So does time away from here. See you."

As Killashandra watched Antona enter the lift, she felt Rimbol's hand sliding up her arm affectionately.

"You feel all right to me," he said, his blue eyes twinkling with amusement. Then he felt her stiffen and suppress a movement of withdrawal. He dropped his hand. "Privacy—sorry, Killa." He stepped back.

"Not half as sorry as I am, Rimbol. You didn't deserve that. Chalk it up to another side effect of singing crystal that they don't include in that full disclosure." She managed an apologetic smile. "I'm so wired I could broadcast."

"Not to worry, Killa. I understand. See you when you get back." Then he made his wobbly way into the yellow quadrant to his quarters.

Killashandra stared after him, irritated with herself for her reaction to a casual caress. She'd had no such reaction to Lanzecki. Or was *that* the problem? She was very thoughtful as she walked slowly to her quarters. Fidelity was an unlikely disease for her to catch. She certainly enjoyed making love with Lanzecki, and definitely he exerted an intense fascination on her. Lanzecki had unequivocally separated his professional life from his private one.

"Rani, huh," she murmured to herself as she put her thumb to the door lock. She entered the room, closing the door behind her, and then leaned against it.

Now, in the absence of background sounds, she could hear the resonance in her body, feel it cascading up and down her bones, throbbing in her arteries. The noise between her ears was like a gushing river in full flood. She held out her arms but the static apparently did not affect her, the carrier, or she had exhausted that phenomenon in herself. "Mineral baths! Probably stink of sulfur or something worse."

Immediately she heard the initial *phluggg* as radiant fluid began to flow into the tank in the hygiene room. Wondering why the room computer was on, she opened her mouth to abort the process, when her name issued from the speakers.

"Killashandra Ree?" The bass voice was unmistakably Trag's.

"Yes, Trag?" She switched on vision.

"You have been restored to the active list."

"I'm going off-world as soon as I can arrange transport, Trag."

Expressionless as ever, Trag regarded her. "A lucrative assignment is available to a singer of your status."

"The Optherian manual?" As Trag inclined his head once, Killashandra controlled her surprise. Why was Trag approaching her when Lanzecki had definitely not wanted her to take it?

"You're aware of the details?" For the first time Trag evinced a flicker of surprise.

"Rimbol told me. He also said he wasn't taking it. Was he your first choice?"

Trag regarded her steadily for a moment. "You were the logical first choice, Killashandra Ree, but until an hour ago you were an inactive."

"I was the first choice?"

"Firstly, you are going off-world in any event and do not have sufficient credit to take you past the nearer inhabited systems. Secondly, an extended leave of absence is recommended by Medical. Thirdly, you have already acquired the necessary skills to place white crystal brackets. In the fourth place, your curriculum vitae indicates latent teaching abilities so that training replacement technicians on Optheria is well within your scope."

"Nothing was said about training technicians. Borella and Concera both have considerably more instructional experience than I."

"Borella, Concera, and Gobbain Tekla have not exhibited either the tact or diplomacy requisite to this assignment."

Killashandra was amused that Trag added Gobbain to the list. Had Bajorn told Trag who had inquired about transport to Optheria?

"There are thirty-seven other active Guild members who qualify!"

Trag shook his head slowly twice. "No, Killashandra Ree, it must be you who goes. The Guild needs some information about Optheria—"

"Tactfully and diplomatically extracted? On what subject?"

"Why the Optherian government prohibits interstellar travel to its citizens."

Killashandra let out a whoop of delight. "You mean, why, with their obsession for music, there isn't a single Optherian in the Heptite Guild?"

"That is not the relevant issue, Killashandra. The Federated Sentient Council would be obliged if the Guild's representative would act as an impartial observer, to determine if this restriction is popularly accepted—"

"A Freedom of Choice infringement? But wouldn't that be a matter for—"

Trag held up his hand. "The request asks for an impartial opinion on the *popular* acceptance of the restriction. The FSC acknowledges that isolated individuals might express dissatisfaction, but a complaint has been issued by the Executive Council of the Federated Artists Association."

Killashandra let out a low whistle. The Stellars themselves protested? Well, if Optherian composers and performers were involved, of course the Executive Council would protest. Even if it had taken them decades to do so.

"And since the Guild's representative would certainly come in contact with composers and performers during the course of the assignment, yes, I'd be more than willing to volunteer for that facet." Was that why Lanzecki had been against her going? To protect her from the iron idealism of a parochial Optherian Council? But, as a member of the Heptite Guild, which guaranteed her immunity to local law and restrictions, she could not be detained on any charges. She could be disciplined only by her Guild. That any form of artistry might be limited by law was anathema. "There've been Optherian organs a long time . . ."

"Popular acceptance is the matter under investigation."

Trag was not going to be deflected from the official wording of the request.

"All right, I copy!"

"You'll accept this assignment?"

Killashandra blinked. Did she imagine the eagerness in Trag's voice, the sudden release of tension from his face.

"Trag, there's something you've not told me about this assignment. I warn you, if this turns out to be like the Trundie—"

"Your familiarity with elements of this assignment suggests that you have already done considerable background investigation. I have informed you of the FSC request—"

"Why don't you leave it with me for a little while, Trag," she said, studying his face, "and I'll consider it. Lanzecki gave me the distinct impression that I shouldn't apply for it."

There. She hadn't imagined *that* reaction. Trag was perturbed. He'd been deliberately tempting her, with as subtle a brand of flattery as she'd ever been subjected to. Her respect for the Administration Officer reached a new level for she would never have thought him so devious. He was so completely devoted to Guild and Lanzecki.

"You're asking me without Lanzecki's knowledge?" She did not miss the sudden flare of Trag's nostrils nor the tightening of his jaw muscles. "Why, Trag?"

"Your name was first on the list of qualified available singers."

"Stuff it, Trag. Why me?"

"The interests of the Heptite Guild are best served by your acceptance." A hint of desperation edged Trag's voice.

"You object to the relationship between Lanzecki and me?" She had no way of knowing in what way Trag had adapted to Ballybran's symbiont. He kept to himself, seeking no companionship at all. He seemed to respect Lanzecki enormously, but so did others. Could Trag be jealous of her close association to the Guild Master? Was he likely to remove a rival if one appeared?

"No." Trag's denial was accompanied by a ripple of his facial muscles. "Up till now, he has not allowed personal consideration to interfere with his judgment."

"How has he done that?" Killashandra was genuinely perplexed. Trag was not complaining that Lanzecki had awarded her another valuable assignment. He was perturbed because he hadn't. "I don't follow you."

Trag stared at her for such a long moment she wondered if the screen had malfunctioned.

"Even if you just go to Rani, it will not be far enough away or long enough. Lanzecki is long overdue for a field trip, Killashandra Ree. Because of you. Your body is so full of resonance he's been able to delay. But your resonance is not enough. If you're not available, he will be forced to cut crystal again and rejuvenate his body and his symbiont. If you have a real regard for the man, go. Now. Before it's too late for him."

Killashandra stared back at Trag, trying to absorb the various implications—foremost was the realization that Lanzecki was genuinely attached to her. She felt a wave of exultation and tenderness that quite overwhelmed her for a moment. She'd never considered that possibility. Nor its corollary: that Lanzecki would be reluctant to cut crystal because he might forget his attachment. A man who'd been in the Guild as long as he had would be subject to considerable memory loss in the Ranges. Had he learned his duties as Guild Master so thoroughly that the knowledge was as ingrained in him as the rules and regulations in a crystal-mad brain like Moksoon's? It was not Lanzecki's face that suddenly dominated her thoughts, but the crisscross tracings of old crystal scars on his body, the inexplicable pain that occasionally darkened his eyes. Antona's cryptic admission about singers who could not break crystal thrall echoed in her head. She puzzled at the assortment of impressions and suddenly understood. She sagged against the back and arms of her chair for support. Dully she wondered if Trag and Antona had been in collusion. Would the subject of crystal thrall have come up at that lunch hour even if Rimbol had not arrived?

There was little doubt in Killashandra's mind that Antona knew of Lanzecki's circumstances. And she did doubt that the woman knew about their relationship. She also doubted that Trag would mention so personal an aspect of the Guild Master's business. Why couldn't Lanzecki have been just another singer, like herself? Why did he have to be Guild Master and far too valuable, too essential, to be placed in jeopardy by unruly affection?

Why, the situation has all the trappings of an operatic tragedy! A genuine one-solution tragedy, where hero and heroine both lose out. For she could now admit to herself that she was as deeply attached to Lanzecki as he was to her. She covered her face with both hands, clasping them to cheeks gone chill.

She thought of Antona's advice, to put down everything—including love; Killashandra writhed in her chair. Antona couldn't have known that Killashandra would so shortly be faced with such an emotional decision. Which, Killashandra realized with a flicker of ironic amusement, was one to be as deeply and quickly interred and forgotten as possible.

One thing was sure—no matter how long the journey to Optheria, it wouldn't be long enough to forget all the wonderful moments she had enjoyed with Lanzecki the man. She squeezed her eyes shut against the pain of encountering him when she returned, and, perhaps, finding no recollection of her in his dark eyes. Nor feel his lips again on her hand . . .

"Killashandra?" Trag's voice recalled her to his watching presence on the viewscreen.

"Now that I know the ramifications of the assignment, Trag, I can hardly refuse it." Her flippant tone was belied by the tears rolling down her cheeks. "Do you go with him to break the thrall?" she asked when her throat opened enough to speak again.

At any other time, she would have counted Trag's startled look as a signal of victory. Maybe if she found someone to sing with, she would also find such a passionate and unswerving loyalty. She must remember that.

"When's the next shuttle to Shanganagh, Trag?" She rubbed her cheeks dry with an urgent impatience. "Tell Lanzecki—tell him . . . crystal resonance drove me to it." As she spun off her chair, she heard herself give a laugh that verged on the hysterical. "That's no more than the truth, isn't it?" Driven by the need just to *do* something, she began to cram clothes into her carisak.

"The shuttle leaves in ten minutes, Killashandra Ree."

"That's great." She struggled to secure the fastenings on the bulging sak. "Will you see me aboard again, Trag? That seems to be your especial duty, rushing me onto shuttles to Shanganagh for unusual assignments all over the galaxy." She was unable to resist taunting Trag. He was the author of her misery and she was being strong and purposeful in a moment of deep personal sacrifice and loss. She glanced up at the screen and saw that it was dark. "Coward!"

She hauled open her door. She decided that slamming it was a waste of a grand gesture. She had just enough time to get to the shuttle.

"Exit Killashandra. Quietly. Up stage!"

Chapter 3

Trag had timed Killashandra's departure well for she and the three crates of white crystal were on board a freighter bound for the Rappahoe Transfer Satellite within four hours of their confrontation. She didn't think about it at the time for she was totally immersed in the strong emotions of self-sacrifice, remorse for her effect on Lanzecki, and a perverse need to redeem herself in Trag's eyes. Even though she had permitted herself to be borne on the tide of circumstance, she kept hoping that Lanzecki might somehow get wind of her defection and abort the mission.

To insure that her whereabouts were known, she rummaged through the shopping area of Shanganagh Base like a mach storm. She bought necessities, fripperies, and foodstuffs, accompanying each purchase with a running dialogue at the top of her voice and spelling out her name for every credit entry. No one could fail to know the whereabouts of Killashandra Ree. After adding a few items of essential clothing to the garments she had stuffed into her carisak, her keen instinct for survival asserted itself in the base's victuallers. She had vivid memories of the monotonously nutritious diet on the Selkite freighter and the stodge supplied by the Trundimoux cruiser. She did have to consider her palate and digestive system.

Sadly, no deferential shopkeeper tapped her on the arm to tell her of an urgent call from the Guild Master. In fact, people seemed to keep their distance from her. A chance glimpse of her gaunt, harrowed face in a mirror provided one explanation—she'd have needed no cosmetic aids to play the part of any one of a number of harried, despairing, insane heroines. At that point her humor briefly reasserted itself. She had often thought that the make-up recommended for, say, Lucia, or Lady Macbeth, or Testuka and Isolde was totally exaggerated. Now, at last having had personal experiences with the phenomenon of losing one's great love through selfless sacrifice, she could appreciate the effect which grief could have on one's outward appearance. She looked awful! So she purchased two brilliant multihued floating kaftans of Beluga spider-silk, and hastily added their fingerlength cases to her bulging carisak, then a travel-case of fashionable cosmetics. She'd nine days to travel on the first freighter and it would only be civil to remedy her appearance.

Then the boarding call for the *Pink Tulip Sparrow* was broadcast and she had no option but to proceed to the loading bay. In an effort to delay the inevitable, she walked at a funereal pace down the access ramp.

"Singer, we've got to get moving! Now, please, hurry along."

She made an appearance of haste but when the Mate tried to take her arm and hurry her into the lock, her body arched in resistance. Abruptly he let go, staring at her with an expression of puzzled shock—his arms were bare, and the hairs on them stood erect.

"I'm awaiting purchases from Stores." Killashandra was so desperate for a last-minute reprieve that any delay seemed reasonable.

"There!" The Mate conveyed frustrated disgust and impatience as he pointed to a stack of odd-sized parcels littering the passageway.

"The crystals?"

"Cartons all racked and tacked in the special cargo hold." He made a move as if to grab her arm and yank her aboard, but jingled his hands with frustration instead. "We've got to make way. Shanganagh Authority imposes heavy fines for missed departure windows. And don't tell me, Crystal Singer, that you've got enough credit to pay 'em." Abruptly she abandoned all hope that Lanzecki, like the legendary heroes of yore, would rescue her at the last moment from her act of boundless self-sacrifice. She stepped aboard the freighter. The airlock closed with such speed that the heavy external hatch brushed against her heels. The ship was moving from the docking bay before the Mate could lead her out of the lock and close the secondary iris behind them.

Killashandra experienced an almost overpowering urge to wrench open the airlock and leap into the blessed oblivion of space. But as she had deplored such extravagant and melodramatic actions in performances of historical tragedy, integrity prevented suicide despite the extreme anguish which tormented her. Besides, she had no excuse for causing the death of the Mate who seemed not to be suffering at all.

"Take me to my cabin, please." She turned too quickly, stumbled over the many packages in the passageway and had to grab the Mate's shoulder, to regain her balance. Ordinarily she would have cursed her clumsiness, and apologized but cursing was undignified and inappropriate to her mood. From the pile, she chose two packages with the victualler's logo, and waved negligently at the remainder. "The rest may be brought to my cabin whenever convenient."

The Mate wended a careful passage through the tumbled parcels as he passed her to lead the way. She noticed that the hair on his neck, indeed the dark body hairs that escaped the sleeveless top he wore, were piercing the thin stuff, all at right angles to his body.

This was no longer an amusing manifestation. Just another fascinating aspect of crystal singing that you *don't* hear about in that allegedly Complete Disclosure! It should be renamed "A Short Introduction to what's really in store for you!" One day, no doubt, she would be in the appropriately damaged state to give All the Facts.

The Mate had stopped, flattening himself against the bulkhead, and gestured toward an open door.

"Your quarters, Crystal Singer. Your thumbprint will secure the door." He touched his fingers to a spot above his right eye and disappeared around the corner as if chased by Galormis.

Killashandra pressed her thumb hard into the door lock. She was pleasantly surprised by the size of the cabin. Not as big as any accommodation she had enjoyed on Ballybran but larger than that closet on the Trundimoux cruiser. She slid the door shut, locked it, and put the packages down on the narrow writing ledge. She looked at the bunk, strapped up to the wall in its daytime position. Suddenly she was light-headed with fatigue. Strong emotion is as exhausting as cutting crystal, she thought. She released the bunk and stretched herself out. She exhaled on a long shuddering sob and tried to relax her taut muscles.

The hum of the ship's crystal drive was a counterpoint to the resonance between her ears, and both sounds traveled in waves up and down her bones. At first her mind did a descant, weaving an independent melody through the bass and alto, but the rhythm suggested a three-syllable word—Lan-zec-ki—so she changed to an idiot two-note dissonance and eventually fell asleep.

Once she got over the initial buoyancy of self-sacrifice aboard the *Pink Tulip Sparrow*, Killashandra vacillated between fury at Trag and wallowing in despair at her "Loss." Until she concluded that her misery was caused by Lanzecki—after all, if he hadn't made such a determined play for her affections, *he* wouldn't have become so attached to her, nor she to him, and she wouldn't be on a stinking tub of a freighter. Well, yes, she probably would. *If* all Trag had told her about the Optherian assignment was true. In no mood to be civil to either the crew or the other passengers, she stayed in her cabin the entire trip.

At Rappahoe Transfer Point, she boarded a second freighter, newer and less unpleasant than the *Pink Tulip Sparrow*, with a lounge for the ten passengers it carried. Eight were male and each of them, including the only attached man, stood quickly at her entrance. Plainly they were aware that she was a crystal singer. Equally apparent was the fact that they were willing to put scruples aside to discover the truth of the space flot about singers. Three of them desisted after their first hour of propinquity. Two more during the first evening's meal. To have one's hair constantly standing on end seems like a little thing but so is a drop of water patiently wearing away a stone. The bald Argulian was the most persistent. He actually grabbed her in the narrow companionway, pressing her close to his body in an ardent embrace. She didn't have to struggle for release.

He dropped his arms and slid away, flushing and trembling. "You're shocking." He scrubbed his arms and brushed urgently at those portions of his body which had been in contact with her. "That's not a nice thing to do to a friendly fellow like me." He looked aggrieved.

"It was all your idea." Killashandra continued on to her quarters. *And another singer legend is spawned!*

The female captain of the third freighter, which she boarded at Melorica, bluntly informed her that, under no circumstances, would she tolerate any short term disruption of the pairing in her all-female crew.

"That's quite all right, captain. I've taken a vow of celibacy."

"What for?" the captain demanded, raking Killashandra with an appraising scrutiny. "Religious or professional?"

"Neither. I shall be true to one man till I die." Killashandra was pleased with the infinitesimal tremor of pathos in her voice.

"No man's worth that, honey!" The captain's disgust was genuine.

With a sad sigh, Killashandra asked if the ship's library had much in the way of programs for single players and retired to her quarters, which had been getting smaller with each ship. Fortunately this was the shortest leg of her space hike to Bernard's World.

By the time Killashandra reached the Bernard's World Transfer Satellite, she entertained doubts about Trag's candor. The journey seemed incredibly long for a modern space voyage, even allowing for the fact that freighters are generally slower than cruisers or liners. She'd logged five weeks of interstellar travel and must somehow endure another five before she reached the Optherian system. Could Trag have done a subtle job recruiting her because no other singer would consider the assignment? No, the fee was too good—besides, Borella, Concera, and Gobbain had been trying for it.

In the orbital position of a small moon, the Transfer Satellite inscribed a graceful forty-eight-hour path about the brilliant blue-and-green jewel of a planet. The satellite was a marvel of modern engineering, with docking and repair facilities capable of handling FSC cruisers and the compound ships of the Exploration and Evaluation Corps, felicitously sited at the intersection of nine major space routes. Fresh fruit and vegetables were grown in its extensive gardens, and high quality protein was manufactured in its catering division: sufficient in quantity and diversity to please the most exacting clients. Stores of basic nutrients were available for five other star-roving species. Additional nodules accommodated small industries and a thriving medical research laboratory and hospital. In the transient quadrant, there were playing fields, free-ball and free-fall courts, spacious gardens, and a zoo housing a selection of the smaller life forms from nine nearby star systems. As Killashandra perused the directory in her room, she noted with considerable delight that a radiant fluid tank was one of the amenities in the gymnasium arc.

Although she was certain that there had been some decrease of the resonance in her body, she ached for the total relief provided by an hour or so in the radiant fluid. She booked the room and, fed up with the reaction of "ordinary" people to her proximity, took the service route to it. She had also decided that she was not going to spend the five weeks on the cruise ship enhancing crystal singer myths. Just then her bruised and aching heart had no room for affection, much less passion. And crystal neutralized passing fancy or pure lust.

If she could reduce the hair-standing phenomenon to a minimum, she intended to adopt a new personality: that of an aspiring young musician traveling to Optheria's Summer Festival, and required by economics to travel off-season and on the cheaper freight lines. She had spent long hours preparing the right make-up for the part, affecting the demeanor of the very young, inexperienced adult and recalling the vocabulary and idiom of her student days. So much had transpired since that carefree time that it was like studying for an historic role. In such rehearsals, Killashandra found that time passed quickly. Now if her wretched body would cooperate . . .

After nine hours of immersions over the course of three days, Killashandra achieved her goal. She acquired a suitable modest wardrobe. On the fifth day on the Bernard's World Transfer Station, in wide-eyed and breathless obedience to the boarding call, she presented her ticket to the purser of the FSPS Liner *Athena*, and was assigned a seat on the second of the two shuttles leaving the station to catch the liner on its parabolic route through the star system. The shuttle trip was short and its single forward viewscreen was dominated by the massive orange hulk of the *Athena*. Most of the passengers were awed by the spectacle, babbling about their expectations of the voyage, the hardships they had endured to save for the experience, their hopes for their destinations, anxieties about home-bound relatives. Their chatter irritated Killashandra and she began to wish she had not posed as a student. As the respected member of a prestigious Guild, she would have been assigned to the star-class shuttle.

However, she'd made the choice and was stuck with it, so she grimly disembarked onto the economy level of the *Athena* and located her single cabin in the warren. This room was the same size as her Fuertan student apartment but, she told herself philosophically, she wouldn't be so likely to step out of character. Anyway, only the catering and lounge facilities differed with the price of the ticket: the leisure decks were unrestricted.

The *Athena*, a new addition to the far-flung cruise line Galactica, Federated, was on the final leg of its first sweep round this portion of the Galaxy. Some of the *oh*'s and *ah*'s that Killashandra breathed were quite genuine as she and other economy class passengers were escorted on the grand tour of the liner. A self-study complex included not only the schoolroom for transient minors but small rehearsal rooms where a broad range of musical instruments could be rented—with the notable exceptions of a portable Optherian organ—a miniature theater, and several large workshops for handicrafters. To her astonishment, the gymnasium complex boasted three small radiant fluid tanks. Their guide explained that this amenity eased aching muscles, overcame space nausea, and was an economical substitute for a water bath since the fluid could be purified after every use. He reminded people that water was still a rationed commodity and that two liters was the daily allowance. Each cabin had a console and vdr, linked to the ship's main computer bank which, their escort proudly told them, was the very latest FBM 9000 series with a more comprehensive library of entertainment recordings than many planets possessed. The FSPS *Athena* was a true goddess of the spaceways.

During the first forty-eight hours of the voyage, while the *Athena* was clearing the Bernard's World system and accelerating to transfer speed, Killashandra deliberately remained aloof, in her pose of shy student, from the general mingling of the other passengers. She was amused and educated by the pairings, the shiftings and realignments that occurred during this period. She made private wagers with herself as to which of the young women would pair off with which of the young men. Subtler associations developed among the older unattached element.

To Killashandra's jaundiced eye, none of the male economy passengers, young or old, looked interesting enough to cultivate. There was one absolutely stunning man, with the superb carriage of a dancer or professional athlete, but his classic features were too perfect to project a hint of his character or temperament. He made his rounds, a slight smile curving his perfect lips, well aware that he had only to nod to capture whichever girl, or girls, he fancied. Lanzecki might not have been handsome in the currently fashionable form but his face was carved by character and he exuded a magnetism that was lacking in the glorious young man. Nevertheless, Killashandra toyed with the idea of luring the perfect young man to her side; rejection might improve his character no end. But to achieve that end she would have had to discard her shy student role.

She discovered an unforgivable lack in the *Athena*'s appointments the first time she dialed for Yarran beer. It was not available, although nine other brews were. In an attempt to find a palatable substitute, she was trying the third, watching the energetic perform a square dance, when she realized someone was standing at her table.

"May I join you?" The man held up beakers of beer, each a different shade. "I noticed that you were sampling the brews. Shall we combine our efforts?"

He had a pleasant voice, his ship-suit was well cut to a tall lean frame, his features were regular but without a distinguished imperfection; his medium length dark hair complimented a space tan. There was, however, something about his eyes and a subtle strength to his chin that arrested Killashandra's attention.

"I'm not a joiner myself," he said, pointing one beaker at the gyrating dancers, "and I noticed that you aren't, so I thought we might keep each other company."

Killashandra indicated the chair opposite her.

"My name is Corish von Mittelstern." He put his beers down nearer hers as he repositioned the chair to permit him to watch the dancers. Killashandra turned ever so slightly away from him, not all that confident of the remission of resonance in her body, though why she made the instinctive adjustment she didn't know. "I hail from Rheingarten in the Beta Jungische system. I'm bound for Optheria."

"Why, so am I!" She raised her beer in token of a hand clasp. "Killashandra Ree of Fuerte. I'm—I'm a music student."

"The Summer Festival." Then a puzzled expression crossed Corish's face. "But they have a Fuertan brew—"

"Oh, that old stuff. I might have to travel off-season and economy to get to Optheria but I'm certainly not going to waste the opportunities of trying everything new on the *Athena*."

Corish smiled urbanely. "Is this your first interstellar trip?"

"Oh, yes. But I know a lot about traveling. My brother is a supercargo. On the *Blue Swan Delta*. And when Mother told him that I was making the voyage, he sent me all kinds of advice"—and Killashandra managed a tinkling giggle—"and warnings."

Corish smiled perfunctorily. "Don't ignore that sort of advice. Fuerte, huh? That's a long way to come."

"I think I've spent half my life traveling already," Killashandra said expansively while she tried to compute how long she ought to have been traveling if her port of embarkation had been Fuerte. She hadn't done enough homework. Though she couldn't imagine that Corish would know if she erred. She took a long sip of her beer. "This is a Bellemere, but it's too sour for me."

"The best beer in the galaxy is a Yarran brew."

"Yarran?" She regarded Corish with keener interest. If Corish came from Beta Jungische, he was a long way from a regular supply of Yarran beer. Killashandra's curiosity rustled awake.

"The Yarran brewmasters have no peers. Surely your brother has mentioned Yarran beer?"

"Well, now, it's possible that he has," Killashandra said slowly, as if searching her memory. "But then, he told me so much that I can't remember half." She was about to giggle again and then decided that, not only did her giggle nauseate herself but it might repel Corish and she wanted to satisfy this flicker of curiosity about him. "Why are you traveling to Optheria?"

"Family business, sort of. An uncle of mine went for a visit and decided to become a citizen. We need his signature on some family papers. We've written several times and had no reply. Now, he could be dead but I have to have the proper certification if he is, and his print and fist on the documents if he isn't."

"And you have to come all the way from Beta Jungische for that?"

"Well, there's a lot of credit involved and this isn't a bad way to go." He enscribed a half circle with his beaker, including the ship as well as the dancers, and smiled at Killashandra over the rim as he sipped. "This Pilsner's not all that bad, really. What have you there?"

She went along with Corish's adroit change of subject and with the beer sampling. Although singing crystal brought with it an inexhaustible ability to metabolize alcohol without noticeable affect, she feigned the symptoms of intoxication as she confided her fake history to the Jungian, whenever necessary embellishing her actual experiences at the Arts Complex. Thus Corish learned that she was a keyboard specialist, in her final year of training, with high hopes that the Optherian Festival would provide her with sufficient data for an honors recommendation. She had credentials of sufficiently high caliber to gain entrance into the Federal Music Conservatory on Optheria where she hoped she'd be allowed to play on an Optherian organ.

"An hour is all I need," she told Corish, blinking in the simulation of advancing inebriation, "for the purposes of my dissertation."

"From what I hear about their precious organ, you'd be lucky to get within spitting distance."

"Even half an hour."

"I hear that only Federal licensed musicians are allowed in the organ loft."

"Well, they'll have to make an exception in my case because I have a special letter from Fuerte's President—he's a friend of my family's. *And* a sealed note from Stellar Performer Dalkay Mogorog . . ." She paused deferentially at the mention of that august personality, who was evidently unknown to Corish, "and I'm sure they'll concede. Even fifteen minutes?" she asked as Corish continued to shake his head. "Well, they'll just have to! I haven't come all this way to be refused. I'm a serious student of keyboard instruments. I won a scholarship to the Federated Sentient Planets Conservatory on Terra. I've been permitted to play on a Mozartian clavier, a Handelian spinet, Purcell's harpsichord, a Bach organ, and a Beethoven pianoforte and—" She hiccuped to mask the fact that she was running out of prestigious composers and instruments.

"So? Which beer do you prefer now?"

"Huh?"

Corish solicitously conducted her to her cabin and arranged her on her bunk. As he drew a light blanket over her, she felt the static leap from her shoulder to his hands. He hesitated briefly, then quietly left.

As Killashandra gave him time to leave her passageway, she reviewed her "performance" and decided that she hadn't dropped from character, even if he had. It was rather nice of him, too, not to have "taken advantage" of her. When she felt secure, she slipped from her cabin and down to the gymnasium level. At that hour, it was empty and she enjoyed an hour's luxuriating in the radiant fluid.

They met the next morning at the breakfast hour, Corish solicitously inquiring after her health.

"Did I fall asleep on you?" she asked with wide-eyed dismay.

"Not at all. I just saw to it that you were safely in your own cabin before you did."

Critically, she held her hands out in front of her. "Well, at least, they're steady enough to practice."

"You're going to practice?"

"I practice every day."

"May I listen?"

"Well . . . it can be quite boring—I have to spend at least an hour on the preliminary finger exercises and scales before I can do any interesting music . . ."

"If I'm bored, I'll leave."

As she led the way to the practice rooms, she wondered if she had slipped up in her characterization. Why else should he be curious enough to want to listen to her practice?

Killashandra was rather chuffed to discover that the old drills came easily to her fingers as she addressed the keyboard with every semblance of true authority. Corish departed after fifteen minutes but she left nothing to chance and played on, making remarkably few errors for someone who had not played in three years.

As she had established her credentials with him, he continued to project the image of an amiable young man on a journey to protect family interests. He sought her out at mealtimes, helped her evade the organizers of team sports, directed her investigations of the caterer's potential with the amused tolerance of the mature traveler, and accompanied her to shipboard activities. On one or two occasions, she had the urge to shock him with her true identity just to see how he might react, but she repressed that whimsy.

Then, after a particularly bibulous evening, when she had taken an extra long radiant bath, she encountered him in the gymnasium. He was sweating profusely, working out against a hefty weight on the apparatus with apparent ease. Stripped as he was for the exercise, Killashandra could appreciate that Corish's lean frame was suspiciously well muscled and fine tuned for his public image.

"I didn't know you were a gymnast!"

"It's only smart to keep fit, Killashandra Ree." He whipped a towel about his shoulders and mopped his face. "Where've you been?"

Killashandra managed a blush of embarrassment, dropping her eyes and affecting mortification.

"I tried that radiant stuff. In the tank," and she pointed vaguely in the right direction. "That blond girl from Kachachurian was saying that it was good for hangovers!" She kicked at the apparatus base with her toe, eyes still downcast.

"Well, is it?"

"I think it is." She allowed some doubt in her tone. "At least that awful spinning has stopped . . . and the nausea!" She put one hand to her head and the other to her stomach. "I think I may have to go back to Fuertan beer. I could always drink as much of that as I wanted. Or is it something to do with traveling in space? My brother did say something about that . . ." She looked up at Corish. "Isn't this a funny time to be working out?"

"That's how I work alcohol out of my system," Corish said, pulling on his shirt. "I'll see you back to your cabin. You really shouldn't be wandering about the ship at this hour. Someone might get the wrong impression about you."

As Killashandra permitted him to escort her back, she wondered why he was rushing her out of the gym. She felt she had deftly accounted for her presence. And naively accepted his explanation. Safely returned to her cabin, she agreed to meet him as usual for breakfast the next morning, and dutifully went to bed.

Waiting for sleep, she reflected on his extraordinary fitness and the stealth in which he kept it. Could Corish possibly be an FSP agent? It struck her as unlikely that the Federation would choose to send only one observer—an inexperienced one at that—into a planetary society that was being investigated. She chuckled to think that, out of the eighteen hundred passengers and crew on the *Athena*, Corish should attach himself to her. Of course, in her eager-student guise, she might constitute an integral part of *his* shipboard cover. Unless he had been advised of her extra assignment by his superiors. If he was a Federal agent, he would also know the capabilities of crystal singers, and the subtler ways to identify them.

No matter! In her concentrated efforts to recall her days as an impecunious and ardent music student, she had been able to shelve the more recent, painful episode. Seriously now, Killashandra considered Antona's advice to record incidents in detail. Who knew when she might find it necessary to adopt the role of the student again?

Chapter 4

As the *Athena* plunged toward the Optherian primary for the deflected hyperbolic pass that would bring it close to the one inhabited planet of the system, the passengers who were disembarking went through the rituals of leave-taking from their shipboard acquaintances. That strange magic of voyaging which could make total strangers into confidantes and lovers had lost none of its potency in the space age.

As they waited in the airlock for the shuttle that would take them to the surface, Killashandra found herself prattling on at Corish about how they must meet and share their adventures: that they couldn't part and never meet again while they were on the same planet. She'd want to know how he'd made out with his uncle and she hoped she'd be able to tell him of her success, invading the Optherian musical hierarchy. Of course that sort of chatter was in character with her role. What astonished Killashandra was that she meant what she said.

"That's very sweet of you, Killa," Corish replied, patting her shoulder in a condescending fashion that returned her instantly to her own personality.

"If I don't get a place at the Music Center hostel, I'll go to the Piper Facility," she said, ducking away from his hand as she fumbled with the fastening on the side pocket of her carisak. She tendered the small plastic card distributed by the Facility with its communit codes. "The Optherian Traveler's Guide says they'll take messages for visitors. You could leave word for me there." She smiled up at him with tremulous wistfulness. "I know that once we leave Optheria, we'll never meet again, Corish, but at least while we're still on the same planet, I was hoping we could stay friends." She broke off, ducking her head and dabbing at her eyes which, on cue, had filled with moisture. She let him have just a confirming glimpse of her teary face, although why she was prolonging their association, she hadn't a notion. One can get too wrapped up in role-playing.

"I promise you, Killa, that I'll leave word at the Piper for you." And Corish put a finger under her chin and lifted her head to his gaze. He had a rather engaging half-smile, she thought, though it wasn't a patch on Lanzecki's. She managed to squeeze out a few more tears on the strength of that comparison. "No need for tears, Killa."

Just then the shuttle clanged against the *Athena*'s side and conversation became impossible with the noise of lock engagement and the excited crescendo of farewells. Then crewmen were officiously directing passengers to move to the port side of the lock. Killashandra was crammed rather tightly between two large men and separated from Corish by another sideways push.

"What's the delay?" one of her cushions demanded.

"They're loading some crates," was the indignant reply. "Must be something special. There're seals and impregtape all over them."

"I shall complain to the Cruise Agent. I was under the impression that people got preference over commodities on this Line!"

As suddenly as it had begun, the press eased off and everyone was shuffling toward the ramp into the shuttle. Killashandra didn't see Corish among the passengers already seated but she couldn't fail to miss three large foam boxes that contained the white crystal, for they occupied the first three rows of seats on the shuttle's starboard side.

"They must be immensely valuable," the first cushion-man said. "Whatever could it be? Optherians don't import much."

"Too right," his companion said in an aggrieved tone. "Why those are Heptite Guild seals."

The shuttle attendant had taken complete control of seating arrangements, peremptorily filling the rows as he backed down the main aisle. He gestured Killashandra to an inside seat and the two cushions obediently settled in the next two. She caught a brief glimpse of Corish as he passed, but he was assigned a seat on the other side of the aisle.

"Not wasting any time, are they?" the first man said.

"Have none to waste in a parabolic orbit," his friend replied.

"There mustn't have been any outgoing passengers."

"Probably not. Optherians don't leave their planet and the tourist season hasn't really started."

A rather ominous rumbling, issuing from the floor plates, startled them. This was quickly followed by additional metallic complaints, causing further vibrations under their feet.

Two distinct thuds signaled the closing of the cargo bays. Then Killashandra felt the air compress as the main passenger lock was shut and secured. Through the skin of the hull beside her, she heard the snick of the grapple release so she was prepared for the stomach-wrenching motion of the shuttle's falling away from the *Athena*. Her seatmates were not and gasped in reaction, clutching the arm rests as the shuttle's engines took hold and pushed the passengers into the foam of their seats.

The transfer from liner to planetary surface was a relatively short run, though Killashandra's seatmates complained bitterly about the discomfort and duration all the way down. Killashandra accounted the landing smooth but the two cushions found fault with that as well, so she was immensely grateful when the port opened again, flooding the shuttle with the crisp clean cool air of Optheria. She inhaled deeply, clearing her lungs of the *Athena*'s recycled air. For all the craft's modern amenities, it had not quite solved the age-old problem of refreshing air without the taint of deodorizers.

No sooner had the first passengers filed into the arrival area than the public address system began a recorded announcement, scrolling through the same message in all major Federated Planets languages. Passengers were requested to have travel documents ready for inspection by Port Authorities. Please to form a line in the appropriately marked alphabetic or numeric queues. Aliens requiring special life support systems or supplies would please contact a uniformed attendant. Visitors with health problems were to present themselves, immediately after Clearance, to the Port Authority Medical Officer. It was the hope of the Tourist Bureau of Optheria that all visitors would thoroughly enjoy their holiday on the planet.

Killashandra was relieved to see that she would be able to present her i.d. in some privacy, for the Inspectors presided in security booths. Those waiting their turn in the queue could not observe the process. She kept glancing to the far right of the line where Corish should be waiting but he was not immediately visible. She caught sight of him just as it was her turn to approach the Inspector.

Killashandra suppressed a malicious grin as she slid her arm and its i.d. bracelet under the visiplate. The blank expression of the Inspector's square face underwent a remarkable change at the sight of the Heptite Seal on his screen. With one hand he pressed a red button on the terminal in front of him and with the other urgently beckoned her to proceed. Quitting the booth, he insisted on relieving her of her carisak.

"Please, no fuss," Killashandra said.

"Gracious Guildmember," the Inspector began effusively, "we have been so concerned. The cabin reserved for you on the *Athena*—"

"I traveled economy."

"But you're a Heptite Guildmember!"

"There are times, Inspector," Killashandra said, bending close to him and touching his arm, "when discretion requires that one travel incognito." The hair stood up on the back of his hand. She sighed.

"Oh, I see." And clearly he did not. He unconsciously smoothed the hair back down.

They had walked the short distance to the next portal, which slid apart to reveal a welcoming committee of four, three men and a woman, slightly breathless. "The Guildmember has arrived!" The Inspector's triumphant announcement left the distinct impression that he himself had somehow conjured her appearance.

Killashandra stared apprehensively at them. They had a disconcerting resemblance to each other, not only a sameness of height and build but of coloring and feature. Even their voices were pitched in the same sonorous timbre. She blinked, thinking it might be some trick of the soft yellow sunshine pouring in from the main reception area. Then she gave herself a little shake: all were government employees, but could any bureaucracy, Optherian or other, hire people on the basis of their uniform appearance?

"Welcome to Optheria, Guildmember Ree," the Inspector said, beaming as he ushered her past the portal, which whispered shut behind them.

"Welcome, Killashandra Ree, I am Thyrol," the first and oldest man said, taking one step toward her and bowing.

"Welcome, Killashandra Ree, I am Pirinio," said the second, following the example of the first.

In unvarying ceremony, Polabod and Mirbethan made themselves known to her. Had they practiced long?

"I am truly welcomed," she said with a gracious semibow. "The crystal? It was aboard the shuttle."

All four looked to her right, left hands rising from their sides at the same instant, to indicate the float appearing through a second portal. Null-gravs suspended float and cartons above the gold-flecked marble floor but proper guidance apparently required six attendants, each wearing an anxious frown of concentration. A seventh man directed their efforts, dancing from one side to the other to be certain that nothing impeded their progress. These citizens of Optheria were reassuringly mismatched in size, form, and feature.

"We four," Thyrol began, indicating his companions with a twist of his hand, "are to be your guides and mentors during your stay in Optheria. You have only to state your wishes and preferences and we—Optheria— will provide."

The four bowed again, like a wave from right to left. The Inspector beside her also bowed. Thyrol lifted one eyebrow and the Inspector, bowing again as he surrendered Killashandra's carisak to Pirinio, formally receded until the portal hissed apart and then closed. Killashandra wondered if the Inspector's euphoria would extend to lesser breeds, those without Guild affiliation, when he resumed his booth in Immigration.

"If you will step this way, Guildmember Ree." Thyrol made another of his graceful gestures.

When she moved to walk beside him, he altered his stride to keep a deferential meter from her. The others fell in behind. Killashandra shrugged, accepting the protocol. Not having to chat with her escort gave her a chance to glance about the shuttle port. The facility was functional and decorated with murals of Life on Optheria: the main attraction of the Summer Festival—the organ—was not depicted. Nor did the vaulted arrivals hall appear to have any catering areas apart from one narrow bank for beverage dispensing. Conspicuous by their absence were curio and souvenir booths. Not even a ticket bank was to be seen. And only one lounge area. At the wide exit, the doors sighed aside for Killashandra and Thyrol, who quickly walked down the wide shallow steps to a broad, intricately patterned apron of flat stones. Beyond was the roadway where the crew had just finished stowing the three foam crates in a large ground effect machine.

Suddenly an arc of light flashed on behind Killashandra and a muted alarm sounded. Guards materialized from inconspicuous booths on both sides of the main entrance and approached the three Optherians of the reception committee who were walking behind Killashandra and Thyrol.

"Please do not be disconcerted, Guildmember Ree." Thyrol waved to the guards and they retreated back into their stations. The arc of light disappeared.

"What was that all about?"

"Merely a security precaution."

"For my leaving the shuttle port?"

Thyrol cleared his throat. "Actually, for Optherians leaving the shuttle port."

"Leaving?"

"This is our vehicle, Guildmember," Thyrol said, smoothly urging her across the flagstone plaza. She allowed herself to be diverted because it was obvious that, whoever *left* the shuttle port was first obliged to *enter*: the alarm would work in both directions. But how could the device distinguish Optherians from other humans? No mutation had been mentioned in her perusal of the *Encyclopedia Galactica* entry for the planet: most ingenious for a warning device to differentiate between residents and nonresidents. But surely it got a bit noisy and confusing when Optherians were escorting tourists to the shuttle port. Or was that the reason for this broad flagstone area? She would have to check on FSP regulations about security measures restricting citizens of their planets.

As her vehicle glided forward, the first of the shuttle passengers began to emerge. On cue, fat accommodation buses filed out of the parking area to the flagstone curb. Craning her neck slightly, Killashandra took due note of the fact that the security system did not respond to the foreigners' exits.

Already the vehicle was climbing out of the valley which contained the shuttle port and the clutter of maintenance buildings. The place looked bleakly ordered and preternaturally neat in comparison to what Killashandra recalled of Fuerte's busy space port. Perhaps when the tourist season started . . . Even the clumps of trees and bushes which softened the harder lines of the buildings had a regulated look. Killashandra wondered how often the plantings had to be replaced. Shuttle emanations had a disastrous effect on most vegetation.

"Are you comfortable, Guildmember?" Mirbethan asked from her seat behind Killashandra.

"Of necessity the shuttle port was placed close to the City," Pirinio took up the conversation, "but is screened by these hills which also absorb much of the noise and bustle."

Noise and bustle, his tone of voice told Killashandra, were the unpleasant concomitants of space travel. "How wise of you," Killashandra replied.

"Optherian's founding fathers planned for every contingency," Thyrol said smugly. "No effort has been spared to conserve our planet's natural beauty."

The vehicle had reached the top of the gap; and Killashandra had an unimpeded view of the broader valley below them, in which nestled the felicitous arrangement of pastel colored buildings, domes, and round towers that comprised Optheria's capital settlement, known as the City. From that height, the impressive view drew a surprised exclamation from Killashandra.

"It is breathtaking!" Thyrol chose to interpret her response his way.

Beautiful was a fair adjective, Killashandra thought, but breathtaking, no! Even at that distance something was too prim and proper about the City for her taste.

"None of the indigenous trees and bushes were removed, you see," Thyrol explained, gesturing with his whole hand rather than a single finger, "when the City was constructed, so that the natural, unspoiled landscape could be retained."

"And the river and that lake? Are they natural features?"

"But of course. Nature is not distorted on Optheria."

"Which is as it should be," Polabod added. "The entire valley is as it was when Man first landed on Optheria."

"The City Architect planned all the buildings and dwellings in the unoccupied spaces," Mirbethan said proudly.

"How exceedingly clever!" Killashandra was wearing the contact lenses recommended for Optheria's sunlight and wondered if the planet would be improved, viewed via augmented Ballybran vision. Just then it was very, very *blah*! Killashandra had to delve a long way for an adequate expression which, tactfully, she did not voice. Would Borella have restrained herself? Would she have noticed? Ah, well, Beauty is said to be in the eye of the beholder! For Optheria's sake, she was glad that someone loved it.

While it might have been laudable of the Founding Fathers to wish to preserve the entire valley as it was when Man first landed, it must have given the architects and construction crews a helluva lot of trouble. Buildings wrapped around copses of trees, straddled brooks, incorporated boulders and ledges. Probably the floors on upper levels were even but it must have been bumpy going at ground level. Fortunately the airfoils of her vehicle were up to the uneven surface in the suburbs but the ride became rather bouncy as they proceeded deeper into the City.

Pausing at the intersection of a huge open square—open except for the many thorn bushes and scrawny trees—Killashandra could not fail to notice that the ground floor of one corner building made uneven arches over repulsively greasy-looking bushes whose thorny branches were obviously a hazard to pedestrians; something was to be said for the curtailment of natural "beauty." She could learn to hate the City quite easily. No wonder some of the natives were restless. Just how did the Summer Festival compensate for the rest of the Optherian year?

Once past the open square, the road climbed gently to a cluster of buildings evidently uninhibited by natural beauties, for they seemed to have an architectural integrity so far lacking in the City.

"It was necessary," Thyrol said in a muted voice, "to add the merest trace of a ramp to ascend to the Music Center."

"I wouldn't have known it if you hadn't told me," Killashandra said, unable to restrain her facetiousness.

"One ought to approach on foot," Pirinio went on in a repressive tone, "but some latitude is permitted so that the audience may assemble punctually." His gesture called Killashandra's attention to the many small switchback paths to one side of the promontory.

Killashandra repressed a second facetious remark which Pirinio's tone provoked. It wouldn't be the installation on Optheria, not the organ, nor the planet which were hazardous: once again it was the inhabitants. Was she always to encounter such intolerant, inflexible, remorseless personalities?

"What sort of local brew do you have here on Optheria?" she asked, keeping her tone casual. If the reply was "none," she'd book out on the next available craft.

"Well, ah, that is, possibly not at all to your taste, Guildmember." Mirbethan's startled reply was hesitant. "No beverages can be imported. I'm sure you saw the notice in the Port Authority. Our brewmasters produce four distinct fermented beverages: quite potable, I'm told. Spirits are distilled from the Terran grains which we have managed to adapt to Optherian soil, but I've been told that these are raw to educated palates."

"Optheria produces excellent wines," Pirinio said rather testily, with a reproving glance at Mirbethan. "They cannot be exported and indeed, some do not travel well even the relatively short distance to the City. If wine is your preference, a selection will be put in your quarters."

"I'll try some of the brews, too."

"Wine *and* beer?" Polabod exclaimed in surprise.

"Crystal singers are required to keep a high blood-alcohol content when absent from Ballybran. I'll have to decide which is the best for my particular requirement." She sighed in patient forebearance.

"I wasn't informed that members of your Guild required special diets." Thyrol was clearly perturbed.

"No special diet," Killashandra agreed, "but we do require larger intakes of certain natural substances from time to time. Such as alcohol."

"Oh, I see," Thyrol replied, although clearly he did not.

Does no one on this repulsive planet have a sense of humor? Killashandra wondered.

"Ah, here we are so soon," Pirinio said, for the vehicle had swung down the curving drive to the imposing main entrance of the largest building on this musical height.

In orderly fashion but in decorous haste, a second welcoming committee formed itself on the wide and shallow marble steps under the colonnaded portico that shielded the massive central doors of the edifice. Although large urns had been planted with some sort of weeping tree to soften the harsh architecture, the effect was forbidding, rather than welcoming.

Killashandra emerged from the vehicle, ignoring Thyrol's outstretched hand. The Optherian's obsequious behavior could quickly become a major irritant.

She had just straightened up and turned to step forward when something slammed hard into her left shoulder and she was thrown off balance against the vehicle. The fleshy point of her shoulder stung briefly then began to throb. Thyrol began to bellow incoherently before he attempted to embrace her in the misguided notion that she needed his assistance.

For the next few moments total chaos erupted: Thyrol, Pirinio, and Polabod dashed about, issuing conflicting orders. The throng of dignitaries turned into a terrified mob, splintering into groups which fled, stood paralyzed, or added their shouts to the tumult. A flock of airborne sleds reared up from the plateau to hover above the Music Complex, darting off on diverse errands.

Mirbethan was the only one able to keep her wits. She tore a strip from the hem of her gown, and despite Killashandra's protestations that she required no aid, bound the wound. And it was she who discovered the weapon, imbedded in the upholstery of the back seat.

"That's a businesslike piece of wickedness," Killashandra remarked as she studied the asterisk-bladed object, three of its lethal blades buried in the seat back. The one which had wounded her pointed outward, a strand of her sleeve material laid neatly along the cutting edge.

"Don't touch it." Mirbethan put out her hand to prevent such action.

"No fear," Killashandra said, straightening up. "Local manufacture?"

"No." Mirbethan's voice took on a note of indignant anger. "An island implement. An outrage. We shall spare no effort to discover the perpetrator of this deed."

There was a subtle, but discernible, alteration in Mirbethan's tone between her first two remarks and the last which Killashandra caught but could not then analyze, for the rest of the committee suddenly recalled that there had been a victim of this "outrage" and more attentions were showered on Killashandra by the concerned. Despite her protestations, she was carried into the vaulting entrance hall of the main building, and whisked along a corridor, lined floor to ceiling with portraits of men and women. Even in her swift passage she noticed that they all smiled in the same tight, smug way. Then she was conducted to a lift while dignitaries bickered about who should accompany her in the limited space.

Once again, Mirbethan won Killashandra's approval by closing the door on the argument. They were met at their destination by a full medical convention and Killashandra was made to lie on a gurney and was wheeled into diagnostics.

At the moment of truth, when the temporary bandaging was reverently unwound from the injury, there was a stunned silence.

"I could have spared everyone a great deal of unnecessary effort,"

Killashandra remarked drily after she glanced at the clean, bloodless cut. "As a crystal singer, I heal very quickly and am not the least bit susceptible to infection. As you can see."

Consternation was rampant, with all the medics exclaiming over the wound, and others cramming forward in an attempt to witness this miracle of regeneration. Glancing up, Killashandra saw the very smug smile on Mirbethan's face, so very like the smiles on the portraits.

"To what agency do you attribute such remarkable healing properties?" asked the eldest of the medical people in attendance.

"To living on Ballybran," Killashandra replied. "As you must surely be aware, the resonance of crystal slows down the degenerative process. Tissue damage regenerates quickly. By this evening this minor cut will be completely healed. It was a clean swipe and not all that deep."

She seized the opportunity to slip off the gurney.

"If we may take a sample of your blood for analysis," the elder medic began, reaching for a sterilely packaged extractor.

"You may not," Killashandra said and again felt a wave of incredulous dismay and surprise from her audience. Was contradiction forbidden on Optheria? "The bleeding has stopped. Nor will analysis isolate the blood factor which slows degeneration," she went on with a kind smile. "Why waste your valuable time?"

She strode purposefully toward the door, determined to end this interlude. Just then, Pirinio, Thyrol, and Polabod arrived, breathless in their haste to rejoin her.

"Ah, gentlemen, you are just in time to escort me to my quarters." And when there were stumbled explanations about receptions and Music Center faculty waiting and the prospect of attendance by the Elders, she smiled gently. "All the more reason for me to change . . ." and she gestured to the torn sleeve.

"But you've not been attended!" Thyrol cried, astonished to see an unbandaged slash.

"Very well, thank you," she said and walked past him into the corridor. "Well?" She swung round to face a throng of very confused people. "Will no one escort me to my quarters?" This farce was beginning to pall.

The corridor, too, had its occupants, mostly in the universal green garb of the medical profession. Therefore, the young man, clad in a dark tunic, his bronzed legs bare to the soft leather ankle boots, stood out among them.

Lanzecki might swear that the Ballybran spore did not confer any psychic enhancement but Killashandra was entertaining severe doubts on that score. She had definitely caught conflicting emotional emanations from Mirbethan, from the other worthies, and now, from this young man—a curious flash of green, annoyance, interest, and anticipation far too strong to be the casual reaction to a visitor. And flash was all it could be, for Thyrol and Pirinio bore down on her, all apologies for their discourtesies real and imaginary. Mirbethan firmly took her place at Killashandra's right, edging the three men out of position and motioning their guest down the hall. When Killashandra was able to glance back to the young man, he was striding down a side corridor, head down, shoulders sagging as if weighed down by some burden. Guilt?

Then she was swept into the lift, down to the guest level, and into the most sumptuous quarters which had ever been allotted to her. Having agreed to descend to the reception as soon as she had changed gave her time for only the most cursory examination of the apartment. She'd been guided through a large, elegant reception room suitable for formal affairs. A smaller room was evidently to be used as a studio or office. They hurried past two bedchambers, one of them quite modern, before she was ushered into a main room so vast that she had to stifle a chuckle. Mirbethan indicated the toilet and the slightly open closet panel where her clothes had been hung. Then the woman withdrew.

Stripping off the torn garment, Killashandra flicked open one of the Beluga spider-silk kaftans which ought to be suitable for any reception: certainly a foil against the predominantly white or pale colors which the Optherians seemed to prefer. Except for that brooding young man.

Killashandra dwelt briefly on him as she washed hastily. Then she couldn't resist a peek into the other hygiene rooms. One contained a variety of tubs, massage table, and exercise equipment while the third boasted a radiant-fluid tub and several curious devices which Killashandra had never before encountered but which left an impression of obscenity.

Back in the bedchamber, she heard a soft rapping at the door.

"I'm ready, I'm ready," she cried, masking irritation with a lilt in her voice.

Chapter 5

That protocol had become an art form on Optheria told Killashandra quite clearly that if there were no rebellious spirits then the entire population had stagnated. At the reception, every faculty member, their subordinates, then every student, all in order of their rank and scholastic standing, filed past her. Mercifully, handshaking was no longer a part of the ritual. A nod, a smile, a mumbled repetition of the name sufficed. After fifty nods, Killashandra felt her smile fixed in her cheeks and her face stiffened into that mode. With her everfaithful quartette, she stood at the top of a massive double staircase, whose white marble flights curved down into a marbled hall below. The ceiling of the vast reception chamber was so high that the murmuring of the assembled crowd was absorbed.

Killashandra had had a glimpse of tables, laden with patterns of plates whose contents were as precisely placed as the plates were, and with beakers of colored liquids. The assembled scrupulously kept their eyes from the direction of the refreshments. Killashandra guessed that they all knew too well the taste and texture of the reception repast.

There were curious patterns, too, in the reception. Five people would take the right-hand staircase, the next five would descend on the left. Killashandra wondered if a steward in some distant anteroom ticked the people off for left and right. There were never more than ten people waiting to be introduced, yet the flow down the hallway was steady despite its apparent randomness.

Abruptly no more people were making their way to the reception line and Killashandra let her cheeks relax, rotating her head on her neck, wriggling her lips and nose in a very undignified manner in order to ease the muscles. One never knows when one's early training as a singer is going to prove useful, she thought, just as she heard a concerted intake of breath from her quartette. Reorganizing her expression, she glanced up the hall in time to observe the ceremonial approach of dignitaries.

The seven figures who processed—and that was the correct verb to describe their advance—were not differently garbed from the other highly placed Optherians, but they wore their pale robes with an unmistakable air of authority. Four men and three women, each wearing the same slight smile upon their serene faces. Faces, Killashandra would shortly note, that had been carefully adjusted by surgery and artifice to enhance that serenity, for only one of the smiles reached the weary, bored, aged eyes.

Elder Ampris, Killashandra was immensely relieved to discover, was the only one of the Optherian rulers with whom she would have much contact. He was currently responsible for the Music Complex. If there should ever be a Stellarity Award given for Best Character Actor among Planetary Rulers, surely Ampris would win it. But for the disparity of expression between eye and face, Killashandra might have missed that gleam of humor and possibly ignored that spontaneous lifting of the heart that occurs when one encounters a kindred spirit. The others, whose names Killashandra promptly forgot, gave her hand one firm shake in welcome, a few words of gratitude for making "so arduous a journey in this moment of planetary crisis," and passed on by, having acquitted their duty. They all waited, without appearing to wait, at the top of the right-hand stair. Then Killashandra felt the almost electric touch of Ampris's hand, looked into his bright and knowing eyes and returned the first genuine smile of the long afternoon.

"We will have time to talk later on, Guildmember. In the meantime, let us gild their afternoon with the gold and scarlet of our presences." His negligent wave took in the whole room, not just the high dignitaries patiently awaiting the dissolution of the reception line.

Thyrol glanced at Killashandra, her hand on Ampris's arm, then he turned to the nearest Elder woman and offered his arm. No fuss, no confusion, no dithering about altered escorts or who would be left to descend alone: everything was already worked out, planned down to the last detail, including the unexpected. For, obviously, no one could have expected Ampris to confer such an honor as his personal escort on Killashandra.

Killashandra wondered if the foodstuffs had been minutely measured, for two bites disposed of each of the four small tidbits, five mouthfuls emptied the wine glass. But she was among the lucky minority who had their glasses refilled and were offered additional canapes.

"This will be over soon," Ampris murmured to her, his lips barely moving. "A proper meal will be served us when the lesser orders have dutifully taken their sip and sup and toddled back to the comfort of their routines."

He spoke with neither scorn nor malice: Ampris was stating a fact about the majority of the assembled.

"Having had their rare treats of standing in the same room with a real live breathing crystal singer?"

"You are that!" Ampris's gaze returned hers with no trace of guile or evasion but he had a definite twinkle in his eye. "Three minutes after you reached the infirmary, the news of your regenerative powers had seeped to the basements."

"Surely you are not housed in a basement?"

Ampris's bright brown eyes twinkled again. "The seat of all knowledge . . ."

"So you can get to the bottom of things?"

"Of course."

"And a position of maximum security?" Killashandra taunted him. Why shouldn't she start at the top with her covert inquiries?

"Security is never a problem on such a well-ordered world as Optheria." He inclined his head to acknowledge the passing of three of the dignitaries circulating the gathering. "Everyone is secure"—he paused—"on Optheria, each knowing his place and his duties. Security is the foundation of the serenity of spirit which typifies this natural world."

Killashandra could find no mockery in his words nor any special inflection in his voice. No sparkle of amusement lit his eye, no cynical expression molded his face, yet Killashandra heard the denial as clearly as if he had phrased it.

"Someone must have had a momentarily troubled spirit to launch that little star-knife at me."

"An island weapon," Ampris said. "We allowed that settlement too much leeway during the early years on Optheria. Its original colonists were, naturally, of our mind, but before we could reestablish contact with them, they had deviated from the original intent. Optheria was to be an autonomous world: not to consist of autonomous groups." Ampris's humorless voice and manner implied the treatment which had undoubtedly been meted out to the dissenters. "The matter of that outrageous attack on your person will be resolved, I can assure you, Guildmember Killashandra."

"I don't doubt that for a moment."

Ampris searched her face. "On an ordered planet, the unusual is always remarkable."

"Ampris, you may not monopolize our distinguished visitor," said a deep grating voice and Killashandra turned to find herself scrutinized by one of the other male Elders. He had the eyes of a scavenger, bright, dark, piercing. His thin, hooked nose did much to encourage the analogy. His skin had a curious lacquered look, crinkling at the edges of his face from whatever minor shift of expression he permitted. His glance dropped briefly to her left shoulder, as if his gaze could penetrate the silk and examine the healing wound beneath.

"Monopoly has never been my passion, Torkes," Ampris said. "My associate, Torkes, holds the Communications Seat on Optheria. We work closely together in our adjacent disciplines. He maintains that Music is dependent on Communications, and I, of course, take the position that Music is independent and without it, Communications would have nothing to disseminate!"

"But of course!" Killashandra mustered a broad and giddy smile with which she favored both men impartially. Ampris accepted her evasion with a slight smile while Torkes bowed as if her ambiguous reply awarded him the decision. "What sort of crystal network does your facility use, Elder Torkes?"

"Crystal?" Torkes's piercing stare was affronted. "We have no funds to waste on that sort of technology. Crystal is reserved for musicians!"

"Really?" And Killashandra caught the barest glimpse of the satisfied reaction from Ampris. Torkes seemed totally oblivious to the implication of his statement. "Even when crystal is a very natural—"

"Crystal is not natural to Optheria. Not a native product, you understand. And we must maintain the integrity of our Charter."

"Indeed? Do you not violate that integrity by using alien instrumentation?"

Torkes dismissed her argument with a flick of his bony fingers. "Music is an art form which we were able to bring with us, within the mind. It is intangible—"

"And what is communication, then? Can it be touched? Smelt? Tasted?"

Torkes stared at her so fiercely that Killashandra was made aware of the fact that not only had she dared to interrupt an Elder but she had argued with him. She sensed rather than saw Ampris's intense amusement then, in the blink of his eyes, when Torkes was faced with the unpalatable realization that a Heptite Guildmember, an invited specialist urgently required by his planet, held equal status with himself.

"Of course," Ampris said, breaking the heavy silence that ensued, "the organ was developed by an Optherian for Optherian purposes and is, in fact, unique to our planet."

"Yes, yes, quite so," Torkes mumbled just as a mellow chime discreetly ended the reception.

Torkes made an adroit escape.

"So, one does not dispute with you Elders here?" Killashandra asked, watching him move off through the throng.

"It is good for us, I assure you," Ampris replied with a chuckle. "Fortunately Torkes is more flexible than he sounds, for when he changes Seats, he becomes totally committed to his immediate responsibility." When Killashandra looked quizzical, he added: "We Elders change our duties every four years, so as not to become too narrow in our understanding of the overview."

"I see."

"Then you are wiser than your years," Ampris said, "for I cannot believe that an administrator who is tone deaf can effectively guide Music: or that an Elder who cannot integrate should have charge of the Treasury. However, the governmental mechanism is so weighty that four years of mismanagement generally produce no more than annoying miscalculations and minor blunders easily corrected. The brilliance of the Founding Fathers of Optheria is once more unquestionably elucidated."

Thyrol appeared, respectfully inclining his upper body at his interruption.

"Elder Ampris, Guildmember Ree, if you will proceed to the dining chamber?"

The beauty of the hall, the elegantly set table and Elder Ampris's earlier comment deceived Killashandra into anticipating a far better meal. Although presented in appealing style, the miniscule portions did not appease Killashandra's heavy appetite. Nor was she offered enough of any one food to make a positive identification of its constituents or savor its taste. The courses were accompanied by beverages which were so bland that the water had more zest to it—and not a brew or a ferment among them. Killashandra's exasperated sigh caught the attention of Elder Pentrom, her right-hand dinner partner.

"Something is amiss?" he asked politely and then stared for a brief moment at her clean plate. He was but halfway through the food on his.

"Doesn't Optheria produce brews, or vintages or something with more taste than these, Elder Pentrom?"

"You mean an *alcoholic* beverage?" he said, as if she had made a particularly obscene suggestion.

Killashandra favored him with a longer look and decided that with his prim mouth, sharp chin, and tiny eyes, no other reaction could have been expected.

"Indeed I do mean alcoholic beverages." He opened his mouth to protest, but before he could utter a word she said, "Alcohol is essential to the proper metabolic function of a crystal singer."

"I have never heard that in all my years as Medical Supervisor of this planet."

"Have you encountered many crystal singers in your career?" Piqued by yet another dogmatic encounter, Killashandra discarded any semblance of tact. These people needed a set-down and she was in the enviable position of being able to give it with impunity.

"In actual fact, no—"

"Then how can you possibly dispute my statement? Or question my requirements? This"—and she waved a scornful hand at the goblet before her—"*bilge*—"

"That *beverage* is a nutritious liquid, carefully combined to supply the adult daily requirements of vitamins and minerals to ensure—"

"No wonder it tastes so revolting. And may I point out that any brewmaster worth his license provides the same vitamins and minerals in a form palatable enough to satisfy the inner man as well."

The Medical Supervisor hitched his chair back, throwing his serviette on the table in preparation for harangue, and suddenly they were the center of attention. "Young woman—"

"Spare me your condescension, Elder," Killashandra replied as she rose gracefully to her feet and glared down at him. She swept the table with a reproving look. "I shall retire to my apartment until such time as my dietary requirements can be met with enough food"—she flipped over her empty plate—"to satisfy my appetite and sufficient alcoholic beverages to keep my metabolism functioning. Good evening!"

In the stunned silence, Killashandra left the room. Doors the size and density of the ones securing the dining chamber did not slam satisfactorily but she had enjoyed her exit so much that she did not miss that part of the finale. In the corridor, she startled minions, lounging against the walls.

"Does anybody know where my apartments are in this mausoleum?" she demanded. When all raised their hands, she pointed to the nearest. "Take me there." When he hesitated and looked anxiously at the door, she repeated her order in a louder and more authoritative tone. He scurried forward, more desirous of avoiding her immediate wrath than courting disfavor of an absent authority.

"Tell me," she asked in a pleasant tone when they had entered a small lift, "is food plentiful on Optheria?"

He cast her a very nervous glance and when she smiled winningly at him, relaxed a little, though he kept as far from her in the carriage as possible.

"There is plenty of food on Optheria. Too much. This year only half the fields may be planted, and I know that early fruit has been left to rot on the vine."

"Then why did I get three mouthfuls at dinner?"

Something approaching levity touched the young man's face. "All the Elders are old: they don't eat much."

"Hmm! That's one explanation. But a good brew or a nice dry vintage would have helped!"

A smile tugged at the young man's lips. "Well, Elder Pentrom was present and he is death on any sort of alcoholic beverage. Says it saps the energy of the young and disrupts thought in the mature."

"And he was my dinner partner!" Killashandra's crow of malice resounded in the enclosed space. "My timing is, as ever, superb! Well, I'm not under his jurisdiction and, if Optheria really needs that organ repaired, the Elders will have to placate me, not him." The young man was obviously shocked. "Tell me," she said in her kindest, most wheedling voice, "you seem to be a knowledgeable fellow, what sort of interesting beverages are produced on this planet?"

"Oh, there are brews and vintages," he assured her promptly and with some pride, "and some rather potent spiritous drinks manufactured in the mountains and the islands—but that sort of stuff isn't permitted in the Conservatory." The lift's doors slid open, and the Optherian bustled out.

"More's the pity." Killashandra strode on down the hallway after her guide. "What do you drink? No, abort the question," and she grinned at his startled glance. "What is the most popular drink?"

"The most popular one on this continent is a brew called Bascum."

"Is Bascum a plant or a person?"

"Person." Her guide was warming to his subject. He indicated they take the left-hand corridor at the junction. "One of the Founding Fathers."

"So his brewery is allowed to function in the face of the Medical Supervisor's displeasure?" Killashandra grinned as he nodded. "I infer from your remarks that there are other popular drinks? Any wines?"

"Oh, yes, the western continent produces some very fine vintages, both white and red, and some doubly distilled liqueurs. I'm not familiar with the wines at all."

"And those islands you mentioned, they go for the spiritous liquors?"

"The polly tree."

"The polly tree?"

"Its fermented fruit makes a brandy which, I'm told, is more potent than anything else in the universe. The polly tree provides foliage for shelter, a fine-grained wood for building, its roots burn for a long time, its bark can be pounded into a fiber which the islanders use for weaving cloth, its pith is extremely nutritious, and its large fruit is delicious as well as nutritious—"

"When it isn't fermented—"

"Exactly."

"And the polly tree only grows on the islands?"

"That's right, and here is your apartment, Guildmember." He opened the door.

"There's no privacy lock on this?" Killashandra had not noticed the lack in her first hurried inspection.

"There is no need for such in the Complex." Her guide appeared surprised at her reaction. "No one would presume to enter without your express permission."

"There are no thieves on Optheria?"

"Not in the *Conservatory*!"

She thanked him for his escort and entered her sacrosanct apartment, closing the door behind her with a sigh of relief. Only then did her eye fall on the table. She exclaimed aloud at the display of bottles of all sizes and shapes, at the beakers, goblets, wine glasses that waited in pristine array on the white cloth. A separate tray offered an assortment of tidbits, nuts, and small wafers. A small chest opened to exhibit chilled bottles and two pottery amphoras.

There was no way the collection could have been assembled and spirited into her apartment in the time elapsed since she stormed out of the dining room. Then she remembered her remarks on the trip from the spaceport. Well, Elder Pentrom might be a prissy, dogmatic, abstemious man, but obviously her every whim was someone's command.

Because her guide had mentioned Bascum, her choice among so many finally settled on the neat brown bottle in the cold chest. She flipped the top off and let the midbrown brew slowly descend into an appropriate beaker. The malty scent that rose to her nostrils suggested good things to come.

"And about time, too," she said, scooping up a random selection of nibbles and sinking into the nearest comfortable seat. "To absent friends!" She lifted her beaker high then took her first sip.

She regarded the brew with respect and delight. "Could Bascum possibly have come from Yarra?" she asked herself. "This might not be so bad an assignment after all!"

Chapter 6

By the time the quick Optherian sunset had finished its evening display, Killashandra had sampled nine beverages, wishing she had someone with whom to share the largesse, especially since there was a prohibition against it. Which brought Corish to mind, and that mythical uncle of his. Unless she could discover how much surveillance she would be having from her discreet quartette—and how easy it would be to outwit it—she didn't want to risk meeting him. Would they think it odd if she left a message at the Piper Facility? Corish had considerably piqued her curiosity and she was somewhat motivated by a desire to show him that two could play the exploitation gambit.

Someone tapped on her apartment door and, when Mirbethan entered on her permission, Killashandra caught the shade of uncertainty in the Optherian's manner.

"Since you're not accompanied by any priss-mouthed ancients, you are welcome. And if that excuse for a meal is a state dinner here, no wonder you're a lean bunch."

Mirbethan flushed. "Since Elder Pentrom graciously accepted our invitation, we are obliged to cater to his dietary preferences. Didn't Elder Ampris mention this to you?"

"He failed to put me in the know. However, all this," and Killashandra waved expansively at the beverage table's load, "makes up for that deficiency, though solid food would assist my investigations . . ."

"There was no time to show you the catering facility." Mirbethan glided to one of the discreet wall cabinets. Its doors opened on a catering unit. "Alcoholic beverages are not included. Students have a distressing aptitude for breaking restricted codes." Killashandra decided that she merely thought she detected a note of tolerant humor in Mirbethan's voice. "That is why we have supplied you with a sampling of the available intoxicants."

"In spite of Elder Pentrom."

Mirbethan cast her eyes downward.

"Tell me, Mirbethan, would you happen to know if Bascum the brewmaster originated from the planet Yarra?"

"Bascum?" Mirbethan looked up, startled, and confused. When Killashandra waved the long-emptied bottle at her, she blushed. "Oh, that Bascum." Now she glided to a second ornate cabinet which opened into a full size terminal, and a panel in the wall slid aside to reveal a large screen.

She typed an entry as Killashandra made a private wager. "Why, how under the suns did you know?"

"The best brewmasters in the galaxy hail from that planet. I haven't sampled everything yet," Killashandra went on, "but I shall be very well suited indeed if you'll undertake to keep me supplied with Bascum's brew."

"As you require, Guildmember. But for now, the concert is about to start in the Red Hall. Only the single manual organ, but the performer was last year's prize winner."

Killashandra was tempted, but she was a shade hungrier and drier than she liked to be. "The Elders are present?" When Mirbethan solemnly nodded, Killashandra sighed deeply. "Convey my apologies on the grounds of travel fatigue . . . and the stress of metabolic readjustment after the assault and the wound." Killashandra ran the silk up her arm, exposing her shoulder where only a thin red line gave evidence of an injury.

Mirbethan's eyes widened significantly and then, with a subtle shift, she inclined a bow to Killashandra.

"Your apologies will be conveyed. Call code MBT 14 if you require any further assistance from myself, Thyrol, Pirinio, or Polabod."

Killashandra wished her a pleasant evening and Mirbethan withdrew. As soon as the door had closed on the woman, Killashandra discarded her languor and made for the catering unit. Once again, Optherian peculiarities inhibited her, for when she called up a menu, there was no scrolling of delectable, mouthwatering selections but a set dinner, with only three choices for the main course. She opted for all three, and immediately the catering unit queried her. She repeated her request and, when the unit wanted to know how many were dining, she tapped in "three." At which point the unit informed her that the apartment was recorded as having a single occupant. She replied that she had guests. Their names and codes were required. She responded with the names of Elders Pentrom and Ampris, codes unknown.

The food was promptly dispensed, two of the meager servings that she had observed in the dining hall. Fortunately the third one was substantial enough to abort the kick that she had been about to bestow on the catering unit.

Once she had solid food in her stomach, she continued her liquor sampling. While not in the least inebriated, thanks to her Ballybran-altered digestion, Killashandra was very merry and sang lustily as she ventured into the hygiene rooms and splashed in the scented water of the bath. She continued to sing, her fancy latching onto a riotous ballad generally rendered by a tenor, as she made her way to the bedroom. A lambent radiance augmented the soft lighting and, curious, she went to the window, observing three of Optheria's four small moons, one near enough for the craters and vast sterile plains to be clearly visible. Entranced, Killashandra broke off the ballad and began the haunting love duet from Baleef's exotic opera, *Voyagers*, which seemed particularly appropriate to the setting.

When a tenor voice joined her on cue, she faltered a moment. Then, despite her astonishment at spontaneity in such a rigidly controlled environment, she continued. *Voyagers* had been her last opera as a student on Fuerte, so she knew it well enough to divert some of her attention from the words. And a fine, rich, well produced voice he had. Might need a bit more support for the G's and A's in the last three measures—she'd be amazed if he could hit the high C along with her—but he had a firm sense of the dynamic requirements and sang with great sensitivity. As the tenor took up the melody, she gathered herself for the taxing finale, delighted to find her singing voice still flexible enough for the dynamics, and the high C. The tenor, with no loss of vibrance, opted for the A, but it was a grand ringing A and she applauded his judgment.

She sustained her note, perversely wishing him to drop but, as it happened, they broke off at the same instant, as if they had had the innumerable rehearsals such inspired singing required.

" 'When shall our paths cross again?' " she asked in the recitative which followed that spectacular duet.

" 'When the moons of Radomah make glorious the sky with measured dance.' " The invisible tenor also had a vibrant speaking voice, and, better yet, an appreciation of the humor in their impromptu performance for she caught the ripple of laughter in his chanted phrases. Did he also find the words, and the opera, a trifle ludicrous in the austere setting of the Optherian Complex?

All of a sudden, the courtyard below was floodlighted. Figures erupted onto the paving, shouting commands for silence. Before she stepped back from the window, Killashandra caught a glimpse of a figure, in a window directly opposite hers but a story above, withdrawing into the shielding darkness. Soprano and tenor exited the stage while the extras made a diligent and vain search for the conspirators.

Killashandra poured herself a full glass of something which its label identified as a fortified wine. This was an odd music center if impromptu singing, particularly of so high a caliber, was answered by punitive force.

She downed the drink, doused all the lights in the suite and, in the milky light of the moons, sought the comfort of her bed. Despite a wish for sleep, her mind ranged through the scenes of the Baleef opera and the sorrows of the star-crossed lovers. She must remember to ask Mirbethan who that tenor was. Fine voice! Much better than the pimple-faced little oaf who had sung the role opposite her on Fuerte!

Morning chimes, soft but insidious, roused her. She lifted herself on one elbow, saw that dawn was just breaking, groaned and, flinging the light coverlet over her head, went back to sleep. A second sequence of chimes, louder, sounded. Cursing, Killashandra strode to the console, coded the number Mirbethan had given her. "Is there any way to stop the wretched chimes in this apartment? Imagine, having to wake up at dawn!"

"That is the way here, Guildmember, but I shall advise Control that your apartment is to be excluded from the Rising Chimes."

"And all others, please! I will not be ordered about by bells, drums, whistles, shrills, or inaudibles. And who possesses that remarkably fine tenor voice?"

Mirbethan shot Killashandra a startled look. "You were disturbed by it—"

"Not in the least. But if that's the quality of natural musical talent on Optheria, I'm impressed."

"The Center does not encourage vocalizing." Mirbethan's cool denial roused Killashandra's instant hostility.

"You mean, that tenor is a reject from your opera school?"

"You misunderstand the situation, Guildmember. All the teaching centers on Optheria emphasize keyboard music."

"You mean, only that organ?"

"Of course. The organ is the ultimate of instruments, combining the—"

"Spare me the hype, Mirbethan." Killashandra took an obscure pleasure in the shock her statement gave the woman. Then she relented. "Oh, I concur that the Optherian organ is a premier instrument, but that tenor voice was rather spectacular on its own merit."

"You should not have been disturbed—"

"Fardles! I enjoyed singing with him."

Mirbethan's eyes rounded in a secondary shock. "You . . . were the other singer?"

"I was." *File that for future reference!* "Tell me, Mirbethan, if only a few of the hundreds who must study at this Center ever attain the standard required to play the Optherian organ, what happens to those who don't?"

"Why, suitable situations are found for them."

"In music?" Mirbethan shook her head. "I'd think that crystal singing would provide a marvelous alternative."

"Optherians do not care to leave their planet, whatever their minor disappointments. You will excuse me, Guildmember—" Mirbethan broke the connection.

Killashandra stared at the blank screen for a long moment. Of course, neither Mirbethan nor any of the quartette knew of her early background in music. Certainly none of them could possibly know of her disappointment, nor how she would relate that to what Mirbethan had just admitted. If you failed to make the grade at the organ, there was nothing else for you on Optheria? There was no way in which Killashandra would buy Mirbethan's statement that frustrated Optherian musicians would prefer to remain on the planet, even if they had been conditioned to the restriction from birth.

And that tenor had sung with absolute pitch. It'd be a bloody shame to muzzle that voice in preference to an organ, however "perfect" an instrument it might be. Hazardous crystal singing might be as a profession, but it sure beat languishing on Optheria. A sudden thought struck her and, with a fluid stride, she went to the terminal, tapped for Library, and the entry on Ballybran. A much expurgated entry scrolled past, ending with the

Code Four restriction. She queried the Files for political science texts and discovered fascinating gaps in that category. So, censorship was applied on Optheria. Not that that ever accomplished its purpose. However, an active censorship was not grounds for charter-smashing, and the Guild had only been requested to discover if the planetary exit restriction was popularly accepted.

Well, she knew one person she could ask—the tenor—if he hadn't gone into hiding after last night's hunt. Killashandra grinned. If she knew tenors . . .

She had breakfasted—the catering unit did offer a substantial breakfast—and dressed by the time Thyrol arrived to inquire if she had rested, and more importantly, if she would like to start the repairs. He tactfully indicated her arm.

"You've apprehended the assailant?"

"Merely a matter of time."

"How many students in the Complex?" she asked amiably as Thyrol led her down the hall to the lift.

"At present, four hundred and thirty."

"That's a lot of suspects to examine."

"No student would *dare* attack an honored guest of the planet."

"On most planets, they'd be the prime suspects."

"My dear Guildmember, the selection process by which this student body is chosen considers all aspects of the applicant's background, training, and ability. They uphold all our traditions."

Killashandra mumbled something suitable. "How many positions are available to graduates?"

"That is not an issue, Guildmember," Thyrol said with mild condescension. "There is no limit to the number of fully trained performers who present compositions for the Optherian organ—"

"But only one may play at a time—"

"There are forty-five organs throughout Optheria—"

"That many? Then why couldn't one of those be substituted—"

"The instrument here at the Complex is the largest, most advanced and absolutely essential for the performance level required by the Summer Festival. Composers from all over the planet compete for the honor and their work has been especially written for the potential of the main instrument. To ask them to perform on a lesser organ defeats the purpose of the Festival."

"I see," Killashandra said although she didn't. However, once she had been admitted through the series of barriers and security positions protecting the damaged organ, she began to appreciate the distinction Thyrol had made.

He had taken her to the rocky basements of the Complex, and then to the impressive and unexpectedly grand Competition Amphitheater which utilized the natural stony bowl on the nether side of the Complex promontory. Some massive early earthfault and a lot of weathering had molded the mount's flank into a perfect semicircle. The Optherians had improved the amphitheater with tiered ranks of individual seating units, facing the shelf on which the organ console stood. This was accessible only from the one entrance through which Thyrol now guided Killashandra. With a sincere and suitable awe, Killashandra looked about her, annoyed that she was gratifying Thyrol's desire to impress a Guildmember even as she was unable to suppress that wonder. She cleared her throat, and the sound, small though it was, echoed faithfully back at her. "The acoustics are incredible," she murmured and, as Thyrol smiled tolerantly, heard her words whispered back. She rolled her eyes and looked about her for an exit from the phenomenal stage.

Thyrol gestured to a portal carved in the solid rock on the far side of the organ console. From his belt pouch he extracted three small rods. With these and his thumb print, he opened the door, the sound reverberating across the empty space. Killashandra slipped in first. As familiar as she was with auditoria of all descriptions, something about this one unnerved her. Something about the seats reminded her of primitive diagnostic chairs which used physical restraints on their occupants, yet she knew that people would cross the Galaxy to attend the Festival.

Lights had come up at their entry and illuminated a large, low-ceilinged chamber. Taking up the floor space in front of the innocuous interlinked cabinets that made up the electronic guts of the Optherian organ were the prominent sealed crates containing the white crystal. Overhead harnesses of color-coded cables formed a ceiling design before they disappeared through conduits to unknown destinations.

Thyrol led the way to the large rectangle containing the shattered remains of the crystal manual.

"How, in the name of all that's holy, did he manage that?" Killashandra demanded after surveying the damage. Some of the smaller crystals had been reduced to thin splinters. In idle wonder she picked up a handful of the shards, letting them trickle through her fingers, ignoring Thyrol's cry of alarm as he grabbed her wrists and pulled her hands back. The tiny cuts inflicted by the scalpel-sharp crystal briefly oozed droplets of blood then closed over while Thyrol watched in fascinated horror.

"As you can see, the merest caress of crystal." She twisted her hands free of Thyrol's unexpectedly strong grasp. "Now," and she spoke more briskly, looking down at the mess in the bottom of the cabinet, "I'll need some tools, some stout fellows, and stouter baskets to remove the debris."

"An extractor?" Thyrol suggested.

"There isn't an extractor built on Ballybran or anywhere else that wouldn't be sliced to ribbons by crystal shards in suction. No, this has to be cleaned in a time honored fashion—by hand."

"But you . . ."

Killashandra drew herself up. "As a Guildmember, I am not averse to performing *necessary* manual tasks." She paused to let Thyrol appreciate the difference. She had done more than enough shard-scrapping on Bally-bran to undertake it here on Optheria.

"It is only that security measures—"

"I would, of course, accept your assistance in the interests of security."

Thyrol hastily adjourned to a communication console. "What exactly do you require, Guildmember?"

She gauged the volume of broken crystal in the cabinet. "Three strong men with impervometallic bins of approximately ten-kilo volume, triple-strength face masks, durogloves, fine-wire brushes, and the sort of small, disposable extractor used by archaeologists. We have to be sure to glean every particle of crystal dust."

Thyrol's eyes bugged out a bit over the more bizarre items, but he repeated her requirements, and then turned up very stiff indeed when he was subjected to questions by the staff. "Of course, they have to be cleared by Security, but they are to be here immediately, properly geared to assist the Guildmember!" He broke off the connection and, his face blotched with displeasure, turned to Killashandra. "With so much at stake, Guildmember, you can appreciate our wish to protect you and the organ from further depredations. If something should happen to the replacement crystal . . ."

Killashandra shrugged. From what she had seen of Optherians, "once bitten, twice shy" described their philosophy. She ran her hand across the instrument nearest her, glancing around at the rest of the anonymous equipment. "This is a more complex device than I'd been led to believe." She turned and presented a politely inquiring expression to Thyrol.

"Well, ah, that is . . ."

"Come now, Thyrol, I am scarcely connected with the subversives."

"No, of course not."

Killashandra diverted Thyrol's attention from realizing that he had covertly admitted the existence of an underground organization by turning, once again, toward the front of the chamber and pointing at the access panel to the keyboard. "Now the actual keyboard is beyond that panel, so the right-hand box houses the stops and voicing circuitry. And is that," she pointed to the largest unit, "the CPU? The induction modulator and mixer must be in that left-hand cabinet."

"You are knowledgeable about organ technology?" Thyrol's expression assumed a wary blankness. For the second time since her arrival, Killashandra perceived empathic emanations from an Optherian: this time a strong sense of indefinable apprehension and alarm.

"Not as much about organs as I do about interface techniques, sensory simulators, and synthesizer modulators. Crystal singing requires a considerably wide range of experience with sophisticated electronic equipment, you know."

He obviously didn't or he wouldn't have nodded so readily. Killashandra blessed her foresight in utilizing the sleep-teaching tapes she had copied from the *Athena*'s comprehensive data retrieval system. Her answer reassured Thyrol and the shadow of his fear slowly dissipated.

"Of course there is a double handshake between the program," and he tapped the black case by him, "and the composition memory banks. Composition," and he walked from one to the other, his hand lightly brushing the surfaces, "of course leads directly into the recall excitor stimulator, for that uses the memory symbology of the median individual member of any audience so that a composition is translated into terms which have meaning to the auditors. Naturally the subjective experience of a program for Optherians would differ greatly from the experience a non-human would have."

"Of course," Killashandra murmured encouragingly. "And the information from the crystal manual goes? . . ."

Assuming the pose of a pompous lecturer, Thyrol pointed to the various units in flow sequence. "Into the synapse carrier encoder and demodulator multiplexer, both of which feed into the mixer for the sensory transducer terminal network." Beaming with pride, he continued, "While the composition memory bank primarily programs the sensory synthesizer, the feedback loop controls the sensory attenuator for maximum effectiveness."

"I see. Keyboard to CPU, direct interface with manual and synapse carrier encoder, plus the double handshakes." Killashandra hid her shock—this emotion manipulator made the equipment at Fuerte look like preschool toys. Talk about a captive audience! Optherian concertgoers hadn't a chance. The Optherian organ could produce a total emotional override with a conditional response unequaled anywhere. And a sufficient gauge of the audiences' basic profile could be ascertained by matching ID plates and census data. Killashandra wondered that FSP permitted any of its citizens to visit the planet, much less to expose themselves to full-scale emotional overload at Festival time. "I can see why you'd need many soloists. They'd be emotionally drained after each performance."

"We recognized that problem early on—the performer is shielded from the full effect of the organ in order to retain a degree of objectivity. And, of course, in rehearsal the transducer system is completely bypassed and the signals inserted into a systems analyser. Only the best compositions are played on the full organ system."

"Naturally. Tell me, are the smaller organs amplified in this fashion?"

"The two-manual organs are. We have five of them, the rest are all single manual with relatively primitive synthesizer attentuator and excitor capability."

"Remarkable. Truly remarkable."

Thyrol was not blind to the implied compliment and looked about to smile as the outside door opened to admit the work party. Behind them came three more men, their stance and costume identifying them as security. The work party stopped along the wall while the security trio tramped stolidly down to where Thyrol and Killashandra stood by the sensory feedback transponder.

"Elder Thyrol, Security Leader Blaz needs to know what disposition is to be made of the debris." He saluted, ignoring Killashandra's presence.

"Bury it deep. Preferably encapsulated in some permaform. Sea trench would be ideal," Killashandra answered and was ignored by the security leader, who continued to look for an answer from Thyrol. Abruptly Killashandra's captious temper erupted. She slammed her right hand into the leader's shoulder, forcefully turning him toward her. "Alternatively, insert it in your anal orifice," she said, her voice reasonable and pleasant.

With a wave of astounded gasps sounding in her ear, she made her exit.

Chapter 7

As Killashandra started across the stage to retrace her steps to the Complex, she decided that that was the last place she wanted to go in her state of mind. After all, Trag had chosen her because she could be more diplomatic than Borella. Not that Borella mightn't have handled that security fardleface with more tact, or effectiveness. However, the Optherians were stuck with her and she with them, and just then she didn't wish to see one more sanctimonious, self-righteous, smug Optherian face.

She strode to the edge of the stage, peered over at the ten-foot drop to the ground, saw the heavy doors at each end of that level and made her decision. She lay at the edge, swung her legs down, gripping the overhang, and let go.

Her knees took the jar and she leaned against the wall for a moment just as she heard the men emerge from the organ room.

"She'll have gone back to the Complex," Thyrol said, breathless with anger. He hurried across the stage, followed by the others. "Simcon, if you have offended the Guildmember, you may have jeopardized far more than you have protected . . ." The heavy door closed off the rest of his reprimand.

Somewhat mollified by Thyrol's attitude and pleased with her timely evasion, Killashandra dusted off her hands and moved toward the clearly marked exit door at the outer edge of the amphitheater. Even the soft sound of the brushing was echoed by the fine acoustics. Grimacing, Killashandra stepped as cautiously and as silently as she could toward the exit. The heavy door had the usual push-bar on the inside, which she depressed, holding her breath lest it be locked from a control point. The bar swung easily out. She opened it only wide enough to permit her egress and it closed with a *thunk* behind her. Its exterior was without handle or knob for reentry and a flange protected it from being forced open—if such a circumstance ever arose on perfect Optheria.

Killashandra now found herself on a long ledge which led to one of the switchback paths she had seen yesterday, though this one was at the rear of the Complex. From that height she had a view of an unpretentious area of the City, to judge by the narrow streets and the small single-story buildings crowded together. Between it and the Complex heights lay a stretch of cultivated plots, each planted with bushy climbing plants and fenced off from its neighbors, and most of them neat. In several, people were busily watering and hoeing in the early morning sunlight. The rural scene served as a restorative to Killashandra's exacerbated nerves.

She began her descent.

As she reached the valley floor, her nose was assailed by the unmistakable aroma of fermenting brew. Delighted, Killashandra followed the odor, squeezing past an old shed, traversing the narrow path between allotments, nodding polite greetings to the gardeners who paused in their labors to regard her with astonishment. Well, she *was* wearing a costume which marked her as alien to Optheria, but surely these people had encountered aliens before. The aroma lured her on. If it tasted half as good as it smelled, it would be an improvement on the Bascum brew. Of course it could *be* Bascum, for breweries were often situated in suburbs where the fumes would not irritate the fastidious.

She reached the dirt road that served as main artery for the settlement, deserted at that morning hour except for some small, peculiar-looking animals basking in the sun. She was aware of being watched, but as that was only to be expected, she continued her inspection of the unprepossessing buildings facing the road. The brew-smell continued to permeate the air but intensified to her right. Common sense indicated that the wide gray structure on the far side of the road some thousand meters away was probably the source. She headed there.

As she walked she heard doors and windows open behind her, marking her passage to her objective. She permitted herself a small smile of amusement. Human nature did not change and anything new and unusual would be marked in a society as dull and repressed as she suspected Optheria's was.

The brew-smell was almost overpowering by the time she reached the gray building. An exhaust fan was extracting the air from the roof, its motor laboring. Although there was no sign or legend on the building to indicate its purpose, Killashandra was not deterred. A locked front door, however, did pose an obstacle. She rapped politely and repeated her knock when it brought no immediate response. Thumping on the door also produced no results, and Killashandra felt determination replace courtesy.

Was brewing illegal in Optheria's largest city? Or could it be brewing without due license? After all, Bascum originated on Optheria and might have a monopoly. To be sure, she hadn't paid much attention to what plants were being so carefully tended in the gardens. Home industry? Thwarting the ever vigilant and repressive Elders?

Quickly she stepped around the building and toward its rear, hoping to find a window. She caught a glimpse of a running juvenile body and heard it raise its voice in warning. So she raced around the corner to find the rear doors folded back on a scene of much industry as men and women supervised the bottling of a brew from an obviously improvised vat. The young messenger took one look at her and fled, ducking down the nearest alley.

"May a thirsty stranger to this planet have a sample of your brew? I'm perishing for lack of a decent glass."

Killashandra could, when she exerted herself, be smoothly charming and ingratiating. She'd played the part often enough. She glanced from one stony expression to the next, holding her smile.

"I'll tell you it was some shock to discover this planet doesn't import anything spiritous or fermented."

"Shuttle got in yesterday," someone in the group said.

"Too early for tourists."

"Those clothes aren't local."

"Nor island."

"I'm not a tourist," Killashandra inserted in the terse comments. "I'm a musician."

"Come to see the organ, have you?" The man's voice was so rich in contempt, disapproval, cynical skepticism, and malicious amusement that Killashandra tried hard to spot him in the hostile group.

"If I can judge by my reception above, that sour lot permits few favors. A body really needs a brew here." Again she fortified her smile with winning charm. And licked dry lips.

Later, in reviewing the scene at her leisure, Killashandra decided that it might have been that unconscious reflex that won her case. The next thing she knew an uncapped bottle was thrust at her. She reached to her belt pouch for the Optherian coins she had acquired on the *Athena* but was curtly told to leave off. Money didn't buy their brew.

Although some had turned back to their job, most watched while she took her first sip. It was rich despite its clandestine manufacture, slightly cool, undoubtedly improved by a proper chilling but superior to the Bascum and almost on a par with Yarran.

"Your brewmaster wouldn't happen to be of Yarran origin?" she asked.

"What do you know of Yarra?" Once again the question was posed anonymously though Killashandra thought the speaker was on her left, near the vat.

"They make the best beer in the Federated Sentient Planets. Yarran brewmasters have the best reputation in the Galaxy."

A rumble of approval greeted this. She could feel the tension ease though the work continued at the same swift pace. Above the rattle of bottles, and the noise of crating the full containers, Killashandra heard a gasping wheeze to her right, on the roadway, and then a dilapidated vehicle, its sides scarred and rusting, pulled up to the open door.

Immediately crates were loaded into it, Killashandra helping, for she'd finished her bottle and wondered how she could wheedle another, others, from them. Thirst properly quenched, she'd find it easier to deal with the reproaches of Thyrol and the others. No sooner had the load bed been filled than the vehicle moved off and another, equally disreputable, slid into its place. Of course this patently unauthorized operation proved conclusively to Killashandra that the population of Optheria had not all stagnated. But how much of a minority did they constitute? And did any of them actually wish to leave Optheria? Some people enjoy thwarting their elected/established/appointed governments out of perversity rather than disloyalty or dislike.

When the third transport had been loaded, only a few crates remained. And the vat and its attendant paraphernalia had been dismantled and reassembled in different form entirely. Killashandra gave the brewers full marks for ingenuity.

"You expect a search?"

"Oh yes. Can't mask brewing completely, you know," said a sun-wrinkled little man with a twinkle in his eye. He offered Killashandra a second bottle, gesturing to the loaded vehicle in explanation of his generosity.

As she inadvertently glanced in the same direction, Killashandra noticed that his workers, each laden with a crate, were disappearing up and down the street and into the alleys. Just audible was an odd siren. He cocked his head at the sound and grinned.

"I'd take that with me, were I you. Won't help you to be found in my disreputable company."

"You'll be making another batch soon?" Killashandra asked wistfully.

"Now *that* I couldn't say." He winked. The siren became more insistent and louder. He began to fold over the doors.

"What's the quickest way back to the City?"

"Over two ranks and then to your left." He closed the last lap of the door behind him and she heard the firm click of the lock.

The vehicle with the siren was moving at a good clip so Killashandra made rapid progress in the direction the brewer had indicated. She had just reached the next parallel road when she heard the sound of air brakes engaging and considerable shouting. She ducked around the corner and was on another deserted block. When she heard the pounding of booted feet, she realized that she might not have time to explain her possession of the illegally brewed beer if she was caught out on the streets.

The first door she approached was locked and her quick rap met with no response. The second door was jerked open just as she got to it. She needed no urging to step into the sanctuary. Indeed, not a moment too soon for the searchers came pounding around the corner and stormed past the door.

"That was a bit foolish, if you ask me," said the woman beside her in a hoarse accusation. "You may be an alien but that wouldn't matter to *them* did they apprehend you down here." She gestured for Killashandra to follow her to the rear of the little house. "You must have some thirst to go roaming about Gartertown in search of quenching. There are places which legally serve drink, you know."

"I didn't, but if you could tell me—"

"Not that the hours you can drink are that convenient, and our brew's superior to anything out of the Bascum. The water, you know! This way."

Killashandra paused because a crate of the illegal bottling was sitting in the middle of the floor of the rear room, right by a section of flooring which had been removed.

"Give me a hand, would you? They might do a house-to-house if they're feeling particularly officious."

Killashandra willingly complied and, when the crate was stored, the section replaced, the hiding place was indistinguishable.

"Don't like to rush a body's enjoyment of a brew, but . . ."

Killashandra would have preferred to savor the second bottle, but she downed it in three long swallows. The woman took the empty and chucked it toward the disposal. With a loud *crunch* the evidence was disposed of. Killashandra drew her fingers down the corners of her mouth, and then belched yeastily.

The woman took a position by her door, ear to the panel, listening intently. She jumped back just as the door swung in wide enough to admit a tall figure.

"They were recalled," the man said. "And there's some sort of search going on in the City—" He broke off then because he had turned and caught sight of Killashandra standing in the doorway.

She was as motionless with surprise as he for she recognized him, by garb and stance, as the young man from the infirmary corridor. He recovered first while Killashandra was considering the advisability of dissembling.

"You're making this far too easy," he said cryptically, striding up to her. Surprised, she saw only his fist before a stunning blackness overcame her.

She roused the first time, aware of a stuffy atmosphere, the soreness of her jaw, and that her hands and feet were tied. She groaned, and before she could open her eyes, she felt a sudden pressure on her arm and her senses reeled once more back into unconsciousness.

She was still tied when she woke the second time, with an awful taste in her mouth and the tang of salt in her nostrils. She could hear the hiss of wind and the slap of water not far from her ears. Cautiously she opened her eyes a slit. She was on a boat, all right, in an upper berth in a small cabin. She was aware of another presence in the room but dared not signal her consciousness by sound or movement. Her jaw still ached though not, she thought, as much as on her previous awakening. Whatever drug they had given her was compounded with a muscle relaxant, for she felt exceedingly limp. So why did they bother to keep her bound?

She heard footsteps approaching the cabin and controlled her breathing to the slow regularity of the sleeper just as an outer hatch was flung open. Spray beaded her face. A warm spray so that her muscles did not betray her.

"No sign?"

"No. See for yourself. Hasn't moved a muscle. You didn't give her too much, did you? Those singers have different metabolisms."

The inquisitor snorted. "Not that different, no matter what she said about alcoholic intake." Amusement rippled in his voice as he approached the bed. Killashandra forced herself to remain limp though anger began to boil away the medically induced tranquillity as she reacted to the fact that she, a member of the Heptite Guild, a crystal singer, had been kidnapped. On the other hand, her kidnapping seemed to indicate that not everyone was content to remain on Optheria. Or did it?

Strong fingers gripped her chin, the thumb pressing painfully on the bruise for a moment, before the fingers slid to the pulse-beat in her throat. She kept her neck muscles lax to permit this handling. Feigning unconsciousness might result in unguarded explanations being exchanged over her inert body. And she needed some before she made her move.

"That was some crack you fetched her, Lars Dahl. She won't appreciate the bruise."

"She'll have too much on her mind to worry about something so minor."

"Are you sure this scheme is going to work, Lars?"

"It's the first break we've had, Prale. The Elders won't be able to fix the organ without a crystal singer. And they've got to. So they must apply again to the Heptite Guild to replace this one, and that will require explanations, and that will bring FSP investigators to this planet. And there's *our* chance to make the injustice known."

What about the injustice you did me? Killashandra wanted to shout. Instead she twitched with anger. And gave herself away.

"She's coming round. Hand me the syringe."

Killashandra opened her eyes, about to argue for her freedom when she felt the pressure that brooked no argument.

Her final awakening was not at all what she had been expecting. A balmy breeze rippled across her body. Her hands were untied and she was no longer on a comfortable surface. Her mouth tasted more vile than ever, and her head ached. She controlled herself once more, trying to sort out the sounds that reached her ears. Wind soughing. Okay. A rolling noise? Ocean waves breaking on shore line not far away. The smells that accosted her nostrils were as varied as the wind and wave, subtle musty floral fragrances, rotten vegetation, dry sand, fish, and other smells which she'd identify later. Of human noises or presences she had no input.

She opened her eyes a fraction and it was dark. Encouraged, she widened her vision. She was lying on her back on a woven mat. Sand had blown onto it, gritty against her bare skin, under her head. Overhead, trees bent their fronds, one sweeping against her shoulder in a gentle caress. Cautiously she lifted her torso, propping herself up on one elbow. She was no more than ten meters from the ocean, but the high-tide mark was safely between her and the sea, to judge by the debris pushed into an uneven line along the sand.

Islanders? What had Ampris said about the islanders? That they'd had to be disciplined out of autonomous notions? And the young man of the corridor who had assailed her. He had been suntanned. That was why his skin was so dark in comparison to the other onlookers.

Killashandra looked around her for any sign of human habitation, knowing that there wouldn't be any. She had been abandoned on the island. Kidnapped and abandoned. She got up, absently brushing the sand off her as she swung about, fighting her conflicting emotions. Kidnapped and abandoned! So much for the prestige of the Heptite Guild on these backward planets. So much for another of Lanzecki's off-world assignments!

Why hadn't she left a message for Corish?

Chapter 8

Killashandra grimaced as she crossed off yet another week on the immense tree under which she had erected her shelter.

She sheathed the knife again and involuntarily scanned the horizon in all directions, for her polly tree dominated the one elevation on the island. Once again she saw distant sails to the northeast, the orange of the triangles brilliant against the sky.

"May their masts snap in a squall and their bodies rot in the briny deep!" she muttered and then kicked at the thick trunk of the tree. "Why don't you ever fish in *my* lagoon?"

Morning and night she threw in her hook and line and was rewarded by wriggling fish. Some she had learned to throw back, for their flesh was either inedibly tough or tasteless. The small yellowbacks were the sweetest and seemed to throw themselves with selfless sacrifice on her hook.

The bronzed young man had not stranded her without equipment. When dawn had come on that bleak first day, she had discovered hatchet, knife, hooks, line, net, emergency rations in vacuum pack, and an illustrated pamphlet on the resources of the ubiquitous polly tree. She had cast that contemptuously to one side until boredom set in three days later.

For someone who had been as active as Killashandra, enforced idleness was almost a crippling punishment. To pass the time she had retrieved the pamphlet and read it through, then decided to see if she could make something out of this so-universal plant. She had already noticed that many of the tree's multiple trunks had had satellite trunks removed at an early age. Her manual said that these were cut for the tender heart or the soft pith, both nutritious. Was the locals' interference with "nature" one of the reasons for their discipline by the mainland?

And how far away was the mainland? She couldn't even hazard a guess as to how long she had been unconscious. More than a day, at the least. She wished she'd studied the geography of Optheria more closely, for she couldn't even guess at the location of her island on the planet's surface. In her first days, she had prowled the island's perimeter ceaselessly, for there were neighboring ones tantalizingly visible even though they were also small. Hers at least boasted a bubbling spring that flowed from its rocky source mid-island into the lagoon. And, if she could trust her judgment, hers was the largest in the cluster.

Before she immersed herself in polly tree studies, she had swum to the nearest of the group. Plenty of polly trees but no water. And beyond that islet more were scattered in careless abundance across the clear aquamarine sea—some large enough to support only a single tuft of polly trees. So she had returned to her island, the best of a bad lot.

Working with her hands and for a varied diet did not prevent Killashandra from endless speculations about her situation. She had been kidnapped for a purpose—to force an investigation of Optherian restrictions. The FSP, much less her own Guild, would not tolerate such an outrage. *If*—and here her brief knowledge of the Optherians let her down—the Optherians admitted to FSP and the Heptite Guild that she *had* been abducted.

Still, the Elders needed an operative organ by the time of the Summer Festival, and to do that they needed a crystal singer to make the installation. The crystal they had, but surely they wouldn't attempt such a delicate job. Well, it wasn't *that* delicate, Killashandra knew, but the crystal would prove difficult if not handled properly. So, grant that the Optherians would be searching for her, would they think to search on the islands? Would the islanders be in contact with the Ruling Elders about the terms of her ransom? If so, would the extortion be successful?

Probably not, Killashandra thought, until the Ruling Elders had abandoned any hope of finding her within the next two months. Of course, that could throw their timetable off. It would take nearly three months for a replacement Guild Member to reach Optheria, even if the Optherians admitted the loss of the one already dispatched to them. On her own part, she'd be stark raving lunatic if she was left on this island for several months. And if the Optherians acquired another singer to install their wretched white crystal, that didn't mean that they'd continue their efforts to find *her*!

After much deliberation, silent as well as vocal, Killashandra decided that the smart thing to do was rescue herself. Her kidnapper had overlooked a few small points, the most important of which was that she happened to be a very strong swimmer with lungs well developed from singing opera and crystal. Physically, too, she was immensely fit. She could swim from island to island until she found one that was inhabited, one from which she could be rescued. Unless all the islanders were in on this insidious kidnap scheme.

The hazards that she must overcome were only two: lack of water was one, but she felt that she could refresh herself sufficiently from the polly fruit—the tree flourished on all the islands she could see. Two, the larger denizens of the sea constituted a real problem. Some of them, cruising beyond her lagoons, looked deadly dangerous, with their pointed, toothy snouts, or their many wire-fine tentacles which seemed to have an affinity for the same yellowback fish she favored. She had spent enough time watching them to know that they generally fed at dawn and dusk. So, if she made her crossings at midday, when they were dormant, she thought she had a fairly good chance to avoid adding herself to their diet.

Three weeks on the island was long enough! She had a few of the emergency food packets left and they would be unharmed by a long immersion.

Following the directions in her useful little pamphlet, she had made several sturdy lengths of rope from the coarse fiber of the polly tree, with which she could secure the hatchet to her body. Her original clothing was down to shreds which she sewed with lengths of the tough stem into a halter and a loin cloth. By then she had become as tan as her abductor and was forced to use some of the oilier fishes to grease her hide for protection. She would coat herself thoroughly before each leg of her swim to freedom.

Having made her decision, Killashandra implemented it the next day at noon, swimming to her first destination in less than an hour's time. She rested while she made up her mind which island of the seven visible would be next. She found herself constantly returning to the one farthest north. Well, once there, none were far away if she decided she'd overshot the right line to take.

She made that island by mid-afternoon, dragging herself up onto the narrow shore, exhausted. Then she discovered some of the weak points in her plans: there weren't many ripe polly fruits on the island; and fish wouldn't bite on her hook that evening.

Because she found too few fruits, she was exceedingly thirsty by morning and chose her next point of call by the polly population. The channel between was dark blue, deep water, and twice she was startled by dimly seen large shapes moving beneath her. Both times she floated face down, arms and legs motionless, until the danger summoned by her flailing limbs had passed.

She rested on this fourth island all the rest of that day and the next one, replenishing her dehydrated tissues and trying to catch an oily fish. To her dismay, she could only attract the yellowbacks. Eventually she had enough of them to provide some oil for her raddled skin.

On her voyage to the fifth island, a fair sized one, she had her worst fright. Despite the sun's being at high noon, she found herself in the midst of a school of tiny fish that was being harvested by several mammoth denizens. At one point she was briefly stranded on a creature's flank when it unexpectedly surfaced under her. She didn't know whether to swim furiously for the distant shore or lie motionless, but before she could make a decision the immense body swirled its torpedo tail in the air and sounded. Killashandra was pulled under by the fierce turbulence of its passage, and she swallowed a good deal more water than she liked before she returned to the surface.

As soon as she clambered up on the fifth island, she headed for the nearest ripe polly fruit only to discover that she had lost her hatchet, the last packets of emergency rations, and the fish hooks. She slaked her thirst on overripe polly fruit, ignoring the rank taste for the sake of the moisture. That need attended to, she gathered up enough dry fronds to cushion her body, and went to sleep.

She woke sometime in the night, thirsting for more of the overripe fruit which she hunted in the dark, cursing as she tripped over debris and fell into bushes, staggering about in her search until she had to admit to herself that her behavior was somewhat bizarre. About the same time she realized that she was drunk! The innocent polly fruit had been fermenting! Given her Ballybran adaptation, the state could only have been allowed by her weakened constitution. Giggling, she lay down on the ground, impervious to sand or discomfort and fell into a second drunken sleep.

Much the worse for her various excesses, Killashandra awoke with a ghastly headache and a terrible need for water. Number five was a much larger island than her other way stops and she was searching so diligently to relieve her thirst that she almost passed the little canoe without its registering on her consciousness.

It was only a small canoe, pulled up beyond the high tide mark, a paddle angling from the narrow prow. At another time and without her urgent need, Killashandra would not have ventured out on the open sea in such a flimsy craft. But someone had already brought it from wherever they came so it could as easily convey her elsewhere, too. Her need for water diminished by this happy discovery, Killashandra climbed the nearest polly tree and, hanging precariously on to the ridged trunk, managed to saw through several stems with her short knife blade.

She didn't waste time then, but threw the fruit into the small craft, slid it into the gentle waves, and paddled down the coast as fast as she could, just in case the owner should return and demand the return of his canoe.

While she no longer needed to wait until noon to cross to the next island in her northern course, Killashandra's previous day's fright made her cautious. She keenly felt the loss of her hatchet. But good fortune continued to surprise her for, as she paddled around a narrow headland, she spotted the unmistakable sign of a small stream draining into the sea. She could even paddle a short way up its mouth and did so, pausing to scoop up a handful of sweet water before she jumped out of the canoe and pulled it out of sight under the bushes. Then she lay down by the water and drank until she was completely sated.

By evening, just before the sun suddenly settled below the horizon in the manner characteristic of tropical latitudes, she stood out on the headland, deciding which of the island masses she would attempt to reach the next day. The nearest ones were large, by comparison, but the distant smudge lay long against the horizon. The water lapped seductively over her toes and she decided that she had fooled around with the minor stuff long enough. With the canoe, a fair start in the morning, and plenty of fruit in her little craft, she could certainly make the big island, however distant.

She had the foresight to weave herself a sun hat, with a fishtail down her back to prevent sunstroke, for she wouldn't have the cooling water about her as she had while swimming. She had no experience with currents or riptides, nor had she considered the possibility of sudden squalls interrupting her journey. Those she encountered halfway across the deep blue stretch of sea to the large island.

She was so busy trying to correct her course while the current pulled her steadily south that she was unaware of the squall until it pelted against her sunburned back. The next thing she knew she was waist deep in water. How the canoe stayed afloat at all, she didn't know. Bailing was a futile exercise but it was the only remedy she had. Then suddenly she felt the canoe sinking with her and, in a panic lest she be pulled down, she swam clear, and had no way to resist the insidious pull of the current.

Once again the stubborn survival instinct came to Killashandra's aid, and wisely she ceased struggling against the current and the run of the waves, and concentrated on keeping her head above water. She was still thrashing her arms when her legs grated against a hard surface. She crawled out of the water and a few more meters from the pounding surf before oblivion overcame her.

Familiar sounds and familiar smells penetrated her fatigue and allowed her to enjoy the pangs of thirst and hunger once again. Awareness of her surroundings gradually increased and she roused to the sound of human voices raised in a happy clamor somewhere nearby. She sat up and found herself on one end of a wide curving beach of incredible beauty, on a harbor sheltering a variety of shipping. A large settlement dominated the center of the harbor, with commercial buildings at the center gradually giving way to residences and a broad promenade that paralleled the beach before retreating into the polly plantations.

For a long time Killashandra could only sit and stare at the scene, rendered witless by her great good fortune. And then not at all sure what her next step should be. To arrive, announcing her rank and title, demanding transport back to the City? How many people had been privy to her abduction? An island weapon had made the first assault against her. She had better go cautiously. She had better act circumspectly.

Yes, indeed she should, she realized as she stood up and found herself without a shred of clothing on her body. Nudity might not be appreciated here. She was too far away to notice how much or how little clothing the happy group on her side of the bay was wearing. So, she would get close enough to discover.

She did that with little trouble, and also discovered abandoned clothing, shirts and long, full skirts of decoratively painted polly fiber as well as undecorated underskirts. So she took several of those, picking from different piles, and a conservatively marked shirt and dressed herself. She also filched several packets of food, spoiling someone's picnic lunch but filling the void in her belly. No footwear had been left on the beach, so she concluded that bare feet would not be distinctive and her soles were sufficiently callused now not to trouble her. The off-white of her underskirts set off the fine brown of her tanned skin.

She tucked her knife under the waistband, then set off on the well-marked path toward the main settlement.

Chapter 9

What Killashandra required most was a credit outlet. She would need more clothing—a proper, decorated overdress—if she was to blend in with the islanders. As well, she needed some sort of accommodation and enough credit to get her back to the mainland or wherever the City was located.

None of the commercial buildings facing the harbor appeared to have credit outlets, though all had intake units. One of them had to, or this planet was more backward than she'd previously thought. Every inhabited planet utilized the standard credit facilities.

She had a bit of a fright, too, while she was making her initial reconnaissance—the sight of herself in a reflective surface. Sun had streaked the top layer of her dark hair almost blond, had bleached her eyebrows to nonexistence. This, plus the deep brown of her tan, altered her appearance so that she had almost not recognized herself. The whites and the intense green of her eyes with the filtering lenses were emphasized by the tan and dominated her face. The exertions of the last few days had thinned all the flesh which she had acquired with easy living on the voyage. She was as gaunt as if she'd been in the Crystal Ranges for weeks. Furthermore she felt like she had. Why was it, when she was tired, she still felt the crystal surging through her bones?

There was only one other building on the waterfront, set off a little from the others, looking rather more prosperous. A factor's residence? She made for it, having little choice, ignoring the covert glances of the few pedestrians. Was the community so small that any stranger was remarkable? Or was it indeed her lack of the proper attire that occasioned their scrutiny?

She recognized the building's function as soon as she climbed the short flight of stairs to the wide verandah which surrounded all four sides. The smell of stale beer and spirits was manifest, as well as a burned-vegetable odor, pungent and not altogether unpleasant. It was always good to know where the brew was served.

The main room of the tavern was empty and dark and, despite the sea breezes wafting through, stank of a long night's drinking. Chairs were neatly piled on the tables, the floor had been swept and glistened wetly to one side, where mop and pail propped open a door. She gave the room a sweeping glance, which stopped at the reassuring shape of a credit outlet.

Hoping she could make her transaction in private, she glided across the floor on her bare feet. Slipping her i.d. under the visiplate, she tapped out a modest credit demand. The sound of the outlet's whirring and burping was unnaturally loud in the deserted room. She grabbed the credit notes, compressing them quickly into a wad in one hand while she tapped out the security code that would erase the transaction from all but the central credit facility on the planet.

"Ya wanted something?" An unshaven face peered around the half-open door.

"I got it," Killashandra said, ducking her head and making a speedy exit before she could be detained.

While this island town had more in the way of merchandise establishments that catered to fishermen and planters, she had marked the soft goods store in her search for the credit outlet. It was unoccupied and automated so that she didn't need to manufacture explanations to a salesperson. It only struck her then that in none of the shops on the waterfront had she seen human attendants. She shrugged it off as another island oddity. She bought two changes of the brightly decorated, and rather charmingly patterned, outer garments, additional underskirts—for custom apparently demanded a plethora of female skirts—sandals of plaited polly tree fiber, a matching belt and pouch, and a carisak of a similar manufacture. She also got some toilet articles and a tube of moisturizing cream for her dry skin.

The little shop boasted a rather archaic information unit, a service Killashandra needed almost as badly as credit. She dialed first for hostel information and was somewhat daunted by the fact that all the listed facilities were closed until the Season. Well, she'd slept on island beaches for nearly four weeks and come to no harm. She queried about eating places and found that these also were closed until the Season. Irritated because she didn't wish to spend time gathering food in a large settlement, she tapped out a request for transport facilities.

Quite an astonishing variety of ships were available for charter: for fishing, pleasure cruising, and underwater assisted exploration "with requisite official permits. Travel documents are required for passengers or cargo. Apply Harbor Master."

"Which I can't do until I know more about this place," Killashandra muttered as a stately woman entered the premises. "And how many in sympathy with my kidnappers."

"Did you find all you needed?" the woman said in a liquidly melodic voice, her large and expressive brown eyes showing concern.

"Yes, yes, I did," Killashandra said, surprised into a nervous response.

"I'm so glad. We don't have much here yet. No call, with everyone making their own, and the Season not started." She tilted her head, her long thick braid falling over her shoulder. Her fingers moved to check the position of the blossom twisted into the end of the plait. Her smile was luminous. "You've not been here before?" The question was asked in such a gentle voice that it was almost a statement of fact and not an intrusion on Privacy.

"I just came in from one of the outer islands."

"That's lonely." The woman nodded gently.

"Lost my canoe in that squall," Killashandra said and began to embroider slightly. "Came ashore with nothing to my name but my i.d." She flashed her left wrist at the woman who nodded once again.

"If you're hungry, I've fresh fish and greens, and there's whiteroot to make a good fry."

"No, I couldn't," Killashandra began, even as her mouth was watering. When the woman tilted her head again, a broad smile spreading across her serene features, Killashandra added, "But I certainly would appreciate it."

"My name is Keralaw. My man is mate on the *Crescent Moon*, been gone four weeks and I do miss company." She rolled her eyes slightly, her grin twisting upward another fraction of an inch so that Killashandra knew very well what Keralaw missed.

"My name is Carigana." Killashandra suppressed her amusement; the former owner of that name would be livid at her presumption.

Keralaw led her to the back of the shop, through the storage section to the living quarters in the rear: a small catering area, a small toilet room, and a large living room that was open on three sides, screened against the depradations of insects. The furnishings consisted of low tables, many pillows, and hammocks secured to bolts in the ceiling. Of the modern accoutrements there was only a small screen, blank, with a fine coating of dust and a very primitive terminal. On the one solid wall hung a variety of spears, their barbed heads differing in design and weight, a small stringed instrument, a hand drum that looked well used, four wooden pipes of different lengths and circumferences, and an ancient tambourine, its trailing ribbons sun-faded to shades of gray and beige.

Keralaw led her through this room, out the screened door to the rear and to a stone hearth. Checking the position of the sun over her shoulder, Keralaw altered the arrangement of a mirror and a bright metal sheet to her satisfaction and began to arrange the fish and whiteroot on the sheet.

"Won't be long with the sun right in position. Beer or juice?"

"Island brewed?"

"Best there is." Keralaw's smile was proud. She went to the heavy bushes growing beyond the solar hearth and, pushing them aside, disclosed a dull gray container a meter high and half that wide. Lifting its heavy insulated lid, she extracted two beaded bottles.

"Been a long time dry," Killashandra said, receiving her chilled bottle with considerable anticipation. She flipped back the stopper and took a swallow. "*Whhhhoooee* but it's good." And it was—the equal of a Yarran! But Killashandra stopped herself from making that comparison aloud just in time, smiling instead at Keralaw.

Already the sun was broiling their lunch and the smell was a suitable accompaniment to the taste of the cool beer. Killashandra began to relax. Keralaw tossed the greens into a wooden bowl, slipped two wooden platters to the hearth side, along with two-tined forks and knives with intricately carved handles accentuating the natural dark grain of the wood, and divided the now completed meal.

"That was what I needed most," Killashandra said, closing her eyes in a sincere appreciation for the simple but satisfying meal. "I've been living too high off the polly tree!"

Keralaw chuckled fruitily. "You and your man farming? Or are you fishing for the gray?"

Killashandra hesitated, wondering what cover story wouldn't become an embarrassment later. She felt a curious reluctance to mislead Keralaw.

Keralaw reached over and touched Killashandra's forearm, just the barest touch, her mobile face suddenly expressionless.

"Don't need to tell me, woman. I been out in the islands and I know what can happen to humans out there. Sometimes the credit ain't worth the agony getting it. I won't pry." Her smile returned. "Not my place to, anyhow. You picked a good day to land on Angel Island. Schooner's making port this evening!"

"It is?" Killashandra picked up the cue to wax enthusiastic.

Keralaw nodded, pleased to surprise. "Beach barbecue and a keg of beer for sure! That's why the harbor's so deserted." She chuckled again, an earthy rich laugh. "Even the little ones are out foraging."

"Everyone contributes to the barbecue?"

Keralaw nodded, her smile wide with anticipation. "How well do you weave polly?" she asked, tilting her head sideways. When Killashandra groaned, Keralaw looked sympathetic. "Well, perhaps you cut and strip while I weave. Chore goes fast in company."

With fluid gestures, she collected a hatchet hanging from a nail under the eaves and a large cariall, which she handed to Killashandra. With a grin and a jerk of her head, she indicated the way.

The expedition suited Killashandra in many ways: Keralaw could supply her far more information than any terminal, however well programmed, and the little one in Keralaw's shop was intended for tourists and had limited memory. Killashandra could doubtless discover just how closely the Harbor Master stuck to the letter of the law in granting travel permits. Just like the Optherians to need to know who went where and when. Though why they bothered, since their citizens weren't allowed *off* the planet, Killashandra couldn't see. She also needed more general information about the islanders and their customs if she was going to pass as one that evening.

For her purposes, the barbecue couldn't have come at a better time; with everyone relaxed by a full belly and plenty of beer, she could discover more about the islanders' politics and, just possibly, something about her abduction.

By the time they had returned from the polly plantation that evening, both laden with platters and baskets woven at speed by Keralaw's deft hands, Killashandra knew a great deal more about island life, and had tremendous respect for it.

The easygoing gentleness of the style would be abhorrent to the persnickety mainlanders. In the early days of their subjugation of the islanders, the mainlanders had even tried to prohibit the use of the polly tree in their strict adherence to the letter of their Charter. The polly tree itself worked against the restriction, for it grew with such rapidity and profusion that pruning back the plantations was absolutely essential. The casual islander habit of cutting as needed to provide the essentials for daily life prevented overgrowth. The vigorous polly tree would take root on even a square meter of soil, which accounted for its proliferation in the islands.

Killashandra had been hard pressed to cut and strip enough polly fronds to keep up with Keralaw's agile weaving but the crystal singer learned as she watched and, to support her adopted identity, wove a few baskets herself. The manufacture, which seemed to be easy when one watched an adept, took considerable manual strength and dexterity, which, fortunately, Killashandra possessed. Seeing the clever way in which Keralaw finished off her mats and baskets taught Killashandra the necessary final touches that spoke of long practice.

As they passed a small freshwater lake on their way back, Keralaw suddenly dropped her burden, shucked her clothing, and dashed into the water. Killashandra was quick to follow. Nudity was not, then, a problem. And the soft water was refreshing after the concentrated work of the day.

The tantalizing aroma of roasting meat reached them as they neared Keralaw's dwelling. She rolled her eyes and smacked her lips appreciatively.

"Mandoll's the cook!" Keralaw said with satisfaction. "I can smell his seasoning anywhere in the islands. Porson sure had better catch him a smacker to go with it. Nothing better than long beef and smacker. Oho, but we eat good tonight!" She rolled her eyes again in anticipation. "We'll drop these off," and she swung the tangle of baskets on their string, "and then we get us pretty. A barbecue night's a *good* night for Angel Island!" And she winked broadly at Killashandra, who laughed.

Two barbecue pits had been dug on the beach front. In one a very long animal carcass was slowly turning over the sizzling coals. Four men were good-naturedly attempting to raise a massive fish onto the spit braces, urging each other to greater effort while the onlooking women taunted them for weakness.

Prominently centered on the beach was a long low table, already being laid with garlands of flowers, baskets of fruit and other delicacies which Killashandra couldn't identify. An immensely plump woman, with a most luxurious growth of hair spilling down to her knees, greeted Keralaw with delight, chattering about the quantity and quality of the baskets and plates, and then fell silent, cocking her head inquiringly at Killashandra.

"Here is Carigana, Ballala," Keralaw said, taking Killashandra's arm. "In from the outer islands. She wove with me."

"You picked the right time to come," Ballala said approvingly. "We have some good barbecue tonight. Long beef *and* a smacker!"

Suddenly a siren split the air with a hoot that occasioned loud cheers from everyone on the beach.

"Schooner's on the last tack. Be here right quick," Keralaw said and then began smoothing her arm in an absentminded way.

Killashandra cast it a quick look—all the fine hair was standing up. Killashandra rubbed her own brown arms to deflect comment. But Keralaw apparently did not notice the phenomenon.

"Come, Carigana, we must get pretty now."

Getting pretty meant decorating their hair with the scented flowers that grew on the low bushes under ancient polly trees. There seemed to be a community of possessions on Angel Island, for Keralaw visited several back gardens to find the colors she wanted for her own long tresses. And she had decided that only the tiny cream flowers would do as a garland for Killashandra's head, since Killa's hair was not long enough to braid. Keralaw offered to trim the dried ends, tutting over the exigencies that had deprived Killashandra of so many amenities on her distant island.

Then Keralaw decided that they'd have time to make some wreaths of the fragrant blossoms. Fortunately Killashandra was able to delay starting a wreath until she saw how Keralaw began hers and then the two twisted and tucked the stems in comfortable silence. Eventually, festive sounds drifted back to their ears from the beach and then cheering broke out.

"Schooner's in," Keralaw cried, jumping to her feet, her braids bouncing their floral tips against her waist. She grabbed Killashandra's hand, jerking her up. "Pick yourself a handsome one, Carigana. Of course, they're all handsome on the schooner," she said with an earthy giggle. "And away in the morning with no harm done, coming or going."

Killashandra followed willingly, clutching her wreaths in her hand, hoping her crude manufacture would not break apart from the jostling.

There could be few sights more impressive than a schooner sailing effortlessly into the beautiful azure waters of a harbor under an evening sky rich with sun-tinged clouds, while colorfully dressed and beflowered people lined the pier and the beach. The odors of a delicious meal permeated the air and all present were happily anticipating an evening spent in joyful pursuits—of all kinds. Killashandra had no wish to resist the enticements so lavishly available and she cheered as hard as the rest of the inhabitants of Angel Island as sailors on the yardarms reefed the sails while the schooner glided toward the pier, and the shoremen waited to secure the lines tossed to them. She jumped about, yelling at the top of her lungs, as everyone else was doing, waggling at arm's length her wreaths, as seemed to be the custom.

Then, suddenly, out of the crowd two men stood apart, grinning at the enthusiastic display but not joining in. Killashandra gasped, clutched the wreaths close to her face and stared, incredulous.

Corish von Mittelstern of the Beta Jungische system, purportedly in search of his uncle, was standing next to the bronzed young man of the corridor who had abducted and abandoned her on a miniscule island in the middle of nowhere!

Even as she reacted to their presence, she saw Corish was glancing about the crowd. Before she could duck, his gaze touched her face . . . and passed on without a blink of recognition.

Chapter 10

Shock rooted Killashandra in the sand. She ignored the surge of the islanders toward the pier, the vanguard already throwing their wreaths about the disembarking sailors. Fury that Corish didn't recognize her—and relief that he didn't—warred in her. To judge by his deep tan, Corish had been in the islands as long as she had. He looked comfortable in the shorts and sleeveless half-vest that the island men preferred, though his was modestly decorated. Not so the one Lars Dahl wore, which was thick with many-hued embroidery.

Common sense quickly tempered her initial strong reactions. She hadn't recognized herself in the mirror, why would Corish or Lars Dahl? Further, neither man could logically have expected to see Killashandra Ree on the beachfront at Angel Island. She relaxed from the tense half-poised stance she had assumed.

"Come on, you'll want to catch a good one," Keralaw said, tugging Killashandra by the sleeve. She paused, seeing the objects of Killashandra's riveted attention. "Lars Dahl is very attractive, isn't he? But he's committed to the Music Conservatory—the first Angel Islander to be admitted!"

"The other one?" Killashandra stood fast, though Keralaw plucked urgently at her to move.

"Him? He's been around the last few weeks. A pleasant enough man but . . ." Keralaw shrugged diffidently. "Come on, now, Carigana, I want a live one!"

Now Killashandra permitted herself to be drawn, holding her breath as first Corish then Lars Dahl looked toward them. When there was still no sign of recognition from either man, Killashandra grinned, then waggled her fingers at them and brandished the wreaths invitingly. Lars Dahl smiled back, gesturing a good-humored rejection of her offer before he renewed his conversation with Corish.

As Corish did not turn away, she swung her hips in her best imitation of a seductress, and cast one last longing look over her shoulder before Keralaw was hauling her through the crowd toward the approaching sailors.

Joyfully Keralaw deposited her garlands on a lean, brown-black man and, with a half-reproachful, half-apologetic glance at Carigana, accompanied him toward a distant section of the beach in the gathering dusk. Other couples had the same idea while many more made for the barbecue area and the kegs of beer, and jugs of fermented polly fruit in jackets of woven

316

polly fronds which were now being circulated. Many of the islanders had paired off, and the disappointed drifted back to the imminent feast, all still in the best of good spirits.

"What about garlanding me?" a male voice grated in her ear.

Killashandra turned her head toward the speaker, only far enough to catch the stench of his breath, before she deftly avoided his importunities with a giggle, slipping past a group of women. He paused there and someone less fastidious crowned him. Killashandra continued to glide forward and toward the shadows cast by the polly trees growing above the high tide line. The joyous sensuality of the islanders amused and frustrated her. Crystal resonance was slowly abating, and consequently her body's normal appetites were returning.

Corish and Lars Dahl were still deep in conversation at the water's edge. She was level with them now, though shadowed from their notice, and she could observe unobtrusively. She sank to the warm sand, the unused garlands fragrant in her loose grip. Ignoring the happy roistering at the barbecue pits, she concentrated on the two men.

What could be of such fascination to them in the midst of all this jollity? Her original instinct about Corish had been correct: he was an FSP operative. Unless she was fooling herself and his association with the impertinent Lars Dahl was a coincidence. She doubted that vigorously. Did Corish know that Lars Dahl had abducted her? And why? Had Corish taken some covert part in that kidnapping? Had Corish known who she was? Killashandra chuckled to herself, amused by the possibility although everything pointed to Corish having accepted her in the role she had played for him. Then she thought of how her earlier shipmates had reacted to the knowledge that she was a crystal singer. She doubted that Corish was less a man, particularly in his ease on the *Athena*, who would not make the most of his chances.

Keralaw had said that Lars Dahl was the first Angel Islander to reach the Music Conservatory. That explained his presence in the infirmary corridor, and his unconventional clothes, for the islanders appeared to prefer the browns and tans that emphasized their sunned skins. Why had he appeared so unexpectedly in Gartertown? Though he certainly maximized his opportunities. Had the original note of dissatisfaction with Optheria originated in these islands? That appeared logical, now that she had seen the different styles and standards, and had heard Elder Ampris's disparaging remarks about the islanders' early rebellion against the Optherian authoritarianism.

A shout went up by the long beef pit, and people surged toward it, platters in hand. The aroma was tantalizing and slowly Killashandra rose to her feet. A full stomach was unlikely to improve her understanding of the puzzle, but it wouldn't hinder thought. Corish and Lars Dahl seemed to have succumbed to the enticement as well.

In that instant, Killashandra decided to approach her problem in a direct fashion. Altering her direction, she intercepted the two men.

"You've had your natter," she began, mimicking Keralaw's throaty drawl and speech pattern, "now enjoy. Angel's a good island for feasting." She flung one garland on Corish, the other about Lars Dahl's neck, making her smile as seductive as possible. Before they could respond, though neither removed her flowers, she linked her arms in theirs and propelled them toward the pit, grinning from one to the other, daring them to break away.

Corish shrugged, smiled tolerantly down at her, accepting her impudence. Lars Dahl, however, covered her hand on his arm and, just then, their thighs brushed and she lurched against him, abruptly aware of receiving an intense shock. Startled, she glanced up at Lars Dahl, his face illuminated by the pit fires, his lazy smile appreciating the contact shock they had both felt. His long fingers curled tightly around hers with a hint of possessiveness. His blue eyes sparkled as his gaze challenged her. His arm fastened hers to his smooth warm waist as Killashandra candidly returned his glance. He sidestepped suddenly, pulling Killashandra with him so that she had to drop Corish's arm.

"I've certainly done enough talking," he said, grinning more broadly at the success of his maneuver and maneuvering. "Corish, find yourself another one. You're mine, aren't you, Sunny?"

Corish gave a slightly contemptuous snort but continued on while Lars Dahl stopped, swinging Killashandra into a strong embrace, his hands caressing her back, settling into her waist to hold her firmly against him as he bent his head. The flowers were crushed between them, their fragrance spilling into her senses. With an inadvertent gesture of acceptance, Killashandra's hands slid up his bare warm chest, her fingers caressing the velvet skin, taking note of the strong pectoral muscles, the column of his throat. His lips tasted salty, but firm, parting hers as he settled his mouth against her, and once again the shock of their contact was almost like . . . crystal. Hungrily Killashandra surrendered to his deft kiss, trying to meld her body against the strong, lean length of him. She altered her arms, stroking the silky skin of his hard-muscled back, all her senses involved in this simple act.

They parted slightly, his hands still caressing her, one hand on the bare skin beneath her shirt as she gently stroked his shoulders, breathless and unable to leave his supporting arms. If his embrace had begun as perfunctory, it wasn't now. There was about his grasp a sense of astonishment, wonder, and discovery.

"I must know your name," he said softly, tipping her chin up to look into her eyes.

"Carigana," she managed to remember to say.

"Why have I never seen you before?"

"You have," she said with a rich, suggestive chuckle, amused by her own presumption, "but you are always too busy with deep thoughts to see what you look at."

"I am all eyes now . . . Carigana." A slight tremor in his soft tone sent one through her body, as his hands renewed their grip, encouraging her body to conform to his.

Part of her mind recognized the sincerity in his voice while another section wondered how she could make the most of this encounter. All of her didn't care what else happened to either of them if they could just enjoy this one evening. She was so hungry . . . it had been months since she'd made love.

"Not yet, sweet Sunny, not yet," he said, determinedly but gently disengaging himself. "We've the whole night before us," and his low voice lilted with promise. "You'll know I cannot absent myself so soon. And we'll both be the stronger after a good meal"—his laughter rippled with sensuality—"for our dalliance."

She let herself be swung again to his side, his arm tucking hers against his ribs, his warm hand stroking hers as he guided her to the barbecue pits. She had no argument against his so firm decision. Although she murmured understanding, she seethed with abruptly interrupted sensations, forcing herself to an outward amity. Perhaps it was as well, she told herself, as they collected platters from one of the long tables and joined those awaiting slices of roasted meat. She'd need time to recover and buffer herself against the charisma of the man. He was as potent as Lanzecki. And that was the first time she'd thought of the Guild Master in a while!

What did Lars mean in saying she'd know why he couldn't absent himself so soon? How important was he within the island society, aside from being its first citizen to get into the Conservatory?

Then they were in the midst of the eager diners, with Lars exchanging laughing comments, teasing acquaintances, his rich lilting laughter rising above theirs. Yet he kept a firm grip on Killashandra and she tried to compose her expression against the surprise in the women's faces and the curiosity of the men. Who was this Lars Dahl when he wasn't kidnapping crystal singers?

Once thin slices of the juicy meat had been served them, Lars Dahl escorted her back to the table and they sank to the sand. Lars kept his left hand lightly on her thigh as he filled their plates from the foods displayed in the center of the table: breaded fried fish bits, steaming whiteroots, chopped raw vegetable, large yellow tubers which had been baked in polly leaves and exuded a pungent spiciness. He snagged a jug as it was being passed and filled their cups, deftly pouring without losing so much as a drop. Killashandra was aware of furtive glances the length of the table for Lars Dahl's partner. She looked for Keralaw for her support but there was no sign of her friend. Nor could she discern any animosity in the scrutinies. Curiosity, yes, and envy.

"Eat. I guarantee you'll need your strength . . . Carigana."

Though she gave him a gleaming smile, she wondered why he had hesitated with the name, as if he was savoring the sound of it, the way he had rolled the *r*s and lengthened the final two *a*s. Was he dissembling? Had he recognized her? He knew she'd been injured by that island star-knife . . .

She almost pulled away from him, startled by a sudden knowledge that *he* had thrown that vicious starblade at her. She shook her head, smiling to answer his sudden quizzical look, and applied herself to the heaped food. His hand soothed her thigh, the fingers light and caressing.

You sure can pick 'em, Killashandra, she thought, pulled by intense and conflicting emotions. She couldn't wait to roll with him, somewhere in the warm and fragrant plantation, with the surf pounding in rhythm with her blood. She wanted to solve the conundrums he represented, and she was determined to resolve each one to her advantage—and furious that he didn't even recognize the woman he had first injured and then abducted.

Yet, with all apparent complaisance, she sat, smiled, and laughed at his rather clever comments. Lars Dahl seemed to miss nothing that went on about him, and ate hugely. A beaming plump man wearing half a dozen garlands passed about a platter of the black flesh of the smacker fish, nudging Lars Dahl with a lewd whisper for his ear only, while Lars was lightly kneading her thigh, and then the plump man winked broadly at her, dumping a second slice of the fish onto her plate.

She was indeed grateful for the second slice of the smacker for it was succulent and highly unusual in taste, having nothing oily or fishy about it. The fermented polly juice was more subtle than the overripe fruit she had eaten on the island. Lars kept her cup filled, though she noticed that he only sipped at his while appearing to imbibe more freely than the level in his cup suggested.

When she admitted that she could eat no more of the cooked foods, he carefully picked one of the large, dark red melons, and, with one hand—someone called aloud with a quick guess as to where his other hand was—he split it with his knife, glancing expectantly at her. Out of the corner of her eye she had seen another woman so served scoop the seeds from her halved melon. Laughingly she did the same service, settling Lars's half in his plate before taking her own. Then, before she could lift her spoon, he had made a thin slice which he lifted to her lips. The flesh of the melon was the sweetest she had ever tasted, velvety, dripping with juice once the flesh was pierced. He took his first bite on top of hers, his even, strong teeth leaving a neat semi-circle all the way to the rind.

It was not the first time eating had been part of her love-making, but never before so many, even if all the pairings were performing much the same ritual. Or was that why the air was electric with sensuality?

"A song, Lars. A song while you can still stand on your feet."

Suddenly there was the loud roll of drums and tambourine, and applause, while half a dozen stringed instruments strummed vigorously to presage the advent of evening entertainment. Then the applause settled into a rhythmic beat and the feasters began to chant.

"Lars Dahl, Lars Dahl, Lars Dahl!"

Giving her thigh a final squeeze, Lars Dahl rose to his feet, spreading his arms for silence, smiling compliance at the chanters and abruptly the clamor ended, a respectful silence awaited his pleasure.

Lars Dahl lifted his head, a proud smile curving his lips, as he surveyed his audience. Then, taking one backward step, he raised his arms and hit an A, clear, vibrant, beautifully supported. Utterly astounded, Killashandra stared up at him, the half-formed suspicion solidifying into confirmation just as his voice glided down the scale. There couldn't be two tenor voices of similar caliber on one planet. This was her unknown tenor of that spontaneous duet. Fortunately Lars Dahl took the expression on her face as pleasure in his performance. He swung into a rollicking sea ballad, a song as gay, as nonchalant as himself, a song that was instantly recognized and appreciated by his audience.

At the verse, voices joined his in harmony, people swaying to the tempo of the song. Hastily Killashandra joined in, mouthing words until she learned the simple chorus. She took good care to sing in her alto register. If she could recognize his tenor, he'd know her soprano. And she didn't want him to be tipped to her true identity—at least not until morning. Now she relaxed into the music, letting her alto swell in a part singing she hadn't enjoyed since her early adolescence on Fuerte. Suddenly she remembered family outings in the summer in the mountain lakes, or at the ocean shore, when she had led the singing. Was that what Antona had had in mind for Killashandra to keep as enriching memories? Well, there were aspects of even those mellow evenings which Killashandra would have as soon forgot. For her older brothers had always teased her about screeching at the top of her lungs, and showing off and preening herself in public.

Even before this evening, Killashandra had been aware that some melodies seem to be universal, either recreated within a planet's musical tradition or brought with the original settlers and altered to fit the new world. Words might be changed, tempo, harmony, but the joy in listening, in joining the group singing was not: it struck deep nostalgic chords. Despite her musical sophistication, despite her forswearing that same background, there was no way Killashandra could have remainded silent. Indeed, not to participate in the evening would have marked her as antisocial. For the Angel Islanders, singing was a social grace.

Nor was the singing simple, for the islanders added embellishments to choruses and songs, six-part harmonies and intricate descants. Lars Dahl functioned as both stage manager and conductor, pointing to the people expected to rise and sing or perform on their instruments: performing to a high degree of musical competence on such unexpected instruments as trumpet, a woodwind that looked like a cross between an oboe and an ancient French horn, and on a viola with a mellow, warm tone that must have arrived with the early settlers. The hand drums were played with great skill and showmanship, the three drummers executing a whirling dance in time to their intricate rhythms.

Even when the rest of the audience was not actively participating,

their attention was rapt, and their reaction to the occasional mistake immediate and understanding. There were songs about polly planters: one sung
by two women, humorously itemizing the necessary steps to make one
polly plant produce everything needed by their family. Another tune, sung
by a tall thin man with a deep bass voice, told of the trials of a man bent on
catching an ancient grandaddy smacker fish which had once demolished
his small fishing boat with a negligent flick of its massive tail. A contralto
and a baritone sang a sad haunting ballad on the vicissitudes of gray fishing and the vagaries of that enormous and elusive quarry.

"You've dallied long enough, Lars, you and Olav sing it now," a man
demanded from the shadows at one point. A wave of cheering and hand-
clapping seconded that order.

Grinning amiably, Lars nodded, beckoning to someone seated to Killashandra's left. The man who came to stand beside Lars had to be related
to him for their features were similar, if differently arranged. Though the
older man had a thin, long face, the nose was the same, and the set of the
eyes, the shape of the lips, and the firm chin. Neither man could really be
called handsome, but both exuded the same unusual quality of strength,
determination, and confidence that made them stand out as individuals.

A respectful silence fell and the instruments began the overture. Killashandra had a good musical memory: she could hear a composition once
and remember not only the theme, if there was one, but the structure. If she
had studied the score in any detail, she would know the composer and performances, what different settings or arrangements the music had had over
the years, and possibly which Stellars had performed it and where.

Before the men began to sing, she recognized the music. The words
had been altered but they suited the locality: the search for the lost and
perfect island in the mists of morning, and the beautiful lady stranded
there for whose affections the men vied. Lars's beautiful tenor paired well
with the older man's well produced baritone, their voices in perfect balance with each other and the dynamics of the music.

Nevertheless, at song's end Killashandra stared at Lars in amazement. He had the most outrageous gall . . . until she also remembered that
he had been required to sing it, however appropriate it might also be to her
circumstances. And Lars Dahl had not had the grace to look abashed.

Why should he? The performer in her argued with her sense of personal outrage. The music was beautiful, and so obviously a favorite of the
islanders that the last chorus trailed off into reverent silence.

Then the baritone held out his hand, into which was placed a twelve-
stringed instrument that he presented to Lars Dahl.

"The Music Masters may not have approved your composition for
the Summer Festival, Lars, but may we at least hear it?"

Plainly the request distressed Lars Dahl, for his mouth twitched and
he had ducked his head against the compelling level gaze. Nevertheless, he
took a deep breath, reluctantly accepting the instrument. His lips were
pressed into a thin line as he strummed a chord to test the strings. Lars did

not look at Olav, though he could not refuse the older man's request, nor did he look out at the audience. His expression was bleak as he inhaled deeply, concentrating onward to the performance. The rankling disappointment, the pain of that rejection, and the sense of failure which Lars had experienced were as clear to Killashandra as if broadcast. Her cynical evaluation of him altered radically. She was possibly the only one in the entire assembly who could empathize, could understand and appreciate the deep and intense conflict he had to overcome at that moment. She also could approve heartily of the professionalism in him that unprotestingly accepted the challenge of an excruciating demand. Lars Dahl possessed a potentially Stellar temperament.

Despite her proximity to him, she almost missed the first whispering chords which his strong fingers stroked from the strings. A haunting chord, expanded and then altered into a dominant, just like the dawn breeze through the old polly tree on her island of exile. Soft gray and pink as the sky lightened, and then the sun would warm the night-closed blossoms, their fragrance drifting to beguile senses: and the rising lilts of birds, the gentle susurrus of waves on the shore, and the lift in the spirit for the pleasure of a new day, for the duties of the day: climbing the polly for the ripe fruit, fishing off the end of a headland, the bright sun on the water, the rising breeze, the colors of day, the aroma of frying fish, the somnolence of midday when the sun's heat sent people to hammock or mat . . . an entire day in the life of an islander was in his music, colored and scented, and how he managed that feat of musical conjuring on a limited instrument like a twelve-string, Killashandra did not know. How that music would sound on the Optherian organ was something she would give her next cutting of black crystal to hear!

And the Music Masters had rejected his composition? She was beginning to understand why he might wish to assassinate her, and why he had kidnapped her: to prevent the repair of the great organ and, perhaps other less worthy compositions, from being played by anyone. And yet there was nothing in her brief association with Lars Dahl, in this evening's showmanship, even in his reluctant acquiescence to the demands of his island, to suggest such a dark vengeful streak in the man.

When the last chord, heralding moon-set, had faded into silence, Lars Dahl set the instrument down carefully and, turning on his heel, stalked away. There were murmurs of approval and regret, even anger in some faces, a more complimentary reaction to the beauty of what they had been privileged to hear than any wild applause. Then, people began to talk quietly in little groups, and one of the guitars tried to repeat one of the deceptively simple threnodies of Lars's composition.

With a glance to be sure no one was observing her, Killashandra rose to her feet and slipped out of the flickering torch light. Adjusting her eyes to the night, she saw movement off to the right and moved toward it, almost turning her ankle in one of the footprints that Lars's angry passage had gouged in the soft sand.

She saw his figure outlined against the sky, a dark tense shadow.

"Lars . . ." She wasn't sure what she could say to ease his distress but he shouldn't be alone, he shouldn't feel his music had not been appreciated, that the totality of the picture that he had so richly portrayed had not come across to his listeners.

"Leave me—" his bitter voice began, and then his arm snaked out, and catching her outstretched hand, pulled her roughly to him. "I need a woman."

"I'm here."

Holding tight to her hand, he pulled her into a lope. Then, pushing at her shoulder with his, he guided her at right angles to the beach, up toward the thick shadow of the polly grove on the headland, near where she had beached that morning. When she tried to slow his headlong pace, his hand shifted to her elbow. His grip was electric, his fingers seemed to transfer that urgency to her and anticipation began to course through her breast and belly. How they avoided running into a polly tree trunk, or stumbling over the thick gnarled roots, she never knew. Then suddenly he slowed, murmured a warning to be careful. She could see him lift his arms to push through stiff underbrush. She heard the ripple of a stream, smelt the moisture in the air, and the almost overpowering perfume emanating from the creamy blossoms before she followed him, pushing through the bushes. Then her feet were on the coarse velvet of some kind of moss, carpeting the banks of the stream.

His hands were urgent on her and the initial physical attraction she had felt for him was suddenly a mutual sensation. He put her at arm's length, staring down at her, seeing her not as a vessel from which he expected the physical relief, but as a woman whose femininity had aroused an instinctive and overpowering response.

"Who are you, Carigana?" His eyes were wide with his amazement. "What have you done to me?"

"I've done nothing yet," she replied with a ripple of delighted laughter. No one else had awakened such a response in her, not even Lanzecki. And if Lars had somehow sensed the crystal shock in her, so much the better: it would enhance their union. She had been celibate far too long and he was partly to blame: the consequences were for both to enjoy. "Whatever are you waiting for, Lars?"

Chapter 11

A light, almost tender, finger touch on her shoulder, just where the star-knife had sliced her flesh, roused Killashandra from the velvet darkness of the deepest sleep she had ever enjoyed. She felt weightless, relaxed. Despite her having led an uninhibited private life, Killashandra was inexplicably possessed by shyness, a curious reluctance to face Lars. She didn't want to face him, or the world, quite yet.

Then she heard the barest ripple of laughter in the tenor voice of her lover.

"I didn't want to wake up either, Carigana . . ."

Loath to perpetuate any lies between them, she almost corrected the misnomer but she found it too difficult to overcome the physical languor that gripped her body. And an explanation of her name would lead to so many more, any of which might fracture the stunning memory of the previous night.

"I've . . . never . . ." He broke off, his finger tracing other scar lines on her forearms—crystal scar (and how could she explain those at this point in a magical interlude)—down to her hands where his strong tapered fingers fit in between hers. "I don't know what you did to me, Carigana. I've . . . never . . . had a love experience like that before." A rueful laugh that cracked because he couldn't keep it soft enough to match his whisper. "I know that when a man's been troubled, a normal reaction is to seek sexual relief from a woman—any woman. But you weren't just 'any woman' last night, Carigana. You were . . . incredible. Please open your eyes so that I can see you believe what I'm saying—because it is true!"

Killashandra could not have ignored the plea, the sincerity, the soul sound in his voice. She opened her eyes. His were inches away and she was gripped by an overpowering surge of love, affection, sensuality, empathy, and compassion for this incredible and talented young man. Relief was mirrored in the very clear blue of his eyes: a morning-lagoon-in-sunlight clear blue, as vivid as the sea could sometimes be. Relief and the sudden welling up of tears. With the shuddering sigh that rippled down his body, so close to hers, he dropped his head to the point of her shoulder, just above the knife-scar. When, at length, he confessed that he had caused it, she would willingly forgive him. Just as she was willing to forgive him her abduction, for whatever marvelous reason he might submit. After last night, how could she deny him anything? Perhaps last night had been such

325

a unique combination of emotional unheavals that a repetition was unlikely. The prospect made her smile.

As if he sensed her responses—he had certainly sensed them last
night—he lifted his head again, anxious eyes searching her face. She saw
that he was not unscathed, for his lower lip was red and puffy as he tried
to echo her smile.

Then she chuckled, tracing the line of his mouth with an apologetic
finger.

"I don't think I can ever forget last night happened, Lars Dahl."
Would she ever find adequate words to record *this* on her personal file at
Ballybran? She let her finger drop to his jaw. His grin became more self-
confident, and his fingers squeezed hers lightly. "There's one problem . . ."
His face tightened with concern. "How long will it take us to recover to try
it again?"

Lars Dahl burst out laughing, rolling away from her.

"You may be the death of me, Carigana."

Once again Killashandra ardently regretted using that particular
pseudonym. She desperately wanted to confess everything and hear her
own name on his lips, in his rich and sensual voice.

"Like last night?"

"Oh my precious Sunny," he replied, his voice altering from spontaneous laughter to urgent loverliness as he rolled back to her, his hand
gently cupping her head, fingers stroking her hair, "it was almost a death
to leave you."

That he might be quoting some planetary poet, she discarded as un-
worthy. Her body and mind echoed the sentiment. Their exhausted sleep
had been like a little death, it had overtaken them so completely.

With total unconcern for aesthetics, her stomach rumbled alarmingly.
They suppressed a laugh and then let their laughter blend, as they enveloped each other in loving arms.

"C'mon, I'll race you to the sea," Lars said, his eyes sparkling with
amusement. "A swim to cool us off." He rose lithely to his feet, offering her
a hand.

It was only when the light blanket fell from her body that she realized
its presence. And noticed the small basket to one side of the clearing, the
unmistakable neck of a wine jug protruding from the lazy stream.

"I woke at dawn," Lars said, hands on her shoulders as he gently inclined forward to kiss her cheek. "The wind was a touch chilly. So I got a
few things for us. Could we spend today together and alone?"

Killashandra leaned lovingly against him for a moment. "I feel remarkably unsocial." She wanted nothing more.

"You'll barely look at me!" Lar's voice rippled with amused complaint.

Her hands began to caress him as his were gentle on her arms. Almost guiltily they broke apart. Laughing, they joined hands and pressed
through the bushes toward the seashore.

The sea was calm, the waves mere ripples flopping over at the last moment onto the smooth, wet sand. The water was soothing, soft against her body. Finally hunger could no longer be denied and they sprinted back to the secret clearing, patting each other dry, carefully avoiding the sorest spots. That morning Lars had acquired fresh fruits, bread, and a soft savory cheese as well as some of the flavorful dried fish that was an island specialty. There was wine to wash it all down. Lars had also had the wit to "borrow" from Mama Tulla's wash line a voluminous and comfortable kaftan for her and a thigh length shirt for himself.

They were both hungry enough to concentrate on eating, but they smiled whenever their eyes met, which was often. When their hands touched as they hunted in the basket for food, the touch also became a caress. When all the food had been eaten, Lars excused himself with grave courtesy and pushed through the bushes. Trying to suppress giggles, Killashandra did the same. But when she returned to the clearing, Lars was making a couch of polly fronds and sweetly scented ferns. In silent accord, they lay down, spread the light blanket over their weary bodies and, hands lightly clasped, surrendered to fatigue.

Once again the sensation of light fingers stroking the crystal scars roused Killashandra.

"You were a long time learning to handle polly, weren't you?" he said, his teasing tender.

She sighed, hoping she could somehow, and, with reasonable truth, evade his natural curiosity about her. She daren't risk a full disclosure even in the euphoria which still enveloped them.

"I came from the City. I'd no choice about an island life or an education in polly planting."

"Must you go back to the City?" Apprehension roughened his voice, his fingers tightened on hers in an almost painful grip.

"Inevitably." She turned her face against his arm, wishing it were bare and she could taste the skin covering the strong arms that had held her with such love: which must hold her once again in love, preferably for a long, long time. "I don't belong here, you know."

"I didn't think you did," and his reply was amused acceptance, "once you dropped the Keralawian accent." She warned herself to watch what she said. "Where *do* you belong, Carigana?"

"Besides in your arms?" Then the honesty of the moment began to close in on her. "I don't really know, Lars." These moments were out of context with any previous part of her life on Fuerte or Ballybran: totally divorced from Killashandra, Crystal Singer. Pragmatically she knew the euphoria would end all too soon but the desire to prolong it consumed her. "How about you, Lars? Where do you belong?"

"The Islands don't actually hold me any more. I've come to realize that over the past few months. And I think that my father recognizes it, too. Oh, I'm partner in an interisland carrier service that's reasonably profitable—useful to the islanders certainly." He grinned. "But three years in the City at the Complex taught me discipline, order, and efficiency and the easy way of islanders irritates me. I can't see me settling in to City life, either . . ."

Killashandra raised herself on her elbow, looking down at his face. The muscles were relaxed but the strength and character in his features were not the least bit diminished.

"Aren't you going to appeal the Master's decision?" Her fingers traced his clearly defined left brow.

"No one appeals their decision, Carigana," he said with a contemptuous snort. Then he drew both eyebrows together: her finger followed to caress away his scowl. "They did, damn their souls to everlasting acid, have the incredible gall to suggest that, if I performed a slight service for them, they might reconsider. And like a childish fool I believed them." Incensed by his memories, he swung to a sitting position, arms clasping his knees tightly to his chest, his mouth in a bitter line. "A real fool but so desperate to have my composition accepted—not so much for my own prestige as to prove that an islander could succeed at the Complex and to vindicate the support the islanders had given me during those years." He twisted his torso around to face her. "You'd never guess what this slight service was."

"I wouldn't?" Killashandra was quite certain what he would say.

"They wanted me to make an assault on a visiting dignitary. Possibly the most important person to set foot on this forsaken mudball."

"Assault? On Optheria? On whom? What visiting dignitary?" Killashandra was astonished at the surprise and concern in her voice, a genuine enough response to Lars's shocking statement.

"You heard that Comgail had died, shattering a manual of the Festival Organ?" When she nodded silently, he continued. "You may not know that the damage was deliberate." It was easy for her to react suitably, for a death involving crystal would not have been painless. "There are a lot of people who believe that they—we," and he grinned humorlessly, admitting to his complicity, "have an inalienable right to leave this planet in order to achieve professional fulfillment. And that right should be enjoyed by more than disappointed composers, Carigana. This restriction is stagnating intelligent people all over this world. People who have tremendous gifts which have no channel whatever on this backward *natural* mudball.

"So, it was decided to manufacture a situation that would require the presence of an extraplanetary official. An impartial but prestigious person who could be approached to register our protest with the FSP. Oh, letters have been smuggled out but letters are ineffective. We're not even sure that they reached their destinations. What we needed was someone who could be *shown* examples of this stagnation, talk to people like Theach, Nahia, and Brassner, see what they have been developing in spite of strictures of federal bureaucracy."

Lars gave a rueful laugh. "It's rather depressing to realize how little Optheria requires. The founding fathers wrought too well. We're a population expert in making do with the meanest possible natural resources. Good old polly!

"It was Comgail who proposed what had to be done to force the government to bring in a foreign technician. A manual on the Festival Organ would have to be shattered. The Government would be forced to have that replaced in time for the Summer Festival tourists.

"Did you ever realize how dependent the Government is on tourism?" His eyes glinted with malicious amusement. "Theach researched the economics. He can do the most phenomenal computations in his head—that way, there's no written proof of his alienation from the Optherian way of life! That tourist income is absolutely essential to purchase the high tech items which cannot be manufactured here. And without which all the federal machinery would grind to a halt. Even the barrier arc at the shuttleport is fashioned from imported components.

"Mind you, Comgail did not intend to be a martyr. But he didn't draw back when the moment was on him. So the Government was forced to apply to the Heptite Guild for a complete and very expensive new crystal manual. And this is where Comgail's sacrifice becomes relevant; he was also the only technician on Optheria capable of installing the replacement. They'd have to have the services of—at the very least—a highly skilled technician or ideally a crystal singer to make the repair. Once the crystal singer was on Optheria, we'd make sure there'd be an opportunity to present our desperate situation and ask that it be submitted to the FSP Council. A singer has access to the Council, you know."

"Go on, Lars . . ." A nasty suspicion began to form in Killashandra's mind, recalling Ampris's snide remarks about islanders.

He inhaled, closing his eyes briefly against unpleasant memories. "The crystal singer arrived on the *Athena* the day after my audition. Only the Elders weren't sure of her identity."

"That sort of i.d. cannot be forged, Lars."

He gave a contemptuous snort. "I know it, you know it, but you must also know how paranoid our Elders are. And Torkes is now in Communications." Again his words elicited a nodded reaction from her. "Oh, the urgency behind this slight favor was subtly presented to me. A crystal singer is known to have great recuperative powers. A minor scratch would be no inconvenience to a crystal singer but would unconditionally reveal an imposter. Since islanders are known," his voice dripped with sarcasm, "to live primitive and violent lives, accustomed to handling dangerous weapons, it was thought that I was admirably suited to perform this small favor for the Masters, in return for their reevaluation of my composition."

"And did they promise you immunity from reprisal as well?"

"I'm not quite that naive, Carigana. They did not require a frontal assault. So, I picked a window on the upper story where I'd have a good view of the arrival. I've been winning competitions with the star-blades since my father first allowed me one. A simple flick and the blade angles at the right trajectory. It caught her on the arm. I think a little higher than I'd planned for she moved just as I had completed the throw." His expression was chagrined and he gave Killashandra a quick defensive glance. "Oh, she was all right, Carigana. I scooted round to the infirmary the back way and she was walking out of the surgery without so much as a bandage showing." He smoothed her arm reassuringly. "Crystal singers really do heal with unbelievable speed. She seemed more annoyed with her escort than the incident.

"The next morning, of course, I was told that on due reconsideration, the Masters had to abide by their original decision. The omnipotent, omniscient Masters, speaking from their immense and encyclopedic knowledge of all forms of music and their total understanding of the universe and Man's sublime relationship with the Natural World, do not believe that this facet of Optherian life needs to be celebrated at any point in the year, certainly not during the Summer Festival when off-worlders might possibly hear something evoking a valid Optherian subculture and more original than variations on the usual pre-predigested pap that 'accredited' composers churn out."

"Stupid, insensitive, unimaginative, flatulent fardlings!" Killashandra's derision was slightly colored by hearing the details of the "outrageous" attack, and by the realization that her instinct about Ampris's specious assurance was quite valid. "They're so old they've lost the energy enthusiasm requires; they couldn't possibly recognize imagination."

Lars smiled at her vehemence. "So, despite all their promises and assurances, I was given a ticket back to Angel as a reward for my unmentionable service, and told to be out of the City on the evening oceanjet. Guardians were there to be sure I boarded, which I did. After a stroke of incredibly good luck."

He turned his face fully to her then, his lips lightly compressed as if controlling amusement, and the sparkling of his eyes indicated that he had considered confiding in her. As much as she hoped that he might, she wished fervently that he would not. For his honesty would require the similar courtesy from her.

"Lars, I don't mean to be a spoil-sport, but something occurred to me. A star-knife is an island blade, isn't it?"

"Yes . . ." He regarded her, suddenly alert.

"And if an island blade was responsible for wounding the crystal singer—even if it healed rapidly—would that not prejudice her against listening to your problem?"

"A good point. The Elders don't miss many tricks, but that ploy would not have worked. Nahia and Brassner were going to speak for us."

"*Were* going?"

"Yes, I did say that I had a stroke of good luck," and he clasped her hand with a firm grip, his clear blue gaze fixed on the thick bushes. "Nahia and Brassner will now have an even better chance to present our situation." He sounded so confident that Killashandra would have given much to be privy to his plans. "You'll see."

"Since I'm being candid, let me tell you that you've been rather indiscreet confiding in me, Lars. You don't know me—"

"Don't *know* you?" Lars threw back his head and guffawed. He clasped her to him, rocking her in his arms, roaring with laughter. "If I don't, young woman, no one ever will."

"You know what I mean. Who were you talking to last night on the beach? He's not an islander."

"Oh, him? Corish von Mittell-something. No, he's not an islander. In fact, he could be very useful . . ." Lars paused a moment in thought, and then shrugged it off. "He's looking for an uncle. Father asked me to help him, take him on my next swing through the islands. Frankly I don't think the uncle came this far out: doesn't sound like a man who'd want this sort of life style."

"Are you sure this Corish is who he says he is?"

Lars eyed her with some interest. "Father's sent for an i.d. verification. We're not so haphazard as all that in these islands, you know. There've been snoopers before. Father's got a sixth sense about the breed and that Corish tilted it. Oh, he says he came in on the *Athena,* and he sounded as if he'd made the trip on her." Then he added in another tone altogether, "I'm glad you worry about my safety."

He smoothed back her sun-bleached hair, fingering the strands before he patted them in place, his whole face softening as once more he fell in her thrall. Then he relaxed, lying back again, hands under his head, his eyes intent on her face, a very tender smile playing at the corner of his lips. "Anyway, everyone on Angel dislikes federal interference as much as we do. I studied under a master of heresy. My father. The duly appointed harbor master of the Angel Island archipelago and federal representative. If you can't lick 'em, join 'em."

"Your father's the harbor master?"

Surprise registered blankly on Lars's face. "Of course. Don't tell me you didn't know that?"

"I do. I didn't."

"So, if you really insist on going back to the City, you'll have to be very nice to me." He was smiling as he gently reached for her arms to bring her down to him.

"Oh?"

"*Very* nice to me."

"Are you able for it?"

He settled her into the curve of his arm, her head pillowed on his shoulder, his cheek against her hair.

"When you are, beloved." Then he yawned and, apparently, between one breath and the next, fell asleep. For another long moment, Killashandra heard the singing in her blood and for once did not regret its murmur. She repositioned her arm on his chest, placidly noting that the fine hairs across Lars's pectoral muscles stirred upright. Well, they had more energy than he or she did. She closed her eyes and was also claimed by sleep.

Shouts startled them awake: the cheerful calls and laughter of people fishing on the beach. Killashandra couldn't hear what was so exciting, but Lars smiled.

"A yellowback school has been forced into the cove." He embraced her enthusiastically. "Once they've caught what's needed, we'll get our"—he looked about for the angle of sunlight—"our dinner. Hungry yet?"

"Hungry enough to go right out there bold-faced . . ." She made as if to rise, for her belly was almost painfully empty.

He pulled her back flat beside him, kissing her half-formed protest into silence. His eyes were unsmiling as he then gently stroked her cheek.

"My dear girl, with those bruises on you, I'd be hauled up in front of the Island Court and charged with rape."

"What about the marks on you?"

"You resisted my improper advances—"

"And you made enough of those—"

"Precisely what the bruises say. So, since I have a reputation to maintain in this community, we will remain secluded." He emphasized this decision with a gentle kiss. Then he stroked her hair back from her forehead, his fingers lingering in the soft gold-streaked mass. "I don't wish to share you yet, share even the sight of you with anyone. If I believed the ancient tales of witchcraft, sorcery, and enchantment, I'd name you 'witch,' so I would. But you're not . . . though I am completely spellbound . . ." His fingers became insistent, and his expression was an urgent appeal. "D'you think you could possibly bear me . . . if I'm very careful . . ."

She chuckled and linked hands behind his head to bring his lips to hers.

The fishers were long gone before they finally got around to fishing. Together they waded out through the gentle tide.

"Stay here, Carigana," Lars directed, "and make a basin of your skirt."

She did, first wringing water from the voluminous folds. Lars was thigh deep in the water when he suddenly bent down and scooping with both hands sent water, and fish, flying at her. She missed the first lot, laughing at her ineptitude, but neatly caught two fish in the second. After three more catches, she had to hold up her skirt lest the active yellowbacks flip out. Lars splashed back to inspect her catch, grinning at his success and her bemusement.

"This one's too small." He released it. "Two, four, six, seven. How many can you eat? Shall I get more?"

Before she could answer, he dove back toward his vantage point, and peered down into the clear water. With one last mighty heave, three big yellowbacks were sent flying in her direction. She cheered when she caught them in her skirt, closing the makeshift net and running awkwardly through the wavelets to the shore before any of the squirming fish could escape.

Helping her secure the bundle, Lars laughingly escorted her back to the bushes surrounding their secluded clearing.

"You clean 'em and I'll get firing, and see what else I can scrounge," he said as he held the bushes back for her to enter.

Gutting fish was not one of Killashandra's favorite chores, but she had finished half the catch before she realized it, washing them clean in the little brook. Lars was back as she slit the last one. In one crooked arm, he held twisted polly fronds that provided a quick hot fire, and another basket swung from his right hand. He found rocks by the stream to enclose their fire, hauled a frying sheet from the basket, and set out oil, seasonings, bread, fruit, and another pot of the soft island cheese.

The quick tropical night had settled upon the island, enclosing them more securely in their clearing as they finished their supper, licking the last of the juices from their fingers.

"Going to be nice to me?" Lars asked, leering dramatically at her.

"Maybe I'll just stay in the islands." Killashandra surprised herself with the longing in her voice. "There's all I could possibly need just for the taking . . ."

"Even me?"

Killashandra looked up at him. Despite his light words, his voice held a curious entreaty.

"I would be a right foolish dolt to consider you part of the taking." She meant it, for quixotic though the man might appear, she sensed that Lars had an unshakable integrity which she, or any other woman, would have to recognize and accept.

"We could stay in the islands, Carigana, and make a go of the charter service." Lars, too, was caught in the same thrall which infected her resolve. "Sailing's never dull. The weather sees to that. It could be a good life, and I promise you wouldn't have to hack polly!" His fingers caressed her hands.

"Lars . . ." She had to set the record fair.

He covered her lips with his hand. "No, beloved, this is not the time for life-shaping decisions. This is the time for loving. Love me again!"

Chapter 12

The idyll lasted another full day and into the early morning of the third, during which time Killashandra would have been quite willing to forego all the prestige of being a crystal singer to remain Lars's companion. A totally impossible, improbable, and impractical ambition. But she had every intention of enjoying his companionship as long as it was physically possible. She was haunted by memories of Carrik and, as such traumas can, they colored, and augmented, her responses to Lars.

It was the change in the weather which necessitated their return to society. The drop in barometric pressure woke Killashandra just before dawn. She lay, wide awake, Lars's lax arms draped about her, his legs overlapping hers, wondering what had returned her so abruptly to full consciousness. Then she smelled a change in weather on the early morning breeze. It had not occurred to Killashandra that her Ballybran symbiont would be agitated by other weather systems. And she pushed her sensitivity as far as she could, testing what the change might herald.

Storm, she decided, letting symbiotic instinct make the identification. And a heavy one. In these islands a hurricane more likely than not. A worrisome phenomenon for a reasonably flat land mass. No, there were heights on what Lars had termed the Head. She smiled, for yesterday, in between other felicitous activities, he had given her quite a history and geography lesson pertinent to the island economy.

"This island gets its name from the shape of the land mass," he explained and drew a shape on the wet sands with a shell. They had just emerged from a morning swim. "It was seen first from the exploratory probe and named long before any settlers landed here. There's even a sort of a halo of islets off the Head. We're at the Wingtip. The settlement lies in the wing curve . . . see . . . and the western heights are the wings, complete with the ridge principle. This side of the island is much lower than the body side. We've two separate viable harbors, north and south, the angel's outstretched hands completing the smaller, deeper one. My father's offices are there, as the backbone sometimes interferes with reception from the mainland. You can't see it from here because of Backbone Ridge, but there's rather an impressive old volcano topping the Head." He grinned mischievously, giving Killashandra an impression of the devilish child he must have been. "Some of us less reverent souls say the Angel blew her head when she knew who got possession of the planet. Not so, of course. It happened eons before we got here."

Angel was not the largest of the islands but Lars told her that she'd soon see that it was the best. The southern sea was littered, Lars said, with all kinds of land masses: some completely sterile, others bearing active volcanoes, and anything large enough to support polly plantations and other useful tropical vegetation did so.

"We were a race apart from the mainlanders, and we've remained so, Carigana. *They* listen to what the Elders dish up for them, dulling their minds with all the pap that's performed. Islanders still have to have their wits about them. We may be easygoing and carefree, but we're not lazy or stupid."

She had discovered an unexpected pleasure in listening to Lars ramble on, recognizing that his motive was as much self-indoctrination as explanation for her benefit. His voice was so beautifully modulated, uninhibited in its expressiveness that she could have listened to him for years. He made events out of small incidents, no matter that all were aimed at extolling the islands, subtly deprecating mainland ways. He was not, however, an impractical dreamer. Nor was his rebellion against mainland authority the ill-considered antagonism of the disillusioned.

"You sound as if you don't want to leave Optheria even if you are trying to pave the way off for these friends of yours," Killashandra was prompted to remark late that second evening as they finished a meal of steamed molluscs.

"I'm as well off here as I would be anywhere else in the galaxy."

"But your music—"

"It was composed to be played on the Optherian organ and I doubt that any other government allows them to be used, even if the Elders and Masters would permit the design to be copied." He shrugged off that consideration.

"If you could compose that, you have a great gift—"

Lars had laughed outright, ruffling her hair—he seemed fascinated by the texture of her hair.

"Beloved Sungirl, that took no great gift, I assure you. Nor do I have the temperament to sit down and create music—"

"Come on, Lars—"

"No, seriously, I'm much happier at the tiller of a ship—"

"And that voice of yours?"

He shrugged. "Fine for an island evening sing-song, my girl, but who bothers to sing on the Mainland?"

"But, if you get the others off the planet, why don't you go, too? There are plenty of other planets that would make you a Stellar in a pico—"

"How would you know?"

"Well, there have to be!" Killashandra almost screamed in her frustration with the restrictions imposed by her role. "Or why are you trying to crack the restriction?"

"The height of altruism motivates me. Besides, Sunny, Theach and Brassner have valid contributions to make within the context of the galaxy. And once a person has met Nahia, it's obvious why she must be let free. Think of the good she could do."

Killashandra murmured something reassuring since it was called for. She felt an uncharacteristic pulse of jealousy at the reverence and awe in Lars's voice whenever he mentioned this Nahia. Lars had perfectly healthy contempt for Elder and Master alike, indeed all federal officials with the exception of his father. And while he spoke of the man with affection and respect, Nahia occupied a higher position. Quite a few times Killashandra noted a nearly imperceptible halt in the flow of Lars's words as if he exercised a subtle discretion, so subtle that all she caught was its echo. Just as he had stopped short of admitting the abduction of the crystal singer. And, now that she understood his motivation, she marveled at his quick-witted opportunism. Did the others in his subversive group know what he had done? Had they approved of it? And what would the next step be? She could just imagine the furor caused in the Heptite Guild! Or maybe she was supposed to rescue herself? Which she had.

Lars was weather-sensitive, too, for she had only just completed her analysis when he woke, equally alert. With a loving tug at her hair and a smile, he stood up, sniffing at the breeze now strong enough to ruffle his hair, turning slowly. He stopped when he faced in the direction she had.

"Hurricane making, Carigana. Come, we'll have a lot to do."

Not so much that they didn't start the morning with a quick passage at arms, not the least bit perfunctory despite the brevity. Then they had a quick swim, with Lars keeping a close watch on the dawn changes in the sky.

"Making up in the south so it'll be a bad blow." He stood for a moment as the active waves of the incoming tide flounced against his thighs. He looked southwest, frowning and, dissatisfied by his thoughts, started inshore, taking her hand as if seeking comfort.

She thought nothing of his brief disappearance as she cleared up the camp site. Lars pushed his way past the bush screen, an odd smile on his face as he came up to her, two garlands of an exceptionally lovely blue and white flower in his hands. "This will serve," he said cryptically, gently draping one around her neck. The perfume was subtly erotic and she stood on tiptoe to kiss him for his thoughtfulness. "Now you must put mine on."

Smiling at his sweetness, she complied and he kissed her, exhaling a gust as if he had acquitted himself nobly.

"C'mon now," and he gave her the basket, slung the blanket with their clothing over his shoulder, and grabbing her hand, led her back through the underbrush.

Though the sun was not yet up over the horizon, there was considerable activity on the beach when they arrived. Torches were lit outside all the waterfront buildings, and torchlit groups of scurrying people pushed handcarts. Bobbing lights on the harbor, too, indicated crews on their way to anchored ships. The schooner was gone but Killashandra had not really expected to find the big ship still at Angel Island.

"Where can they take the boats?"

"Around to the Back. We'll just check to see how much time there is before the wind rises. There'll be a lot to do before we can take the *Pearl Fisher* to the safe mooring."

Killashandra glanced up and down the picturesque waterfront, for the first time seeing just how vulnerable it was. The first line of buildings was only four hundred meters from the high-tide mark. Wouldn't they be just swept away in hurricane driven tides?

"They often are," Lars startled her by saying as they strode purposefully toward the settlement. "But mostly polly floats. After the last big blow, Morchal salvaged the complete roof. It was floating in the bay, he just dried it out and reset it."

"I should help Keralaw," Killashandra suggested tentatively, not really wanting to leave his side but ignorant of what island protocol expected of her in the emergency. Lars's hand tightened on her elbow.

"If I know Keralaw she has matters well in hand. I'm not risking you from my side for an instant, Carigana. I thought I'd made that plain."

Killashandra almost bridled at the possessive tone of his voice but part of her rather liked the chauvinism. She had too hearty a respect for storm not to wish to be in the safest place during one. Common sense told her that was likely to be in Lars Dahl's company.

Men and women were filing in and out of the tavern. Lars and Killashandra entered and found a veritable command post. The bar was now dispensing equipment and gear which Killashandra could not readily identify. Along the back wall, the huge vdr screen was active, showing a satellite picture of the growing storm swirling in from the south. Estimated times of arrival of the first heavy winds, high tide, the eye, and the counter winds were all listed in the upper left hand corner. Other cryptic information, displayed in a band across the top of the screen, did not mean much to her but evidently conveyed intelligence to the people in the bar. Including Lars.

"Lars, Olav's on line for you," called the tallest of the men behind the bar, and he jerked his head toward a side door. The fellow paused in his dispensations, and Killashandra was aware of his scrutiny as she followed Lars to the room indicated.

However rustic the tavern looked from the outside, this room was crammed with sophisticated equipment, a good deal of it meteorological, though not as complex as instrumentation in the Weather Room of the Heptite Guild. And all of it printing out or displaying rapidly changing information.

"Lars?" A young man turned from the scanner in front of him and, screwing his face in an anxious expression, almost pounced on the new arrival. "What are you going to do—"

Lars held up his hand, cutting off the rest of that sentence, and the young man noticed the garland. He threw an almost panic stricken look at Killashandra.

"Tanny, this is Carigana. And there's nothing I can do with this storm blowing up." Lars was scrutinizing the duplicate vdr satellite picture as he spoke. "The worst of it will pass due east. Don't worry about the things you can't change!" He gave Tanny a clout on the shoulder but the worried expression did not entirely alter.

Killashandra kept the silly social smile on her face as Tanny accorded her the briefest of nods. She had a very good idea what, or rather whom, they were discussing so obliquely. Her. Still trapped, they thought, on that chip of an island.

"Tanny's my partner, Carigana, and one of the best sailors on Angel," Lars added, though his attention was still claimed by the swirling cloud mass.

"What if the direction changes, Lars?" Tanny refused to be reassured. "You know what the southern blows are like . . ." He made an exaggerated gesture with both arms, nearly socking a passing islander, who ducked in time.

"Tanny, there is nothing we can do. There's a great big polly on the island that's survived hurricanes and high tides since man took the archipelago. We'll go have a look as soon as the blow's gone. All right?"

Lars didn't wait for Tanny's agreement, guiding Killashandra back into the main room. He paused at the counter, waiting his turn, and receiving a small handset. "A light one will do me fine, Bart," he added and Bart set a small antigrav unit on the counter. "Most of what I own is either on the *Pearl* or on its way back to me from the City. Grab a couple of those ration packs, will you, Carigana," he added as they walked out on the broad verandah where additional emergency supplies were being passed out. "Might not need them but it's less for them to pack to the Ridge."

As Lars turned her west, away from the settlement, she caught sight of Tanny, watching them, his expression still troubled. The wind was picking up and the water in the harbor agitated. Lars looked to his right, assessing the situation.

"Been in a bad one yet?" he asked her, an amused and tolerant grin on his face.

"Oh, yes," Killashandra answered fervently. "Not an experience I wish to repeat." How could Lars know how puny an Optherian hurricane would be in comparison to Passover Storms on Ballybran. Once again she wanted to discard her borrowed identity. There was so much she would like to share with Lars.

"It's waiting out the blow that's hard," Lars said, then grinned down at her. "We won't be bored this time, though. My father said that Theach came with Hauness and Erutown. I wonder how they managed the travel permits?" That caused him to chuckle. "We'll know how the revised master plan is working."

Killashandra was very hard put to refrain from making any remarks but, of a certainty, waiting out this blow would be extremely interesting. She might not be getting on with the primary task of her visit to Optheria, but she was certainly gaining a lot of experience with dissidents.

His place was on a knoll, above the harbor, in a grove of mature polly trees. It reflected an orderly person who preferred plain and restful colors. He produced several carisaks which had been neatly stored in a cupboard, and together they emptied the chest of his clothes, including several beautifully finished formal garments. He cleared his terminal of any stored information and when Killashandra asked if they shouldn't dismantle the screen, he shrugged.

"Federal issue. I must be one of the few islanders who use the thing." He grinned impiously. "And then not to watch their broadcasts! They can never appreciate that islanders don't need vicarious experiences." He gestured toward the sea. "Not with real live adventures!"

The pillows, hammocks, what kitchen utensils there were, the rugs, curtains, everything compacted into a manageable bundle to which Lars attached the antigrav straps. The entire process hadn't taken them fifteen minutes.

"We'll just attach this to a train, grab something to eat and then get the *Pearl* to safety." He gave his effects a gentle shove in the proper direction.

When they returned to the waterfront, Killashandra saw what he meant by train. Numerous personal-effects bundles, all wrapped and weightless, were being attached to a large floater on which families with small children perched. As soon as it had reached capacity, the driver guided it away, along a winding route toward the distant Ridge.

"Catch you next trip, Jorell?" Lars called to the man steering the harbor boat out toward the anchored ships.

"Gotcha, Lars!"

"There's Keralaw," Killashandra said, pointing to the woman who was ladling hot soup from an immense kettle into bowls.

"You can always count on her hospitality," Lars said and they altered their path to meet her.

"Carigana!" Keralaw paused in serving a family group and waved one arm energetically to catch their attention. "I'd no idea where you'd—" She halted, eyes goggling a bit at the garland about Killashandra's neck, staring at Lars's matching one. Then she smiled. She patted Killashandra's arm approvingly. "Anyway, I put your carisak with mine on the float to the Ridge. Will I see you two there?" Her manner bordered on the coy as she handed them cups from the bag at her side, and poured the hot soup.

"After we've sailed the *Pearl* to the Back," Lars said easily, but Killashandra thought his expression a trifle smug, as if he liked surprising

Keralaw. He blew on his soup, taking a cautious sip. "As good as ever, Keralaw. One day you must pass on your secret recipe. What'll Angel do in a crisis without you around to sustain us!"

Keralaw made a pleased noise, giving him a dig in the ribs before she sidled up to Killashandra. "You did better on the shore than I did from the ship!" she murmured, winking and giving Killashandra an approving dig in the ribs. "And," she added, her expression altering from bawdy to solemn, "you're what he needs right now."

Before Killashandra could respond to that cryptic comment, Keralaw had moved off to the next group.

"With Keralaw in the know," Lars said between sips, "storm or not, the rest of the island will be informed."

"That you and I have paired off?" Killashandra gave him a long stare, having now decided what the special blue garlands must signify in island custom. It was presumptuous of him, but then, he was also presuming her acquaintance with island ways. The account, when rendered from her side, was going to be heavy. "You're remarkably well organized here . . ." She let her sentence dangle, implying that she'd been elsewhere to her sorrow.

"Angel's not often in the direct path, and the storm may veer off before it hits, but one doesn't wait until the last moment, not on Angel. Father doesn't permit inefficiencies. They lose lives and cost credit. Ah, Jorell's back. Hang on to your cup. We'll need them later."

The harbor skip waited for them and its other passengers in the choppy waters. Lars bent to rinse out his cup and Killashandra followed suit, before swinging over the gunwales of the water taxi. Willing hands pulled them aboard.

There was a lot of activity on those ships still left in the harbor, but many had already started for the safety of the protected bay. Lars chatted amiably with the other passengers, naming Killashandra once to everyone. The approaching storm worried them all, despite the well-drilled exodus. It was considered early in the season for such a big blow: odds were being given that it would veer west as so many early storms tended to do; relief was felt that neither of the nearer two moons was at the full, thus affecting the height of the tides. The pessimist on board was sure this was the beginning of a very stormy winter, a comment which caught Killashandra's interest. Winter? As far as she knew, she'd arrived in Optheria in early spring. Had she missed half a year somehow?

Then the taxi pulled alongside a sleek-lined fifteen meter sloop-rigged ship, and Lars was telling her to grab the rope ladder that flopped against its side. She scrambled up, almost falling over the life-railing, which she hadn't expected. Then Lars was beside her, cheerfully shouting their thanks to Jorell as he deftly hauled the ladder inboard and began to stow it away.

"We'll rig the cabin before we sail," Lars said, nodding astern toward the hatch.

Killashandra didn't know much about ships of this class but the cabin looked very orderly to her, arranged as it was for daytime use. She went to the forward cabin, and decided that she had been in the top right-hand bunk. She turned back, to approximate the view she would have had, and decided that the *Pearl Fisher* had conveyed her to that wretched little island.

"Update!" Lars said as he came down the companionway, talking to the handset. He listened as he did a cursory inspection of the nearest cupboards, smiling as he turned toward her. "Alert me to any changes. Over."

He put the handset down and, in one unexpected sweep, hauled her tightly into his arms. His very blue eyes gleamed inches above her face. His face assumed the expression of a sex-mad fiend, his eyes wide in exaggerated ferocity, as he bent her backward in one arm, his other hand stroking her body urgently. "Alone, at last, m'girl, and who knows when next we have the privacy I need to enjoy you to good advantage!"

"Oh, sir, unhand me!" Killashandra fluttered her eyelashes, panting in mock terror. "How can you ravish an innocent maid in this hour of our peril?"

"It seems the right thing to do, somehow," Lars said in a totally different tone, releasing her so abruptly she had to catch herself on the table. "Curb your libido long enough for me to make the bed you're about to be laid in." He flipped the table onto its edge, gestured for her to take the other side of the seat unit which pulled out across the deck.

Simultaneously they fell onto the bed, and Lars began his assault on her willing person.

The summons of the handset brought them back to reality that had only peripherally impinged on their activities. Lars had to steady himself in the lurching ship to reach the handset. He frowned as he heard the update.

"Well, beloved, I hope you're a good sailor, for it's going to be a rough passage around the wing. That storm is hurrying to meet us. Neither a veer nor a pause! Grab the wet weather gear from that cupboard. Temperature's falling and the rain's going to be cold."

Fortunately Lars gave clear instructions to his novice crew and Killashandra coped with her tasks well enough to gain his nods of approval. The *Pearl Fisher* was fitted to be sailed single-handed, with the sheet lines winched to the cockpit and other remotes to assist in the absence of a human crew. Lars beckoned Killashandra to join him in the stern as the anchor was lifted by remote. Another hauled the sloop's mainsail up the mast, Lars's pennon breaking out as the clew of the sail locked home.

The wind took the sail, and the ship, forward, out of the wide mouth of the harbor, which was now clear of all craft. Nor did there seem to have been anyone to notice their delay. The beach was empty of people. The shuttered shops and houses had an abandoned look to them. The tide was already slopping into the barbecue pits and Killashandra wondered just how much would be left on the waterfront when they sailed back into Wing Harbor.

Killashandra found the speed of the *Pearl Fisher* incredibly exhilarating. To judge by the rapt expression on his face, so did Lars. The fresh wind drove them across the harbor almost to its mouth, before Lars did a short tack to get beyond the land. Then the *Pearl* was gunwhale deep on a fine slant as she sped on a port tack toward the bulk of the Wing.

It was an endless time, divorced from reality, unlike cutting crystal where time, too, was sometimes suspended for Killashandra. This was a different sort of time, that spent *with* someone, someone whose proximity was a matter of keen physical delight for her. Their bodies touched, shoulder, hip, thigh, knee, and leg, as the canting of the ship in her forward plunge kept Killashandra tight against Lars. Not a voyage, she realized sadly, that could last forever but a long interval she hoped to remember. There are some moments, Killashandra informed herself, that one does wish to savor.

The sun had been about at the zenith when they had finally tacked out of the Wing Harbor. It was westering as they sailed round the top of the Wing with its lowlands giving way to the great basalt cliffs, straight up from the crashing sea, a bastion against the rapidly approaching hurricane. And the southern skies were ominous with dark cloud and rain. In the shelter of those cliffs, their headlong speed abated to a more leisurely pace. Lars announced hunger and Killashandra went below to assuage it. Taking into account the rough water, she found some heat packs which she opened, and which they ate in the cockpit, companionably close. Killashandra found it necessary to curb a swell of incipient lust as Lars shifted his long body against hers to get a better grip on the tiller.

Then they rounded the cliffs and into the crowded anchorage which sheltered Angel's craft. Lars fired a flare to summon the jitney to them, then he ordered Killashandra forward with the boat hook to catch up the bright-orange eighty-two buoy to starboard. He furled the sail by remote and went on low-power assist to slow the *Pearl* and avoid oversailing the buoy.

Buoy eighty-two was in the second rank, between two small ketch-rigged fisherboats, and Killashandra was rather pleased that she snagged the buoy first try. By the time Lars had secured the ship to ride out the blow, the little harbor taxi was alongside, its pilot looking none too pleased to be out in the rough waters.

"What took you so long, Lars?"

"A bit of cross-tide and some rough tacks," Lars said with a cheerful mendacity that caused Killashandra to elbow his ribs hard. He threw his arms about to forestall further assaults. Indeed they both had to hang on to the railings as the little boat slapped and bounced.

For a moment, Killashandra thought the pilot was driving them straight into the cliff. Then she saw the light framing the sea cave. As if the overhang marked the edge of the sea's domination, the jitney was abruptly on calmer waters, making for the interior and the sandy shore. Killashandra was told to fling the line to the waiting shoremen. The little boat was sailed into a cradle and this was drawn up, safely beyond the depredations of storm and sea.

"Last one in again, eh Lars?" he was teased as the entire party made its way out of the dock and started up the long flight of stairs cut in the basalt. It was a long upward haul for Killashandra, unused to stairs in any case and, though pride prevented her from asking for a brief halt, she was completely winded by the time they reached the top and exited onto a windswept terrace. She was relieved to find a floater waiting, for the Backbone towered meters above them and she doubted her ability to climb another step.

Polly and other trees lined the ridge, making a windbreak for the floater as it was buffeted along, ending its journey at a proper station-house. Killashandra had profited by the brief rest and followed Lars's energetic stride into the main hall of the Backbone shelter.

"Lars," called the man at the entrance, "Olav's in the command post. Can you join him?"

Lars waved assent and guided Killashandra to an ascending ramp, past a huge common room packed with people. They passed an immense garage, where hundreds of packets resembling some strange form of alien avian life dangled weightless from their antigravs.

There was a storm chill in the air and Killashandra was aware of symbiont-generated inner tension as her body sensed the impending arrival of the hurricane.

"The command post is shielded, lover," Lars said, catching her hand in his and stroking it reassuringly. "Storm won't affect you so much there. I feel it myself," he added when she looked up in surprise at his comment. "Real weather-sorts, the pair of us!" The affinity pleased him.

They reached the next level, predominantly storage to judge by the signs on the doors on either side of the wide corridor. Lars walked straight for the secured portal at the far end, put his thumb on the door lock which then slid open. Instinctively Killashandra flinched, startled by the sight of the storm-lashed trees, and the unexpected panoramas, north and south, of the two harbors. Lars's hand tightened with reassurance. On both sides of the door, the walls were covered by data screens and continuous printout as the satellites fed information to the island's receivers. The other three sides of the command post were open, save for the circular stairs winding down to the floor below.

Olav was on his feet, walking from one display to the next, making his own estimate of the data. He looked up at Lars and Killashandra, noting with the upward lift of one eyebrow the bruised garlands they wore. He indicated the circular stairway and made a gesture which Killashandra read as a promise to join them later.

They crossed the room, Lars pausing to read the displays at the head of the staircase. He made a noncommital grunt and then indicated that she should precede him. Therefore she was first in the room, grateful that only large windows north and south broke its protection from the elements without, while a fire burned in a wide hearth on the eastern wall. The western wall was broken by four doors, the open one showing a small catering area. But Killashandra's attention was immediately on the occupants of the room, three men and the most beautiful woman Killashandra had ever seen.

"Nahia! How dare you risk yourself!" cried Lars, his face white under his tan as he brushed past Killashandra. To her complete amazement, he dropped on one knee before the woman, and kissed her hand.

Chapter 13

A startled expression crossed Nahia's perfect features at Lars's obeisance. She shot a quick look at Killashandra, managing to convey her embarrassment even as she tried to lift Lars from his knee.

"My friend, this will not do," she said kindly, but firmly. "Only think what effect such a gesture could have on an Elder or a Master—and yes, I do most certainly know your opinion of those worthies. But Lars, such histrionics could damage our goal."

Lars had by now risen to his feet. With a final few pats to his hand, an oblique apology for her public admonition, she withdrew from his grasp, moving past him toward Killashandra. "Whom have you brought with you, Lars?" she asked, smiling tentatively as she extended her slender hand to Killashandra. "Who wears your garland?"

"Carigana, lately a polly planter," Lars replied, stepping back to Killashandra's side and taking her other hand firmly in his.

It was one way of apologizing for his effusive welcome of another woman but it was Nahia herself who effectively dissolved Killashandra's incipient hostility. The touch of her hand had a soothing effect, not a shock or a jar, but a gentle insinuation of reassurance. Nahia's eyes were troubled as she regarded Killashandra, her lips curving upward in a slight smile which blossomed as she felt Killashandra's resistance to her dissipate. Then a little frown gathered at her brows as she became aware of the lingering crystal resonance within Killashandra. It was the crystal singer's turn to smile reassurance and an acknowledgment of what Nahia was: an empath.

Killashandra had heard of such people but she had never encountered one. The encyclopedia had not hinted the psi talents were an Optherian quality. It could be a wild talent and often was. In Nahia it was combined with unexpected beauty, integrity, and an honesty which few citizens of the Federated Sentient Worlds could project without endangering their sanity. Lars had been correct in his statement that Nahia's especial talents would be a galactic asset. She was Goodness personified.

Nahia looked with gentle inquiry at Killashandra, struggling to identify the elusive contact with crystal. Killashandra smiled and, with a final light pressure on Nahia's fine-boned hand, released her and leaned slightly against Lars.

At this point, the other men stepped forward to greet the newcomers.

"I'm Hauness, Nahia's escort," said the tallest of the three, an attractive man whom Killashandra judged to be in his mid-thirties. His handclasp was strong but not crushing and he, too, exuded a charm and personality that would have been instantly apparent in any group—at least any group that did not contain Nahia. Or Lars. "Believe me, Lars, we had no report of such rough weather when we embarked on this journey but—"

"There are matters we must discuss with you, no matter what the risk." Erutown was the oldest, and bluntest. His manner suggested that he tended to be a humorless pessimist. He gave Killashandra's hand one brief shake and dropped it. "And there was no risk—in the weather—when we started." He hovered, his upper body inclined away from Killashandra even as his feet shifted, as if he wanted to separate Lars from Killashandra and plunge into the "matters to be discussed" as quickly as possible.

"Theach," said the third man, giving Killashandra a brief, self-effacing nod.

He was the sort of nondescript human being, mild mannered, with undistinguished features, who can be encountered almost anywhere in the human population, and promptly forgotten. Only because she had heard of his mathematical abilities from Lars did Killashandra give Theach any sort of an inspection and thus noticed that his eyes were brilliant with intelligence: that he had already assumed she would discount him, indeed, hoped that she would, and was quite willing to accept the sort of dismissal to which he was clearly accustomed.

So Killashandra gave him a saucy wink. She half expected Theach to retreat in confusion as many shy men would, but, smiling, he winked back at her.

Erutown cleared his throat, indicating that now introductions had been made, he wanted to initiate the discussions they had come for.

"I don't know about you, Lars, but I'm starving," Killashandra said, gesturing toward the catering area. "Is it all right to see what's available?" She turned to the others. "May I fix something for you?"

Lars gave her hand a grateful squeeze before he released it. He told her to find what she fancied and he'd have the same but the others demurred, gesturing toward the low table where the remains of a meal could be seen.

The four conspirators didn't know that Killashandra's symbiont-adapted hearing was uncommonly acute. At that distance they could have whispered and she would have caught what was being said.

"They finally sent the message two days ago, Lars." Erutown's baritone was audible above the noises Killashandra was making in the catering unit.

"Took them long enough," Lars said in a low growl.

"They had to search first. And search they did, uncovering a variety

of minor crimes and infringements which, of course slowed them down."
Hauness was amused.

"Any one of us caught?"

"Not a one of us," Hauness replied.

"Cleansed us of some very stupid people," Erutown said.

"She is safe, isn't she, Lars?" Nahia asked in gentle anxiety, a graceful
gesture of her hand indicating the darkening southern horizon.

"She should be. All she needs is enough sense to climb the polly tree."

"You ought to have contacted us before you acted so impulsive-
ly, Lars."

"How could he, Erutown?" Nahia was conciliatory. Then she gave a
little chuckle. "Impulsive but it has proved such an extremely effective
gambit. The Elders have been forced to reapply to the Heptite Guild."

"They haven't admitted that the crystal singer has been abducted?"

"As no one has confessed to committing such a heinous crime, how
could they?" Hauness asked reasonably, his voice rippling with amusement. "Elder Torkes has been hinting dark words about that islander
assault—"

Lars let out a burst of sour laughter for which Erutown growled a
warning, looking over his shoulder at Killashandra who was well out of
sight in the catering area.

"What you don't know, Lars," Hauness went on, "is that the crystal
singer had had an altercation with Security Leader Blaz and stalked out of
the installation before *any* repair had been accomplished."

Lars emitted a low whistle of delighted surprise. "Is that why she was
wandering about Gartertown? I had wondered!"

"Erutown may not approve, and some of the others were appalled at
your action, Lars, but there is no doubt," and Hauness overrode Erutown's
disapproving murmurs, "that the action will require embarrassing inquiries when the second crystal singer arrives."

"As long as it also requires an appeal to the Council," Lars said.
"Now what else brought you here so unexpectedly?"

"As I said, the search for the crystal singer exposed some unsuspected flaws in our organization. Theach and Erutown must ruralize. Have
you another suitable island?"

Lars paused, staring at Hauness, and then the others. Erutown
scowled and looked away but Theach regarded him with a smile.

"Some of my scribblings were discovered, and as I am already under
threat of rehabilitation . . ." Theach shrugged eloquently.

When Lars looked to Erutown for an explanation, the man did not
meet his gaze.

"Erutown was denounced as a recruiter," Hauness said. "Not his
fault."

"It was, if I was daft enough to recruit such soft-bellied cowards!"

Lars grinned. "Well, I could put you ashore with the crystal singer." Something increased his mirth out of proportion to the joke, though Hauness grinned and Nahia tried to control unseemly mirth at Erutown's expense. "The island's big enough and she might even be grateful for company."

"I would be easier in mind about her safety if Erutown and Theach *were* there," Nahia said. "The hurricane will have frightened her badly."

"I don't like the idea," Erutown said.

"Actually, if she thinks you've also been kidnapped . . ." Hauness suggested, then gestured to dismiss his notion at Erutown's negative response.

"I wouldn't object," Theach said. "One doesn't know much about crystal singers, except that they heal quickly and indulge in an unusual profession."

"You?" Erutown snorted contemptuously. "You'd probably drown yourself thinking up more theories."

"When I initiate a session of theoretical thinking, I take the precaution of seating myself in some secure and secluded spot," Theach said in amiable reprimand. "An island would suit me very well indeed."

"You'd starve!"

"No one can starve on a polly island." Theach turned for confirmation to Lars, who nodded.

"You have to work at it, though," Lars amended. "For at least a few hours every day."

"Despite a misapprehension current about my absentmindedness, I have found that intense thought stimulates an incredible appetite. Since eating replenishes both body and the mechanics of thought, I do pause now and again in my meditations to eat! If I have to gather the food myself, I shall also have had that beneficial exercise. Yes, Lars," and Theach smiled at the islander, "I begin to think that an island residence would provide me with all I require: seclusion, sustenance, and sanctuary!" He sat back in the chair, beaming at his circle of friends.

"How many know you and Erutown are in the islands?" Lars asked seriously.

"Nahia has been working very hard lately, Lars," Hauness said. "She was granted a leave of absence: I took my annual holiday and announced our intention of cruising the coast. There are friends who will vouch for our presence in mainland waters. Besides, who would expect us to brave a hurricane?"

"We boarded the jet from the seaside without being seen the night before she sailed," Erutown added. "What Elder would suspect Nahia's involvement with renegades?"

"If they had any sense whatever," Nahia said in a crisp tone that surprised Killashandra with its suppressed anger, "how could they fail to realize that I sympathize deeply with repressions, frustrations, and despairs which I cannot avoid feeling! With injustices not all the empathy in the world will ease."

A moment of silence followed.

"Is your woman to be trusted with any of this, Lars?" Hauness asked quietly.

Suppressing a flare of guilt at her duplicity, Killashandra decided that it was time to join the group before Lars perjured himself.

"Here, this should satisfy, Lars," she said, approaching the others with a purposeful stride. She set before him a generous plate of sandwiches and hot tidbits which she had found in the food storage. "You're sure I can't get anything for you?" she asked the others as she began to gather up the used plates and cups.

Erutown gave her a sour glance, then turned to watch the roiling cloud formations of the approaching storm. Theach smiled absently, Hauness shook his head and settled back next to Nahia who had leaned back in the couch, eyes closed, her beautiful face relaxed.

When Killashandra returned with her own serving, Lars and Hauness were absorbed by the satellite picture of the approaching hurricane, displayed on the vdr. It would be a substantial blow, Killashandra had to admit, but not a patch on what Ballybran could brew.

Storm watching could be mesmerizing, certainly engrossing. Theach was the first to break from the fascination. He reseated himself at a small terminal and began to call up equations on the tiny screen. There was a tension to the line of his back, the occasional rattle of the keys that proved he was still conscious, but there were long intervals of total silence from his corner during the next few hours.

"It's not going to be a long one at its current rate," Lars remarked when he had finished eating. "The eye'll be on us by night."

"Is it likely to make the mainland?"

"No. That is, after all, eight thousand kilos off. It'll blow itself out over the ocean as usual. You only get our storms when they make up in the Broad, not from this far south."

So, Killashandra thought, she was in the southern hemisphere of Optheria, which explained the switch in seasons. And it explained why this group felt themselves secure from Mainland intervention and searches. Even with the primitive jet vehicles, an enormous distance could be traversed in a relatively short time.

It struck Killashandra that if Nahia, Hauness, and the others could travel so far, so could the Elders, especially if they wanted to implicate islanders. Or was that just talk? If, as Lars had admitted, Torkes had set him up to assault her in order to verify her identity and was using that assault now to implicate the islanders, would it not be logical to assume that some foray into the islands would be made by officialdom? If only to preserve their fiction?

Killashandra closed her mouth on this theory for she had gleaned it

from information she had overhead surreptitiously. Well, she'd find a way
to warn Lars, for she had a sudden premonition that a warning was in order. From what she had seen of the Elders, reapplying to the Guild would
be a humiliating embarrassment to their sort of bureaucracy. Unless—and
Killashandra smiled to herself—they took the line that Killashandra Ree
had not arrived as scheduled. How tidy it could be made, the Elders able to
suppress any reference to the reception in her honor. However, Lanzecki
would know that she had gone, and know, too, that she would not have
evaded the responsibility she had accepted. And there would be computer
evidence of her arrival—even the Elders would have a hard time suppressing that sort of trail mark. Not to mention her use of the credit outlet on
Angel. This could be very interesting!

She must have dozed off, for the couch had been comfortable, the
day's unusual exercise exhausting, and watching the weather screen soporific. It was the lack of storm noise that woke her. And a curious singing
in her body which was her symbiont's reaction to drastic weather changes.
A quick glance at the screen showed her that the eye of the storm was
presently over Angel Island. She rubbed at her arms and legs, sure that the
vibration she felt might be discernible. However, Nahia had curled up on
the end of the long couch, Hauness, one arm across her shoulders, was also
asleep, head back against the cushions. Theach was still diddling, but
Erutown and Lars were absent.

She heard voices and steps on the circular stair and made a dash for
the toilet. She distinguished Lars's distinctive laugh, a bass rumble from
his father, and a grunt that could be Erutown, and some other voices. Until
the eye had passed and the symbiont had quieted, Killashandra wanted to
avoid everyone, especially Lars.

"Carigana?" Lars called. Then she heard him approach the toilet and
rap on the door. "Carigana? Would you mind fixing some hungry storm
watchers more of those excellent sandwiches?"

Under ordinary circumstances, Killashandra would have had a tart
rejoinder but catering would solve the more immediate problem.

"Just a moment." She splashed water on her face, smoothed back her
hair, and regarded the blossoms about her neck. Strangely enough they
were not dead, their petals were still fresh despite the creasing. Their fragrance scented her fingers as she opened the crushed flowers and spread
them back into their original shapes.

When she opened the door, Nahia and Hauness were making their
way toward the catering area.

"They only want to talk weather," Nahia said with a smile. "We'll
help you."

The others did talk weather, but on the communits to other islands,
checking on storm damages and injuries, finding out what supplies would
be required, and which island could best supply the needs. The three caterers served soup, a basic stew, and high-protein biscuits. In the company of
Nahia and Hauness, the work was more pleasant than Killashandra would

have believed. She had never met their likes before and realized that she probably never would again.

The respite at the storm's eye was all too brief, and soon the hurricane was more frightening in its renewed violence. Though it was a zephyr in comparison to Ballybran turbulence, Killashandra rated it a respectable storm, and slept through the rest of it.

A touch on her shoulder woke her, a light touch that was then repeated and her shoulder held in a brief clasp. That was enough to bring Killashandra to full awareness and she looked up at Nahia's perplexed expression. Killashandra smiled reassuringly, attempting to pass off the storm resonance still coursing through her body. As Lars was draped against her, she moved cautiously to a sitting position and took the steaming cup from Nahia with quiet thanks. Killashandra wondered how the man had been able to sleep with her body buzzing.

Other storm watchers had disposed themselves for sleep about the room. Outside a hard rain was falling and a stout wind agitated the rain forest but the blow had become a shadow of its hurricane strength.

"We had orders to wake people as soon as the wind died to force five," Nahia said and extended a second hot cup to Killashandra for Lars.

"Has there been much damage? Many injuries?"

"Sufficient. The hurricane was unseasonably early and caught some communities unprepared. Olav is preparing emergency schedules for us."

"Us?" Killashandra stared at Nahia in surprise. "Surely you're not going to risk being seen and identified here?"

"These are my own people, Carigana. I am safest in the islands." Serenely confident, the beauty returned to the catering area.

Lars had awakened during that brief interchange although he hadn't changed his position. His very blue eyes were watching her closely, no expression gave her a hint of his mood. Lazily he caressed her leg. Gradually his lips began to curve in a smile. What he might have said, what thoughts he held behind those keen eyes he did not share with her. Then he touched the garland she still wore, carefully unfolding a crushed petal. "Will you be crew for me? We won't have much time together southbound. Tanny, Theach, and Erutown sail with us, and we'll be dropping off supplies here and there . . ."

"Of course I'll come," Killashandra said eagerly. She wouldn't miss the trip for the world. Only . . . how would Lars take her deception? Would she lose him? Well, she didn't have to admit that she was the crystal singer they had incarcerated on the island!

The winds out of the Back Harbor were brisk enough to be dangerous, but the well laden *Pearl* settled down to her task like the splendid craft she was. Erutown was the nonsailor among them and took to a bunk in the forward cabin until the motion sickness medication had taken effect. Theach had appropriated the small terminal, smiling with absentminded good humor at his shipmates, before he resumed his programming.

Now that Tanny was on his way, he was as cheerful a companion as one could wish. Nor was he impatient with Killashandra as a crewmember. They had set sail once the winds had dropped to force three, one of the first of the larger sailing vessels to leave haven. Others were being loaded and crewed for their relief voyages. After the enforced idleness of the storm, it was good to be physically active. Killashandra didn't mind the wet weather nor the tussle with wind as she and Tanny made periodic checks of the deck cargo.

Fresh water and food were unloaded at the first stop, and some emergency medical supplies. The *Pearl* had carefully motored past the debris floating in the small harbor: roofs, the sides of dwellings, innumerable polly trees, fruit bobbing about like so many bald heads. That sight had startled Killashandra and she had nearly exposed her ignorance of island phenomena to Tanny. The inhabitants had taken refuge on the one highland of the island, but they were already hauling salvageables from the high tide mark and the water. They cheered the arrival of the *Pearl*, some wading out to float the watertight supplies in to shore. The exchange was completed in the time it took the *Pearl* to turn about and head back to the open sea.

And that was the routine at a half-dozen smaller islands. Killashandra had had a long look at the charts and the compass; they were taking a long arcing route, "her" island being the farthest point of their journey to the southwest.

The waters were studded with islands, large, small, and medium. All showed the devastation of the storm, and on most the polly trees were still bent over from their struggle with the hurricane: on some of the smaller islands, the trees had been uprooted. As no one made a comment on this waste, Killashandra could not ask how soon polly would reestablish itself.

In answer to a faint emergency call, they eventually sailed into the harbor of a medium-size island that had lost its communications masts and had been unable to make contact with Angel. Lars and Tanny went ashore there, leaving Killashandra in conspicuous sight while Erutown and Theach remained below. Some of the urgently needed items could be supplied from the extras on board and Lars contacted Angel for the rest.

As they finally lifted anchor and sailed onward, Tanny's rising excitement was communicated to Killashandra. She could recognize nothing, but if they were indeed near the island of her incarceration, she had swum *away* from nearby help. As they approached the next landfall, she didn't need Tanny's shout of relief to know they had reached "her" island; the huge polly tree in the center was a distinctive landmark. Not only had the tree survived but also its siblings or offspring, and the little hut she had made in their shelter. Lars had to restrain Tanny from diving into the breakers and swimming ashore in his eagerness to reassure himself.

"I don't see anyone!" Tanny cried as the *Pearl* motored toward the beach. "Surely she could hear the engine!"

"Is this where you want to dump us?" Erutown growled, surveying the uprooted polly, the wind-depressed trunks of more, and the storm debris on the once white sands.

"Oh, you'll be luxuriously situated, I assure you," Lars said. Killashandra had decided that Lars and Erutown were in basic disagreement on too many counts. Lars was delighted to deposit the man out of the way for a while. "We've solar-power units for Theach's equipment, all sorts of emergency camp gear, and plenty of food should you tire of the stuff the island and the sea provide."

"And a hatchet, a knife, and a book of instructions?" Killashandra asked. She was not above priming her surprise.

"There speaks the polly planter." Grinning, Lars flipped the toggle to release the anchor, cut off the engine, and gestured Tanny overboard. He was halfway up the heights to the shelter before the others had made the beach.

"There's no one here, Lars. Ye gods, what shall we do? There's no one here!" Tanny screamed.

Consternation smoothed Lars's features and he set off up the slope at speed. Killashandra followed at a more leisurely pace, wondering whether she would ease their fears. One look at the terror and hopelessness of Tanny's face, and a second one at the shock on Lars's eroded her need for revenge. Erutown and Theach were on the beach, out of hearing.

"You don't know very much about crystal singers, do you, Lars . . ."

He swung around, stared at her, trying to assimilate her words. Tanny reached his conclusion first and sat heavily down among the storm-strewn polly fronds, his expression incredulous.

". . . If you thought I'd just sit here until it suited you to retrieve me."

Chapter 14

Any discussion of *that* would have to be postponed. Theach and Erutown reached the height, looking about them for their fellow exile. Unable to look in Killashandra's direction, Tanny shot one horrified glance at Lars as the latter smoothly invented a note that she had been removed from the island by a passing vessel. He even flourished a piece of paper from his pocket as he commented that he was glad she was safe.

"That tears it," Erutown said gloomily. "We'll all be in trouble."

"I doubt it. A very good friend of ours skippered that ship," Lars replied without a blink. "She can't go anywhere without my knowledge." Tanny made a strangled sound and Killashandra grinned, choking on her laughter. "There's nothing you could safely do without jeopardizing yourself at this point, Erutown. It isn't as if you'll be out of touch," and Lars handed the man a small but powerful handset. "The frequency to use for any contact is 103.4 megahertz. All right? You can listen in on any of the other channels but communicate only on the 103.4."

Erutown agreed with ill grace, hefting the set doubtfully. With a sideways grin at Killashandra, Lars handed over hatchet, knife, and polly book.

"There now, you're completely equipped," Killashandra said cheerfully. "You'll find that a polly island is quite restful." She glanced maliciously at Tanny and Lars. "Everything you require—polly for food, fish in the lagoon for sport and a change of diet, and a fine reef to prevent the omnivorous from dining on you. You're far better off than I was on my polly island, I assure you." Tanny squirmed, noticeably discomfited.

"Oh, we'll do fine, Carigana." Theach grinned as he began to unpack the solar reflectors.

Lars chuckled, linking his arm in hers, and swinging her down the slope to the beach.

"C'mon, Tanny, I want to be at Bar Island before sundown."

What with the routine necessary to up anchor and maneuver the *Pearl* through the one gap in the reef, there wasn't time for discussions until they were once again under full sail and beating due north for the Bar Island.

"Tanny, I think you'd better go below," Lars began, signaling Killashandra to join him in the cockpit. "What you don't know won't hurt you—"

"Who says?" Tanny growled.

"Fix us some grub, will you? All this excitement gave me an appetite. So," and once Tanny had slammed the hatch closed, Lars turned expectantly to Killashandra, "could I have some explanations?"

"I rather think a few are due me!"

Lars cocked an eyebrow, grinning sardonically at her. "Not when you must have figured out many of the answers already if you're half as smart as I think you are." Lars slid a finger across the scar on her arm, then he reached for her hand and held it up before her face, his thumb rubbing against the crystal scars. " 'I came from the City.' Indeed!"

"Well, I did . . ." she said, deceptively meekly.

"Your best line, you witch, was the one about your having had no choice about coming to the islands!" Lars could not contain his mirth then and tilting his head back, roared with laughter.

"I wouldn't laugh if I were you, Lars Dahl. You're in an unenviable position in my files." She tried to sound severe but couldn't.

His eyes were still brimming with humor when he abruptly switched mood. He touched the garland. "Yes, I am rather. And on Angel Island. For one thing, according to island tradition, this announces us handfasted for a year and a day."

"I had guessed that the garlands signified more than your loving wish to adorn my person." The words came out more facetiously than she meant for she ached with a genuine regret. Lars's steady blue eyes caught her gaze and held it. He waited for her explanation.

"With all the will in the world to continue what we started, I don't have a year and a day here, Lars Dahl." The words left her mouth slowly, unwillingly. "As a crystal singer, I am compelled to return to Ballybran. Had I understood yesterday morning precisely what these blooms meant, I would not have accepted them. Thus does ignorance wound the giver. I am . . . tremendously attracted to you as a man, Lars Dahl. And in the light of what I have been told, heard, and overheard," she gave him a faint smile, "I can even forgive you that idiotic abduction. In fact, it would have been far more humiliating for me to have been caught in a raid on a bootleg brewery. What you cannot know is that I wasn't sent to Optheria merely to repair that organ—I am here as an impartial witness, to learn if restriction to this planet is popularly accepted."

"Popularly accepted?" Lars lifted half out of the cockpit seat in reaction. "What a way to phrase it! It is the most singularly unpopular, repressive, frustrating, discouraging facet of the Optherian Charter. Do you know what our suicide rate is? Well, I can give you hard statistics on that. We made a study of the incidents and have copies of what notes have been left by the deceased. Nine out of ten cite the hopelessness and despair at having no place to go, nothing to do. If you're lucky enough to be unemployed on Optheria, oh, you're given food, shelter, clothing, and assigned stimulating community service to occupy you. Community service!— Trimming thorn hedges, tidying up hillsides, dusting boulders in the roadways, painting and repainting federal buildings, stuffing the faces and wiping the bottoms of the incontinent at both ends of life. Truly rewarding and fulfilling occupations for the intelligent and well educated failures that this planet throws upon the altar of the organ!"

He had been emphasizing his disgust with blows of his fist to the tiller, until Killashandra covered his hand with hers.

"Which one of our messages got through? It's been like tossing a bottle message into the Broad Sea with precious little hope of its ever floating to the Mainland."

"The complaint originated with the Executive Council of the Federated Artists' Association, who claim a freedom of choice restriction. A Stellar made the charge, though I wasn't told which one. His principal concern was with the suppression of composers and performers." She gave him a wry grin.

Lars raised his eyebrows in surprise. "It wasn't me who sent that one." Then he seemed to take heart, his expression lightening with renewed hope. "If one appeal got through, maybe others have, and we'll have a whole school of people helping us—And you'll help us?"

"Lars, I'm required to be an impartial—"

"I wouldn't dream of prejudicing you . . ." His twinkling eyes challenged her as he threw his free arm about her shoulders, nibbling at her ear.

"Lars, you're crushing me. You're supposed to be sailing this ship . . . I've got to think how to go on from here. To be candid, I really don't have much more than your word that there is a widespread dissatisfaction, and not just a few isolated instances or personal grudges."

"Do you know how long we've been trying to reach the Federated Council?" Now Lars gestured wildly in his agitation. "Do you know what it will mean to the others when I tell them one message *has* got through, and someone is actually investigating?"

"There's another matter that we have to discuss, Lars. Is it advisable to *tell* them, or would it be wiser for me to continue covertly?" His jubilation subsided as he considered her question. "I suppose the suicide file would be acceptable as valid evidence. Has the restriction matter ever been put to the vote here?"

"A vote on Optheria?" He laughed sourly. "You haven't read that abominable Charter, have you?"

"I scanned it. A boring document, all those high-flown phrases turned my pragmatic stomach." Before Killashandra's eyes rose the vision of tortured architecture coping with "natural formations" so as not to "rape" the Natural World. "So there is no referendum mechanism in the Charter?"

"None. The Elders run this planet and, when one of them keels over and can no longer be resuscitated, a replacement is appointed—by the remaining undefunct Elders."

"No rising from the ranks on merit here?"

"Only in the Conservatory, and for especially meritorious composition and exceptional performance ability. Then one might possibly, on rare occasions, aspire to reach the exalted rank of a Master. Once in a century, a Master might possibly gain an appointment to the Council of Elders."

"Is that what you were after?"

Lars gave her a wry grin. "I tried! I was even willing to assault you to gain favor and show them what a good, useful, boy I was."

He snorted at his gullibility.

"Granted, I haven't heard an approved composition, much less yours, played on the sensory organ," Killashandra began in casual accents, "but I was tremendously impressed by your performance the other evening. The musical one."

"The time, the place, the ambiance . . ."

"Not so fast, Lars Dahl. I was a trained musician before I became a crystal singer. I can be a critical auditor . . . and when I heard your music, I didn't know you as well as I do now, so that is an unbiased assessment. If by any chance the Stellar who lodged the complaint with the Artists' Association had had you in mind, I second his concern."

Lars regarded her with a genuine surprise. "You would? What music training did you have?"

"I studied for ten years at the Fuerte Music Center. Voice."

Lars nearly lost his grip on the tiller and before he had altered the course, the *Pearl* yawed in the rough seas, throwing Killashandra against him. "*You* were the soprano that night?"

"Yes." She grinned. "I recognized your tenor at the barbecue. Where did you learn Baleef's *Voyagers*? And the *Pearl Fishers* duet? Certainly not in the Conservatory."

"My father. He'd brought some of his microlibrary with him when he came to Optheria."

"Your father is naturalized?"

"Oh, yes. Like yourself, he didn't come to the islands by choice. If we mention your true identity to no one else—and what *is* your true name? Or don't crystal singers give them?"

"You mean to say you don't know the name of the woman you assaulted and then abducted?" Killashandra pretended outrage.

Lars shook his head, grinning at her with an almost boyish mischief.

"Killashandra Ree."

He repeated the syllables slowly, then smiled. "I like that much better than Carigana. That was a rather harsh name to say endearingly. The *ells* and the *sh* are sweeter."

"Possibly the only sweet thing about me, I warn you, Lars."

He pointedly ignored that remark. "My father must know who you are, Killashandra. It will give him new heart for I'll tell you frankly, he was far more discouraged about those arrested in the Elders' search than he let on to the others. Nor"—he paused, only then aware of the water sloshing in the cockpit about their toes—"nor do I like deceiving Nahia. She doesn't deserve it."

"No, she doesn't. Though I have the feeling she already has a good idea that I'm not the island maid I've been portraying."

"Oh? Was she at that reception in the Conservatory?"

"No, but she sensed the crystal resonance." Killashandra stroked her arm explanatorily. Lars caressed her then.

"You mean, that's what I've been feeling whenever we touch?"

Killashandra gave him a reassuring smile. "Not entirely, lover. Some of it is a perfectly spontaneous combustion."

Lars guffawed at that, embracing her once again.

"Shouldn't I bail or something?" she asked as the chill sea water splashed over her toes. His arm restrained her.

"Not just yet." He frowned, glancing off to port, not really seeing the sprouts of islets as he corrected their course a few points easterly. "However, if we tell my father and Nahia who you are—"

"Hauness, too?"

"What Nahia knows, Hauness does, and safe enough in both their hands. But then what? Hard copy on the suicide files is rapidly available. But I should insist that you meet with other groups to prove unquestionably that the arbitrary restriction to Optheria is not popularly acceptable."

"I'm glad you agree to that."

"In doing that, you will also need to avoid the Elders. It wouldn't do for them to discover you blithely treading the cobbles at Ironwood or the terraces of Maitland."

"You never told them you'd kidnapped me, so why couldn't I visit other communities?"

"Because you've now been missing for five weeks. How would you explain such an absence, much less why you haven't repaired their precious Festival organ?"

"I'd've done that if that wretched security officer hadn't been in his flatulent dotage! My absence is easy to explain. I just don't explain it." She shrugged diffidently.

Lars sniggered. "You don't know how much our Elders dislike mysteries—"

"You have seen me playing a humble island maid, Lars. Try seeing me as a highly indignant and aristocratic member of the Heptite Guild." As she spoke, her voice became strange, disdainful, and Killashandra pulled herself arrogantly erect. Lars started to remove his arm from her shoulders in reaction to the transformation. "I'm *more* than a match for Ampris or Torkes. And they need my services far too much to annoy me again."

"I'm obliged to mention that they've sent for a replacement—"

"I know that."

"How could you?"

Killashandra grinned at him. "Crystal singers have preternaturally acute hearing. You and your little band of conspirators were only across the room from me. I heard every word."

Lars momentarily let the tiller slip but Killashandra grabbed it and steadied the helm.

"A second crystal singer might be all to the good, depending on who they send. But we've time to spare—it'll take nearly ten weeks to get another singer here. I happen to need the contract money so I'll repair their damned organ. Maybe this time, I'll get the kind of help I need." A thought suddenly struck Killashandra. "By all that's holy, I'll get you!" She prodded Lars's chest with her forefinger.

Lars snorted with derision. "I'm the last person welcome in the Conservatory!"

"Ah, but you will be welcome—as the man who rescued this poor abandoned crystal singer from durance vile!"

"What?"

"Well, that would answer why I've been absent. But, of course, I never set eyes on my abductor so I can't say who it might be." Killashandra fluttered her eyelashes in mock horror. "There I was, taking a stroll to compose myself after that horrible confrontation with an officious oaf and *wham! bang!* I'm coshed on the head and wake up, all alone, on a desert island, heavens knows where!" Killashandra got into the part with a faked swoon. "I'm less of a ham with a properly respectful audience, I might add. But there I am. Lost! Who knows who the dastards are—using a plural will suggest a whole group of conspirators, you see—And then you . . ." Killashandra laid a delicate hand on Lars's arm. His eyes were bright with mirth and he had his lips pressed together against distracting laughter. "You—loyal despite your terrible disappointment"—and Killashandra put her hand to her breast and breathed hard—"rescued me and insisted on returning me to the safety of the City, to install the crystal manual so that the priceless organ will be ready for the Summer Festival. Thus currying favor with the powers that be—which, in view of your subversive activities, is a very good idea—and saving them the cost of another expensive crystal singer. We are very expensive to hire, you see. And I have the impression that the Elders are credit-crunchers."

Lars began to chuckle, rubbing his chin as if he was visualizing those moments of triumph.

"If you can be trusted not to overact"—he ducked as she shook her fist at him—"you know, it might work."

"Of course it will work! I was able to gauge audience reactions to a pico. And more than just give you a well-deserved return for their meanness and chicanery to you, I'll pretend that I'm so very nervous about a repetition of assault and battery that I'll need you by my side *all* the time."

"I think," Lars began, slowly, thoughtfully, "Father and the others will like this plan."

"Oh?"

Lars gave a rueful snort. "I got rather soundly told off for acting in a unilateral fashion when I abducted you, you know. My father is a mild mannered man most of the time—"

"Then let us by all means present this idea to him—them. And by the way, speaking of mild-mannered men, what do you know about Corish von Mittelstern?"

"The man looking for his uncle?"

"That's the one."

"Well, he's not an Optherian agent if that's what you're worried about. We checked him for residue."

"Checked him for what?"

"D'you recall the arc at the shuttle port? That's to prevent Optherians from leaving the planet. The arc is set to detect a mineral residue that is present in our bone marrow. There's absolutely no argument with the port guards if you try to enter the shuttle port. They just shoot."

"And that's activated by any Optherian passing the sensors?"

"Even visitors who've stayed long enough to absorb sufficient trace to be detected." Lars's expression was sour. "Like my father."

Killashandra half heard that comment, as she was thinking back to her exit from the port. Thyrol had been right beside her and the alarm hadn't gone off for them, though it had when the rest of the Optherian quartette had passed.

"Strange, that," she said half to herself. "No, Corish isn't Optherian. He came out on the *Athena* with me. But I've a very good notion that he's an FSP agent of some sort. I mean, what good is just one impartial observer if the object is to change the *status quo* of an entire planet? Even if I am a crystal singer."

"Did Corish know that?"

"No." Killashandra chuckled. "To Citizen von Mittelstern I was a brash and impulsive music student traveling cheap to the Summer Festival!" When Lars gave her a puzzled look, she laughed. "Being a crystal singer entails some rather curious disadvantages which are not relevant to the more important discussion at hand."

"I don't know much about crystal singers—"

"What you don't know won't hurt you," she said, waggling a finger under his nose. "But I'd very much like to know more about Corish, and if there is a missing uncle."

"Why didn't Corish recognize you on the beach?"

"The same reason you didn't. And he didn't know me all that well," she added, a bit amused by Lars's reaction. "He rather obviously, at least to me, cultivated the company of an innocuous and silly young music student. And one or two other anomalies alerted me."

"I'd encountered a few of those creatures recently myself," Lars remarked in a reproving drawl.

"I did the best I could with the background material I had."

Lars pulled her as close to him as the tiller allowed. "Your only mistake, now that I think back on it, were your comments about singing. *Every*one in the islands sings. But voice is not an instrument for real music . . . according to the Masters."

Killashandra began to sputter indignantly. "That in itself proves how stupid they all are!"

Lars laughed in delight at her reaction and then drew his feet up as the water began slopping up their calves.

"Tanny!" he shouted. "On the deck, on the double."

The hatch was opened so quickly in response to his call that Killashandra wondered how long the young man had had his ear to the wooden panels.

"Haven't you found us something to eat yet? About time." For Tanny held up two heavy soup mugs. "Give it over and start bailing."

Chapter 15

I t took quite a bit of persuading on Killashandra's part to reassure Tanny that she intended no reprisals against him for his very minor part in her abduction. Lars explained that he had managed to sneak her on board the ocean jet with the help of another friend who merely thought Lars's latest girl friend had had a shade too much new brew.

"One for the girls, are you, m'bucko?" Killashandra had asked in an arch tone.

Lars nodded at her garland. "Not any more, Sunny! I've made an honest woman of you!"

That exchange did more to reassure Tanny than any other argument Killashandra had presented. That and the fact that she was perfectly willing to help bail out the cockpit.

Bar Island was reached just before sunset, with enough time to unload the emergency supplies. The Bar Islanders had been directly in the hurricane's path and suffered more damage than any of the other islands on their sweep. Two men, a woman and a young child had internal injuries which the medical facilities of the smaller settlement could not treat adequately. Lars immediately offered them passage on the *Pearl Fisher*, giving Killashandra a guarded and rueful grin of regret. Nor did they have a chance to be private that night. Everyone pitched in to finish constructing temporary communal shelters, and Killashandra found herself once again plaiting polly fronds, pleased that her deftness caused no questions. When a halt was called at midnight, Killashandra was far too tired to do more than curl up gratefully against Lars on the sand, her head pillowed on his arm, and fall asleep.

At first light of a sullen day, the injured were floated on bladder rafts to the *Pearl*, carefully hoisted aboard, then secured in the cabin bunks. Killashandra was given instructions by the medic for the administration of necessary drugs and care. The patients had been sedated for the voyage, so he expected no problems.

As soon as she could, Killashandra went up on deck. She found care of the sick and injured a distasteful necessity and the faint odor of antiseptics and medicine made her slightly nauseous. She said nothing about her disinclination, uncharacteristically wanting to sustain Lars's good opinion of her. He was bent over the chart display on the small navigational terminal, plotting the most direct course for Angel Island's North Harbor where the main medical facility was situated.

"Tide and wind are in our favor this morning, Killa," he said, reaching his arm about her waist and drawing her in to him without taking his eyes from the display. He tapped for an overlay of the route he had chosen and she could see how it made use of the swift channels between the islands and the fuller morning tide. "We'll be in North before we know it." He made a final correction and laid in the course. Now the display cleared to show him the compass headings and the minimum required tacking to slip into the swift current just beyond Bar Island's western reef. "Is the spinnaker set, Tanny?"

"Aye, aye skipper," the young man called from the bow as Killashandra watched the vivid red and orange sail belling out briefly over the bowsprit before the wind caught it.

There's an exhilaration to sailing a fast, trim ship, with a following wind and a current to assist smooth passage. The *Pearl* slipped into the flow as effortlessly as a slide down a greased pole. The sea was almost calm, and gunmetal green-gray, not quite the same color as the gray sky.

"Lucky it's today instead of yesterday," Killashandra said, settling herself in the cockpit beside Lars. He had the tiller on its upper setting so that he could see forward without the cabin blocking him.

"They're all secure below?"

"Secure and asleep! I'll check on the half hour."

They sat together enjoying wind, sea, and sail while Tanny coiled lines and set all fair. Then he joined them in the cockpit, maintaining the companionable silence.

Just before noon, sailing smartly on the same westerly current that had nearly defeated Killashandra, they rounded the Toe and tacked eastward to sail right up to the large North Harbor pier at the elbow of the Angel. When Lars had been able to estimate his time of arrival, he had called it in, so medics and grav units were waiting for the injured. Killashandra, dutifully checking every half hour, had had no problems with her patients but it was an immense relief to turn them over to trained medical technicians.

"Father wants a word with us," Lars said quietly in Killashandra's ear as they watched their passengers being trundled away. "Tanny, anchor the *Pearl* at buoy twenty-seven, will you? And keep her ready. Don't know where we'll have to go next. Stay on the page, okay?"

Tanny nodded, his expression rather strained, as if he was relieved to stay on the *Pearl*, whose eccentricities he could cope with and understand.

If the Wing Harbor on the south side of Angel Island had appeared rustic and homely to Killashandra's eyes, North Harbor was the antithesis: that is, within the framework of the Charter's prohibition against raping "a Natural World." The colorful buildings set up above the harbor behind sturdy sea walls utilized manmade materials and modernistic surfaces in some sort of tough, textured plastic and made a good deal of plasglas so no vista would be hidden from the occupiers. If the architecture lacked warmth or grace, it was also practical in a zone where wind speeds could make a dangerous missile out of a polly branch.

Lars guided Killashandra up a ramp that climbed to the top of the Elbow, where a dormered structure commanded views of the main harbor as well as the smaller curved bay that featured the old stratovolcano that was the Angel's Head. A small sailing craft was tacking cautiously through the Fingerbone reefs at the end of the Hand. From the different colors in the sea, Killashandra could distinguish the safer, deeper channel, but she didn't think she'd like to sail that in a ship as large as the *Pearl*.

To her surprise, the first person they saw as they entered the Harbor Master's office was Nahia. She had been using the terminal and upon their entry she half rose, her expression eager for Lars's news of the stranded crystal singer.

"We needn't have worried ourselves for a moment about our captive, Nahia." Lars strode up to the empath and, before she could protest, kissed her hand.

"Lars, you simply must stop that," Nahia protested, giving Killashandra a worried glance.

"Why? I only do you a courtesy you fully deserve!"

Would Nahia comfort Lars, Killashandra wondered, after she had departed Optheria?

"The woman is all right, isn't she, Carigana?" Nahia was by no means reassured by Lars's droll comment.

"Never better," Killashandra replied affably. She wondered why Lars was drawing the game out when he had specifically said he didn't wish to deceive Nahia. She gave him a sharp glance.

"Where's Father?"

"I'm here, Lars, and there's trouble on its way," the Harbor Master said, appearing from the front office. "I'm only grateful we had the hurricane, for it slowed down the official transport. There's to be a full search of the Islands. Torkes leads it so it'd be the height of folly to protest or interfere."

"Then isn't it fortunate that the crystal singer has been rescued," Killashandra said.

"She has?" Olav Dahl looked about, even to peering outside, seeking the woman.

Unerringly now, Nahia turned her worried face toward Killashandra, her eyes widening.

"And, Olav Dahl, by your courageous son, who found her abandoned on an island while he was on a hurricane rescue mission in the vicinity."

"Young woman, I—" Olav Dahl began, frowning at her light tone.

"You are Killashandra Ree?" Nahia asked, her beautiful eyes intent on Killashandra's face.

"Indeed. And so grateful to the loyal upright Optherian citizen Lars Dahl that this much-abused crystal singer feels secure only in his presence." Killashandra beamed fatuously at Lars.

Nahia's slender hands went to her mouth to suppress her laughter.

"I presume that in your official capacity you can inform the official vehicle of the felicitous news?" Killashandra asked Olav Dahl, smiling encouragingly at him to coax a less reproving response.

Olav Dahl regarded Killashandra with an expression that became more and more severe, as if he didn't believe what he was hearing, didn't condone her levity, and quite possibly would not accept her assistance. Slowly he sank onto the nearest desk for support, staring at her with amazement. Killashandra wondered that this man could be Lars's father until suddenly a smile of great charm and pure mischief lightened his countenance. He got to his feet, one hand outstretched to her, radiating relief.

"My dear Guildmember, may I say how pleased I am that you have been delivered from your ordeal? Have you any idea at all who perpetrated this outrage on a member of the most respected guild in the galaxy?"

"None under the sun," Killashandra replied, the epitome of innocent bewilderment. "I left the organ loft, rather precipitously, I hasten to add, because of a distressing incident with an officious security captain. I hoped that a stroll in the fresh air might compose my agitated spirits. When all of a sudden—" She brought her hands together. "I think I must have been drugged for a long time. When I finally regained consciousness, I was on this island, from which your son fortuitously rescued me only this morning!" Killashandra turned, fluttering her eyelashes at Lars in a parody of gratitude.

"I find that absolutely fascinating, Killashandra Ree," said a totally unexpected newcomer. Lars half crouched as he whirled toward the doorway framing Corish von Mittelstern. "Evidently your credentials were far more impressive than you led me to expect. So you're the crystal singer who was dispatched?"

"Oh, and have you found your dear uncle?"

"Actually, I have." Corish, his lips twitching with the first real amusement she had seen him exhibit, gestured toward Olav Dahl.

Lars was not the only one who stared at his father. Nahia gave a silvery laugh.

"It was too amusing, the confrontation, Lars," Nahia said, chuckling. "They were circling the truth like two hemlin cocks. It was all I could do to retain my composure, for, of course, Hauness and I have known Olav's history. It didn't take me very long to perceive that Corish was not looking for the man in the hologram."

"I could hardly brandish Dahl's real likeness in case I jeopardized him. I'd memorized his facial characteristics so I thought I'd recognize him once I did see him." Then Corish turned to Killashandra. "He hadn't altered as much as you had. I didn't recognize you at all, with your hair and eyebrows bleached and a good few kilos lighter. If it matters," and Corish gestured at the matched garlands, "this is an improvement over the mawkish music student."

"So are you Council or Evaluation?" Killashandra shot a triumphant glance at Lars. "Olav's no more your uncle than I am. That inheritance business was very thin."

"For you, perhaps," and Corish inclined his body toward her, and his manner turned starchy at her criticism, "but you'd be surprised at how effective it was. Especially with Optherian officials who might get their percentage out of it." Corish made an age-old gesture with his thumb and forefinger. "Since all off-planet mail is censored, and not always delivered to the addressee, such a problem is peculiarly applicable to Optheria."

"I withdraw my comment." Killashandra nodded graciously and then seated herself in the nearest chair. "Do I also assume that Olav has been a—misplaced—agent?"

"Inadvertently detained," Olav replied on his own behalf, with a nod to Corish. "My briefing was at fault, on a point no one had considered at headquarters. To wit, the mineral residue, which is what trapped me here. And which provides the Optherians with such simple means of preventing unauthorized departure from this planet. The exile has not been without profit to me," and he smiled warmly at his son, "though my time was not spent in activities of which the Council wholeheartedly approve. 'If you can't lick 'em, join 'em' is useful advice." He winked at Killashandra, who gave a crow of laughter. "However, you appear to be remarkably tolerant of the abuse you have suffered at my son's hands."

Killashandra laughed. "Oh, yes, since it has afforded me the chance to investigate a complaint."

"Oh?" Olav exchanged glances with Corish.

"Lodged by a Stellar of the Federated Artists' Association."

"Really?" Nahia clapped her hands together in delight, grinning at Lars with triumph. "I told you they were a good choice."

Corish had straightened up in his chair. "You . . . were also told to investigate?"

"Oh, yes, but the organ repair should have been the priority!" And she gave Lars a stern glance.

"We can discuss this at a later time," Olav said, raising his hand for silence. "We have a much more immediate problem in the imminent arrival of an official search party."

"I've outlined the way to deal with that, haven't I?" said Killashandra.

"To what purpose?" Olav asked. "Not that I am not grateful for you forgiving my rascally son . . ."

"I think that would be my preeminent task, Olav Dahl," Killashandra replied with a grim smile. "I don't know which Elder supervises Security on this planet, but from what I have seen, your son is probably first on their list of suspects whether or not they've any evidence at all."

"Oh, I agree, Olav," Nahia said.

"Will Security believe your explanation?" Corish asked skeptically.

"What?" Killashandra rose in a flowing movement, drawing herself up to her full height, in a pose of haughty self-confidence. "Refute the statement of a crystal singer, a member of the Heptite Guild, a craftsman whose services are vital to the all-important tourist season? You must be joking! How, under which ever name you hold sacred, can they challenge what I say? Besides," she said, relaxing and flashing a friendly smile, "I have every confidence in Lars's ability to lend credence to the account. Don't you?"

"I must say, when you assume that pose, Killashandra, I'd hesitate to contradict you." Corish rose to his feet. "But now, I think that Nahia and I had better join Hauness and prepare to disappear. If they credit Killashandra's explanation, they'll not be likely to mount a twenty-five-hour radar watch, will they? So we won't have that problem to contend with."

Nahia had returned to the console, and was taking some hard copy from the retrieval slot. "I've all the charts we need, Olav, and my thanks for your suggestions. Just in case, I think we will take the devious course through the islands and then double back north. Lars, Olver survived the purge and you can contact us through him when you need to." Corish had her by the arm and was drawing her toward a rear exit. "May I hope to see you again, Killashandra?"

"If that is at all possible, officially, yes, of course, and I look forward to the occasion." Abruptly, annoyed at her stilted phrases, Killashandra stepped forward and swiftly embraced Nahia, kissing her on both cheeks. She stepped back, rather surprised at her uncharacteristic effusiveness until she saw the pleasure in Nahia's brilliant eyes and smiling face.

"Oh, you are kind!"

"Don't be ridiculous!" Killashandra replied fiercely, and then smiled with embarrassment. She felt Lars take her elbow and squeeze it gently.

"Should I need to contact you, Killashandra," Corish added, opening the door and all but pushing Nahia out, "I'll leave a message at the Piper Facility. As I already have." The door closed behind them with an emphatic slam.

"Come," Olav said, striding toward his front office. "We'll signal the jet. Fortunately, the return of the *Pearl* has been entered in the Harbor log and not too much time will have elapsed before we inform them of this good news." Olav paused in front of the huge console, frowning slightly at Killashandra. "You are certain you wish to go through with this? It could be dangerous!"

"Far more dangerous for them," Killashandra said with a snort. "To have put me in such a situation in the first place." Then she laughed. "Just think, Olav, with Lars's confession that Torkes and Ampris hired him to 'assault me,' to prove my identity, how they have compromised themselves."

"I actually had not considered that aspect." He turned to the console and began to send out the message.

The jet cruiser responded instantly with a request for visual with which Olav instantly complied.

"Look pleased but humble, Lars," Killashandra muttered before she turned to the screen, once more the haughty and arrogant crystal singer.

"Elder Torkes, I must protest! It is over five weeks since I was abducted from the City—a City, I might add, in which I had already been assaulted though I had been told in unequivocal terms that Optheria was a 'secure' planet, where everyone knew his place, and no unusual activities were condoned or permitted." Killashandra stressed the words as sarcastically as possible, enjoying the shock on the Elder's face. "Yet I could also be insulted by a minor and officious idiot, *and* kidnapped! I could be abandoned on this dreadful world. And it has taken you all this time to come to the islands which you yourself told me were populated by a dissident group. Dissident they might be, but courteous they are, and I have been made to feel far more welcome in these islands than I was during your pompous, ill-provisioned reception. I will also inform you, if you haven't already heard from them, that my Guild will take a very dim view of this whole incident. In fact, reparations may well be required. Now, what have you to say to me?"

"Honored Guildmember, I cannot adequately express our horror, our concern for you during your terrible ordeal." Those in the Harbor Master's office saw the effort which Elder Torkes was forced to make to moderate his own manner. "I don't know how the Council can ever redeem itself in your eyes. Anything we can do—"

"I suggest that you begin by expressing gratitude to the young man who rescued me after that frightening hurricane—Why, I thought I'd be swept to sea and drowned during the night. This is the young man," and ruthlessly Killashandra pulled Lars beside her. Torkes's face was unreadable as he inclined his head in the curtest possible recognition. "He's the skipper of the—what did you say your boat's called, Captain Dahl?"

"The *Pearl Fisher*, Guildmember."

"I might add that he took considerable risk to himself and his vessel to put in to that island. The monsters in the lagoon and all about it were in some sort of frenzy. The storm does that, he told me. But I was so relieved to see another human after all that time . . . Look at me! I'm a sight! My hair, my skin! I'm nothing but skin and bones!"

"Our estimated time of arrival is 18:30, Guildmember. Until that time, the Harbor Master will be able to attend to your comfort to the limits of his facilities." Torkes regained some of his usual repressive manner as he eyed Olav Dahl significantly.

"Begging your indulgence, Elder Torkes, but the Guildmember insisted that you be contacted before any personal comfort was seen to. We are hers to command until your arrival."

The picture was cut off at the cruiser screen. No sooner was it blank than Lars seized Killashandra in his arms, whirling her about the communications room, roaring his approval.

"His face! Did you see how he had to struggle to control himself, Killa?"

"You'll break my ribs, Lars—Leave off! But you can see how easy it is—"

"When you have one of the most prestigious Guilds in the FSP to back you," Olav said, but he was grinning as broadly with satisfaction at the confrontation as Lars was.

"Well, you have the FSP Council—"

"Only if they are in the position to acknowledge me," Olav reminded her, raising a hand in contradiction. "Which they are not, as my mission here was covert. The Council does not interfere with planetary politics when no other planet or system is affected. Optheria could not be approached on an official basis, you know. The FSP had ratified their Charter."

"With you to explain all about the lack of popular acceptance of the restriction, surely—"

"My dear Killashandra Ree, the situation on Optheria cannot be altered by one man's testimony, especially a man who could by planetary laws to which he is now subject under intergalactic regulations, be tried and convicted of treasonous acts."

"Oh!" Killashandra's elation drained away quickly.

"Don't concern yourself with this problem now, my friend—for I count you one," Olav said, gripping her on the shoulder. "I am grateful for what you have already achieved." He took Lars's shoulder in his other hand, smiling with great affection at his son. "Ever since we saw the cruiser jet on the screen, I'd been wracking my brains on how to protect Lars from interrogation by Torkes. You have scuttled that plan, but do not deceive yourself that all will be fair sailing."

"It was a superb performance, Killa! When I tell the others—"

"Softly, Lars, softly," Olav said, "Torkes has had enough to swallow. Give him no more on your peril. Now, Killashandra, we must do the courteous for you, and lavish you with suitable gifts and personal services—"

"Teradia, of course, Father. And I'll advise her about our visitors— and their preferences." Lars grimaced with distaste.

"Yes, I'll warn her you're coming up and then I'll organize appropriate festivities."

"Why waste a barbecue on Torkes? He doesn't eat!" Killashandra said in disgust.

"But you do, Killashandra, and it's *your* return to civilization that we're celebrating!" Lars squeezed her about the waist.

"One point, Lars," and Olav laid a restraining hand on his son's arm as he reached and removed the garland from his neck. "I am sorry, but these would bring unwelcome questions." He reached for Killashandra's and she hesitated before giving it to him.

"Not half as sorry as I am." She walked out of the building, Lars following quietly behind her.

Chapter 16

Teradia's house was situated on one of the upper levels facing North Harbor, and as they hurried up the steep, zigzag stairs that linked the terraces, Killashandra saw that much of the debris occasioned by the hurricane had already been removed. Groups of young people were unhurriedly staking polly trees upright and replanting those young pollys which had been entirely uprooted. Others were pruning bushes or restoring bedding plants.

"Are there any snakes in this paradise?" Killashandra asked when they paused at the first level to let her catch her breath.

"Snakes? What are those?" Lars asked, humoring her.

"Normally, a long, slender, legless reptile—only I meant humans with unpleasant characteristics." She made a weaving, sinuous gesture with her hand, and grimaced with distaste. "Surely the Elders make use of informers and spies."

"Oh, they do. Most of whom report themselves to us and pass back such information as we want the Elders to have." Lars grinned as his fingers caressed her arm. "It's not naive of us; islanders stick together. The Elders can give us little that we lack—except the freedom to leave the planet. To be sure, not many of us would leave: it's having the option to do so. And my father has a small detector so that people posing as tourists can be quickly identified. Father has a theory that only a certain type of personality is attracted to such an infamous occupation, and they often give themselves away. Strangely enough, by not singing!" He gave her a mischievous grin. "I was relieved to hear you singing lustily at the barbecue."

"I nearly didn't because, if I could recognize your tenor, you might have spotted me as that midnight soprano. So I sang alto. But, Lars, isn't Nahia in jeopardy for being here? Someone might just slip up and mention her presence?"

Lars took her by the elbows and pulled her against him, unconcernedly stroking her hair. "Beloved Sunny, Nahia would be protected under any circumstances but, as it happens, only my father, you, and the people she came with, know she was on this island during the hurricane. Her party's ocean jet has been secreted in another of the Back caves, unseen by anyone. It's still there and won't emerge until we've had a chance to jam the cruiser's surveillance systems. Nahia and Hauness will use the islands to screen them from any possibility of detection when the cruiser takes you—all right, and me—back to the Mainland. Satisfied? I told you my father is efficient. He is.

"There will also be no one here tonight from Wing Harbor who might inadvertently remember the girl Lars Dahl had as his partner."

"But—"

"No one in Wing will feel slighted: they're all too busy with storm damage. Every building on the waterfront collapsed. And Wingers avoid Elder inspection as they would a smacker school."

Killashandra did feel relieved by his explanations. She was rather pleased, too, as she reviewed her confrontation with Torkes. Nor would she fail to be exceedingly cautious in the presence of any of the Elders. Torkes would never forgive her for that tongue-lashing, and she knew that he would do everything he could to rank the others against her if a second confrontation was to occur. Still, she was glad she had launched her frontal assault on the fardling tyrant.

"We shan't leave anything to chance, however, Sunny," Lars went on as they climbed to the last terrace level. "If sun-bleached hair and eyebrows alter your appearance enough to deceive an FSP agent—"

"Corish was not expecting me to be on that beach, any more than you—"

"Then Teradia can restore your beauty. With more sophisticated clothes, and that hauteur of yours, you'll be every inch the crystal singer." Lars halted, swinging her into his arms again. No one was in sight. "Will the impressively beautiful crystal singer still favor her island lover?" He smiled down at her, but tension caught at the corners of his gray-tinged eyes.

"Don't tell me you—who braves hurricanes, Elders, and Masters—feared my ranting?" She soothed the creases from his eyes. "I assume a role, Lars Dahl, from some opera or other. I play no role with you, no matter under what circumstances. Believe me. Let's not lose a moment of what we have together!"

She stood on tiptoe to kiss him and the hunger they both felt made them tremble.

"How are we going to make out, Killa, on board that cruiser? And back on the Mainland?"

"Oh, citizen!" Killashandra laid her hand gracefully against her bosom, fluttering her eyes, as much to keep back the tears as to embellish her assumed character. "When I trust to you my safety, where else shall you be but with me, wherever I go, even in my bedchamber? And have you seen where they quartered me in the Conservatory? You'll see, Lars. It will all be arranged *my* way!"

By then they had reached an establishment with a modest sign spelling out "Teradia" in graceful lettering. Teradia herself greeted them, a woman as tall as Lars, with a supple, willowy figure, and densely black hair very intricately braided. Her skin was olive and flawless, the pale green pupils of her eyes appeared luminous: she was a superb testimonial to her establishment.

"Olav Dahl wants the very best for you, Killashandra Ree, and I myself will see to your care."

"I'll supervise," Lars interrupted. "The bleaching must be . . ."

With a quick movement, Teradia placed one hand across Lars's chest and eased him away from Killashandra, a look of mild disdain on her elegant features. "My dear boy, clever you may be in some of the ways of pleasing a woman, but this is *my* art . . ." she began to draw Killashandra away with her, "and you will allow me to practice it. Come, Guildmember, this way."

"Teradia, that's not fair." Lars pushed through the door in pursuit. "I'm Killashandra's bodyguard—"

"Here I guard her body, though from the look of her skin and hair, you've done a poor job—sun-bleached, dry-skinned, waterlogged child."

"Teradia!"

For the first time Killashandra had seen her lover rattled; she looked more keenly at Teradia. There was a twinkle in the woman's eyes, though her expression did not soften at his exasperation.

"It is, of course, as the Guildmember wishes . . ."

"How do you do it, Teradia?"

"Do what?"

"Quell him."

Teradia shrugged delicately. "It is easy. He has been reared to respect his elders."

"What?" Killashandra peered more closely at Teradia's face.

"She's my grandmother," Lars said with a disgusted growl.

"My compliments, citizen," Killashandra replied, trying not to laugh at Lars's discomposure. "I shall have your artistry to support me this evening—"

"And me!" Lars was emphatic.

So, under Lars's eyes and occasionally with his help and company, Killashandra was soaped and bathed and massaged and oiled, and repairs to hair and nail accomplished, Killashandra fell asleep during the massage and later Lars fell asleep while Teradia tinted Killashandra's hair and dyed her eyebrows dark again.

"It does make a considerable difference in your appearance," Teradia said, surveying her handiwork. "I'm not certain which becomes you more," she added thoughtfully. "You are a striking woman in either guise. Now," she went on so briskly that Killashandra did not have to make any reply to this assessment, "we don't have everything back from hurricane storage, but I know exactly where I put several unusual gowns that would suit your style and rank. Come this way, into the dressing room."

Killashandra looked over her shoulder at the slumbering Lars.

"If he fell asleep in your presence, he is far more tired than he would ever admit, Killashandra Ree. We will leave him so until he is needed to escort you back to Olav Dahl."

By the time Teradia had garbed Killashandra to her satisfaction, which had nothing, Killashandra realized, to do with her own, Lars had awakened. He executed a double take at the vision before him, presented a properly stunned expression before he began to smile then nod with approval.

"In there," Teradia said, flicking her fingers to direct him to another dressing room in the shop portion of her establishment. "We can't have a shabby escort. Not that any will notice you."

Killashandra began to frown, then the woman winked slowly and grinned. "That one is too sure of himself by half."

"He'll need it," Killashandra said sadly.

"Oh?"

But before Killashandra could say anything more, an unclad Lars had stormed into the room, waving a heavily embroidered, tissue thin, blue shirt and equally thin blue trousers.

"If you think I'm parading about like a stud on sale! When did I ever have the need to display—"

In one long stride Teradia reached the room, and scooped up a pair of blue briefs that had evidently fallen to the floor. She flourished them under his nose and then pushed him back into the room.

"Well, if that's the case . . ."

Killashandra stifled her giggles.

"You only wanted to take the limelight . . ."

He poked his head around the door. "Not when I know Torkes's proclivities. Then again," he paused in the act of withdrawing his head, "he probably has the cruiser packed with his boys so I'm safer here than in City."

"Who needs the bodyguard then?"

"Shall we have a mutual assistance pact? I read those were once very popular."

"Done!"

Lars slammed open the door, strode across the room, and gathered her into his arms, beaming down at her.

"If you spoil her dress or make-up . . ." Teradia's mock anger subsided as she became aware of the atmosphere between them.

Lars ached to kiss Killashandra as badly as she wanted to have his lips on hers. He sighed deeply and let her go. "You look regal, Killashandra! But I think I liked you even better on the beach at Wing! Then you were mine alone to enjoy!" His voice was low, his words meant for her, his sentiment unhindered by his grandmother's presence. "You have outdone yourself, Teradia." He pulled the woman close, and kissed her cheek.

Killashandra felt relief that there would be another sane and well-adjusted person to help Lars when she had returned to Ballybran.

"Now we had better go, Killashandra. The cruiser will have docked!"

Killashandra thanked Teradia as warmly as she could, wishing that the woman did not dismiss so casually her genuine gratitude.

As they started to retrace their steps to the Harbor Master's residence,

Killashandra was instantly aware of an alteration in the ambiance. Far below the squat bulk of the cruiser jet did much to explain the change, looming as it did, gross and menacing, its white ovoid hull diminishing the graceful fishing vessels. The slanted superstructure, the little nodules of its armaments, and the sprouting whiskers of its communications and surveillance equipment added to its menacing presence.

Killashandra unconsciously hugged Lars's arm. "That is a very deadly looking machine. Do they have many of those?"

"Enough!"

"Can Nahia and Hauness escape it?"

Lars chuckled, relieving his own tension and reducing hers. "The *Yellowback* is smaller and faster, highly maneuverable and could slip through reefs that would ram the cruiser. Once they're away, they're well away."

Killashandra could see the coming and going on the ramp leading to Olav's—people bearing tables, chairs, seating cushions, baskets of fruit, jars, several men staggering under loads of provender. Killashandra had been expecting another beach barbecue, with its pleasant informality. It had not occurred to her that there might be no beach at North Harbor, nor would the Elder have been entertained in the casual setting she had so much enjoyed at Wing. She groaned.

Lars squeezed her hand. "What's wrong?"

She gave a gusty sigh. "State occasions! Formality! Scrapes and smiles and total boredom."

Lars laughed. "You'll be surprised. Pleasantly."

"How will your father get away with it?"

Lars grinned at her. "You'll see."

What she first saw was the disposition of guards, lining the route up from the harbor, spaced neatly and stiffly about the Residence, and armed. She had seen very few stun rifles in her life but she could recognize them.

"What was he expecting? Civil war?"

"Elders usually travel with a considerable entourage. Especially in the islands. We are so aggressive, you see." Lars spoke with deep sarcasm and she took in an anxious breath. "Oh, don't worry, Killa. I'll be circumspect. You'll not even recognize me as your impetuous lover."

She cocked an eyebrow at him. "I'll expect a return of that lover as a reward for my evening with Torkes. And why is it Torkes? I thought he was in charge of Communications."

Lars choked back a loud laugh, for they had neared the first sentry. "Elder Pedder is afflicted with motion sickness."

The sentry who had been watching them approach from the corner of his eye suddenly pivoted, ported his weapon, and stared with impartial malevolence at them. "Who goes there?"

"The crystal singer, you fool," Killashandra replied in a loud and disgusted tone. "With her bodyguard, Lars Dahl." When Killashandra would have proceeded she was stopped by the weapon. "How *dare* you?" She darted forward, grasped the weapon by its muzzle, and levered it forcefully to the ground. The surprised young sailor panicked and relinquished his weapon. "How *dare* you threaten a crystal singer? How dare you threaten *me*?"

Killashandra was seized by a violent surge of real anger at the archaic and inane formality. She didn't hear Lars trying to soothe her; she barged past two more sentries who came to assist their mate; she would have gone through the officer who came hurrying up the ramp, flanked by three additional guards on either side. She paused momentarily, seething at this additional obstacle. The officer had either encountered Elders in a tearing fit or he instantly recognized an elemental force. He barked an order, and the barricade suddenly became an escort which fell in behind the officer and Lars, who had managed to keep at Killashandra's heels as the enraged crystal singer stormed forward to the Residence, seeking the initiator of this additional affront.

Here Lars took the lead, adroitly indicating the way. She heard an exchange of urgent shouts. She had a confused vision of more guards snapping to attention, and another pair hastily opening the elaborately carved wooden doors—which despite her involvement in anger, she recognized as magnificent panels of polly wood. Then she was in the formal reception antechamber of the Residence, and she remembered thinking that the tip of this iceberg was the business end. She continued her angry progress right to the shallow tier of steps that led down to the main level. With an alert and wary expression, Olav was halfway across the floor to greet her. Behind him Elder Torkes was seated on a high wooden chair, members of his staff standing about the room, conversing with several islanders.

Automatically, Killashandra gave the assembled one quick glance before she proceeded toward Torkes. "Did I spend weeks on a deserted island to be stopped and questioned by an *armed* minion? To have a *weapon* thrust in my face as if I were an enemy? I"—and Killashandra nearly bruised her breastbone as she thumped herself with rigid fingers—"I am the one who has been assaulted and abducted. I am the one who has been at jeopardy and you—" Now she pointed an accusing finger at Torkes, who was regarding her in a state of shock. "You have been safe! Safe!"

Afterwards Lars told her that she had been magnificent, her eyes visibly emitting sparks, her manner so imposing that he had been breathless with astonishment. What operatic role had she been using?

"I wasn't," she'd replied with a rueful smile, for the effect of her dramatic entrance had more than satisfied her rage. "I've never been so angry in my life. A *weapon*? Pointed at *me*?"

Torkes heaved himself out of his chair, his expression that of a man confronting an unknown and dangerous entity and uncertain which course to take. "My dear Crystal Singer—"

"I am not your dear anything."

"Your experiences have unnerved you, Guildmember Ree. No aggression was intended against you, merely—"

"—Your wretched, suffocating need for protocol and an irrelevant show of aggression. I warn you"—and she waggled her finger at him again—"I warn you, you may expect the most severe retribution"—she caught herself; in her rage, she had been on the point of revealing too much to Elder Torkes—"from my Guild, reparation for the callous and undignified way in which I have been treated."

Torkes regarded her finger as if it were some sort of deadly weapon in itself. Before he could assemble a suitable reply Olav was at Killashandra's elbow, offering a glass of amber liquid. "Guildmember, drink this . . ." His baritone voice, so soothing and conciliatory, penetrated her ranting. She knocked back the drink, and was rendered momentarily speechless. The shock of the potent beverage effectively restored her to discretion. "You are understandably overwrought, and have been needlessly upset, but you are safe here, now, I do assure you. Elder Torkes has already initiated the most thorough investigation of this terrible outrage and personally supervised your security here on Angel Island."

Olav's tactful reassurances gave her the time to regain use of her throat and vocal cords. Her throat was on fire, her stomach throbbing, and her eyes watered. Which seemed a good cue to develop. She allowed her tears to flow and reached weakly for Olav's hand to support her. Instantly she felt Lars take her right arm, and the two men led her to the other elaborate chair in the chamber, seating her as if she were suddenly fragile.

"I am overset. Anyone would be, enduring what I have," Killashandra said, using her sobbing to purge the last dregs of anger, for she estimated that she'd worked that pitch long enough. "All alone, on that wretched island, not knowing where I was, if I'd ever be rescued. And then the hurricane . . ."

A second glass was proffered. When she glared at Olav, he winked. Nevertheless, she sipped cautiously. Polly wine.

"Please accept my apologies, Elder Torkes, but that ridiculous weapon was the last straw." Her voice died away but she managed to sound reasonably sincere. Then she smiled weakly at the nonplussed Elder, and fluttered her eyelashes at his attendants. They seemed afflicted by some sort of paralysis. It afforded Killashandra considerable satisfaction that she had managed to confound an entire Optherian crew. They had stood in great need of such a lesson. She relaxed into the cushioned back of the chair.

"There isn't an islander in this Archipelago who would do you any injury, Guildmember," Olav continued, now offering her a finely stitched handerkerchief. "Especially after the news of your devoted nursing of the Bar Island injured. When I consider how unselfishly you volunteered to assist, and you only an hour away from being rescued, why, we are all in your debt."

Shielding her face from Torkes with the handerkerchief, Killashandra looked up at Olav. She blotted the last of the tears she could manage to squeeze out. She had received his message. She gave a sniff, then exhaled in a huge sigh.

"What else could I do? Their need was far greater than mine for I had suffered no real physical injury. It was excellent therapy," and she managed that on a rush of breath, "for me to tend those less fortunate than I. And I do feel safe with you, Harbor Master, and with Captain Dahl!" She touched each man on the arm, favoring them with a tremulous smile. Lars managed to give her shoulder an admonitory pinch which, she felt, indicated that she had milked this scene for all it was worth. "I hope you didn't encounter that ferocious storm on your way here, Elder Torkes?"

"Not at all, Guildmember. In fact," Torkes cleared his throat nervously, "we didn't set out until sure that the hurricane had dwindled. I ought to have listened to Mirbethan's representations, Captain"—he turned to the senior officer behind him—"for she offered to accompany us, Guildmember, on the slim chance that we would discover you here."

"How very kind of her."

"She would have been an ideal companion to settle your nerves, Guildmember."

"Yes, she was most considerate but, though I appreciate her willingness, I now insist on someone . . ." she waved a negligent hand in Lars's direction, "who is capable of managing himself in difficulties. I have seen Captain Dahl in action, fighting to bring his ship close enough to take me off that island, and in dealing with high seas, and injured people." And that should be the end of that notion. Had it been Mirbethan's? Or Ampris's? From whichever source, she'd not spend credit on it.

"If I may suggest it, Guildmember, would you be feeling recovered enough to dine now?" Olav asked, deftly changing the subject. "Or should Captain Dahl escort you to the quarters prepared for you here in the Residence?"

"Why, yes," Killashandra said, extending her hand to Lars and smiling graciously at Olav, "I think that perhaps hunger is at the root of my deplorable temper. I'm not usually so easily upset, citizens." Now that the scene had been played, she *was* ravenous and hoped that Olav's hospitality would be to the standard she expected. It was, and she was seated on Olav's right at the beautifully appointed banquet table. Torkes was opposite her, Teradia appearing at his right hand. Evidently she had merely had to change her gown. Killashandra did wonder how she had arrived so promptly. Other charmingly dressed ladies partnered the officers of Torkes's retinue and from some discreet corner delicate music wafted to the diners' ears.

The food was sumptuous, a feat, considering the island had so recently been in the throes of a hurricane. As Killashandra sampled the many dishes presented, she realized that the components were not as varied as the manner in which they had been prepared. Polly—fruit, pulp, and heart—was the basis of nine dishes. Smacker was served as a chowder, boiled, broiled, fried in a delicious light batter and in a rich piquant sauce. The largest yellowbacks she had yet seen had been lightly broiled with slivered nuts. A succulent mollusc was offered, grilled with a dollop of some flavor enhancer. There were salads of greens, moulded salads of some jellied vegetable, fruit, and fish.

From the way in which Torkes's officers filled their plates, and re-filled them when the dishes were presented a second time, they weren't used to eating. Torkes was abstemious by comparison although a fair trencherman away from Elder Pentrom's dietary regimen. He did not refuse the wine, either, though his two senior captains did.

When the first hunger was appeased, Torkes addressed Lars, his ex-pression far too bland to be as affable as he sounded.

"Just where did you discover the Guildmember, Captain Dahl?"

"On a polly islet slightly east of Bar Island. I don't normally pass by for it's a bit off the regular trade route, but with the higher tides to give me clearance over the reef in that area, I could take a bit of a short cut to Bar, which I aimed to reach before sunset."

"Do you have this islet marked on your charts?"

"Of course, Elder Torkes. I will show you its location immediately af-ter dinner." Lars had one hand on her thigh under the table and gave her a reassuring squeeze. Had his father tipped him off as he had her? "As well as the entry in my log which verifies the position."

"You keep a log?"

"Of a certainty, Elder Torkes. The Harbor Master is most insistent on such details which are, in my view, an integral part of responsible seamanship."

Farther down the table, an officer nodded his head in agreement. Torkes returned to his meal.

"What is this delicious fish, Harbor Master?" Killashandra asked, in-dicating the smacker.

"Ah, that is one of the island delicacies, Guildmember," and Olav launched into an amusing description of the habits of the tropical behe-moth and the dangers of capturing it. In his tale he managed to touch on the strength and bravery of smacker fishermen and their dedication to an unenviable task. Much of the smacker catch went to feed the Mainland.

With such innocuous tidbits and discourse, the meal finished. Imme-diately upon rising from the table, Elder Torkes told Lars Dahl that now was the time to show him the islet.

"We can call up the information right here," Olav said, going to the elaborate sideboard of the dining room. One section of its flat surface im-mediately transformed to display a terminal while the island seascape above slid to one side exposing a large screen.

Killashandra, watching Torkes obliquely, saw him stiffen until Olav merely gestured for Lars Dahl to retrieve what documents he needed. Within a moment, a small-scale chart of the entire Archipelago dominated the screen. Lars tapped keys and the chart dissolved to a larger-scale one of Angel Island, then flowed left toward Bar Island, slightly upward, and in another adjustment, magnified the chosen islet, complete with its protect-ing reefs, quite isolated from other blobs of polly-treed islands.

"Here, Elder Torkes, is where I discovered the Guildmember. Fortunately, whoever abandoned her left her where there is a good fresh spring." He now magnified the islet so that its topographical features were apparent.

"I'd a bit of a shelter on the height," Killashandra said.

"Here," Lars agreed and pointed.

"And mercifully I was high enough there to be out of reach of the hurricane tides—just barely—I fished in this lagoon, and swam, there, too, because the larger things couldn't pass over the reef. But, as you can see, gentlemen, I could not even have swum to an occupied island for help!"

One of Torkes's officers noted the longitude and latitude of the islet.

"Just thinking about it again distresses me." Killashandra turned to Olav. "That was a magnificent dinner to be served so soon after a hurricane, Harbor Master. And it was such a pleasure, for me especially," and she graciously gestured, "to have so much variety to choose from and enjoy. Now, I would like to retire."

"Guildmember, there is much to discuss—"

"We can discuss it just as easily in the morning, Elder Torkes. It has been a long and exhausting day for me, remember. We left Bar Island with the injured at dawn and it's now midnight." She turned from the Elder now to Olav. "I am quartered tonight in the Residence?"

"This way." Olav and Lars immediately escorted her to the inner wall where a lift door slid aside. "Let me assure you that this is the only way into the living section of the Residence. This will be guarded well tonight." He peremptorily gestured for the guard to be posted.

"Elder Torkes, this is the first time that we have been privileged to entertain members of the Council," Teradia said, her deep voice tinged with awe as she took Torkes's arm and began to lead him back to the reception room.

Olav bowed over Killashandra's hand, smiling as he came erect and gestured her into the lift. The door slid shut on Killashandra and Lars and, with an exaggerated sigh of relief, Killashandra leaned against him.

He made a quick sign with his hand, his eyes busy on the ceiling pane.

"I am totally exhausted, Captain Dahl." So, Torkes had had the area monitored. That would make it exceedingly awkward for her and Lars.

The lift made a brief, noiseless descent and then the door slid open to a scene that caught her breath. The wide window gave onto moonlit harbor. An aureole of bright light illuminating the ancient stratovolcano as a second moon rose behind it. Of one accord, they stood for a long moment in appreciation of the beauty.

As Lars led her down to the short corridor toward two doors at its end, he glanced at the chrono on his wrist. Killashandra had time to notice the grin on his face before all the lights went off. Simultaneously she saw three short blue flashes, two along the corridor and a third one at the first door.

"What—" she began in alarm, but then the lights came on and Lars took her in his arms.

"Now we're safe!"

"You blew the monitors?"

"And his ship's systems. Father's got a way with electronics and . . ." he swung her into his arms and impatiently strode toward the first door, which slid open to their approach. "I'm about to have my way with you."

Which, of course, was exactly what Killashandra had been hoping for.

Chapter 17

Abreakfast tray in hand, Teradia appeared early next morning. Killashandra found she was in a large room brightly lit by sunlight reflected from the surface of the harbor. How the woman maintained her perfect grooming and serene composure Killashandra would have given much to know. Perhaps it had something to do with the experiential tranquillity of advanced years, although "old" in the physiological sense did not seem to apply to Teradia.

"And what of the day, oh bringer of delights?" Lars asked, settling pillows behind Killashandra. "Olav didn't miss a trick last night, did he?"

"He's still playing them this morning." Teradia smiled faintly. "May I compliment you on last night's performance, Killashandra? You were spectacular. I don't think anyone on Torkes's staff had ever witnessed its like."

"I was consumed with righteous wrath," Killashandra replied. "Imagine, someone pointing a weapon at me! A crystal singer!"

Lars soothingly stroked her arm and poured out the steaming morning beverage. "What's Olav up to today then?"

Teradia seated herself on the edge of the wide bed, folding her hands together in her lap, the faint smile still tilting the corners of her full lips. "As you surmised, the power failure effectively crippled the cruiser, since Olav had so courteously suggested that they hook up to the land facilities and spare the cruiser's batteries. When it went, Torkes was quite upset, worrying about you, Guildmember, and thinking this was another attempt on your safety. Of course, the lift wouldn't operate, and an inspection party quickly discovered that this apartment cannot easily be scaled from the ground, so they posted guards on the waterfront. That's why your sleep was undisturbed." She lowered her eyes briefly. "Olav worked with the cruiser's engineers all night, to discover the trouble in our generators which, as you might suspect, had suffered previously undetected damage from the hurricane. All is now restored, except, of course, the units which were overloaded!" She pointed out the several char marks where walls met the ceiling. "And, of course, the blown chip was discovered to be water damaged. Your father has a genius in that area. But I think you had both better put in appearances shortly. There are suitable garments for you both in the dressingroom and I have been requested to deliver necessities for you to the cruiser, Killashandra."

Teradia rose in one lithe movement, hesitated, and then moved to Killashandra's side. "You can have no idea how I enjoyed seeing an Elder rendered speechless. An excellent strategy on your part. Keep them off balance and guessing. They don't have any experience with that!" Then Teradia laid her soft fragrant cheek against Killashandra's and before the crystal singer could react, had glided out of the room and closed the door.

"You *have* made an impression," Lars said. "I'll tell you about Teradia's experience with the Council and you'll understand what she meant. I never would have thought of complaining about that sentry nonsense," and Lars gave an exasperated sigh, "but then, I'm used to it. It must be . . ." He searched for the appropriate word, shrugged when he couldn't find it. "How remarkable not to need weapons or guards. Is it the case on Ballybran, or did that felicitous state exist on your Fuerte, too?"

"Both. On Fuerte for lack of aggression, and on Ballybran because everyone's too busy in the Ranges cutting crystal. We know our place and are secure in it," she paraphrased, mimicking Ampris's voice. "Lars, how are we going to fuse the monitors at the Conservatory? They'll have installed them, I know."

"You could always throw another tantrum."

"No thank you. Fits of temper are exhausting."

"Oh, is that truly why you're tired today?"

"Pleasure never tires me. Now let's eat and dress. I've just been attacked by a case of circumspection."

A few minutes later they emerged onto the reception floor with no further delays. An officer immediately leaped to his feet at their arrival, stammering queries about Killashandra's rest, apologies for any inconvenience caused by the power failure, and obsequiously requesting Killashandra and Captain Dahl to join the Harbor Master and Elder Torkes in the communications room.

Olav Dahl looked tired but there was a merriment in his eyes as he asked if all her needs had been satisfied. She reassured him, then turned to Torkes and affected surprise at his evident fatigue, fussing at him graciously.

"If the Guildmember is agreeable, I should like to depart immediately," Torkes replied, when the amenities were completed. He eyed her as if he expected her to demur.

"I left unfinished—even unstarted, to be totally candid—" she said, "the task which brought me to Optheria. I am more eager than you can imagine to complete the organ's repair and depart. I'm sure we will all feel relieved when I'm safely homebound."

Patently Elder Torkes could not be more in agreement, although he kept throwing skeptical glances at Killashandra as he made his farewells to Olav Dahl. Lars kept in the background. Meanwhile sailors in Council uniform had formed up into a guard of honor all the way from the Residence down to the pier where the cruiser's boat awaited its distinguished passengers.

Just as she reached the top of the steps, Killashandra looked up at the terraces, at the polly trees, the dwellings, at the old volcano on the Head, at the fishing skiffs serenely clearing the harbor, and she didn't want to leave Angel Island. Someone touched her arm and there was Olav with two garlands in his hand.

"Indulge me in an island custom, Guildmember." He draped the fragrant blossoms about her neck. Killashandra had just recognized the blooms as those with which Lars had handfasted her, when she saw Olav bestow one on his son. "Discharge your duties assiduously to the protection of the Guildmember's person, my son, and return to us only when you have seen her safely to the shuttle port!"

Before Killashandra could say anything in acknowledgment, Olav had stepped back. So, she could only smile her gratitude for his vote of confidence and proceed to the waiting boat. Impatiently she brushed aside the tears in her eyes before anyone could notice, and took a seat under the awning amidships. She was not surprised when Lars did not elect to join her for she could well imagine that he had been equally astonished by Olav's farewell.

She sat staring at the squat bulk of the cruiser, and liked it less the nearer she got to it. Nor did her opinion change during the three-day voyage back to the City. The Captain, a dour man named Festinel, was waiting at the top of the gangplank and escorted her himself to her cabin, explaining that her bodyguard would be quartered in the next cubicle, within hearing distance. She did not groan but saw this trip would be a repetition of the Trundimoux voyage. Well, she had survived that, too. Lars came along the companionway at that point and was greeted almost effusively by Captain Festinel.

During the evening meal, it was apparent from Festinel's deference to Lars that the man had been impressed by the islander's seamanship, or rather, the false account of his rescue of Killashandra from the dangerously positioned islet of exile. Killashandra added only her physical presence to the officers' mess. She was tired. She could feel muted crystal resonance in her body, though it was insufficient to raise the hair on those nearby. She was pleasant when addressed but limited her answers, contenting herself with enigmatic smiles. Elder Torkes kept shooting her wary, surreptitious glances but did not engage her in conversation. Which satisfied her. Keep him guessing about her, and off balance. Only how were she and Lars to have any sort of normal relationship if her quarters in the Conservatory were monitored?

On the crowded cruiser there was no way for them to have a private word or even the chance of a caress. Abstinence after the feast did nothing for her temper. So, preoccupied, she didn't notice the subliminal whine until the second evening, when she twitched all through dinner, rubbing at her neck and ear. Something was wrong.

"You're very unsettled tonight, Guildmember," Lars said finally, having endured her contortions throughout dinner. He spoke quietly, for her ears only, but his voice carried.

"Nerves—No, it's not nerves. Does this cruiser use a crystal drive?" She spoke in a loud, accusing tone, looking to Captain Festinel for her answer.

"It does, Guildmember, and I regret to inform you that we are experiencing some difficulty with it."

"It urgently needs to be retuned. As soon as you're in port. The way it sounds right now, it'll be broadcasting secondary sonics by morning."

"The engineer has been monitoring an uneven drive thrust but it should see us safely to the Mainland."

"You have reduced speed?"

"Of course, Crystal Singer, the moment the instrumentation recorded resonance."

"What is the matter with the cruiser?" Elder Torkes asked, only then aware of the nature of the discussion.

"Nothing for you to worry about," Killashandra said curtly, without glancing in his direction, for she was rubbing that side of her neck. She felt Lars stiffen beside her, and heard the tiny intake of her left-hand partner's breath. "I hope." She rose. "The whine is subsonic but highly irritating. Good evening, gentlemen."

Lars followed her and for a miracle they were alone in the companionway as he escorted her to her cramped quarters.

"Is it monitored?" she asked him in a low voice. He nodded.

"Do you require any medication to sleep, Guildmember?"

"Yes, if you can find some polly wine, Captain."

"The steward will bring a decanter to your quarters."

With a bottle of that inside her, Killashandra slept in spite of the increasingly audible distortion. The next morning, the noise was almost audible. Even Lars was affected. She was relieved when Captain Festinel requested her presence on the bridge. And concerned when she was shown the drive printout. Festinel and his engineering officer were justifiably concerned.

"We were due for an overhaul when this emergency came up, Guildmember. The Broad Sea had more turbulence than we had anticipated, putting a strain on the compensators as well as the stabilizers, especially at speed." The Captain was flatteringly deferential so Killashandra nodded as he made his points, and frowned wisely at the printout as if she knew what she was seeing. Fortunately the bridge was buffered against crystal noise as the rest of the ship was not, giving her a respite from the sound. Until she put her hand on the bulkhead and felt it coursing through the metal.

"The drive is losing efficiency," Killashandra said, recalling the phrases which Carrik had used at the shuttle port on Fuerte, and obscurely pleased with herself that her memory remained lucid for that period, now so completely divorced from her present life.

"Frankly, I'd prefer heaving to and having a good look at the crystal drive, but our orders are to proceed with all possible speed to the Mainland." The Captain shrugged and sighed.

Killashandra decided against reassuring him. The drive was souring: she didn't need the printouts to tell her that. But she had only the one experience on which to base an opinion and had no intention of ruining the image she had projected by a bad guess.

Then Captain Festinel asked hesitantly, "Do you really *hear* crystal resonance?"

Killashandra was aware of the expectant hush in the bridge as junior and senior officers, not to mention Lars at her side, waited for her reply.

"Yes, indeed. Like a dull ache from my earbones to my heels. If it were any louder, you'd find me asking for a life raft!"

"We know so little about your profession . . ."

"It is one like any other, Captain, with its dangers, its rewards, an apprenticeship to pass, and then years of refining one's skills." Killashandra was conscious, as she spoke, of one set of ears listening more keenly than others. She dared not look at Lars. "One facet of my training was retuning soured crystals." She made a rueful grimace. "Not my favorite occupation."

"Are there any prerequisites for the profession?" the older engineer asked, as he looked up from the printout.

"Perfect and absolute pitch is the one essential."

"Why?" Lars asked, surprised by that unexpected condition.

"We're called crystal singers because we must tune our subsonic cutters to the dominant pitch of the crystal we cut from the Ranges. A dangerous and exhausting task." She held out her hands so that all could see the fine white scars that crisscrossed the skin.

"I was told," Lars said in an amused drawl, "that crystal singers have amazing recuperative powers."

"That is quite true. Crystal resonance apparently slows the degenerative processes and accelerates the regenerative. Crystal singers retain their youthful appearance well into their third century."

"How old are you, Guildmember?" a brash young voice asked.

Frowning, the Captain turned about to seek the source of such insolence but Killashandra laughed. "I am a relatively new member of the Heptite Guild, and in my third decade."

"Are you able to travel anywhere you wish?" Did she detect a note of yearning?

"All crystal singers travel," she said with commendable restraint and then realized that her statement was hardly politic on Optheria. She had shown few examples of the tact for which Trag had chosen her. "But we always return to Ballybran," and she tried to make it sound as if going home was more desirable than traveling far away. No sense in arousing hopes on Optheria, especially in the presence of the cruiser's senior officers. "Once a crystal singer, always a crystal singer!"

In the same instant the printer extruded an impatient sheet, Killashandra felt a stab of crystal shock travel painfully from her heelbone to her ears.

"Kill the drive," she shouted as the Captain was issuing the command.

Breathless from the unexpected peaking, Killashandra sagged against Lars. "Congratulations," she said, hoping the sarcasm would hide the pain in her bones, "you have just lost one of your crystals. What are they? Blues?"

"Greens," the Captain replied with some pride, "but the same crystals since the cruiser was commissioned."

"And Optheria will spring credit for organ crystals with considerably more alacrity than for plebeian greens, huh?" Festinel nodded solemn affirmation. "Engineer, I request permission to inspect the crystal drive with you. My apprenticeship in tuning crystals may be of some use here."

"Honored, Guildmember." He strode to the communit. "Damage report!"

"Sir," came the disembodied voice from the bowels of the cruiser, "casing blown, foam applied, no injuries."

"As you were!"

An acrid stench, a combination of odors arising from the intense heat on the crystal casing and on the foam, was still being exhausted by fans when Killashandra, Engineering Officer Fernock, and Lars reached the drive deck. The captain had hurried to inform Elder Torkes of the delay. Killashandra winced as she caught residual echoes from the other crystals of the drive. Or perhaps more than one element had blown. That could happen.

Fernock quickly directed his men to sweep up the now hardened foam and remove the cover. The durametal had been fractured by the explosion and came off in pieces.

"See if stores have a replacement." Fernock's expression suggested this was unlikely. "I'd not want to drive unshielded crystal."

"There'd be no problem so long as the remaining brackets are secure," Killashandra said, reasonably sure that she was correct. After all, there was no shield at all around black crystal. And they generated far more power than greens.

Suction was used to clean foam from the intact blocks but both Killashandra and Fernock warned the seaman to stay away from the fragmented shaft.

"Bracketing came adrift," Killashandra announced, remembering her manners enough to look to Fernock for confirmation.

"You're right. See, here?" Fernock pointed to the lopsided bracket at the green's base. "Now how could that happen?"

"You said the seas were turbulent. And that you were overdue an overhaul. Doubtless the discrepancy would have been seen and corrected. No fault of yours, Officer Fernock."

"I appreciate that."

"All right, then . . ." Killashandra squatted by the drive, reached for the shattered green crystal.

"What are you about, Guildmember?" Fernock grabbed her wrist and Lars moved forward.

"Well, until this crystal is moved, we won't." And she again reached for the crystal.

"But you've no gloves and crystal—"

"Cuts clean and heals quickly. For me. Allow me, Fernock."

The man continued to protest, but he made no further attempt to stop her. The first splinter did not cut her. Fortunately the broken bracket also made it easier for her to lift out the pieces. She pointed to a metal oil-slop pail and when it was fetched, she laid the crystal in it. She removed the remaining portions with only one slice, when the final fragment resisted her initial pull. She held up her bleeding hand.

"Behold, before your marveling eyes, the incredible recuperative powers of the crystal singer. One of my professions' few advantages."

"What is another?" Lars asked.

"The credit!" She reached for the suction device. "This won't be good for anything, and *no one* is to touch it on its way to the disposal unit." She depressed the toggle and made sure that the few loose slivers were cleared. "I'll check all the brackets to be sure none are loose. More problems are caused by faulty bracketing than anything else."

That was a tedious enough process but it was her own safety she was ensuring, hers and Lars's. With Fernock and Lars handing her the appropriate tools, she released each bracket in turn and reseated the five squat crystal shafts remaining. Then she struck each in turn for tone. They were all G s, of course, in a crystal drive, and to her intense relief, each emitted a pure unblemished tone. She glanced up at Lars, to see him nod at the true G she had just sung. He had not been the only one fascinated by the process. There had been a constantly changing if discreet audience on the catwalk above the drive floor. As well. This would only enhance the image of the crystal singer. And it might just safeguard her against any more nonsense from the Elders.

"There now, Mr. Fernock," she said at last, arching her back against the crick cause by awkward positions. "I think you can safely proceed with reconnections. I don't think there's any danger if the load is properly apportioned. A five-shaft drive should generate enough power to get us to the Mainland." She held up the hand that had been profusely bleeding an hour before. "See? All better."

"Guildmember, do you know how long it would have taken me and my men to make such repairs?"

"I couldn't begin to guess, Mr. Fernock, but do get on with the job." She smiled at the disconcerted officer and then, with Lars a step behind her, retraced her steps to the upper deck.

"Citizen, you're too much for this island boy."

"Huh! I was showing off . . . again," and, leaning backward on one hand, kissed him lustily. Just in time to avoid the exchange's being witnessed by Captain Festinel, who was hurrying to check on repairs. "You were a very deft assistant, Captain Dahl. I must ask for your help with the organ repair." She sedately continued her ascent.

"Surely, just perfect pitch—" Lars began as they returned to the wardroom.

"—Perfect and absolute—"

"—As you say, isn't the only requirement for your profession?"

"The major one. Ballybran is a Code Four planet—"

"What does that mean? I'm an island lad from a iggerant planet," and Lars's voice was rich with contempt.

"Dangerous. Singing crystal is rated a 'highly dangerous' profession, limited to Type IV through VIII bipedal humanoids . . ."

"Are there any other kinds?"

"Don't alien life forms come for the Festival? The Reticulans are avid musicologists though I could never come to terms with their croons as music."

"Are they the ones that look like an assembly of twigs on a barrel?" The wardroom was empty and Lars swung her into his arms, kissing her passionately, stroking her body, murmuring endearments. But knowing that they could be interrupted at any time inhibited Killashandra's response, even as she yearned for more. At a scraping sound, they broke apart, Killashandra sliding breathlessly into the nearest chair.

"What a delightful description of Reticulans! The barrel is mostly windbag but I've never been close enough to discover which of their pseudopods are the pipes."

Lars stopped pacing, for the noise in the companionway had ceased, and he came back to fondle her.

"A candidate for Guild membership has to pass Physical Fitness Test SG-1, Psychological Profile SG-1—which you'd never pass if you continue to do *that*, Lars—and Education Level 3."

"I'm not applying to the Guild, only applying a member . . ."

This time the footsteps stopped and the door was slid back. Mr. Fernock entered, smiling broadly when he saw the occupants.

"We'll be underway in ten minutes, Guildmember, thanks to your invaluable assistance. And we'll be able to make a reasonable enough speed on five shafts to reach our destination on time."

"How marvelous," Killashandra said in a languid drawl. Marvelous was not really the way she felt, considering the inner turmoil Lars's caresses had stimulated. She couldn't get to the City and the Conservatory fast enough.

Chapter 18

Fortunately Lars was equally frustrated by their lack of privacy and made no further overtures. Perversely, Killashandra missed them. The cruiser had broken out flags and a full honor guard for the ceremonial and triumphant return. Killashandra steeled herself for yet another protocologically correct reception. She reflected on what scene she could produce to shorten the tedium, and debated whether or not a scene would produce any advantage. She had made several points. Unless she had sufficient provocation, she decided to leave well enough alone. For now. She might need to produce an effect to gain privacy within her suite.

For she was determined to enjoy Lars without any surveillance for whatever time remained to them. She could, of course, stretch out the organ repair as long as she wished. Or her instruction of technicians. She could include Lars in that program. He had the perfect—and absolute—pitch to tune crystal as well as the strength and manual dexterity required. She must do everything she could to make him indispensable to the Elders, for whatever protection that could provide him, since he didn't seem at all interested in leaving Optheria. Even if that were possible.

"We're near enough for you to have a spectacular view of the City Port," Lars said, interrupting her reflections.

"A 'natural' port?" She smiled.

"Completely, though not nearly as good a natural harbor as North."

"Naturally."

"Captain Festinel awaits your arrival on the bridge."

"How courteous! Where's Torkes?"

"Burning up a few communications units with orders. He was incensed that you had to bloody your hands on the drive of a mere cruiser."

"Doesn't he value his skin as much as I do mine?"

Her entry rated salutes, rigid attention from the seamen and a smile and a warm handshake from Festinel. She politely accepted his effusive thanks and then pointedly turned to watch the rapidly approaching shoreline.

The City Port bustled with activity: small water taxis skipping across the waves, larger barges wallowing across their swells, and coastal freighters awaiting their turn at the piers which, with their array of mechanical unloading devices, were anything but "natural." The cruiser's velocity had moderated considerably now that it was in congested waters.

Ponderously it approached the Federal docking area, where sleek courier vessels bobbed alongside two more squat cruisers.

Killashandra had no difficulty identifying their berth—it was crowded with a welcoming committee, all massed white and insipid pale colors, blurred faces turned seaward, despite the glare of the westering sun, which was full in their eyes. The cruiser swung its bow slightly to port and the drive was cut, momentum carrying the big vessel inexorably to the dock and the grapples clanked against the hull, bringing it to a halt with a barely perceptible jolt.

"My compliments on a smooth docking, Captain Festinel—and my thanks for an excellent voyage." Killashandra made gracious noises to all the bridge staff and then swept out to get the rest of the tedious formalities over.

"Ampris!" Lars grunted as they reached the portal. Beneath them the gangway was extruding the few meters to the dock.

"Of course, and my quartette lined up like the puppets they are. I think I am developing a splitting headache. All that crystal whine, you know." She raised her hand to her forehead.

"See what line Ampris takes first." Lars's face was set, his nostrils flaring a little as he settled his respiratory rate.

Killashandra suppressed a perfectly natural surge of repugnance for a man who had ordered an assault on her, then hypocritically assured her that the culprit would be punished . . . How could she punish Ampris? The method she had employed with Torkes would not work; Ampris was too wily.

The gangplank had locked in place, the honor guard was arranged, Elder Torkes appeared, the welcoming committee began to applaud and, every inch the gracious celebrity, Killashandra descended. Mirbethan took a step forward, anxiously scanning Killashandra's face for any sign of the "ordeal." Thyrol, Pirinio, and Polabod all bowed low but permitted Elder Ampris to do the honors.

"Guildmember Ree, you cannot imagine our elation when we learned of your safe deliverance—" Then Ampris caught sight of Lars, whom he was patently not expecting.

"This is Captain Lars Dahl who rescued me so boldly, and at no small risk to himself and his vessel. Captain Dahl, this is Elder Ampris." Killashandra took the plunge, pretending ignorance of any previous contact between the two men. "I am forever indebted to Captain Dahl, as I'm sure the Council of Elders must be, for delivering me from that wretched patch of nowhere."

Lars saluted crisply and impassively as Elder Ampris executed the shallowest of acknowledgments.

"The Harbor Master at Angel Island has detached him from duty there to be my personal bodyguard." Killashandra gave an elegantly delicate shudder. "I won't feel safe without his sure protection."

"Quite understandable, Guildmember; however, I think that you'll find *our* security measures—"

"I felt quite secure within the Conservatory, Elder Ampris," Killashandra said demurely. "I seem to be only at risk when I leave its sanctuary. I assure you I have no desire to do that again."

"Security Leader Blaz—"

"I'll not have that officious oaf near me, Elder Ampris. He's the reason I was put in jeopardy. The man has no intelligence or tact. I don't trust him to spit in the right direction. Captain Lars Dahl is in charge of my personal security at my personal insistence. Have I not made myself clear?"

For a second Elder Ampris looked about to argue the point, but the moment passed. He inclined his head again, forced his face into a grim smile, and then gestured toward the waiting vehicle.

"Why this vast throng?" Killashandra asked, smiling graciously about her.

"Some of the winning composers and prospective performers for this year's Festival and final-year students."

"All waiting for the organ to be repaired?"

Elder Ampris cleared his throat. "Yes, that is true."

"Well, I shan't delay them any longer than necessary. Especially since Captain Dahl proved so capable in assisting me with the cruiser drive."

Ampris stopped midstride and stared first at her, then incredulously at Lars.

"Yes, weren't you informed that the cruiser had drive difficulties this morning? One of the crystals shattered. I still have a slight headache from the distortion. Naturally the ship could not proceed without emergency repairs. And while that was merely a matter of removing the shards and resetting the brackets on the undamaged crystals, it does require steady hands, a keen eye and ear. Captain Dahl was far more adept than the cruiser's engineer. And he has the perfect and absolute pitch required. I think he will prove an admirable assistant, one in whom I certainly repose complete trust. You do agree, I'm sure." They had reached the vehicle now. "You first, Captain Dahl, I shall want Elder Ampris on my right."

Lars complied before the Elder could blurt out a protest and Killashandra settled herself, smiling as warmly as possible at Ampris, just as if she hadn't delivered a most unpalatable request.

The quartette settled itself in the seats behind them and the vehicle left the dock area. Ports required much the same facilities throughout the galaxy. Fortunately nature had conspired in favor of human endeavors, so warehouses, seamen's hostels, and mercantile establishments were not quite so tortuously situated in City Port as in the City proper. The Music Conservatory on its prominence was visible as soon as the Port gave way to an agricultural belt. From this approach, Killashandra could see the lateral elevation of the Festival auditorium and the narrow path that led to the suburb Lars had called Gartertown. She wondered if there'd be a new brew soon. Maybe Lars could collect a few bottles for her?

The drive was in the main a silent one, with Ampris stewing beside her and Lars stiffly silent. The strained atmosphere began to affect her, causing her to wonder if she really were doing the right thing for Lars. Yet if she hadn't taken pains to divert suspicion from him, he'd be running with a threat of rehabilitation hanging over him. Had she erroneously assumed that he was as eager to continue their relationship as she was? Olav had wreathed them both with the handfast garlands. Surely that act held significance. She'd best have it out with Lars as soon as possible.

After what seemed a long time, they drew up at the imposing entrance to the Conservatory.

"I dispensed with the formality of a welcoming throng, Guildmember, in the interests of security." Elder Ampris got out of the car and turned to give her a steadying hand.

"I have no fear of a second assault, Elder Ampris," she said taking his dry clasp and smiling ingenuously at him, "with Captain Dahl beside me. And, you know, after the courtesies I received at the hands of the islanders, I'm beginning to think that that attack, as well as my abduction, were made to seem island-instigated. I can't imagine an islander being jealous of anything on the Mainland."

Lars had emerged from the car, but his expression was devoid of reaction. The skin on Ampris's face was taut with the effort of controlling his. "With your comfort in mind, Guildmember, perhaps you might prefer to eat in your suite this evening."

"That is so thoughtful, Elder Ampris. Resetting a crystal drive is an exhausting process. So many fiddling things requiring fine muscle coordination and complete concentration." She sighed wearily, turning slightly to smile apologetically at Mirbethan and the others. "I want to be well rested to attack that repair tomorrow. Oh, Thyrol? With Captain Dahl to assist me, I won't need any other helpers."

She took Lars's arm and ascended the shallow steps to the main entrance. She felt him quivering but for which of several reasons she couldn't have told without glancing at his face. And she didn't dare do that. "Do you know the way to my quarters, Captain Dahl?"

"If I may just escort you," Mirbethan answered, hastening to lead the way.

"I was never in this part of the Conservatory, Crystal Singer," Lars said as they entered the imposing main lobby.

"You've been to the Conservatory, Captain Dahl?" Killashandra asked.

"Yes, Guildmember, I studied here for three years."

"Why, Captain, you have unexplored capabilities. Are you then a singer?"

"Vocal music is not taught at the Conservatory: only the organ."

"Really, I would have thought the planet's main Conservatory would exploit every musical potential. How odd!"

"Do you find it so, Guildmember?"

"In other parts of the FSP, vocal arts are much admired, and a Stellar soloist highly respected."

"Optheria places more value on the most complex of instruments." Lars's tone was of mild reproof. "The sensory organ combines sound, olfactory and tactile sensations to produce a total orchestration of alternate reality for the participant."

"Is the organ limited to Optheria? I've never encountered one before in all my voyaging."

"It is unique to Optheria."

"Which certainly has many unique experiences for the visitor."

Mirbethan's pace, and her erect back, seemed to reflect at once her approval, and shock, at their conversation.

"Why, then, Captain Dahl, if you have studied to use the organ, are you sailing about in the islands?"

"Because, Guildmember, my composition was ah . . . not approved by the Masters who pass judgment on such aspirations, so I returned to my previous occupation."

"To be sure, I am selfishly glad, Captain—for who would have rescued me had you not been in those waters?" Killashandra sighed deeply just as they turned the corridor into the hall she did recognize. "Mirbethan?"

The woman whirled, her expression composed though she was breathing rather rapidly.

"By any chance, I mean, I know I've been gone a good while, but I do hope that those beverages . . ."

"Your catering facility has been completely stocked with the beverages of your choice."

"And the chimes have been turned off?"

Mirbethan nodded.

"And the catering unit instructed to supply proper-size portions of food without requiring additional authorization?"

"Of course."

"Thank you. I, for one, am starving. Sea air, you know." With a final smile, Killashandra swept through the door Lars held open.

By the time he had shut it, she had discovered four ceiling surveillance units in the main salon. "I am quite weary, Captain."

"With due respect, Guildmember, you did not eat much of the evening meal, perhaps a light supper—"

"The variety on the catering unit seems geared to student requirements . . . unless you, having spent time here, can make a suggestion."

"Indeed I would be delighted to, Guildmember." Lars located several more as they moved through the suite to the two bedrooms. He peered into the first bathing room and grinned broadly at her. "May I draw you a bath?"

"An excellent idea." She strode to what was evidently the one room that had been left unmonitored.

Lars began filling the tub, having turned the taps on full.

He reached into his tunic and extracted an innocuous metal ball. "A deceiver, Father calls it. It distorts picture and sound—we can be quite free once it's operating. And when we leave the suite,"—he grinned, miming the device returned to his pocket—"it'll drive their technicians wild."

"Won't they realize that the distortion only works when we're here?"

"I suggest that tomorrow you complain about being monitored in the bedroom. Can we cope with just one free room?" He began to undress her, his expression intense with anticipation.

"Two," Killashandra corrected him with a coy moue as the bright and elegant overall Teradia had chosen for her fell in a rainbow puddle at her feet.

It was, of course, thoroughly soaked with the water displaced when Lars overbalanced her into the tub.

When they had sated their appetites sufficiently, Killashandra idly described wet circles on the broad expanse of Lars's chest. "I think that with the best motives in the world, I have placed you in an awkward situation."

"Beloved Killashandra, when you sprang that," and he aptly mimicked her voice, " 'I have no fear of being assaulted with Captain Dahl beside me,' I nearly choked."

"I felt you quaking, but I didn't know if it was laughter or outrage."

"And then suggesting that someone else had instigated the attack to implicate islanders—Killashandra, I wouldn't have missed that for anything. You really got mine back on the flatulent fardling. But watch him, Killa. He's dangerous. Once he and Torkes start comparing notes . . ."

"They still have to get that organ fixed in time for all those lucky little composers to practice their pieces. I'm here and even if a replacement is coming, it's the old bird-in-the-hand."

"Yes, and they've got to have done all the Mainland concerts to ensure a proper Optherian attitude toward visitors."

"Proper attitude? Mainland concerts? What do you mean?"

Lars held her slightly away from him in the capacious bath, reading her face and eyes.

"You don't know? You don't really know why that organ is so important to the Elders?"

"Well, I do know that the set-up will produce an intense emotional experience for the listener. It verges on illegal manipulation."

Lars gave a sour laugh. "Verges? It *is*. But then you would only have seen the sensory elements. The subliminal units are kept out of sight, underneath the organ loft."

"Subliminals?" Killashandra stared at Lars.

"Of course, ninny. How do you think the Elders keep the people of Optheria from wanting any of the marvels that the visitors tell them about? Because they've just had a full dose of subliminal conditioning! Why do you think people who prefer to exercise their own wits live in the islands? The Elders can't broadcast the subliminals and sensories."

"Subliminals are illegal! Even the sensory feedbacks border on illegality! Lars, when I tell the FSP this—"

"Why do you think my father was sent to Optheria? The FSP wants proof! And that means an eyeball on the illegal equipment. It's taken Father's group nearly thirty years to get close enough."

"Then you weren't here just to learn to play that blasted thing?"

"Playing the blasted thing is the only way to get close enough to it to find out where the subliminal units are kept. Comgail did. And died!"

"You're suggesting he didn't suicide?"

Lars shook his head slowly. "Something Nahia said during the hurricane confirmed my suspicion that he hadn't. You see, I knew Comgail. He was my composition tutor. He wasn't a martyr type. He certainly wanted to live. He was willing to risk a lot but not his life. Nahia mentioned that he'd asked Hauness to provide him with rehab blocks. A good block—and Hauness is the best there is—prevents the victim from confessional diarrhea and a total loss of personality. Comgail had been so above reproach all the time he'd been at the Conservatory that not even a paranoid like Pedder would have suspected him of collusion with dissidents. But, for shattering the manual, Comgail'd automatically be sent to rehab. He had prepared himself for that. He wasn't killed by a crystal fragment, Killa, he was murdered by it. I think it was because he had found the access to the subliminal units."

"Subliminals!" Killashandra seethed with horror at the potentially total control. "And he found the access? Where? All I need is one look at them—"

Lars regarded her solemnly. "That's all *we* need—once we find them. They've got to be somewhere in the organ loft."

"Well, then"—Killashandra embraced him exuberantly—"wasn't I clever to insist that you and I handle the repairs all by ourselves."

"If we're allowed!"

"You've the jammer." She rose from the deep bath, Lars following her. "Say, if your father's so clever with electronics, why hasn't he figured a way to jam the shuttle port detection arch?"

Lars chuckled as she dried him, for once more interested in something other than his physical effect on her.

"He's spent close to thirty years trying. We even have a replica of the detector on Angel. But we cannot figure a way to mask that residue. Watch out for my ears!" She had been briskly toweling his hair.

"Does the detector always catch the native?"

"Infallible."

"And yet . . ." She wrapped her hair in a towel. She pointed to the jammer and then proceeded to the salon. Lars followed, the jammer held above his head like a torch, a diabolical gleam in his eye as he waved it at each of the monitors he passed. "Yet when Thyrol came out right with me, the detector didn't catch *him*. And passed me."

"What? No matter how many people pass under it, it will always detect the native!"

"It didn't then! I wonder if it had anything to do with crystal resonance."

"You mean in you?"

"Hmmm. It's not exactly something we can experiment with, is it? Prancing in and out of the shuttle port."

"Hardly—and we're half a world away from the only other one."

"Well, we can worry about that later. After we've found the access and after we've repaired that wretched organ! Now," and she opened the doors of the beverage store with a flourish, "what shall we drink with our supper?"

Chapter 19

Killashandra woke before the chimes, which did not sound in her suite but were nevertheless audible from the adjacent sections of the Conservatory. She woke refreshed and totally relaxed, and cautiously eased herself away from Lars's supine body so that she might have a better view of his sleeping form. She felt oddly protective of him as she propped her head on one hand and minutely inspected his profile. Thus she noticed that the tips of his long eyelashes were bleached and the lid itself was not as dark as the surrounding skin. Fine laugh, or sun, lines fanned out from the corners to the temple. The arch of his nose just missed being too high, too thin, being balanced by fine modeling and length. His cheeks wore a dusting of freckles which she hadn't noticed before. And several dark brow hairs were out of line as the brow curved around the eye socket. Several hairs bristled straight up at the inner edges of brows that would almost meet when he frowned.

She liked best his wide lips, more patrician than sensual. She knew the havoc they could raise with her body and felt they were perhaps his best feature. Even in sleep, the corners raised slightly. His chin was rather broader than one was aware when his face was mobile, but the strong jawline swept back to well-shaped ears, also tan, with a spot of new sunburn about to peel on the top skin.

The column of his neck was strong and the pulse beat in his throat. She wanted to put her fingertip on it and almost did before retracting her hand. He was more truly hers when asleep, untouched by stress, relaxed, his rib cage barely moving.

She loved the line of his chest, the smooth skin clothing smooth pectoral muscle, and once again she had to repress the wish to run her hand down the shape of him, to feel the fine crisp hair on his chest. He was not hirsute and she found that much to her preference as well, his legs and arms having only a fine dusting of blond hairs.

She had seen handsomer men but the composition of his face pleased her better. Lanzecki—now that was the first time she'd thought of him in days—actually was the more distinguished in looks, heavier in build. She decided she preferred the way Lars Dahl was put together.

She sighed. It was easier to be philosophical about Lanzecki. Would she have been as easily resigned to that loss if she hadn't met Lars Dahl?

She had broken off with Lanzecki for his own good, but she hadn't "lost" him, for she would return to Ballybran. Once she'd left Optheria . . .

For a moment her emotions hovered above a new abyss of despair and regret. And for the first time in her life, the thought of bearing a man's child crossed her mind. That was as much an impossibility as remaining with Lars, but it emphasized the depth of her emotional involvement with the man. Perhaps it was just as well that no child was possible, that their liaison would end when this assignment was over. She surprised herself! Children were something other people had. To feel that desire was remarkable.

Optheria, for all its conservatism and alleged security, had unexpected facets of danger. Not the least of which were her adventures so far. She could hardly fault Trag, or rail at the *Encyclopedia Galactica*. Facts she had had. What couldn't have been foreseen were the astonishing predicaments which had entangled her. And the fascinating personalities.

More extraordinary still, she remembered all too vividly, and with just a trace of chagrin, her rantings and ravings and desperations when she'd left Ballybran, a sacrifice to the Guild for Lanzecki's good. Now, when contemplating a much deeper and irreversible loss, why was she so calm, fatalistically resigned, even philosophical. How very strange! Had her loss of Lanzecki inured her to others? Or was she mistaking her feelings for Lars Dahl? No! She'd remember Lars Dahl for the rest of her life without benefit of data retrieval.

The second chimes rang faintly across the open court outside the windows. Faint but sufficient to waken Lars. He was as neat on wakening as he was in sleep. His eyes opened, his right hand searched for her body, his head turned and his smile began as he located her. Then he stretched, arms above his head, back arching toward her as he extended his legs and then on the top of his extension, suddenly retracted himself, drawing her against him, to complete a morning ritual which included the exercise of their intimate relationship. Each time, they seemed to discover something new about themselves and their responses. She particularly liked Lars's capacity for invention, stimulating as it did heretofore unsuspected originalities in herself.

As usual hunger roused them from these variations.

"Breakfast here is the heartiest meal," Lars said cheerfully, striding quickly for the catering unit. "You'll like it."

Killashandra saw that he had left the jammer behind him, and she followed him at a quick trot, holding the device up to distort anything else he might say.

He laughed. "We'd best leave them something to hear. A discussion of breakfast must be sufficiently innocuous."

Killashandra settled in one of the chairs near the catering unit, swiveling her hand as she looked at the little jammer. If only some way could be found to mask that mineral residue in Optherians! Blank out the detector.

"You know," Killashandra said as they ate, sitting companionably together on the elegant seating unit, "I simply cannot understand this concentration on one instrument—albeit a powerful one—but they're wiping out more than ninety-nine percent of the FSP's musical traditions and repertoire, as well as stultifying talents and potential. I mean, your tenor is formidable!"

Lars shrugged, giving her a tolerant side glance. "Everyone sings—at least in the islands, they do."

"But you know *how* to sing."

Lars cocked an eyebrow at her, still humoring what he felt was her excessive fascination with a minor ability.

"Everyone knows how to sing—"

"I don't mean just opening the mouth and shouting, Lars Dahl. I mean, projecting a voice, supporting it properly on the breath, phrasing the music, carrying the dynamic line forward."

"When did I do all that?"

"When we did that impromptu duet. When you sang on the beach, when you did that magnificent duet from *The Pearl Fishers*."

"I did?"

"Of course. I studied voice for ten years. I—" She shut her mouth.

"Then why are you a crystal singer instead of one of these famous vocal artists?"

A surge of impotent fury, followed by a wave of regret, and then a totally incomprehensible loathing of Maestro Valdi—the moment that had changed her life—rendered Killashandra speechless.

Lars watched her, his mild curiosity turning to concern as he saw the emotions in her stormy eyes and face. He put a hand on her bare thigh. "What did I say to distress you so?"

"Nothing you said, Lars." She dismissed all that from consideration. It was over and done with. "I had all the requirements to be a Stellar, except one. A voice."

"Ah, now." Lars pulled back in indignation.

"I'm quite serious. There's a flaw, a noticeable and unpleasant burr in the voice that would have limited me to secondary roles."

Lars laughed now, his white teeth gleaming in his tanned face, his eyes sparkling. "And you, my beloved Sunny," he kissed her lightly, "would never settle for being second in anything! Are you first among crystal singers, then?"

"I don't do badly. I've sung black crystal, which is the hardest to find and cut properly. In any event, there aren't degrees among singers. One cuts to earn enough credit for the things one needs and wants." Now why wasn't she being totally honest with Lars? Why didn't she confess that the sole aim of most crystal singers was sufficient credit not to have to sing crystal—to leave Ballybran for as long as possible?

"I wouldn't have thought crystal singers are so much like islanders," Lars surprised her by saying. "Well, you cut for what you need and want, much as we fish or plant polly, but all we really need is available."

"It's not quite the same thing with crystal," Killashandra said slowly, glad she had been less than honest. Why disillusion Lars needlessly? On so many worlds, in so many minds, there were so many misconceptions about crystal singers, she had not realized how much a relief it was to find an unbiased world—at least one unbiased with respect to her Guild.

"Cutting crystal seems more dangerous than fishing." He stroked her scarred hand. "Or learning polly."

"Stick to fishing, Lars. Crystal's hazardous to your health. Now, we'd best apply ourselves to fulfill my Guild contract with these fardling fools. And maybe shake them out of their organic rut!"

They dressed and then Killashandra entered the number Mirbethan had given her. The woman seemed immensely relieved to accept the call and said that Thyrol would be with them directly.

"D'you suppose he slept in the hall?" Killashandra murmured to Lars as she answered the polite scratching on the hall door. Lars shook his head violently, then held up his hand while he deactivated the jammer and pocketed it. "Good morning, Thyrol. Lead on." She gestured peremptorally, smiling at Thyrol before she noticed two burly men in security uniforms. "I have no need of them!" she said coldly.

"Ah . . . they will not interfere, Guildmember."

"I'll make sure of that, Thyrol. I will need the duragloves—"

"Everything you requested before your unfortunate disappearance is in the organ loft."

"Oh, very well then. It's gathered dust long enough. Lead on!"

Once again the instinctive reaction to tiptoe and maintain silence affected Killashandra as they emerged onto the stage of the Festival auditorium. She glanced at Lars to see if he was similarly affected. He grimaced slightly and she noticed that his active stride perceptibly altered. She did not miss the almost covetous way he frowned at the covered organ console. And wondered what she could do about *that*! She had been entranced with the music he played on the twelve-stringed instrument, and she was eager to hear it with organ amplification. Or would that be too cruel an imposition?

As Thyrol used his keys on the panel to the loft, Killashandra wondered if among them were the keys that would allow access to subliminal mechanisms. All three on that ring were apparently needed to open the loft door. Or would someone of Thyrol's rank even know about such a refinement? She presumed it was limited to Elder rank only, or maybe a Master or two. They'd need someone with a hefty dab of imagination and energy to create subliminal images. Unless the subliminals reflected the inflexibility of the Elders' attitudes toward everything, which was also logical— Why search for a template when one was oneself the ultimate role model?

The necessary equipment was indeed in the loft, neatly stacked against one side of the long wall. Lars maintained an attitude of casual indifference after giving the room a sweeping glance. Killashandra noted the monitor buds, caught Lars's glance and gave him a nod. She waited until his hand disappeared into his pocket and then bent over the open console and the glittering shards of crystal.

"Lars Dahl, grab a mask and some gloves, and bring that bin over here. And a mask and gloves for me. I don't fancy inhaling crystal dust in these close quarters." Then she looked up at the burly men taking up so much space in the loft. "Out!" She flicked her fingers at them. "Out, out, out, out! You're taking up space and air."

"This room is well ventilated, Guildmember," Thyrol began.

"That is not the point. I dislike observers peering at my every move. There's no need for *them*. Certainly no one can get in or out of here. They can stand on the other side of the door and repel boarders! In fact, Thyrol, without meaning offense, your absence would oblige."

"But—"

"You'll only be hovering. I'm sure you have more important duties than hovering! And you're a distraction—Or, are you one of those I'm to teach crystal installation?"

Thyrol drew back, affronted by the suggestion, and without further protest retired from the loft.

"Now," Killashandra began, not even watching the man leave, "the first thing we must do is clear the shards. Stick to the larger pieces, Lars Dahl. My body deals with cuts more easily than yours. Hang up that lid. We'll put the pieces on that before transferring them to the bin. Crystal has a disastrous habit of spraying shards when it bounces . . . Shouldn't want unnecessary accidents to mar this procedure."

"Why'd you want the jammer on in here? Guild secrets?" Lars's voice was muffled by the mask.

"I just want them to understand that monitors won't work around me. I was brought up on a planet that respects privacy and I'm not allowing Optherians to violate that right. Not for all the sensory organs on this narking world. Besides, how else can we search for the access? It would look far odder if suddenly their scanners don't work, than if they haven't worked from the start. Now, let's do what we came for."

It was slow work, especially once Lars had cleared the larger pieces. The extractor could be used only in short bursts; continued suction expelled tiny splinters right through the bag. For that reason, the bag had to be emptied and brushed out after each burst.

"It'd be easier with two of these, wouldn't it?" When Killashandra nodded, Lars strode to the door panel, slid it open, and issued the request. Killashandra heard a murmured reply. "Now, I said! We don't have time to wait for the request to go through Security. By the First Fathers! Does everything have to be authorized by Ampris? Move it! Now!"

Killashandra grinned at him. Lars's return grin was pure satisfaction.

"If you knew how often I've wanted to bark at a Security man—"

"I can't honestly imagine you making meek—"

"You'd be surprised at what I'm willing to do for a good reason." He gave her a singularly wicked look.

A case of the extractors was delivered in half an hour by an officer whom Lars later told Killashandra was Blaz's second in command, but not a bad fellow for all of that. Castair had been known to look the other way during student romps which Blaz never would have permitted.

"Guildmember," Castair began, as Lars took the case from him, "there's some problem with the monitoring system in here."

"There is?" Killashandra straightened up from the console, glancing about her.

Castair indicated the corner nodules.

"Well, I don't want someone distracting me while I'm doing this. Your repairs can wait. We certainly are not damaging anything!"

"No, of course not, Guildmember."

"Then leave it for now." She waved him off, bending back to the tedious cleaning before he had left.

"Perfect pitch is not the only talent required to sing crystal." Lars's comment startled Killashandra as she finally stood erect, arching her back against tight muscles.

"Oh?"

His expression was a mixture of respect and something else. "A crystal singer has total concentration and an absence of normal human requirements—such as hunger!"

Killashandra twisted her wrist to look at the chrono and chuckled, leaning against the unit behind her. It was mid-afternoon and they had been working steadily since nine that morning.

"You should have given me a nudge."

"Several," Lars said drily. "I only mention it now because you're looking a bit white under your tan. Here." He thrust a heatpak at her. "I do not have your dedication so I sent for food."

"Without authorization?" Killashandra broke the seal on the soup, aware that she was very hungry indeed.

"I took a hint from your manner and pretended they had no option but obedience." He shook his head. "Are all crystal singers like you?"

"I'm pretty mild," she said, sipping carefully at the now heated soup. Lars passed her a plate of small sandwiches and crackers. "I only act the maggot when circumstances require. Especially with this lot of idiots." She lifted and rotated one shoulder to ease back muscles. Lars came to her side, pushing her away from her perch, and began to massage her back. His fingers unerringly found the tension knot, and she murmured her gratitude. "I hate this part of working in crystal so I'd rather get it over and done with as fast as possible."

"How crucial is the clean sweep?"

Killashandra sang a soft note and the crystal shards answered in a nerve-twitching dissonance.

Lars shook convulsively at the sound which, in spite of being soft, took time to die away. "Wow!"

"White crystal is active, picks up any sound. Leave so much as the minutest particle of crystal dust and it'll jam the manual and produce all kinds of subharmonics in the logic translator. It'd really be easier to start with a brand new manual case but I doubt they'd have spare parts. Which reminds me—the ten brackets that I've cleared are all spoiled." She picked one up, turning the clamping surface so that the scratches picked up the light. "Tighten one of these on a new crystal and you'd create uneven stresses through the long axis of the crystal, introducing spurious piezo-electric effects and probably a flaw in next to no time."

Lars took the bracket from her, hefting it in his hand. "They're no problem. Olver can do them."

Instinctively Killashandra looked up at the monitors as Lars mentioned his contact. She dragged at the fabric of Lars's sleeve and pointed to the surveillance buds, where traces of black had mysteriously appeared to make an aureole about each unit. "Now what did that?"

Killashandra chuckled and pointed to the white crystal. "A secret weapon for you when I leave. Sing white crystal to whatever room you're in and blast the monitors." She reached for one of the larger pieces Lars had cleared away and hefted it. "We'll just save some of this for you. I wonder if Research and Development know about this application of white."

Suddenly Lars had his arms about her, his face buried in her hair, his lips against her neck. She could feel the tension in him and caressed him with gentle hands.

"Oh, Sunny, must you leave?"

She gave him a twisted, rueful smile, gentling the frown from his face with tender fingers. "Crystal calls me back, Lars Dahl. It's not a summons I can ignore, and live!"

He kissed her hungrily and as she responded they both caught the slight sound, swiveling away from each other, as the door slid open.

"Ah, Elder Ampris," Killashandra said, "your arrival is most opportune. Show him the bracket, Lars Dahl," and when Ampris regarded this unusual offering with amazement, "run your fingers over the clamping edge . . . carefully . . . and feel how rough it is. We're going to need some two hundred of these, for I'm not about to trust new crystal in old brackets. All I've removed so far have been scratched just like that one. Will you authorize the order—and designate it as urgent?"

Killashandra snapped her mask back over her face and picked up the brush. Then she swore.

"I could also use a handlight of some sort. Some of this wretched stuff is like powder."

Elder Ampris peered in and she heard his intake of breath. She straightened, regarding him passively, seeing the stern accusation in his eyes.

"Let me demonstrate, Elder Ampris, the need for meticulous care." She hummed, more loudly than before, and took great delight in its effect on the man. "Sorry about that." She resumed work.

"I came to inquire, Guildmember, how soon the repairs would be completed."

"Since the idiot who smashed the manual put his heart in the destruction, it's going to take a lot more time than it did for me to remove one shattered crystal from the cruiser drive—if that's the comparison you were using." Killashandra sighed, and looked disconsolately at the crystal ruin. "It's slow going because of the nature of crystal and because, as you perceived, every smidgeon has to be cleaned out. That's all we've achieved today . . ."

Elder Ampris shot a sour glance at Lars. "More helpers?"

Killashandra gave a bark of laughter. "Just find me a vacuum capable of sucking up crystal dust and we'd clear this in an hour. Or, supply me with a brand new case!" And she gave the one before her a dismissive slap with her hand. Crystal pinged, Lars and Ampris winced. "Gets to you, doesn't it? Well, Elder Ampris, that's where we stand. Now, if you'll excuse me, the nitty gritty doesn't get done by talking about it." She picked up her brush but Ampris cleared his throat.

"A dinner and concert have been arranged for your enjoyment this evening," he said.

"I appreciate the courtesy, Elder Ampris, but until I have finished this, I wouldn't feel right about taking any time off for mere entertainment. If you'll send us in some more food—"

"Guildmember," Lars interrupted, "with all due respect, Elder Ampris is not . . . I mean, it is hardly his responsibility . . ."

"What are you trying to say, Captain?"

Ampris, his eyes glinting with the first glimpse of the humor she had seen from him since that long-ago reception, held up his hand, relieving Lars of the necessity of explanation.

"If the Guildmember is willing to forgo pleasure to complete her task, I feel I may serve as messenger for her requirements."

"Apparently everything I require has to be authorized by you anyway. Seems silly to waste time with all those intermediate stages." Killashandra grinned at Ampris without a sign of remorse. "Would you not have a word with them out there, or Thyrol? Speed things up tremendously. Oh, and don't forget, I need two hundred of those brackets. And the handlight. Lars, you go with him and get it, will you? It has to be small enough not to hamper sight, and I'd prefer a tight beam."

They left and she returned to work. When Lars came back with several handbeams, his eyes were bubbling with humor.

"Your wishes are his commands, Oh mighty Guildmember, Oh sweeper of the white crystal specks! Orders were issued to all the boys out there," and he jerked his thumb at the closed door panel, "that anything you request is to be secured as fast as possible."

"Hmmm. Bring one of those lights to bear on this corner, will you, Lars?" She flicked the brush and disclosed tiny granules that glittered in the light. "See? The fardling things are pernicious! I'll get 'em, every last speck!"

When the sumptuous dinner was wheeled in to them some time later, she grumbled but stopped working.

"Is crystal singing some kind of disease?" Lars asked conversationally.

"You sail. Do you call a halt in the middle of a storm? Do you leave off fishing in the midst of a school to nap?"

"It's not quite the same thing—"

"It is to me, Lars. Be of good cheer. The bracketing will be relatively easy and you can help me do that."

Despite her protests, Lars carried her out of the organ loft just before midnight. When they reached her suite, she insisted that they had better have a good soak, to be sure none of the crystal dust had penetrated their clothing. In the bath, he had to hold her head above water, for she kept falling asleep.

It took nearly four days to ensure that no speck of crystal dust remained in the case. By the time they arrived each morning, new monitor buds had been installed. So the first thing that Killashandra did on entering the organ loft was to hum a happy tune, charging the white crystal shards to do their duty and blast the fragile sensors.

On the third day, the new brackets were delivered and Killashandra set Lars Dahl to checking each one under a microscope. Fourteen were rejected for minor flaws. After the visit of Elder Ampris, they had no visitors. Thyrol would conduct them every morning to the loft, unlocking it and inquiring after their needs. Excellent meals were delivered at the appropriate hours. Assured of uninterrupted privacy, with easily disabled monitors, Lars had the freedom to undertake a very patient examination of the room, searching for the location of the subliminal equipment.

On the fourth morning, as Thyrol led them across the stage, Killashandra noted a curious discrepancy. The loft room did not extend the entire length of the stage behind the organ console. She silently counted her paces to the door. When Thyrol had closed the panel and Lars had activated the jammer, she paced out the width of the room.

"In-ter-est-ing," she said, her nose against the far wall. "This room is only half the length of the stage, Lars. Does that suggest anything to you?"

"It does, but there is no corresponding door on the other side of the console!" He joined her in her scrutiny of the blameless wall. "The subliminals have to be linked to the main frame data bases. I wonder . . ."

She followed his inspection of the cables that festooned the ceiling, pausing where they ran alongside the wall.

"Just a little minute," he said, his eyes wide with discovery, and he spun one of the impervo tubs to a position just under the cables.

He had to crane his neck, half stooped against the ceiling, but he gave a low and triumphant whistle. When he jumped down, he gathered Killashandra in his arms and whirled her about, crowing with exultation.

"The wall drops—how I don't know, but there is just the slightest gap at the top, where no one would think to look for it. And three very heavy cables go through the wall."

Lars replaced the tub before he began to inspect the corner joint. Once again he gave an exultant *yip*.

"The whole wall must move, Killa—but how?"

"That large a mass sinking into the floor might be a touch noisy."

"If we knew the mechanism . . ." He felt along the corner, then the floor, pressing and tapping.

"That's far too obvious, Lars. Stupid they are but never obvious. Try for an extrusion on one of the units, underneath 'em, inside . . ." She ran searching fingers under the one nearest her, finding nothing but a rough edge on one corner which produced a gouged finger. "*Ach*, I haven't the patience for this sort of nonsense right now. You go ahead. I'll finish this last bit of cleaning."

By the time their lunch was brought in, Lars had found nothing more. The units that could be opened had been opened with no result. Lars stewed and fussed all through the meal at his inability to resolve the problem.

"What sort of form do the security measures generally take on Optheria? Bureaucracies tend to find a reliable mechanism and stick with it," Killashandra suggested, with only half her attention on that part of the problem since she was so close to clearing the manual case for the next task.

"I can find out. Would you mind being left alone this evening?" He grinned at her, stroking her arm gently. "You'd be a mite conspicuous where I want to go."

"And where would that be?" she asked with an arch glance of mock disgust.

"I've got to acquire a few more clothes," and he twitched the fabric of his shirt, not as gaudy as that of most island designs but certainly noticeable amid the drab garb of the city dwellers. "Talk to a few people. Lucky for us, it's nearing the time of year when the subliminals wear off and normal student appetites revive. I might be late, Killa,"—he made a grimace of regret—"We don't have as much time together . . ."

She kissed the pulse in his throat. "Whenever you return then. That is, of course," and she had to add a light touch to relieve the tension in her throat, "if the guards pass you in."

Chapter 20

"A nd?" Killashandra prompted Lars the next morning as they break-fasted. Despite a valiant effort to stay awake, she had been asleep when he returned and he was showering when she was awakened by the distant chimes.

"I got clothing, all right enough," Lars admitted with a frustrated sigh. "The Elders' search and seizure for you was far more comprehensive than our visitors," and despite the jammer he was taking no chances, "had led us to believe. Or perhaps knew. Anyone—anyone who has been booked even for a pedestrian offense—was drawn. Half a dozen students were sent on to rehab without benefit of Inquiry."

"Olver?"

Lars ran his fingers through his hair, scratching his head vigorously as if to erase his despondency. "How he escaped I don't know and neither, I gather, does he. We didn't exchange more than a few signs." Lars pro-pelled himself from his chair, pacing, head down. "It could very well be that the Elders have marked him and are playing a waiting game."

"Are Nahia and Hauness safe?"

Lars gave her a quick and grateful smile for that concern. "They were holding clinics in Ironwood," he waved his hand to the north, "at the time of your disappearance. The City, Gartertown, and the Port took the brunt of search and seizure. And Security then used your disappearance as an excuse to take known dissidents in protective custody."

"How many are?"

"In protective custody? My dear Guildmember, such figures are never made public."

"An informed guess? Suicide is one form of social protest, the size of the p.c. population another one."

Lars shook his head. "Hauness might be able to find out," and Lars resumed his head shaking, "but I wouldn't risk getting in touch with him right now."

Killashandra stared at Lars Dahl for a long moment, a sinking sensa-tion that had nothing to do with hunger cramping her guts.

"And I have made you as vulnerable as any of those already in p.c., haven't I?"

Lars shrugged and grinned. "If you hadn't named me your rescuer, I'd be tucked away in a rehab cubicle right now spinning out my brains."

"After I've gone?"

Lars shrugged again, then gave her an impudent wink. "All I need is a half-day's start on 'em. And once I've made the islands, there isn't an S & S team that can find me if I don't wish to be found."

He sounded so confident that, for a moment, Killashandra almost believed him. As if he sensed her doubt, he leaned over her in the chair, his eyes more brilliantly blue than ever, his lips upturned in a provocative half smile.

"Beloved Sunny, if it wouldn't sound mawkish, I'd say that meeting you has been the high point of my life so far. And confounding Elders Torkes and Ampris are adventures to lighten my darkest hour—"

"Which might yet be in a rehab booth!"

"I know the risk, and it's been worth it, Killa!" He kissed her then, a light brief touch of his lips to hers but it set her blood ringing as quickly as crystal.

"Speaking of Elders," she began in an attempt to shake off her anxiety, "we begin to bracket crystal today." She rose from the chair with a determined effort, then saw his expression. "All right—I grant you, learning to bracket and tune crystal won't advance you in the Elders' files, but those are useful skills anywhere else in the FSP."

Lars laughed. "Had we but worlds enough and time—"

Killashandra let out a great guffaw. "Malaprop!" But outrageous humor made a better start to a tricky day than gloom.

Lars was every bit as quick to learn and adept in the use of his strong hands as Killashandra had thought he'd be. To set the white crystal in the brackets, she asked Thyrol the height of the stroke of the padded hammers. They already had six in place by the time Elder Ampris appeared in the loft, Thyrol hovering anxiously behind him in the open door. Killashandra noticed, first, the breath of sweet fresh air and she flicked a quick glance at the intruders as they stood there. Lars was holding the crystal dead still.

"You'll feel just the slightest surface tension and a slippery, almost electric, tension when the clamps are tight enough. Tell me when you do."

She tightened the brackets, keeping both little fingers under the crystal so that she could sense that surface tension.

"Now!" Lars said.

"Right on!" She struck the crystal with the tone hammer, and the rich deep note spun through the air, drifting out and causing the two door guards to risk a quick peek into the loft. A muted and discordant response came from the covered tubs of crystal shard. Then she straightened up and turned to the observers. "And that's how it's done, Elder Ampris."

Ampris's bright brown eyes glittered as he arranged his mouth in a smile which she took to mean approbation.

"The lower octave is always easier, for some reason, to set and pitch," Killashandra went on affably. "We're making excellent progress."

"And?"

Killashandra heard a curious vibration in that single word. Elder Ampris was overly eager to have this installation completed and it could not be simply to allow performers practice time. He also exhibited an uncharacteristic nervousness; his fingers rubbed against his thumb.

"I think we'll have the entire manual finished by tomorrow evening. Set the next pair of brackets, will you, Lars Dahl, while I watch." Killashandra stepped away from the cabinet, stood next to Elder Ampris. "He's quick and deft and once I'm sure he's doing it right, we'll work both ends against the middle."

Ampris regarded her with a blink, his mind evidently jumping to another application of that phrase. His stiff and pleased smile forewarned her. "You will then perhaps be delighted to have trained assistance."

"Trained?" Killashandra glanced at Lars who had also suspended motion, catching the smugness in Ampris's dry tone.

"When we could not find you anywhere in the City, Guildmember, we apprised your Guild of your disappearance. And requested a . . ." Ampris's smile took on a faintly apologetic twist, "replacement. Our need, as I'm sure you appreciate, is urgent."

"It takes nearly ten weeks to get from the Scoria system to the Ophiuchian."

"Not by FSP courier ship." Ampris inclined his head briefly. "Your Guild values you highly, Killashandra Ree . . ."

"Surely you've communicated news of my rescue?"

Ampris spread his hands deferentially. "But of course. But we did not then know how promptly the Heptite Guild would respond. The courier ship has entered our atmosphere and at this very moment is landing at the shuttle port."

"Trag!" And there was no doubt at all in Killashandra's mind that that was who had been dispatched.

"I beg your pardon."

"Lanzecki would have sent Trag here."

"This man is capable?"

"Eminently. However, the more we can do now, the sooner Trag and I will finish. If you'll excuse me, Elder Ampris?" And Killashandra signaled Lars to continue. "Our last request to you, Ampris,"—although Ampris had not yet stirred from his vantage point—"those tubs of crystal shard could now be removed to wherever I—or Trag—will be instructing the trainees. Some of the larger pieces can be useful but they are a considerable nuisance sounding off in here."

"Yes, we should want to restore the monitors within this room, Guildmember, now that the organ is nearly repaired." Ampris flicked his hand at Thyrol who then issued the appropriate order to the guards. Killashandra did not dare glance in Lars's direction.

"Don't bounce the tubs about," Killashandra warned, as the guards shuffled out with the first one.

"There now," Killashandra said when the door had slid shut leaving them alone, "the shards'll be more accessible to us now. We can purloin the ones we want. Can you get your hands on a small plasfoam pouch?"

"Yes. Who's this Trag?"

"The best person they could possibly have sent. Lanzecki's Administration Officer." Killashandra chuckled. "I'd rather him than an army, and certainly I'd rather him than any other singer they could have chosen. And a courier ship. I am flattered."

"Somehow Ampris is too pleased with this development."

"Yes, and fretting with impatience." Killashandra mimicked his hand gesture and Lars nodded grimly. "Is it just that he wants the organ done? Or us out of the loft for good?" She swiveled slightly so that she was facing the wall they could not shift. "Why?" She bit one corner of her lip, trying to solve its mystery. Then, with an exclamation, she ran her hands around the casing of the manual, picked up the lid and examined it closely.

"What are you looking for, Killa?"

"Blood! Did you see any discoloration on the shards you handled?"

"No—If Comgail was killed by," and he gestured at the newly placed crystal spires, "there would have been blood somewhere here!"

"Was there only the official version of Comgail's end?"

"No. I had a chance to speak with one of the infirmary attendants and she said that he was covered in blood, crystal fragments had pierced eyes, face, and chest."

"With a little help, perhaps? But do you know for certain that it was Comgail who shattered the manual?"

Lars nodded slowly, his eyes gray and bleak, his face expressionless.

"And he had mentioned earlier that he knew the access to the subliminal units was through the organ loft?"

Again Lars nodded and both stared at the wall.

"Comgail did all the maintenance on the Festival organ?" At Lars's impassive nod, Killashandra scrubbed at her face with one hand. "Did Ampris ever compose or perform?" she asked in angry exasperation.

The look of total surprise on Lars's face gave her the answer.

"No wonder he's been bouncing about here," Lars cried, seizing Killashandra and hugging her with the excess of his jubilation. "No wonder he's been so eager to get the manual repaired. He can't get to the subliminal units until it is. He can't alter the subliminals for this year's concerts. Oh, Killa! You've done it."

"Not quite," Killashandra said with a laugh. "I'm only hypothesizing that the manual provides the unlocking mechanism. We've no idea what sort of music key he'd use. It could be anything—"

"No, not anything," Lars cried, shaking his head and grinning, his eyes vividly blue again. "I'd stake my life I know what he'd use—"

"I wish you wouldn't use a phrase like that," Killashandra murmured.

Lars gave her a reassuring grin and went on. "Remember what you said about bureaucracy finding one mechanism that suited them? Well, Ampris's one and only Festival offering utilizes a recurrent theme."

"But everyone on the planet would know it then."

"What difference would that make? You'd still have to have access to this manual, wouldn't you?"

"True. What's the theme?"

"It's a real thumpety-dump," and he da-da-ed the notes to Killashandra's utter amazement.

"Not only is it thumpty-dumpety-dump, it's complete and utter plagiarism. Ampris lifted that theme from an 18th Century composer named Beethoven."

"Who?"

Killashandra lifted her hands in exasperation. "Enough of this idle speculation, Lars, we've got to finish the organ as fast as possible."

"What about Trag?"

Killashandra shook her head. "Trag is no threat to us. If we could just get the bass notes finished, we'd have something to show him. I hope." She dropped a set of brackets into Lars's hands and took another for herself. "You wouldn't happen to know the signature of Ampris's composition?" When Lars shook his head, she cursed briefly and then began to chuckle. "We'll just try the original one!"

Because they were rushing, nervous with anticipation and hope, hands sweating from tension, it seemed to take three or four attempts to place each of the next three crystals. Lars was muttering imprecations by the time Killashandra could test the third one. No sooner had she struck the crystal than the door panel slid open and the aperture was filled by Trag's bulky figure.

"Trag, I bless your timely arrival. We're both fingers and thumbs trying to set this manual. A fresh hand and a sane mind will work wonders!"

Trag gave her a nod of his head and stepped inside, giving Lars a cursory glance before his attention was completely taken by a critical appraisal of their endeavors. Killashandra ignored the entrance of Ampris, Torkes, Thyrol, and Mirbethan, who filed slowly into the room in Trag's wake. Trag picked up the tuning hammer and struck each of the crystals.

Trag merely nodded his head. Lars made a noise of protest but Killashandra shot him a warning glance. The fact that Trag had no comments to make was all the approval she required, knowing better than to expect overt praise from him. For a *very* fleeting moment, however, she was seized with a totally irrational desire to throw her arms about Trag's neck, a notion which she quickly suppressed without revealing it by so much as a grin.

Elder Torkes, resembling the scavenger bird more faithfully than ever, seemed about to step forward, then, apparently, changed his mind as if aware of how Trag's bulk diminished his stature to insignificance.

"You have only just arrived, Guildmember, and as it is now midday, refreshment has been prepared for you," Torkes began with scant courtesy.

Trag dismissed the offer. "You gave the Guild to understand the matter was of the most urgent."

"We need to eat," Killashandra said tartly. "Just send us in some food, please, someone," and she picked up more brackets as Trag removed the next crystal from its bed of plasfoam. "We might even finish this today if given the chance to work without interruption."

"Not quite," Trag amended in his deliberate fashion as he held the crystal up for inspection in the ceiling light. Satisfied he lowered it, his gaze traveling beyond to the fascinated observers. "If you please?" And he extended his hand toward the door.

Killashandra, her eyes on Lars's blank face, had to fight not to chortle at the aura of dismay, fury, and shock emanating from the four high ranking Optherians. But her hands were free of both sweat and tremble and, with Lars carefully tightening the matching bracket, they were ready to fasten it the moment Trag inserted the crystal in place. The door panel *whooshed* over the rectangle of sunlight. Killashandra tightened her bracket just as Lars finished his. Trag took up his hammer for the ceremonial tap and the D, mellow and clear, broke the silence of the room.

"Just two more, Trag and I believe we'll have something to show you," Killashandra said, reaching for more brackets. "This is Lars Dahl."

"A lover posing as a bodyguard! A young man with highly suspicious credentials," Trag said bluntly, his hooded stare fixed on Lars.

Killashandra held up a hand to restrain any understandable outburst from Lars but he only smiled, inclining his head in brief acknowledgment of the description.

"According to Elder Ampris or Torkes?" Killashandra asked, grinning at Trag as she faced him squarely.

Trag focused his attention on her. Had she not been so positive of her own righteousness, she would have been hard pressed to maintain her composure beneath that basilisk stare.

"I will hear your explanation, then, for I warn you, Killashandra Ree, the Guild looks with disfavor on a member who abrogates her contractual obligations for whatever personal reasons obtain . . ."

Killashandra stared at Trag incredulously.

"I was given two assignments here, Trag, by you—"

"The secondary assignment was considerably less important than the primary—" Trag's big hand indicated the unfinished installation.

"The two are more closely linked than you or Lanzecki imagined when the Guild accepted that contract. But then abduction ought not to be a high-risk-factor on well-ordered, conservative secure Optheria. Right? Ever aware of my primary obligation," Killashandra allowed some of her outrage to color her voice, "I swam dangerous channels from one island to another in order to escape the one I was dumped on. Confounding all parties and managing thus to return to my primary contractual obligation."

Trag merely raised his eyebrows.

"Tell me, Trag, what is your opinion of subliminal conditioning?"

Trag's bleak eyes widened fractionally. "The Council of the Federated Sentient Planets has declared any form of subliminal projection morally criminal and punishable by expulsion from the Federation."

"Then if I were an Elder," Lars said in a quiet, faintly amused tone, "I wouldn't be so quick to accuse anyone else of having highly suspicious credentials."

"If you will assist us to install the next two crystals, Trag, I believe we may be able to prove our allegation," Killashandra said.

"If you cannot prove this allegation, Killashandra Ree, you are liable to severe discipline and censure."

"Then isn't it convenient that I'm right?"

"Guildmember, I have been subjected to subliminal conditioning," Lars said, as if he sensed her minute uncertainty. Trag turned his penetrating stare on the islander.

"The insidiousness of subliminal conditioning, Lars Dahl, is that the victim is totally unaware of the bombardment."

"Only if he is unprepared, Guildmember. My father, late an agent of the Federated Council, was able to safeguard me, and other friends, against electronically induced subliminals. Which, I might add, are particularly adaptable to the heavy emotional experience of the sensory organ."

"Late an agent?" Killashandra fancied she saw some diminution of Trag's intractability.

"Trapped here by the same restraint which keeps Optherians from competing in galactic enterprise," Lars replied. "Contact with the Federated Council has only just been reestablished after nearly thirty years—"

She and Trag heard the minute sound at the same instant and assumed suitable poses of interrupted labor when the door panel slid open. Mirbethan escorted the lunch table which the security guard wheeled in.

"If you'll just leave it there, Mirbethan," Killashandra gestured with a hand full of brackets while Trag and Lars bent over an already sited crystal, "we'll take a break shortly."

"Not the one they expect, either," Lars murmured when the door panel had closed. Trag favored him with another unnerving stare. Lars returned it equably, with a slight bow toward the manual case. "After you, Guildmember."

"Why three more crystals?" Trag asked.

"This loft is half the size of the available space behind the organ console on stage," Lars said. "We think the subliminal programming equipment is hidden behind that wall, and accessed by a musical key activated from this manual. We have reason to believe that Comgail, who is alleged to have smashed the crystal," Trag's eyebrows raised, "was killed because he had discovered that musical key, not because he was injured by the shards or because he had destroyed the manual. That would have only got him sent to rehab."

"Who is responsible for the subliminal programming?"

Lars grinned maliciously "My own personal candidate is Ampris; he is musically trained."

"It wouldn't take musicality to strike notes in the right sequence," Trag said.

"True, but he knows as much about the organ as every performer must and he became head of the Conservatory about the time the subliminal conditioning started. It began shortly after my father arrived, and he was here to investigate the first request for the revocation of the planetbound restriction. Then, too, Torkes has always favored the propaganda control of population. But what one Elder does, the others invariably condone. And subliminal conditioning sustains them in their power."

"Arrange for me to meet your father, Lars Dahl."

Lars grinned. "His credentials are as suspicious as mine, Guildmember. I doubt we could reach him. In any event, we are here, close to the damning proof of what we suspect. Surely a bird in hand—"

"Bird?" The word exploded from Killashandra, a result of the tension she felt and a combination of surprise and respect for Lars's sterling performance under Trag's unnerving scrutiny.

"Perhaps the analogy is wrong," and Lars shrugged diffidently. "Well, Guildmember? Have I my day in court, too?"

"Three more crystals?" Trag's manner gave no indication of his thoughts.

"Two more," Killashandra said, "if we are using the original key."

Trag made a barely audible grunt at that comment before he reached for the next crystal and motioned Lars to place his bracket.

Killashandra could not keep her mind entirely on the task at hand for she suddenly realized just how much rested on the truth of the dissidents' contentions. Had she indeed allowed a sexual relationship to cloud her judgment? Or favorable first impressions from Nahia, Hauness, and the others to color her thinking? And yet, there was Corish von Mittelstern, and Olav Dahl. Or was that convoluted situation carefully contrived? She might be out on a limb, the saw in her own hand, she thought as she delicately tightened the bracket on the second crystal. She didn't dare look at Lars across the open case as they straightened up.

Expressionless as ever, Trag handed Lars the tuning hammer. Lars gave Killashandra a rakish and reassuring grin and then tapped out the sequence: da da da-dum, da da da-dum. For one hideous moment nothing happened and Killashandra felt the last vestige of energy drain from her body with the groan she could not stifle. A groan that was echoed by a muted noise and a slight vibration in the floor. Startled, she and Lars looked down but Trag remained with his eyes fixed on the ceiling.

"Clever!" was his comment as the wall sank slowly and, to their intense relief, noiselessly apart from the initial protest. "Clever and utterly despicable." As soon as the descending wall reached knee height, Trag swung over it, Lars right behind him.

For a heavy man, Trag moved with considerable speed and economy of motion. He did a complete circuit of the room, his eyes sweeping from one side to the other, identifying each bank in the complicated and extensive rack system, and the terminal which activated the units. He completed his circuit at the three heavy cables that provided the interface between the two sets of computers.

"No one has been in here for some time," he said finally, noting the light coating of dust on the cabinets.

"No need, Guildmember."

"You may address me as Trag."

Lars grinned triumphantly at Killashandra, where she stood, resting her ear against the door panel. Nothing must interfere at this critical moment.

"Trag. The yearly dose for Optherians occurs shortly before the Festival season begins, and the tourists arrive. All Optherians are given the 'opportunity and privilege,'" and Lars's voice was mildly scornful, "of attending the preliminary concerts for the current year's Festival selections. The Mainlanders get their dose then, to keep them contented while the tourists are here. Then, the tourists get theirs, which includes sufficient Optherianisms to prevent them from accepting messages from strangers for posting once they return to their homes. Some don't, you know, having fallen for the vastly superior and secure Optherian natural way of life."

Trag dropped his gaze from the fascinating cable. "How many escape these conditioning sessions?"

"Not many Mainlanders, though there are a few who independently discovered the subliminal images." Lars turned to Killashandra. "Nahia, Hauness, Brassner, and Theach. Over the last ten years, they've been able to warn those they felt could be trusted."

"Do the Elders know that some escape?" Killashandra asked.

"There is a head check at the concerts which simultaneously registers with the Central Computers."

"But islanders don't go to concerts, do they?" Killashandra said with a chuckle. It was a relief to know that she had occasion to be amused. It had looked very grim for a bit there, with Trag coming on strong as Guildmember.

"I think it is time to end such pernicious subjugation," Trag said. He took from his biceps pocket a hand-unit of the sort used to check programming systems, and placed it on the nearest cabinet. "It should be a simple matter of reprogramming the master sensory mixer to bypass the subliminal generator. That would inhibit the subliminal processor, yet leave no physical trace of alteration." Taking from the same pocket a heavy compound knife of the kind favored by crystal singers for field use, he opened the heaviest cutting blade. He sliced carefully at the plastic cable cover, peeling it back to expose the multicolor flex package.

Killashandra watched as Trag set the system checker against the flex, taking a preliminary reading. As he pondered the results, she could not restrain a glance at the subliminal room. The devices were so repugnant to her, abusing every precept of the individual privacy which had been her birthright on Fuerte, that she felt besmirched just looking at them.

"If there's no power . . ." Lars began, his hand half-raised in caution.

"I have had sufficient experience with this sort of equipment, Lars Dahl." Trag entered instructions on the hand unit, noted the display on the rectangular vdr, and a muscle twitched in his cheek. "The subroutine of the subliminal will function on any dummy test, and indicate the programming modes selected under their program listing, but I am placing a security lock," and with those words he put the device firmly against the thick red-coded cable and depressed the main key, "on it now. I don't have the equipment necessary to generate a program for propaganda detoxification."

"That's too bad," Killashandra said with heartfelt dismay.

"There!" Trag said. "And unless they know exactly what I've done to inhibit the subliminal processor, the alterations can't be reversed. Let the Optherians program that computer for whatever images they wish. None will reach the minds of the people they intend to pervert!" Trag pulled hard on the plastic coating and then pressed it firmly back around the cables. Killashandra could not see where the cable had been entered.

"And you'll bear witness to the Federated Council?" Lars was taut as he eagerly awaited Trag's reply.

"We shall all bear witness to the Council, young man," Trag replied.

Lars nodded but his smile was wry. "It will be the crystal singers' word that will be credited, Guildmember Trag, not that of an islander whose motivations are suspect."

"Even if he could leave the planet, Trag," Killashandra said. "Remember the arc at the shuttle port? Didn't it glow blue and erupt guards with weapons?"

Trag nodded. "Except when I passed under it."

"That arc detects a mineral deposit in Optherian bones," Lars said, "and in those of anyone here for more than six months. Which is what caught my father originally."

Trag dismissed that difficulty with a flick of his hand. "I have a warrant in my possession to arrest the party or parties responsible for the Guildmember's abduction, which would take you past their reprisals."

"You came well prepared, Trag," Killashandra said with a rueful smile. "But you'd have to bring the entire population of the Archipelago if you named Lars Dahl abductor."

When Trag turned to Lars for affirmation, he nodded. "I hadn't planned on leaving Optheria," Lars said, with a slightly embarrassed grin, "and I'm sure my father is more than willing to, but you'd need an entire liner to remove those who'd be vulnerable. The Optherian Elders have been waiting for years for an excuse to search and seize the adult population of the islands. They'd all end up in rehab. Unless, of course, you also have the authority to suspend every government official on this charge."

Trag was silent for a long moment, regarding Lars steadily. Then he exhaled slowly. "I was given broad powers by the Federated Council but not that broad." His lower jaw jutted out slightly. "Had there been any suspicion of this . . ." He paused, his contempt for once visible in his expression. "Let us not reveal this knowledge prematurely."

Carefully they removed every trace of their entry. Neither man had touched the cabinets or files, so covering their tracks took little time. Meanwhile, Killashandra repositioned herself at the door panel, listening for sounds of approach.

Trag reexamined the cables he had clipped, checking from all angles to be sure the incision would escape all but the most critical inspection. He gave the room a thorough survey and then, apparently satisfied, looked expectantly at Killashandra and Lars.

"Well, close it!"

Killashandra gave a burst of puzzled laughter, more shrill than amused.

"How?"

Lars chuckled as he took the hammer from her nerveless hand. "Find something he likes . . ." He tapped out the Beethoven sequence again. The wall immediately responded by closing, giving the barest *thunk* as the panel met the ceiling. Trag gave the cable housing a final glance and dismissed it with a shrug.

"I suggest you eat something, Killashandra. You're too pale. Probably the effect of combining both assignments for your Guild. Lars Dahl, set the next bracket."

Chapter 21

It was well that they had completed their investigations, for Elder Ampris returned twice, the first time issuing an unrefusable invitation to a quiet dinner with several of the Elders who were most anxious to meet the Guildmember.

"Which means you'd better eat before you go," Killashandra told Trag when Ampris had left them. "Especially if Elder Pentrom, a medical man with interesting views on nutrition, is attending." She made a very small circle—thumb and forefinger overlapping—to indicate the size of the portion. "Trag, do you drink?"

Trag peered up at her. "Why?"

"The worthy Elders, Pentrom in particular, are currently under the impression that members of our profession must daily consume alcohol in substantial quantities to assist their unusual metabolism."

Trag slowly straightened from the manual. His expression bordered on the incredulous. "Oh?"

"They are so frail, these Elders of Optheria"—Lars made a derogatory comment—"that I should dislike causing any of them distress. Prematurely, that is."

"Or exposing yourself as a calculating fraud?" Lars suggested.

"Occasionally it is useful to spawn a helpful myth about our profession. Otherwise we'll be stuck with water which, despite its high mineral content, is not purified because of the Optherian lust for nature untampered. It tastes as if it was decanted from the tank of the first long-range starship. The beer here is not bad."

A flicker crossed Trag's usually inscrutable face. "Yarran beer?"

"Unfortunately no." Trag's preference raised him further in her estimation. "The Bascum brew is potable while the better beer is illegal." She shot a knowing glance at Lars who grinned back at her.

"They generally are. Your advice is timely, Killashandra," Trag said, then appropriately sounded the B-flat.

Thirty-four crystals were in place when Elder Ampris appeared for the second time late that afternoon. There was no disguising the elation in his eyes at their progress. He was seething with the most excitement she had yet seen an Elder exhibit. Had he despaired of running up this year's dose of indoctrinal conditioning on his subliminal program?

"We will finish this tomorrow," Trag told Elder Ampris, "with a further day to tune the new manual into the system, and to check the other three manuals for positive feedback. One minor detail on which Killashandra was unable to reassure me: Was the organ in use when the manual was destroyed?"

"I believe it was," Ampris replied, his lids dipping to conceal his brown eyes. "I will of course confirm this. After the deplorable desecration, I myself conducted an inspection of the other manuals to be sure they were undamaged."

"Elder Ampris, Killashandra Ree and I would consider ourselves derelict in our Guild obligation to Optheria if we failed to assure ourselves, and you, that your Festival organ is in full and complete working order."

"Of course," Ampris managed through clenched teeth. Then, in an abrupt alteration, he smiled tightly. "Most thorough of you."

"Can we turn on the main organ console from here?" Killashandra asked, wondering what had caused Ampris's sudden change. "I admit that I am quite eager to hear it in all its glory."

Ampris regarded her for a long moment before his thin lips widened in the original smile.

"For you to appreciate fully the versatility of the Festival organ, you need some measure of comparison. Therefore I am delighted that you are able to attend this evening's concert which will be performed on the two-manual Conservatory instrument."

"Yes, of course." Killashandra let pleased affability ooze through her voice. "Now that this installation is nearly completed, and with Trag here, I realize how much tension I've been under. It is always so much easier to share responsibilities, isn't it, Elder Ampris?" she added gaily.

He murmured something and withdrew. Trag looked at her expectantly.

"When the inevitable can no longer be avoided, it is always wise to accept it gracefully." She grimaced. "Though I have to admit I *despise* student concerts."

Lars grinned. "Oh, you won't be getting the students tonight, Killa. And in view of what you told me of the origin of Ampris's party piece, I eagerly await your critical appraisal. Are you at all musical, Guildmember?" he asked Trag.

"Frequently." Trag carefully replaced the tools in their case, gestured for Lars to close the crystal container. Killashandra covered the manual, and taking a hair from her head, wet it and laid it carefully across one corner of the lid. Trag gave a snort that she translated as approval.

"Hair of the dog that bit?" Lars asked.

"Where do you get these sayings?" Killashandra demanded, rolling her eyes in exaggerated dismay. Then she pointed to his pocket.

"I'd like to have a close look at that device," Trag said. Lars withdrew the little jammer.

"Trag, I'm trying to get them to believe that it's me distorting their monitors."

Trag surprised Killashandra by placing his hand flat against her shoulder blade. "Not any more. But I would qualify. Sensible of you."

"How many of the myths about crystal singers are derived from sensible precautions?" she asked Trag. "Or survival techniques?" Trag shrugged indifferently.

Lars deactivated the device as Killashandra opened the door panel and the three left the loft. Killashandra watched Trag to see if the acoustics of the Festival auditorium affected him. Trag did not so much as alter his firm stride or respond to the echoes his vigorous pace produced. The guards had to scurry to keep up with them.

Once inside the guest suite which Trag was to share with them, Lars switched on the jammer before he passed it over to Trag.

"They've been replacing the monitors in the organ loft every day but a trill of crystal and they shatter," Killashandra told Trag as she made her way to the beverage counter. "A cold glass of the Bascum, Trag?"

"Please." Trag returned the jammer to Lars. "What sort of detector do they have at the shuttle port?"

"Isotope scanner," Lars said with a grimace. "The popular theory is that the detector is set off by a rare isotope of iron peculiar to Optherian soil. Once the residue of the isotope builds up in the bone marrow, it tends to be self-perpetuating. There've been unsuccessful attempts to neutralize the isotope and jam the scanners but nothing works." Then he scowled. "All the guards are rehabs and never miss. Trying to get past them is an effective form of suicide. There is also a stun field that operates in the event that another concerted attempt is ever made to gain entry to the port."

"I was met by four Optherians . . ." Trag began.

"Who had been passed in. Oh, authorized personnel come and go but they are very careful to display their authorization to the guards."

Killashandra had punched up sandwiches which she now passed to the men.

"We don't have much time before dinner and the concert, and I need a bath," she announced, her mouth half full of sandwich.

"So do I." Lars followed Killashandra, taking the jammer with him after an apologetic nod to Trag. "Trag is no threat to us, huh?" Lars murmured sarcastically, once they were in the unmonitored bathroom.

Killashandra shrugged and grimaced. "I didn't think he'd cut up that stiff, but then, neither of us knew what lies the Elders were spinning. And the Guild does have a reputation to maintain, especially if they had to call in the FSP to get a cruiser for a fast trip here. But," she added, rather pleased, "it means they cared."

"I felt I was talking to a brick wall, Killa, until it came down." Lars ran his fingers through his thick hair. "What would you have done if it hadn't, Killa?"

"Well, it did and Trag has been converted. Now all we have to do is get word to your father. Just how many people would we have to get to safety? I mean, if Trag has that warrant for party or parties . . ."

Lars framed her face with his hands, grinning down at her. "No matter how broad that warrant, Killa, it wouldn't extend to all those who really need our protection. Nahia, Hauness, Theach, Brassner, and Olver are just the most important. Why—"

"Couldn't some just disappear into the islands?"

Lars shook his head.

"Then we'll have to hold tight somehow until Trag reports the subliminal conditioning to the Federated Council. The Fleet Marines would land, in force, and the Elders would be sampling rehab. You're safe as long as I'm here—and stop shaking your head. Look, Trag can return, now that the organ is repaired and I'm unabducted—"

"Is the cruiser still here?"

"Oh, I rather doubt it."

"Then unless he can recall it, he's surfaced on Optheria until the next liner and that's not due for at least two weeks."

"Two more weeks!" Killashandra realized that she had taken for granted the same constant space traffic that frequented Shanganagh Moon Base.

"What? Have my charming presence and inspired coupling worn thin now that you have a fellow crystal singer to pair you?"

"Trag? You think—Trag and I? Don't be funny! Listen to me, young man, there's a lot you don't know about crystal singers!"

"I'd like the time to find out." His reply was wistful even if the kiss he gave her was not. And her response to his embrace temporarily suspended less urgent matters, even the bath.

Fortunately, by the time Trag knocked peremptorily on the bathroom door, they were both dressed.

"Coming," Killashandra responded in a trill, bestowing one last kiss on Lars before she hauled open the door. Sweeping dramatically into the main room with Lars a step behind her, she was delighted to see Trag, a half-empty glass of beer in his hand, in the company of Thyrol, Mirbethan, and Pirinio. Facetiously wondering if Polabod had been loaned to another quartette, she greeted them graciously, exclaiming her eagerness to attend the evening's concert and, at long last, hear an Optherian organ.

Dinner was served in the same chamber that had charmed Killashandra. The charm was enhanced this time by the fact that Elder Pentrom was missing from the guest roster. Trag was monopolized at one end of the table by Elders Ampris and Torkes, who engaged him in very serious discussions, while Mirbethan did her best to introduce unexceptional topics into conversation at the other. Thyrol, Pirinio, and two very meek older women instructors completed the buffer between the Elders and the distinguished and newly arrived Guildmember Trag.

"Elder Torkes," Trag said in a well-pitched voice that carried to every part of the dining room after he had sipped the beverage in his glass, "my metabolism requires the ingestion of a certain quantity of alcohol daily. What have you to offer?"

After that, Killashandra didn't bother straining her ears to hear what information, or misinformation, might be exchanged. Fortunately the portions served them were considerably more generous, if unexciting to the palate, than her first dinner there, so that hunger was assuaged.

There was no reason to dally at the festive board so, immediately after the sweet course was finished, Mirbethan led the way to the Conservatory Concert Hall. Those already assembled rose to their feet at the entrance of the distinguished visitors.

"Like lambs to the slaughter," Lars whispered in her ear.

"Wrong again!" she whispered back, then composed her features in a gracious expression. Until she had a good look at the seating.

The organ console, of course, dominated the blue and white stage. Golden curtains were richly draped to complete the frame which was bathed in a gentle glow of diffused light. They walked up a slight ramp to the orchestra floor where Mirbethan smilingly turned and gestured toward their chairs.

Bloody inquisition, Killashandra thought to herself. Upholstered in a mid-blue velvety fabric, the chairs were bucket shaped, semirecumbents equipped with broad arm rests, sculptured to fit wrist and hand for proper sensory input. Killashandra did not expect to find an easy repose for over each seat was a half hood, no doubt containing additional sensory outlets. As Lars might remark, the occupants of the seats were sitting ducks.

Nevertheless, and because it was consonant with the role she had adopted, Killashandra expressed delight over the "ambiance of the hall," the charming decor, and the unusual seating. She counted fifteen rows extending up and into the shadows behind her, all of them filled. She counted the front-row seats on her side of the entrance as fifteen so that some four hundred and fifty people, the complement of the Conservatory, were about to be entertained.

She took her seat but because of the tilt and the arm rest, the only part of her that could touch Lars was her foot. She angled so that she could touch his. She felt a return pressure which gave her far more reassurance than she should need or had expected to gain from such a minimal contact.

The house lights dimmed and Killashandra was filled with a perturbation she had never experienced before at what was usually the most enjoyable, anticipatory moment of a performance.

A woman swirled out onto the stage, her robes flowing out behind her. She bowed quickly to the assembly and took her place at the organ console, her back, with its pleated draperies, illuminated by the spotlight. Killashandra saw her lift her hands to the first manual and then all the lights went out as the first chord was played.

Killashandra all but kicked Lars as she recognized the music. In most Conservatories, a man named Bach would have been credited with its composition. On Optheria it was unlikely that any sheep safely grazed. Then the sensory elements began their insidious plucking. It was well done, the scent of new grass, spring winds, tender green, soothing color, bucolic fragrances and then—Lars's foot tapped hers urgently but she had already caught the image of the "shepherd," a glamorized Ampris, a kindly, loving, affectionate, infinitely tender shepherd, gazing for that one moment upon members of his "flock."

Had Trag failed? Disappointment and a keen flare of apprehension suffused Killashandra. She forced herself to recall that first glimpse of this smaller theater. There had to be a second subliminal generator behind this organ console. Indeed, there was probably one attached to every one of these insidious instruments. How would they disconnect them all? A second image, of a grieving Ampris, saddened by a misdemeanor of his flock— saddened but infinitely tolerant and forgiving—capped her disgust with the entire exercise.

Killashandra caught all of the images that were broadcast, as sharp and as clear as if a hologram had been suspended for inspection of a tri-d screen. The subliminals seemed etched on her retina. Something to do with her symbiont's rejection of this superimposition?

When the lights came up, Killashandra elected to seem to be affected by the performance as she should have been.

"Guildmember?" Mirbethan asked in a soft eager voice.

"Why, it was charming. So soothing, such a lovely scene. I declare that I could smell new grass, and spring blossoms." Lars tried to step on her toe. She struggled up out of the clutch of her seat and peered around him. "Why, Lars Dahl, it is everything you told me it would be!" He tapped twice, getting her message.

A second performer strode out on the stage, his manner so militant that Killashandra laid a private bet with herself: one of the Germans or an Altairian, if Prosno-Sevic's bombastic compositions had been composed before the Optherians had settled this planet.

The music was an uninspired melange of many of the martial themes, each new one buffeting the captive audience so that she found herself twitching away from the onslaught of the music, and wondering if she would survive the subliminals. She did, but her eyeballs ached with visions of Torkes and an improbably robust Pentrom urging the faithful onto the path to victory and planetarianism, defending the credo of Optheria to the death.

An audible sigh—of relief?—preceded the applause of this selection engendered. So the audience was being soothed to trust, encouraged to resist subversive philosophies: now what, Killashandra wondered?

An alarmingly thin and earnest young man, swallowing his Adam's apple convulsively as he crossed the stage, was the next performer. He looked more like a wading bird than a premier organist. And when he took his seat and lifted his hands, they splayed to incredible lengths, making the soft opening notes ludicrous to Killashandra's mind, especially when she recognized the seductive phrases of a French pianist. The name escaped her momentarily but the erotic music was quite familiar. She held her breath against the first image and choked on the howl of laughter as the subliminal image of Ampris-the-seducer was superimposed, in reds and oranges, on the viewers' abused senses. Fortunately, the notion of Ampris making love to her, or anyone, was so bizarre that the eroticism—even magnified by scent and sensory titillation—failed to achieve its full effect. Lars's continual tapping—was he succumbing to the illusion, keeping the beat, or trying to distract her from the powerful sensuality—against her toe kept reminding her how perilous their position was at the moment.

Bolero! The name returned to her as the lights came up. And fury at this arrant manipulation set a flush in her cheeks that matched those in Mirbethan's as the delighted woman turned to inquire breathlessly how Killashandra had enjoyed the concert.

The seats were all tilting forward, releasing their occupants once more into the cold cruel world of reality.

"I have never so totally experienced music before in my life, Mirbethan," Killashandra said in ringing, heart-felt tones. What she felt in her breast was not what the performance was expected to generate. "A balanced and professional performance. The artists were magnificent. Excellent adaptations to the Optherian organs."

"Adaptations? Oh, no, Guildmember, this was the first performance of three brilliant new compositions," Mirbethan said and Killashandra could only goggle at her.

"That music was totally original? Composed by the performers?" Killashandra's surprise was misinterpreted by Mirbethan as the proper expression of awe. Lars squeezed her arm warningly and she managed to contain her outrage.

"A truly brilliant concert," Trag said, joining them as the audience was dispersing. "An experience I would not willingly have foregone."

Never having heard so much warmth in his voice, Killashandra looked sharply at Trag. Surely, if her symbiont had protected her . . . Now she stared at Trag's flushed face, his bright eyes, and noticed that a smile had reshaped his lips. Killashandra grabbed at Lars's arm, before anyone else could see her dismay, she pulled them both into the crowd, away from Trag and the two Elders who escorted him.

"Easy, Killa," Lars murmured in her ear. "Don't give it away. Not now!"

"But he—"

His hand twisted her fingers cruelly, reminding her of the danger they were in.

"That last piece will send them all to their beds, alone if necessary," Lars continued, breaking up the sentence into quick short phrases as he hurried her away from the hall. "No one is expected to linger. Not after that dose of eroticism." They turned a corner, Killashandra accepting Lars's direction. "Trag's coming."

"Don't you understand? No one here composed that music. It was all stolen!"

"I know, I know."

"Yours wasn't stolen. It was original. The only bloody original music I've heard on this fardling mudball!"

"Shush now, Killa. Only one more corridor and we're home safe and then you can rant and rave."

"I get the cold shower first."

"What, and waste the music?"

She tried to kick him but they were walking so fast she would have lost her balance if she'd succeeded.

"I will not be manipulated . . ." and the last word she roared in the privacy of their suite. She was hauling the Beluga spidersilk kaftan over her head as she reached the bathroom door and, flipping on the cold water, stood in its frigid torrent until she could feel her flesh shriveling. Lars pulled her out, handing her a towel as he took her place.

"I think it's a shame to waste all their hard work and effort—"

"Did you want to go to bed with an image of Ampris?" she demanded at the top of her voice.

"Oh, I saw Mirbethan," Lars said ingenuously, toweling himself dry.

"Mirbethan?"

"Yes, didn't you know that was why she was included in your welcoming committee? She's bi—"

"What?" Killashandra screeched that at the top of her lungs.

"Compose yourself, Killashandra Ree," said the cool voice of Trag from the doorway. "You and Lars Dahl are in every bit as much danger as you thought. We must talk."

Chapter 22

"First," Trag said as Killashandra and Lars joined him in the main room, and he pointed to the monitors. Lars held up the jammer. "Very good. Secondly, I need to hear an account of your adventures here, Killashandra. Then I can separate the fact from the fiction presented by Ampris and Torkes. Both are clever men."

"A drink, Killa?" Lars asked and his voice was rough with either anger or anxiety.

"I would appreciate something stronger than that tasteless beer, please, Lars Dahl," Trag said.

"My pleasure, Trag."

Killashandra could feel the tension release in her belly and she let out a lungful of air as Trag's courteous request gave her a reassuring measure of his attitude. She took a quick pull at the polly liqueur which Lars handed her before he sat on the couch, not touching her but with one arm protectively along the back. She began with her arrival on the *Athena* and her suspicions about Corish. Nor was she any less than candid about the fit of pique with Optherian bureaucracy which had led her to leave the Conservatory grounds, her subsequent kidnapping, escape, and her second meeting with the young islander. She was as forthright about Lars's effect on her sexuality as she was about the impact Nahia, Hauness, and Theach had had on her sympathies. Crystal singing tended to peel off unnecessary veneers and conditioned attitudes, not that she had been afflicted by many, having been raised on Fuerte.

During her recitation, Trag had sipped his drink, any reaction hidden by his hooded eyes. He finished the last of the polly liqueur which Lars had elected to serve him as she concluded the summary and he gestured politely to Lars for a refill.

"They are clever, those old men, but they have not dealt with crystal singers before," Trag said. "They have outsmarted themselves this time. Whom the Gods would destroy, they first make mad."

Killashandra regarded Trag in mild astonishment and then Lars, wondering if his habit was contagious. But Trag's adage was eminently applicable.

"Or think themselves impervious to the slings and arrows of outraged fortune," Lars said with a mischievous grin. Killashandra groaned in protest.

"Tomorrow I shall offer to realign the Conservatory instrument," Trag said. "I distinctly heard a burr—the first sign of a souring crystal."

"Will they permit you?" Killashandra asked.

"They are greedy. And they have no qualified crystal tuner until we have trained some. I have already resolved the point that the Guild contracted to supply the crystals and technical assistance, without reference to the number of appropriate technicians supplied. Therefore no further sum is to be paid by them. Until they received that reassurance from me, they were trying to make out that you were in breach of contract—"

"In breach? Me? When they placed me in jeopardy? First by hiring an assailant to prove my Heptite origination? Then they hinder me in the execution of my assignment? And they malign my competence?" Killashandra quickly switched to malicious amusement. "Not that they will really appreciate the level of competence we have exhibited! Nor the caliber of the technical assistance they've bought!" She grinned at Trag. "So, what other knotty problems did you solve at dinner?"

"Your incorruptible dedication to your Guild."

"What!" Killashandra's irritation rekindled. "Of all the—"

Trag held up his hand, a gleam in his eye that suggested to Killashandra that he was enjoying her discomfiture. Firmly she controlled herself. It didn't help to notice, out of the corner of her eye, that Lars was struggling to suppress his own amusement.

"Coming as I do from Guildmaster Lanzecki's office, I am," Trag paused unexpectedly, shooting a glance at Killashandra which she could only interpret as sly, "above reproach. I am also male. Apparently the Elders trust few women in any but the most traditional or subordinate capacities. I assured them that not only were you Guildmaster Lanzecki's first choice for such a delicate and crucial installation, but you were mine as well."

Killashandra sniffed but gave him a long hard look, to remind him exactly why Killashandra Ree had been Trag's first choice.

"Your praise, Guildmember, is only surpassed by your concern for the welfare of the Guild," she said demurely.

"In a matter affecting the Guild reputation, I am, too, incorruptible," Trag replied, neatly parrying her thrust.

"So tomorrow are Lars and I permitted to continue with the Festival organ?" Trag nodded. "And you will reorganize the second instrument?"

"In the best interests of the guiding precepts of the Federated Sentient Planets Council, yes, I certainly shall. Otherwise I assure you that these Elders would not receive unreimbursed and gratuitous services from the Heptite Guild."

"Bravo!" Lars called.

"Their greed blinds them," Trag said. "So, following a recent example, we shall take the opportunity that is presented," he added, nodding toward Lars who returned the compliment. "Basically they have trite minds. Security, pride, and sex! Imagine! Inflicting such prurience on tonight's audience."

Killashandra regarded Trag with mild astonishment. The man was positively garrulous, volunteering comments not to mention uncontracted services. Or was he simply responding to the backlash of that maladroit rendition of the *Bolero*? She'd have thought Trag made of sterner stuff, especially since he'd been forewarned of the subliminals.

"Oh, that's a common diet for the Conservatory," Lars said. "For the masses, they have other themes, sometimes so indigestible I wonder how they can be swallowed, even conditionally. Mainlanders are often subjected to a spectrum ranging from xenophobia," Lars began ticking the subjects off on his fingers, "a fear of races in their own territories, to claustrophobia to nip any budding interest in space-faring, to fear of disobedience, fear and disgust of acts that are 'unnatural,' fear of committing an illegal action, rational or not. They've even constructed a negative-feedback loop to inhibit thinking along lines the Elders have suddenly decided are subversive. A dislike of the color red was achieved a year or so ago.

"Then," and Lars was really warming to his subject, "the tourists get a different menu: love of the simple life, very little eroticism—which would follow, wouldn't it? All sorts of nebulous goodnesses to be obtained by staying on here. Immense credit balances are constantly flashed luringly at the most bizarre moments. Naturally the disadvantages aren't mentioned at all."

"No lecture on Full Disclosure?" Killashandra shot Trag a glance but he ignored her.

"Have you a reliable contact in the Conservatory, Lars?" Trag asked him.

"I wouldn't dare contact any of them after tonight's subliminal messages. I could try the marketplace—"

Trag shook his head. "It was politic to agree with Ampris and Torkes that you, Killashandra, have undoubtedly fallen under this young man's insidious spell." He raised his hand at Killashandra's guffaw. "Neither of you are to be allowed to leave the Conservatory without escort. For your safety, of course, Killashandra."

"Of course!"

"What works in your favor, though, in this infatuation—"

"Trag!"

"I'm not Ballyblind, Killashandra," Trag said in a stern voice, "and, if the Elders consider you two self-absorbed to the exclusion of other, more treacherous activities, it is a safeguard, however tenuous. At least while we are still on Optheria." Trag turned to Lars. "Once we leave, Lars Dahl, you are in grave jeopardy."

Lars nodded and, when Killashandra closed her fingers about his, he smiled down at her. "All I need is a half-day's start on any pursuit; no one will ever find me in the islands."

Trag managed to look skeptical without changing a muscle in his face. "Not this time, I think. This time the islanders are to be disciplined to a final and total obedience to the Optherian Council."

"They have to catch us first," Lars said calmly, although anger flared in his eyes and his fingers tightened on Killashandra's. In an abrupt change he shrugged. "The threat of wholesale reprisal is scarcely new."

"Trag has that warrant . . ." Killashandra suggested but caught the obstinate set of Lars's face.

"May I remind you, Killashandra," Trag said, "that a Federated Council warrant is not a writ one exercises with impunity. If I am forced to use it, Lars, and whoever else it includes, would be charged with your abduction and subject to the authority of the FSP Council."

"If I don't press charges, once they're off Optheria—"

"If you perjure yourself in a Council Court, Killashandra Ree, not even the Heptite Guild can rescue you from the consequences."

"I repeat, and listen to me this time," Lars interrupted firmly, jiggling Killashandra's arm for her attention, "I only need a head start and there isn't a captain on this planet who could catch me. Look, Trag, it's not your affair, but if you're willing to disorganize the Conservatory projector, would you consider doing others? There are quite a few two-manual organs on the Mainland. To have two sabotaged will already be a considerable boon, but the more Mainlanders who are freed from subliminal manipulation, the more chance we'd all have of surviving until the Federated Council moves.

"The Elders can blandly puff on about disciplining islanders, but first they have to jizz enough Mainlanders up to the point of a punitive action. Mainlanders are a passive bunch, after so many years of the pap they've been subjected to." He grinned maliciously. "You saw last night which of the three pressures the audience responded to the most—Not the martial pride. So, psyching a punitive force up would take time, a clever program, and sufficient audience saturation. The smaller the net the subliminals cast, the longer it will take the Elders to mount any sort of expedition to the islands.

"Now," and Lars leaned forward urgently, "you and Killa have to make a report to the Federated Council? Well, I would find it hard to believe that any Council acts fast. Right?"

Trag nodded. "Speed is determined by the physical threat to the planet involved."

"Not to the population?" Killashandra asked, surprised at Trag's emphasis.

Trag shook his heavy head. "Populations are easy to produce, but habitable planets are relatively scarce." He indicated that Lars should continue.

"So, your report will be considered, deliberated upon, and then?"

"It may indeed take time, Lars Dahl, but the Federated Council has outlawed the use of subliminal conditioning. There is absolutely no question in my mind that action will be taken against the Optherian Elders. A government which must resort to such means to maintain domestic satis- faction has lost the right to govern. Its Charter will be revoked."

"There's no danger that you and Killashandra will be restrained from leaving?" Lars asked abruptly.

"Why should we be? Can they have any suspicion that someone knows that they maintain control by illicit means?"

"Comgail did," Killashandra said, "even if he was killed before he could pass on the information. Whoever killed the man must wonder if Comgail had accomplices."

Lars shook his head positively. "Comgail's only contact was Hauness and Hauness didn't reveal that until after Comgail's death. I knew that some drastic measure was planned. Not what it was."

"Tell me, Lars," Trag asked, "does any one suspect that you are aware of the subliminals?"

Lars shook his head vigorously. "How? I always pretended the cor- rect responses after concerts. Father didn't warn me until I was sent to the Mainland for my education. His warning was accompanied by a descrip- tion of the retribution I would suffer, from him as well as the Council, if I ever revealed my knowledge unnecessarily." Lars grinned. "You may be sure I told no one."

"Besides your father, who knows?" Trag asked. "Or don't you know that?"

Lars nodded. "Hauness and his intimates. As a trained hypnothera- pist, he caught on to the subliminals but had the sense to keep silent. It is quite possible that others in his profession know it, but if they do, they don't broadcast it either. What could they do? Especially when I doubt that many Optherians know that subliminals are against Federated Law!" The last was spoken in a bitter tone. "Who would suspect that music, the Ulti- mate Career on Optheria, can be perverted to ensure the perpetuation of a stagnant government? Then there was the almost insoluble problem of try- ing to get word off Optheria, to someone with sufficient status to get Coun- cil attention. Complaint from people who could be considered a few maladjusted citizens—and every society has some—carries little weight.

"It was Hauness who devised a way to get messages off Optheria for us. Posthypnotic requests—yes, yes, I know; and don't think it was an easy matter for him to violate his ethics as a physician-healer, but we were get- ting desperate. A suggestion to receive and later mail a letter from the nearest transfer point seemed a minor infraction. I am certain that Hauness only capitulated because Nahia was suffering so much distress. She had to cope with such a devastating increase of suicide potentials. She's an em- path, Trag—"

"You must encounter Nahia, Trag, before you leave Optheria," Kil- lashandra said, twining her fingers reassuringly about Lars's. He gave her a quick and grateful glance.

"That's why, if you would go to Ironwood to check out the organ there, you would surely encounter Nahia and Hauness," Lars said eagerly.

"I would?" Trag asked.

"Quite likely, if you were suddenly taken ill."

Trag regarded him steadily. "Crystal singers do not succumb to planet-based diseases."

"Not even food poisoning?" Lars was not to be deterred.

"And that's a likelihood if you eat often with the Elders. Or do I mean starvation?" Killashandra remarked.

"That way, you can warn Nahia and Hauness, and they can alert others." Lars leaned forward, eagerly waiting for Trag's decision. "I couldn't save myself at the expense of my friends."

"How large a group do you have, Lars Dahl?" Trag asked.

"I don't know at the moment. We had about two thousand, and more were being investigated. The Elders' search and seize to find Killashandra reduced our ranks considerably." Regret for having provoked the Elders to such action colored Lars's expression. He squared his shoulders, accepting that responsibility. "I fervently hope more sacrifices will not be required."

"Do your islanders perpetrate many outrages on the Mainland?"

"Outrages on the Mainland?" Lars burst out laughing. "We leave the Mainland to stew in its own juice! If you wish to punish an island child, you threaten to send him to a Mainland school. What crimes were being laid on our beaches?"

"Crimes hinted at darkly but never specified, apart from the attack on Killashandra—"

"Ampris instigated that—" Killashandra said angrily.

"And her abduction."

"And I have laid that firmly on the shoulders of unknown malfeasants. I thought they'd bought that."

"They might have if the attachment between you and Lars Dahl was not so apparent, almost as if you were in resonance with each other. However," and Trag went on quickly, "Torkes contended that young Lars Dahl could scarcely have found you so conveniently if he had not known where you were. The islands being so numerous and widespread he does not accept coincidence."

"I think Torkes is in for a large surprise on the mechanics of coincidence," Killashandra said in her most caustic tone. She had poured another stiff drink for herself, trying to dull anger and indignation. "Trag, I don't see why the Federated Council cannot act expeditiously—"

"This planet is not threatened by destruction."

"Our much vaunted Federated Council is not much better than the Elders Council, is it?"

"I will do everything in my power, Lars Dahl, to ensure the physical and psychological integrity of your adherents," Trag said. "And if that includes servicing every instrument on this planet, I will do that, too." A slight shift of the alignment of his lips gave him an appearance of smiling. "Greed provokes me. And all this talk has made me thirsty. What is this?" he asked, obliquely requesting a refill.

"The fermented juice of the ubiquitous polly fruit," Lars said, serving him. "The Elders may complain about the islands but they are its best customers."

"Tell me again about the security arrangements at the shuttle port," Trag went on. "A liner is due in two weeks' time. I should like to have you both on it."

"There's more chance of sailing a straight course in the islands, Trag," Lars said, shaking his head discouragingly. "If anyone had been able to discover a flaw in the security curtain at the shuttle port, it would have been done. My father had the unique honor of adjusting the screens to prevent a mass attack. Father came here on a short-term contract to provide security micro-units for the Optherian Council. Father was co-opted by the Federated Council because of his expertise with micro-chip installations. The Federation wanted him to find out why another agent had never reported back to them. But, while he was installing the chips, he didn't have much luck with the covert assignment. So when the Optherians offered him the shuttle port contract, he took it. No one mentioned the fact that three to four months was the longest it was safe to stay on Optheria without getting trapped. When he realized that he was, and even he couldn't get past the shuttle port curtain, he talked himself into his position as Angel Island Harbor Master. Far enough away from the shuttle port to satisfy the Elders, and far enough away for him to feel safe from them."

"How is cargo transferred?" Trag asked.

"What little there is is unloaded through the main passenger lock, which is operated by the shuttle pilots, true and loyal, uncorruptible citizens of Optheria. The only way into the shuttle port is past the detector's arc. And if the detector is set off without first presenting the right pass to those rehabbed guards," he made a popping sound, "you're dead."

"Ah, but Thyrol was right beside me as we left the port, Lars," Killashandra said, "and the arc did not go off. Yet you say that it goes off whenever the mineral residue is detected."

"Crystal resonance might mask or confuse the detector," Trag remarked, choosing his words slowly. "For the same thing occurred, and with Thyrol beside me, when I exited the port."

"Why don't we just boldly go under the fardling arc then? Both of us with Lars between."

"You no longer resonate, Killashandra," Trag said.

"Besides, that only helps me, Killa. I won't leave the others vulnerable to the Elders' reprisals."

"Impasse!" Killashandra threw her hands out in disgust but she had to admire Lars's stand. "Wait a minute. I may not resonate, but white crystal does. Trag, they blow out the monitors at the sound of an *A*. Won't crystal resonance affect other piezoelectrical equipment? I know it'd be folly to try to blow out the shuttleport detector . . ."

"That's been tried, too, Killa." Lars interrupted her with a rueful grin.

"Trag?—If crystal resonance provides a mask . . ."

"I should not like to put it to the test and fail."

Killashandra turned to Lars. "You said something about your father being able to detect Council agents. Does he have a unit?"

"A small one."

"If we had it, we could test crystal resonance with it. We've got all those crystal shards, Trag, and you know how interactive white is."

"First we have to contact my father," Lars said with an ironic laugh, "then get him and the device here. Oh, it's not large but certainly not something you carry barefaced through City streets." But, even as Lars spoke in pessimistic terms, it was clear to Killashandra that she had revived his hopes. "All the more reason, Trag, for you to get to Ironwood and make contact with Nahia and Hauness. They've got the oceanjet. They could discreetly bring Father and the device as far as Ironwood."

"There are no other embarkation clearances at the shuttle port?" Trag asked.

Lars shook his head slowly. "No other beside the security curtain has ever been needed. You forget, Trag, that loyal, happy, natural Optherians have no desire to leave their planet. Only tourists, who can buy tickets anywhere, so long as they've enough credit."

"Then," and Trag got to his feet, carefully putting the glass down on the nearest surface, "patently I must oblige both you and the greedy Elders. Good night."

Killashandra watched, wondering if the polly had got to the impervious Trag but his step was as firm and unswerving as ever. She saw that Lars was watching his progress, a very thoughtful expression on his face.

"If this idea works, Killa," he said, taking her in his arms, his eyes on that distant prospect, "is there enough crystal to get six or seven people off Optheria?"

"Don't hope too hard, Lars!" she cautioned him, her head against his shoulder, her arms about him. "Nor can we schedule a mass exodus on the next liner without giving the whole scheme away. But if crystal resonance fools the scanner, the most vulnerable people will get free. The Festival season hasn't even started. When it does, a few one-way passengers could go out on each flight." She looked up and caught the bleak look on his face. "Lars, dance with me?"

"To a distant drum?" he asked with a rueful grin, but he shortly sloughed off depression.

The next morning Killashandra woke to the second chimes and to an interesting idea.

"Lars, Lars, wake up."

"Why?" and he attempted to pull her back down on the bed, murmuring suggestions.

"No, I'm serious. We responded to the subliminals last night, didn't we? How long are they supposed to be effective?"

"Huh? I dunno. I've never . . . Oh, I see what you mean!" And he sat

up, linking his arms about his raised knees and considering the implications. "We never took last night's performance into our deliberations, did
we?" He rubbed his chin thoughtfully, then grinned at her. "I'd say we
could work this to our advantage. Security, pride, and sex, huh!" Lars began to laugh, a mirth which developed into such a paroxysm that he fell
back on the bed and hauled his knees up to his chin to relieve the muscular
cramp of uncontrollable laughter.

Trag appeared in the doorway, pointed to the ceiling monitor and,
when Killashandra pointed to the jammer on the table, he came in and shut
the door, regarding Lars expressionlessly.

"We got conditioned last night, Trag," Killashandra said by way of
explanation as she hauled her coverall on. "I don't think I should overdo it,
but if Lars wants to act disaffected with me, it will lull Ampris and Torkes
into thinking their programming's effective. Even on a crystal singer. Trag,
I could even stay on here . . . not want to leave Optheria. I'm a musician. If
last night is the best they can do, just lead me to a keyboard! I'll show 'em
some sensory music that'll knock 'em in the aisles."

Trag shook his head slowly from side to side. "Risky for any number
of reasons which I shouldn't have to enumerate."

Brushing laugh tears from his eyes, Lars was still grinning broadly as
he reached for his clothes.

"So what was so funny?" Killashandra asked.

"Mirbethan as a sex image when I have you!"

"I'm not sure I needed to know that!" Killashandra stalked into the
main room and up to the catering unit. She punched out her selection so
hard that the tab stuck and a succession of beverage cups paraded out. Fortunately the mechanism was programmed against excessive use and the
emergency panel flashed "quota" at her as the depressed button snapped
out again.

"Put Ampris in my place and what do you have?" Lars wanted to
know and his voice was just a shade repentant.

"Nausea." She handed him a cup from the plentiful supply waiting
on the catering facility.

Chapter 23

They had just finished eating when the communit blipped. Killashandra flicked open the channel. Mirbethan appeared, looking both annoyed and hesitant. Killashandra schooled her face to courteous inquiry.

"My apologies for disturbing you so early, Guildmember . . ." she did not continue until Killashandra had murmured reassurance, "but a citizen has been most persistent in trying to contact you . . . We have assured him that you are not to be disturbed by trivia. He insists on speaking with you personally and his attitude borders on the insolent." Mirbethan closed her mouth primly on the verdict.

"Well, well, what's his name?"

"Corish von Mittelstern. He says that he met you on board the *Athena*." Mirbethan obviously doubted this.

"Indeed he did. A pleasant young man who knows nothing of my Guild affiliation. Put him through."

Corish's image immediately replaced Mirbethan's. He was frowning but his expression cleared into a broad smile once he saw Killashandra.

"Thank Krim I got you, Killashandra. I was beginning to doubt that you ever existed, with that Conservatory playing it so cosy. I never heard of a Conservatory monitoring the calls of a student."

"They're very careful and they prefer your complete dedication to your studies here."

"You mean, you've been allowed to play on one of those special organs?"

Killashandra affected a girlish giggle. "Me? No. But I heard the most marvelous recital on the Conservatory's two-manual sensory organ last night. You wouldn't believe how versatile it is, how powerful, how stimulating. Corish, you've simply got to get to one of the concerts before you leave. The public ones will be starting soon, they tell me, but I could see if it's possible to get you to one here at the Conservatory. You really have to hear the Optherian organ, Corish, before you can possibly understand what it's like for me." Someone pinched her arm. Well, maybe she was overdoing it a trifle but enthusiasm was not out of order. "Have you found your uncle yet?"

Corish's expression altered from the skeptical to the dolorous. "Not yet."

"Oh, dear, how very disappointing."

"Yes, it is. And I've only two more weeks before I'm scheduled to leave. The family is going to be upset about my failure. Look, Killashandra, I know you're studying hard, and this is a chance of a lifetime for you, but could you spare me an evening?" Killashandra gave Corish full marks for a fine performance.

"Oh, Corish, you sound so discouraged. Yes, I'm sure I can wangle an evening out. I don't think there's a concert tonight. I'll find out. I'm not a prisoner here."

"I should hope not," Corish said stiffly.

"Look, where can I reach you?"

"The Piper Facility," Corish replied as if there were no other suitable place in the City, "where you *said*," and he emphasized the word, "that you'd leave a message for me. I was concerned when there'd been no word at all from you. Food's not bad here but they won't serve anything drinkable. Typical traveler hostel. I'll see if they can recommend some place a little more Optherian. This isn't a bad world, you know. I've met some sterling people, very helpful, very kind." Then his expression brightened. "You check and leave word at the Facility only if you can't make it. Otherwise, come here at seven thirty. You have enough funds for ground transport, don't you?" Now he was the slightly condescending, well traveled adult, older sibling.

"Of course I do. You sound just like my brother," she replied cheerfully. "See you!" And she broke the connection, turning to Trag and Lars. "That sort of solves one problem, doesn't it?"

"Does it?" Trag asked darkly.

"I think so," Lars replied. "Corish has an unlimited travel pass, issued by Elder Pentrom. His credentials must have come from very highly placed Federationists for that kind of assistance."

"More likely, 'his uncle' is due to inherit a sizable hunk of credit of which the Optherian government will get its own share," Killashandra suggested. Lars nodded. "And if his cover has been that good, it's unlikely the Elders have tumbled to his true identity so he could get in touch with anyone we need, including Olav Dahl! Or Nahia or Hauness."

"What concerns me," Lars said, his eyes clouded with anxiety, "is why he's getting in touch with you right now. He must have come back to the City from Ironwood—and Nahia and Hauness. Maybe they're in jeopardy. So many people were picked up on the search and seize . . ."

Killashandra put a reassuring hand on Lars's arm. "I think somehow Corish would have managed to intimate that."

"I think he did by not admitting to finding his uncle."

"If he admitted to having found his uncle," Trag said, unexpectedly joining forces with Killashandra to reassure Lars, "he would no longer have any need to use that travel pass, and if he's as good a Council agent as he seems to be, he wouldn't surrender that option."

Lars accepted that interpretation with a nod of his head and pretended to be reassured.

"We'll know soon enough," Killashandra said kindly.

"Well, when you meet Corish this evening," Lars said, "walk to whichever restaurant he's been recommended. That way you have some chance of open talk. The Piper is certain to recommend The Berry Bush or Frenshaw's. Neither are far from the Piper, but both restaurants are run by Optherians, loyal and true to the Elders, so you'll be under observation. The food's pretty good." Lars gave her an encouraging grin.

"Then I'm taking the jammer, too. Got to keep them thinking it's me that causes the static. Well, they should have had enough time to digest Corish's innocuous conversation." So Killashandra tapped out a sequence on the communit. "Mirbethan, is there a concert tonight? I shouldn't want to miss any but von Mittelstern has invited me to dinner tonight, and I've accepted. I don't want him to come charging up here and discover I'm more than the simple music student he thinks me, so I'll settle his doubts."

Whatever Mirbethan thought was disguised by her reassurances that no concert was scheduled.

"Then please arrange transport for me this evening. By the way, when is the next concert? I'm fascinated by the organ effects. Fabulous concert last night. The most unusual one I've ever attended."

"Tomorrow evening, Guildmember." Mirbethan's reply was gracious, but Killashandra noticed the slightly smug turn to the woman's faint smile.

"Good." Killashandra broke the connection. "Offense is the best defense, Guildmember," she added, turning to Trag. "You didn't have to promise the Elders that you'd discipline me for my emotional aberration, did you? Well, then, it's business as usual for me in a normal fashion which means I come and go, whether they trail me or not. Right? And since I'm disaffected with you," and Killashandra kissed Lars's cheek, "I'll go alone. Unless, Trag, you want to come and meet Corish."

"I might, at that," Trag said, half-closing his eyes a moment.

"That gives me the chance to moon after Mirbethan," Lars said slyly.

Killashandra guffawed and wished him luck.

"Now let us attend our duties," Trag said, gesturing for Killashandra to precede them to the door.

When they reached the Festival Auditorium, a large contingent of security men was loosely scattered about the stage, concentrated near the organ console, which was open. Two men were fussing about the keyboard but Killashandra couldn't tell whether they were dusting or adjusting the keys. Suddenly Elder Ampris detached himself from the gaggle and took a few steps forward to meet them.

"Don't overdo it, Killa," Lars murmured at her, aiming a slightly fatuous grin at the Elder.

"After last night, Elder Ampris, I wonder at my audacity in suggesting that I play on any Optherian organ," she said, and felt Lars's admonitory pinch on the tender inside flesh of her arm. Unnecessary, she felt, since she had forced herself to employ a meek and sincere tone of voice.

"You enjoyed the concert?"

"I have never heard anything like it," she said, which was no more than the truth. "Truly an experience. Mirbethan tells me there'll be another one tomorrow evening. I do hope that we'll be invited?"

"Of course you are, my dear Killashandra," Elder Ampris replied, his eyes glittering almost benignly at her.

She limited herself to a happy smile and continued on to the organ loft door.

"A word with you, Elder Ampris," Trag began, his anxious frown attracting the Elder's instant attention.

Killashandra and Lars continued into the organ loft.

"You pinched far too hard!"

"You wouldn't fool me, Killa!"

"Well, I did fool him," and hiding her gesture from observation, she pointed to the hairless corner of the manual cabinet.

"Jammer on?" she asked.

"The moment I finished pinching."

"Brackets, please!"

They had already positioned the first of the final slender crystals when Trag and Elder Ampris entered.

"Only five more crystals and this installation is complete," Trag was saying to Ampris. "I know that Killashandra is well aware that these upper register notes require the finest tuning." Killashandra nodded, receiving his tacit message. "I will check the brackets on that sour crystal in the Conservatory organ and be back here in time for the tune-up."

Killashandra was hoping that Elder Ampris would leave them to the task but he elected to remain, observing every movement. Killashandra hated to be overseen under any circumstances, and to have Ampris's gimlet eyes on her made the hairs on the back of her neck rise. She was annoyed, too, because Ampris's presence put the damper on any conversation between herself and Lars. She had enjoyed the bantering exchanges which relieved the tedium and tension of this highly precise work. So she felt doubly aggrieved to be denied a morning of matching wits with Lars Dahl. They would have so little time left to enjoy each other's company.

Therefore, it gave her a great deal of vicarious pleasure to spin out the last final bracketings, giving Trag ample time to make his alterations on the Conservatory program. And deliberately irritating Elder Ampris with her persnickety manipulations. He was in a state of nervous twitch when she and Lars tightened the last bracket.

"There!" she said on a note of intense satisfaction. "All right and tight!" She picked up the hammer and, seized by a malicious whimsy, struck the first note of the Beethoven motif. Out of the corner of her eye, she saw Ampris start forward, one hand raised in protest, his face drained of all color. She went up the scale, and then, positioning the hammer on the side of the crystal shafts, descended the forty-four notes in a glissando. "Clear as the proverbial bell and not a vibration off the true. A good installation, if I say so myself."

Killashandra slid the hammer into its space in the tool-box and brushed her fingertips lightly together. She released the damper on the striking base of the crystals and replaced the top. "I don't think we'll fasten it just yet. Now, Elder Ampris, the moment of truth!"

"I would prefer that Guildmember Trag—"

"He can't play! Doesn't even read music," Killashandra said, deliberately misinterpreting Elder Ampris. Lars pinched her left flank, his strong fingers nipping into the soft flesh of her waistline. She would have kicked back at him if she could have done so unobserved. "But I suppose you would feel more secure if he was to vet the completed installation," she added, giving Ampris a timorous smile more consonant to someone in the thrall of subliminal conditioning than her previous declaration.

Trag's reappearance was fortuitous.

"Just as I suspected, Elder Ampris, a loose bracket on the middle G. I checked both manuals thoroughly."

Ampris regarded Trag with a moment's keen suspicion. "You don't play," he said.

"No."

"Then how can you tune crystal?"

Killashandra laughed aloud. "Elder Ampris, every would-be crystal singer has perfect and absolute pitch or they can't get into the Heptite Guild. Guildmember Trag doesn't need to be a trained musician. Guild Master Lanzecki isn't either. One of the reasons I was chosen for this assignment is because I am—and trained in keyboard music. Now, Trag, if you will inspect the installation?" She and Lars lifted off the cover.

Trag was not above giving Ampris a second fright for he tapped out three of the Beethoven notes in the soprano register before altering the sequence to random notes. Then he did each note in turn, listening until the exquisite sound completely died before hitting the next crystal.

"Absolutely perfect," he said, handing her the hammer.

"Now, with your permission, Elder Ampris," Killashandra began, "I would like to use the organ keyboard." When she saw his brief hesitancy, she added, "It would be such an honor for me and it would only be the sonics. After last night's performance, I would be brash indeed to attempt any embellishments."

Bowing stiffly to the inevitable, Elder Ampris gestured for her to proceed from the loft. Not that she could have done anything to damage the actual organ keyboard, and live, with so many security guards millimeters from her. As she took her seat, pretending to ignore the battery of eyes and sour expressions, she decided against any of the Beethoven pieces she remembered from her Fuertan days. That would be risking more than her personal satisfaction was worth. She began to power up the various systems of the organ, allowing the electronic circuits to warm up and stabilize. She also discarded a whimsical notion to use one of Lars's themes. She flexed her fingers, pulled out the appropriate stops, and did a rapid dance on the foot pedals to test their reactions.

Diplomatically she began with the opening chords of a Fuertan love song, reminiscent of one of the folk tunes that she'd heard that first magical night on the beach with Lars. The keyboard had an exquisitely light touch and, knowing herself to be rather heavy handed, she tried to find the right balance, before she began the lilting melody. Even playing softly and delicately, she felt, rather than heard, the sound returning from the perfect acoustics of the auditorium. The phase shield around the organ protected her from the full response.

Playing this Festival organ was an incredible, purely musical experience as she switched to lowest manual for the bass line. For her as a singer, keyboards had been essential only as accompaniment, tolerated in place of orchestra and choral augmentation. She might have been supercilious about the Optherian contention that an organ was the ultimate instrument, but she was willing to revise her opinion of it upward. Even the simple folk song, embellished with color, scent and "the joy of spring," she thought sardonically, was doubly effective as a mood setter when played on the Optherian organ. She was sorely tempted to reach up and pull out a few of the stops that ringed the console.

Abruptly she changed to a dominant key and a martial air, lots of the bass notes in a sturdy thumpy-thump, but half-way through she tired of that mood, and found herself involved in the accompaniment to a favorite aria. Not wishing to spoil the rich music by singing, she transferred the melodic line to the manual she had just repaired, taking the orchestra part in the second manual and the pedal bass. The tenor's reprise naturally followed, on the third manual, mellower than the soprano range. From that final chord, she found herself playing a tune, filling in with a chorded bass, and not quite certain what tune it was when she felt someone pinch her hip. Her fingers jerked down the keys just as she realized that it was Lars's melody she was rehearsing. She made the slip of her fingers into the first music that came to mind, an ancient anthem with distinct religious overtones. She ended that in a flourish of keyboard embellishments and, with considerable reluctance, lifted her hands and feet from the organ, swiveling around on the seat.

Lars, being nearest, took her hand to ease her to the ground from the high organ perch. The pressure of his fingers was complimentary, if the arch of his eyebrows chided her for that slip. It was the surprise on Elder Ampris's face that pleased her the most.

"My dear Killashandra, I had no idea you were so accomplished," he said with renewed affability.

"Woefully out of practice," she said demurely, though she knew that she had struck few wrong notes and her sense of tempo had always been excellent. "Almost a travesty for someone like me to play on that superb organ, but I shall remember the honor for the rest of my life." She meant it.

There was a general sort of highly audible reshuffling as the security men permitted a handful of hesitant new arrivals closer to the console. Some nervous clearings of throats and foot scufflings also echoed faithfully about the auditorium.

"Balderol's students," Elder Ampris murmured by way of explanation. "To practice for the concerts now the organ is repaired."

At a glance, Killashandra decided there must be nine security men for each student. She smiled kindly, then noticed out of the corner of her eye that a solid line of the biggest security men stood shoulder to shoulder in front of the door to the organ loft. Were they glued to their posts?

"Well, let's leave them to it," she said brightly. "Don't you have some students for Trag and myself? To learn crystal tuning? They must have perfect and absolute pitch, you know," she reminded Elder Ampris as they left the stage. Her voice sounded dead as her final words were spoken in less resonant surroundings.

"That is not scheduled until tomorrow, Killashandra," Ampris said, mildly surprised. "I had thought that you and Guildmember Trag should take this opportunity to see the rest of the Conservatory."

That was not high on Killashandra's list of priorities but since she was momentarily in Ampris's good graces, she should make an effort to stay there. She was not best pleased when Ampris turned the projected tour over to Mirbethan, excusing himself on the grounds of urgent administrative duties. Instead of proving to Ampris that sublimation worked on crystal singers, she had to watch Lars proving it to Mirbethan while she tried to attach herself to Trag. At first Trag remained his inscrutable self but suddenly altered, attentive to her explanations of this classroom, that theory processor, when the small theater had been added, and which distinguished composer had initiated what ramification on the Festival organ. Had Lars brazenly pinched the impervious Trag? As she trailed behind the trio, now inspecting the cheerless and sterilely neat dormitories, she would have been glad enough to receive Lars's pinch.

If she had herself been more receptive, she would have been impressed by the physical advantages of the Conservatory for it was exceedingly well organized and equipped in terms of practice and classrooms, library facilities, processing terminals. There was even a library of books, donated by the original settlers and subsequent visitors. The actual Conservatory had been designed as a complete unit and built at one time, only the Festival Auditorium added on at a later date although included in the original plans. In design it was a complex far superior to Fuerte's Music Center, which had sprawled in extensions and annexes with no basic concept. There was, however, more charm in a corner of Fuerte's Music Center than in any of the more elaborate and pretentious chambers of Optheria's Conservatory.

"The infirmary is this way." Mirbethan's unctuous voice broke through Killashandra's sour reflections.

"I've been there," she said in a dry and caustic tone and Mirbethan had the grace to look embarrassed. Then she gave Lars a penetrating look which he returned with an impudent wink. "And I'm hungry. We didn't eat any lunch in order to get the installation completed."

Mirbethan was full of apologies and, when both Trag and Lars said they were sure the Infirmary was of the same high standard as the rest of the premises, she led them back to their quarters.

Once inside, Lars ostentatiously activated the jammer and Killashandra heaved a sigh of relief. She hadn't realized how tense she'd become.

"I'm hungry, that's all, I'm hungry," she told herself as she made her way to the caterer.

"Where did you find the subliminal unit, Trag?" Lars asked, pausing at the drinks cabinet.

"Under the stage, but keyed by the same motif. For clever men, the Elders can be repetitive."

Killashandra gave a contemptuous snort. "Probably can't remember anything more complicated at their advanced ages."

"Don't make the mistake of underestimating them, Killashandra," Trag said solemnly as he poured himself a brew.

"Let them have that privilege," Lars added. "Sententious bastards. We're down to Bascum, Killa."

"Well, that goes well with the fish, which seems the only thing left on today's menu."

Lars guffawed. "It always is. Take the soup instead," he said in a tone that suggested dire experience. "And don't, Killa, play my music again in the Conservatory," he added, waggling a finger at her. "Balderol heard me practice often enough."

"I won't say I'm sorry," Killashandra replied. "It just happened to develop from the previous chord. It's probably the most original music ever played on that organ if what we heard last night is standard."

"They don't want originality, Killa," Lars said with a twist to his smile. "They want more of the same that they can orchestrate to mind-penetration. Trag, what did Ampris say about your doing the provincial organs?"

"I haven't suggested it. Yet. There has been no opportunity."

Lars looked anxious. "I'm the one who's greedy now. Disabling their program in the City is a big step forward because so many provincials make the trek here in order to say they've heard the Festival organ. But *they're* not the ones who'd be recruited to Ampris's punitive force. So they're the ones we want to keep unaffected this year."

"Who else has access to the organ lofts?" Trag asked.

"Only . . . Ah!" Lars's expressive face altered to triumph. "Comgail never got the chance to make his annual inspection of the other facilities. And maintenance is Ampris's responsibility, not Torkes. He'll have to use you and Killa, Trag. He hasn't anyone else. And he certainly wouldn't entrust maintenance to the puff heads you're supposed to initiate into the art of crystal tuning."

"Especially not you, Lars," said Killashandra with a laugh.

"Let's not continue that part of the farce, Killa," Lars said.

"Why not?" asked Trag. "I think you must realize that we will not leave you on this planet, no matter how cleverly you could hide yourself amid your islands, Lars Dahl. Crystal tuning is a universal skill."

"So is sailing, Trag."

"But let us continue as we have started. Farce or not, it keeps you in our company and safe."

"Trag, are you recruiting?" Even to herself, Killashandra sounded unnecessarily sharp.

Trag turned his head slowly to look at her, his heavy features expressionless. "Recruiting is not permitted by the FSP, Killashandra Ree."

She snorted. "Neither is subliminal conditioning, Trag Morfane!"

Lars looked from one to the other, grinning at this evidence of unexpected discord. "Here, here, what's this?"

"An old controversy," Killashandra replied quickly. "If all the provincial organs need at least basic maintenance, then you and I, Trag, are the only qualified technicians on Optheria. Ampris will have to ask you, for I can't see him asking me, and that solves that problem, doesn't it?"

"It should," Lars replied, grinning at her for her change of subject and the facile solution.

"We shall see," Trag added, rising to refill his glass.

"I need a bath," Killashandra said, rising. "After a morning spent with Ampris, I feel unclean!"

"Now that you mention it," Lars murmured and followed her.

A stolid security man drove the small ground vehicle that evening. Its plasglas canopy gave her an unobstructed view of the City in its tortured sprawl as she was driven sedately down from the Conservatory prominence. The spring evening was mild and the sky cloudless. Quite likely, Killashandra thought, she was seeing the City at its best, for spring growth hazed most of the vegetation with a delicate green, gold, or fawn brown, providing some charm to the otherwise sterile buildings. The residential dwellings often sported vines, now sprouting a bright orange leaf or blossom.

Most of the traffic was pedestrian, though a few larger goods-carrying vehicles intersected their route through the winding streets of the City. There seemed to be no visible roadway controls but her driver slowed to a complete halt at several cross streets. At one, she received incurious glances from the several pedestrians halted on the footpaths. Doubtless all good Optherians were at home with their families at that hour, and the few people that Killashandra did pass looked glum, anxious, or determined. It occurred to Killashandra that she missed the light-hearted islanders with their ready smiles and generally pleasant behavior. She'd seen very few genuine or lasting smiles in the Conservatory: a perfunctory movement of the lips, a show of teeth but no genuine delight, pleasure, or enthusiasm. Well, what else could she expect in such a climate?

She spotted the Piper Facility before the driver turned up the broader thoroughfare to it. It hung, block-square and utilitarian, like hostels anywhere, even Fuerte. She had once thought the native orangy-red sandstone of Fuerte garish and common but she could feel almost nostalgic for its hominess. Certainly the relaxed and random designs of Fuertan architecture were a patch above Optheria's contorted constructions.

The timepiece above the entrance of the Piper Facility flashed a big 1930 as the driver reduced the forward speed of the vehicle. Precisely then, the main door slid aside and Corish, looking tanned and expectant, emerged. Immediately he saw Killashandra, he smiled a warm and enthusiastic welcome.

"Right on the dot, Killashandra, you've improved!" he said, giving her an unnecessary assist out of the vehicle.

"Thank you, driver," Killashandra said. "I really need to stretch my legs, Corish. Let's walk to the restaurant if it isn't far. I felt awfully conspicuous where so few people use ground transport."

"Have you paid him?" Corish asked, reaching into his belt pouch.

"I told you I could," she began in a sulky voice and made shooing gestures at the driver. The man reengaged the drive and the vehicle slid slowly away. "I'm being monitored, Corish, and we need to talk," she said, cocking her head up at him with an apologetic expression on her face.

"I thought so. I'm told to try the Berry Bush so I expect it's got monitors in the utensils. This way." Corish cupped his hand under her elbow, guiding her in the right direction. "It's not far. I'm only just back from Ironwood."

"Lars is in a swivet about Nahia and Hauness."

"They're all right . . ." And Corish's tone of voice added *so far*, "but the search and seize continues! Hauness is convinced that the Elders mean to rouse a punitive expedition against the islands. In spite of your safe return."

"Torkes doesn't believe in coincidence. More important . . ." and Killashandra broke off, stunned by the look of pure hatred on the face of a woman passing by. Killashandra glanced around but the woman had not paused or accelerated her pace.

"More important?" Corish prompted, his hand impelling her to keep pace with him.

With an effort, Killashandra redirected her attention, but an afterimage of the intensity of that expression burned in her mind.

"The Elders use subliminal conditioning."

"My dear Killashandra Ree, that is a dangerous allegation." Corish tightened his fingers on her arm, shocked by her statement. He looked about, to see if any of the few passers-by could have overheard.

"Allegation, fardles! Corish. They blasted last night's audience with it," she said, only barely able to keep her intense indignation at the conversation level. "Security, pride, and sex was the dose. Didn't Olav mention subliminals to you? He knows about them."

Corish set his mouth in a grim line. "He mentioned them but he could provide me with no proof."

"Well, I can swear to it, and so can Trag. He disconnected the processor on the Festival organ yesterday—while we had the chance—and the Conservatory instrument today." She cast him a snide sideways glance. "Or should we have waited until tomorrow night so you'd have firsthand experience?"

"Of course I trust Trag's evidence . . . and yours." He added the last in an afterthought. "How were you able to find the equipment? Wasn't it well hidden?"

"It was. Shall we say a joint effort—the murdered Comgail, Lars, and Trag. It wasn't crystal that killed Comgail, and I never could see how it had, but a desperate man. Probably Ampris. There'll be enough witnesses to testify before the Federation Council. Nahia and Hauness, too, if we can get them out."

"You'll never get Nahia to leave Optheria," Corish said, shaking his head sadly. He gestured for them to make a right turn at the next junction. The smell of roasting meats and frying foods greeted their nostrils, not all of it appetizing. But this was clearly a catering area. Open-front stalls served beverages and a pastry-covered roll—with a hot filling to judge by the expression of a man cautiously munching one.

"If we could get anyone out," Corish said gloomily. "They're all in jeopardy now."

"Which is why we want you to contact Olav and get him and . . ."

A change in air pressure against her back gave Killashandra only a second's warning but she had turned just enough to deflect the long knife descending to her back. Then a second knife caught her shoulder and she tried to roll away from her assailants, hearing Corish's hoarse cry.

"Lars!" she shouted as she fell, trying to roll away from her attackers. *"Lars!"* She had become too used to his presence. And where was he when she really needed him? The thought flitted even as she tried to protect herself from the boots kicking her. She tried to curl up, but hard rough hands grabbed at arms and legs. Someone was really attempting to kidnap her, even with Corish beside her. He was no bloody use! She heard him yelling above the unintelligible and malevolent growls of the people beating her. There were so many, men and women, and she knew none of them, their faces disguised by their hatred and the insanity of violence. She saw someone haul back a man with a knife raised to plunge into her, saw a face she knew—that woman from the street. She heard Corish howling with fury and then a boot connected with her temple and she heard nothing else.

Chapter 24

O f the next few days, Killashandra had only disconnected memories. She heard Corish arguing fiercely, then Lars, and under both voices, the rumble of Trag who was, she thought even in her confusion and welter of physical pain, laying down laws. She was aware of someone's holding her hand so tight it hurt, as if she didn't have enough wounds, but the grasp was obscurely comforting and she resisted its attempt to release hers. Pain came in waves, her chest hurt viciously with every shallow breath. Her back echoed the discomfort, her head seemed to be vibrating like a drum, having swollen under the skull.

Pain was something not even her symbiont could immediately suppress but she kept urging it to help her. She chanted at it, calling it up from the recesses of her body to restore the cells with its healing miracle, especially the pain. Why didn't they think about the pain? There wasn't a spot on her body that didn't ache, pound, throb, protest the abuse that she had suffered. Who had attacked her and why?

She cried out in her extremity, called out for Lars, for Trag who would know what to do, wouldn't he? He'd helped Lanzecki with crystal thrall. Surely he knew what to do now? And where had Lars been when she really needed him? Fine bodyguard he was! Who had it been? Who was the woman who hated her enough to recruit an army to kill her? Why? What had she done to any Optherians?

Someone touched her temples and she cried out—the right one was immeasurably sore. The pain flowed away, like water from a broken vessel, flowed out and down and away, and Killashandra sank into the gorgeous oblivion which swiftly followed painlessness.

"If she had been anyone else, Trag, I wouldn't permit her to be moved for several weeks, and then only in a protective cocoon," said a vaguely familiar voice. "In all my years as a physician, I have never seen such healing."

"Where am I going? I'd prefer the islands," Killashandra said, rousing enough to have a say in her disposition. She opened her eyes, half-expecting to be in the wretched Conservatory infirmary and very well satisfied to find that she was in the spacious bed of her quarters.

"Lars!" Hauness called jubilantly. His had been the familiar voice.

The door burst inward as an anxious Lars Dahl rushed to her bedside, followed by his father.

"Killa, if . . . you knew . . ." Tears welling from his eyes, Lars could find no more words and buried his face against the hand she raised to greet him. She stroked his crisp hair with her other hand, soothing his release from uncertainty.

"Lousy bodyguard, you are . . ." She was unable to say what crowded her throat, hoping that her loving hand conveyed something of her deep feeling for him. "Corish was no use, after all." Then she frowned. "Was he hurt?"

"Security says," Hauness replied with a chuckle, "he lifted half a dozen of your assailants and broke three arms, a leg, and two skulls."

"Who was it? A woman . . ."

Trag moved into her vision, registering with a stolid blink that her hands were busy comforting Lars Dahl. "The search and seize stirred up a great deal of hatred and resentment, Killashandra Ree, and as you were the object of that search, your likeness was well circulated. Your appearance on the streets made you an obvious target for revenge."

"We never thought of that, did we?" she said ruefully.

The movement to her right caused her to flinch away and then offer profuse apologies, for Nahia was moving to comfort the distraught Lars.

"So you took the pain away, Nahia? My profound thanks," Killashandra said. "Even crystal singers' nerve ends don't heal as quickly as the flesh."

"So Trag told us. And that crystal singers cannot assimilate many of the pain-relieving drugs. Are you in any pain now?" Nahia's hands gently rested on Lars's head in a brief benison, but her beautiful eyes searched Killashandra's face.

"Not in the flesh," Killashandra said, dropping her gaze to Lars's shuddering body.

"It is relief," Nahia said, "and best expressed."

Then Killashandra began to chuckle, "Well, we achieved what I set out to do in meeting Corish. Got you all here!"

"Far more than that," Trag said as the others smiled. "A third attack on you gave me the excuse to call a scout ship to get us off this planet. The Guild contract has been fulfilled and, as I informed the Elder's Council, we have no wish to cause domestic unrest if the public objects so strongly to the presence of crystal singers."

"How very tactful of you." Belatedly remembering caution, Killashandra looked up at the nearest monitor, relieved to find it was a black hole. "Did the jammer survive?"

"No," Trag said, "but white crystal, in dissonance, distorts sufficiently. They've stopped wasting expensive units."

"And . . ." Killashandra prompted, encouraging Trag since he was being uncharacteristically informative.

He nodded, Olav's grin broadened, and even Hauness looked pleased. "Those shards provide enough white crystal to get the most vulnerable people past the security curtain. Nahia and Hauness will organize a controlled exodus until the Federated Council can move. Lars and Olav come with us on the scout ship. Brassner, Theach, and Erutown are to be picked up by Tanny in the *Pearl Fisher* and leave with Corish on the liner—"

"Corish?" Killashandra looked about expectantly.

"He's searching most thoroughly for his uncle," Hauness said, "and attending the public concerts which have been hastily inaugurated, to soothe a disturbed public."

"What's the diet?"

"Security, pride, reassurance, *no* sex," Hauness replied.

"Then you didn't get to the other organs, Trag?"

"Corish suggested that some should be left in, shall we say, normal operating condition as evidence, to be seen by the Federal Investigators."

"What Trag doesn't say, Killashandra," replied Nahia, a luminous smile gently rebuking the other crystal singer, "is that he refused to leave you."

"As the only way to prevent the Infirmary from interfering with the symbiont," Trag said, bluntly, disclaiming any hint of sentiment. "Lars thought to send for Nahia to relieve pain."

"For which I am truly grateful. I've only a tolerable ache left. How long have I been out?"

"Five days," Hauness replied, scrutinizing her professionally. He placed the end of a hand-diagnostic unit lightly against her neck, nodding in a brief approval of its readings. "Much better. Incredible in fact. Anyone else would have died of any one of several of the wounds you received. Or that cracked skull."

"Am I dead or alive?"

"To Optheria?" Trag asked. "No official acknowledgment of the attack has been broadcast. The whole episode has been extremely embarrassing for the government."

"I should bloody hope so! Wait till I see Ampris!"

"Not in that frame of mind, you won't," Trag assured her, repressively stern.

"No more of us for the time being," Hauness said, nodding significantly to the others. "Unless Nahia . . ."

Killashandra closed her eyes for a moment, since moving her head seemed inadvisable. But she opened them to warn Hauness from disturbing Lars, who was still kneeling by the bed. He no longer wept but pressed her hand against his cheek as if he would never release it. The door closed quietly behind the others.

"So you and Olav can just walk into the scout ship?" she asked softly, trying to lighten his penitence.

"Not quite," he said with a weak chuckle, but, still holding her hand, he straightened up, leaning forward, toward her, on his elbows. His face looked bleached of tan, lines of anxiety and fear aging him. "Trag and my father have combined their wits—and I'm to be arrested by the warrant Trag has. Don't worry," and he patted her hands as she reacted apprehensively, remembering Trag's remarks about using the warrant. "Carefully worded, the warrant will charge me with a lot of heinous crimes that weren't actually committed by me, but which will keep Ampris and Torkes happy in anticipation of the dire punishment which the Federated Courts dispense for crimes of such magnitude."

Killashandra grabbed tightly at his hands, ignoring the spasm of pain across her chest in her fear for him. "I don't like the idea, Lars, not one little bit."

"Neither my father nor Trag are likely to put me in jeopardy, Killa. We've managed a lot while you were sleeping it off. When we're sure that the scout ship is about to arrive, Trag will confer with Ampris and Torkes, confronting them with his suspicions about me—in your delirium you inadvertently blew the gaff. Trag is not about to let such a desperate person as me escape unpunished. He has held his counsel to prevent my escaping justice."

"There's something about this plan that alarms me."

"I'd be more alarmed if I had to stay behind," Lars said with a droll grin. "Trag won't give the Elders time to interfere, and they'll be unable to protest a Federal Warrant when a Federation scout ship is collecting me and you and Trag. The beauty part is that the scout's the wrong shape to use the shuttle port facility. Its security arrangements require open-space landing anyhow. That way my father has a chance of boarding her."

"I see." The scheme did sound well-planned, and yet some maggot of doubt niggled at Killashandra—but her unease could well arise from her poor state of health. "How did Olav get invited here?"

"He'd been called in by the Elders on an administrative detail. Why so few islanders attend concerts!" Lars had regained considerable equilibrium and he rose from his knees, still holding her hand, to sit beside her on the bed.

"Who did attack me, Lars?"

"Some desperate people whose families and friends had been scooped up by that search and seize. If only I'd been free to get into the marketplace, Olver would have warned me of the climate of the City. We'd have known not to let you walk about."

"As Corish and I left the Facility, a woman who gave me such a look of hatred—"

"You were spotted long before she saw you, Sunny, driving down from the Conservatory. If only I'd been with you . . ."

"Don't fret about *ifs*, Lars Dahl! A few aches and pains achieved what the best laid plans might have failed to do."

Lars's face was a study in shocked indignation.

"Do you know how badly you were hurt? Hauness wasn't kidding when he said you could have died from any one of those wounds, let alone *all* of them together." He held her hand in a crushing grip. "I thought you were dead when Corish brought you back. I . . ." A sudden look of embarrassment rippled across his stern face. "The one time you really needed a bodyguard, I wasn't there!"

"As you can see, it takes a lot to kill a crystal singer."

"I noticed, and don't wish to ever again."

Unwittingly he had reminded them both of the inescapable fact that their idyll was nearly over. Killashandra couldn't bear to think of it and quickly evaded further discussion of that.

"Lars," she said plaintively, "at the risk of appearing depressingly basic, I'm hungry!"

Lars stared at her in consternation for a moment but he accepted her evasion and his understanding smile began to replace the sadness in his eyes.

"So am I." Lars leaned forward to kiss her, gently at first and then with an urgency that showed Killashandra the depths of his apprehension for her. Then, with a spring in his step and a jaunty set to his shoulders, he went in search of food.

Killashandra did have to endure the official apologies and insincere protestations of the Elders, all nine of them. She made the obligatory responses, consoling herself with the thought that their days were numbered, and she would shorten that number as much as possible. She pretended to be far weaker than she actually was, for once the symbiont began its work, her recovery was markedly swift. But, for official visits, she managed to assume the appearance of debility so that her convalescence had to be supervised by Nahia and Hauness, skilled medical practitioners that they were. This gave the conspirators ample time to plan an orderly and discreet exodus of people in jeopardy from Elderly tyrannies.

Olav had smuggled his miniature detector unremarked into the Conservatory as a piece of Hauness's diagnostic equipment. At first they had been bitterly disappointed when it responded to Lars's proximity, despite his pockets being full of white crystal shards. If Trag approached with Lars, the device remained silent, so Killashandra's theory that crystal resonance confused the detector was correct. But her resonance was gone and, with the imminent arrival of the scout ship, there would be no chance for Trag to usher a few refugees past the security curtain at the shuttle port arch.

Fortunately Lars also remembered that Killashandra had disrupted the monitors by singing the crystal fragments. These, resonating discordantly as the wearer hummed, fooled the detector. It was then only a matter of experimentation to discover just what quantity of crystal provided adequate shielding. Perfect pitch was actually a handicap, the more out-of-tune the note, the more the white crystal reacted, and deluded the detector.

A week after the attack, Olav had no further excuse to stay at the Conservatory, and left, it was said, for the islands. He had been able to convince the Elders of his determination to send more islanders to the public concerts. Actually, he stayed in the City and made a few minor but important alterations to his appearance. The next day, he reported to Hauness

and Nahia in Killashandra's suite, bearing documents that proved him to
be the qualified empath whom Hauness and Nahia had drafted from their
clinic to attend Killashandra. Now that Killashandra was recovering, they
wished to return to their other patients in Ironwood.

"Nahia's the one who ought to be leaving," Lars had bitterly objected. "She's the most vulnerable of us all."

"No, Lars," Trag had said. "She is needed here, and she needs to
be here for reasons which you might not understand but for which I esteem her."

Trag's unstinted approval of the woman did much to placate Lars but
he told Killashandra that, in leaving, he keenly felt himself the traitor.

"Then come back with the Revision Force," she said, more than a little irritated by Lars's self-reproach on this and other issues. She immediately regretted the suggestion at the look of relief in Lars's face. But it was a
solution which could resolve many of Lars's doubts, especially when she
knew he loved his home world and would be happy enough sailing the
Pearl Fisher around the islands. She was somewhat relieved that Lars
would be happy on Optheria once the government had been changed.
"The Federation will need people with leadership potential. Trag says it
usually takes a full decade before a new provisional government is appointed, much less ratified by the Federation. You might even end up a
bureaucrat."

Lars snorted derisively. "That's the most unlikely notion you've had.
Not that I wouldn't like to get back here unprejudiced. I'd like to make
sure the change is going to be beneficial."

"And ensure that you had official permission to sail about in your
beloved islands." She managed to keep the bitterness out of her voice for
she could think of many things that a man with Lars's abilities and talents
could do, once free to move about the galaxy. It rankled that her body was
not sufficiently mended to add that argument to verbal ones. Lars was
treating her as if she were fragile. He was gentle and affectionate. His caresses, though frequent, were undemanding, leaving her frustrated. He
was so solicitous of her comfort that she was frequently tempted to wreak a
bit of violence on him. Although her jagged, red scars looked more painful
than they were, a lover as considerate as Lars had always been would be reluctant to approach her. The symbiont couldn't work fast enough for her.
But would it have repaired her *before* the scout ship brought them to the
Regulus Federation Base? She tried to overcome her desire for Lars and to
ignore the fact that time was running out for them both.

It was too soon and not soon enough when Mirbethan communicated
the imminent arrival of the scout ship, the CS *914*. Then she was called
upon to witness Trag's confrontation of Lars, in the presence of the astonished, and delighted, Elders Ampris and Torkes as the Guildmember, imposing in his righteous indignation and wrath, accused Lars Dahl of
infamous acts against the person of Killashandra Ree, and displayed the

Federal Warrant. Against Killashandra's loud cries of distress and disillusionment over her erstwhile lover's felonies, Ampris and Torkes struggled to contain their exultation over the arrest.

Trag's timing was superb and his manner so daunting that, with the Federal scout ship landed in the shuttle port valley, the Elders were left with no option but to permit the arrest and the deportation of their erring citizen. There was no doubt they were delighted, though deprived of the joy of punishing him, that the Federal justice due to be meted out to Lars Dahl would be far more severe than their Charter allowed them. Among the others vindicated by this unexpected climax was Security Officer Blaz, who clamped restraints on Lars's wrists with undisguised satisfaction.

What was supposed to have been a dignified farewell to their auspicious guests was hastily cancelled by Ampris, waving off the various instructors and senior students gathered on the steps of the Conservatory. Presently only Torkes, Mirbethan, Pirinio, and Thyrol were left.

Lars was strong-armed by Blaz into the waiting transport and it was difficult for Killashandra not to react to that treatment. Or deliver an appropriate parting shaft at the officious Blaz. But she was supine on the grav-stretcher guided by the disguised Olav and she had to concentrate on looking ill enough to require the services of an empath.

When Torkes stepped forward, obviously about to say something which would nauseate her, she forestalled him. "Don't jostle me when you load this floating mattress," she irritably warned Olav.

"Yes, let us not unnecessarily prolong our leave-taking," Trag said, giving the float a little push into the ground transport. "Scout pilots are notoriously short-tempered. Is the prisoner secure?" Trag's voice was the cold of glaciers as he glanced back at his prisoner, and Security Captain Blaz growled a reassurance. He had insisted on personally turning over this felon to the scout captain.

It was a silent journey, only Blaz enjoying his circumstances. Lars affected an appropriate dejected, fearful pose, not looking up from his hand restraints. From her position, Killashandra could see nothing but the upper stories of buildings and then sky, and they passed so fluidly she experienced motion sickness; she spoke severely to her symbiont until the reaction disappeared. Trag was staring stolidly out the window on the seat in front of her, and Olav was beyond her view. Rather an ignominious departure to all appearances. And yet, a triumphant one, considering what she and Trag and Lars had accomplished.

She contented herself with that reflection but it was with considerable relief that she saw the spires of the shuttle port appear, approach, and pass by as the transport was driven to the landing site of the scout ship. It was on its tail fins, ready for take-off; the mobile scout pilot waited for her passengers by the lift on the ground.

"There is no way I am going up that," and Killashandra pointed to the lift, "in this," and she slapped the grav-stretcher.

"Guildmember, you have been—" Olav began firmly.

"Don't 'Guildmember' me, medic," she said, raising up on her elbow. "Just get me off this thing. I'll leave this planet as I got on it, on my own two feet."

The transport stopped and Trag and Olav were quick to get her float out.

"Chadria, Scout Pilot of the CS *914*," said the trim woman in the Scout Service blue, walking forward to lend an unobtrusive hand. "My ship's name is Samel!" A smile lurked in her eyes but fled as Security Officer Blaz hauled Lars unceremoniously out of the transport and roughly propelled him to the lift.

"Where do I stow the prisoner, Scout Pilot Chadria?" he said in an ill-tempered growl.

"Nowhere until the Guildmembers are settled," Chadria replied. She turned to Killashandra. "If you're more comfortable on the float—"

"I am not!" Killashandra swung her legs over the side of the float, and Olav hastily adjusted its height so that she only had to step off it to be erect. Lars moved forward but was hauled back to Blaz's side and she could see him tensing in rebellion. "Trag!" The man supported her around the waist. "Permission to come aboard, Chadria, Samel!"

"Permission granted," scout and ship replied simultaneously.

The unexpected male voice, apparently issuing about his feet, startled an exclamation out of Blaz. A small, superior smile twitched at Lars's lips, hastily erased but reassuring to Killashandra.

She let herself be conducted to the lift by Trag and the medic, wondering how Olav would be able to stay if Blaz continued in his officious manner. There was no hint of uncertainty in either man's face so she decided to let them worry about such a minor detail. She remembered to salute the ship as she stepped aboard.

"Welcome, Killashandra, Trag. And you, gentle medic." The ship spoke in a baritone voice which rippled with good humor. "If you will be seated, Chadria will be up in just a moment."

"How are we going to get rid of Blaz? And keep Olav?" Killashandra whispered urgently to Trag.

"Watch," Samel said and one of the screens above the pilot's console lit up, displaying a view of the lift.

"I'll take control of this fellow, now," Chadria was saying as she pulled a wicked little hand-weapon from her belt. "I was told to secure quarters aboard. And there's nothing he can do to escape a scout ship, Officer. Get on there now, you."

The observers could see the conflict in Blaz's face but Chadria had pushed Lars onto the lift and stepped on the platform with her back to Blaz so that there was no room for him to accompany them, and no way to dispute the arbitrary decision with someone's back. That maneuver confused Blaz just long enough. The lift ascended quickly, Blaz watching uncertainly.

"Permission to board?" Lars said, grinning in at Killashandra.

"Granted, Lars Dahl!" Samel replied, and Chadria stepped beside Lars in the airlock, punching out control sequences. The lift collapsed and secured itself, the airlock door closed, Lars and Chadria stepped into the cabin while the inner door slid shut with a final metallic *thunk*. An alarm sounded.

On the ground, Blaz reacted to the claxon, suddenly aware that the medic was still on board and not quite sure if that was in order. The transport driver shouted at him as the ship's drive began to rumble above the noise of the take-off alarm, and Blaz had no recourse but to retreat to safety.

"Oh, that was well-done!" Killashandra cried and, finding her legs a bit unstable in reaction to the final moments of escape, she sank onto the nearby couch.

Trag thumbed the bar that released the restraints on Lars's wrists and Lars stumbled to enfold Killashandra in his arms.

"Everyone, take a seat," Chadria warned, sliding into the pilot's gimballed chair. "We were told to make it a fast exit," she added with a grin. "Okay, Sam, they're secure. Let's shake the dust!"

Chapter 25

Killashandra's complacency about their confrontation with the Federated Council on Regulus Base altered drastically as the CS *914* began its final approach to the landing strip. The building which housed the administrative offices for that sector of the Federated Sentient Planets covered an area slightly more than twenty klicks square.

Chadria cheerfully informed her passengers that there was as much again in subterranean levels as above ground, and some storage areas delved as much as a half a klick below Regulus's surface. Monorail lines connected the sprawling offices with the residential centers thirty and forty klicks away, for most of the workers preferred the nearby valleys and the many amenities available there. Regulus was a good post for everyone.

From a distance, the profile was awe inspiring. The random pattern of rectangular extrusions above the mass of the complex was silhouetted against the light green early-morning sky. Even Trag was impressed, a reaction which did nothing to assuage Killashandra's growing sense of doubt. She inched as close to Lars as possible and felt him return the pressure in an answering need for tactile reassurance. But he was nowhere near as tense as she was. Perhaps she was just hypersensitive due to her recent ordeal. As they approached, the building dominated the landscape to the exclusion of any other features on Chinneidigh Plain. Skimmers could then be seen landing and taking off at the myriad entrances, each embellished with official symbols depicting the department housed within.

"We're cleared to land at the Judicial Sector," Chadria said, swinging about in her gimballed chair. "Don't look so worried." She grinned up at the three. "They don't leave you hanging about here for weeks on end. You'll know by midday. It's anticipation that gets to you, and waiting!"

Killashandra knew that Chadria meant to reassure them, for both brain and brawn partners had been excellent hosts, with stories scurrilous and amusing, and stocks of exotic foods and beverages in the scout ship's well-stocked larder to tempt every taste. With exquisite tact, the others had left Killashandra and Lars to enjoy their own company for the week in which the CS *914* hurtled from one corner of the sector to the Regulan planet at its center. Courtesy, however, had dictated to both Lars and Killashandra that they join the others at mealtimes and for evening conversations, and the occasional rehearsals of Lars's defense against the warrant's charges. Trag and Olav had begun a friendly competition over a tri-dimensional maze game which could last up to a day between well-matched players. Chadria and Samel had teamed up against the two men in another contest, one of multiple-choice, which could be expanded to include Lars and Killashandra whenever they chose to play.

There was a strange dichotomy about that journey: the tug between learning more of each other's minds and sating their bodies and senses sufficiently to cushion the imminent parting. On the final day, it was more than Killashandra or Lars could endure to make love: instead they sat close together, one pair of hands linked, playing the maze game with an intensity that bordered the irrational.

Now Chadria swung back to the screens as their progress to the landing site closed with the linear diagram Samel displayed on the situation screen. Killashandra could not restrain the small gasp nor her instinct to clutch at Lars's hands as the two positions matched and the scout ship settled to the ground.

"Here we are," Samel said in a tactfully expressionless tone. "Ground transport is approaching. Glad to have had you all aboard and I hope that Chadria and I will meet you again."

Chadria lifted her long frame from the chair, shaking hands with each one in turn, clasping Killashandra's with an encouraging smile and giving Lars an impish grin before she kissed his cheek in farewell. "Good luck, Lars Dahl! You'll come out on top! Feel it in my bones."

"Me, too," Samel added, and opened the two lock doors.

Killashandra wished that she felt as positive. Then, suddenly, there was no way to evade the inevitable. They picked up their carisaks and filed out. Trag and Olav took the lift down first, permitting Lars and Killashandra a few moments' privacy.

Killashandra didn't know what she had expected but the ground transport was a four-seat skimmer, remote controlled, the purple-gold-and-blue emblem of the FSP Judiciary Branch unobtrusively marking the door panel. She took in a deep breath, looking off to the massive tower of the entrance. As she had done for several days, she repeated to herself that "justice would prevail," that the much edited wording of the warrant would support their hopes. And that the disclosure of subliminal conditioning would result in the swift dispatch of a revisionary force to overthrow the Elders' tyranny on Optheria.

But one Killashandra Ree, one-time resident of the planet Fuerte, barely four years a member of the Heptite Guild, had had no encounters at all with Galactic Justice, and feared it. She had never heard or known anyone who had been either defendant or plaintiff at an FSP court. Her ignorance rankled and her apprehension increased.

Silently the four settled into the skimmer and it puffed along on its short return journey. It did not, as Killashandra half expected, stop at the imposing entrance. It ducked into an aperture to one side, down a brightly lit subterranean tunnel, and came to a gentle stop at an unmarked platform.

There a man built on the most generous of scales, uniformed in the Judicial Livery, awaited them. In a state of numbness, Killashandra emerged.

"Killashandra Ree," the man said, identifying her with a nod, not friendly but certainly not hostile. "Lars Dahl, Trag Morfane, and Olav Dahl." He nodded politely as he identified each person. "My name is Funadormi, Bailiff for Court 256 to which this case is assigned. Follow me."

"I am Agent Dahl, number—"

"I know," the man said pleasantly enough. "Welcome back from exile. This way." He stepped aside to allow them to enter the lift which had opened in the wall of the platform. "It won't take long."

Killashandra tried to convince herself that his manner was reassuring if his appearance was daunting. He towered above them and both Lars and Trag were tall men. Killashandra and Olav were not many millimeters shorter but she had never felt so diminished by sheer physical proportions. The lift moved, stopped, and its door panel slid open to a corridor, stretching out in either direction, pierced by atriums with trees and other vegetation. Gardens seemed an odd decorative feature of a Judicial building but did nothing to buoy Killashandra's spirits. She rearranged her fierce grasp on Lars's fingers, hoping that Funadormi did not see it and that he did, to show this human representative of the Courts that Lars Dahl had her total support.

Funadormi gestured to the left and then halted their progress at the second door on the left, which bore the legend "Grand Felony Court 256."

Killashandra reeled against Lars Dahl, Trag behind him placed a reassuring hand on his shoulder, and Olav straightened his lean frame against the imminent testing of a scheme that had been entered rather lightheartedly.

Funadormi thumbed open the panel and entered. It was not the sort of chamber Killashandra would have recognized as judicial. She did recognize the psychological testing equipment for what it was, and the armbands on the chair beside it. Fourteen comfortable seats faced that chair and the wall screens and a terminal which bore the Judicial Seal. A starred flag of the Federated Sentient Planets bearing the symbols indicating the nonhuman sentient species was displayed in the corner.

The door panel *whooshed* shut behind them and Funadormi indicated that they were to be seated. He faced the screen, squared his shoulders, and began the proceedings.

"Bailiff Funadormi in Grand Felony Court 256, in the presence of the accused, Lars Dahl, remanded citizen of the planet Optheria; the arresting citizen, Trag Morfane of the Heptite Guild; the alleged victim, Killashandra Ree, also of the Heptite Guild; and witness for the accused, Olav Dahl, Agent Number AS-4897/KTE, present at this sitting. Accused is restrained under Federal Sentient Planet Warrant A-1090088-O-FSP55558976. Permission to proceed."

"Permission is granted," replied a contralto voice, deep and oddly

ANNE MCCAFFREY

maternal, definitely reassuring. Killashandra could feel her muscles unlock from the tenseness in which she had been holding herself. "Will the accused Lars Dahl be seated in the witness chair?"

Lars gave her hand a final squeeze, smiled with a cocky wink at her, rose, and took the seat. The Bailiff attached the arm cuffs and stepped back.

"You are charged with the willful abduction of Heptite Guild member Killashandra Ree, malicious invasion of the individual's right to Privacy, felonious assault, premeditated interference with her contractual obligation to her Guild, placing her in physical jeopardy as to shelter and sustenance, deprivation of independent decision and freedom of movement, and fraudulent representation for purposes of extortion. How do you plead, Lars Dahl?" The voice managed to convey an undertone of regretful compassion, and an invitation to confide and confess. Highly sensitized to every nuance, Killashandra wondered if, by some bizarre freak, the Judicial Branch might actually be guilty of a subtle use of subliminal manipulation in that persuasive voice.

"Not guilty on all counts," Lars answered quietly, and firmly, as he had rehearsed.

And, Killashandra reassured herself, he was not, by the very wordage that Trag and Olav had cleverly employed.

"You may testify on your own behalf." The request was issued in a stern, uncompromising tone.

Although Killashandra listened avidly to every word Lars said in rebuttal and in explanation, tried to analyze the terse questions put to him by the Judicial Monitor, she was never able to recall the next few hours in much detail.

He was completely candid, as he had to be, to discharge the accusations. He explained how Elder Ampris, superior to Lars Dahl, student in the Conservatory and as a ruling Elder of the Optherian Council, had approached him, citing the dilemma about Killashandra's true identity and the request to wound her, resolving the quandary. His reward was the promise of reconsidering Lars's composition. The point that Lars had been coerced to perform a personally distasteful act by an established superior was accepted by the Court. To the charge that the abduction was premeditated, Lars explained that he had come upon the victim unexpectedly in an unprotected environment and acted spontaneously. He had, it was true, rendered her unconscious but without malice. She had not even suffered a bruise. She had been carefully conveyed to a place of security, with tools and instructions to provide daily food and shelter, so that she had been in no physical jeopardy. As she had left the premises of her own volition, she obviously had not been denied independence of decision and movement. He had not fraudently represented himself as her rescuer for she had not required rescue, and she had requested his continued presence as a safeguard against further physical violence from any source on Optheria. He had not premeditated any interference on her contractual obligation to her Guild for he had not only assisted her in repairing the damaged manual, her preemptive assignment, but he had also provided her with conclusive evidence to resolve the secondary assignment. He therefore restated his innocence.

After Lars gave his testimony, Killashandra was called to the chair and had to exercise the greatest degree of control to suppress signs of the stress she felt. It didn't help to know that the sensitive psych equipment would record even the most minute tremors and uncertainties of its subject. That was its function and the results which the Monitor then analyzed against the psychological profile of each witness. Objectively she was pleased that her voice didn't quaver as she supported Lars's testimony on each count, managing to publicly absolve him from felonious assault as he was, in fact, acting even when he abducted her in her best interests, contractually and personally. She kept her answers concise and unemotional. Subjectively she had never been so terrified of any experience. And the equipment would record that as well.

Trag and Olav had their turns in the witness chair. Each time the subliminal manipulation was mentioned, there was significant pause in the flow of questions, though there was no hint of how this information was being received and analyzed by the Judicial Monitor, since, in point of law, this part of everyone's testimony was irrelevant to the case at hand.

When Olav resumed his seat between Trag and Lars, the Bailiff approached the screen. They could all see the activity of the terminal but the pattern of its flashing lights disclosed nothing. Killashandra, holding Lars's hand, jumped an inch above her chair when the contralto voice began its summation.

"With the exception of felonious assault, the charges against the accused, Lars Dahl, are dismissed." Killashandra swallowed. "Criminal intent is not apparent but disciplinary action is required by law. Lars Dahl, you are remanded into the custody of the Judicial Branch, pending disposition of the disciplinary action. You are further remanded for examination of the charge of subliminal manipulation against the Elders of Optheria. Olav Dahl, you are seconded to assist these investigations, which have now been initiated. Trag Morfane, Killashandra Ree, have you anything to add to your recorded testimonies on the charge of subliminal manipulation by the Elders of Optheria?"

Having already been as candid as possible, neither crystal singer could expand on the information already on record. And Killashandra did not quite understand the matter of disciplinary action for Lars and the remand orders.

"Then this session of the Grand Felony Court of Regulus Sector Federation is closed." The traditional *crack* of wood against wood ended the hearing.

Perplexed by the legal formulas, Killashandra turned to Lars and his father.

"Are you free, or what?" she demanded.

"I'm not quite sure," Lars said with a nervous laugh. "It can't mean much. Everything else was dismissed, wasn't it?" He looked to Olav and was sobered by his father's solemn expression.

"He has been remanded," the Bailiff explained kindly, taking Lars by the arm. "I interpret the judgment to mean that the Court has dismissed all charges but Lars Dahl's physical assault on you in the matter of your abduction. Disciplinary action is always short term. On the second remand charge, the Court requires further discussion of the allegations about the use of subliminal conditioning by the Optherian government. If these are proved correct, then it is likely that the disciplinary action will be suspended. I can give you hard copy of the precedents involved, indeed of the entire trial, if you wish." When Lars nodded a perplexed affirmation, "Then I shall program them for your quarters. If you gentlemen will come with me?"

A panel at the back of the seating area opened and it was toward this that Funadormi gestured Lars and his father.

"Come with you?" Lars cried, trying to break from the Bailiff's grip.

Shock and surprise briefly immobilized Killashandra and before she could make a move to reach Lars, the Bailiff, securely holding her lover, had him nearly to the open door.

"Wait! Please wait!" she screamed, falling over the chairs in her haste.

"You two have been dismissed. Justice has been served! Arrangements for your transport have been made and the ground vehicle programmed to take you to the appropriate site."

"But—Lars!" Killashandra's cry of protest was made to the immense back of the Bailiff which was disappearing through the aperture, totally eclipsing Lars. Olav hurried anxiously after, adding his protests. *"Lars Dahl!"* she screamed, every fear alerted to his unexpected departure. The panel closed with a final *thuck* just as Killashandra reached it.

"Justice has been served?" she shrieked, beating the wall with impotent fists. "What justice? What justice? LARS DAHL! Couldn't they let us say good-bye? Is that justice?" She wheeled on Trag who was trying to silence her tactless accusations. "You and your fool-proof verbiage. They've charged him after all. I want to know why and what does disciplinary action mean for a man who's put himself on the line for a whole benighted fardling useless planet?"

"Killashandra Ree," and both crystal singers turned in astonishment as the voice issued unexpectedly from the wall. "During your evidence, your psychological reactions exhibited extreme agitation and apprehension—unusual when compared to your official profile—which have been interpreted as fear of the accused, despite your generous testimony to his actions against you. Disciplinary action will prevent the accused from any future acts of felonious assault."

"WHAT?" Killashandra could not believe what she had heard. "Of all the ridiculous interpretations! I love the man! I *love* him, do you hear, I was frantic with worry *for* him, not against him. Call him back. There's been a dreadful miscarriage of justice."

"Justice has been served, Killashandra Ree. You and Trag Morfane are scheduled to leave this Court and this building immediately. Transport awaits."

The silence after that impersonal order provoked a thunder of tinnitus in her skull.

"I don't believe this, Trag. This can't be right. How do we appeal?"

"I do not believe that we can, Killashandra. This is the Federal Court. We have no right of appeal. If there is one available to Lars, I am certain that Olav will invoke it. But we have no further right. Come. Lars will be taken care of."

"That's what I'm fardling afraid of," Killashandra cried. "I know what penalties and disciplines the Judicial Branch can use. I had Civics like any other school-child. I can't go, Trag. I can't leave him. Not like this. Not without any sort of a . . ." Tears so choked her that she could not continue and a sudden disastrous inability to stand made her wobble so that Trag only just kept her from falling.

She didn't realize at first that Trag was supporting her out of the room. When she found them in the hall, she tried to wrench herself out of Trag's grasp but there was someone else by then, assisting Trag and between the two of them, she was wrestled into the lift. She struggled, screaming imprecations and threats, and although she heard Trag protesting as sternly as he could, she was put in padded restraints. The ignominy of such a humiliating expedient combined with fear, disappointment, and her recent physical ordeal sent Killashandra into a trembling posture of aggrieved and contained fury.

By the time they reached the shuttle transport to the Regulus transfer moon, she had exhausted her scant store of energy and crouched in the seat, sullen and silent, too proud to ask for her release from the restraints. She let Trag and the medic lead her where they would, and didn't protest when they undressed her for immersion in a radiant fluid tank. Legitimate protest and recourse denied her, she submitted to everything then, despairing and listless. Over and over she reviewed her moments in the witness chair, when her body, the body which had loved and been loved so by Lars, had betrayed them both with false testimony. She was appalled at that treachery, and obsessed by the horrifying guilt that she, herself, her anxieties and idiotic presentiments, had condemned Lars on the one count which had not been dismissed by the Court. She could never forgive herself. Somehow, sometime, she would be able to face Lars, and beg his forgiveness. That she promised herself.

All the way back to Ballybran, she said not a single word to anyone, nodding or shaking her head in answer to the few questions that were put directly to her by officials. Trag supervised her meals, immersed her in radiant fluid whenever such facilities were available, and remained by her side during her wakeful hours. If he resented her silence or interpreted it as an accusation, he gave no indication of regret, remorse, or penitence. She was too immersed in her obsession with the outrageous circumstances of Lars's betrayal to try to explain the complexities of her depression.

By the time she and Trag had completed the long journey to Ballybran's surface, Killashandra was completely restored to physical health. She paused only long enough in her quarters to check, as she had begun to do toward the end of the trip, with galactic updates. There was no further word on the Optherian situation beyond the original bulletin announcing the arrival of Revision troops on the planet to "correct legislative anomalies." She refused to consider what that statement might mean for Lars. Dumping her carisak, she changed into a shipsuit. Then she headed for the Fisherman's bailiwick and, with a voice grown gruff from disuse, demanded her sonic cutter. While waiting for him to retrieve it from storage, she checked with Meteorology and, with a twinge of satisfaction, learned that the forecast predicted a settled period of weather for the next nine days.

She backed her sled out of its rack herself, though she could see the wild protesting signals of the duty officer trying to abort her precipitous departure. As soon as she was clear of the Hangar, she poured on the power and, in an undeviating line, fled for the Ranges.

It was all part of the miserable web of ironic coincidence that she found black crystal again in the deep, sunless ravine in which she had hoped to bury herself and her grief for the reason and manner of her parting with Lars Dahl.

Epilogue

Stolidly Killashandra watched, arms folded across her breasts, as Enthor reverently unpacked the nine black crystal shafts.

"Interstellar, at the least, Killashandra," he said, blinking his eyes back to normal vision as he stepped back to sigh over the big crystals. "And this is all from that vein you struck last year?"

Killashandra nodded. Not much moved her to words these days. Working the new claim, she had quickly recouped her losses on the Optherian contract; Heptite rules and regs had required her to part with a percentage of that fee to Trag. She accepted that as passively as she had accepted everything since that day in Court on Regulus. Not even Rimbol had been able to penetrate her apathy, though he and Antona continued their attempts. Lanzecki had spoken pleasantly to her after her first return from the Ranges, complimented her on the new black crystal vein but their early relationship could never have been revived even if Lanzecki had persisted.

She didn't see him. She saw no one but Lars, a laughing Lars, garland-wreathed, his blue eyes gleaming, teeth white in his tanned face, his bronzed body poised on the deck of the *Pearl Fisher*. She woke sometimes, sure she felt his hand on her hip, heard his voice in the whisper of the wind in the deep ravine, or in the tenor of warming crystal at noon, when the sun finally touched the cliff. She made two attempts to succumb to crystal thrall but each time the symbiont had somehow pulled her back. Not even that enchantment was powerful enough to break through her emotions, obsessed as she was by the guilty betrayal of her body in the witness chair on Regulus.

She had kept informed of the situation on Optheria and often, on the nights brilliant with crystal song, she composed letters to Lars, asking to be forgiven that betrayal. She wrote imaginary letters to Nahia and Hauness, knowing that they would be compassionate, and intercede for her with Lars. In her better moments, common sense dictated that Lars would not have held that bizzare psychoanalysis against her for he, of them all, knew how much she treasured and admired him. But he had not heard her impassioned plea to the Court, and she doubted if "I love you" had been included in the hard copy of the hearing transcript. And he had other plans for the rest of his life.

She frequently entertained the notion of returning to Optheria to see how he was getting on, even if she never made actual contact with him. He might have found another woman with whom he could share his life on Optheria. Sometimes she returned from the Ranges, full of determination to end her wretched half-life, one way or another. She had more than enough credit for a fiercely expensive galactic call: ironically through some of the black crystal she had herself cut. But would she reach Lars on Optheria? Maybe, once he had completed that disciplinary action and his subordination to the Federal investigation of Optheria, he had found another channel for his abilities and energies. Once he discovered his freedom to travel the stars, they might have won him from his love of the sea.

At her most rational, she recognized all the ifs, ands, and buts as procrastinations. Yet, it was not exactly an unwillingness to chance her luck that restrained her: it was a deep and instinctive "knowing" that she must remain in this period of suspension for a while yet. That she had to wait. When the time was right, action would follow logically. She settled down to wait, and perfected the art.

"You're in early, too, you know," Enthor was saying to her. "Storm warnings only just gone out."

"Aren't those good enough?" Killashandra asked. "No need to risk life and limb, is there?"

"No, no," Enthor hastily assured her.

Killashandra had, in fact, answered the storm warning her symbiont had given her. She was used to listening to it because it so often proved the most accurate sense she had.

"You've enough here to spend a year on Maxim," Enthor went on with a sly sideways glance. "You haven't gone off in a long time, Killashandra. You should, you know."

Killashandra shrugged her shoulders, glancing impassively at a credit line that would once have made her chortle in triumph. "I don't have enough resonance to have to leave," she said tonelessly. "I'll wait. Thanks, Enthor."

"Killa, if talking would help . . ."

She looked down at the light hand the old Sorter had put on her arm, mildly surprised at the contact. His unexpected solicitude, the concern on his lined face nudged the thick shell which encased her mind and spirit. She smiled slightly as she shook her head. "Talking wouldn't help. But you were kind to offer."

And he had been. Sorters and singers were more often at loggerheads than empathetic. The northeaster which her symbiont had sensed swept a fair number of singers in from the Ranges to the safety of the Complex. The lift, the hall, the corridors were crowded but she wended her way through, and no one spoke to her. She didn't exist for herself so she didn't exist for them.

The screen in her quarters directed her to contact Antona. There usually was a message from the medical chief waiting for her. Antona kept trying to make a deeper contact.

"Ah, Killa, please come down to the Infirmary, will you?"

"I'm not due for another physical?"

"No. But I need you down here."

Killashandra frowned. Antona looked determined and waited for Killashandra's acquiescence.

"Let me change." Killashandra brushed at the filthy blouse of her shipsuit.

"I'll even give you time to bathe."

Killashandra nodded, broke the connection and, unfastening the suit as she made her way to the hygiene room, switched on the taps. Though once—fresh in from the Ranges—she might have done, she didn't luxuriate in the steaming water. She made a quick but thorough bath, and put on the first clean clothes she found. Her hair, close cropped for convenience, dried by the time she reached the Infirmary Level. Her nostrils flared against the smell of sickness and fever, and the muffled sounds reminded her of her initial visit to Antona's preserve. A new class must be passing through adjustment to the Ballybran symbiont.

Antona came out of her office, her color high with suppressed excitement.

"Thank you, Killa. I've a Milekey Transition here whom I'd like you to talk to, reassure him. He's positive there's something wrong." Her words came out in a rush, as she dragged Killashandra down the hall, and thrust her through the door she opened. Impassively, Killashandra noted the number: it was the same room she had so briefly tenanted five years before. Then the occupant rose from the bed, smiling.

"Killa!"

She stared at Lars Dahl, unable to believe the evidence of her eyes for she had seen his phantom so often. But Antona had brought her here so this vision had to be real. Avidly she noted each of the tiny changes in him: the lack of tan, the gauntness of his shoulders under the light shirt, the new lines in his face, the loss of that twinkle of gaiety that had been a trademark of his open, handsome expression. He had subtly aged: no, matured. And the process had brought him distinction and an indefinable air of strength and the patience of strength and knowledge.

"Killa?" The smile had dropped from his face, his half-raised hand fell to his side as she failed to respond.

Imperceptibly she began to shake her head, and tentatively, certain that he would vanish if she admitted to herself that he was flesh, bone, and blood, her hands began to lift from her sides. Inside her body the cold knot into which all emotion and spirit had been reduced began to expand, like a warm draught through her veins. Her mind reverberated with one exultant conclusion: he was there, and he wouldn't be if he hadn't forgiven her.

"Lars?" Her voice was a whisper of disbelief but sufficient reassurance to propel him across the intervening space. Then, as if he found their reunion as incredible as she, he folded her carefully into his arms.

Momentarily she lacked the strength to return the embrace but burrowed her head into the curve of his shoulder and neck, inhaling the smell of him, and exhaling into the tears she had kept bottled for the eternity in which they had been parted.

Lars swept her up in his arms, and carried her to the chair, where he cradled her, appalled at the wildness of her sobbing and comforting her with kisses, caresses, and strong embracings.

"That fardling machine that served justice was never told we were emotionally attached, the one piece of information that no one but us would have thought relevant," he said, releasing in talk the tension he had endured all through the process of getting to this point when he would be ready, and able, to meet her again. "Then Father found out what had happened and he moved the entire Department to revoke that judgment on the basis of misinterpretation of your psychological response. Poor sweet Sunny, so worried about me she messed us both up." To her surprise, he chuckled. "You didn't know that the only reason that disciplinary action was entered against me was the Court's attempt to satisfy what they took to be a suppressed desire for revenge in you. Justice was being served, blind as it was. Father finally reached a human in authority, swore blind to half a dozen psych-units that he himself had hand-fasted us on Angel Island and got the action revoked. D'you know, that Court Bailiff was a narding construct! No wonder I couldn't move when he grabbed me. Then, when we did understand our rights, Trag had already departed with you.

"I guess you were pretty upset."

At such a massive understatement of fact, she managed to nod, trying not to laugh at the absurdity, but she couldn't stop weeping. It had built up quite a head and it ought to prove conclusively to Lars, if he needed any, just how much she had missed him. She had waited so long to be in his arms, to hear his rich and pleasant tenor voice, and the sort of nonsense he was likely to speak. He could have been speaking gibberish and she'd have been content to listen. But he was also telling her the things she would have asked about him, what she needed to know to put some color in the past dreadful year.

"Then Father, Corish, and I spent two months processing material for the Council. Theach, Brassner, and Erutown had come out with Corish and they got assigned to the Revision Corps until someone in the Council took a closer look at the equations which Theach was idly calling up on his terminal." Lars smiled tenderly as he delicately blotted tears from her cheeks, then kissed her forehead for such an un-Killashandraish display of sentimentality. "So he landed on his feet, as usual. Five more people, including the brewmaster of Gartertown, whom you might remember," he added, tapping her nose as he teased, "got out on the next liner and are being resettled. What had worried Nahia and Hauness was what refugees would

do once they got off Optheria, but there seems to be a resettlement policy. Not that Optherians have all that many skills to offer the advanced
societies.

"Father and I got drafted to brief the actual Revision Force. You see,
right after that infamous hearing, several more agents were sent in to play
tourist during the Summer Festival. Good job we left some two-manuals
intact. They came back, reporting that they were subjected to blatant subliminal conditioning at public concerts in Ironwood, Bailey, Everton, and
Palamo. One thing Father and I emphasized was that the Revision Forces
had better wait until after The Festival or they'd have a bankrupt planet as
well as a disorganized one. So Optheria got its annual chance to acquire
revenue," and Lars grinned with great satisfaction, "and the Elders hadn't
twigged to the fact that no subliminal messages were going out on either of
the big Conservatory organs. Leaving the Mainlanders quite willing to accept anything said about them.

"When we've spare time, I've got some tapes of the actual landing
and the takeover. Four Elders had fatal seizures but Ampris, Torkes, and
Pentrom will answer to the Supreme Judiciary for their infamous, felonious, malicious, premeditated, and illegal manipulation of Optherian
loyalties.

"The Revision Forces are well installed now on Optheria . . ." He
looked out with the unfocused gaze of someone imagining a scene and was
briefly sad. He bent to kiss Killashandra again, noting that her tears had
abated and her breath was no longer taken in ragged gasps.

"Why didn't you go with them?"

"Oh, I was given many arguments why I should. Even a rather complimentary commission. Father returned, but I rather thought he wouldn't
leave Teradia for long. To my surprise, Corish went, and of course
Erutown and Brassner. I had other plans."

Killashandra shook her head in sad rebuke. "If I'd known what you
planned to do . . ." Her gesture included all that his presence in the Infirmary signified.

Lars hugged her tightly to him. "That's why I didn't mention them.
Besides," and he gave her a raffish look, "I hadn't really made up my
mind."

"How did Trag recruit you then?"

Lars raised his eyebrows in surprise. "He didn't. It is illegal to recruit
citizens for the highly dangerous Heptite Guild. Didn't you know? Candidly, my beloved Sunny, I was much impressed by Trag's integrity. It was
refreshing to find an honorable and trustworthy man. It was yourself who
did the recruiting, Killa. You were the embodiment of the undeniable advantages of being a crystal singer. Your vibrant youth, charm, invulnera-
bility, indefatigable energy, and resourcefulness. Then all those diversified
assignments, space travel, credit, not to mention the chance to see a Galaxy
I had been denied all my reckless youth—"

"You're mad." Vitality returned to Killashandra in the form of exasperation with his flamboyance, and such relief that she was once again in its presence. "Did you listen to one word I told you about the *dis*advantages? Didn't you pay attention to any of the details in the Full Disclosure, and that isn't the half of what does happen? As you'll find out. How could you be so blind?"

"None so blind as will not see, eh, Killa, my lovely Sunny? My pale Sunny, my beloved. Is there no sun on this planet that you are so wan?" He began to kiss her in a leisurely fashion. "I admit I did hesitate. Briefly." His eyes sparkled with his teasing. "Then I ran the entry on Ballybran itself. That decided me."

"Ballybran? Ballybran decided you?" Killashandra wriggled about in his arms, astounded. Not that she understood why she had such ambivalent reactions to his decision in the first place. He was here! How had she, and that conniving symbiont of hers, known that he would come? Because she didn't think that he wouldn't? Long absent, she felt the caress of crystal along her bones.

"Of course, Sunny. Now if you'd thought to mention earlier on that Ballybran has seas—"

"Seas?" Killashandra put a hand on his forehead. He must be feverish. "Seas!"

"All I've ever needed for perfect contentment is a tall ship and a star to sail her by." He held her as her temper began to rise, though she didn't know if he was mauling that obscure quotation or not. "And then, too, Ballybran has you, beloved Sunny!" His tenor voice dropped to an intense and passionate whisper, his eyes were an incredible brilliant blue, dominating her immediate vision. His arms encompassed her in a grip that reminded her of sun-warmed beaches and fragrant breezes and—"Show me, crystal singer, all that Ballybran has to offer me."

"Right now?"

Crystal Line

To my good friend
ELIZABETH MOON
teacher extraordinaire

Chapter 1

" ' **A**nd a star to steer her by,' " Killashandra Ree shouted to herself. Not that Lars Dahl could have heard her over the roar of the sea crashing against the bow of the *Angel* and the humming tension of the wind through the sail stays and across the sloop's mainsail.

She pointed to the first star of the evening in the darkening eastern sky and looked back at him to see if he was watching her. He was and nodded, his grin showing his very white teeth against his very tan skin. She was nearly as dark as he was after their circumnavigation of the main continent of Ballybran. But Lars always *looked* the complete captain, especially as he was standing now—his straddled legs bracing his long lean body on bare feet against the slant of the deck, strong hands firmly on the spokes of the wheel as he kept the *Angel* on the starboard tack under tight sail. The stiff breeze had ruffled his sun-bleached and salt-encrusted hair into a crest, much like the ritual headdress of a primitive religion.

They had plenty of sea room between the *Angel* and the jagged stones of the shore, but soon—all too quickly—they would reach the headland and the harbor that served the Heptite Guild headquarters.

Killashandra sighed. She almost didn't want this voyage to end—and yet this kind of voyage, therapeutic though it was, was not quite enough to ease the surge of crystal in her blood. Lars, not having sung as long as she, was in better shape; but they *had* to strike a good lode of crystal on this next trip into the Ranges and make enough to get off-world for Passover, which was, once again, nearly upon them. She devoutly hoped that their sled was repaired and ready for the Ranges.

Killashandra gritted her teeth, remembering the ignominy of having to be *rescued* when their sled had been buried by a rockslide! Hauling the crushed sled out of the Ranges had sliced a hefty hunk out of their credit balance. The crystal they had cut before the rockslide—which had been preserved in containers sturdy enough to resist collapse—had been sufficient to pay the huge repair bill, but there hadn't been enough credit left for them to take an off-world jaunt while the refit was being done. Once again the *Angel*, and the ever-challenging seas of Ballybran, had rescued them from the ping of crystal in their blood and the boredom of the Heptite Guild quarters.

But, by all the holies, Killashandra swore, this time they would sing good crystals—if they could possibly find that wretched lode again. Communication crystal was always valuable. If they could just cut one set quickly and without foul-ups! She wanted to get off-planet, and *this* time Lars was not going to talk her into going to yet another water world. There *were* other planets that could prove just as interesting. If she didn't get to choose once in a while, she might just seriously consider finding another partner. There was that stocky young redhead with weird eyes and a roguish grin—he reminded her of someone. She grimaced into the wind. The need for "reminders" was becoming more frequent for her. She had been singing crystal a long time now, and she knew very well indeed that her memory was eroding; what or how much she was losing she didn't know. She shrugged. As long as she didn't forget Lars Dahl, nor he her . . .

The *Angel* was nearly round the massive headland, and Killashandra could just see a slice of the eastern face of the great Heptite Guild cube that loomed large from all directions even though it was kilometers inland. The good mood that had sustained her abruptly altered.

"Back to the old grind," she muttered, anticipating Lars's next words.

"Back to the old grind, huh?" Lars bellowed, and she rolled her eyes and gave herself a shake.

Damn! *Knowing* what would come out of his mouth because they had shared so much, so intensely, was also beginning to irritate her. Or maybe all she and Lars needed was new stimulation. He found enough in their sea trips, but suddenly she realized that these were no longer enough for her. She grimaced again. How long was too long?

Lars bellowed for her attention, motioning for her to join him in the cockpit. With cautious but practiced steps she made her way astern, balancing against both wind and the slant of the *Angel*, turning her head against spray and the occasional high wave that broke across the deck.

As she came even with him, Lars reached out an arm and hooked her to his side, smiling down at her, contented in the elements of the sea/wind/ship, even if the end of their voyage was now in sight. She let herself be held against his long, strong body. She knew him so well! Was that such a bad thing for a crystal singer? Especially when memory began to erode? She glanced up at Lars's profile, elegant despite his peeling nose: Lars Dahl, the constant factor in her life!

"Hey, Killa, Lars! Lanzecki wants to see you soon as you dock," the harbor master yelled as he caught the line Killa deftly threw at him. He bent it neatly about the bollard as she ran aft, leaping lightly onto the marina slip, stern line in hand.

"Ya heard me?" he roared.

"Sure, I heard."

"We both heard," Lars added, grimacing at Killa.

Then, from long-established habit, Killashandra ducked down the companionway to check that everything in the cabin had been stowed properly, her chore as Lars had motored into the harbor. Satisfied, she threw their duffels topside, following more circumspectly with the bag of nondegradable trash.

Lars had shut down the engines and was checking the boom crutch to be sure it was properly secured.

"I'll keep an eye on the boat for ya," the harbor master said anxiously. Singers were not expected to dally when the Guild Master sent for them. This pair made their own rules, but he wasn't about to receive debits for their impudence.

"Sure you will, Pat," Lars said reassuringly as he checked the mast stays, "but old habits die hard. You'll run her in"—he jerked his head toward the spacious boathouse—"if there's a bad blow?"

Pat snorted, jamming his hands indignantly into his jacket pockets. "And when haven't I?"

Lars scooped his duffel bag off the deck and, leaping neatly from the *Angel* to the pier, gave Pat a grateful grin and a clout for the reassurance. Killashandra was a step behind him, adding her nod of appreciation before she matched Lars's stride for stride up the ramp to the wharf. They took the nearest scooter and turned its nose inland, to the Guild Complex.

By the time they had parked the scooter, entered the residential section of the Complex, and taken a lift to the executive floor, nineteen other people had informed them, in tones varying from irritated malice to sheer envy, that Lanzecki wanted to see them.

"Fardles!" Killashandra said, stressing the *f* sound against her teeth and lips. "What's up?"

"Hmmm, we are not in favor with our peer group," Lars said, his expression carefully bland.

"I've got a bad feeling," Killashandra muttered for his ears only.

Lars gave her a long searching look, just as the lift halted at the executive floor. "You think Lanzecki might have one of those choice little extra jobs for us?"

"Uh-huh!"

Then, in step, they swung left to Lanzecki's office. The first thing Killashandra noticed was that Trag was not in sight. A slender man rose from Trag's accustomed place: he bore the fine scars of healing crystal scores on face, neck, and hands, but Killashandra couldn't remember ever seeing him before.

"Killashandra Ree?" the man asked. He looked from her to her companion. "Lars Dahl? Don't you ever turn on your ship communit?"

"When we're in the cabin," Lars answered pleasantly enough.

"Weren't in it much, not with only two to crew her through some nasty storms," Killa added with mock contrition. "Where's Trag?"

"I'm Bollam." He gave the odd shrug of one shoulder and tilt of his head that told them that Trag was no longer alive. "You know your way?"

"Intimately," Killashandra snapped over her shoulder as she strode angrily around him and toward the door to Lanzecki's sanctum. She didn't like Trag being dead. He had taught her to retune crystal during her apprenticeship, and she vaguely remembered other remote things about him, mainly good. Bollam didn't look like the sort of personality who could manage the duties that Trag had so effortlessly—and unemotionally—executed. If she were Lanzecki, she wouldn't trust that dork-looking weed as a partner in the Ranges. Fardles, she didn't have half that many scars on her arms, and she'd been singing crystal for . . . for a long time!

Slapping the door plate with an angry hand, she pushed through as soon as its identifying mechanism released the lock. She strode across to where Lanzecki was leaning over a worktop.

"You do have a communit aboard that boat of yours," he began before she could take the initiative.

"Ship," Lars automatically corrected Lanzecki.

"When we turn it on," Killashandra said simultaneously. "What's so earth-shattering?"

Lanzecki tossed the stylus he had been using to the worktop and, straightening, gave the pair a long look. Killa felt something twist inside her. Lanzecki's face looked drawn and—aged. Had Trag's death been that recent?

"In the 478-S-2937 system in the Libran area of space, they've found what they think might be a new version of crystal, opalescent, but purported to be considerably more complex than Terran opals or Vegan firestones, either clear or opaque."

He clicked on the viewing screen, fast-forwarding it so that the exploration ship zoomed in speedy orbit, landed, and early-evaluation processes went at an ever-increasing kaleidoscopic rate.

"Ah! Here!" And Lanzecki pressed for normal speed. "Planet's a shell with an immense cavern system—geologists suggest that the planet cooled too fast."

"No oceans?" Lars asked.

Lanzecki shook his head, and Killa grinned, a trifle sourly, for that was always Lars's first question about a new planet: Were there seas to sail?

"Underground deposits of ice neither drinkable nor," the Guild Master added with a rare display of broad humor, "sailable."

"Damn!"

"Ah!" Killa said, as the vid angled up and a coruscation of what appeared to be liquid was reflected back. The angle altered, and Killa and Lars became aware that the liquidity was actually the reflection of what appeared to be a band of Lanzecki's medium blue opalescent stone.

Abruptly Lanzecki fast-forwarded to another extrusion, this time a deeper blue in a wider band that was almost a complete rib, vaulting across the ceiling from one side of the cavern to the other, nearly to the floor on both sides, seemingly spread from the "pool" in the center of the roof. Curiously, the color seemed to flow as if it were forcing itself downward on both ends, striving to reach the base.

"This is taken with only existing light," Lanzecki said, his tone laced with amused interest. "The planet has a very slow rotation, taking nearly forty standard hours to complete one diurnal revolution. This was taped in dawn light. Full noon is blazing."

Lars was more vocal in his admiration. "All this one stone, or a vein?" he asked, sounding awed.

"Well, *that* is another matter no one has been able to ascertain," Lanzecki said dryly.

"Oh?" Killa wasn't sure she liked the possibilities becoming apparent in the situation.

"Yes, these tapes are several years old. Every member of the exploration team died within four months of landing on Opal."

"Opal?" Killashandra asked, staving off the gorier details she was sure Lanzecki would give them.

He shrugged, his lips twitching briefly. "The team named it."

"Not knowing it would be their memorial?" Lars commented wryly.

"Happens."

"How did they die?" Lars asked, hitching one leg over the corner of the worktop and settling himself there.

"Not nicely. When the deadman alarm went off, broadcasting a contamination code, the Trundimoux who investigated took every precaution. They recovered the tape cassette in the airlock along with the ship's log and a small chunk of *unflexing* material which turned out to be part of that coruscating stuff. There were notes from the geologist and the doctor of the stricken ship in the log entries. They concurred in the opinion that they had acquired a lethal dose of something on Opal, and it could well have been from contact with the stone. The log said that to get this sample, they had to laser out the stone around it, as they couldn't detach it in any other way." Lanzecki paused for effect. "The survey guys have identified cesium, gallium, rubidium, and lesser quantities of iron and silicon in the sample. There are also several radioactive isotopes, indicating that at some point the sample included a radioactive element, but we found no trace of one to identify. Odd thing was that the sample did not have the coruscating look of the parent body. Trag thought it had died, being excised from the main body."

"Trag went?"

Lanzecki looked away from them for a long moment before he answered. Then he made eye contact first with Killashandra, then with Lars.

"The Ballybran symbiont will heal our bodies and reduce degeneration to a very slow crawl, but eventually it, too, loses its resilience. Trag has been on the Guild Roll a long, long time. He knew his symbiont protection was waning. When the Guild was asked to send a representative on the premise that the Ballybran symbiont might protect a Heptite member, Trag volunteered. Presnol put him through exhaustive tests and discovered that the symbiont was still active. Trag insisted that he had protection enough to be safe."

There were many in the Guild who called Lanzecki "the Stone-face." Even Killashandra had once made the mistake of thinking him emotionless, but later events had corrected that misjudgment. The stony look now was masking at least regret, if not something deeper. Lanzecki had depended on Trag for more than just partnership when he had to cut crystal.

"He spent unshielded time with the stone and suffered no ill effects."

"Then what killed him?" Killashandra demanded.

Lanzecki gave a snort. "Some damned fool respiratory ailment he caught on the voyage back." A twist of his right shoulder indicated his dislike of such an ignoble ending. "Presnol did consider the possibility that contact with the stone had further reduced his symbiont protection, and tissue examination proved that Trag certainly hadn't contracted the same, or a similar, disease to that which affected the geological ship's personnel." Lanzecki paused again. "In his report Trag was confident that the Ballybran symbiont would protect crystal singers, and that further investigations should be carried out by the Heptite Guild. He reported a *resonance* from the stone, unlike anything he ever encountered in the Ranges—unlike but similar."

Killashandra folded her arms across her chest, ignoring the quavering expression on Lars's face. "And you want us to explore the possibilities?" she finally asked.

"Yes."

Lars caught her gaze, blinking his left eye in their private code of interest. Killa made Lanzecki wait for their answer.

"How much?"

Lanzecki gave her a shark's grin. "We have quoted them a . . . substantial fee for the services of a Heptite Guild team."

"Ooooh, then the Powers that Be are really interested," she said. When Lanzecki nodded, she went on, "And you have a price in mind—for us, as well as the Guild?"

"I am able to offer you fifty thousand credits. You'd be off-planet during Passover—and you should have more than enough time to complete the investigation before the frenzy overtakes you."

Killashandra dismissed that aspect as she rapidly considered the monetary enticement and decided that the Guild must have asked for twice or three times that amount.

"We wouldn't take less than ninety thousand for that sort of hazardous work." She flicked a quick glance at Lars. Even the fifty thou would take them anywhere in explored space for as long as they could stand being away from Ballybran.

Lanzecki inclined his head briefly, but the slight upturn of his lips told Killa that he had expected her to haggle. "Sixty. The Guild will have expenses . . ."

"You should have asked for those above and beyond the danger money," Killashandra said with a snort of contempt. "Eighty-five."

"We might have to keep you in isolation on your return from Opal . . ."

"Why else have I been paying dues all these years? And don't you trust Trag's evaluation?"

"As I always trusted him. He was, however, only in the chamber with the stone for a relatively short period."

"How long?" Lars asked.

"Three weeks."

"And you want us to believe that it didn't affect the symbiont?"

"Presnol says not. A simple bronchial infection killed him. Those on the exploration ship—examined by remote probe—died of a rampant lymphatic leukemia which no medication available to any nonaltered humans could combat. There were no indications of lymphatic failure or alteration in Trag."

"Three weeks might not have been long enough for the problem to develop."

Lanzecki shook his head. "Not according to the data in the log of the medic on board the exploration ship. Initial symptoms of fatigue, headache, *et cetera*, appeared in the second week after contact."

Killashandra kept staring at Lanzecki. After the Trundimoux black-crystal installation—a traumatic memory she hadn't been able to eradicate—and some other little special assignments, the memories of which had been reduced over the years to feelings of annoyance rather than specific complaints, Killashandra had an innate distrust of any Lanzecki assignments.

"Eighty buys our time and effort," she told him with terse finality.

"*Plus* . . ." Lars held up his hand, entering the bidding for the first time. "A half percent of Guild profits arising from viable merchandising of this as a product."

"*What!*" Lanzecki's blast of surprise startled Lars off his perch.

Killashandra threw her head back in a burst of laughter as he pulled himself back up onto the worktop. "Boy, you're learning!"

"Well, I don't see why not," Lars told her, but he was watching Lanzecki's face. "If we're risking our asses for the Guild, we should see some of the profits!"

"It may be nothing more than a pretty stone!" Lanzecki bit out the words.

"Then there'd be no royalty to be paid."

"It could be sentient," Killashandra put in.

"Whose side are you on?" Lars demanded.

But Lanzecki grinned.

"Done!" And before either crystal singer could protest, he caught Killashandra's hand and slapped it down on the palm pad, effectively registering her agreement. Then he extended the unit to Lars Dahl, who grinned broadly and made a show of wriggling his fingers before placing them down on the pad.

"We could have held out for more," Killashandra said with some disgust.

Lars parted his lips in a broad grin. Bargaining was usually her province, and she was very good at it. He was rather pleased with his initiative in adding the percentage: not too much for Lanzecki to reject out of hand, but if the rock proved useful, they could easily never have to cut crystal unless they needed to renew the symbiont. Still, eighty thousand credits and a royalty was enough to salve pride and greed.

"So, if unaltered humans can't land on this planet, how do we?" Killashandra asked.

"Brain ship's been allocated."

"Our old friends Samel and Chadria?" Lars asked. The names titillated Killashandra's memory but produced no further recall.

Lanzecki gave Lars a patient stare. "Not them."

Killashandra winced, for his attitude plainly indicated that that pair were no longer alive. She wondered, but only briefly, how long ago their demise had occurred. Brain ships had life expectancies of several hundred years. Could she have been cutting crystal for *that* long?

"They had an awkward accident," Lanzecki amended, and Killashandra relaxed. "I'll inform the Agency that you've taken the contract."

"So there've been no tests or assays or anything completed on this stone? Even by Trag?" Lars asked. "Discounting its effects on humans."

"Trag felt it was sentient."

"Trag did?" Killashandra was astounded. "Then it is."

"And you treat that as a possibility only, Killashandra Ree," Lanzecki said, sternly waggling a blunt finger at her.

"You bet!" She began to feel better about the assignment. If blunt ol' thick-skinned conservative Trag had felt something, she rather supposed that she and Lars would have much better luck. "A silicon sentience has been postulated."

"Will it say it's sorry it killed the team?" Lars asked sarcastically, crossing his arms over his chest.

"Does crystal?" Killashandra responded with a snort.

"At least crystal sings," was Lars's soft rejoinder.

To Lars, Lanzecki passed a flimzie and a thin tape cassette. "That's all we have on the silicon, and the relevant log entries."

"So when do we go?"

"Your transport, the BB-1066—" He held up his hand when Killashandra started to interrupt him. "The Brendan/Boira. Boira's on sick leave, so Brendan's willing to undertake the journey."

"Truly a B-and-B ship," Lars said dryly.

"And I suppose you expect us to depart immediately?" Killashandra asked irascibly.

Lanzecki nodded briefly. "Brendan's been *patiently* waiting your return."

"We just got in," Killashandra protested.

"From a holiday," Lanzecki pointed out.

"Holiday?" Noting Lars Dahl stiffen on his corner of the worktop, she grinned impudently. "Well, from one point of view, but I'd like time to get the salt off my skin and a bit of crystal out of my blood."

"A tub—a double one"—Lanzecki's grin was malicious—"and sufficient radiant fluid are aboard the 1066. With eighty thou to your credit, you can surely see your way clear to a precipitous departure. Everyone you might know—bar Presnol—is out in the Ranges."

Killashandra sniffed her displeasure at what seemed suspiciously close to being part of a maneuver to shanghai them.

"If you'd bothered to keep in contact, you'd've had more time," Lanzecki pointed out.

"C'mon, Killa," Lars said, dismounting from his perch and draping an affectionate arm about her shoulders.

"I suppose our sled isn't ready?" she said, eyeing Lanzecki sourly.

"It is." Lanzecki never took kindly to any suggestion of Guild inefficiency. "And you'll earn more from this—"

"As well as easy credit for the Guild," Killa put in.

"Not to mention that we're the best ones for this little errand," Lars added.

"That, too," Lanzecki unexpectedly conceded. "Only this time"—his pointed finger stabbed in Lars's direction—"I want on-the-site accounts recorded in Brendan's memory circuits from the moment you land on Opal."

"This time," Killashandra said, smiling in saccharine obedience, "you'll have 'em. We'll just dump our gear and grab a few personal things from our quarters."

"Brendan's stocked your usual brands, and being a B-and-B ship, he's amply supplied with more than the usual trip paraphernalia. Leave for Shanganagh from here. *Now.* There's a shuttle waiting."

Killashandra unslung her duffel and launched it at Lanzecki, who neatly caught it. Lars merely slipped the webbed carry strap from his shoulder.

"Everything needs cleaning," he said.

Lanzecki nodded. "Get out of here!" The phrase combined imperative order as well as gruff farewell.

So they left Lanzecki's office. Being more diplomatic than his partner, Lars nodded briefly to Bollam, who stared back with no response.

"Once in a while Trag'd smile," Lars muttered in Killa's ear as the door slid shut behind them.

"I don't *like* the idea of that dork going out into the Ranges with Lanzecki," she muttered, scowling.

Lars made a comforting noise in his throat. The Guild Master was in the unenviable position of having to keep as much memory current as possible to manage the intricacies of his position. But he also had to renew contact with crystal periodically or lose the vitality of his symbiont, despite being a virtual prisoner on Ballybran.

As they entered the lift and pushed the shuttle-level plate, Killashandra's frown deepened. Lanzecki wasn't stupid. So Bollam must have more substance or intelligence or skill than his appearance suggested. But she couldn't help fretting. Lanzecki was one of those unfortunate singers who became so rapt by the song of the crystal they cut that they could be totally lost to the thrall. A partner was essential to such singers; they dared not sing crystal alone, or they risked never returning from the Ranges. Antona had once told Killashandra that it was an infrequent enough manifestation, more often accompanying the Milekey Transition, the mildest form of adjustment to the Ballybran symbiont.

Lanzecki had always put off cutting crystal as long as he possibly could, even with Trag to accompany him and bring him safely back from the Ranges. Sometimes, as at one time he had done with Killashandra, he could establish an intimate relationship with someone whose body was singing with crystal pulse; that contact supplied surrogate reinforcements, staving off the need for true crystal. Killashandra did remember her interview with Trag, who had all but physically manhandled her off the planet to force Lanzecki out to the Ranges for a thorough revitalization of his symbiont. Would this Bollam have that sort of loyalty to his Guild Master?

The lift door slid back into the brightly banded corridor that led to the shuttle bays. The blinking orange ready light steered them to the waiting ship.

The pilot waved urgently to them to hurry, but as they passed him on their way into the vessel, he glowered and pinched his nostrils.

"You reek! Where have you two been?"

"Oh, around and about," Lars said with a grin.

"If I wasn't under orders to—"

"Well, we are all under orders to," said Killashandra, sliding into the backseat of the otherwise vacant transport, "so the sooner you get us to Shanganagh, the faster you lose the stink of us."

"Can't be too soon for me," the pilot said sourly, slamming the door to his cabin after a brief pause to be sure they had buckled up.

Lars grinned at Killashandra. "Shall we stuff our old socks somewhere?"

They would have, too, but the pilot had taken their suggestion and their takeoff was the most perpendicular Killashandra had ever experienced. They were jammed so forcefully back into their cushioned seats that she swore she felt the flexible plastic turn rigid. It was the shortest trip she remembered making.

As soon as the shuttle had locked on to the Shanganagh Moon facility, the lock opened with such unusual dispatch that there was no misinterpreting the urgent invitation to depart.

"The B-and-B is one level above, Bay Eighty-seven," the pilot's voice said over the com.

"You are above all a courteous gentleperson, skilled in the performance of your appointed duties," Lars said facetiously.

"I'm what?" was the startled comment that followed them down the lock ramp.

"They must have lowered entrance standards," Killashandra remarked. "I'm first in the bath."

"Lanzecki said it's a double," Lars reminded her.

At the end of the lock tunnel they took turns placing their palms in the ID plate, and the aperture irised open into the corridor.

They encountered no one, which was slightly unusual as Shanganagh was a major stopover point, as well as the Guild's main display and testing center. It also had supply and servicing facilities for vessels of any size.

"You don't suppose that antsy pilot warned everyone off until we've passed and the corridor's been fumigated?" Lars asked.

Killashandra snorted, frowning, and lengthened her stride. "I shall, however, be very grateful for the tub."

"Last one in . . ." Lars began, but then they saw the plate above Bay 87 blinking orange.

"He warned the B-and-B we were here!"

"Last one in . . ."

"*After* we make our duty to Brendan," Killa said quellingly. Of all the myriad manifestations of humans, altered or otherwise, she most respected shell people—to a point of reverence. There was something awesome about knowing that a human being, residing within the main titanium column, ran all the ship's functions and *was* the ship in a way an ordinary pilot could never be. The combination of a shell person with a mobile partner, known as a "brawn," made B&B ships the elite of spacegoing vessels. Traveling with Brendan was truly an honor.

"Of course!" Lars murmured.

As soon as they entered the lock, the panel behind them slid shut.

"Permission to come a—"

"Oh, I never stand on ceremony when I'm solo, kids," said a pleasantly resonant baritone voice. "Don't you ever answer your communit? I've been sitting here on the moon long enough to pick up cobwebs."

"Sorry, Brendan," Lars said, giving as respectful a bow to the titanium column that encased Brendan's shelled body as Killashandra did.

"Ah! A tenor!" Brendan said with delight.

"And he can sing!" Killashandra said. Crystal singers might require perfect pitch, but that did not always accompany a good singing voice or any real musicality.

"So who's going to be last in the tub?" Brendan asked.

"Which way?" the two singers demanded.

"And when can we get under way?" Lars asked, stripping his salt-stiffened garments off. He nearly tripped out of the shorts, trying to keep up with Killa, who had less to shed.

"We are!" Laughter rippled in Brendan's voice. "I don't waste time."

Then he laughed again as Killa elbowed Lars to prevent him from getting to the ladder to the tub rim. Lars merely vaulted up and neatly immersed himself in the thick viscous fluid just as Killa slid into the tub. They gave simultaneous sighs of relief as the liquid covered them. Moments later they found the armholds and secured themselves against the pressure of takeoff.

"You're sure you're under power?" Killa asked after a long interval of bracing herself against a shock that never came.

"Most certainly." Abruptly a screen in the corner of the small cabin lit up with a spectacular view of Shanganagh and Ballybran receding at an astonishing speed. "And about to initiate the Singularity Drive. I think you will find that being immersed in radiant fluid will reduce the discomfort the effect often gives you soft shells."

"Never thought of that before," Lars said.

"Here we go," Brendan said, and everything altered before the eyes of the two singers.

Killashandra squeezed her eyes shut against the Singularity Effect. She did not like seeing the decomposition and re-formation of space as the Singularity Drive "surfed" them—Lars liked the nautical analogy—down the long funnel of "interspace" from one relative spatial point to another. And yes, the radiant fluid did reduce that nauseating feeling of falling in on oneself, spinning and yet deprived of any sense of one's own position relative to that spin.

Then they were through.

"Does the fluid help?" Brendan asked solicitously.

"You know," Lars said in surprise, "I do believe it does. Killa?"

"Hmmmm! How many more of these jumps do we have to make to get to Opal?"

"Only two more."

Killashandra groaned.

"Something to eat, perhaps?" Brendan suggested. "I took on all your favorite foods."

Killa rallied hopefully. "Yarran beer?"

Brendan chuckled. "Would I forget *that*?"

"Not if you're as smart a brain as you're supposed to be," Lars said. Disengaging his arms, he pushed himself to the ladder. "You want anything else, Killa?" he asked as he clambered down.

What else she wanted required two trips by Lars, but in the end they were both well supplied. Brendan had even acquired flotation trays for them to use while immersed.

"I think this trip'll be sheer luxury," Killa murmured quietly to Lars.

Brendan heard her anyway. "I'll do my part," he said.

"Ah, Brendan ..." she began, and was rewarded by a knowing chuckle.

"Just tell me when I'm off-limits and I'll chop the audio system," the ship said.

"Will you really?" Killa asked, trying to keep skepticism out of her tone.

"Actually," Brendan went on conversationally, "if I didn't, Boira would haul off the panel and disconnect *me*. Now there's a gal that likes her privacy . . ."

"How's she doing?" Lars asked.

"Oh, she's regenerating nicely."

The two bathers exchanged glances.

"Do we solicitously ask what happened, or shall we keep our noses short?"

A long silence ensued. "I won't say she was foolish, or stupid—just very unlucky," Brendan said with so little expression that the two would have had to be tone deaf not to appreciate how distressed he was at his partner's injuries. "I was only just able to get her to proper medical assistance in time. It will take a while, but she will completely recover."

"She's been a good partner?" Killa asked gently.

"One of the best I've had." And then his voice altered, not too brightly or lilting falsely. "One tends to nurture the good ones carefully."

"Even if there is only so much one can do?" Killa made it not quite statement, not quite query.

"Exactly. Now, shall I leave you to enjoy your bath in peace?"

Lars and Killa once again exchanged glances. Lars's yawn was not feigned.

"I'm going to have to get some tub-sleep," he said. "Can you monitor this contraption so we don't inadvertently go under?"

"Of course." And by Brendan's tone, the two singers realized they had struck the right attitude with him.

"I could probably sleep a few weeks . . ." Killa said.

"At which point you'd be a wrinkled prune," Lars replied caustically.

"I shall not permit that desecration of your most attractive self, Killashandra Ree," Brendan said in a flirtatious tone.

"Now, wait a mo—" Lars yawned. "—ment, Brendan. This one's mine, you rotten baritone."

Brendan chuckled, a sound that had odd resonances due to the artificial diaphragm he needed to speak or laugh.

"Go to sleep, Lars Dahl. You're no match for me in your present semi-somnolent state."

Killa yawned, too, and jammed her arms deeper in the straps, tipping her head back against the padded rim of the rub. She never knew which of them fell asleep first.

Chapter 2

"**W**hat a cheese hole!" Lars said in a disgusted tone. Killashandra said nothing. She didn't dare express what she felt about the planet Opal. And especially about Lanzecki for taking advantage of their greed, and need to be off-planet. Only the thought that she and Lars were making eighty thousand credits for this kept her from exploding.

Well, that and wanting to keep Brendan's good opinion. He had turned out to be the most excellent of escorts. Not only did he sing good baritone, but he had the most astonishing repertoire of lewd and salacious, prim and proper cantatas and languishing lieder. He wasn't as fond of opera as Killa was, but he knew all the comic operettas, musicals, lilts, pattern songs, and croons, and a selection of the best of every decade back to the beginning of taped music. He also had the most amazing and catholic files.

"Boira's a mezzo, you see, and while I can only sing the one voice . . ."

"Is the ship who sings . . . whatsername?"

"Helva? Yes, she still is, but no one knows where." Brendan had chuckled. "There's a reward if she's spotted, but I don't know a ship worth its hull who'd tell."

"But couldn't she sing *any* range?"

"So legend has it," Brendan had replied, amused. "It's possible. I could make modifications to my diaphragm and voice production, as she did, but frankly, it'd be damned hard to match the 834. Then, too, Boira *likes* me being baritone."

"Can't fight that," Killashandra had said, grinning at Lars.

But now they were orbiting Opal and musicality was irrelevant.

The pock-holed orb was more moon than planet, one of a dozen similar satellites weaving eccentric patterns about the primary. Opal had no atmosphere and only seven-tenths standard gravity. Its primary still emanated the unusual spectrums, coronal blasts, and violent solar winds that had so adversely affected its dependent bodies. Exploration HQ had decided that circumstances might possibly have resulted in unusual metals. Artifacts from some long-gone alien civilizations had been composed of previously undiscovered metallic components—some not kind to human hands but workable by remote control—that had proved to be invaluable to modern metallurgy, electronics, and engineering. Since those first discoveries, such substances continued to be assiduously sought. Which was why this star system had been surveyed.

"Leaving no turn unstoned," Bren had quipped.

According to the log, the now-deceased team had also discovered some very interesting slag on one of the outer satellites of Libran 2937, samples of which were still being analyzed—and their possible uses extrapolated from the all too small supply.

"Where did the geological survey land, Bren?" Lars asked.

"Their landing of record," Bren began, "is . . . right . . . below us." He magnified the image on his main screen, and the iridescent nauseous green paint that exploration teams used to mark their sites became clearly visible.

Lars and Killashandra turned to examine the close-up of the site, which was being displayed on one of the smaller bridge screens.

"Shall we?" the ship asked in a wry tone.

"Ach! Why not!" Lars said.

"We've time to eat," Killa said, feeling hunger pangs though she was certain they had eaten not too long before.

"Is it that time?" Lars asked with a startled expression. "We've done nothing but eat since we came aboard."

"They used to term it singing for your supper," Brendan added. His chuckle ended abruptly. "Oh, I see. You mean, your home planet's going through one of its Passover periods?"

"It was due to," Killa said. "It must have started. That's the only time we can't stop eating."

"Hmmm. Well, we've plenty aboard," Brendan replied soothingly.

Killashandra grimaced. "But we're going to have to suit up to move around down there, and suit food's not very satisfying."

Lars considered this aspect of the unusual hunger of their symbionts at Passover time: an urge that would overtake their bodies no matter how far they were from Ballybran, since it was generated by the symbiont, ever in phase with its native planet. "We could work in shifts, one of us eat while the other explores."

"No! Absolutely not," Brendan vetoed firmly. "As a team always. How long do you last between snacks?"

Killa laughed. "Snack? You've never seen a singer eat!"

"Well, tell me how much and I can deliver it to the lock so you don't have to unsuit completely to assuage your need."

Killa brightened. "That's a thought."

"We'll certainly give it a try," Lars said with a grin. "Now, just let's see if we can plan our excursions around our appetites." He accessed the log files of the fateful geology ship.

"How about I land you near the biggest of the vaults? This one!" Bren suggested, calling up the most remarkable of the liquidlike ribs. "That's not the landing of record, but it's certainly the most interesting site they found. Of course, I'm far more flexible than the *Toronto* was. We can pit hop as much as we need—while you're chowing down a good feed."

"Then there's the problem of the Sleep," Killa said, making a sour face.

"Oh?" Brendan prompted.

"Yes. Having stuffed ourselves like hibernators, we then sleep for the duration of the actual Passover."

"Or rather, our symbionts force us to sleep during the combined transit of the three moons," Lars explained.

"How long?"

Lars shrugged. "A week. That's why we stock up so heavily."

"For a week's sleep?"

Lars shrugged, then grinned at Brendan's column. "Not my choice."

"Then you eat again?" Brendan asked solicitously.

"Just before we fall asleep, even the sight of food makes us nauseous. That's generally how we know we'd best get into a comfortable position," Lars explained.

"Most unusual," Brendan said mildly, "though I've heard *and* encountered weirder ones."

"You're most reassuring," Killashandra said dryly.

"I try to be. You'd best belt in," he added. The main screen was showing their precipitous approach to the pock-marked moon. Seeing that, the two singers hastened to obey.

Brendan was an excellent pilot—as he *was* the ship, to all intents and purposes. As he neatly deposited them on the *soi-disant* surface of Opal, Lars and Killa applauded in the traditional manner. Then they concentrated on eating the enormous meal the ship served them—items that Brendan knew they particularly liked and in quantities that should have daunted a normal appetite.

"You really do stow it away, don't you?"

Killa and Lars were too busy stuffing themselves to give any reply other than a distracted "Hmmm . . ."

At last they were replete; and, groaning a bit, they squeezed into their vacuum suits. Killashandra found herself wishing, if only for a moment, that "space suits" had not evolved to be quite so lean and efficient. But these suits were perfect for non-atmospheric exploration. The close-fitting shell provided the wearer with a nearly impervious second skin. Fine controls for digital manipulations were available; sanitary arrangements were as unobtrusive as possible. The helmet afforded complete head mobility and visibility; the tubes for eating and drinking were housed at the neck rim. The oxygen unit fit snugly across the shoulder blades and down to the end of the spine, which it also served to protect. Helmet, digital, and arm lights illuminated a wide area around the wearer. Versatile tools attached to special rigs on the belt and stowed in thigh and leg pouches gave them additional external resources.

"I've stocked your suit packs with a rather tasty high protein, followed by a sweet confection that might just relieve hunger pangs," Brendan began.

"No matter what you feed us, mate, we'll have to come back for more than any suit could supply," Lars said as he and Killashandra entered the airlock. "All right now, Bren, let us out."

They had both studied the log records of the *Toronto*, so they knew to turn left as soon as they exited the outer lock.

"Humpf," Killa said, training her arm light on the fluorescent line the previous expedition had painted on the porous shell. "Nice of them, considering."

"They expected to return," Lars remarked quietly.

"I see the markings," Brendan said in an oblique reminder to narrate their progress more explicitly.

"For posterity then," and Killashandra began the running commentary as they followed the guideline down steps that had been cut by their predecessors. There was even a line sprayed across a low threshold to warn them where to bend and, hunching over, they started down the short passage into the larger chamber.

"Hey, there's light ahead," Lars said, and turned off his beams. "A sort of blue radiance," he went on, gesturing for Killa to extinguish her lamps.

The light source did not actually illuminate the passage, but the glow was sufficient to guide them to its source.

As they entered the big cavern, they were both speechless for a moment. Luminescence cascaded in flinders of brilliance—like sparks, except that they didn't shoot out of their parent substance. The material that arced across the high ceiling seemed to flow, dark blue and dark green and then silver.

"I am not there," Brendan reminded them politely.

Lars turned on his helmet light, and immediately the radiance was quenched. Where the helmet beam touched, the material writhed with bands of black and dark blue and dark green. Almost, Killashandra thought, as if rushing blood to heal a wound. Did light on this lightless world constitute a threat or injury? She wondered if the sun's rays—unfiltered, with no atmosphere to reduce ultraviolet and infrared—penetrated the cavern to the jewel? For jewel it appeared to her, one graceful long sweep of jewel, a living necklace across the vault of the cavern. Or was it a tiara?

"It's the most beautiful thing I've seen in a long time," she murmured. "And I've seen some magnificent crystal." She paused, frowning. "I also don't know why or how, but I agree with Trag, Brendan. This jewel junk is alive. Who knows about sentience—but definitely a living organism!"

"I agree with that," Lars said quietly, then began to examine the chamber while Killashandra concentrated on the gem cascade.

"It's grown, too, Brendan, since the team was here four or five years ago. It's made a complete hoop across the ceiling from floor to floor," Killashandra went on.

"And down into the next cavern, if there is one," Lars added, kneeling to shine the pencil-thin line of his forefinger light where the shimmering opalescent seemed to penetrate the floor of the cavern. The jewel itself darkened and seemed to contract, to retreat from the light source.

"To the basement level for housewares and utensils," Killashandra recited in the tone of a robotic lift device, feeling a need to dispel the unusual sense of reverence that the chamber evoked in her. *"No!"* she cried in sudden fear as she saw Lars reach out to touch the narrow descending— tongue? facet? finger? probe? tentacle?—of the opalescent.

Lars turned his helmeted head toward her, and his white teeth flashed a grin. "Let's not be craven about this. If the symbiont protects me, it protects me. After all, I'm suited . . ."

"Use an extendable," Brendan said in a tone remarkably close to command. "The material of your suit is only guaranteed impervious to *known* hazards."

"Good point, Lars," Killashandra added.

He gave a shrug and snagged a tool from his belt. A light pass of the instrument across the coruscating extrusion gave no results. Then he prodded it gently—and suddenly jerked back his arm.

"Wow!"

"Report?" Killa reminded him.

First he looked at the tool. "Well, I'm glad you stopped me, Bren." He turned the implement toward Killa. She tongue-switched the magnification of her visor and saw that the end had melted, blurring its outline.

"Hot the material is, but it gave on contact," Lars said.

"Pliable?" Brendan asked.

"Hmmm, flexible, maybe, or able to absorb intrusions," Killa suggested. "Or is it semiliquid, like mercury, or that odd stuff they found on Thetis Five?"

"So far, except for your observation that the, ah—" Brendan paused. "—semiliquid has spanned its cave in the four years since discovery, you have trod in the same path the geologists did. They also melted a few instruments trying to probe it."

"I know, I know," Lars said, "but I like to draw my own conclusions." He passed his gloved hand over the material several times, being careful not to touch it. "Any heat readings on record?"

"None, and I'm getting none either from the instrumentation you're carrying," the ship responded, sounding slightly disgusted.

"Any movement?"

"Negatory."

"Can you give us a reading on whether the ground beneath us is solid or not, Brendan?" Killa asked.

"You are currently standing on the intersection of three caves approximately two meters below you. Two of them are large, the other is small, less than half a meter in width and height. My readings corroborate the expedition's report that this satellite is riddled with cavities, probably right down to what used to be its molten core, in irregular layers and with equally irregular cavities."

"Can you keep a scan on possible spots too thin to bear any weight?" Killashandra had a quick vision of herself falling through level after level of cinder.

"Monitoring" was the ship's response.

Killa realized she had been holding her breath and expelled it. That allowed her stomach to mention it was empty, so while she made a confident circuit of the cavern, she sucked up the ration. In several places and with great care, she placed her gloved hand on the walls; her wrist gauge gave not so much as a wiggle. The ambient temperature of the cavern was the same as that on the satellite's surface. But there was something she was missing. Unable to think what that was, she shrugged and sucked on her tube.

"Hey, this glop's not bad, Bren," she said.

"Not eating already?"

"On the hour, every hour," Lars answered. He hunkered down by the visible end of the material and poked, careful not to let his chisel touch the glowing substance as he scraped out a semicircle. He gave a grunt. "It's going down. But where? Any access to the next level, Bren?"

"I think so," the ship answered after a bit. "Sort of a maze, but your suits have tracers on 'em, so I can keep track and direct you. Go out the way you came in . . ."

Following his directions, they traveled one of the more tortuous routes they had ever followed, accustomed as they were to the vagaries of sly crystal in the Milekey Ranges on Ballybran.

"I'm glad we don't have to stay too long in this place," Killa muttered, shining her lights around. The passageways seemed darker than ever after the subtle radiance of the jewel-junk cave. She preferred to have as much light around her as possible in dark burrows. The rock around them seemed to absorb their lights. "You eat it," she growled as she walked.

"What? Me? Oh, you mean the rock?" Lars asked. "Yeah, it does sort of soak it up. Speaking of which . . ."

"Not you, too!" Brendan exclaimed, almost sputtering. "It's scarcely two hours since you consumed an immense meal."

"Hmmm, true!"

"Humpf."

"We can last about another hour, I think," Lars said, and grinned as Killa glanced back at him. Would Brendan catch the teasing note?

"At this rate," Brendan replied trenchantly, "we'll be here for months! Turn obliquely right now, and watch that it *is* oblique—there's a hole!"

"Whoops, so there is," Killa said, teetering on the edge as her hand and head lamps outlined the even deeper blackness. Then, as she swung right, the comforting arch of a passageway was visible. "Nice save there, Bren. And what have we here but another cave!" Her tone was richly facetious. "And," she added, as she shone both lamps in a swing, "our little creepy-crawly has fingers in this pie, too."

Lars stepped around her and walked up to the glittering nubbin just entering the roof of this cavity. He dropped the beam of his light to the floor, and they could both see a small pile of debris. Lars hunkered down and, with the end of his hammer, carefully prodded the mound, examining the end of the tool when he had finished.

"Nope, not a melt. More like simple dust."

"Take a sample," his partner suggested.

"Take a sample of the rock, too," Brendan added.

"Now, look a'that," Killa said, holding her light steady on the opposite wall, where the liquid opal had intruded as well. "How many layers of this cave complex did the geologists explore?"

"At the original landing site, they penetrated several miles below the surface before they could proceed no further, but not here. However, records indicate that, in the cave above, the arch of the junk was incomplete. Nor do they mention that it penetrated below the first level in the landing site."

"Fascinating!" Killa commented. "How many such manifestations were recorded, Bren?" Dammit, she had studied those reports only last night and she couldn't recall the details.

"In nine of the twenty-three sites explored, they observed this opalescence. By then they hadn't found anything else particularly noteworthy, so they decided to proceed to the next system on their route when . . ."

"Hmmm, yes, indeed, when!"

"You'd think it would grow up, out of the core," Lars mused, "instead of down from the surface."

"If it *is* indigenous," Brendan suggested.

Lars and Killa were silent a moment, considering that theory. "Well, being alien to this system would answer why it's topside instead of down below," Lars remarked.

"Is there a way to prove alien origin?" Killa asked.

"If you could find a sample that'll submit to examination, possibly," the ship replied wryly.

"Suppose we explain that this won't hurt?" Killa was feeling waggish at this point. Faint from hunger, maybe. She sucked on the tube and got a mouthful of something rather more sweet than she liked. But it did depress the hunger pangs. "An alien substance? Hmm. Wherever could it have originated?"

" 'There are more things in heaven and earth, Horatio . . .' " Brendan intoned in a marvelously sepulchral note.

"Nonsense, Bren, there's usually a scientific explanation for *every*-thing," Killa said sharply. The very idea of something like the opal just "dropping" in made her slightly nervous. They hadn't discovered *anything* about it yet. And it had killed a whole exploratory team.

"I wonder," Lars said slowly, "if a quick freeze might not work to get us a sample."

"Work how?" Killa asked, her mind taken off both stomach and apprehension.

"I can't imagine how this stuff generates heat enough to melt an alloy as tough as the chisel, but maybe liquid nitrogen . . ."

"Wouldn't hurt to try," Bren said. "Fight liquid with liquid?"

"Have you got some?" Killa asked, again surprised.

"My dear Killashandra Ree, this ship has everything!" Bren's voice was smug. "My inventory shows that there are two cylinders of liquid nitrogen in storage. I have both spray and stream nozzles that will fit the standard apertures."

"Hmmm."

"I'll have one ready when you return for your next meal," Brendan added at his driest.

"And more luminescent paint, too," Lars added as the last drop dribbled out of his marking tube.

They retraced their steps very carefully, feeling the cindery crunch of the surface under their booted feet. Again something teased at the back of Killa's mind but refused to be identified.

The promised meal awaited them in the airlock, and they could barely wait until the iris had cycled shut and the oxygen level was adequate before they undid their helmets and attacked the food.

"Oh, this is good, Bren," Killa said, gobbling down refried steakbean and reaching for the orange-and-green milsi stalks of which she was particularly fond. Lars, as usual, was munching on grilled protein.

"Is indeed," Lars mumbled.

"You'll notice the nitro tank?" Brendan asked pointedly.

"Hmmm . . ." Killashandra waved a forkful of beans at it. "Appreciate that."

"And the marker tubes?"

It was Lars's turn to reply. "Thanks."

"You're welcome." Brendan sounded a trifle miffed.

"Can't help this," Lars added, glancing up apologetically at the airlock's optic.

Brendan's sigh was audible. "No, I suppose you can't, really. I've just never seen any bodies consume so much food in such a short time. And you're both bone-thin."

"Symbiont," Killashandra managed to say, one hand cramming as many of the bright green vegetable spheres into her mouth as would fit, while she scooped up more milsi stalks in the other. "You'll never see a fat singer," she added after swallowing her mouthful.

Oddly enough, the compulsion to gorge eased off about the time they were mopping up the plates with a yeast bread that was one of Brendan's specialties. Though as a shell person, he was nourished entirely by the fluids pumped into the titanium capsule that contained his stunted body, still he was fascinated by food and did most of the catering, even when Boira was on board.

Replete, Killashandra and Lars exchanged the depleted catering packets in their suits for fresh ones, donned their helmets, picked up the extra equipment, and exited the B&B to resume their explorations.

"Why are we trying to carve a hunk out of the junk?" Killashandra asked as they made their way back to the lower cavern.

"We were sent here to investigate the stuff, *in situ*, make recommendations as to its possible value, and/or usefulness," Lars said. "And see what makes it luminesce. Any report on whether or not the hunk of the junk grew in captivity, Bren?"

"No. I mean, no mention of increase in the sample; however, the report said, once excised, the specimen lost all iridescence."

"The junk doesn't like light," Killa said thoughtfully. "Could be it has to have darkness to sparkle. Or there's something in the composition of this planet that makes it iridescent?"

"And some element that makes it expand, grow, flow, whatever it does," Lars remarked, equally thoughtful. "Down the sides and to the next level. All in four years or so."

"Never heard of anything that *grew* in such a deprived environment as this," Killa said with a snort.

"Well, we ain't seen everything yet, have we?" Lars responded equably.

A ten-second spray of liquid nitrogen turned the entire stalactite colorless, and when Lars gave it a sharp chop with his rock hammer, the end—a piece the length and width of his gloved hand—fell to the ground. Through her boot soles, Killashandra felt a sharp shaking, unexpected and severe enough to unbalance her.

"Did you feel that, Lars?"

"Indeed I did!" Lars had flailed his arms briefly to steady himself.

"Feel what?" Brendan asked sharply.

"A tremor, a shake, a quake. Did you register anything?" Lars asked.

"Hmm. Well, there is a minute blip on the stability gauge. Not enough to set off a stabilizer alarm."

"Look!" Killa shone her light to the opposite wall, and the two singers saw that the other intrusion had disappeared. "A definite reaction to our action. The Junk has enough sense to retract from peril?"

"Sense or reflex?" Lars asked, scooping the colorless stalactite into the duraplas specimen sack he had pulled from his thigh pocket. "Let's see how *far* it's retracting."

Guided by Bren and moving as fast as was safe in the dark maze, they returned to the first chamber. The opalescence was subtly muted, and they had to turn on their suit lights. Then they could see that the Junk had noticeably contracted on both sides of the wall, though the farther "rib" was longer than the one from which they had taken the stalactite. They saw no other change in the central portion of the rib.

"Hey, look, Lars, a channel," Killa said. She pointed to the faint shadow on the wall where the Junk had been. "It makes a channel. Does it absorb rock as it extrudes?"

"Could it be making the caves?" Lars asked. That stunned both listeners into silence.

"Total absorption?" Brendan asked, puzzled. "Most beings excrete some waste material."

"This Junk makes a waste of space," Killashandra replied, grinning at Lars. "I can't see any movement now, but it sure moved incredibly fast in the twenty-odd minutes it took us to get back up here. Getting tape on this, Bren?"

"You bet."

"Well, then, let's try some comparison," Lars said. He motioned for Killashandra to follow him. "The first team found nine such phenomena? Well, let's go see the next one."

"I'm hungry again," Killashandra added apologetically.

Brendan made an exceedingly gross sound, but he had more food ready for them when they reached the airlock. They ate while he changed sites.

And that became the routine of the next ten hours. Search and eat. Eat while searching. At first Brendan had clever, often hilarious comments to make about their "starvation diet," but then he became as fascinated as they by what could only be called the "behavior" of the Junk.

At each of the five sites they investigated, they found that the opalescence had diminished in size from the mass that the geologists had recorded.

"Hey, you two, I'm calling a rest period. Your vital signs are becoming erratic."

"With all the food we're ingesting?" Killa said, half teasing. "Now that you mention it—whoops!" She tripped and fell forward into Lars.

"Now that you mention it," Lars continued, steadying her, "I could curl up for a hundred or so hours."

"Hunger would uncurl you in about three," Brendan replied. "Chow's up!"

They waited long enough before eating to insert their suits in the cleanser and shower themselves. Bren did manage to keep them awake long enough after they had eaten to get to their bunk.

But the next morning, as he served an enormous breakfast, the two singers were alert and keen to examine the remaining locations. By comparing the exploration notes with the present state of the ribbing, they saw distinct differences: less alteration the farther the opalescence was from the rib they had sampled.

"Is this a mass defection, migration, withdrawal?" Lars asked, puzzled.

"Pinch me, you pinch us all?" Killa responded.

"How could one piece of Junk communicate with the others?" Brendan asked.

"That's the easy one," Killa said with a grin. "Through the rock mass. We felt that tremble. Maybe that's communication."

"I'll credit that," Lars said, "but where is the Junk retreating *to*? Anything show up on the scopes, Bren?"

"Visualize me shrugging," the ship said drolly, "because I *have* checked all my systems for malfunction. The Junk refuses to have its picture taken. There isn't so much as a black blob registering on the walls of any of the caverns you've been in. But the Junk's very much *in situ*."

"Wait a minute, team," Killashandra said, a grin deepening. "I know what I missed . . . crunch underfoot. There's no debris or rubble or pebbles or anything in the caves!"

Lars blinked and lowered his head, frowning as he thought over her remark. "No, you're right, there isn't. Only that small pile of dust."

"Where the rib finger had wormed its way down. It may *eat* its way down."

"I could draw a comparison between your appetites and the—hey!" Brendan protested as Killa lobbed a pencil file at his titanium panel.

"I wonder what it does eat," Lars said. "Shall we whip up some appetizing bits and pieces for it to sample?"

"Didn't the explore team do that, Bren?" Killa asked.

"No, they did not." Bren's voice rippled in amusement. "After they seemed to lose tools to its melt process."

"I don't remember a mention of that," Killa said, frowning. She had only just reviewed the reports during breakfast.

"I gather that by inference, Ki," Brendan said. "And the inventory."

"So, what shall we offer up in sacrifice to the Junk God in the Grotto?" Killa asked.

"A bit of this, a bit of that," Lars said. "Can I have a walk through your spare-parts hold, Bren?"

"And can we return to our first cave?" Killa asked, speaking from an impulse she didn't quite understand. "I'm beginning to feel guilty about carving off that hunk of the Junk. We really ought to make restitution by letting it have first crack at our offerings."

That was granted, and Brendan told them what to take, and graciously offered what little garbage was left from preparing their meals, as well as other samples of protein and carbohydrate. The two resumed their now-clean suits, packed the tube wells for their snack, checked the oxygen tanks, snapped on their helmets, and cycled through the airlock.

"You know, you're right about rubble out here and none in the caves," Lars remarked.

As soon as they saw the blue light, they doused their suit lamps.

"The crunch stops here," Lars added as he strode onto the smooth surface of the cavern. "I don't think it's retracted further, Killa. What d'you think?"

"Hmm. We should have thought to mark it. We can reach this far tip . . ." She took out a sample as she made her way across. "Copper, Bren," she said. Using forceps and stretched at full length upward, she laid the copper on the surface. Then she yanked her arm back. "Muhlah! Talk about hungry. And see, Lars, there's a definite pulse that's copper-toned, running all the way back to the hub. Fascinating . . ."

By the time they exhausted the contents of their sacks, the Junk had accepted every single offering, the metallic ones with noticeable alacrity and reaction.

"Omnivorous."

"Not grateful though," Killa added. "Not so much as a centimeter has it expanded. Humpf."

Lars regarded the central mass. "No, but I think it's brighter. Should we see if any of the others are more receptive?"

She was standing in a pose of thoughtfulness, one arm across her chest, propping the elbow of the gloved hand supporting the tilt of her helmet. "I'm thinking!"

"Are you?"

"And what are you thinking?" Brendan asked.

Killashandra began slowly, formulating her thoughts as she spoke. "I think we ought to return the piece we took. I don't think we ought to carve up the Junk."

Lars regarded her for a long moment. "You know, I think you're right. That should put us in their good . . . gravel? dust?"

"Cinder?" Killa offered coyly.

"Well, we'll just do that wee thing then. Especially as it isn't doing us a blind bit of good as a specimen."

"Which reminds me. When we excised that bit of stalactite, there was that shaking. Was that just a tremor, or an incredibly rapid beat of some kind?"

"A percussive-type signal?" Lars asked.

"Ah, like some primitive groups who wished to make long-distance communications," the ship said. "I'll analyze. Never thought of that." There was a pause during which lights and flicks of messages crossed the main control screen. "Ah, indeed! Spot-on, Killa. The tremor does indeed parse into a variety of infinitesimal pulses of varying length."

"We need some drumsticks, Bren," Killa said, grinning at Lars.

He put his hands on his hips in an attitude of exasperation. "Neither of us could rap *that* fast."

"So we'll be *largo*, but it'll be a beat. We can at least use rhythm to see if we'd get any sort of response. Open some sort of a communications channel to this intelligence."

"Intelligence? The retreat could be no more than a basic survival impulse."

"Impulse is the word," Bren said. "I have no wood in my stores, but would plastic do?"

"Anything strong enough to beat out a pulse . . . Maybe we can get an 'in' to our Junk."

Lars groaned at her whimsy, but he was quite ready to return to the ship and take delivery of two pairs of taper-ended plastic lengths. He gave Killa one pair and, with the other, practiced a roll on the bulkhead of the airlock.

"A little ragged," she said.

"Who's had time to practice for the last seventy years?"

Killashandra frowned in surprise that Lars would even mention a time span. Most singers ignored time references. Seventy years? Since they had been singing duet? Or since they had last done much instrumentalizing? She really didn't want to know which. Unlike herself, Lars often input material to his private file. And after a session in the Ranges, he also accessed his file. She couldn't remember when she had thought to add anything to hers. She shook her head, not wanting to think about *that*. She had far more important things to do than worry about relative time—it was rhythmic time she had to play with right now.

"We are armed and ready," she said flippantly, holding the sticks under her nose as she had seen ceremonial drummers do on some old tape clip. "Front and center, and forward into the fray."

" 'We go, we go,' " Lars sang out.

Long-forgotten neurons rubbed together properly, and Killashandra came out with the beginning of that chorus, altering it slightly to suit their circumstances. " 'Go, we heroes, go to glory/we shall live in song and story . . .' "

" 'Yes, but you *don't* go!' " And Brendan's baritone entered the chorus.

" 'We go! We go!' " Lars toggled the airlock to open, awkwardly hanging on to his drumsticks as he resettled his helmet. Killashandra fastened hers.

" 'Yes, onward to the foe!' " Brendan sang melodiously.

" 'We go! We go!' "

And then the airlock completed its cycle and they could *go* back out into the darkness of Opal. They marched into the nearest of the Junk caves and came to a military abrupt halt.

"All right, Ki," Lars said, "where—and what—do we beat?"

"Let's see if we can get its attention. Do we both happen to know a ceremonial roll?"

"I do." Lars proceeded to beat it out.

"Show-off. Now, let's do it together." They did, heads up to see if there was any reaction in the Junk.

"I think you got through," Brendan said. "A hemi-semi-demiquaver of a response, but definitely just after your roll duet."

Lars grinned drolly at Killashandra. "Having said that, what do we say next?"

"Howdy?"

Hunger drove them from the cave, and once they got back into the B&B, sheer fatigue required them to stay. They had beat every tempo they knew, with all the power in their arms, until their muscles had protested. Brendan kept reporting reaction, and once or twice, a repeat—at a much faster speed—of what the two crystal singers had just tapped out. Other patterns of response made no sense to Brendan. But as Killa and Lars re-boarded the ship, he told them that he was trying to figure out any code, or pattern, in the Junk's response to their rolls. When he started to tell them, they begged a reprieve.

"Save it, will you, Bren?" Lars said, an edge to his voice.

"Sorry about that. You've seemed indefatigable. I was beginning to think you were crystal analogues. You have, after all, only been on the go today for twenty-seven hours. I'll reprise after you've had some sleep. And I mean, *sleep*."

"Wicked little man," Killashandra said, struggling out of her suit and tiredly cramming it into the cleanser. Lars had to prop himself up against the wall to balance while he pulled off his suit.

As she stumbled into the main cabin, she yawned, feeling those twenty-seven hours in every sinew in her body—and especially in her weary hands. "I'm almost too tired to eat," she said, but roused herself when the aromas of the feast Brendan had prepared wafted through the main cabin.

"I'm *never* too tired to eat during Passover," Lars announced, and picked up the biggest bowl. He half collapsed into the chair, then settled back with a plate on his chest so he didn't have so far to reach to get food into his mouth. "Can you analyze any particular response from the Junk?"

"In all the caves, it has stopped retreating," Brendan said. "And while I do perceive a definite pattern in the rhythm of its tremors, that's the problem. You could never rap fast enough to 'speak' to them, and they can't seem to slow down enough to 'speak' to you."

"How about us recording something, and you play it back at their tempo, Bren?" Killa asked. "Use one of your extendable tools to hammer the message home?"

Lars tipped respectful fingers in her direction for that notion. "Yeah, but what exactly are we trying to tell them?"

Killa shrugged, her mouth too full to answer just then. She swallowed. "We're singers, not semanticists. I think we've done very well!"

"I concur," Brendan added stoutly. "There are specialists who could handle it from here, now you've established an avenue."

"Yeah, but what about the disease?"

"The specialists do not need to exit their vehicle. I've just monitored the dust your suits left in the cleanser's filters. I can find no contaminants. So the planet must be safe enough. Remember, the geologists had that specimen on board to examine, and I doubt they thought of keeping it shielded."

"You know," Killashandra began, interrupting herself with a great yawn. "We forgot to put the piece back." Her head lolled back.

They fell asleep as they were, half-empty plates balanced on their chests. Brendan decided that he had not been scrupulous enough in monitoring them today—he'd been as fascinated as they had by their attempts to communicate with the Junk. In future, he must remember that singers had phenomenal powers of concentration, as well as appetite.

Then Brendan noticed that weary fingers had left splotches on chairs and carpet. Though he could send the cleaner 'bot to attend to floor spillage, he resigned himself to spots on the chairs until they reached port again. Not that Boira was any neater all the time. He dimmed the lights and raised the ambient temperature, since he couldn't exactly arrange covers for them. Being a ship had a few limitations in dealing with passengers who insisted on falling asleep *off* their bunks.

He was also obscurely delighted by their resolve to restore the specimen to the Junk. It was one thing to take samples of inanimate objects, but to do so to a living, feeling, communicating sentience was quite another matter in his lexicon. Singers were not as insensitive and unfeeling as he had been led to believe. In fact, his opinion of the breed had been raised by several singular leaps.

He must remember to mention it—adroitly, of course, for even to *imply* that he had had his doubts about this mission, and them, was embarrassing. He had a lot to relate to Boira when she was restored to him.

Chapter 3

As soon as they returned to the original site with the excised "finger," Killashandra and Lars noticed the increase of the luminescence.

"Well, we fed it, didn't we?" Killa said. "Big Junk looks fatter, too, don't you think?"

Lars shrugged. "Brendan?"

"Ambient light has increased in your present location, but, as you both know, I can read nothing of the Junk itself."

"It should look fatter after all we gave it to eat yesterday," Killashandra repeated, more to herself than to the others.

"I don't see as much expansion on the rib we cut, though," Lars remarked, peering up at it. That extrusion had not moved from the position into which it had retracted.

"Muhlah! I hope we haven't done irremedial harm," she said with genuine remorse.

"The other end had no trouble absorbing what we gave it to eat. Maybe it can . . ." Lars began.

"Can, can, cannibal?"

"Omnivorous, certainly," Lars replied wryly.

"It didn't exactly 'eat,' it sort of absorbed substances," Killa said.

Lars took the "finger" out of the duraplas sack with duraplas calipers and reached up, his extended arm not quite long enough. "Damnation!"

"If you hoist Killa to your shoulders, Lars, that will give you sufficient height," Brendan said.

Lars eyed his partner. She was a lean-bodied woman, and long in the leg.

"C'mon, lover boy, play acrobat. That'll be dead easy in point-seven gravity."

"Just don't wriggle around on my back. Be careful of my oxygen tanks."

"Hmmm. You've got a point. Whoops!"

Lars handed her the tongs and the "finger," then ducked under her legs and, in an athletic heave, raised her from the ground.

"*Don't* obscure my vision!" he exclaimed. Involuntarily, she had grabbed at his helmet before he steadied her with his hands on her belt.

"Two steps forward, and one slightly . . ." Killa caught her balance.

"To the left and . . . here we are. Steady!" Even with his almost two-meter height, she had to stretch to reach the end of the rib.

"You're wiggling!"

"Am not! I'm stretching. You're the one who's wiggling. To your right half a step. There!" And she whistled in disbelief as, before her very eyes, the Junk turned even more liquid and flowed over the amputated piece, reabsorbing it. Lars started to waver. "Hey!" She dropped the tongs and clung to him. "Don't move!"

"*I'm* not moving!" And suddenly Lars was down on one knee, Killa falling forward off his shoulders.

"Wooof!" she muttered as she lay sprawled on the ground, automatically checking the panel of lights that ringed the bottom of the helmet join. They were all green, not a flicker into the orange.

"You okay, Ki?" Brendan asked, his tone anxious. "That was a quake, not a tremor!"

"Quite a thank-you!" Killashandra got to her feet.

"Certainly a reaction," Brendan said. "Lars?"

"Oh, I'm all right," Lars replied, checking both knees. "Well, lookee there," he added, pointing to the ceiling. "Come home, all is forgiven!"

Neither could see a demarcation on the rib end.

"Absorption? Not the same reaction though," Killashandra said, "as it gave when we offered it merely metal. Should we recommend that the other piece be returned?"

"After four years or more?"

"It's worth a try—as a peace offering." She grinned at the deliberate pun. Lars groaned.

"It would establish human *bona fides*," Brendan said. "That the people who return it have recognized the attempt as mutilation?"

"Not merely amputation for the sake of investigation," Killa said in a caustic voice.

"So? What do we do for an encore?" Lars asked.

Killa shrugged. "Have we been in all the caves that have Junk?"

"All those recorded," Brendan said.

"And we still haven't found the source, if there is one?"

"That wasn't in our brief, was it?" Lars asked, brushing his gloved hands. "We were to discover if this stuff had some commercial value to the Heptite Guild."

"It doesn't belong under the Guild's aegis. It's sentient," Killa said with more vehemence than she intended.

"We don't know that for a fact," Bren said, "but while it may not be animal, it doesn't appear to be mineral in the strict definition of the word."

"I'll go along with that," Lars said, turning to his partner.

" 'And beings animalculus,' " Killa murmured. "There's something . . ." She struggled with the vague notion she was trying to verbalize and then shrugged. "I dunno, but one sure thing, you can't mine it the way we can crystal, or other gemstones and ores. What's your opinion, Brendan?"

"I'm a minder, not a miner."

"Yes, but you've been a big help."

"As a caterer . . ."

"Yuckh!" The very thought of food suddenly nauseated Killashandra. She and Lars locked eyes. "Oh, blast it."

"I'd say the timing was pretty good," Lars said.

"You're ready for the Sleep phase?" Brendan asked.

"Undeniably," Killa said, moving toward the exit of the cavern. "We've done what we were supposed to, and now it's up to the xenos! This isn't a Heptite matter. So . . ." She looked expectantly toward her partner. "Where are we going to spend all those lovely credits we've just earned, Lars? And if you say 'water world,' I'll excise a few chunks of you."

Following close behind her, Lars rapped her helmet. "No, it's your turn to pick."

"I'll pick *after* I've slept on it," Killashandra said.

"In a week I'll be out of this system," Brendan said. "Which way do I go?"

"Turn left then straight on till morning," Killa said facetiously.

"If that's your wish, it is my command," the ship said.

Once back aboard the ship, the lingering odors of previously delectable meals made them gag.

"You weren't joking, were you?" Brendan said. "Ah, you can restrain the compulsion?" he added urgently.

"Don't worry. We never disgrace ourselves," Lars said grimly, depressing his nausea as he stripped off the suit and stuffed it in the cleanser.

Killashandra had a very set look to her face and swallowed constantly as she peeled off not only her suit but the mesh undergarment.

"Hey!" Lars had not taken off his briefs and stared after her as she strode—regally, he thought—across the lounge.

"Brendan won't mind," Killa said absently.

"Indeed I don't, but I find it difficult to see that all that food—"

"Don't!" Killa held both hands up toward his column. "Don't even *think* that word!" She gagged and hurried to their cabin and into the sanitary unit.

"Anything I can get you?" the ship asked solicitously as Lars hurried after his partner.

"Not a damned thing, Bren," Lars said resignedly.

Killa was already in the shower, sluicing her body down, staggering occasionally as even the mild force of the water unbalanced her. When Lars entered the enclosure, they clung to each other, until they had soaped and soaked themselves clean.

Wrapping the generous towels about their bodies, they reeled to the wide bunk and, with groans of immense relief, crawled on and sprawled across it. As Brendan watched, their limbs relaxed despite what he considered to be uncomfortable postures. They were oblivious to any externals.

"These crystal singers don't do anything by halves. As bad as Boira in some respects." His voice echoed in the silent living quarters.

Delicately, as a mother will carry her sleeping babe to its cot, the Brendan/Boira-1066 lifted off Opal, though his passengers wouldn't have stirred no matter what G force he used in takeoff. A week of sleep? Well, if he "turned left"—now why was that sentence vaguely familiar—made one Singularity Jump and headed straight on, he would reach the Lepus sector, which offered the system Nihal. The primary was G2, and it had an inhabited third planet. Taking that route, Brendan would also have the chance to get a closer look at the very red Mira variable R. Leporis. Boira would be interested in his observations of that anomaly.

Serendipitously, it occurred to him that he was under no obligation to return immediately to Regulus Base. From the last report piped to him, Boira had another six or seven weeks to go in rejuvenation and then time in rehab and retraining. He really didn't have to take another short-term assignment or jump about on a courier route: they'd cleared all 1066's indebtedness with the bonus and danger money from the assignment that had put Boira in hospital.

But was the Nihal system where Killashandra *meant* to go? She'd told Lars that she'd pick *after* she'd had some sleep. Brendan accessed his galactic encyclopedia. Nihal's third planet had some unusual recreational facilities and was regarded as an ideal honeymoon planet. Killa and Lars were well past that stage of a partnership, but they might still appreciate a place like that for the extended vacation they intended to take from Ballybran and singing crystal. If he *had* misinterpreted her remark—and Killa's somewhat incoherent directions had sounded a bit like a quotation—they could change their minds when they woke up.

Then he remembered to do the medscans that he had been programmed to carry out, to insure that the symbiont was indeed protecting the singers. What would the Heptite Guild do if they had been contaminated? Exile them? Where? In those Crystal Ranges, until the next storm took care of the problem? The Guild was known to be ruthless, arrogant, and powerful. This pair had been the best company he'd had the entire time he'd been solo—he'd hate to see them mistreated . . . or worse. But just as the dust of their suits had shown no contaminants, neither did their bodies. Reassured, he added the medical data of this latest investigation to the private file.

"Nihal? Never heard of it," Killashandra said between sips of the fruit beverage she had requested of Brendan. Lars was still slumbering beside her.

"That's where we're going on the heading you gave me."

"What heading?" Killashandra skewed around on the wide bunk until she could see through the open cabin door to his column.

" 'Turn left then straight on till morning,' " Brendan's search through his library files had made him no wiser.

"Shards! That wasn't a direction, Bren."

"So you *were* quoting?"

Killashandra snickered. "And you couldn't find the source? How far back do your files go? No, abort that. I don't want to know. It's from an old children's story, and I didn't even remember that I remembered it. And that spurious direction leads us to Nihal? What's there?"

"A rather nice climate, temperate to cold, recreational, excellent—ah, can I use the *f*-word now?"

"Food? Oh, yeah, but we won't need anything more than liquids for a day or two."

"So was that a direction from your subconscious?"

Killashandra finished the last of her drink and yawned. "I'll know when we get there. How long did I sleep?"

"Five days."

"Wake me in another two, huh?" And she was asleep before Brendan could propose that he stay with them a while longer.

"Have a brain ship as our private yacht?" Lars exclaimed, sipping a clear soup.

"Well, I would have to ask you to pay for fuel, supplies, and landing fees," Bren answered tentatively. "You see, Boira and I have bought ourselves free . . ."

Lars recalled that the brain ships could do so, working off the immense debt with Central Worlds occasioned by their early childhood care and the cost of the ship itself. Some partners never did discharge the debt, but a good pair could earn enough in bonuses to do so. "My sincere congratulations on that feat, Brendan!"

"But I don't want to go into our savings."

"Medical expenses high?" Lars asked solicitously. Most humans complained about services singers never required.

"Oh, that! Repairs and injuries are part of our contract, and the contractor has to pay the full tab of Boira's rejuv since they neglected to inform us of the hazards inherent in the assignment." Bren sounded both irritated and smug. "So, all her expenses are paid. I just have to—well, sing for my supper."

"How long a contract did you have with Heptite?"

"To the conclusion of your investigations plus travel time to return you to Shankill Moon Base and me to my base."

"And you wouldn't *object* to carting us about?"

"If you defray my costs . . ."

"Sure, we can do that. Any sailing on this Nihal planet?"

"It's more known for its mountain sports."

"Oh!" Lars took the last gulp of his soup, yawned, and settled back down under the thermal beside Killashandra. "Lemme sleep on it, wouldja, Bren? 'S a great ideeeeee . . . ah . . . mmm."

When Killashandra woke from her second sleep, she woke alert, with that sense of having slept deeply and well—and of being mildly hungry. She rolled out of the bunk so as not to rouse Lars and made it to the sanitary facility before she burst. She showered and shrugged into the loose, colorful striped robe she preferred to wear in transit.

She paused by the broad bunk to see how Lars looked—his face was no longer gaunt so she thought he'd awaken soon. As soon as she had closed the door and was out in the short corridor, Brendan gave her a good-morning.

"Is it?"

"Well, it is morning, Nihal time, early morning."

"Oh! Yes, Nihal, of course. That G2—straight on till morning. How far away is it, Bren?" She was in the galley now, making herself a hot caffeine-rich drink.

"Relatively not far at my present speed."

"And it's not a water world?"

"It has water, of course, but mountain sports are featured."

"Hmmm, in that case, I'm not averse to it. Haven't done any hiking or skiing or climbing in—well, I can't remember when."

"There are lakes . . ."

"Lakes don't fascinate Lars as much as seas do," Killa said with some feeling.

"There are seas, but not much traffic on them. The fishing is limited to shoreline nettings, though there are said to be some very tasty bivalves."

"Hmmm. You know, I'm hungry but not ravenous, if you appreciate the distinction."

"I appreciate the distinction, Ki." Brendan chuckled. "What might you be hungry for?"

Aware that she couldn't overburden her system, she settled on a light meal of juice and cereal, which she took from the galley into the main room.

"Shards! But we get to be sloppy eaters, don't we," she said with chagrin, noticing the food stains on the arm of her usual chair. "Anything I can use to wash these out, Bren? I don't really want to hand you back to Boira in less than the condition you arrived in. That's not shipshape."

"And Bristol fashion?"

Killa laughed. Then she noticed the view on the main screen. "Muhlah! What's that?"

"Ah, that is the very red Mira variable R. Leporis. It has a four-hundred-and-thirty-two-day cycle. A type N, and with any luck, we'll see it at its hottest. The pulsations should be magnificent as it begins to contract."

Killa squinted. "It's very bright."

"I can darken the screen if it is visually uncomfortable."

"Hmmm, would you? Ah, thanks. That is undoubtedly the very reddest object I've ever seen. What are you seeing?"

"The emission spectra. Stupendous!"

They both, in their separate ways, considered the spectacle blazing light-years away but so vivid.

"Of course, if you find nothing of interest on Nihal Three, I'd be happy to take you elsewhere."

Killashandra snapped her fingers. "Just like that?"

"It's like this, Ki," and Brendan explained what he had offered Lars.

The crystal singer whooped and fell against the back of the chair in a paroxysm of laughter.

"Our own brain ship? Acting the yacht? You've got a deal, man!" She gasped the phrases out between spasms of laughter and ended up wiping her eyes of tears. "You really mean it?" she asked, turning toward Brendan's column.

"I wouldn't suggest it if I didn't."

"Don't huff, Bren, honestly, I didn't mean to offend. But don't you cost a lot?"

"I only need fuel, landing fees, and whatever supplies you and Lars require. To be sure, my larder's a bit bare right now."

"I can well imagine. You were champion to feed us as you did, Bren. I haven't eaten better during any Passover I can remember." Then practicality gripped her. "I think you'd better tell me just how much your fuel and general landing fees run to. We got a great fee for risking skin and symbiont on Opal, but . . ."

Brendan then ran through some figures for her so that she realized the idea was feasible. In fact, downright exciting.

"Of course, we've got to get our report back to Lanzecki. Does Nihal Three have black crystals?"

"It does."

A shiver ran up Killashandra's spine. She didn't like to use black-crystal communications. One of the few crystal singers who could locate and cut black crystal, she was unusually sensitive to its presence in cut or raw form. Especially since she had installed the black-crystal communications system for the Trundimoux: she had never managed to bury the memory of the soul-shattering shock of activating the king crystal. She had asked Lanzecki about that lingering pull, but he hadn't had any answers. Whatever it was, it made her wary of actually *using* black crystal— especially when she wanted to forget crystal for a while.

"There are significant bodies of water down there," Killashandra said as Brendan approached their destination.

"We can go somewhere else," Lars said to pacify her. "I didn't choose Nihal Three, remember. It was your 'straight on till morning' . . ."

His partner glowered at him.

"The chief recreational activity of the planet Sherpa is mountain climbing," Brendan said, raising his voice to distract them. "Downhill and cross-country skiing, skidoo and other snow-based sports, canoeing and kayaking on only designated rivers, trekking on foot or mounted, hunting and fishing. The catering is deemed one of the highlights of the planet and, indeed, wears the Four Comets of Gastronomical Excellence."

Killashandra groaned.

"A little exercise would improve your appetite," Brendan remarked. "Although I never thought I'd have to say that to the pair of you!"

Lars chuckled, and even Killa managed a grin. Then Lars regarded her queryingly, his expression blandly conciliatory.

"Oh, all right. We do mountain sports first," she said in assent, then waggled her finger at him. "I might do some canoeing, but you're on the bow paddle."

"Landing fees are moderate," Brendan said happily. "This won't cost you much," he added cheerfully. "You can send in your report, and I can get an update on Boira's condition. Ah, I'm getting a signal. Oh, really?" he added in surprise. "Penwyn, how good to hear your voice!" To the astonished singers, he added, "The planetary manager was in my class! I'm very glad we decided to come here."

Although Killashandra worked on the official report with Lars, she let him take it to the Communications Center. When they had passed it in the ground vehicle on their way into the settlement, she had experienced the frisson in her guts that told her she had cut the system's king crystal. She had returned as quickly as possible to the B&B. Now, in an atavistic burst, she scrubbed the food stains off the chairs while she waited for Lars to return. When he seemed to have been gone rather longer than the dispatch of a message should have taken, she began to feel ill used, then irritated and finally worried.

"This isn't an overregulated planet, is it? Crystal singers aren't forbidden?" she asked Brendan.

"Not at all. It's a very loosely settled place, though there's a fair competition between recreational facilities to attract visitors. Penwyn handles what administration there is and arbitrates any disputes, as well, but it's an orderly world."

At last Lars came back with promotional holos crammed into every pocket of his shipsuit. He was plainly delighted as he dumped them onto the worktop by the viewer and gestured dramatically to Killashandra.

"Take your pick! Reports filed—state of the art comtower, I'll tell you that, with your friend, Penwyn, handling the transmission, Bren. Guess you won't mind how long we're away, will you?"

"Hmmm, no, of course I won't," Brendan answered vaguely. He was busy chatting up Penwyn.

During the day that it took the two crystal singers to decide where to go first—eventually they settled on cross-country skiing to get their muscles limbered up for downhill runs—they didn't hear much from Brendan.

"Must be making up for the last fifty years," Lars said.

"Must you measure time!" she replied in a burst of irritation. What did *time* have to do with anything? It was *today* that mattered, and how well they spent it, how much they enjoyed it, or, if they were working in the Ranges, how much they could cut in a day!

Lars regarded her in surprise and then apologized in such a perfunctory manner that he aggravated her further. The lingering stress put a bit of a damper on their journey to the resort Killashandra had chosen. But once at the 'port that serviced the area—a long narrow valley amidst the most magnificent mountain scenery—her mood lifted.

The 'port was above the snowline in the mountainous rim of Sherpa's main continent, Nepal. They were collected at the door by the soberly welcoming rep of the snotel they had booked into.

"I am Mashid," he told them, making a low, respectful bow. Dark almond-shaped eyes did not so much as blink as he continued his greeting. "I have been appointed to see that your sojourn with us is all that you desired."

Killashandra and Lars exchanged quick looks.

"We're remarkably easy to please," Killa said, "so long as you don't show me any large bodies of water." She dug Lars in the ribs.

"All water at this altitude is frozen," Mashid replied stolidly.

"What do we drink then?" Lars asked with a bare twitch of his lips. "Melted snow?"

"Drinking water"—and Mashid's attitude toward drinking *that* was contemptuous—"is of course supplied as needed from protected reservoirs."

"I was joking," Lars said.

"As you wish." Mashid tendered another bow. Sweat had appeared on his forehead, for he was bundled in furs and thick fur-topped boots.

"Lead on," Lars suggested, gesturing to the door. He and Killashandra had bought outerwear suitable to the mountain climate but, though it had been pricey in the spaceport shop, neither jacket was as lush as Mashid's apparel. They learned later that he had caught, tanned, and made his own garments as most of the mountain people here did.

Turning with yet another bow, Mashid led them outside to an animal-drawn sleigh, brightly painted in orange and black stripes with the name of their snotel blazoned in huge letters on its sides. A pair of antlered, rough-coated beasts were harnessed to it, stamping their cloven hooves in the snow. They were nearly as long as the sleigh.

Lars and Killashandra were gestured into the passenger seat, and an immense fur robe was deftly tucked about them. Mashid swung expertly up onto the driver's seat and flicked a whip at the rumps of the beasts. The speed of their departure nearly gave Lars and Killashandra whiplash.

The pace was exhilarating; so was the crisp air, and the unusual method of transportation. Killa laughed aloud in sheer delight. She couldn't remember ever seeing so much snow before. She almost asked Lars if they had and then, as abruptly, didn't want to know: she wanted less to know if she had seen snow than if Lars could remember if they had. Then he turned a happy smile to her and it didn't matter. She was here, with Lars, and they had months before they had to even *think* of crystal and Ballybran. She was then totally distracted by the cold wind nipping at her ears and clamped her gloved hands together to protect them.

In the four months at the snotel, they attempted every single snow sport available, including races on single skis and on sno-bikes down almost vertical slopes. They missed being buried in an avalanche by the length of a ski; they skate-danced, snow-surfed and -planed, and went spelunking through ice and rock caverns of incredible beauty. They absorbed Mashid's instructions and improved on them, until eventually they surprised approval—even compliments—from the sturdy Nepalese, who began to view their near-indestructibility with awe. They doubted he had ever met crystal singers before or knew that their minor bruises, lacerations, and contusions healed overnight, leaving them fully able to cope with the new day's ordeals. They almost regretted leaving him behind in the mountains.

But they had done all they could of the snow sports, and so they moved from the mountains to the vast bowl of the internal plains of Nepal. There they did take to the water and acquired a new guide without the imperturbability of Mashid. With him, they canoed through tortuous canyons on flumes of water, shooting dire-toothed rapids.

Once in a while they checked in with Brendan, who informed them that he was quite content and they needn't hurry. So they hunted for two months in the lake districts with a party of mixed planetarials, and rode and camped along the coastline for a month with another, during which time Lars so pointedly said nothing about sailing that Killashandra was sure she would burst with not hearing the words he didn't speak.

"We've done everything else," Killashandra said the night before they were to turn inland, back to the vicinity of the spaceport. "We really can't leave Sherpa without sailing, can we?"

"Can we not?" Lars retorted placidly.

"If you wanted to, we could."

"Wrong," he said, and with his index finger pressed her nose in. "If you wanted to, we could."

Perversely, she ducked away from him and rolled off the bed, unaccountably annoyed with his self-sacrifice.

"It was my turn to pick," she said in a savage tone.

"Hey, honey-love . . ." Lars sprang from the bed to catch her in his arms, his face anxious. "Don't be like this. It *was* your turn to pick the place and activities, and I've enjoyed everything we've done together."

She struggled in his arms, furious with his acquiescence, even with his concern.

"Hey, hey . . ." He tried to gentle her, pulling her against his bare body. "Need a radiant bath?" He stroked her to judge crystal resonance in her body.

"I don't need one. I don't need crystal that badly yet. Ahhhhh!" And her irascibility disappeared as she arched in his arms. "Crystal! We didn't try crystal."

"*Try* crystal? Where? What are you talking about, Killa?"

"We never gave the Junk any crystal."

"It would have absorbed—oh, I see what you mean!" He blinked in sudden comprehension. "D'you really think Ballybran crystal wouldn't be absorbed by the Junk?" he asked, catching a bit of her excitement despite his skepticism. "What good would that do?"

"Communication. A lot easier than rapping out rhythm. There'd be a useful link with it, if nothing else." Killashandra was as tense with eagerness as she had been with irritation.

"We've done our job," Lars protested. "We've acquitted the assignment . . ."

"But we didn't find out anything."

"We found out that Junk is not a Heptite concern."

"But we didn't try crystal!" she repeated, struggling to release his grip.

"Well, if it means that much to you, let's see what Brendan says about taking us back there—with crystal. There, there, love-heart." Lars soothed her with hand and voice until she relaxed against him again. "Only where will we get some Ballybran crystal here?"

"They've black crystal . . ."

"Huh? You think they'll loan black for this escapade?"

Killa glared at him. "It's not an escapade. It's a point of investigation we neglected to make."

"Well, if they use black crystal, they use others," Lars said, releasing her and marching to the comconsole. "And if they use others, they also abuse them and there'll be sour crystal somewhere on this planet. We can offer to retune, and take the slivers as part of our fee."

"We can't give the Junk sour crystal."

"I don't think anything would give it indigestion," Lars remarked, pausing as he punched in Brendan's on-planet code. "Any scraps large enough can be tuned to some sort of pitch. You know, it might be fun to tune crystal when we don't have to."

Brendan was willing enough to return to Opal, though Killashandra could hear the reservations in his tone.

"I can't hang about there *too* long," he said, "and get you back to Ballybran in time to collect Boira. She's doing splendidly in rehab and retraining." Pride in his partner's recuperation colored his pleasant voice.

"That's very good news indeed, Bren," Killa said, meaning it. "We just want to see what effect *our* crystal might have on the Junk."

"It'll probably gulp it down like it did everything else and lick its chops at the taste."

"Only sound has any effect on Ballybran crystal," Killashandra said with considerable pride. "And there's no sound on an airless planet."

"Possibly," Brendan said. "And we didn't try diamond either."

"Ballybran crystal's tougher than any diamond ever compressed from carbon!"

"My, we are loyal!" Lars said facetiously.

Killashandra gave a sniff. "Well, there isn't any substance like Bally-bran crystal anywhere else in the universe."

"Except"—and Lars's eyes glinted with teasing—"possibly the Junk!"

Crystal resonance *was* beginning to get to Killashandra as Brendan took them back to the Opal system in one Singularity Jump. It had started when she and Lars retuned to a minor fifth the sour dominant midblue crystals that Penwyn had procured for them. As Lars had thought, there were quite a few soured crystals on the planet. Though Penwyn didn't ask them to, they tuned them all—the work of three days for such experienced singers—and he canceled Brendan's landing fees. But the sessions had an effect on Killashandra, and she spent a full day in the radiant-fluid tub.

"I'm fine, I'm fine," she insisted to Lars and Brendan when they were too solicitous of her. "Being near black always does it."

Lars desisted then and must have told Brendan to leave off inquiring, for neither of them said another word until the BB-1066 landed near the Big Hungry Junk—as Killa dubbed it—with the sweet-tuned slivers of crystal that they had salvaged.

"Old home week," she said with unforced gaiety as they suited up.

"Do we know what we're doing, Killa?" Lars asked as he settled his helmet on his head.

"No."

"D'you know why you're doing it?"

"No."

"Maybe the Junk *is* sentient."

"You mean, some sort of psionic emanations?" Killashandra was not only skeptical but incredulous.

"Why else would you have such a harebrained notion to feed Bally-bran crystal to an opalescent rib?" he demanded.

"I got the notion on Sherpa, not in the cave. I could have understood some sort of a connection if I'd thought of it then."

"You probably did," Lars replied. "You just forgot it. And don't snap at me over your *lapsus memoriae*! Let's get this experiment on the pad."

Even as he spoke he touched the lock release and it cycled open. Oxygen left the airlock with a whoosh. They stepped out onto Opal's cindery hide and followed the bright paint markings to Hungry Junk's precinct.

"Hey, improvement," Lars said as soon as they had descended to the level of the cavern. The blue radiance, edging toward white, made their suit lights unnecessary. "Wow!"

"Wow what?" Brendan asked when the silence went on for fifty seconds.

"You're sure your instrumentation doesn't read anything?" Lars asked.

"Not a thing. What occasioned your unusual exhortation?" Brendan asked flippantly.

"We fed it too much," Killashandra replied softly.

"Naw," Lars said, "but we fed it good."

"Tell me, do!" was Brendan's slightly sarcastic response.

"Sorry, Bren," Killashandra replied, "but it's a bloody shame you *can't* see. Junk's covered the entire cave, and there are long fingers that we'll probably find have descended to the next level. It's more beautiful than ever, all colors now, reds and oranges and yellows, as well as the blues, dark greens, and purples that it originally had. They seem to flow in and out of patterns . . ."

"Like fractals," Lars added, sounding oddly languid. "I could watch—hey, what'd you do that for?" She had given him such a push that he had nearly lost his balance.

"You were becoming thralled. Junk's hypnotic," Killa said, her voice sharp. "Maybe even addictive."

"*Should* we give it crystal then?" Lars asked, his tone crisp and alert again.

"That's what we came to do. So let's do it!"

"All the crystals to old Hungry Junk?"

"No, just one," Killashandra said. "Let's see what happens."

She pointed to a large swag of the Junk that was flowing toward the floor. Lars took the largest crystal, the B-flat, and, holding it in the calipers, inserted the blue. Junk obligingly flowed over it.

The two crystal singers held their breath as they watched.

"*Yup!*" Killashandra let out a triumphant crow. "It can't eat crystal."

"It can't?" Brendan asked. "What's it doing?"

"Holding it in its cheek," Lars said flippantly, grinning at Killashandra, "having a good taste." The Junk was rippling back and forth across the crystal insertion, going through all the colors of its visible spectrum without altering the outline of the cube. Then it seemed to push the cube upward, toward the crown in the center of the ceiling. Though apparently drawn deep into the opalescence, the crystal patently retained its integrity.

"Now what?" Brendan asked when the singers had nothing further to report.

"Look!" In astonishment Killashandra pointed to the half-open sack of crystals at her feet. They pulsed from midblue to dark and then paled. "Damn!" She dropped to her knees beside them. "Are they singing? Can't hear a bloody thing."

Tentatively Lars placed the tip of his gloved finger on the faceted surface of the nearest one.

"Vibration all right!" He grinned in triumph. "Communications established?"

"Could be, but pulsations and color alterations are no more intelligible than drum codes—until a code or even a language can be established. And semanticists we are not," Killashandra said, a degree of regret in her voice.

"Then let us by all means leave it to the experts," Brendan said. "Around such an unknown quantity, I find that I get almost as nervous for you as I do for Boira."

"Why, thanks, Bren," Killashandra said, touched by the ship's concern. "But I don't think we're in any danger."

"You are edible," he replied succinctly.

Killashandra laughed and Lars grinned at her.

"I wonder if any of the other Junk has expanded."

"We only fed this one," she replied. "Let's go see."

Lars picked up the remaining crystal, which continued to glow until they had entered the airlock and Brendan had lifted from the immediate vicinity of Big Hungry. They checked the other locations and found that no other formation had increased as significantly as Hungry Junk, although all had begun to flow downward again.

"Got anything on board to feed the starving?" Lars asked.

"In point of fact, I do," Brendan said. "Penwyn had nonrecyclable wastes he did not care to dispose of on-planet . . ."

"Dirty stuff?"

"Obliging I am; stupid I'm not! No, most of it's clean litter from the spacefield. I thought we might use the refuse to better effect."

"Indeed we can," Killa said, pleased. "I think the Junk's starved too long."

Lars was dubious. "We might be making more problems . . ."

"We might," she said with a shrug, "but I can't *not*."

"I've kept a file on the metallic and organic content of what we're feeding it," Brendan said.

"Then we do a comparison, a standard scientific practice," Lars replied, dismissing his reservations. "We feed four metallic and four organic."

It was tiring work, even in .7 gravity, distributing and feeding eight very hungry opalescents. As they trudged back to the 1066, both singers felt a curious satisfaction in the heightened glow and vigorous flow as the Junk ingested their meals.

When they had finished, the two singers returned briefly to the Big Hungry to check on the crystal.

"Not even Junk can eat Ballybran crystal," Killashandra said proudly.

"The cubes you left in the lock, however," Brendan remarked, "have remained dormant."

"Too bad we didn't have any dirty waste to give the Junk," Lars said, "to see if it could digest half-lifes."

Killashandra regarded him warily. "You do want to live dangerously, don't you?"

"Well, I don't think we've done any lasting harm. How long can one good meal last Junk? I think we leave this to the experts. Singers we are; scientists we're not."

"We're a lot smarter than that exploratory team who found Junk," Killa said.

"Are we?"

"Who can say at this juncture?" Brendan said, deftly diverting an argument with his outrageous pun. Lars and Killa groaned in unison as he went on. "You've done more than you were required to. And, while I hate to press you . . ." he added tentatively.

"Yes, yes, of course," Killashandra said, suppressing any comment on the fact that he was indeed pressuring them. "You're anxious to collect Boira."

"I think we've got more than enough to prove to Lanzecki that we earned our fee," Lars added, giving her a meaningful nod.

She exhaled restively, swinging her arms indecisively. But the men were right: they'd done more than was expected even if *not* what had been anticipated, finding a Heptite use of the Junk. Its fate would now be decided by others.

Lars moved to the exit arch, and with one more backward look at the surging flow of the Big Hungry's questing "finger," she followed. But the feeling that they hadn't done enough remained with her.

Chapter 4

The BB-1066 returned them to Shankill Moon Base and deposited them with many expressions of pleasure at their company and hopes to see them again. Wryly Killashandra heard the undertone of polite impatience in his courtesies and nudged Lars to hurry the disembarkation process. Brendan wanted to return, full speed, to Regulus Base, where he would be rejoined by Boira.

They had the pencil files of their report for Lanzecki in their carisaks, which bulged with souvenirs from their months on Sherpa.

Periodically Killashandra cleared out her storage space of items that she could not remember acquiring. Now she couldn't recall if she had corners into which to stuff the new additions. She hated discarding her belongings until they brought back no memories of where they had been used. When she did get rid of things, she preferred to do it when Lars wasn't around. His memory was much better than hers, and he could remember where and when clothes or equipment had been purchased. And why.

They caught the first shuttle down to Ballybran. It was half-full of singers. To the three she recognized she gave a brief nod; Lars smiled at most, though he did not get a response from all.

"Sometimes they act as if they're going to their own executions," he said.

Evidently he said that often enough that her reply was automatic: "Sometimes they are."

That was true enough to be sobering. There was no chatter, no merriment, no laughter at all, and very few grins when singers returned to the planet on which they earned enough to indulge in whatever fancies rocked their jollies. The ambience today was enough to depress anyone—except Lars, who was smiling tenderly at the screen's magnificent view of the broad oceans on the day side. He must be the only singer who enjoyed another aspect of the Guild homeworld, Killa reflected. He was smiling because he could look forward to sailing again.

"You kept your word," she murmured to him. "You choose the next one."

He grinned absently at her. "Hope Pat put her back in the water after Passover."

"We won't have time now for a cruise."

His hand covered hers on the armrest, and his smile was tender and deeply affectionate. "I like the 'we,' Sunny!" His fingers squeezed, and she, too, was suffused with loving warmth for him. They did make a very good team! Then he exhaled. "Lanzecki'll probably have us both out in the Ranges before the morning."

The shuttle was crossing into the night zone as it spiraled down to Ballybran's surface.

"More than likely." Killashandra felt no resistance to the prospect. The *need* to sing crystal had become more insistent during the last leg of their return voyage.

When she had last checked their credit balance, it was sizable enough to reassure her against any eventuality—not finding one of their old lodes of good crystal, a sudden storm flushing them out of the Ranges, even more damage to the sled, though *that* she intended to avoid. The last accident had caused her extreme aggravation. So asinine to have been caught in an avalanche! Lars had maintained that no blame could be attached to them; she railed that they ought to have checked the stability of the projection that had decided to drop on their sled.

She even remembered the piercing, almost pitying, look he had given her. "Look, Killa, you can't be everything in the Ranges. You've got weather sense that has saved our hides more times than I care to count; you're a superb cutter, and you've never cracked a crystal pitching it. Neither of us is geologist enough to have known that projection was unstable. Leave it!"

She remembered his reassurance now. More vivid and embarrassing was her remembered ignominy at having to be hoisted out of the Ranges. She would be grateful when that memory was expunged from her mind by her return to the Ranges. Soon enough only Lars would have access to the embarrassment. Time after time, she had heard him making reports to his private file. He wasn't likely to tease her about the avalanche—she'd give him that—but she almost wished he wouldn't commit *every damn* detail to electronic memory.

The shuttle landed them, and everyone filed out glumly. Only Lars seemed in good spirits. Then the port duty officer signaled to Lars and Killashandra.

"Lanzecki said you're to report to him immediately, forthwith and now!"

"When have I heard that before?" Lars replied with a grin, clipping Killashandra under the elbow as he guided her toward the lift that would take them to the executive level.

As they entered the administration office, Bollam gave them a brief nod of acknowledgment.

"I really don't like that man," Killa murmured to Lars as she placed her hand on the door plate. "He's a dork! A real dork! I wouldn't trust him in the Ranges, and *I* don't have Lanzecki's problem."

Lars jiggled her elbow to move on as the door slid open. It was as if the Guild Master hadn't moved from the position in which they had last seen him. Except, Killa noticed as he raised his head at their approach, he looked more tired and less . . . less substantial. She shook the notion out of her head.

"Good work," he said, nodding at them.

"*Good* work?" Killa was astonished. "But the Junk isn't something the Guild can use."

Lanzecki shrugged. "One less complication. And this Junk of yours couldn't digest Ballybran crystal?" That was more a proud statement than a question, and a slight smile pulled at the corner of Lanzecki's thin mouth.

He was aging, Killa thought, noticing thin vertical lines on his upper lip, the deeper marks from nose to mouth, and the discoloration under his eyes.

"You're working too hard," she said. Lanzecki raised his eyebrows inquiringly. "That dork at the door's no help. You need someone more like Trag. He was efficient—"

She stopped, seeing Lanzecki's expression alter to a courteous mask that rebuked her for her impudence.

"Look, anything we can do to help?" Lars asked. He glanced at Killashandra, not for permission but for her to reinforce his offer of assistance.

Lars never had learned the lesson Moksoon had taught her—that one asked, and expected, no help from anyone in the Ranges. Only . . . the Cube was not the Ranges.

"Neither of us *has* to get out for a while yet," she replied, though it wouldn't be long before an undeniable urgency began to pulse through her veins. Helpfulness and cooperation were not singer characteristics, but even she could remember being obliged to—and alternately infuriated by—Lanzecki's demands on her, and on herself and Lars. However, she was currently grateful for the benefits of the intriguing Junk assignment, and thus in a mood to be generous.

"I appreciate that very much indeed."

"Isn't there *anyone* else more suitable than Bollam?" she demanded.

Lanzecki shrugged. "He has his uses. Now . . ." He turned immediately to red-sheeted Priority notices. "These can no longer be ignored, Lars. And Killa, Enthor's gone and his replacement needs to be overseen. You've a finely tuned sense for crystal's potential. Can you see your way clear to assisting in the Sorting Shed until the woman's less tentative? She's got to be more confident that her judgment's right. I can't be hauled in to mediate her evaluations with disgruntled singers."

Killa made a face. "So I'm Trag's stand-in?"

Lanzecki gave her a level look. "In that aspect of our craft, you were always his superior."

"Well, well," she said, and would have teased him had she not seen the flicker in his eyes that suggested she restrain her flippancy. "Any singers due in?"

"The Tower says that five are on their way back. Storm gathering over the southeast tip of the Ranges. Met says it's just a squall."

Killa snorted in disgust. Even "just a squall" on Ballybran could be mortally dangerous to any singers caught in it. The high winds that gusted over the canyons stroked mind-blowing resonances out of the crystalline Ranges.

"Who's the new Sorter?"

"Woman name of Clodine," Lanzecki replied. "Don't ride her, Killashandra. Her main fault is being new at the game."

Lars cocked an eyebrow at her and winked conspiratorially. She caught the warning that she would do more good to be patient. She shook her hair back over her shoulder in denial of the reminder and, on her mettle, strode out of the room.

Clodine greeted Killashandra with a nervous blend of gratitude and caution. Sorters, whose particular adjustment to the Ballybran symbiont affected their vision to the point where they did not need any mechanical aid to see intrusions and flaws in crystal, did not suffer the memory deterioration that singers did. Each of the other four Sorters on duty gave Killashandra a pleasant nod or wave as she made her way to Clodine's station—a station that had been Enthor's since before Killa had become a member of the Heptite Guild. She would miss him, too: they'd had some spectacular arguments over his evaluation of the tons of crystal she had presented for his inspection. But she had known him to be exceedingly competent, and fair. The opinion had survived throughout all her trips in the Ranges. Two faces she always remembered, no matter how crystal-mazed she was: Enthor's and Lanzecki's.

Clodine would have to be very good indeed to replace Enthor in Killashandra's estimation. Ironic to find herself in the position of teaching the woman all the skills she herself had learned from the old Sorter. But Killa *did* know crystal.

The tall, slender girl—Killa judged her to be young in real chronology—kept blinking, her eyes going from one state to the other. Involuntarily she shuddered when the magnification of her enhanced sight made what should have been ordinary images unnerving to behold. She was an attractive girl, too, which might be why Lanzecki had enlisted Killa's aid. There had been a time when Killa would have been intensely jealous of anyone who took Lanzecki's interest, but those days were a long time back in the decades that had not included Lars Dahl. Clodine had lovely blond hair, a lot of it, neatly confined in a thick net. She had the fair complexion of the genuine blonde, and midbrown eyes with light flecks. Yes, very attractive. Some of Killa's unexpected anxiety for Lanzecki's aging dissipated. He still had an eye for a pretty girl and a lissome shape.

"I'm Killashandra Ree," she said, holding out her hand to Clodine. That was a habit most humanoid worlds had adopted, and she had been doing it so much on Sherpa that it had become natural. Singers fresh out of the Ranges never touched anyone if they could help it. Crystal shock sometimes had an adverse affect on others. But Clodine was too new to Bally-bran to notice anything out of the ordinary. "Lanzecki sent me down as backup to this grimy lot on their way in. He doesn't want to scare you off the job at too early a date."

The crystal singer noticed that the worn scales and equipment that had served Enthor for so many decades had been replaced. Even the metal worktop, once scraped and scored by hundreds of thousands of cut-crystal forms, was pristine.

Clodine gave a tentative smile, and her eyes flicked into the alter state and then back again. "Oh, Gods, I'll never get the hang of it."

"Make your eyes very round when you want to stay in normal visual mode," Killashandra said in a low voice, aware that the other Sorters were watching them.

Clodine tried to smile *and* widen her eyes, then groaned because her eyes altered despite her efforts.

"It's surprising how soon you will become accustomed to the alteration," Killashandra said in her most sincere "buck up there" tone. "Ah, here they come!"

"They do?" Clodine looked up at the wraparound screens that showed the as-yet empty Hangar where the singers' sleds would land. The latest batch of Guild apprentices waited there to help unload the precious crystal. The Met screens showed that the squall, having wreaked brief havoc in the Ranges, was passing harmlessly out to sea, half a continent away. The Hangar crew was lounging about. When storm systems raged close to the Guild's massive cube, their duties became far more urgent and perilous—even to closing the great Hangar doors to incoming singers rather than risk damage to those already safe inside. More times than she cared to remember—probably many more times than she *could* remember—Killa had been the last singer to get in over the interlocking jaws of the great portal.

"See?" Killa said, directing Clodine's attention to the long-range screen where the first of the incoming sleds was just now visible as a speeding blip.

"Oh!" Clodine blinked nervously and, shaking her head in distress, looked about to weep.

"Relax," Killa drawled, and pushed herself up to sit on the brand-new worktop. "They're a good half hour out—unless they've had a good scare!" She grinned in amusement and saw Clodine relax a bit. "Where you from?"

"I don't imagine you've ever heard of my home system . . ." the Sorter began apologetically.

"Try me," Killa replied with a laugh.

"A planet named Scartine—"

"In the Huntsman system," Killashandra said, oddly pleased by the girl's delight in her knowing. "Nice place. Good currents in the Great Oceans."

"You've *sailed* on Scarteen?"

"I've sailed—" Killa paused, censored the ennui in her tone, and smiled kindly at the child. "—on most worlds that are hospitable to our species."

"You sail? I mean, sheet-sail, not motor cruise?"

"Wind-sail, of course." She flicked one shoulder, consigning motor cruising to a suitable nadir. "And you'll find there's good sailing here, too. In fact, if we've time before we go out in the Ranges, my partner and I would be happy to take you out on our ship, show you some of the tricks of sailing Ballybran's currents and coasts."

"Oh, would you?"

Once again, Lars's avocation won her unexpected friendship. Killa sighed and filled in the time until the sleds arrived with sea tales that were honorably unembellished. They didn't need to be! Sorters might not need to leave Ballybran as often as singers, but they took holidays—especially during Passover storms. It didn't hurt to reassure the girl that there was more to life as a Heptite Guild member than remembering to widen her eyes to avoid blinking to crystal-gaze.

Clodine was, as Lanzecki suspected, suffering only from inexperience in dealing with Range-crazed singers. Killashandra's presence quelled the other singer's urge to argue with Clodine's estimate of his crystals—which were a rather good midgreen, currently in scarce supply, so even without arguing he got a better price than Killa knew he had anticipated. He would have had no cause to berate a Sorter, new or experienced, but arguing price with the Sorter got to be an ingrained habit with singers. Some Sorters enjoyed persiflage, and/or getting the better of the singer.

Timing was so often the deciding factor in the value of a cut. If the market was glutted, the price was understandably low. Some colors were always worth the premium price, like black crystals, which were so valuable as communications links. The pale pinks were always low market, but a fine seven-shaft cut of even pink could be valuable in an industrial complex.

When the singer had left, grumbling desultorily, Killashandra touched Clodine's shoulder and grinned at her woeful expression.

"He's all wind and piss. Most of us are. You know your grading, the latest market price is what's on your terminal. Don't let 'em hassle you. Part of it's coming in sudden from the Ranges without as much as you thought you would cut this time out: *I'm* always sure I should have been able to cut longer and more. Most of it's pure singer cussedness. Ignore it, considering the source! Enthor train you up?" she added, for something of the way Clodine had handled the crystal reminded her of the old man.

"Yes." Clodine's eyes widened in astonishment. "How did you know that?"

Killa sniffed. "Enthor loved crystal. He passed that on to you. Remember that the next time a singer gives you a hard time. You"—Killashandra prodded Clodine lightly in the chest—"love crystal. I can see that in how you handle it. Singers"—she turned her thumb into her own sternum—"invariably *hate* crystal."

"You do?"

"For all that it does for us and to us, yes." And, feeling that that sounded like a great exit line, Killashandra left the Sorter Shed.

Lars had not returned to their apartment. She gave herself a long soak in the water tub; then, wearing a loose robe, she began to unpack the carisaks that had been delivered while she was overseeing Clodine. When she got hungry and Lars still hadn't returned, she tapped out a "where is" code on the terminal.

"Here," Lars's voice responded as his features formed on the screen.

"Where?"

"Lanzecki's," he replied, as if she should have known. "C'mon up."

Puzzling over that, Killa changed and returned to the Guild Master's domain.

The pair were sitting at the table where Killa had often dined alone with Lanzecki. There was a third place set, and as Lanzecki gestured her to be seated, Lars rose and met her halfway, giving her a quick embrace and kiss.

Wondering what this was all about, Killa smoothly took her place.

"We waited," Lars said, and he nodded at the array of sumptuous-looking dishes.

"How did Clodine do?" Lanzecki asked, forestalling any query from her.

"She's fine. I told her not to let singers get up her nose. Enthor trained her. She loves crystal. I told her singers hate it. Opened her eyes!" Killa grinned.

"In more ways than one, I trust?" Lanzecki said, quirking his eyebrow. He was being Lanzecki-the-man, as he had been in their old loverly days—a pose he had never before assumed in Lars's presence. For some reason it disturbed her.

"Well, that's the trick, isn't it?" she replied, knowing better than to show her surprise. "Widening the eyes to prevent the alteration? She was only nervous."

"Anything good in?" Lanzecki asked.

Killa regarded him coolly. The Guild Master ought to have been the first to know the answer to that question.

"Lars and I have been discussing the Junk to the exclusion of all else." Lanzecki raised his wineglass in a toast to her, then included Lars. "Interesting ... Junk. I'm almost sorry I have to turn the matter over to the proper authority."

"Junk's sentient," Killa said flatly, helping herself to food.

"Too bad sentience isn't a marketable commodity," Lanzecki said.

"Have some milsi stalks!" he added, passing her the plate and changing the subject.

"What under the suns were you and Lanzecki up to for half a day?" she asked Lars as she swung her legs up onto the sleeping surface of their bedroom.

He yawned mightily, stepping up off the floor and walking to the pillowed end, where he folded down and began to wriggle into a comfortable position.

"The Junk mostly, and speculation as to whether or not it could use the crystal as a comlink. I doubt it. And this and that." Lars punched a pillow into the right contours and stuck it under his head, watching her as she rolled up against him. He lifted one arm, a tacit invitation to nestle against him. She did. "He misses Trag."

"Did you find out what crystal-crazed notion made him pick that dork in Trag's place?"

She settled her cheek against Lars's smooth chest. At some point he, too, had bathed, for his skin exuded a subtly spicy odor. Lanzecki preferred spicy scents. What could these two be dreaming up together? she wondered. Lars had never used to tolerate Lanzecki at all, he'd been so possessive of her.

His fingers lazily trailed across her back, and she forgot about all other concerns and began to stroke him where it would do the most good. Somehow, despite being reasonably sure that Brendan's shipboard manners were impeccable, they had never quite been able to abandon themselves on the 1066. They proceeded to indulge each other shamelessly.

Uninhibited loving was the best!

The communit buzzed until they woke, or rather until Lars waved his hand at the panel and accepted the call.

"Lars? Can you spare me the morning?" Lanzecki asked.

Killashandra groaned at the sound of his voice, but she didn't quite take in the message. She flattened her body against the bedding and determinedly resumed her interrupted slumbers. So when she did wake, she wasn't quite certain what had happened to Lars. There was no residual heat left where his body had been.

She roused, washed, and ordered food. As usual, the latter triggered an interruption.

"Killa? I'm up in Lanzecki's office."

"Humph! What's he got you doing now?"

She could hear the amusement in Lars's voice. "Actually, he's got me interested in spite of myself, and you know I'm not an admin type."

"No, you're not."

"Don't be so sour, Sunny. It's a bright day, and we don't have to go cut crystal—yet!"

"Well, I can't say as I mind that . . ." Killa said, as much because that was the expected answer. Then she began to wonder. "Lars, what are you—" But the call had been disconnected at his end.

More curious than disgruntled, Killa finished her meal, dressed, and went up to Lanzecki's office. There, the mere sight of Bollam, hunched over his terminal, annoyed her. His frantic look and his sudden intense interest in the contents of his screen added to her aggravation.

She couldn't resist twitting him. "Lost something, Bollam?"

"Ah, yes, that is, no! No, I'm merely not sure under what category Trag filed the pencil data files."

"Try the first four letters of whatever file you're hunting, the year if you know it, and hit Search." She meant to be facetious and was irritated that her advice seemed to solve his problem. She caught a glimpse of his relieved smile as she continued on her way into the office.

"Haven't you two moved?" she demanded as she saw them in positions similar to yesterday's.

"I never knew just how much power the Guild wields," Lars said, beckoning to her in an airy fashion.

"You ought to," Killa said, scowling at Lanzecki. "We trade rather heavily on it whenever we leave Ballybran."

"I don't mean as singers, Killa, but the Guild as a force in interstellar politics. And policies."

"Oh?"

"And all without having to leave Ballybran! Whoever needs to speak to the Heptite Guild *must* come here!" Lars chuckled with an almost boyish delight. Lanzecki wore just the slightest smile as he glanced over at her.

To Killashandra that cynical amusement meant that Lanzecki was building to something devious. She cocked her head at him. He shook his head very slightly in denial.

"I've a meeting later today, Killa. I'd appreciate it if you and Lars would sit in on it."

Killa jerked her finger over her shoulder in the direction of Bollam. "He's your assistant."

The fleeting shift of Lanzecki's dark eyes told her that he didn't expect much of Trag's replacement, and his lack of such expectation worried her all the more.

"Yesterday Enthor, today Trag?" she asked, mockingly.

"I'd appreciate your counsel," he said, bending his upper body just slightly toward her in an unexpected bow.

She wondered if he knew that that deference would insure her support. Probably. Lanzecki had usually been able to read her, at times better than Lars did. She realized then that she usually compromised with Lars more than she would have with Lanzecki. But then, she wanted to. She trusted Lars Dahl more than she had ever trusted Lanzecki, even when they had been passionate lovers. Or maybe because of that!

"Bollam? Have you got those trade figures?" Lanzecki called out.

"Still working" was the all too quick reply.

A look of pained patience crossed Lanzecki's face.

"I remember Trag's system," Killa said, turning on her heel and re-tracing her steps to the worktop where Bollam was plainly unable to find the relevant pencil files. "Move over," she told the flustered man. "Now, who's coming?"

"The Apharian Four Satellite Miners League," he said, both resenting her usurpation and relieved that finding the documentation was now someone else's responsibility.

She typed "Apha4SML.doc" and obediently the recalcitrant entry blossomed across the screen. Bollam groaned.

"I did, I tried that. I really did."

"The library banks know an authoritative punch when they get one," she said, shrugging. She tapped a deliver.

"He wants the Interstellar Miners League, as well."

"What year?"

"Twenty-seven sixty-six."

Killa frowned. Twenty-seven sixty-six? *When* had she left Fuerte, storming out off her native planet with that crystal singer—ah, what *was* his name? Had it been 2699? Or 2599? She shook her head in irritation, then concentrated on tapping out the required sequence. The new files joined the others in the delivery slot. She was a lot better at his job than Bollam was. She gave him not even a look as she gathered up the files and brought them in to Lanzecki and Lars.

Lanzecki gave her a grateful smile as he began feeding them into the reader slot. He folded his arms across his chest as the first one came up on the monitor.

Feeling an obligation to assist the Guild Master, Killa stayed on, as Lars did. She accessed additional data when Lanzecki asked for it, ignoring Bollam when he hovered in an attempt to figure out how she found files so easily. At first it amused her that Lars and Lanzecki worked together so ef-fortlessly. She wondered that, at times, Lanzecki seemed to defer to Lars's opinions. Certainly he tapped them into his own notes.

Then the representatives arrived for the meeting, properly attired against breathing Ballybran air. Lanzecki, hands on the backs of Killashan-dra and Lars, steered them into the conference room.

The Apharian Miners League wanted to extend their communica-tions link in the asteroid belt they were currently working. They could not afford black crystal.

"Black crystal isn't needed for belt communits. Blue will do as well and is half the price," Lanzecki said. "Here are specifications and cost." He inserted a pencil file in the screen reader, and specs and relative costs were displayed on the large monitor for all to see.

"Even that's out of our budget," the head delegate said, shaking his helmeted head.

"I doubt it," Lanzecki said bluntly. A tap of his finger and their trade figures replaced the spec / cost data.

Another delegate, a woman with sharp features and narrow-set eyes, glared first at the screen and then at him. "How did you obtain restricted data?"

"I particularly like to assemble 'restricted' data," Lanzecki replied.

"You could go to a green-crystal connection," Lars suggested. "Of course, there is a longer time lag in communication, especially for any distant units. The blue link is unquestionably faster. Basically you get what you pay for. The option is always yours."

Though Killashandra kept her expression bland, she was amused by Lars's hard-line pose. She had rarely seen that facet of his personality. He was as cool and uncompromising as Lanzecki. An interesting development.

"At present we have the necessary blue-crystal cuts such an installation would require," Killa said smoothly. She gave a little shrug with one shoulder. "Who knows when we'd have sufficient green. It's not an easy color to cut. Nearly as elusive as black. Which we also don't have on hand. You might have a long wait for quality black crystal."

"We can't *afford* that quality crystal," the woman said, almost spitting the words out over her helmet mike. "But we did expect that, in making the effort to come here and outline our need, you might be amenable to a deal."

Lanzecki cleared his throat dismissively. "Your League has nothing this Guild requires. The Guild has what you require, and at the advertised price." He rose. "You either take it or do without. It's up to you."

Lars and Killa moved to bracket him.

"Wait!" The head of the delegation said, his expression anxious. "You don't understand. We've had accidents, deaths, problems, all due to a lack of adequate communications. We must have a reliable comsystem."

"Blue is available. You can wait for green, if that's all you can afford." Lanzecki spoke with no emotion whatever. He really didn't care one way or another.

Killashandra saw hatred sparkle in the eyes of the woman.

"My husband and my two sons died in an accident . . ."

Lanzecki turned halfway to her and inclined his head. "A singer died and two more were seriously injured acquiring the blue crystal. We have both lost, and we can both gain."

"You heartless—" The woman launched herself at Lanzecki, screaming other epithets in her frustration at his diffidence.

Lars intercepted her neatly even as Killashandra moved to interpose her body to protect Lanzecki's back.

"Lideen, don't!" the leader said, reaching her first. He grabbed her by the arms and passed her to the other members of his party. He took a deep breath before he went on. "Guild Master, I do recognize that sentiment has no place in business."

"In either yours or mine," Lanzecki replied with cool courtesy.

"You singers have crystal for blood! Crystal for hearts!" Lideen yelled as the other two miners' reps hauled her out of the room.

"The Guild does not make deals," Lars added. "The integrity of our price scale has to be maintained. Two options are currently open to you. You can, of course, wait until there is a glut of blue crystal on the market, which would bring the price down, but there is no downward market forecast on blue crystal at the moment. Or you can install green when it is available. Your credit balance indicates that your League is able to fund either. It's up to you to decide."

As Killashandra followed Lanzecki and Lars to the door, she sneaked a look over her shoulder and saw the hesitation on the leader's face. He wanted the crystal badly; he knew he could pay for it; he was just trying it on as standard operating procedure. But he had obviously never approached this Guild before. Quite likely, there would be an order from the Apharian League before the Apharians departed Shankill Moon Base. Someone should have warned them not to haggle with Lanzecki and the Heptite Guild. Most people knew that. Still, there were always those who would chance their arms to save a few credits. Only this group had forgotten that mining crystal was not so very much different from mining asteroids: the result of failure bore the same cost.

She shrugged.

"Damn fools," she heard Lanzecki say as she closed the door to the conference room.

He stalked across to the table at which he and Lars had been working, slammed a new file into the reader slot, and stared at the display.

That wasn't like Lanzecki, and Killashandra blinked in surprise. Lars gave an imperceptible shake of his head; she shrugged and dismissed the matter.

By the seventh day, when Lars hadn't mentioned going out into the Ranges, she did.

"Did those Apharians order? Or should we concentrate on finding some green crystal?" she asked when he finally appeared late that evening.

"Huh?"

Lars's mind was clearly on other matters. She felt excluded and that made her irritable. They were partners, close partners, and shared everything.

"I thought we came back to cut crystal, not sit around playing diddly with pencil files."

He gave her one of his quick, apologetic grins. "Well, we can depart in a day or two."

She raised her eyebrows, trying for a light touch.

"Are you aiming to take over from Bollam?"

"From Bollam?" He stared at her in amazement, then laughed, pulling her into his arms. "Not likely, when I've the best partner in the whole Guild. It's just that—well, I can't help being flattered when Lanzecki keeps asking my advice, now can I?"

"I don't mean to denigrate your advice, but that's not like Lanzecki."

"Too true, Sunny, too true," he said with a sad sigh. "I'd hazard that he misses Trag more than he'd admit."

"Then why did he take on such a want-wit as Bollam! There must be someone more qualified!"

Lars grinned at her vehemence and rocked her close in his arms. "Did you *find* anyone to replace him over the last few days?"

She pushed him away, glaring reprovingly at him. She had thought her search discreet enough.

"Oh, there's little going on here that Lanzecki doesn't hear about sooner or later. He said to tell you that he appreciated your efforts. Bollam suits his needs."

Killa swore.

"Hey, I wouldn't mind a late-night snack," Lars said, hauling her with him to the catering unit. "And yes, the Apharians ordered the blue, still registering complaints about the cost and issuing veiled statements about unethical access and invasion of commercial privacy and all that wind and piss."

Two days later Killashandra and Lars lifted their sled out of the Hangar and headed east, toward the Milekey Ranges. Behind them a second sled departed, but immediately struck out on a nor'easterly course.

"That's Lanzecki's," Killashandra said in surprise.

"Yes, that's why he's been working such long hours, to clear all current business. He'll be the better for a spell in the Ranges. That's all he needs, really."

"But with Bollam?"

"I'll grant you that I've qualms, but who knows? Bollam might turn out to be a top-rank cutter. Or why would Lanzecki shepherd him?"

"Shepherd him?" Killa blinked. "Bollam's not been blooded in the Ranges yet?" She recalled the first crystal scars on Bollam's hands and arms. "He's cuts enough."

Lars grinned. "I heard tell that he was the clumsiest apprentice they ever had on the Hangar floor. He's lucky to find anyone to shepherd him, the number of singers he annoyed dropping crystals when he was unloading sleds."

Killa muttered uncomplimentary epithets about Bollam.

"I suppose that sort of duty does fall with Lanzecki," Lars went on with a sigh, "shepherding the ones no one else will take to initiate."

"I don't envy him the job, that's for sure."

"Nor I." Lars turned to grin at her, his eyes deep with affection. "But then, I had the best of all possible partners."

"You!" She faked a cuff to his jaw. She could, and did, envy Bollam the chance to be shepherded by Lanzecki on his first trip into the

Ranges: the twit didn't deserve such an honor. Odd, though; she would have thought Lanzecki would have blackmailed someone else to shepherd Bollam, reserving his own talents to take the rough edges off the man once he had been exposed to the Ranges.

"Where'll we head, partner?" Lars asked her as they entered the Milekey.

Killashandra grimaced. The usual ambivalence surged up in mind and body. A singer cut crystal in order to leave the Ranges as frequently as possible. But a singer also had to renew herself with the crystal she cut. The more she cut out of a certain lode, the easier it was to find later. If she went off-planet for any length of time, that attraction diminished. But a singer had to go off-planet to ease the crystal pulse in her blood. Cutting too much was almost, not quite, as much a hazard as cutting too little. With Lars, she had often been able to cut just enough, which was the main advantage of singing duet.

"Can you remember where we cut those greens a couple of trips back?"

Lars gave her a long thoughtful look.

"What's wrong?" she asked. "We have cut greens, and with none available it seems sensible to get top market price on something."

"Why don't we go for black?"

"You know how hard it is to find black, good black," she replied in a cranky tone. She didn't *want* to cut blacks—ever.

"Green it is," he said, and slightly altered the sled's course. "Our marker may have faded a lot," he went on. "Lots of storms have passed over since we cut green."

"Not that many!"

He said nothing and accelerated the sled. "It'll be a while. Settle down."

She watched the jagged pinnacles of the Range. Paint splotches, old and new, indicated claims. Once she would have recognized markers by their color and pattern. She didn't try anymore. Theirs was a black and yellow herringbone design, which Lars had thoughtfully painted on the console. She often cursed that choice, because it was hell to paint the pattern on uneven rock surfaces, but she had to admit that the black and yellow herringbones had high visibility.

The sled plowed through the skies, the sweep of peak and pinnacle flowing past her in an almost mesmerizing blur. Below a relatively fresh paint splotch, she caught the metallic glitter of a sled half-hidden under a canyon overhang.

"They ought to watch out," she murmured under her breath. "Ledges can fall down on top of you."

"What say, Sunny?" Lars asked, and she grinned as she waved at him to ignore her.

It was late in the morning when he began to circle the sled. "Think I found one," he said, bringing them down to hover over the spot.

"Are you sure?" Killa squinted down at rocks bearing the barest hint of color: the herringbone pattern was all but indistinguishable.

"Sure as I can be. Shall we put down and see what we remember of the site?"

"We certainly have to renew the marker," she said, annoyed that the paint, which was supposed to have a long sun-life, had faded so badly. Markers were what kept other singers from usurping claims. A claim was circular in shape, with a radius of a half kilometer radiating from the painted logo. No one was supposed to enter a space so marked. As further protection, the mark was not required to be at the lode itself—or even anywhere near. The lode could be right at the edge of the enclosed space and still be claimed by the singer.

"Paint first, look later," Lars said, calling the order.

They painted and then took a meal break, all the while looking around the circle, hoping to trigger recollections of this particular site.

"We've got to go down," Killa said after she had swallowed her last mouthful. "Nothing's familiar at this height."

"Eeny, meeny, pitsa teeny," Lars chanted as he circled up from the peak. At "teeny" Lars left the circle in that direction, bringing the sled down into the small canyon. He grinned at Killa: a random choice had often proved lucky. He neatly parked their vehicle in the shadow cast by the higher side, and she nodded approval of his caution. They would be hidden from an aerial view until the morning.

She was first out of the sled, running her fingers along the uneven rock walls of the canyon and hoping to catch a trace of crystal resonance. Or find the scars of a previous working.

Lars struck off in the opposite direction. They met on the far side, having seen nothing to indicate that this canyon was the one they were looking for.

"Shall we go left or right?" Lars asked as they got back into the sled.

"Off the top of my head! Right!" Killashandra said after a moment's sober thought. "Not that that's any indication."

But she turned out to be correct—for in the narrow ravine to the right of their first landing they came across evidence of cutting.

"I'd know our style anywhere," Lars said.

"You mean yours," she replied, settling in to another of their long debates as they returned to the sled and unpacked their sonic cutters.

"We'd do better if we waited until the sun hits them," Lars said.

"No better or no worse. Hit a C."

Inhaling deeply, he sang a fine powerful true mid-C, his eyes sparkling at her, daring her as he so often did. She sang out a third above his note, as powerfully as he had. Sound bounced back at them, making them both flinch at the undertones.

"Some of it's cracked," Killa said, but, as one, they moved toward the resonating point. "Green, from the power in its echo."

"I told you I remembered where we'd cut green."

Once at the side of the ravine, they sang the pitch notes again and set their cutters to the sound. Killa indicated the cut she would make and set herself for the first wrenching scream of cut crystal. No sooner had she set the cutter than Lars set his a handspan to the right.

The first set cleared away the imperfect crystal to reveal a wide vein of fine green.

"Shards, but those Apharians are going to be furious when they hear about this," she said, slicing away additional marred quartz.

"What'll we try for?"

"Communit sizes, of course," she said with a snort.

Once the debris cleared, they sang again in case they had to retune the cutters, but Lars's C and her E rang clearly back at them. Together they placed their cutter edges and, taking a simultaneous breath, turned on the power.

Chapter 5

Darkness forced them to stop with twelve fine crystals cut and stored in the padded carrier case carefully strapped in the cargo bay. Quietly, from the ease of long practice, they made a meal and ate it. Then, continuing their rituals, they washed—there would come days when crystal song would override such habits. While Lars made entries in the sled's log, Killashandra pulled down their double bunk and got out the quilts. They were both ready to settle at the same time.

The morning sun, stroking the Ranges awake, provided an alarm no singer could resist: the insidious chiming of crystal as the first rays dispelled the chill of night. The notes were random, pure sound, for only perfect crystal could speak on sunlight. The ringing stirred senses and awoke desires as it grew louder and more insistent. Killashandra and Lars simultaneously turned to each other. She could see his smile in the shadowy cabin and answered it, lifting her arm to his shoulders, eager for the touch of his bare skin against hers. It seemed to Killashandra that as their lips met an arpeggio rippled through the air, excitingly sensual, deliciously caressing, ending on a clear high C that shivered over them just as their bodies joined.

This was the real reason men and women sang crystal together—to hear such music, to experience such sensations and such ecstasy as only crystal could awaken on bright, clear mornings. Such unions made up for all the mundane squabbles and recriminations between partners when crystal cracked or splintered and a whole day's work might lie in shards at their feet. There was always the prospect of the incredible combination of sound and sensation in sunlit crystal to reanimate their relationship.

"We must get moving, Sunny," Lars murmured, making an effort to move. Too languorous with remembered passion, Killashandra murmured a throaty denial and shaded her eyes from the sun splashing into the cabin.

"C'mon now. Hell, we'll be having a spate of good clear weather," he said, pushing her toward the edge of the bunk. "We can afford to do a little work today. I'll start breakfast. Your turn in the head."

He used the light jocular tone that he knew Killashandra would accept. As she rose and stretched luxuriously, she glanced enticingly over her shoulder at him.

"That won't work on me today, Sunny," he said wryly and gave her a slap across the buttock. Sometimes the sight of her at full stretch was enough to tempt him, despite the fact that they both knew a repeat performance once the sun had risen would be less satisfying than the first.

She strutted sensually across to the head, flirting with him, but he only laughed and stuck his right leg into his coverall, pulling the garment up past his unresponsive member. She grabbed her own clothes and slid open the door. As he took his turn, she finished making the substantial breakfast they would need to fuel them for working crystal all day. On clear days, singers rarely stopped to eat, cutting as long as there was light enough to see where to place their blades.

Killashandra recalled, without remembering when, that there had been a time or two when she had cut throughout a double-moon night: the times when she had struggled to cut enough to afford passage off the fardling planet to get some respite from crystal song.

They had been profitably working that vein for five days when Killashandra's weather sense began to pluck at her consciousness.

"Storm?" Lars knew her so well.

She nodded, and set her cutter for a new level. "Not to worry yet."

"Nardy hell, Killa, we've got eight crates of the stuff. No sense in taking a risk. And the marker's new enough to draw us right back here after the storm."

"We've time. Sing out," she told him in a tone that was half command, half plea. "Greens aren't easy to find, and I'm not about to quit when there's still time to cut. The storm could ruddy well splinter this vein to nothing good enough to spit at."

Lars regarded her levelly. "Just let's not cut it too fine!"

"I wouldn't let you get storm-crazed, lover."

"I'm counting on it. I think this tier's going to be minor key," he added, humming a B-flat and hearing the same tone murmur back at him.

"I'll make mine E, or would A be better?"

He nodded crisp agreement for the A, and they sang, cutting as soon as they heard the answering notes the crystal flung back at them, its own death knell.

But storm sense caught at Killashandra again, not long after they had crated the nine crystals of that cutting.

"I think we're going," she told him, hefting the cutter in one hand and bending her knees to take one handle of the crate. He did the same, and she set a rapid pace back to the sled. As Lars settled the crate into its strappings, Killa racked up both cutters and took the pilot's seat, closing hatches and starting up the engines.

Lars peered out the window of the right-hand side and muttered a curse. "Angle of the wall's wrong. Can't see anything. Where's it coming from?"

"South." Just then the weather-alert klaxon cut in. It got one hoot out before her hand closed the toggle.

"You're ahead of the best technology the Guild can beg, borrow, or steal, aren't you?" Lars grinned at her, proud of her ability.

"Yup!"

"Don't get cocky."

"It's going to be a bad one, too." She shifted uneasily in the seat, her bones already responding to the distant stroking of the crystal. "I swear, the longer I cut, the more sensitive I get to the intensity of weather systems."

"Saves our skins, and our crystal."

She lifted the sled vertically, and as they rose above the sheltering walls of the ravine, storm clouds could be seen as a smudge of dark, roiling gray on the horizon. She veered the sled about to port and lifted above the higher cliffs, hovering just briefly over their paint mark, satisfied that it would survive this storm and a few more before wind-carried abrasives scoured the rock clean again.

They were nearly out of the Ranges when their communit lit up.

"Mayday, Mayday," cried a frantic voice.

"Mayday? What the—" she demanded indignantly, leaning to one side to close the connection.

Lars's hand masked the plate. "That's Bollam's voice."

"Bollam?" Killashandra stared at him in puzzlement: the name meant nothing to her.

"Lanzecki's new partner," Lars muttered, and responded. "Yes, Bollam?"

"It's Lanzecki, I can't get him to stop!"

"Take the crystal out of his hand," Killashandra said angrily. It irritated her that she still couldn't place this Bollam fellow.

"He's not holding crystal. He's cutting and he won't stop. He won't listen. He's—he's thralled."

"You dork, of course he is, that's why he doesn't cut often. It's your job to stop him. That's why he takes a partner into the Ranges," Lars replied, his tone still reasonable.

"But I've tried, I've tried everything. He's bigger than I am!" Bollam's voice had turned to a distressed whine.

"Knock his feet out from under him," Lars said, concern deepening in his expression.

"I tried that, too."

"Cross-cut with your cutter. Tune it off-pitch, queer his note," Killa roared, becoming more incensed with this dork's stupidity. Where had Lanzecki found such an ineffectual partner?

"I can't. I don't know how to cross-cut. This is my first time in the Ranges. *He* was shepherding *me*!" Now there was grievance and indignation in Bollam's voice. That particular tone triggered the appropriate memory in Killashandra's mind: it was exactly how Bollam had sounded when he couldn't find the Apharian files.

"So this is why Bollam suited him," Killashandra said, bitter with the realization of exactly what Lanzecki was doing.

Lars stared at her, jerking her arm to pull her around to face him. "Turn the sled. We've got to try."

"No." She reset her hands on the yoke, gritting her teeth against the pain that suddenly scored her and the tears that threatened to blind her. "No, we can't! Rules and Regs! Mayday means nothing on Ballybran!"

"Nothing?" Lars roared at her. "Lanzecki's been our friend, your lover! How can you abandon him?"

"I'm *not* abandoning him," Killashandra shrieked back, glaring her anger, her hurt, the pain of *knowing* what Lanzecki wanted! "Get out of there, Bollam," she bellowed at the communit. "Save your own skin. You can't save his."

"But I can't just *leave!*" Bollam sounded shocked, horrified at this heartless advice. "He's the Guild Master. It's my duty . . ."

"There is no such duty in the Rules and Regs, Bollam. There never was and there never will be. Get out of there, Bollam, while you still can. *Leave Lanzecki.*"

"I don't believe I'm hearing you say this," Lars cried.

She swiveled around at him, tears streaming down her face, her throat closing so that she was momentarily deprived of speech.

"He wants it this way," she managed to choke out. Then she swallowed hard on her grief and glared straight into Lars's appalled face. "Consider, Lars, would there be any other logical reason why Lanzecki would team up with a dork like Bollam? A novice in the Ranges? Physically too weak to knock him out of thrall? We haven't the right to interfere. We owe Lanzecki his choice."

She hooked her elbows through the yoke so that Lars would have to break her arms to get control of the sled. But he didn't try. He sat staring at her as she sent the sled roaring out of the Ranges, using every ounce of thrust in its powerful new engines.

"Lanzecki *intended* to opt out?"

"Singers have that option, Lars," she said in a voice as low as his. Her throat thickened again, her eyes stinging with tears. It was a hard reality to accept, but she didn't doubt for a moment—now—that that had been Lanzecki's intention. She could even hear his deep voice replying to her puzzled query about Bollam: that the man had his uses. She ought to have *known* what Lanzecki was about and tried to—tried to what? Talk a tired man out of ending a life that had grown too tedious with responsibility, too tiresome with problems, too lonely with his longtime partner dead? "He's been Guild Master for centuries."

Lars was silent until, behind them, they could both hear storm wail creeping inexorably nearer.

"Then is that also why he was so intent on me understanding Guild politics?" Lars asked, softly, shakily.

"What do you mean by that?" she demanded.

"I'm not sure I know," Lars replied, raising his hands in doubt. "It was just that—well, Lanzecki knew you and—whenever we were in from the Ranges, he sought out our company, but I always thought it was you . . ." His voice trailed off.

"Don't get any ideas, Lars Dahl," she said coldly, harshly. "You may be a Milekey Transition . . ."

"So are you."

"But there's no way I'd be Guild Master." She glared at him, willing him to respond in the same vein. "Damn it, Lars, you're my partner. And there's a lot more to being Guild Master than understanding the politics of the job."

"That is true enough," he replied in a muted voice, his eyes looking directly ahead as they passed over the last hills before the Cube.

The flight officer signaled them to park their sled near Sorting with the other half-dozen vehicles that had fled the storm. Killashandra killed the engines and turned to Lars.

"Start with the crates, will you? I'll report," she said bleakly.

"I will, if you want me to," Lars offered, suddenly human again in his unexpressed sympathy.

"No, I was pilot."

The flight officer, a lanky lean man whom Killashandra didn't recognize at all, was trotting in her direction, signaling her to wait for him.

"Were you within range of Bollam? The one Lanzecki was shepherding?"

"Yes," Killashandra said so flatly that the man blinked in surprise. "He couldn't break Lanzecki out of thrall. We told him to get the hell out of the Ranges."

"You mean . . ."

The cargo officer arrived at that point, her face grim.

"I mean Lanzecki *chose*!" Killashandra dared the flight officer to argue her point.

"You're sure, Killa?" the cargo officer asked.

Killashandra rounded on her, away from the accusing eyes of the flight officer.

"Why else would he choose a dork like Bollam? And a novice? Too inexperienced to know how to break thrall and too physically insignificant to be a threat!"

The cargo officer bowed her head, her eyes closed.

"I don't understand . . . Were you near enough, Killashandra Ree, to reach them in time?" the flight officer demanded.

"I accepted Lanzecki's choice. You'd better."

With that Killashandra turned on her heel, returning to her sled at a pace that was nearly a run. Behind her she could hear the flight officer arguing with Cargo, whose low and curt rejoinders told Killashandra that she, at least, accepted Lanzecki's option.

As she helped her silent partner unload their cut, she knew that Lars's feelings about that option were ambivalent. The news seemed to seep through from the Hangar into Sorting, and conversations were muted, arguments over crystal prices conducted in low tones. When the Sorter told them how much they had earned for the green, Killashandra felt none of the elation such a figure should have elicited. Lars only arched his eyebrows, nodded acknowledgment, and turned away. The Sorter shrugged. Dully, Killashandra followed Lars to the lifts. She did listen to the Met report that was being broadcast, even in the lifts, since weather had top priority with most singers. Nothing was said about missing sleds. Nothing ever was.

"That's a relief," Killashandra muttered as the report concluded. The storm had been one of those quick squalls, fierce in its brief life, its only damage that of taking Lanzecki's life in its fury. "We can be back out in the Ranges by tomorrow evening."

"Fardles, Killa!" Lars rounded on her. "Lanzecki's not even found and—"

Her livid expression stopped his words. "The sooner I'm in the Ranges, the sooner I'll forget."

"Forget Lanzecki?" Lars was stunned.

"Forget! Forget!" The lift door opened and she ran down the hall to their apartment. She heard him following her and wasn't even grateful.

As she slammed into their quarters, she could hear the radiant fluid slopping into the tub. Pulling off her coverall and boots, she stumbled into the room and clambered into the bath. The fluid was no more than calf-deep, so she stood under the spigot and let it roll down her back and shoulders. Dimly she heard Lars's voice, updating his records. She began to curse, so that she couldn't possibly hear a word he said.

All the resident staff of the Cube were quiet and depressed the next noon when Killashandra and Lars reached the dining room. While Killa filled her tray from the alcohol-drinks dispenser, Lars kept looking around, peering at the faces of those sitting in alcoves. Seeing his discreet search for Bollam recharged Killa's vexation.

"Lanzecki opted out, Lars," she said in an intense low voice, jerking him to her side. "What're you drinking?"

"Yarran!" His voice was flat.

"Yarran? This is no time for beer! This is the time to get paralytic drunk!"

He gave her a bitterly amused look. "I thought you wanted to be back in the Ranges tomorrow morning. With a hangover?"

"With the most massive hangover I can acquire between now and then," she told him savagely, and downed the first of the many triple-measure glasses on her tray, pressing for a refill as she tossed the empty glass into the recycler.

"You may just go out alone, then," he said. Taking the Yarran beer from the slot, he left her standing there.

Surprised, she watched him maneuver among the tables, heading for the far alcove where the two Hanger officers were sitting. She hadn't thought Lars had a masochistic streak in him. Or maybe he just had to find out if Bollam had somehow managed to get Lanzecki into the sled and back to the Cube.

The dork couldn't have managed it, or the nonsingers of the Guild wouldn't be so deep in drink. Now that she had looked around, she could see that most of them were as badly gone as she would like to be. She downed another triple and, moving carefully so as not to slosh a drop of liquid anesthesia, made her way toward Lars. The stench of ketones was almost overpowering. These people must have been drinking steadily since the news got out.

"Oh, he'll live," Cargo was saying as Killashandra approached the table. "That's not saying how much good he'll be." She glanced up at Killashandra and, with a brief inclination of her head, indicated that the singer could join them. The flight officer clearly did not agree with that invitation. "Oh, leave it, Murr. You haven't been here long enough to *know*. You did as you should, Killa," she added and patted the cushion beside her. Her eyebrows lifted at the sight of so much liquor on the tray. She raised her mug of coffee. "Happy hangover!"

Suddenly Killashandra lost any taste for the boozing she had planned. Her stomach roiled and growled. She sat down, hands limp in her lap, and stared across at Lars, wanting his reassurance and understanding even more than she had ever wanted to cut black crystal. He pointedly ignored her, and the tears began to stream down her face.

"You did right, Killa. You did," Cargo said softly, and clasped her fingers on the singer's forearm, squeezing briefly with a gentling firmness before releasing. "Didn't she, Lars Dahl?" she added sternly.

Lars looked at Cargo, unable to avoid his partner's tear-streaked face. He closed his eyes, exhaling in defeat. "Yes, if you say so, she did."

"Look here, Dahl." Cargo leaned across the table, her face fierce. "I do say so. If you want, you can ask Medical. They could see." And she waved her hand in the general direction of the Infirmary wing where damaged singers were tended until such time as hearts in crippled bodies stopped and empty minds went dark. "*I* could see!" And her tone was fierce. "Murr here didn't know Lanzecki in his prime as I did, and Killa did! And Killa knew him better than most. Face it, Murr, Lars, she did the right thing. Don't know why that ass Bollam even qualified—except he was probably too craven, or too shitless scared to step back after Disclosure, when he heard all the risks he'd be taking on Ballybran. He had a lousy Transition, as if the symbiont working into his bloodstream also discovered it hadn't made a great choice of a home body, and we never thought he'd end up a singer!" The scorn in her voice gave unexpected ease to Killashandra's anguish. "Certainly not as Lanzecki's partner!"

"Lanzecki was shepherding him . . ." Lars said, trying to find some perverse justification.

Cargo snorted bitterly. "When Lanzecki said he'd shepherd the geek,

I knew I wouldn't ever see Lanzecki back in the Hangar, Lars. And I told you that, didn't I, Murr?"

"I just don't understand why," Murr said. "Everyone's saying he was the best Guild Master we've ever had . . ."

"There've only been four," Cargo replied.

"Four?" Murr was staggered. "But the Guild's been going close to seven hundred years!"

"Hmmm, so it has, and I've been Cargo for nearly two and a half hundred."

That silenced Murr completely—he stared at the woman as if he expected her active body and attractive face to crumple into dust if he so much as blinked. Despite her grief, Killashandra was amused.

"What did Medical know about Lanzecki?" Lars asked, his expression as bleak as ever. Somehow, though, Killa sensed that his antagonism toward her had eased.

Cargo shrugged. "What happens to all of us eventually? The symbiont is weakened past restoration, and degeneration finally starts. All a fast downhill ride then." That was when she noticed Murr's expression and grinned. "Never fear, Murr, you're stuck with me a while yet. Me and my symbiont are in great shape."

"It doesn't say in Rules and Regs," Lars began after watching Murr try to assume a normal attitude, "how a new Guild Master is elected."

"No, it doesn't," Cargo agreed, frowning slightly. "But, like I say, the problem doesn't come up very often."

Killashandra sent a fierce glare at Lars. The slight grin that tugged at one corner of his mouth did not reassure her.

"It'll take time," Cargo added indifferently. "Politics is involved. What else is new? They have to choose someone acceptable to the majority of the long-term customers."

"Who's 'they'?" Lars asked.

"I dunno." Cargo shrugged again. "Maybe one of the Instructors knows." She looked around the big room. "None of them appears to be sober enough to ask. I gotta get back to work. Do I put your sled into a ready slot? That storm's cleared off."

Killashandra didn't dare look at Lars.

"Yes, we'll be out again tomorrow," he said, and she sagged against the cushions with relief. But her relief was very short-lived as she remembered that Cargo had estimated it would be a long time before the new Guild Master was chosen.

So she didn't get drunk to blunt her acute sense of loss at Lanzecki's death. She endured it as Cargo and Lars did, as Murr couldn't. But she drank glass for glass of Yarran beer with them. A singer could drink Yarran beer for days and barely blunt sensitivities. She heard that Bollam had survived with what wits he originally possessed intact. He had been badly crystal-cut when the rescue ship had found his crashed sled, but he had made it past the storm zone before losing control. What she hated Bollam for was that crystal had wiped all his memories of Lanzecki. She couldn't wait to get out in the Ranges and hope for the same respite. A few days cutting in the Ranges, and one could forget just about anything.

Lars was up before her the next morning, their gear all packed, and silently they made their way to the Hangar. Cargo lifted her hand in acknowledgment; Flight Officer Murr raised his only to give them the go-ahead. Some trainee gave them a formal release.

As if the sled were on some kind of giant spring whose pull could not be resisted, they flew directly back to the black and yellow chevron of the green crystal.

"We shouldn't have gone direct," Killashandra remarked to Lars as he passed over the marker.

"Sky's clear," he said, with a diffident shrug. It was. No other singer was aloft to see the direction they took, direct or oblique.

When they landed in the little canyon, they both knew the vein had been damaged. They spent the rest of the day trying to cut down into clear color.

"Fardles, it's gone, Lars, leave it," Killa said when decades upon decades of experience finally surfaced to remind her how pointless their efforts were. "Green cracks the worst of all when a vein's been exposed."

He kicked at the shards underfoot to relieve his frustration and led the way back to the sled. They stayed there the night, but when crystal song woke desire in them, it was only crystal that spoke, not their hearts.

It took them a week to search the full circle of which that chevron was the center. They found a very light pink, but it wasn't worth the effort of turning on their cutters. They had withdrawn from each other as never before, and Killashandra cursed silently, craving to cut crystal and relieve the tension. Even Lars might forget—at least lose the edge of painful memory—if they could just cut.

Perversely the weather stayed fair, but summer had Ballybran in its thrall and baked the Ranges. As they searched for crystal, they also looked for the deepest, most shadowy canyons in which to spend the night and get some relief from the unmitigated heat.

"I could almost welcome a storm," Lars said. "Unless we can find some water, we're going to have to go back."

"No! Not until we find crystal."

He shrugged, but they did find water, a deep pool under an overhang where water had oozed out of the more porous rock and been collected in the shade. They filled the tank, then stripped and bathed, washing their clothing where a tiny stream trickled out of the pond. The relief was physical, not mental, but they were more in charity with each other than at any time since Bollam's voice had shattered their rapport.

Late the next morning Lars, whose turn it was to pilot the sled, spotted an almost invisible black and yellow chevron.

"What do you think? We cut here?" he asked.

"I don't remember, don't care, I'd even cut pink, so long's we cut *something!*"

"Eeny, meeny, pitsa teeny," and Lars aimed the sled sou'sou'east to a narrow gorge with high walls on the north side. There was a V-shaped notch in the eastern lip. "That looks familiar."

"It's a cut all right." She had both their cutters unracked before Lars landed the sled, and pausing only long enough to grab a water bottle, she half ran to the fracture, slipping on old shards to reach the site. "It's the black, Lars, it's the black!"

Depression lifted from her, and she even remembered to be cautious as she climbed to the top of the shelf. Lars sang out a fine strong C, and she could feel the crystal's response even through the thick soles of her boots. She cut the first shaft, then struggled with Lars when he had to wrest it out of her hands, for it thralled her as black crystal usually did. She was weeping when she saw him nestle the black in the padded crate. He slapped her hard, three times across the face, and she leaned against him, grateful.

"It's all right, Sunny. It's all right," he murmured, caressing her hair briefly. "Now, let's cut. For Lanzecki. He did like to see us bring in the blacks."

"Yeah, but he's not going to make me link 'em! No way will he talk me into linking again!"

She was figuring where to cut next, and how many they could get out of this fine black crystal, so she didn't see the peculiar way Lars looked at her.

Clodine gave them top market price on their five crates of black. There was enough for two planetary systems—if any could afford the price of black-crystal communits—and some nice single pieces that might just chord into current installations as auxiliaries. Clodine was full of praise for their work.

"No one cuts the way you two do. I didn't realize singers could be so individual, but you are, you know," she said, slightly shy with embarrassment but sincere in her compliment.

"Where'll we go, Lars?" Killashandra asked. "I think it's your choice."

"I think you're right," he replied, laughing. He was himself again, she knew, but she didn't know why she thought he hadn't been.

Back in their quarters, as usual she plunged directly into the tub while he updated his file.

"That didn't take you long," she said. It seemed only a few moments before he came into the room. Usually an update took him a quarter of an hour.

Still clothed, he was looking in a puzzled fashion at a printout. He held it so she could see the message.

"Report to Conference? What does Lanzecki want you to do *now*?" She hauled at his hand. "You've got to bathe first. We reek!" She laughed because the smell of him could always arouse her no matter how rank he was.

"Lanzecki?" He sighed, his eyes sad, and she wondered what was wrong. "I'd better go find out. This message is several days old."

"He can wait. He has before."

Lars peeled off the perspiration-stained and crystal-sliced overall. "I'll shower. I'll be back as soon as I know what this means." He crumbled the message in a wad and lobbed it at the recycler.

"Oh, Lars! We've got to make plans . . ."

"You start. Just find us a water world that we haven't been to, Sunny," he said, but she sensed his tone was forced.

And so it would be, being required to report so immediately to Lanzecki after a month in the Ranges. Hot summer, at that. It would take several long baths to cleanse her skin of accumulated sweat and dust. Fardles, how she hated Ballybran in the summer. Even her hair had been baked off her head; she fingered the inch-short strands. No, the memory surfaced: they had cut each other's hair scalp-close at one point because they had been so hot and their hair so filthy.

She sank to her chin; the radiant fluid was heavy against her skin, drawing out the vibrations that seemed to throb in every pore. She was tired. She didn't know how Lars was finding the energy to answer Lanzecki's summons. She did remember to pull the shoulder harness from its alcove and get her arms through it. That way, if she did fall asleep, she wouldn't slip beneath the fluid. A singer could drown that way. She had too much awareness of danger to fall into *that* trap the way . . . She paused, unable to remember who it was who had been in danger.

She was just beginning to feel clean when Lars came swinging into the bathroom. He stood for a moment on the threshold, taking her in, and then began the grin she knew too well meant he was about to say something he knew she wouldn't like.

"There's a terminal patient waiting escort at Shankill, Killa," he said, drawling the words out.

She groaned. "And you volunteered? Why does Lanzecki always pick on us?"

He pointed his index finger at her, lifting his eyebrows and grinning rather sheepishly, and she groaned again.

"He picked *me* again?"

An odd expression flashed across Lars's face, and his brows leveled again. "*I* picked you." He strode over to the bath, hooking a towel in one hand as he passed the rack. He held it up for her. "This is a real bad one. She wasn't diagnosed properly and the symbiont is the only chance she has."

Killashandra heaved herself out of the bath, ignoring the entreaty in his eyes and the set of his lips. She stalked to the shower stall, the radiant fluid sleeting off her body with every step. She turned the water shower on full blast. From the curtain of water she glared at him, turning slowly to be sure the fluid rinsed off completely. Slamming the lever in the opposite direction, she deigned to take the towel from his hand. And sighed.

"Does Lanzecki need singers so badly he'll recruit the moribund?" she asked flippantly, drying herself, deliberately making the actions sensual. Catching that same odd expression on her partner's face, she realized that dalliance was the last thing on his mind then.

"She hails from a planet named Fuerte. *I* thought you'd be the best representative the Guild could send."

She caught the slight emphasis of the personal pronoun. A second flippant remark was on her lips when she sensed that Lars really wanted her to take this assignment.

"Shuttle's waiting, Killa," he said gently. "She doesn't have much time."

"Shards! Why me?" She flipped the towel away, examining her body. "I don't even have a recent scar to show off. I couldn't prove the positive rejuvenation of the symbiont. Much less," she added with a wry smile, "much less that I originated on Fuerte."

"She doesn't have much time." Lars gave her his one-sided grin, though his blue eyes remained sad. "And you're much better at Disclosure than anyone else I know."

Grumbling to herself, nevertheless Killashandra went to the closet and dragged out the first clean shipsuit she saw, thrusting her feet through the pant legs, shoving her arms down the sleeves, and closing the front as she used her toes to hook boots from the floor. She jammed her feet into them.

"Where've they stashed her?"

Lars's arm came around her shoulder and he nuzzled her ear, kissing fondly but with no hint of sensuality. "In Recruitment."

"Recruitment?"

He nodded. "You'll understand when you get there. Now go!"

In fact, he walked her to the lift and gave her another kiss when she exited at the shuttle level. Killashandra wasn't happy about Lanzecki preempting Lars's assistance, but she didn't really mind about her assignment—she had done it before.

The Ballybran symbiont was the last chance for those whose illnesses could not be cured by modern techniques. In a galactic civilization, minor human mutations could result in major immune reactions to relatively innocuous viruses that refused to respond even with an immense pharmacopoeia and therapeutics cunningly developed from old-world reliables and alien innovations. Exposure to the Ballybran symbiont had proved remarkably effective in almost every single case—at least the ones that reached the planet before the organ damage had gone past the point of retrieval. The obvious deterrent was that the patient then had to take up whatever new life the symbiont provided—and not always that of crystal singer, since that required perfect pitch. But crystal singing was not the

only career available on Ballybran. Support skills and professions were always welcomed. Killa wondered what skills this new candidate might
have. Maybe replace that dork in Lanzecki's office?

Lanzecki's personal shuttle was parked at the bay, and the pilot
ceased lounging the moment she emerged from the lift, gesturing to her
urgently to hurry. She gave him a smile, since he appeared to know her.

"What's the gen on this candidate?" she asked as she strapped herself in.

He nodded briefly and completed the formalities with Traffic Control, but he didn't answer until they had cleared Ballybran's atmosphere.

"The daughter of some planetary official . . ."

"Fuerte."

"Yeah, that's the place. Medic says they got her here just about in
time. Some bug's doing nasty things to her spinal cord."

Killashandra gave a shudder.

"The irony is that she was trying to find a vaccine for the same
infection."

"She's medical?" Medically trained personnel were valuable on
Ballybran, despite the symbiont's benefices.

"Research and Development. Not enough R and very little D," he
added.

Shankill Base cleared them immediately to the Guild portal.

"I'll wait," the pilot said with a nod as he opened the shuttle's lock.

The recruitment director, a rather portly and impressive-looking
man, seemed immensely relieved at her arrival.

"This way, Killashandra Ree," he said. "They oughtn't to have left
this so long," he added with a mixture of annoyance and criticism. "She
may not make it."

Killa started to give a facetious response, but limited herself to a shrug.

"This way," he said, gesturing her away from the interview rooms toward one of the larger accommodations. "We *have* completed all the necessary formalities . . ."

"Then why—" She broke off, for he had palmed the door open and
she was momentarily startled by the number of people crowded into the
room. From the expressions on their faces, she began to understand some
of the problems. The candidate was on a float, to one side of the room, a
medic hovering anxiously and fussing with the dials of the support system
that evidently kept the girl alive. Five people whose faces were tanned by
Fuertan sun and anxious with fear rushed toward her, each addressing her
with such urgency that she could understand nothing.

"Which of you are her parents?" Killashandra asked. "I can plainly
see who's the applicant."

Two stepped forward while the other three looked displeased at being excluded.

"I am Governor Fiske-Ulass," the man said, "Donalla's father, and
this is her mother, Dian Fiske-Ulass."

"So what's your problem?"

The man gave a twitch to his shoulders that suggested to Killa that he was rarely in the position of petitioner and found it unacceptable.

"We find that we are unable to accompany Donalla to Ballybran . . ."

"You may—if you wish to remain with her," Killa said drolly.

Irritation flickered in his eyes, but he went on, regarding her with growing suspicion. Fuertan officials hated being challenged.

"That there is absolutely no guarantee that this—this unusual symbiosis will cure her . . ."

The medic spoke up from the side of the room. "It *was* her option, Governor. Her option when she was still able to speak. She maintains that position."

Killa made eye contact with the medic. "She can no longer speak?"

"She *can* communicate," the medic replied, sending a glance at the governor, who flicked his fingers in repudiation of that statement.

"How?"

"If you have been in attendance on an invalid, you learn to interpret requirements . . ."

The governor snorted in dismissal, and the mother stifled a sob. Killa nodded her head in acceptance, however, and waited for the medic to continue.

"One blink of the eyelids is no, two is yes." She stepped away from the float, gesturing Killa to see for herself.

"Everyone blinks," the governor said.

Killa ignored him and approached the patient. Looking at the bleached white face, lines of long suffering and pain drawn on the papery-looking dry skin, Killashandra felt a stab of sympathy for this wreck of a human being. Her head was braced, and Killa had to bend slightly over her to see her eyes, light blue, alive and vivid in a sickly yellow that should have been healthy white.

"Is Ballybran symbiosis what you wish?" she asked.

The eyelids closed firmly once, then twice, and then the eyes held Killa's glance with an appeal that was crystal clear.

"What's the prognosis without symbiont?" she asked the medic.

"How she's held on to life this long is beyond me," the medic murmured. "A few more days at the most, and that's close to miraculous."

"And there's been full Disclosure, to which Donalla has agreed," Killa asked, lightly stressing the girl's name as she regarded the recruitment officer.

He nodded. "In strict accordance with regulations. But the parents have to sign in her place, since she is unable to. That's also regs."

"So what *is* your problem?"

"We've heard tales . . ." the mother blurted out while her husband glared suspiciously at Killashandra.

"That the symbiont changes people into monsters?" Killashandra asked, and knew that, indeed, that was their fear.

She snatched an ampoule from the medic's pack, smashed it against the table, and, to the horrified astonishment of those in the room, deliberately gouged her forearm with a shard of the broken glass. The lacerations were satisfactorily long and bled profusely.

"A monster that heals in minutes," Killa said, holding out her arm so that all could see how quickly the symbiont worked to stem blood flow and repair tissue. "Sign!" she said to the parents in her most imperious tone. "You've got thirty seconds before I leave . . . without her and her last chance to live."

It didn't take Dian Fiske-Ulass that long to reach for the document and scrawl her signature. She held the stylus out to her husband. "What *other* chance has Donalla got?" she cried.

"None," the medic said firmly, and closed her lips over whatever else she would have added.

With a shrug of angry resignation, the governor took the stylus and scribbled his name, illegible, but embellished with rather fancy amendments. "There! You've taken my only daughter from me."

"And you're *governor* of Fuerte?" Killa asked with contempt and then turned to the medic. "Let's get her aboard the shuttle. The Guild Master sent his personal craft." She shot a jaundiced look at Fiske-Ulass.

The others trailed after the float, Dian beginning to sob, the governor trying to recover his public image by appearing sternly resolved.

As soon as the pilot saw them in the corridor, he moved forward to take the front end of the float from Killa, who gently took the other position from the medic.

"Give me your code and I'll let you know the outcome," she told her.

The medic jerked her head back at the retinue. "They're all staying on the station until . . ."

Killashandra snorted. "Our head medic will communicate all details to you. What's your name?"

The medic gave her a very odd smile. "Hendra Ree."

"Ree? You're a relative?" When the medic nodded, her eyes dancing a bit, Killa went on. "So you knew I was here?"

"You're something of a family legend, and I mentioned you, and Ballybran's symbiont, to Donalla when her condition disimproved," the medic told her as they maneuvered the float into the shuttle.

"Legend?" Killashandra asked, surprised, for she hadn't expected *her* family to remember her at all, considering she had left home in the company of an infamous crystal singer. She strapped in the handles of the float.

"Even in today's sophisticated tech societies, legends have their place."

"No, sir, not even in shuttle," they could hear the pilot saying. "Not unless you want to stay. Shards, the air in here was processed on Ballybran. You're getting enough just saying your farewells."

Instantly the governor backed out, restraining his wife from setting foot over the threshold.

The medic gave a little snort, tugged to be sure the straps were secure, and then, in a swift movement, bent to kiss Donalla's cheek. "Good luck, kid!" she whispered.

Hendra turned slightly as she left the shuttle and gave Killa a good-luck sign and a broad grin. Was that what you did when you met a family legend? Killa wondered.

"Let's move it," Killashandra said, belting into her seat as the pilot slipped into the control chair.

As soon as he was released from the satellite dock, he contacted Heptite HQ, telling them to be ready to receive the terminally ill applicant.

The medical team was squeezing through the portal before it was fully dilated. As they angled the float out, Killashandra noticed the tear streaks down the sick girl's pallid face.

"You're okay, Donalla?" she asked.

The eyelids closed twice, each time squeezing out tear drops, oddly emphatic in a bizarre fashion.

"I'll keep in touch, kid!" Killa added as the medical team whisked the girl away to the waiting lift.

Donalla wouldn't be in the Infirmary, but in one of the candidate rooms until she became infected by the symbiont. Killa hoped that it wouldn't take long for a body already so weakened and stressed by illness. There was an aura of courage about Donalla that Killa respected, and she hoped that the girl's stupid, bias-ridden parents hadn't dallied away her last hope of life.

She nodded her thanks to the pilot and then strode to the nearest communit, asking for Lars Dahl.

"You got her?"

"Let's hope in a timely fashion. She's pretty far gone."

Lars gave a grunt. "All the easier for the symbiont to get to work—according to Medical."

"By the way, being Fuertan was no help!" Killa grinned at his look of query. "Except for the medic."

"That's right, keep me guessing."

"It appears," Killa said with a chuckle, "I'm a family legend."

"And all the time you thought you were a black sheep," Lars replied with a suitably dour expression.

"All this time I thought I had been expunged from the Ree genealogy."

"Well, well! Life has its little surprises, does it not?"

"When one can remember them!"

Chapter 6

Thinking that a legend ought to be compassionate or kindly or at least welcoming, Killashandra accompanied Donalla to her new quarters. Green-garbed medical personnel hovered, checking dials and hooking up remote life-support gear.

Presnol, the Guild's senior medical officer, huddled over the record printout, tsk-tsking, occasionally swearing, and looking extremely displeased with what he saw.

"Why do they leave it so late?"

"Miracles occur with every passing second," Killa said.

"Well, it's been left bloody late," Presnol repeated with a fierce scowl. "Why, her throat muscles aren't even strong enough to operate an implant. How does she communicate?"

"One blink is no, two are yes."

Presnol was clearly appalled. "What backwater planet spawned her?"

Killa grinned. "A mudball named Fuerte. However, there's not a thing wrong with her ears."

Presnol swore again, his skin darkening with embarrassment. Then his expression cleared to a thoughtful look. "Hmmm, I certainly hope the symbiont can do its trick. With her background, she'd be invaluable in the labs."

Lowering her voice, Killa asked, "How long before you see any transitional traces?"

"In her weakened state, it won't take long. It better not take long."

"Here, symbiont. Nice symbiont, come here please," Killa said in a discreet whisper, as if calling a recalcitrant animal, then grinned wickedly at Presnol.

"That's about it." Then Presnol went up to the float, his expression blandly friendly. "I'm Presnol Outerad, head medical officer. I've read your files, and there's every chance that, in your current state, the symbiont has already entered your system. We will know fairly soon, once it has had a chance to filter through your blood, but I hesitate to subject you to unnecessary phlebotomies. There are several degrees the Transition can take. Of that I must apprise you. I think we all hope"—his gesture took in Killashandra—"that you enjoy one of the gentler forms." His grin was more friendly than professional. "I'd like to stay on in attendance, if you don't object?"

Killa was relieved by Presnol's manner and explanations. But then,

Antona had trained him out of the false heartiness that some medical personnel affected. He was also dealing with someone medically trained, and the usual medic-patient interface would have been insulting. Her respect for Presnol rose. She saw Donalla blink firmly once.

"Very good. In your condition a monitor wouldn't be adequate. However, if you become aware of any increase in discomfort, a rapid eyelid motion will attract my instant attention. You could experience . . ." And as he began to enumerate the manifestations, Killa saw Lars at the doorway, watching the scene, his expression somber.

Deciding that Donalla couldn't be in better hands, Killa tiptoed away.

"We could wait a little while, couldn't we, before we go off-planet?" she asked Lars.

He regarded her with no expression whatever for a long moment, and then gave her a quick hug. "We certainly should wait to see how Donalla makes out. Being a fellow Fuertan and all . . ."

He ducked before she could pummel him.

The symbiont took very little time installing itself in Donalla's immune-deficient body. Speech returned first, and she indulged in a near-hysterical spate of weeping, which was certainly understandable and relieved her of a backlog of stress. Weeping could be quite therapeutic, Presnol remarked when he reported to Lars and Killa, as pleased as if he had had more to do with it than the symbiont.

"Back from the jaws of death, and all that," he said proudly.

Killa exchanged glances with Lars, and they both managed not to laugh.

"What's her alteration?" Lars asked.

Presnol regarded him blankly. "How on earth could we know that yet? Why, she's barely—"

"Back from the jaws of death, Lars," Killa said, struggling to keep her expression bland. "How can she possibly know how she's changed?"

"Point." Lars's lips twitched. "We'll look in on her later," he added, and blanked the screen.

Killa let loose the giggle she had been controlling. "The jaws of death, indeed!"

When they came to visit, Donalla was sitting up, propped by pillows, able to move her head and even to raise one limp, wasted hand in greeting.

"I'd hoped to be able to thank you in person, Killashandra Ree," she said.

Although her voice was low, it was a rich, warm contralto. Killa wondered if the woman was actually musically inclined and might have come out of Transition as a singer.

"Why? We Fuertans have to stick together in this alien environment," Killashandra replied genially, appropriating one of the guest chairs while Lars took the other.

Two days had improved Donalla Fiske-Ulass considerably. Her face had lost its gaunt, wasted look; her hazel eyes had gained a sparkle, her skin a healthier color; her lips were pink and less pinched. In fact, from a death's-head she was quickly turning into a rather attractive woman. Perhaps even pretty, and Killa shot a glance at Lars, who, as he had often told her, liked to look—only look—at pretty women. "Easier on the eyes than ugly ones." But there was nothing in his expression other than attentive concern and interest.

Donalla dropped her eyelids, covering either embarrassment or confusion.

"I didn't even know about the Heptite Guild until Hendra mentioned it, and you."

Killa shrugged. "Why should you?"

"It would have saved me a great deal of stress if I *had* known more about Fuertan notables."

Killa snorted just as Lars said, with a mischievous glint in his eyes, "And here you always gave me the impression you were a renegade, Killa!"

"I suppose in time even renegades become respectable," Killa said diffidently. But she was irritated: she couldn't remember any details of her departure from Fuerte. Except that she had been very glad to go. Perhaps it was just as well that she *had* forgotten the circumstances. Maybe she hadn't *wanted* to remember. Being a crystal singer made that easy enough.

"You told me that you almost didn't make it off the planet with Carrik," Lars said. He turned to Donalla. "Were you given the usual misinformation that crystal singers are wicked, dangerous, eager to entice the unwary into their lairs, corrupting the innocent?"

Donalla gave a little smile, her eyes glinting slightly. "No, but then my informant was a relative, as much of a renegade as I guess you were, Killashandra. She thought you were daring and adventurous. She was thrilled with the chance to meet you, you know."

"Really?" Killashandra was amused. That hadn't come across in Hendra's brief conversation with her, but they had had other priorities at the time. "Certainly I managed to escape Fuerte."

"It's changed since you were there," Donalla said loyally.

"It would have had to," Killa said dryly. She changed the subject. "Presnol tells me you're over the worst of the Transition."

Donalla managed another of her semi-smiles. "I'm unaware of any Transition . . ."

"That's it exactly," Killa said, rather pleased. "The symbiont was kind to you. You won't be bedridden much longer."

"I'm deeply grateful for that, I assure you. I just wish that I'd been allowed here earlier when the extent of my paralysis was appreciated."

"Just like Fuertans to resist the inevitable," Killa said.

"My parents only wanted the best for me," Donalla said.

Lars rose then. "Let's not tire her, Killa."

Obediently Killa followed his lead, although Donalla protested that she enjoyed company—especially now that she could talk again.

"I've a lot of catching up to do."

"We have, too," Lars said cryptically, guiding Killashandra out of the room.

"What did you mean by that?" she asked him when they were walking down the corridor.

He said nothing, pretending to concentrate on the Met reports as he guided her down the corridor to the lifts to the administrative level. When she realized that their destination was Lanzecki's office, she tried to pull away from him.

"Oh, no! I'm not falling for one of Lanzecki's deals. And you're daft if you let him talk you into anything. We're in good credit, Lars. We can coast for a while. What we need to do is get out in the Ranges again. We've hung about far too long."

"We don't have to worry about Lanzecki," Lars said in a tight voice. "He's not involved, Killa. Come in, please."

She couldn't withstand the entreaty in his voice; she entered the anteroom warily, looking about her.

Trag's desk was empty. Killashandra frowned, realizing vaguely that she wouldn't have seen Trag anyway. Splinters of recall suggested that there had been someone else, someone she didn't like. Lars had his hand on her back now and was propelling her into the office. It was empty. She looked about, wondering where Lanzecki had gone. Lars released her and, striding around the desk, sat down in the Guild Master's big chair.

"Killashandra Ree," Lars began in a tone she had never heard him use before: part entreaty, part frustration, and part anger. "You've simply got to recognize that Lanzecki is dead. You knew that two months ago. You even insisted that no one try to rescue him from Bollam . . ." She recognized that name and put an unattractive face to it. But Lars wasn't finished. "Have you got that lodged in your head? Finally? Lanzecki is dead."

Killashandra stared at Lars, uncomfortably aware that this was something else she had conveniently managed to forget. She shouldn't forget who was Guild Master. He was the most important person to a crystal singer, to all Heptite Guild members.

"There has to be a Guild Master . . ." she began, floundering badly as the discomfort swelled and brushed against concepts and images that she didn't want to remember.

"There is a Guild Master, Killashandra." Lars's tone was kind, soothing, his expression concerned. "I am the Guild Master now."

"*No!*" She backed away from the desk.

He jumped to his feet and came around the desk, arms outstretched to her, his expression both desperate and supplicatory.

"I know you've been resisting it, Sunny. I know that you've suppressed the fact of Lanzecki's death, but it is a fact. It's also a fact that I've been appointed Guild Master in his place. I would like you to be my executive partner in this, as you have been my partner in the Ranges."

Killashandra shook her head at him, more and more forcefully as she resisted the sense of his statements. How could Lars become Guild Master? That was absurd. He was *her* partner. They sang crystal together. They were the best duet the Guild had ever had. They *had* to return to the Ranges and sing crystal. With Lanzecki dead it was more important than ever that *they* sing crystal—black crystal, green crystal, blue! A Guild Master didn't have the time to sing crystal. Lars had to sing crystal with her. He couldn't be the Guild Master.

"I know, Sunny," Lars went on more kindly. "His death *is* hard to take. He was such a force for us all. I'd like to be as good a leader, but I want—I need—your help. You're incontestably the best singer the Guild has. You know more about singing crystal than anyone else, and you can explain what you know. Many can't articulate or convey the information they have locked in their brains. You can. Hell, you taught me!" He grinned with wry flattery. "That's only one reason why I need your cooperation and your input." He had come close enough to take her in his arms, trying with his clever hands, to which she had always responded, to soothe her distress and somehow stroke her into acceptance of the hard truths he had given her.

"There, there, Sunny. I see now that I was wrong to let you forget what you didn't want to remember just because I could always remember for you. But now I don't have that luxury. And I *need* you as my partner more than ever."

"But I'm a crystal singer. I'm not a—an office flunky."

Lars gave a brief laugh. "You think Trag was a flunky?"

"Trag was—Trag," Killa finished lamely, casting about for any rebuttal he would accept as her refusal. Lanzecki was Guild Master. He had been and would be. Trag . . . She wasn't Trag. She wasn't anything like Trag.

"I know it'll take getting used to, Sunny, but accept the reality. Accept me as the Guild Master. I know I'm not Lanzecki, but each Guild Master puts his own stamp on the Guild, and I've got some positive, if bizarre, ideas on how to improve—"

"That's why Lanzecki monopolized you so much," she said in petulant accusation. "That's why you had so many meetings with him!"

"Believe me, Killa, I didn't *know* what Lanzecki was doing. I had no idea that he was briefing me to take over for *him*. But he did think my ideas had merit . . ."

Killa stared at the man who had been her constant companion to the point where she could not envision life without him at her side. She stared at his familiar face and wondered that she knew so little about him.

"You could have said no," she whispered, appalled by what he was saying, and by what he wanted of her. "You didn't *have* to accept the appointment."

"Lanzecki suggested it with terms I couldn't refuse."

"You *want* to be Guild Master!" she accused him.

He shook his head slowly, a sad smile on his lips. "No, Sunny, I didn't *want* to be Guild Master. But I am, and I'm going to improve the Guild, and every kicking, screaming resisting member will benefit."

"Benefit? I don't like the sound of that." She stepped back from him. "What's wrong with the Guild the way it is? Who do you think you are to *change* it?" Her voice rose, shrilling with the growing sense of panic that enveloped her. "You're not Lanzecki! You've never cared about the Guild before. Just sailing. That's all you care about—sailing and seas and ships . . ." And, whirling, she ran from the office.

"Killa, love, let me explain!" he called after her.

She bashed at the lift buttons, begging the door to open and get her out of there. Lars was a seaman, not a Guild Master. Lanzecki was. He always had been. The stable, safe, and secure pivot of her life in the Guild. The door slid open and she jumped inside the car, pounding the panel to make the door close before Lars could reach her. He was going to talk her into this, too, because he could always convince her that his suggestions would work. She wouldn't let him wheedle her into an *office* job. He would keep her out of the Ranges, keep her from cutting crystal, and she would end up like Trag—with less and less symbiont protection. That's what had killed Trag: no protection.

She had to protect herself against Lars now. He would talk her into doing something she did not want to do. The Guild didn't need to be changed! It had run perfectly well for centuries. What could possibly need changing? Well, she wasn't going to help. Best cutter in the Guild, huh? Just the kind of soft talk that had gotten Lars his way with her too often! Make her a stand-in for Trag, would he? She wasn't old sobersides Trag, critical, unswerving, duty-bound. She was Killashandra Ree. She always would be! The door opened again, and she fled. At first she didn't realize where she was; then, when she recognized the Hangar floor, she gasped with relief. She mustn't let Lars catch up with her.

She'd lose herself in the Ranges and then Lars, the Guild Master, wouldn't be able to find her. She'd go as deep as she could, past any claim they had made together. She'd find new ones, ones he didn't dream existed. She'd cut and cut and she'd show the Guild Master that she was too important a cutter to be restricted to an *office*!

She was only peripherally aware that the flight officer was trying to tell her something. She repeated her urgent request for her sled. When he seemed recalcitrant, trying to restate his message, she barged past him, running toward the racks where sleds were stored. Hers was in the first rank, so she climbed to it, palmed the cabin door open, and settled herself in the pilot's seat. She checked the engines, slipped on the headpiece, and heard the babble from Operations.

"I want clearance and I don't want any nonsense. I have got to get out into the Ranges. Is that understood?"

Suddenly the voices that were trying to dissuade her went silent. There was a long pause during which she revved the engines and clenched and unclenched her hands on the yoke, waiting for her release. She'd go without it if she had to. She was reaching for the propulsion toggle when the silence ended.

"Killashandra Ree, clear to go," said a tenor voice, flat with a lack of emotion. "Good luck, Singer!"

She was in such a swivet to depart that she didn't realize that it wasn't the flight officer who had released her. She eased the sled out of the rack and headed for the open Hangar door. Once clear, she pointed the nose of the sled north. She allowed the merest margin of distance before she engaged the drive. The relief of her escape diminished the discomfort of gravitational pressure as the sled obediently shot forward, shoving her deep in the cushioning.

The first storm caught her still looking for a possible site. She didn't return to the Guild. She headed farther north, skipping across the sea away from the storm, and settled on the North Continent to wait out the heavy weather. She slept most of the interval, then returned to the Ranges and continued her search.

Lack of supplies, especially water, finally drove her back. She stayed only long enough to replenish her stores, ignoring all suggestions from both the flight and cargo officers, both of whom were desperately trying to delay her. Lanzecki probably had something in mind for her, and she didn't want any part of it.

"It isn't Lanzecki, Killa," Cargo insisted, her expression troubled. "Donalla—"

"I don't know any Donalla." And Killashandra brushed past the woman and slid into her restocked sled and closed the door firmly.

As she maneuvered the sled out of the Hangar, the flight officer kept wildly pointing to his headphones, wanting her to open up her comline, but she ignored him and sped away, taking a zigzag course at such speed that no one could track her.

She finally found crystal—deep greens in dominants. She was still cutting when the alarms in her sled went off. That made her stop— briefly—and consult her weather sense. For the first time it had not given her advance notice. Or had it? She'd had a few sessions with crystal thrall lately. Perhaps . . . But it was only the first of the warnings. She had time.

She almost didn't, for the last of the greens, a massive plinth, thralled her, and only the lashing of gale-force winds broke the spell by knocking her off balance and out of the trance.

Frantic to load her cartons, for she obviously hadn't bothered to for several days, she worked against the slimmest margin ever. Luck barely hung on to the fins of her sled, for the crash came on the very edge of the storm, near enough for a crew to rescue the crystal and her battered body. The sled was a write-off.

"Whaddid I cut? How much did I earn?" were Killashandra's first coherent questions when she finally roused from accident trauma.

"Enough, I gather, to replace your sled, Killa," a female voice said.

Killashandra managed to open her eyes, though her lids were incredibly heavy to raise. It was hard to focus, but gradually she was able to distinguish a woman's face.

She retrieved a suitable name with effort. "Antona?"

"No, not Antona. Donalla."

"Donalla?" Killa peered earnestly, blinking furiously to clear her sight. She didn't recognize the face. "Do I know *you*?"

"Not very well." There was a slight ripple of amusement in the tone. "But a while ago you saved my life."

"I don't remember cutting crystal with anyone."

"Oh, I'm not a singer. I'm a medic. Do you remember anything at all about helping persuade my parents to let me come to Ballybran?"

"No." When Killa began to shake her head to emphasize the negative, she experienced considerable pain. "I've had little to do with recruitment," she said repressively. "I sing crystal. I don't entice people to it."

"You didn't entice me, Killashandra Ree, but you did give my parents incontrovertible proof that the Ballybran symbiont heals. Fast."

"It has to, doesn't it, to keep singers in the field? I nearly bought it this time, didn't I?"

"As near as makes no never mind," said a man's voice. That one was familiar—and panic welled up in her. Him she didn't want to see. That much she remembered. She turned her head away from the direction of the voice—the Guild Master's voice.

A hand clasped her fingers warmly, the thumb caressing the back of her hand with an intimacy she found both reassuring and insidious. She tried to pull away and hadn't the strength to do so.

"Mangled yourself rather extensively, Sunny. I've always been afraid that would happen. If I'd been there . . ."

Infuriated, she did manage to snatch her hand free. "You weren't. You were in an office. Where the Guild Master has to stay!" She chewed the words out spitefully, and when she saw his face come into her line of vision, she raised her arm, despite the pain, to cover her eyes. "You had your chance to cut crystal with me. Go away." She flung her arm in his direction in an effort to strike him.

"I think you'd better go, Lars. Your presence is definitely not reassuring. She's incoherent."

"On the contrary, Donalla, she's most coherent."

"Please, Lars, don't take her seriously. Not now. She's in considerable pain despite the symbiont."

"She'll survive?"

"Oh, most certainly. The lacerations are healing quickly, and the leg bones are almost completely joined. Strained tendons and pulled muscles take a little longer to mend."

"Let me know when she's . . . herself again, will you, Donalla? And suggest . . ."

"I'll keep you informed, Lars, and I won't suggest anything right now. It would be totally inappropriate."

Killashandra moved restlessly, subconsciously resenting the friendliness of the exchanges, the subtle inference of a relationship between the two speakers: this Donalla and the man she did not want to acknowledge at all.

"I'm giving you something to put you out a while longer, Killashandra," the woman said, and Killa felt the cold of a spray on her neck. "You'll be better when you wake."

"Nothing's ever better when you wake."

It was morning when next she woke, or so the digital on the wall told her. Day, month, and year were never a function of Heptite timekeepers. And, as the Infirmary was deep in the bowels of the Guild, shielded against the ravages of Passover storms, a wall hologram reflected the external weather. Somehow a bright clear morning seemed blasphemous to Killashandra. She groaned. But the bed sensors had already picked up the alteration in her sleep pattern, and the door opened, a bright face peering around it.

"Hungry?"

"Ravenous," Killa said with a groan. Hunger also seemed a travesty to her, and she buried her face in the pillows.

"Be right back."

Food did set immediate needs to rights. Sitting up to eat also emphasized her recuperation. She didn't hurt, though her limbs felt very stiff. She examined her arms and legs and ran wondering fingers down the whitening scars that showed how horrific her wounds had been. Inevitably that reminded her that she had crashed the sled. She couldn't quite face that yet, so she heaved herself out of bed and went into the bathroom to run a deep tub of hot water, full of aromatics to ease the lingering stiffness. Finally, refreshed as well as more flexible, she settled at the room terminal and tapped out her personal code. Ignoring the line that invited her to update her memory data, she accessed her credit balance. For a moment her spirits sank. There wasn't enough to replace the sled.

Wait a minute. There was not enough credit to replace the sled she had crashed, but that one had been a double. She wasn't singing duet anymore. She had enough for a single, maybe not top of the line, but sufficient to get her back into the Ranges and, if she bought just basic rations, enough supplies for a month. She tapped out a query about her cutter. If she had banjaxed the cutter, she would be in heavy debt. Not for long, she assured herself. Not for long. She'd cut—blacks again—and show him! She dialed the cutter's facility, but no one answered. She couldn't remember the current one's name and stewed over that. She called up the Admin roster to see who it was: "Clarend nab Ost" rang no bells and, evidently, answered no calls to his or her quarters. Fortunately the girl arrived with lunch to distract a growing sense of frustration.

By the time she had finished the second hearty meal, she had also managed to contact Clarend nab Ost, who had a few choice words to say about someone who would leave her cutter unracked, crash, and then expect the tool to be ready to go. She hotly insisted that she *always* racked her cutter.

"So how come it was stuck in the cargo hatch door?" he asked snidely.

That silenced her. She was far more appalled by that lapse than she was about crashing the sled or her own injuries. So she apologized profusely, and Clarend finally ended his tirade against careless, derelict, wanton, blasé, feeble-minded, lack-witted singers and their sins, errors, and shame. Then he told her in a less trenchant tone that he hadn't quite finished repairs and he couldn't vouch for its continued efficiency if she abused it her next time in the Ranges and she was bloody lucky she had a cutter at all the way she'd treated it.

Oddly enough, the episode made her feel somewhat better: things were normal when one got properly chewed out by a technician for blatant irresponsibility. She called the Hangar and asked how long she would have to wait for a replacement single.

"I've enough credit—unless you've jacked the cost up again," she told the supply officer.

"The very idea of our benefiting by your misfortune! Single, you want now? I thought—"

"You're not keeping up with the gossip, Ritwili," she said so angrily that there was a long silence. "Haul one out of stock and commission it, provision it. Basic rations for a month. I should be out of here soon."

"Not quite 'soon,' " interrupted the medic who had overheard the last of her conversation.

Killa frowned: the woman looked familiar . . . and yet unfamiliar. Killashandra shrugged, unable to prod recall.

"In case you've forgotten, I'm Donalla Fiske-Ulass, a fellow planetarian from Fuerte," the woman said, advancing to the bed. Her voice ended on an upnote of inquiry.

Killa sighed and shook her head. "I don't remember. Don't expect me to."

"Oh, I do. I expect that the woman who saved my life should remember the fact," Donalla said blandly, shoving her hands in the pockets of her clinical coat. She was a very attractive woman, slender without being thin—although the idea of thinness tweaked Killashandra's memory. Her hair was curly and short, and framed a delicate-featured, clever face. She had lovely eyes and exuded an air of authority and competence. "Especially when I consider myself under obligation to you."

"There're no obligations in the Guild," Killa reminded her.

"Among singers, no, because you lot are, and have to be, competitive, dedicated, and woefully single-minded." Donalla grinned again. "So you'll allow me to discharge my obligation to you."

"I said, I don't recognize that there is one."

"You could if you remembered it," Donalla insisted, and something in the almost wheedling tone made Killashandra wary.

"I avoid people trying to do me good," she said in a flat and, she hoped, discouraging voice.

Donalla perched on the edge of the bed and regarded Killashandra for a moment. "That's because you haven't heard what the good bit is."

"Do I have to?" Killa sighed resignedly.

"Yes, because the Guild Master has asked me to approach every singer on this matter."

"Oh, he has." Killa set up an immediate resistance to the notion.

Donalla laughed lightly, as if she recognized the reaction and had expected it. "Hmmm, yes, well. Quite a few singers have taken me up on my offer."

"Enough of the jollying. Inform me in words of one syllable."

"Don't be churlish, Killashandra Ree." There was a caustic tone to Donalla's voice now that made Killashandra regard her with surprise. "Since I recovered my health here, I've tried to figure a way around the most important drawback that all singers face."

"How kind of you!" Killashandra gave a supercilious snort.

"Kindness had little to do with it. An efficient use of singers' time and energies does. Singers lose memory function every time they go into the Ranges. They lose crucial details of the precise location of valuable sites."

"Detail maybe, but not the resonance that'll lead you right back to a good claim," Killashandra said, shaking her head to dismiss Donalla's faulty logic.

"Only if you go right back into the Ranges. How much more convenient it would be to *recall* the exact locations by accurately remembering the relevant landmarks."

"And leave such information around for other singers to access? No way! Try another on me."

"I'm not *trying* anything on you. I've already had notable success in accessing memory in crystal-mazed singers' minds."

"You've what?" Killashandra sat up, fury building in her at such an intrusion. Who did this woman think she was?

"I had the Guild Master's authority, and it's—"

"Get out of here. I don't want any part of such a scheme. That Guild Master of yours must be out of his gourd to permit such harassment. That's the worst example of privacy invasion I've ever heard."

"But so much information can be restored," Donalla said urgently, bending toward Killashandra in an effort to win her over. "So much lost memory can be retrieved."

"I haven't lost anything I want retrieved." Killashandra was a decibel away from a shout. "Go peddle your nonsense to someone else, Donalla. Leave me alone!"

"But I want to *help* you, Killashandra," Donalla said, switching tactics.

"I don't need that kind of help. Now go, or do I have to throw you out? I'm well enough to do so, you know." And she half rose from her chair.

Donalla pushed off the edge of the bed and took a step back, flustered. "You'll be helping Lars Dahl as well, you know. Not to mention your Guild."

"Spare me the sentimental violin passage, Donalla. Loyalty is another commodity singers lack and don't need!" Killashandra completed her rise in one fluid movement, delighted that her body would respond so readily. She grabbed Donalla by the arm, turned her toward the door, and forcefully ejected her from the room. "And don't come back."

"If you'd only listen . . ." Donalla began, but Killa shut the door on her entreaty.

"Regression isn't painful!" The woman was incredible, shouting through a closed door at her. With one twist of the volume control, Killa turned on to full whatever program was on the in-room entertainment, drowning out Donalla's voice. Then she threw on the door privacy lock.

For a long moment she seethed, letting the music, some sort of a baroque chorus, roll over her. The song was familiar to her. She picked up the soprano line, surprised and pleased to be able to add words to the notes. She broke off singing when, even to herself, her voice sounded harsh and strident.

Well, wouldn't it? When she was being harassed by a silly bitch who had made a unilateral decision about what Killashandra Ree "needed"? Only Killashandra Ree could make those decisions. She had earned that right, by all the holies! Ridiculous woman! Absurd notion—reviving useless baggage of memories. And the Guild Master agreed?

Killa exhaled in disgust, reviewing what Donalla had said. Her memory might be faulty, but she had been reading voices for years. She snorted again, remembering tonalities and inflections that told her more than Donalla might have intended. The woman had said Lars's name in a tone that indicated more than casual acquaintance with him, intimating a relationship that was more than work-oriented. They were a fine pair, they were! Well suited! If she'd known the woman would take on this way, behaving like a conscience, she'd've let her die in the Recruitment Room!

"There, too, I *can* remember—when I want to!" Killa muttered to herself. Then she laughed as she heard the childish petulance in her voice. She remembered the important things, like how to fly a sled, how to locate claims, how to cut—and, most important of all, she generally remembered *what* to cut in order to get top market value on her crystal. What more did she need to remember? The petty details of everyday life? The trivia that clogged the brain and got in the way: the incidents that humiliated or enraged, the bilge, bosh, claptrap that happened while traveling, things inconsequential when one would only be visiting the world once?

What about remembering the new world?

If it was worthwhile, interesting, or exciting, I'll remember it, she told herself.

Will you?

I can, if I want to! I can!

She slept away the afternoon and awoke to hear a tentative tapping on her door. It was the bright little infirmary aide wanting to serve her dinner. She ate heartily, trying to ignore the fact that someone had gone to the trouble of ordering a selection of her favorite foods. That would pad the charges for her Infirmary usage. Ah, well. She'd always paid for exotics, and the Yarran beer did go down a treat!

She didn't see the irritating Donalla over the next three days but had several sessions with therapists, who worked to help her regain full muscle tone. She retrieved her cutter from Clarend, who warned her again to remember—*remember*—that she couldn't abuse her cutter again or she would have to replace it. She took possession of a sparkling brand-new sled.

"I won't tell you how many you've banged up over the years, Killa," Ritwili told her in a sour tone as he extended the purchase order for her signature. "And stocking it took the rest of your credit. You're in the red right now—so cut well!"

She paused long enough to contact Clodine and find out what crystal she ought to look for.

"Someone's wanting those deep amethysts and, of course, any black you stumble across," Clodine said with a grin. "You've a natural affinity for them anyway, and blacks are always needed."

"Yeah." Killa wasn't all that happy with her affinity. She liked the money from blacks but not cutting them solo. They tended to thrall more easily than any other color. "I'll remember that."

She was not the only singer departing the Guild Hangar that day: fifteen others were making ready and each of them was determined to be the last one out and thus not only see the direction every other singer was taking but conceal his or her own ultimate destination.

Disgusted, Killashandra gave up waiting. At this rate, it would be dark before she made any significant progress into the Ranges. Noting the marks of age and misuse on most of the other vehicles, she realized that with her new sled, she could easily outfly any of them. She asked, and received, clearance, along with a heartfelt thanks from the flight officer, who was losing patience with the dilatory singers.

"Blinding damn paranoid, the lot of 'em," he muttered, forgetting to close the circuit.

"You better believe it," Killa said with a laugh, and eased her new vehicle through the Hangar's immense outer doors.

The exchange put Killashandra in a good mood, which improved even more when she heard five other singers demanding clearance. Well, she'd show them!

Capriciously she zipped off at a speed inappropriate for her proximity to the Hangar, laughing at the flight officer's irate reprimand. Running at a recklessly low altitude over the uneven terrain of the foothills, she built the sled up to maximum power as fast as she dared.

"Try to follow me now, you dorks! Shatter yourself on the hills trying!"

She let out a musical hurrah as the ground hurtled past her. Lyrics to the aria deserted her, but she sang on, using vowels and singing at the top of her lungs, reveling in her renewed freedom.

Chapter 7

Killashandra came in from the Milekey Mountains with a load of blue-quartz prisms and cylinders in A-sharp or higher. She had always worked well solo in the upper registers, which gave her a distinct advantage over most crystal singers.

She made it into the Hangar on a windy blast from the oncoming storm. Cutting it fine again, but she grinned at having made it without harm to herself or her sled. That was all that mattered: coming back in the same state of mind or body as she had gone out. Still, and in the back of her mind, she allowed herself to be relieved that her recklessness had not exacted a penalty.

Being one of the last in, she had to wait for Clodine to be free to assay her crystal. It was a long wait, especially with every nerve in her body screaming for the radiant fluid that would reduce the resonance to a mild discomfort. The storm outside seemed to stroke her body to an intense pitch. She shuddered from time to time, but managed to survive the waiting.

When Clodine told her she had hit the top of the market, she could feel the physical relief course through her despite storm scream.

"I've been due a change of luck," she said, wincing as she remembered the last week in the Ranges. The sun had been fierce on the scars of her cuttings, half blinding her, and the scream of crystal had sliced through her mind as she had cut. But she had been desperate to hack enough cargo to get off-world for a while—away from crystal song, far away, so her mind would have a chance to heal. "How much?"

Clodine peered up at her from her console, a little smirk bending the left corner of her mouth. "Don't you trust me anymore, Killa?"

"At this point, I wouldn't trust my own mother—if I could remember who she was," Killa replied. She forced a smile for Clodine on her grimy lips and tried to relax. Clodine was her friend. She would know how badly Killa needed to get away from Ballybran and crystal whine. "Is it enough?"

Clodine altered her enhanced eyes and gazed at Killashandra almost maternally. "You've been a singer long enough, Killa, to know when you've cut sufficient crystal."

"Tell me!" With totally irrational fury, Killashandra brought both fists down on the counter, jarring the crystal and startling Clodine to blink into enhancement. Immediately she relented. "I'm sorry, Clodine. I shouldn't shout at my only friend. But . . ."

"You've enough," Clodine said gently. She reached to grasp Killa's arm encouragingly, but drew back her fingers as if she had been burned. The Sorter's expression altered to sadness. Then her gaze switched to someone over her shoulder.

Killashandra jerked her head slightly sideways to see who had joined them. It was the Guild Master. She looked back at Clodine, ignoring the man as she had done for a long time now.

"Killa," he said, his tenor voice pitched to concern, "that was cutting it too close by half. You shouldn't work solo for a while. Any singer in the Guild would partner you for a couple of runs."

"I'll work as I please," she said, forcing her wretchedly tired body into a straight and obstinate line. "I'm not so ancient that I can't scramble when I have to."

The Guild Master pointed to the weather displayed on the back wall of the Sorting Shed, and despite herself, Killashandra followed his finger. She maintained a show of diffidence, but she felt cold fear in her belly. She hadn't realized the storm was that powerful: twelve-mach-force winds? Had her weather sense betrayed her? Lost its edge? No, but she *had* been deeper in the Ranges than she realized when she started out. She could well have been caught out over crystal. But she hadn't. And she had safely brought in enough crystal to get off-planet again.

"A good blow," she said with a defensive shrug and a wry twist of her lips, "but it's going to knock hell out of my claim."

The Guild Master touched her shoulder lightly; he did not pull away from her as Clodine had. "Just don't go back solo, Killa." She dipped out from under his hand. He continued, "You've sung crystal a long time now. You kited in here just ahead of a mach-twelve storm and one day you'll stay just that moment too long and—poof!" He threw his hands up, fingers wide. "Scrambled brains."

"That's the time, Guild Master," she said, still with her back to him, "that I get some of my own back."

She saw the pity and concern in Clodine's eyes.

"With your ears ruptured and your mind a balloon? Sure, Killa. Sure. Look, there're half a dozen good cutters who'd double you any time you raised your finger. Or don't you *remember*"—and the Guild Master's voice turned soft—"how much you made singing duet . . ."

"With Lars Dahl!" Killashandra made her voice flat and refused to look around.

"We worked well together, Killa." His voice was still soft.

"How kind of you to remember, Guild Master."

She turned away from the counter, but he stepped in front of her.

"I was wrong, Killashandra. It's too late for you to cut duo. Crystal's in your soul." He strode out of the shed, leaving her standing there.

She tried to be amused by the accusation—but, from him, it cut like crystal. As if she would want to sing duet again. Especially with Lars Dahl. She cast her mind back, trying to recall some details of those halcyon days. Nothing came. They must have happened a long, long time ago: many storms, many Passovers, many cuts past.

"Killa?"

At the sound of Clodine's voice, Killashandra jerked herself back to the present: the tote was up on the screen—and the news was good. Even with the Guild tithe, she had enough to keep out of the Ranges for close to a year. Maybe that would be enough to take crystal out of her soul.

The Guild Master had to be wrong about that! He had to be! She thanked Clodine, who seemed relieved that her friend's mood had altered.

She stopped in the Hall long enough to tap in her name and get a locator keyed into her quarters. It had long since stopped irritating her that she couldn't remember where she lived in the great cube of the Heptite Guild. She merely let the locator guide her. The mach winds seemed to follow her, echoing through the lift and the corridor. The key vibrated more imperiously in her hand and she hurried. The sooner she immersed herself in the radiant bath, the sooner she would be rid of the angry pulsing of crystal in her blood.

No, it wasn't in her blood. Not yet.

So there were men willing to cut duo with her, were there? Well, Guild Master, what if it's not just any man who is acceptable to *me*? The door to her quarters sprang open as she neared it, so she began to trot. It was going to take so long to fill the radiant bath. Somehow there ought to be a way to trigger that amenity from afar, especially for singers as crystal-logged as she was. Once, someone—what was his name?—someone had done her that courtesy and she had always returned to her room to find the tub full.

As she turned the corner into the sanitary facility, she was amazed to see the tap running the viscous liquid in a bath that was nearly full. But that someone—she pulled at memory even as she pulled off her grimed jumpsuit—was long dead. She was eternally grateful to whoever had started the bath. The Guild Master? Not likely. What had been that other man's name?

She could abuse her mind no longer with pointless attempts to remember. With an immense sigh of relief, she eased into the liquid, feeling it just slightly heavy against her skin, filling her pores. Her flesh gratefully absorbed the anodyne and she placed her head into the recess, slipping her legs and arms into the restraining straps. She forced muscle after weary muscle to relax, willing the resonances to stop echoing through her bones.

She must have slept: she had been exhausted enough to do so. But she felt slightly better. This would be a four-bath cleansing, she decided, and let the used fluid out.

"Dispenser!" she called, loudly enough to activate the mechanism in the other room, and when it chimed its attention, she ordered food. She waited until the second chime told her the food was ready. "Now if they'd only invent a 'bot to bring it to me . . ."

In her past, she hadn't had to worry about that detail, had she? That much she remembered. She crawled out of the tub, setting it for refill, and, flinging a big towel about her, she made for the dispenser slot, ignoring the puddles made by the fluid that sheeted off her body as she walked. The aroma of the food activated long-unused saliva.

"Don't eat too much, Killa," she warned herself, knowing perfectly well what would happen to her underserved stomach if she did. *That* much she always remembered.

She had a few bites and then forced herself to bring the tray back to the tub, where she rested it on the wide rim. Climbing back into the filling tub, she moved her body under the splash from the wide-mouthed tap. With one hand on the rim, she scooped milsi stalks into her mouth, one at a time, chewing conscientiously.

She really must remember to eat when she was in the Ranges. Muhlah knew her sled was well-enough stocked, and since the provisions were paid for, she ought to eat them. If she remembered.

By her fourth bath, she recollected snatches and patches of her last break. They didn't please her. For one thing, she had come in with a light load, forced off the Range a few klicks ahead of a storm. She had reaped the benefits of that blow this trip, of course—that was the way of it with crystal. If a singer could get back to the vicinity of a lode fast enough, the crystal resonated and told her body where it was. But she hadn't had enough credit to get off-planet, a trip she had desperately needed then—though not half as much as she did now.

She'd had to take what relief she could from a handsome and somewhat arrogant young landsman on the upper continent: tone-deaf, sobersided, but he hadn't been man enough to anneal her.

"Crystal in my soul, indeed!" The Guild Master's words stung like crystal scratch.

She made a noise of sheer self-disgust and pulled herself from the tank, knocking the tray off. She turned to the big wall mirror, watching the fluid sheet off her body, as firm and graceful as a youngster's. Killashandra had long since given up keeping track of her chronological age: it was irrelevant anyway, since the symbiont kept her looking and feeling young. Not immortality but close to it—except for the youth of her memory.

"Now where will I go off this fecking planet this time?" she asked her reflection, and then slid open the dresser panel.

She was mildly surprised at the finery there and decided she must have spent what credit she'd had for pretty threads to lure that unwary landsman. He had been a brute of a lover, though a change. Anything had been a change from Lars Dahl. How dare the Guild Master suggest that she'd better duo! He had no right or authority, no lien or hold on her to dictate her choice!

Angrily Killashandra punched for Port Authority and inquired the destinations of imminent departures from Shankill.

"Not much. C. S. Killashandra," she was told politely. "Small freighter is loading for the Armagh system . . ."

"Have I been there?"

Pause. "No, ma'am."

"What does Armagh do for itself?"

"Exports fish oils and glue," was the semidisgusted reply.

"Water world?"

"Not total. Has the usual balance of land and ocean . . ."

"Tropical?" For some reason the idea of a tropical world both appealed to and repelled her.

"It has a very pleasant tropical zone. All water sports, tasty foods if you like a high fruit/fish diet."

"Book me." Crystal singers could be high-handed, at least on Ballybran.

"Blast-off at twenty-two thirty today," Port Authority told her.

"I've just time then." And Killashandra broke the connection.

She drew on the most conservative garments in the press, then randomly selected a half dozen of the brighter things, tossed them into a carisak, and closed it. She hesitated, midroom, glancing about incuriously. It was, of course, the standard member accommodation. Vaguely she remembered a time when there had been paintings and wall hangings, knickknacks that were pretty or odd on the shelves and tables, a different rug on the floor of the main room. Now there was no trace of anything remotely personal, certainly nothing of Killashandra.

"Because," Killashandra said out loud, as if to imprint her voice on the room, "I'm nothing but a crystal singer with only a present to live in."

She slammed the door as she left, but it didn't do much to satisfy her discontent. She found slightly more pleasure in the realization that, though she might have trouble finding her apartment after a session in the Ranges, she had none finding her way up from the subterranean resident levels to the shuttle bays.

She took the time to get the protective lenses removed from her eyes. It didn't change her outlook much. In fact, Ballybran looked duller than it should have as the shuttle lifted toward Shankill. The storm had cleared away, and she felt a brief twinge as her body ached for the resonances she was leaving, for the dazzle of rainbow light prisms dancing off variegated quartz, for the pure sweet sound of crystal waking in the early morning sun, or sighing in the cold virginal light of one of the larger moons, for the subsonic hum that ate through bone in black cold night.

Then she dealt with the formalities of lifting off-world and was directed to Bay 23, where the Armagh freighter, *Maeve 18*, was docked. She was escorted to her cabin by a youngster who couldn't keep far enough ahead of her—and the crystal resonance that pinged off her—in the narrow corridors.

"Is there a radiant-fluid tub on board?" she asked him with a grim smile at his reaction to her condition.

"In your cabin, Crystal Singer," he said, and then scooted away.

It was a courtesy to call it a tub—it was a two-meter tube, just wide enough to accommodate a body. To reach it one had to perform certain acrobatics over the toilet; and, according to the legend on the dials, the same fluid was flushed and reused. Well, she could count on three to four washes before it became ineffective. That would have to do. She opened the tap and heard the comforting gurgle of the fluid dropping to the bottom of the tub.

From there she flung her carisak to the narrow bunk, shucked off her clothes, and did her acrobatic act, inserting herself just as the flow automatically cut off. There were hand and ankle grips, and she arranged her limbs appropriately, tilted her head back, and let the radiant fluid cleanse her.

She entered the common room for the first time the third day out, having purged sufficient crystal resonance from blood and bone to be socially acceptable. She was hungry, for more than food, a hunger she could keep leashed as far as she was concerned. But the eight male passengers and the two crewmen who circulated in the transit area were obviously affected by her sensuality. There wasn't anyone she wanted, so she retired to her cabin and remained there for the rest of the trip. She had traveled often enough in the shape she was in to practice discretion.

Armagh III's Port Terminal smelled of fish oil and glue. Great casks were being trundled into the hold of the freighter as she bade an impatient farewell to the captain. She flashed her general credentials and was admitted unconditionally to the planet as a leisure guest. She didn't need to use her Guild membership—Armagh III was an open planet.

She rented a flit and checked into the Touristas for a list of resorts. The list turned out to be so lengthy that she merely closed her eyes and bought a ticket to the destination on which her finger settled: Trefoil, on the southeastern coast of the main continent. She paused long enough to obtain a quick change of Armagh clothing, bright patterns in a lightweight porous weave, and was off.

Trefoil reminded her of somewhere. The resemblance nagged at her even as the interoceanic air vehicle circled the small fishing town. Ships tacking across the harbor under sail caused her heart to bump with a curiously painful joy. She knew she must have seen sailships, since the nomenclature—sloop, lateen-rigged, schooner, ketch, yawl—sprang to mind with no hesitation. As did a second pang of regret. She grimaced and decided that such clear recollection might even be an asset on this backward little world.

The landing field wasn't that far from one of the longer wharves, where a huge two-master was moving, with graceful and competent ease, to a berth alongside the port side. That term also came unbidden to her mind. As much because she would not give in to the emotion of the recall as because the ship excited her, she swung the carisak to her shoulder and sauntered down to the wharf. The crew was busy in the yards, reefing the last of the square sails used to make port, and more were bustling about the deck, which glinted with an almost crystalline sheen.

"What makes the decks shine?" she asked another observer.

"Fish oils" was the somewhat terse reply, and then the man, a red-bearded giant, took a second look. Men usually looked twice at Killashandra. "First time on Armagh?"

Killashandra nodded, her eyes intent on the schooner.

"Been here long?"

"Just arrived."

"Got a pad?"

"No."

"Try the Golden Dolphin. Best food in town and best brewman."

Killashandra turned to look at him then. "You pad there?"

"How else could I judge?" the man replied with charming candor.

Killashandra smiled back at him, neither coldly nor invitingly. Neutral. He reminded her of someone. They both turned back to watch the docking ship.

Killashandra found the process fascinating and reminiscent, but she forced memory out and concentrated on the landing, silently applauding the well-drilled crew. Each man seemed to perform his set task without apparent instruction from the captain in the bridge house. The big hull drifted slowly sideways toward the wharf. The last of the sails had now been fastened along the spars. Two crewmen flung lines ashore, fore and aft, then leaped after them when the distance closed, flipping the heavy lines deftly around the bollards and snubbing the ship securely.

Armagh men ran to height, tanned skins, and strong backs, Killashandra noticed approvingly. Redbeard was watching her out of the corner of his eye. He was interested in her all right. Just then, the nearest sailor turned landside and waved in her direction. His teeth were startlingly white against the mahogany of his skin. He tossed back a streaked blond curly mane of hair and waved again. He wore the long oil-shiny pants of his profession and an oddly fashioned vest, which left chest and arms bare and seemed stiff with double hide along the ribs. He looked incredibly muscular.

Why was he waving at her? No, the greeting was for Redbeard beside her, who now walked forward to meet his friend. A third man, black-bearded and tangle-maned, joined them and was embraced by Redbeard. The trio stood facing the ship and talking among themselves until a fearsome machine glided along the rails to their side of the dock. It extruded a ramp out and down and into the deck of the boat, where it hovered expectantly. The two sailors had jumped back aboard, the blond man moving with the instinctive grace of the natural athlete. In comparison, the black-haired man looked clumsy. As a team, they heaved open the hatch. The hesitant ramp extruded clamps that fastened to the deck and the lip of the opened hold. More ramp disappeared into the maw of the ship. Moments later the ramp belt moved upward and Killashandra saw her first lunk, the great oil fish of Armagh, borne away on its last journey.

She became absorbed in the unloading process, which, for all the automated assistance of the machine, still required a human element. The oil scales of the huge fish did not always stay on the rough surface of the ramp belt and had to be forced back on manually. The blonde used an enormous barbed hook, planting it deep in what was actually the very tough hide of the elusive fish and deftly flipping the body into place again. Redbeard seemed to have some official position, for he made notes of the machine's dials, used the throat mike often, and seemed to have forgotten her existence entirely. Killashandra approved. A man should get on with his work.

Yes, especially when he worked with such laudable economy of motion and effort. Like the young blonde.

In fact, Killashandra was rather surprised when the ramp suddenly retracted and the machine slid sideways to the next hold. A small barefoot rascal of a lad slipped up to the crewmen, a tray of hot pies balanced on his head. The aroma was tantalizing, and Killashandra realized that she had not eaten since leaving the freighter that morning. Before she could signal the rascal to her, his merchandise had been bought up by the seamen. Irritated, Killashandra looked landward. The docks couldn't be dependent on the services of small boys. There must be other eating facilities nearby. With a backward glance at her blond sailor, contentedly munching on a pie in each hand, she left the wharf.

As it happened, the eating house she chose displayed a placard advertising the Golden Dolphin. The hostelry was up the beach, set back amid a grove of frond-leaved trees, which also reminded her of something and excited an irritation in her. She wouldn't give in to it. The inn was set far enough around a headland from the town and the wharf so that commercial noise was muted. She took a room with a veranda looking out over the water. She changed into native clothing and retraced her steps along the quiet corridor to the public room.

"What's the native brew?" she asked the barman, settling herself on the quaint high wooden stool.

"Depends on your capacity, m'dear," the little black man told her, grinning a welcome.

"I've never disgraced myself."

"Tart or sweet?"

"Hmmmm . . . tart, cool, and long."

"There's a concoction of fermented fruits, native to this globe, called 'harmat.' Powerful."

"Keep an eye on me then, man. You call the limit."

He nodded respectfully. He couldn't know that a crystal singer had a metabolism that compensated for drug, narcotic, or excess alcohol. A blessing-curse. Particularly if she were injured off-world, with no crystal around to draw the noise of accidental pain from her bones and muscles. Quietly cursing to herself, she knew she had enough crystal resonance still in her to reduce even an amputation to minimal discomfort.

Harmat *was* tart, cool, and long, with a pleasant aftertaste that kept the mouth sweet and soothed the throat.

"A good drink for a sun world," she commented. "And sailors."

"Aye, it is," the barman said, his eyes twinkling. "And if it weren't for them, we could export more."

"I thought Armagh's trade was fish oils and glue."

The barman wrinkled his nose disdainfully. "It is. Harmat off-world commands a price, only trade rules say home consumption comes first."

"Invent another drink."

The barman frowned. "I try. Oh, I try. But they drink me dry of anything I brew."

"You're brewman, as well?"

He drew himself up, straight and proud. "I gather the fruit from my own land, prepare it, press it, keg it, age it."

She questioned him further, interested in another's exacting trade, and thought if she weren't a crystal singer, brewmaking would have been fun.

Biyanco, for that was the brewman's name, chatted with her amiably until the laughter and talk of a large crowd penetrated the quiet gloom of the public room.

"The fishermen," he told her, busying himself by filling glass after glass of harmat and lining them up along the bar.

He was none too soon, for the wide doors of the public room swung open and a horde of oil-trousered, vested men and women surged up to the bar, tanned hands closing on the nearest glass, coins spinning and clicking to the wooden surface. Killashandra remained on her stool, but she was pressed hard on both sides by thirty or so people who spared her no glance until they had finished the first glass and were bawling for a refill. Then she was, rather casually, she felt, dismissed as the fisherfolk laughed among themselves and talked trade.

"You'd best watch that stuff," said a voice in her ear, and she saw Redbeard.

"I've been warned," she answered, grinning.

"Biyanco makes the best harmat this side of the canal. It's not a drink for the novice."

"I've been warned," she repeated, mildly amused at the half insult. Of course, the man couldn't know that she was a crystal singer. So his warning had been kindly meant.

A huge bronzed fist brushed past her left breast. Startled, she looked up into the brilliant blue eyes of the blond sailor, who gazed at her in an incurious appraisal that warmed briefly in the way a man will look at a woman, and then grew cautious.

Killashandra looked away first, oddly disturbed by the blue eyes, somehow familiar but not the same, and disappointed. This one was much too young for her. She turned back to Redbeard, who grinned as if he had watched the swift exchange of glances and was somehow amused by it.

"I'm Thursday, Orric Thursday, ma'am," the redbeard said.

"Killashandra Ree is my name," she replied, and extended her hand.

He couldn't have guessed her profession by her grip, but she could see that the strength of it surprised him. Killashandra was not a tall or heavily boned woman: cutting crystal did not need mass, only controlled energy, and that could be developed in any arm.

Thursday gestured to the blonde. "This is my good friend, Shad Tucker."

Thankful that the press of bodies made it impossible for her to do the courteous handshake, Killashandra nodded to Shad Tucker.

"And my old comrade of the wars, Tir Od Nell." Orric Thursday motioned to the blackbeard, who also contented himself with a nod and a grin at her. "You'd be here for a rest, Killashandra?" Thursday asked. And when she nodded, he went on. "Now, why would you pick such a dull fisherman's world as Armagh if you'd the galaxy to choose from?"

Killashandra had heard that sort of question before, how many times she couldn't remember. She had also heard the same charming invitation for confidences.

"Perhaps I like water sports," she replied, smiling back at him and not bothering to hide her appraisal.

To her surprise, he threw back his head and laughed. She could see where he had trimmed the hairs from his throat, leaving a narrow band of white flesh that never saw sun. His two friends said nothing, but their eyes were on her.

"Perhaps you do, ma'am. And this is the place. Did you want the long wave ride? There's a boat out every dawn." Orric looked at her questioningly. "Then water skating? Submarining? Dolphin swimming? What is your pleasure, Killashandra Ree?"

"Rest! I'm tired!"

"Oh, I'd never think you'd ever known fatigue." The expression in his eyes invited her to edify him.

"For someone unfamiliar with the condition, how would you know it?"

Tir Od Nell roared.

"She's got you there, Orr," he said, clapping his friend on the shoulder. Shad Tucker smiled, a sort of shy, amused smile, as if he hadn't suspected her capable of caustic reply and wasn't sure he should enjoy it at his friend's expense.

Orric grinned, shrugged, and eyed Killashandra with respect. Then he bawled to Biyanco that his glass had a hole in it.

When the edge of their thirst had been satisfied, most of the fisher-men left. "In search of other diversions," Orric said, but he, Tir Od Nell, and Shad Tucker merely settled stools around Killashandra and continued to drink.

She matched them, paid her rounds, and enjoyed Orric's attempts to pry personal information from her.

He was not, she discovered, easily put off, nor shy of giving facts about himself and his friends. They had all worked the same fishing boat five seasons back, leaving the sea as bad fishing turned them off temporar-ily. Orric had an interest in computers and often did wharfman's chores if the regular men were away when the ships came in. Tir Od Nell was work-ing the lunk season to earn some ready credit, and would return to his reg-ular job inland. Shad Tucker, the only off-worlder, had sailed the seas of four planets before he landed on Armagh.

"Shad keeps saying he'll move on, but he's been here five years and more," Orric told Killashandra, "and no sign of applying for a ticket-off."

Tucker only smiled, the slight tolerant smile playing at the corner of his mouth, as if he was chary of admitting even that much about himself.

"Don't let Shad's reticence mislead you, Killashandra Ree," Orric went on, laying a hand on his friend's shoulder. "He's accredited for more than a lunk fisher. Indeed he is." Killashandra felt yet another tweak of pain that she masked with a smile for Orric. "Shad's got first mate's tickets on four water worlds that make sailing Armagh look like tank bathing. Came here with a submarine rig one of the Anchorite companies was tout-ing." He shrugged, eloquently indicating that the company's praise had fallen on deaf Armaghan ears.

"They're conservative here on Armagh," Tucker said, his voice a nice change, soft after Orric's near-bellow. She almost had to sharpen her hear-ing to catch what he said.

"How so?" she asked Shad.

"They feel there is one good way to catch lunk when it's in oil. By long line. That way you don't bruise the flesh so much and the lunk doesn't struggle the way it does in a net and sour the oil. The captains, they've a sense of location that doesn't need sonic gear. I've sailed with five, six of the best and they always know when and where lunk are run-ning. And how many they can bring from that deep."

And, Killashandra thought, bemused by Shad's soft accent, you'd give your arm to develop that sense.

"You've fished on other worlds," she said out loud.

"Aye."

"Where, for instance?"

He was as unforthcoming as a fish—or herself.

"Oh, all over. Spiderfish, crackerjaw, bluefin, skaters, and Welladay whales."

The young man spoke casually, as if encounters with aquatic monsters were of no account. And how, Killashandra wondered to herself, did she know that's what he'd named? Nervously, she glanced to one side and saw Orric's eyes light up, as if he had hoped that the catalog would impress her.

"A crackerjaw opened his back for him on Spindrift," Orric said proudly. "And he flew five miles with a skater and brought it down, the largest one ever recorded on Mandalay."

Killashandra wasn't sure why Orric Thursday wished to extol his friend. But it made *him* more acceptable in her eyes. Shad was too young, anyhow. Killashandra made no further attempt to draw Shad out but turned to Tir and Orric.

Despite a continued concern for her consumption of harmat, Orric kept ordering until full dark closed down abruptly on the planet and the artificial lights came on in the room.

"Mealtime," Biyanco announced in a loud, penetrating voice, and activated a barrier that dropped over the bar. He appeared through a side door and briskly gestured them to a table for four on the other side of the room. Killashandra made no resistance to Orric's suggestion that they all dine together, and she spent the rest of the evening—listening to fish stories—in their company. She spent her night alone—by choice. She had not made up her mind yet.

When the sun came up over the edge of the sea, she was down in the hotel's private lagoon, floating on the buoyant waters, just as the lunk ships, sails fat with dawn winds, slid out to open sea with incredible speed.

To her surprise, Orric appeared at midday and offered to show her Trefoil's few diversions. Nothing loath, she went and found him most agreeable company, conversant on every phase of Trefoil's domestic industry. He steered her from the usual tourist path, for which she was grateful. She abhorred that label, though tourist she was, on any world but Ballybran. Nor did she give Orric Thursday any hint of her profession, despite all his attempts to wheedle the information from her.

It wasn't that she liked being secretive, but few worlds understood the function of crystal singers, and some very odd habits and practices had been attributed to them. Killashandra's discretion and caution was instinctive by now.

Late that afternoon, a bleeper on Orric's belt alerted him to return to the dock: the fishing boats had been sighted.

"Sorry, m'dear," he said as he executed a dipping turn of his fast air-flipper. "Duty calls."

She elected to join him on the wharf, allowing him to think it was his company she preferred. Actually, she wanted to watch the silent teamwork of docking, and see the mahogany figure of Shad Tucker again. He was much too young for her, she told herself again, but a right graceful person to observe.

They had made a quick plenteous catch that day, Killashandra was told as the fishermen drowned their thirsts in harmat at the Golden Dolphin. Tucker seemed unusually pleased, and Killashandra couldn't resist asking why.

"He's made enough now to go off-world," Orric said when Shad replied with an indolent shrug. "He won't go." Orric shook his head, a wry grin on his face. "He never does. He's been here longer than on any other planet."

"Why?" Killashandra asked Shad, then had to hush Orric. "Let Tucker reply. He knows his own mind, doesn't he?"

Shad regarded her with mild surprise, and the indolent look left his blue eyes, replaced by an intensity she found hard to ignore.

"This is a real sea world," Shad said, picking his words in his soft-accented way, "not some half-evolved plankton planet."

He doesn't open his lips wide enough to enunciate properly, she thought, and wondered why he guarded himself so.

"You've lunk for profit, territ and flatfish for fine eating, the crustaceans and bivalves for high livers, then the sea fruits for a constant harvest. Variety. I might buy myself a strip of land and stay."

"You do ship on more than the lunk boats?"

Shad was surprised by her question. "All the boats fish lunk when it runs. Then you go after the others."

"If you've a mind for drudgery," Tir Od Nell said gloomily.

Shad gave Tir a forbearing glance. "Lunk requires only muscle," he said with a sly grin.

This appeared to be an old challenge, for Tir launched into a debate that Shad parried with the habit of long practice.

For the sake of being perverse, Killashandra took Tir to bed that night. She didn't regret the experience, although there was no harmony between them. If it gave her no peace, his vehemence did take the edge off her hunger. She did not encourage him to ask for more. Somewhere, long ago, she had learned the way to do that without aggravating a lover.

He was gone by dawn. Orric dropped by a few hours later and took her to see a sea-fruit farm on the peninsula, ten klicks from Trefoil to the south. When she assured Max Ennert, the farmer, of her experience, they were all fitted out with breather tanks and went submarine.

Enclosed by water, isolated by her trail of bubbles, though attached by guideline to Max and Orric, she realized—probably not for the first time—why crystal singers sought water worlds. Below sea level, there was insulation against aural sound, relief from the play of noise against weary eardrums.

They drifted inches above the carefully tended sea gardens, Max and Orric occasionally pruning off a ripe frond of grape or plum and shoving them in the net bags they towed. They bypassed reapers in a vast sea valley where weed was being harvested. Occasionally, loose strands would drift past them, the fuller, longer ones deftly caught and netted by the men.

Killashandra was content to follow, slightly behind Max, slightly ahead of Orric, craning her neck, angling her body to enjoy as much of the clear-sea view as possible. One or the other man checked her gauges from time to time. Euphoria could be a curse undersea, and they didn't know of the professional immunity she enjoyed.

Perhaps that was why Orric argued with Max at one point, when they had been below some two hours. But they stayed down almost three more before they completed the circuit. As they walked out of the sea at Max's landing, night was approaching with the usual tropical dispatch.

"Stay on, Orric, Killashandra, if you've no other plans," Max said, but the words sounded rehearsed, strained.

She entered the room where she had changed to sea dress and heard Orric's footsteps right behind her. She didn't bother closing the door. He did, and had her in his arms the next instant. She made no resistance to his advance nor did she respond. He held her from him, surprised, a question in his eyes.

"I'm not susceptible to euphorics, Orric," she told him.

"What are you talking about?" he asked, gray eyes wide with innocence.

"And I've submarined on more worlds than Shad has sailed."

"Is it Tucker you're after?" He didn't seem jealous, merely curious.

"Shad's . . ." She shrugged, unwilling to place the young man in any category.

"But you don't fancy me?" He did not seem aggrieved—again, merely curious.

She looked at him a long moment. "I think . . ." She paused then voiced an opinion that had been subconscious till that moment. "You remind me too much of someone I've been trying to forget."

"Oh, just remind you?" Orric's voice was soft and coaxing, almost like Tucker's. She put that young man firmly out of her mind.

"No offense intended, Orric. The resemblance is purely superficial."

His eyes twinkled merrily, and Killashandra realized that the resemblance was not purely superficial, for the other man would have responded in just the same way, amused with her and taking no offense. Perversely that annoyed her more.

"So, dark and mysterious lady, when you get to know me better . . ."

"Let me get to know you better first."

They flitted back to Trefoil, circling over quays empty of any fishing craft.

"Lunk is moving offshore," Orric said. "Season's about over, I'd say."

"Does Tucker really have enough for a ticket-off?"

"Probably." Orric was busy setting the little craft down in dim light. "But Tir needs one more good haul. And so, I suspect, does Skipper Garnish. They'll track school as far as there's trace before they head in."

Which was the substance of the message left for Orric at the Golden Dolphin. So Killashandra, Orric, and Biyanco talked most of the evening with a few other drinkers at the bar.

That was why Killashandra got an invitation to go with Biyanco fruit-harvesting. "Land fruit for harmat," Biyanco said with an odd shudder.

Orric laughed and called him an incorrigible lubber. "Biyanco swears he's never touched sea fruit in his life."

"Never been that poor," Biyanco said with some dignity.

The brewman roused her before dawn, his tractor-float purring outside her veranda. She dressed in the overall he had advised and the combi-boots, and braided her hair tightly to her skull. On the outward leg of their trip, Trefoil nestled on the curved sands of a giant horseshoe bay, foothills at its back. Rain forests that were all but impenetrable swept up the hills, sending rank streamers across the acrid road in vain attempts to cover that man-made tunnel to the drier interior.

Biyanco was amiable company, quiet at times, garrulous but interesting at others. He stopped off on the far side of the first range of foothills for lorries and climbers. None of the small boys and girls waiting there looked old enough to be absent from schooling, Killashandra thought. All carried knives half again as long as their legs from sheaths thong-tied to their backs. All wore the coveralls and combi-boots with spurred clamp-ons for tree-climbing.

They chattered and sang, dangling their legs from the lorries as the tractor hovered above the acid road. Occasionally one of them would wield a knife, chopping an impertinent streamer that had clasped itself to a lorry.

Biyanco climbed farther above sea level by the winding acid road until he finally slowed down, peering at the roadside. Five kilometers later he let out an exclamation and veered the tract-float to the left, his hands busy with dials and switches. A warning hoot brought every climber's legs back into the lorries. Flanges, tilting downward, appeared along the lorry load beds, and acid began to drop from them. It sprayed out, arcing well past the tract-float's leading edge, dissolving vegetation. Suddenly the float halted, as if trying to push against an impenetrable barrier. Biyanco pushed a few toggles, closed a switch, and suddenly the tract-float moved smoothly in a new direction.

"Own this side of the mountain, you know," Biyanco said, glancing at Killashandra to see the effect of his announcement. "Ah, you thought I was only a bar brewman, didn't you? Surprised you, didn't I? Ha!" The little man was pleased.

"You did."

"I'll surprise you more before the day is out."

At last they reached their destination, a permaformed clearing with acid-proofed buildings that housed his processing unit and temporary living quarters. The climbers he had escorted went farther on, sending the lorries off on automated tracks, six climbers to each lorry. They had evidently climbed for him before and in the same teams, for he gave a minimum of instruction before dismissing them to pick.

Then he showed Killashandra into the processing plant and explained the works succinctly.

Each of the teams worked a different fruit, he told her. The secret of good harmat lay in the careful proportions and the blending of dead ripe fruit. There were as many blends of harmat as there were fish in the sea. His had made the Golden Dolphin famous; that's why so many Armaghans patronized the hostelry. No vapid, innocuous stuff came from his stills. Harmat took months to bring to perfection: the fruit he'd process today would be fermented for nine months and would not be offered for sale for six years. Then he took her below ground, to the cool dark storage area, deep in the permaform. He showed her the automatic alarms that would go off if the vicious digger roots of the jungle ever penetrated the permaform. He wore a bleeper on his belt at all times (he never did remove the belt, but it was made of soft, tough fiber). He let her sample the brews, and it amused her that he would sip abstemiously while filling her cup full. Because she liked him and she learned about harmat from him, she gradually imitated drunk.

And Biyanco did indeed surprise her, sprier than she had ever thought him and elated with his success. She was glad for his sake and somewhat puzzled on her own account. He was adept enough that she ought to have enjoyed it, too. He had tried his damnedest to bring her to pitch but the frequency was wrong, as it had been with Tir, would have been with Orric, and this badly puzzled Killashandra. She ought not to have such trouble offworld. Was there crystal in her soul, after all? Was she too old to love?

While Biyanco slept, before the full lorries glided back to the clearing, she probed her patchy memory again and again, stopped each time by the Guild Master's cynical laugh. Damn the man! He was haunting her even on Armagh. He had no right to taint everything she touched, every association she tried to enjoy. She could remember, too, enough snatches to know that her previous break had been as disastrous. Probably other journeys, too. In the quiet cool dark of the sleeping room, Biyanco motionless with exhaustion beside her, Killashandra bleakly cursed Lars Dahl. Why was it she found so little fulfillment with other lovers? How could he have spoiled her for everyone else when she could barely remember him or his lovemaking? She had refused to stay with him, sure then of herself where she was completely unsure now. Crystal in her soul?

Experimentally, she ran her hand down her bare body, to the hard flesh of her thighs, the softness of her belly, her firm breasts. A woman never conceived once she had sung crystal. Small loss, she thought, and then, suddenly, wasn't sure.

Damn! Damn! Damn Lars Dahl. How could he have left her? What was rank to singing black crystal? They had been the most productive duo ever paired in the annals of the Heptite Guild. And he had given *that* up for power. What good did power do him now? It did her none whatsoever. Without him, black eluded her.

The sound of the returning lorries and the singing of the climbers roused Biyanco. He blinked at her, having forgotten in his sleeping that he had taken a woman again. With solemn courtesy, he thanked her for their intercourse and, having dressed, excused himself with grave ceremony. At least a man had found pleasure in her body, she thought.

She bathed, dressed, and joined him as the full fruit bins began spilling their colorful contents into the washing pool. Biyanco was seated at the controls, his nimble fingers darting here and there as he weighed each bin, computed the price, and awarded each chief his crew's chit. It was evidently a good pick, judging by the grins on every face, including Biyanco's.

As each lorry emptied, it swiveled around and joined the line on the tract-float that was also headed homeward. All were shortly in place, and the second part of the processing began. The climbers took themselves off under the shade of the encroaching jungle and ate their lunches.

Abruptly, noise pierced Killashandra's ears. She let out a scream, stifling a repetition against her hand but not soon enough to escape Biyanco's notice. The noise ceased. Trembling with relief, Killashandra looked around, astonished that no one else seemed affected by that appalling shriek.

"You are a crystal singer, then, aren't you?" Biyanco asked, steadying her as she rocked on her feet. "I'm sorry. I wasn't sure you were, and I've not such good pitch myself that I'd hear if the drive crystals were off. Honest, or I'd have warned you." He was embarrassed and earnest.

"You should have them balanced," Killashandra replied angrily, and immediately apologized. "What made you think I might be a crystal singer?"

Biyanco looked away from her now. "Things I've heard."

"What have you heard?"

He looked at her then, his black eyes steady. "That a crystal singer can sound notes that'll drive a man mad. That they lure men to them, seduce them, and then kidnap 'em away to Ballybran, and they never come back."

Killashandra smiled, a little weakly because her ears still ached. "What made you think I wasn't?"

"Me!" He jabbed at his chest with a juice-stained finger. "You slept with *me*!"

She reached out and touched his cheek gently. "You are a good man, Biyanco, besides being the best brewman on Armagh. And I like you. But you should get those crystals balanced before they splinter on you."

Biyanco glanced over at the offending machinery and grimaced. "The tuner's got a waiting list as long as Murtagh River," he said. "You look pale. How about a drink? Harmat'll help—oh, you are a witch," he added, chuckling as he realized that she could not have been as drunk as she had acted. Then a smile tugged at his lips. "Oh-ho, you are a something, Killashandra of Ballybran. I should've spotted your phony drunk, and me a barman all these decades." He chuckled again. "Well, harmat'll help your nerves." He clicked his fingers at one of the climber chiefs, and the boy scampered into the living quarters, returning with glasses and a flask of chilled harmat.

She drank eagerly, both hands on the glass because she was still shaky. The cool tartness was soothing, though, and she wordlessly held the glass out for a refill. Biyanco's eyes were kind and somewhat anxious. Somehow he could appreciate what unbalanced crystalline shrieks could do to sensitive nerves.

"You've not been harmed by it, have you?"

"No. No, Biyanco. We're tougher than that. It was the surprise. I wasn't expecting you to have crystal-driven equipment . . ."

He grinned slyly. "We're not backward on Armagh, for all we're quiet and peaceful." He leaned back from her, regarding her with fresh interest. "Is it true that crystal singers don't grow old?"

"There're disadvantages to that, my friend."

He raised his eyebrows in polite contradiction. But she only smiled as she steadily sipped the harmat until all trace of pain had eased.

"You told me you've only a certain time to process ripe fruit. If you'll let me take the tractor down the rails past the first turn—No . . ." She vetoed her own suggestion, arriving at an impulsive alternative. "How long do you have left before the pick sours?"

"Three hours." And Biyanco's widening eyes she saw incredulous gratitude as he understood her intention. "You wouldn't?" he asked in a voiceless whisper.

"I could and I would. That is, if you've the tools I need."

"I've tools." As if afraid she would renege, he propelled her toward the machine shed.

He had what she needed, but the bare minimum. Fortunately, the all-important crystal saw was still very sharp and true. With two pairs of knowledgeable hands—Biyanco, he told her, had put the driver together himself when he had updated the plant's machinery thirty years before—it was no trick at all to get down to the crystals.

"They're in thirds," he told her needlessly.

"Pitch?"

"B-flat minor."

"Minor? For heavy work like this?"

"Minor because it isn't that continuous a load and minors don't cost what majors do," Biyanco replied crisply.

Killashandra nodded. Majors would be far too expensive for a brewman, however successful, on a tertiary fishing world. She hit the B-flat, and that piece of crystal hummed sweetly in tune. So did the D. It was the E that was sour—off by a halftone. She cut off the resonance before the sound did more than ruffle her nerves. With Biyanco carefully assisting her, she freed the crystal of its brackets, cradling it tenderly in her hands. It was a blue, from the Ghanghe Range, more than likely, and old, because the blues were worked out there now.

"The break's in the top of the prism, here," she said, tracing the flaw. "The bracket may have shifted with vibration."

"G'delpme, I weighed those brackets and felted them proper . . ."

"No blame to you, Biyanco. Probably the expansion coefficient differs in this rain forest enough to make even properly set felt slip. Thirty years they've been in? You worked well. Wish more people would take such good care of their crystal."

"That'd mean less call for crystal, bring the price down, wouldn't it?"

Killa laughed, shaking her head. "The Guild keeps finding new ways to use crystal. Singers'll never be out of work."

They decided to shift the pitch down, which meant she had to recut all three crystals, but that way he would have a major triad. Because she trusted him, she let him watch as she cut and tuned. She had to sustain pitch with her voice after she had warmed them enough to sing, but she could hold a true pitch long enough to place the initial, and all-important, cuts.

It was wringing-wet work, even with the best of equipment and in a moderate climate. She was exhausted by the time they reset the felted brackets. In fact, Biyanco elbowed her out of the way when he saw how her hands were trembling.

"Just check me," he said, but she didn't need to. He was spry in more than one way. She was glad she had tuned the crystals for him. But he was too old for her.

She felt better when he started the processor again and there was no crystal torment.

"You get some rest, Killashandra. This'll take a couple more hours. Why don't you stretch out on the tractor van seat? It's wide enough. That way you can rest all the way back to Trefoil."

"And yourself, Biyanco?"

He grinned like the old black imp he was. "I'm maybe a shade younger than you, Crystal Singer Killashandra. But we'll never know, will we?"

She slept, enervated by the pitching and cutting, but she woke when Biyanco opened the float door. The hinge squeaked in C-sharp.

"Good press," he said when he saw she was awake. Behind, in the lorries, the weary climbers chanted to themselves. One was a monotone. Fortunately they reached the village before the sound could get on her nerves. The lorries were detached, and the climbers melted into the darkness. Biyanco and Killashandra continued on the acid road back to Trefoil.

It was close to dawn before they pulled up at the Golden Dolphin.

"Killashandra?"

"Yes, Biyanco?"

"I'm in your debt."

"No, for we exchanged favors."

He made a rude noise. And she smiled at him. "We did. But, if you need a price, Biyanco, then it's your silence on the subject of crystal singers."

"Why?"

"Because I'm human, no matter what you've heard of us. And I must have that humanity on equal terms or I'll shatter one day among the crystal. It's why we have to go off-world."

"You don't lure men back to Ballybran?"

"Would you come with me to Ballybran?"

He snorted. "You can't make harmat on Ballybran."

She laughed, for he had given the right answer to ease his own mind. As the tract-float moved off slowly, she wondered if he had ever heard of Yarran beer. A chilled one would go down a treat right now.

She slept the sun around and woke the second dawn refreshed. She lazed in the water, having been told by the pug-nosed host that the lunk ships were still out. Biyanco greeted her that noonday with pleasantries and no references to favors past, present, or future. He was old enough, that brewman, she thought, to know what not to say.

She wondered if she should leave Trefoil and flit around the planet. There would be other ports to visit, other fishermen to snare in the net of her attraction. One of them might be strong enough—*must* be strong enough—to melt the crystal in her. But she tarried and drank harmat all afternoon until Biyanco made her go eat something.

She knew the lunk boats were in even before the parched seamen came thronging up the beach road, chanting their need. She helped Biyanco draw glasses against their demand, laughing at their surprise to see her working behind the bar. Only Shad Tucker seemed unamazed.

Orric was there, too, with Tir Od Nell, teasing her as men have teased barmaids for centuries. Tucker sat on a stool in the corner of the bar and watched her, though he drank a good deal of harmat to "unstick his tongue from the roof of his mouth."

Biyanco made them all stop drinking for a meal, to lay a foundation for more harmat, he said. And when they came back, they brought a squeeze box, a fiddle, two guitars, and a flute. The tables were stacked against the wall, and the music and dancing began.

It was good music, too, true-pitched so Killashandra could enjoy it, tapping her foot in time. And it went on until the musicians pleaded for a respite and, leaving their instruments on the bar, swept out to the cool evening beach to get a second wind.

Killashandra had been dancing as hot and heavy as any woman, partnered with anyone who felt like dancing, including Biyanco. Everyone except Tucker, who stayed in his corner and watched . . . her.

When the others left to cool off, she wandered over to him. His eyes were a brighter blue in the new red-tan of his face. He was picking his hands now and again because the lunks had an acid in their scales that ate flesh, and he'd had to grab some barehanded at the last.

"Will they heal?" she asked.

"Oh, sure. Be dry tomorrow. New skin in a week. Doesn't hurt." Shad looked at his hands impersonally and then continued absently sloughing off the dying skin.

"You weren't dancing."

The shy grin twisted up one corner of his mouth, and he ducked his head a little, looking at her from the side of his eyes.

"I've done my dancing. With the fish the past days. I prefer to watch, anyhow."

He unwound himself from the stool to reach out and secure the nearest guitar. He picked a chord and winced; he didn't see her shudder at the discord. Lightly he plucked the strings, twisting the tuning knob on the soured G, adjusting the E string slightly, striking the chord again and nodding with approval.

Killashandra blinked. The man had perfect pitch.

He began to play softly, in a style totally different from the raucous tempi of the previous musicians. His picking was intricate and his rhythm sophisticated, yet the result was a delicate shifting of pattern and tone that enchanted Killashandra. It was improvisation at its best, with the player as intent upon the melody he produced as his only audience.

The beauty of his playing, the beauty of his face as he played, struck an aching in her bones. When his playing ceased, she felt empty.

She had been leaning toward him, perched on a stool, elbows on her knees, supporting her chin with cradled hands. So he leaned forward, across the guitar, and kissed her gently on the mouth. They rose, as one, Shad putting the guitar aside to fold her in his arms and kiss her deeply. She felt the silk of his bare flesh beneath her hands, the warmth of his strong body against hers and then . . . the others came pouring back with disruptive noise.

As well, Killashandra thought as Orric boisterously swung her up to the beat of a rough dance. When next she looked over her shoulder, Shad was in his corner, watching, the slight smile on his lips, his eyes still on her.

He is very much too young for me, she told herself, and I am brittle with too much living.

The next day she nursed what must have been her first hangover in a century. She had worked hard enough to acquire one. She lay on the beach in the shade and tried not to move unnecessarily. No one bothered her until midday—presumably everyone else was nursing a hangover as well. Then Shad's big feet stopped on the sand beside her pallet. His knees cracked as he bent over her and his compelling hand tipped back the wide hat she wore against sun glare.

"You'll feel better if you eat this," he said, speaking very softly. He held out a small tray with a frosted glass and a plate of fruit chips on it.

She wondered if he was enunciating with extra care, for she understood every soft word, even if she resented the gist of them. She groaned, and he repeated his advice. Then he put gentle hands on her, raising her torso so she could drink without spilling. He fed her, piece by piece as a man feeds a sick and fretful child.

She felt sick and she was fretful, but when all the food and drink were in her belly, she had to admit that his advice was sound.

"I never get drunk."

"Probably not. But you also don't dance yourself bloody-footed either."

Her feet were tender, come to think of it, and when she examined the soles, she discovered blisters and myriad thin scratches.

Tucker sat with her all afternoon, saying little. When he suggested a swim, she complied. The lagoon water was cooler than she had remembered, or maybe she was hotter for all she had been lying in the shade.

When they emerged from the water, she felt human, even for a crystal singer. And she admired his straight tall body, the easy grace of his carriage, and the fineness of his handsome face. But he was much too young for her. She would have to try Orric, for she needed a man's favors again.

Evidently it was not Shad's intention that she find Orric: he persuaded her that she didn't want to eat in the hostelry; that it would be more fun to dig bivalves where the tide was going out, in a cove he knew of, a short walk away. It was difficult to argue with a soft-spoken man, who was taller than she by several centimeters, and could carry her easily under one arm . . . even if he was a century or so younger.

And it was impossible not to touch his silky flesh when he brushed past her to tend the baking shellfish, or when he passed her wine-steeped fruit chips and steamed roots.

When he looked at her, sideways, his blue eyes darker now, reflecting the fire and the night, it was beyond her to resist his subtle importunities.

She woke on the dark beach, before the dying fire, with his sleeping weight against her side. Her arms were wrapped around his right arm, her head cradled in the cup of his shoulder. Without moving her head, she could see his profile. And she knew there wasn't any crystal in her soul. She could still give, and receive. For all she sang crystal, she still possessed that priceless human quality, annealed in the fire of his youth.

She had been wrong to dismiss him for what was a mere chronological accident, irrelevant to the peace and solace he brought her. Her body was exultant, renewed.

Her stretching roused him to smile with unexpected sweetness into her eyes. He gathered her against him, the vibrant strength of his arms tempered to tenderness for her slighter frame.

"You crazy woman," he said, in a wondering voice, as he lightly scrubbed her scalp with his long fingers and played with her fine hair. "I've never met anyone like you before."

"Not likely to again." Please!

He grinned down at her, delighted by her arrogance.

"Do you travel much?" he asked.

"When the mood strikes me."

"Don't travel for a while."

"I'll have to one day. I've got to go back to work, you know."

"What work?"

"I'm a guild member."

His grin broadened and he hugged her. "All right, I won't pry." His fingers delicately traced the line of her jaw. "You can't be as old as you make out," he said. She had been honest enough earlier to tell him they were not contemporary.

She answered him with a laugh, but his comment brought a chill to her. It couldn't have been an accident that he could relieve her, she thought, caressing his curving thigh. She panicked suddenly at the idea that, once she had tasted, she could not drink again and strained herself to him.

His arms tightened and his low laugh was loving to her ears. And their bodies fit together again as fully and sweetly in harmony as before. Yes, with Shad Tucker, she could dismiss all fear as baseless.

Their pairing-off was accepted by Orric and Tir, who had his ready credit now and was off to apply it to whatever end he'd had in mind. Only Biyanco searched her face, and she had shrugged and given the brewman a little reassuring smile. Then he had peered closely at Shad and smiled back.

That was why he said nothing. As she had known he wouldn't. For Shad Tucker wasn't ready to settle on one woman. Killashandra was an adventure to him, a willing companion for a man just finished with a hard season's work.

They spent the days together as well, exploring the coastline in both directions from Trefoil, for Shad had a mind to put his earnings in land or seafront. She had never felt so . . . so vital and alive. He had a guitar of his own that he would bring, playing for hours little tunes he made up when they were becalmed in his small sloop and had to take shelter from Armagh's biting noonday sun in the shade of the sail. She loved to look at him while he played: his absorption had the quality of an innocent boy discovering major Truths of Beauty, Music, and Love. Indeed, his face, when he caressed her to a fever pitch of love, retained that same youthful innocence and intent concentration. Because he was so strong, because his youth was so powerful, his delicate, restrained lovemaking was all the more surprising to her.

The days multiplied and became weeks, but so deep was her contentment that the first twinge of uneasiness caught her unawares. She knew what it was, though: her body's cry for crystal song.

"Did I hurt you?" Shad asked, for she was in his arms.

She couldn't answer, so she shook her head. He began to kiss her slowly, leisurely, sure of himself. She felt the second brutal knock along her spine and twisted herself closer in his arms so he wouldn't feel it and she could forget it had happened.

"What's wrong, Killa?"

"Nothing. Nothing you can't cure."

So he did. But afterward, she couldn't sleep and stared up at the spinning moons. She couldn't leave Shad now. Time and again he had worked his magic with her, until she would have sworn all crystal thought was purged . . . until she had even toyed with the notion of resigning from the Guild. No one ever had, according to the Rules and Regs she had reviewed over and over. No one ever had, but likely no one had wanted to. When she *had* to have crystal, she could tune sour crystal. There was always a need for that service, anywhere, on any world. But she had to stay with Shad. He held back fear; he brought her peace. She had waited for a love like Shad Tucker for so long, she had the right to enjoy the relationship.

The next moment another spasm struck her, hard, sharp, fierce. She fought it through a body arched with pain. And she knew that she was being inexorably drawn back. And she did not want to leave Shad Tucker.

To him, she was a novelty, a woman to make love to—now—when the lunk season had been good and a man needed to relax. But Killashandra was not the sort of woman he would build a home for on his acres of seafront. On her part, she loved him: for his youth, for his absurd gentleness and courtesy; because, in his arms, she was briefly ageless.

The profound cruelty of her situation was driven home to her mind as bitterly as the next hunger pain for crystal sound.

It isn't fair, she cried piteously. It isn't fair. I can't love him. It isn't fair. He's too young. He'll forget me in other loves. And I—I'll not be able to remember him. That was the cruelest part.

She began to cry, Killashandra who had forsworn tears for any man half a century before, when the harmony between herself and Lars Dahl had turned chaotic. Her weeping, soft as it was, woke Shad. He comforted her lovingly and complicated her feelings for him by asking no questions at all. Maybe, she thought with the desperation of fearful hope, he isn't that young. He might want to remember me.

And, when her tears had dried on her face, he kissed her again, with an urgency that demanded to be answered. And was, as fully and sweetly as ever.

The summons came two days later. Biyanco tracked them in the cove and told her only that she had an urgent message. She was grateful for that courtesy, but she hated the brewman for bringing the message at all.

It was a Guild summons, all right: a large order for black crystal had been received. All who had sung black crystal were needed in the Ranges. Implicit in the message was a Guild warning: she had been away too long from crystal. What crystal gave, it took away. She stared at her reflection in the glass panel of the message booth. Yes, crystal could take away her appearance of youthfulness. How long would Shad remember the old woman she would shortly become?

So she started out to say good-bye to him. Best have it done quickly and now! Then back to Ballybran and forgetfulness in the crystal song. She felt cold all over.

He was sitting by the lagoon, strumming his guitar, absorbed in a melody he had composed for her. It was a pretty tune, one that stayed in the mind and woke you humming it the next day.

Killashandra caught back her breath. Shad had perfect pitch—he could come with her to Ballybran. She would train him herself to be a crystal singer.

"Don't," Biyanco said, stepping to her side.

"Don't what?" she asked coldly.

"If you really love the boy, Killashandra, don't. He'll remember you this way. That's what you want, isn't it?"

It was, of course, because she wouldn't remember him. So she stood there, beside Biyanco, and listened to Shad sing, watched the boyish intensity on his beloved face, and let cruelty wash hope out of her.

"It never works, does it, Killashandra?" Biyanco asked gently.

"No." She had a fleeting recollection of Lars Dahl. They had met somewhere, off-world. Hadn't they? His had been a water world, too. Hadn't it? Had she chosen another such world, hoping to find Lars Dahl again? Or merely anyone? Like Shad Tucker. Had she herself been lured to Ballybran by some ageless lover? Perhaps. Who could remember details like that? The difference was that now she was old enough not to play the siren for crystal. Old enough to leave love while he was young and still in love enough to remember her only as a woman.

"No one forgets you, Killashandra," Biyanco said, his eyes dark and sad, as she turned to leave.

"Maybe I can remember that much."

Chapter 8

"The Guild has received the biggest order ever requested, to facilitate the colonization and exploitation of seven new systems," the Guild Master told the twenty singers he had called back from their travels. "We must be able to fill these orders for black crystal. All of you"—and his blue eyes settled on one after the other—"have cut black crystal from time to time."

"When I could find it," someone said facetiously.

"The chosen few," another added.

He wasn't really all that much like Shad, Killashandra thought, her mind jumping as much from crystal deprivation as deliberate inattention because it was Lars Dahl who was talking in his Guild Master role. Just because they both have blue eyes and love the sea, that doesn't make them comparable. Or it shouldn't. And if any of us could find black crystal, we would, without him having to order us!

"To facilitate that search," Lars Dahl continued as the screen behind him lit up with a variety of paint emblems, "the Guild is canceling the markers of singers who, for one reason or another, are not actively working in the Ranges." That caused a stir and some consternation. "I should amend that—singers who have been known to bring in black crystal," he went on, raising his voice slightly over the murmuring. "We must follow up every potential source of black crystal."

"Leaving no stone unturned?" the wit asked, rousing some laughter and groans.

Lars Dahl grinned in response. "That's it. Now"—he gestured behind to the screen—"these are the canceled markers. If, however, one of you finds black on the claim of a still-existing singer . . ."

"Can't regress 'em back far enough to tell you where they cut black yet, eh, Lars?" someone asked, ending with a malicious laugh.

Regress? The word reverberated, jogging an uneasy memory, and Killa sat upright, trying to locate the speaker. "Regress"? Why should that word alarm her?

"I'll be forced to use that option, Fanerine, if you sane and active ones can't cut the blacks the Guild is obligated to supply. As I was saying, if an existing singer's claim is worked, there'll be a levy of twenty-five percent on your cut which is to go to the original claimant." He held up his hand to interrupt the sharp protests. "That will include the Guild tithe, so you aren't losing much to gain a viable site. Of course, you have to find it, first." Killashandra rather liked that droll touch. Lanzecki had reserved his humor for private moments. "Now here're copies of these released markers for you to take with you. Secure it somewhere highly visible and *try* to remember why the sheet's there. First comer to any of these reopened claims has possession: mark it with your own colors.

"Most of you realize that we've just had Passover, so that's one hazard that won't interrupt the search. Met says there's a period of stable weather due us—isn't it always after Passover?" His remark generated a few polite chuckles, but Killashandra regarded him stonyfaced.

He shouldn't think he could jolly them into doing the impossible even with that ploy of reopening worked claims that might possibly be black crystal. Why was the Guild "obligated" to supply anything? Worlds should be grateful for whatever the singers cut. She flicked her gaze around the room from one face to the next. Of the twenty, she recognized two or three. She ought to be able to recognize more. The buzz in her body made it hard for her to think. On the other hand, did any of the twenty recognize her? But then, she was seated at the back and hoping to get this meeting over with. She hugged herself, wishing she could squeeze out the itch. Maybe she could sneak out, but there was someone standing right in front of the door. To prevent premature exits?

Resignedly she listened to Lars go through his act, stirring the singers up to do the impossible—find enough black crystal to fill those contracts. Muhlah! She gave a humorless snort. He was doing a good job of communicating the urgency of this search. She couldn't recall another such all-out effort! Or that Lanzecki had ever thrown open unused claims before the paint marker was completely obliterated.

She rose when the others did, but was not unduly surprised when her name was called out. The Guild Master pushed his way through to her.

"Killa, can we let bygones be and cooperate duo on this?" he asked in a quiet voice so that only she could hear him.

She was unnerved to have the regard of those intense and brilliant blue eyes focused on her alone. That was one difference between Shad and Lars Dahl—Shad's eyes were kinder, milder, undemanding. She turned her face away.

Damn that Biyanco! She shouldn't have let herself be persuaded out of a good partner by sentiment. True, even if she had brought Shad back with her, he wouldn't have been ready for a massive search this soon, even had he been lucky enough to have a Milekey Transition. But she would have had such fun shepherding him, deftly guiding him to learn the intricacies of a new trade, watching his sensitive face perceiving new and marvelous things . . . and especially hearing the dawn song of crystal with someone as gentle and loving as Shad Tucker. And how he would have enjoyed the seas of Ballybran! What sort of a ship would he have bought with his first big cut?

"Killa!"

Someone had her by the shoulders, firm hands giving her a shake to focus her attention.

"Killa?"

"What?"

The Guild Master frowned at her with concern. "One thing sure, Killashandra Ree, you've got to get back to the Ranges whether you sing black, green, or pink! You left your return mighty late. How do you stand the itch?" The sudden tender concern in his voice startled her, but she gave no hint of that surprise.

"I'll be all right as soon as I make the Ranges," she said wearily, her spine twisting with crystal hunger.

"If you can in this condition. So I'm not asking permission now. I am coming with you. It'd be outright murder to send you out solo in your present state. I'll meet you at the Hangar. Donalla . . ."

Killa peered at the woman who stepped forward. Her face was vaguely familiar, and although her smile was warm and friendly, Killa felt a flash of anxiety.

"Glad to see you safely back, Killashandra." When Killa recoiled slightly, the woman smiled reassuringly. "We're only going straight to the Hangar. You really can trust me that far, you know."

"I'll need . . ." Killa pulled at the clothes she was wearing—they wouldn't last an hour in the Ranges. "I've no boots . . ."

"Let Donalla take care of the details, Sunny, will you?" The loving tone of the Guild Master was gently supportive.

Some part of Killa was unconvinced, but the other, more dominant need for a respite from the crystal itch made that hesitation short. The hands that replaced Lars's were gentle, warm, and subtly persuasive. It was easier to submit and be guided.

Killa rubbed at her forehead. How could she have let herself get into such a state? She ought not to be led about like a child. Surely, she wasn't that bad, that decrepit? She had walked off the transport ship on her own, hadn't she? Found the shuttle bay with no trouble! Why was she suddenly incapable of managing something as simple as getting to the Hangar? Her feet ought to know the way even if her head didn't.

But she let herself be taken. She really couldn't think straight with all that noise in her head and that buzz along her veins, spiking into her heart and lungs—a crystal shiver that no amount of radiant fluid would reduce, only cutting crystal.

She hated to admit it, even to herself, but the Guild Master had been correct. She had cut it fine. She ought to have started back to Ballybran the day she had felt the first shock of crystal deprivation. And that was what was shorting out her decision-making faculty, too.

Now that she put a reason to her mazedness, she also knew how to cure it: cut crystal! Let it sing through her body, bones, and blood. Let it clear the confusion in her mind and strengthen her flagging energies. Crystal! The worst addiction in the galaxy: difficult to live with and impossible to live without.

She stumbled, and Donalla's helping hand steadied her.

Then the noise and ordered confusion of the Hangar swirled about her. Faces peered at her; large blurred objects moved slowly past. She was gently propelled into a space that shut out much of the noise. Hands turned her body this way and that as she was inserted into a shipsuit; her feet were pushed into the familiar restriction of boots.

"My cutter . . ."

Her right hand was pressed against a hard cold surface, and her fingers, of their own accord, fitted themselves around the grip, slipping into grooves exactly carved to fit her grasp. The tension within her eased further.

She was settled into the appropriate contour chair, and the harness was buckled about her. Passive now, because she didn't have to make any movement or decision, she waited. The air around her smelled familiar— and new, of paint and oil, with enough of the pungent fuel odor to be acrid—and somehow comforting.

A sudden burst of noise, and a wave of fuel- and grease-laden air whooshed across the sensitive skin of her face. Someone had entered the sled, not so much noisily as confidently. She felt the throb of engines revving up, increasing the stink of fuel in the air, which also oddly reassured her. The sled moved forward, and she sighed with relief. Slowly she was pushed back against the seat cushions as the sled gathered speed. Sunlight pierced the windows, too brilliant for her tired eyes, and she made a protest as she closed them against the glare. Had she remembered to put in the refractive lenses? She blinked. She had, but it always took a few seconds for them to alter to the necessary refractory index. The blaze diminished, the backward pressure of takeoff eased, and she opened her eyes, suddenly more aware of her surroundings. Lars's lithe figure occupied the pilot's chair.

"Get some rest, Sunny," he said as he had so often said as they departed the Guild for the Ranges.

Because it was easier to obey than resist, she wriggled into the cushions, dropped her head back against the rest, and let herself slip into sleep.

"Eeny, meeny, pitsa teeny . . ." The old choosing phrase roused her.

"Muhlah! Any time I need to blackmail the Guild Master . . ." she murmured.

Lars laughed, the infectious laugh that had been one of his most endearing traits, and despite herself, she felt her mouth curving up in a grin.

"Works every time," he replied, and when she gargled a denial at him, he amended it. "Well, sooner or later, it works."

She struggled upright in the seat, biting her lip as the movement stirred up the crystal sting that pinched at blood and bone. She was in the

Ranges, and it would ease soon . . . ease when she finally cut again. She released the harness and peered out at the steeples and ridges of deep Range. "Where are we?"

"Scouring the parameters of an old claim."

She frowned and stared at him until recent memory returned. "Oh? Whose?"

Lars grinned. "Such details are irrelevant. The marker's on the list: that's enough."

"Where did you find a statute of limitation in Rules and Regs?"

"In the Guild Master's prerogatives." Lars grinned at her. When she snorted derisively, he added, "Why have the rule and not put it into effect? The Guild has to supply legitimate demands. Like Lanzecki, I use every trick I'm allowed—"

"You're not Lanzecki!"

"Thank you for that vote of confidence," he replied, and the buoyancy had gone out of his voice. After a long silence while she rubbed surreptitiously to ease the crystal sting, he asked, "Is it bad?" His tone held genuine concern.

"I've been worse," she said diffidently—though, candidly, she doubted that. She would have remembered it—and tried to avoid a repetition.

"Ha! Try that on someone who doesn't know you as well as I do, Sunny. Take heart. We're nearly there."

"Where?" Her voice had an edge on it. "Oh, quick! Mark *there!*" And she pointed imperiously to starboard. The evening sunlight had just briefly glinted off crystal shard.

Lars gave an appreciative chuckle. "You may be writhing with crystal itch, but your eye's as keen as ever." He veered to the right, slowing the sled and neatly landing it on the bottom of the ravine. "You're one of the best in the Guild," he murmured as they saw the unmistakable evidence of a cutter's discards.

Killa could not control the trembling that racked her body. She fumbled with the door release, managed it the second time, and half fell from the sled.

"Careful now, Sunny," Lars called, rapidly flicking through essential landing procedures at the console.

She stumbled forward to the shards, crouching to gather handfuls, closing her fingers about them, oblivious to the sharp edges, even grateful for the caressing cut of crystal, grateful to spill blood and ease the sting that made artery, vein, and capillary itch.

"Easy, Sunny, easy," Lars cried, and gripped her firmly by the shoulders, pulling her to standing position.

"Muhlah!" she sighed with relief. "I needed that!"

"I don't think you need go to extremes, however," Lars said dryly. He leaned down and picked up a hunk that had crazed in faulty cutting. He tilted her bloody hands to tip the fragments out and replaced them with the larger, blunter piece. Putting his arm about her, he guided her back into the sled and washed each hand, while she held the shaft against her in the other like the talisman it was. The tiny crystal slices were already healing as he finished.

"You'd better eat, Sunny," Lars went on, still using that gently matter-of-fact tone. And he prepared a meal while she sat rocking the crystal against her, feeling it draw the sting from her, damaged as it was, as contact warmed it to her body temperature.

As she mechanically ate the meal he placed in front of her, she kept up her rocking motion, shifting the crystal to her thighs, bending her knees so the crystal touched her belly. She didn't resist when he put her to bed, letting her wrap herself around the crystal in a semifetal position. And that was how she spent the long night, comforted by crazed crystal.

When crystal song woke her the next morning, the damaged shaft sent out painful emanations. With a cry, she unwound, pushing the crystal from her as if it were polluted. Lars picked it up and flung it from the sled, relieving her of the sudden agony.

Then he spread himself across her body—she was arching in the agony of crystal song, too long away from it to be stimulated in the usual way.

"It'll ease, Sunny, it'll ease . . ." he murmured, struggling to keep her from straining herself in the paroxysms that were shaking her. If she had been alone in such a state, she would have launched herself to the nearby lode. In such disorientation, compelled by the irresistible need to reestablish contact with the ecstasy of sunwarmed singing crystal, she could have done herself a fatal injury.

Writhing against his restraint, she screamed at him, desperate to get to the crystal face and ease the intolerable sting and achings.

"Let me go! I'm begging you, Lars, let me go! I've got to get to—"

"You do and you're dead," he yelled back at her, resetting his hands on her wrists, managing, each time she nearly squirmed free, to cover her body with his and deny her freedom. "Hang on, Sunny. It won't be long now. Just let the sun get up!"

She twisted and bit at him, tried to knee his crotch, but he was quicker, stronger, and fitter than she and evaded her savage attempts to inflict enough pain to get free.

Abruptly the dawn chorus ended as the sun's rays flicked up and over the surrounding ridges and lit the ravine. She sagged against the hands that held her, limp, weeping because the itch was back, intensified. The compulsion to seek crystal, however, had eased. Wearily, she rubbed sweat and tears from her face on the quilt beneath her.

"Let me up, Lars," she said dully.

He kept his grip a moment longer, and then his fingers slowly released her wrists and he slid off her.

"Sorry about that, Killa, but you know I was right."

"Yes, I know," she replied, absently rubbing her wrists before she elbowed herself to a sitting position. "You're sneakier than an Altairian tangler," she said nastily. But the purely physical aches distracted her nerves from the interior throb of crystal sting.

A mug of some warm liquid was thrust at her.

"Drink this. Stuffed full of stimulants," Lars said, and she obeyed.

The beverage coursed down her gullet and seemed to find an immediate path to her armpits and stomach, radiating out from those points to her extremities.

"Thanks, Lars," she said.

He ruffled her hair. "That's my Sunny!"

"I am *not* your Sunny," she said, shooting him a brief dark scowl of denial.

"No, you're not much like *my* Sunny, are you?" His voice had gone expressionless again.

She tried not to care, but perhaps it was as well. "We're here to cut, aren't we? Let's do it."

Stiffly she got to her feet and walked as firmly as she could to the cutter rack. The weight of the tool was almost more than her flaccid arm could support, but just as Lars's hand came to her assistance, she managed to heave the cutter strap onto her shoulder.

"Let's go."

As she descended from the sled onto the rock- and shard-strewn ground, she was vaguely aware that he had slung more than his cutter over his shoulder. By the time she had scrambled to the rock face only fifteen meters from the sled, she was panting with exertion. She paused long enough to catch her breath to sing. She chose an A; heard Lars sing out in C and the face echo it back. Not a strong rebound but enough to encourage her. With her hand flat on the rock, she tried to find the source of the echo.

"It's stronger over here," Lars said, and she closed the distance between them with a leap. "Don't break a leg!" he shouted

She sang A again, and the reverberation rippled through her hand.

"Easy, girl," he said, but she was too busy tuning her cutter.

Old habit guided them both, and Killa managed to hold her cutter against the buck of the subsonic blade through the crystal that had lain hidden since the tectonic pressures had formed it.

"Hold it steady!" Lars's voice penetrated her cutting fever and steadied her just enough so that their initial cut was true. Lars did the underslice as Killa held out eager hands to receive the excision. Her fingers clawed it free, ignoring the lacerations, and she held it up—a form in green, clear and solid.

Sunlight caught it, making it sing in her hands. The shaft sang on and on, its sound coruscating through her skin to bone and blood, flowing down her arms to her body, through her body to her legs, flowing and blotting out the sting with its resonance, leeching the agony of her long absence from the crystal that rejuvenated her.

ANNE MCCAFFREY

When someone wrenched the shaft from her, she screamed and received a hard slap across her face; she dropped to the ground, bruising her knees on the scattered crystal debris.

"*Killa!* You've been thralled!" Lars's voice caught her just as she was about to launch herself at him, a formless silhouette in the haze beyond her crystal rapture.

Slowly she got to her feet, crawling her hands arduously up her legs to straighten a body shaking with fatigue and the residue of thrall. Lars reached out to support her, one hand gently brushing dirt and sweat from her face. Instinctively she leaned into his body, accepting support, unconsciously entreating sympathy, and his arms closed about her, his chin on her head, in the way they had so often stood after a good cutting.

"There, there, Sunny," he said, patting her shoulder and cuddling her. "You needed that. Feel somewhat better?" he asked, tipping her head back and looking down into her haggard face.

"How long did you let thrall last?" she asked, aware of her incredible weariness.

"Considering your condition," he said with a laugh, "most of the day."

She pushed away from him. "You mean, you let me thrall all day long when I could have been cutting? An hour or so at most would have been enough!"

He stepped back from her ire, grinning more broadly now, holding up his hands in mock appeal. "That's more like my Sunny."

"I'm not your Sunny," she said, needing to rant and rave herself back to a more normal humor, disgusted by the limp and nauseating lug she knew she had been.

"Well, then, it's a good deep green, and I cut around you, in case you didn't hear, locked in that thrall."

She both hated and admired Lars in this sort of a mood: far too amenable, far too effective, far too . . . *right*! Shard his soul!

Glaring at him, she sang out a high C, lost it for lack of support in her weakened condition, set her diaphragm muscles, and sang it again. She could hear his A an octave below. The green resonated, and their blades touched its bright surface as one.

When they had excised five shafts, Lars refused to let her pitch for more. He even refused to let her help him carry the carton back to the sled. When they got back and had racked their cutters, he insisted that she needed to wash, however briefly, and when she was obviously unable to stand up under the dribble coming from the shower head, he undressed, too, and supported her.

He made her lie down under the quilt while, buff naked, he made a quick meal for them both. She managed to spoon it into her, but the effort was all she had left and he caught the sagging plate before it tipped over onto the quilt.

"Can't mess it up. It's the only one we've got."

She tried to think of a smart reply to that. Honor demanded that she not let Lars get away with the last word today, but she fell asleep before she could think of something appropriately scathing.

Crystal song woke her and, aware of the warmth of the body beside her, she turned, eager for the benison of relief. She matched the eagerness of her partner, accepting and returning the passion she found. The gentleness and tenderness he displayed reminded her of Shad, and yet, as she opened her eyes, it wasn't Shad's engagingly innocent face that she saw. It was Lars Dahl's.

He gazed down at her for a long moment, his blue eyes dark with unspoken words as he searched her face. When she gave a little impatient twitch, he moved away.

"A better day today, isn't it, Sunny?" he said noncommitally.

"Yes, it is," she said with an equal lack of emphasis as she snagged her clothes from the floor.

It was easy to fall into the old habits. She might rail silently at finding herself accepting their former routine, but it helped. They didn't have much to discuss. Except the cutting.

"We shouldn't stay here," she said after they had finished eating. "Green's not black, and that's what we're after."

"Feeling up to it?" he asked offhandedly.

She shrugged. "I'd rather waste time on looking than on cutting."

"Green's easier to cut to get back into the swing of it."

"Ha! I'm back already."

He cocked an eyebrow at her. "When thrall can hold you for hours?"

"That," she said, snapping her words out, "was *your* fault. I wouldn't have needed more than an hour."

"Ha!" he mimicked her.

But they were already, out of long habit, setting the cabin of the sled to rights to take off.

They bickered with some heat and contempt for the first hour in the air. Some equity was reached when they came across another worn paint mark that bore enough resemblance to one of the released ones for them to land. But as they were surveying the canyons, they caught sight of a sled in one of the gorges and quickly left the area, Killa swearing under her breath.

"What about one of the claims we cut? Aren't there any in the vicinity?"

Lars frowned thoughtfully. "Should be." Then he banged his fist on the console. "If only we could establish some method by which singers could register the location of sites . . ."

"Ha! And have renegades spend weeks trying to break into the program?"

"There are security measures available now that no singer could break."

"Ha! I don't believe you! I won't believe you."

"I know," he said, shrugging away her anger, and grinned over his shoulder at her. "But I'll win 'em over to my way of thinking!"

"That'll be the day!"

"It'll come, Sunny. The Guild has to reorganize. It can't continue to operate on guidelines that're centuries old, incredibly obsolete, and damned naive."

"Naive?"

"It's a rough galaxy we live in. The business ethics that motivated the earliest Guild Masters simply don't exist, and modernization is long overdue."

"Modernization?" Killa swept her hand around the cabin, where sophisticated equipment was installed in small, discreet, and effective packages.

"I don't mean the hardware. I mean"—he jammed a finger to his temple—"the software. The thinking, the ethos, the management."

Killa made a disparaging noise in her throat. "This Guild Mastership has addled *your* software, that's for sure."

"Has it?" He cast her a sideways glance. "I think you'll come to agree that updates are essential."

"Hmmm. Hey, isn't that a marker of ours to starboard . . ."

It was, though nearly rubbed completely off the flat summit. They touched down, as much to refurbish the marker as to see if anything was familiar.

"Vaguely" was Killashandra's verdict. Something nagged at her, something quite insistent. "I think," she began hesitantly, "I think it's black."

"You don't sound sure . . ."

"I think you were also right to ask me if I was up to it." She fought the frisson that racked her.

"We can go back and cut more green."

"No, we're here to cut black and black we'll cut, if it kills me."

"I draw the line at suicide, no matter how badly the Guild needs black right now."

She gave him a wry grin.

What they found was a deep blue crystal, one of the loveliest colors either had ever cut. They got three cartons of it and were back at the sled, filling up their water bottles, when the first twinge of storm warning caught Killashandra. She sucked in her breath at the intensity of it. The crystal deprivation must have made her doubly vulnerable. She caught at the side of the cistern, and Lars reached out to support her.

"What's the matter? And don't you dare say 'nothing,' Killa," he said, eyes piercing hers with his growing recognition of the probable cause. "Storm?" When she nodded, he cursed under his breath. Then he closed the water tap and covered his half-filled canteen, stowing it in place. He took hers from her limp hand and put it away as well. "All right, let's get ready."

"But it's only the—"

"Fardles, Killa, I can tell just from your reaction that it's going to be a bad blow."

"It's only because—"

"I don't care what it's because," he cried, irritably chopping his hand downward to interrupt her. He took her arm and turned her toward the galley. "We're returning, and that's that. I'm not risking you to even the mildest blow. Your head's not on straight yet from deprivation."

Though she protested vehemently, she had to recognize the fact that he was absolutely correct in assessing her state. She wouldn't admit it to him—she argued out of habit. He refused to entertain her contention that they would have enough time to cut at least five; he agreed but discounted the fact that this was the best blue lode they had seen in decades.

"It isn't black," he said, his mouth and eyes angry. "Try not to forget that, Sunny. It's black we need!"

"Then why did we waste time cutting this blue?"

"You thought there was black here!" He was moving around his side of the sled, securing cabinets and stowing oddments away.

"We cut good blue . . ." she began, going meek on him, a tactic that had often worked. "I don't remember how many times you've told me that . . ."

The anger went out of him all at once, and reaching across the narrow space that separated them, he caressed her cheek briefly, his smile penitent. "Sorry, Sunny, no matter how you try to slice it, we're not cutting any more . . . here . . . today."

"It should be a partners' decision, not one way," she said, wondering if he was weakening. "You've never been this arbitrary before."

He gave a weary sigh. "I'm arbitrary now! As Guild Master, I have more than a partner's stake in keeping your brain unscrambled."

"I didn't want you to be Guild Master."

"You've made that clear," he said, and his eyes flashed at her before once again he relented. "We were the best duet the Guild ever had. I've seen the printout of our aggregate cuttings. Impressive!" The smile he gave her was suddenly boyish, and she felt her heart unseize as the Lars she knew so intimately surfaced briefly. "Now let's scramble. I'm not risking you, or me."

In far better charity with each other, they returned to the Guild. By then the storm warnings were far-flung, and sleds from all sectors began pouring into the Hangar. Lars was calling for assistance to unload their crystal just as the flight officer handed him a communit with the message that the call had top priority.

"I'll take ours through Sorting," Killa told him when he looked expectantly at her.

For a moment she watched his tall figure stride to the nearest exit, his head bent as he listened to the priority call. Someone else needing black crystal?

Guild Master's cut also took priority in the Sorting Shed and Killa waved her cartons toward Clodine's stall. She ignored the Sorter's initial nervousness and did her best to be pleasant. It was the cut that helped restore Clodine to their previous easy relationship. The market price of the blues would have been enough to appease the most desperate singer.

Once assured of the hefty credit balance, Killashandra became aware of externals—like the crystal song emanating from her person and her clothes. Jauntily she strode to her quarters. As she palmed open the door, she heard the radiant liquid splashing into the tub and smiled. That was nice of Lars. A good long soak, something to eat, and she would be back to normal. Well, as normal as any crystal singer ever was. At least she had worked free of all that crystal cramp. Good cutting was what she had really needed to cure it.

The moment she toggled the food dispenser, the screen lit up to display Lars's face.

"Killa? That's a handy total on the blues," he said.

"Shards, I wanted to tell you myself," she said, feeling a surge of disgruntlement.

"I've ordered up a meal here, if you'd care to join me . . ." The hesitant tone of his invitation struck her as atypical, but it pleased her that this Guild Master was not as autocratic as Lanzecki had been.

"I think I might at that," Killa said graciously, and canceled the order she had just placed. Dinner with Lars, or for that matter, dinner with the Guild Master, tagged elusive wisps of memory, most of them pleasant.

Looking at the garments in her closet, she picked the one that suited a slightly smug mood and dressed carefully, spending time to comb out her snagged hair and arrange it attractively. She ought to get it cut short again, she reflected. It had been a nuisance in the Range, sweating up and falling into her eyes when she wanted a clear view of her cuts. She peered at her face: she had a tan again, making her eyes brighter, canceling the yellow that had begun to tint the white. She pulled her hands down her cheeks: they were still gaunt, and were those age grooves from her nose to her mouth? She grimaced to smooth them away. Then she frowned. She did look older. She would have to be very careful not to tax her symbiont again as badly as she must have done to look *this* way.

As she entered the Guild Master's offices, the first thing she saw was the empty desk, its surface clear of pencil files or any work at all. She frowned. Trag? No, Trag was gone. Lars had not found a suitable assistant. He would have to. No wonder he had been snapping at her in the Ranges. She knew from the amount of work she had seen Lanzecki get through— and that with Trag's help—that the Guild Mastership was no sinecure. She snorted to herself: Lars had been a damned fool to get roped into the job. She bet he hadn't been sailing once since he had become Guild Master!

"When" was not a word she often used, but it suddenly flicked across her consciousness. *When* had he taken over from Lanzecki? She grunted, canceling that irritating consideration as she continued across the floor to the inner office.

Lars was deep in contemplation of whatever was on his desk screen. He had had time to shower and change; his hair was still damp. To one side, in front of the wide window that overlooked the immense doors of the Hangar, a table had been set, and the enticing odors of some of her favorite foods wafted to her. Becoming aware of someone else in the room, he looked up with a scowl that shifted into a smile as he jumped to his feet.

"Sunny!" He gestured for her to join him at the table, then seated her.

"What are you after now?" she asked, a teasing note in her voice to draw the sting of her cynicism.

"Ah, lovey," he said, dropping a kiss on her cheek before he took his own seat, "give me credit for some altruism."

"Why should I?"

Grinning at her, he searched her face and was evidently satisfied by what he saw. She cocked her head at him.

"So?"

"Eat first, talk later. I'd like to see a little more flesh on your bones before we go out again."

She groaned. "So we're not going back out as soon as the storm clears?"

In place of an answer, he served generous portions of her favorite foods onto her plate. When he started to help himself, she saw that he had ordered the nicco spikes she hated even to smell. He grinned when she twitched her nose in disgust.

"You see, I'm not catering entirely to you, Killa Ree, and no, we're not able to go out immediately. Black crystal's not the only one of our products in demand." He ended the sentence abruptly. "I'd be able to go quicker if you could see your way clear to giving me a little help."

"I thought helping you was finding black. I'll go alone."

"No!" The single word was so forceful that she stared at him in surprise. Lars hadn't used to take such a tone with her. She bristled, but he reached for her arm, shaking some of the milsi stalks from her half-raised spoon, before his touch softened in apology. "No, Killa. Too dangerous. You're not completely over the deprivation and you'd thrall. Especially if you were cutting black alone."

While she still resisted his prohibition, she had to admit that she would be extremely vulnerable to black thrall. She also had to admit that she had been in a terrible state when they had gone out: as near as made no never mind to being a crystallized cripple. They might have been searching for black crystal, but she was bloody lucky they hadn't found any. Green thrall had been deep enough. She owed him a lot for risking his own neck taking her out at all in that state.

"So, what do you need done, Guild Master?" she asked flippantly.

He smiled with genuine relief. "Thanks, Sunny, I really appreciate it."

"So?"

"Eat first," he said. "I can't think when my stomach's clinging to my backbone."

She was hungrier than she had thought and quite willing to concentrate on eating. Odd how a full belly could reduce resistance to unpalatable business.

When they had cleared the last morsel from the platters, Lars leaned back, patting his stomach and smiling.

"That's better. Now, if you could finish rounding up the figures and prices on the accounts I have on the screen, then I can go salve wounded feelings."

"Whose?"

"Clarend and Ritwili have legitimate grievances which must be addressed, and I've a delegation to meet at Shankill that I can no longer postpone."

"I might be better with the delegation than with the files," she suggested warily.

"It's the sort of thing you've done for Lanzecki before. D'you remember the Apharian contingent? Well, I've got the Blackwell Triad looking for favors now. Similar circumstances, similar solution, but I need the account figures on hand."

"Bor-ring," she said, rolling her eyes.

"A lot of what I have to do is boring, and yet . . ." Lars regarded her, his wide mouth curling in a grin. "I rather like finding out how this Guild hangs together against all comers."

Killashandra snorted. "We've a unique product that no one else can produce, no matter how hard they try. We're in control."

"I like that 'we,' Sunny." He reached across the table to fondle her hand. "I'll go heal fractured feelings; you find me figures."

"Just this once, because I owe you," she warned him, pulling her hand away and shaking her finger at him. "Don't think you can rope me into this full time. I'm a singer, not a key tapper! Find yourself a recruit with business training."

"I'm trying to," he said with a sly grin.

Once she became absorbed in the analysis, Killashandra found it more interesting than she had expected. Certainly the scope of the Guild's authority—and its unassailable position as the only source of communication-crystal systems—was wider than she had imagined. Her job—the cutting—was but the beginning of a multitude of complex processes with end uses in constant demand throughout the inhabited galaxy. Deprive a world of Ballybran crystal, and its economy would collapse, so vital were the shafts, and even the splinters, to technology on all levels. The pure research buffos in the labs here kept finding new applications of crystal— even ground shards had uses as abrasives. The more brilliant of the smaller splinters could be made into resonating jewelry, much in vogue again. She wondered how the galaxy had let one Guild gain so much power. What had Lars been on about? Reorganizing? Modernizing? What? The Guild bought state-of-the-art technology in other fields.

Unable to resist the temptation of having unrestricted access to the Guild's master files, Killashandra ran some that she might never again have a chance to discover. Lars had said something about aggregate cutting figures. She wanted to know just how much she, Killashandra Ree, had contributed to the success of the Guild. Once in the ultraconfidential files, those entries were easy enough to find. But the dating of their first duet journey was a shock. They couldn't have been cutting *that* long. They couldn't . . .

She canceled the file and sat looking at the screen, patiently blinking a readiness to oblige her. She couldn't . . .

"Sunny?" Lars's voice on the communit broke through the fugue such knowledge caused. "Sunny, got those figures for me? Sunny? Sunny, what's wrong?"

His voice, concerned and increasingly anxious, roused her.

"I got 'em . . ." She managed to get the words out.

"Sunny, what's the matter?"

"Am I old, Lars?"

There wasn't much of a pause and, later on, she was never sure if there had been any before he laughed. "Old? A singer never gets old, Sunny." His voice rippled with a laughter that sounded genuine to her critical ear. She couldn't even imagine that his amusement was forced. "That's why we became singers. To never get old. Give me those figures, will you, and then I can get back from Shankill and show you just how ageless we both are! Don't get sidetracked by trivia like that, Killa. Now, what are those figures? I'm nearly at Shankill Base. Patch them through, will you?"

Like an AI, she performed the necessary function and then leaned back in the Guild Master's comfortable but too big chair and tried to remember how she could possibly have cut so many tons of crystal over so many decades.

Lars found her there when he returned long after night had fallen over Ballybran. Nor could he, using all his skill as lover or persuader, bring her out of her fugue. He did the only thing possible: took her out into the Ranges again.

She broke out herself when she realized that they were deep in the Milekey Range. On that trip they found the elusive black crystal, a full octave in E that was likely to sing messages around the biggest of the systems vying for comcrystals. But cutting the blacks enervated Killa to the point that she did not argue with Lars when he reluctantly but firmly turned the sled back to the Guild Complex. For the first time it wasn't a storm that drove them in.

Dimly Killa realized that he carried her in his arms all the way down to the Infirmary, refusing any assistance or the grav-gurney. He undressed her himself while Donalla attached the monitors and Presnol fussed over which medication would produce the best results in the optimum time.

"Shard the optimum!" Lars raved. "Juice up her symbiont! Heal her!"

He saw her harnessed into the radiant-fluid bath before he stormed off. She let herself drift then and didn't even wonder how much credit that octave of blacks had earned them.

Chapter 9

"Did you get enough blacks in?" Killa asked Lars the first time she saw him after she began to pull out of the traumatic exhaustion.

"Enough to reduce the clamor a few decibels, Sunny." He bent to kiss her cheek and then pinched it, a gleam of mischief in his eyes. "The ones we cut together were the best."

"Naturally," she said with a flash of her usual arrogance.

"Seen the figures on that octave?" he asked.

"One of my first conscious acts." She leaned into the fingers that stroked her cheek. "I've a bird to pluck with you. You gave me part of those you brought in when you went back out by yourself, and that's not in Rules and Regs. You cut by yourself," she said, scowling at him but well pleased at his generosity.

"Ah, but it's your site. All things being equal, you'd've continued cutting with me until the weather turned."

"So," she said, moving her head slightly back from his caresses and eyeing him speculatively, "what is such charity going to cost me?"

Lars gave a hearty laugh, throwing his head back and tipping the chair away from the bed, balancing it deftly on the back legs. "I wasn't so much charitable as conscious of my administrative edict that those whose claims were cut without their participation would be awarded a settlement."

"I'm an existing and active singer," she said, outraged. "I'm not—not yet, at any rate . . ." And she waved her hand in agitated denial toward the section of the Infirmary that cared for the brain-damaged singers.

"No, of course you're not. The fact remains that I was compelled by press of orders to obtain black crystal from any viable site," he said, solemn for a moment. "And you did cut there earlier with me, so it was only just, meet, and fair that you got your share—especially at the current market price of blacks." He rolled his eyes. "Best ever."

"Yes, it was, wasn't it!" Killa grinned back at him. Blacks always generated top earnings. Their octave had earned her more than she had made in—her mind stumbled over the time factor. Quickly she turned away from such speculations. "Has that octave been processed yet?" She was still annoyed with Donalla and Presnol for not allowing her to access that information. They had kept her restricted to a simple voice-only communit.

"Oooh, as fast as it could be shaped and bracketed. The Blackwell

601

Triad drooled when I made it available to them. Eight was what they needed, and eight matched was a plus. Which they paid for."

"Too right!"

"Terasolli installed them." Lars's grin turned sour. "Then lost himself so well in Maxim's Planet I haven't been able to locate a trace of him. Even with what the pricey establishments on Maxim's charge, he's got enough to lose himself for months."

"I remember going to Maxim's once with you," Killa said, though she could recall no details of the legendary exotic pleasances that the leisure planet offered. Though some singers risked mind and body to cut enough for repeated visits to Maxim's, she couldn't recall any desire to do so.

"Once. No seas, not even lakes, so no sailing." He cocked her a malicious grin. "Which reminds me. Care to get out of here for a few days' R and R? You can crew for me."

"To get out of here I'd even crew!"

Counterfeiting irritation at her gibe, he ruffled her hair into snarls and left, whistling a chanty.

Three days later, when she made her way down to the pier, she was surprised to find Donalla, Presnol, and Clodine already there, carisaks at their feet. She very much resented Lars's extending his invitation to anyone else, much less these three. She had wanted—expected—only his company on board the *Angel*. The ship was more than enough rival for his attention. Then she experienced a second, more disjointing shock when she got a good look at the ship moored to the long pier: it was not the *Angel* she *thought* she remembered clearly, but a craft some ten or fifteen meters longer. A sloop, but a much bigger one. That somewhat explained the extra hands but did not disperse her disgruntlement.

Lars arrived before she got past a stiff greeting to the others. He jogged down the pier, grinning broadly at the success of his surprise.

"She's great, isn't she?" he said, the face boyish and more like the Lars she had known than the Guild Master he had become. "This'll be her maiden voyage. You're the shakedown crew."

Not even Killashandra had the effrontery to blight his pleasure as he shepherded them on board, pointing out the technological improvements and amenities, the spaciousness, the luxury of the several cabins and wardroom, still smelling of varnish, paint, and that indefinable odor of "unused." There was even space for a body-sleeve-sized radiant bath. Killa lost the edge of her vexation when Lars guided her to the captain's cabin, genially waving the other three to pick out their own bunks. There would be much more privacy on *Angel II*—unless, of course, Lars insisted on standing a different watch. Maybe they would have to, for she had no idea how much seamanship the two medics and the Sorter had.

"Like it, Sunny?" Lars said, tossing his duffel to the wide bunk and gesturing around the beautifully appointed cabin. "The rewards of cutting black!"

"Must have cost you every bit you made," she murmured, looking about her appreciatively. "State-of-the-art?"

"She was when she left the boatyard on Optheria." Lars slipped his arms about her waist, enfolding her to him and burying his face in her short crisp curls. "Probably still is, though I waited to sail her until I could have my Sunny aboard. No fun for me to sail without you, you know." He kissed her, then let her go to swing his arms about expansively. "She's a beaut, isn't she? Saw her sister ships on Flag Three and I've lusted after one like her ever since."

"Do the others know how to sail?" she asked, curious and still somewhat resentful.

"They sailed on the old ship a couple of times," he admitted casually. "They don't get seasick, if that's your worry, and, while this baby should run herself, they know their way about a deck."

"Who cooks?" Killa asked, half teasing.

"Whoever's off-duty," he replied gaily, and then hugged her to him. "It's good to have you back on board, lovey. Real good. Now"—and his manner turned brisk—"let's get this cruise under way."

It turned out to be a very good cruise, especially when Killashandra realized that she was a much more capable sailor than any of the others. And, as usual, she responded automatically, and correctly, to any of Lars's orders.

The important things to remember she remembered, she told herself. The rest was chaff, which time would have winnowed out of active memory anyway.

And, as they anchored every evening in a cove and the ship could be rigged to rouse the crew if its monitors received any critical readings, Lars and she spent their nights together in the captain's double bunk.

They fished and ate the panfried catch, sweet and delicate in flavor and flesh. They sailed, or rather Lars did—he would let no one take the helm for very long, even Killa. By the afternoon of the third day out, they encountered some stormy weather. She reveled in it, for it brought back to mind flashes of other storms she had experienced on ships with Lars. It was four days before the pressures of the Guild had to be considered. Lars tried to settle one set of problems that were patched through to him, but since he had no assistant to handle matters during an absence, they regretfully had to turn back.

"I thought you were going to find yourself an aide," Killa said, unhappy at having the halcyon trip truncated.

"I've been trying to find the right personality for the past seven years, Sunny. Isn't easy to find anyone suitable. Oh, there've been a couple of recruits who had some potential, passable as temporaries, but none who had the breadth of experience to be effective executives. I need someone who knows and understands Guild tenets, has or could cut crystal, has managerial skills without being a power freak. Most especially someone I can trust . . ."

"Not to usurp your prerogatives?" Killa asked facetiously.

"That, too," he agreed, grinning at her. "It's not an easy position to fill. I've learned to do as much as I can myself without delegating it to others because, bluntly, singers forget too much."

Killa heard that on several levels and winced. His arm came about her, lovingly tucking her against him, and she felt his kiss on the nape of her neck.

"Worse, they sublimate—Donalla's word—crystal singing into the most important aspect of their lives, which, in many senses, it *has* to be. The disadvantage to that is the balance: they end up with such narrow parameters in which they can function that they're bloody useless for any broader view. They're either singing or they flee *from* singing until they can no longer ignore the need for crystal. That sort of myopia compromises a lot of otherwise good people. Life holds more—hey, Sunny, what's the matter with you?" Killa had stiffened in his arms, and tried to push him away. "Hey, no need to take offense!" He laughed at her and pulled her back into his arms, caressing her until she began to relax. "Silly chunk!"

She made herself soften in his arms because they were nearly back at the Guild harbor, but whether or not he denied it, she felt that his comments had not been as casual as he pretended. And yet . . . nothing in the past few days had suggested to her that there had been any other, subtle alteration to their long relationship. Donalla was patently interested in Presnol, and Clodine apparently had a like-for-like preference.

Then Lars issued the necessary orders to ready the ship for docking, and there was no time for any further conversation. On the one hand, Killa resented that Lars had left her so unsettled with his remarks unclarified, but, on the other, she wanted time to mull over what he *had* said. If the suit fits, wear it, she thought.

With utter honesty, she recognized that she was guilty of compressing her personal parameters into just such a narrow track. Had Lars seen that? Was he hoping that his remarks would jolt her out of that myopia? Only how? Something teased at the edge of her mind. Something important. She couldn't catch so much as a hint.

She sighed and finished cleaning up the galley and removing the last of the perishable foods. Well, maybe she wasn't as myopic as some. She sailed, didn't she? And she could remember seeing more water worlds than any galaxy had the right to offer.

Sailing had given Lars Dahl some respite from the pressures of his responsibility, but the main one had doubled on him—more black crystal was ordered.

"I left instructions that no further orders were to be taken," Lars said, angrily furrowing his brows as he glared at the comscreen. It had been buzzing for his attention the moment he opened the hatch on his private ground vehicle.

"Guild Master, we *never* refuse orders for black," he was told.

"We can't fill the orders we've got," Lars leaned out of the open door. "Donalla, you're going to have to lean on Borella and Rimbol."

The names were vaguely familiar to Killashandra.

"I'll do what I can, Lars," Donalla called back to him, but she shrugged as if she was none too sanguine about success.

"Rimbol? I knew him—I think," Killashandra said as a hazy image of an ingenuous smile on a boyish face flickered in recall. "And Borella . . ." The woman's face was not clear; memory centered on a tall strong body and a badly lacerated leg. "I haven't seen them in a long time," she added.

"You're not likely to, Sunny," Lars said kindly. "They both turned off storm warnings once too often."

"Oh!" She paused, considering that information. "Then how can Donalla lean on them?"

Lars had stowed their two duffels; he strapped into his seat, motioning for Killa to do the same, as he prepared to drive back to the Cube.

"Regression," he replied succinctly.

That was the word.

"What's that?"

"It's an old technique of accessing segments of memories lost on purpose or from brain injury. We don't use but two-fifths of the brains we've got. As Donalla explained, some functions can be switched to unused portions of the mind, and often memories get shunted out of active recall. Off and on, there have been fads of regression, usually to former lives." He chuckled before continuing, an indication of his opinion of such an exercise. "We're using it to tap memory strings. Donalla's research on memory loss suggests that we don't actually lose anything we've seen, heard, and felt. The unpleasant we tend to bury as deep as possible, depending on its effect on our psyches. Oddly enough, good memories get dropped just as thoroughly. Through a careful use of hypnosis, Donalla has been able to reclaim lost knowledge."

"That's illegal!" She saw Lars shake his head at her outburst. "Isn't it?"

"No, it isn't. I had that point clarified. We are the custodians of those husks of former singers, and they get the best physical care we can supply. Some of them, under Donalla's care, have actually been restored as functioning humans."

Killa stared at him aghast. "You can't possibly put them back in the Ranges!"

Lars laughed harshly. "I'm not sadistic, Killa; it's a plus to me if they are able to care for themselves. Some have improved enough to undertake simple duties in the Infirmary."

"That's macabre, Lars," Killa said with a shudder.

"It's also expedient. The Infirmary is damned near full, and I won't short anyone on the care they need if they've totaled their minds. The other problem is that the Guild is not attracting enough new recruits to make up for those losses . . ."

She felt both anger at him and a stirring of terror. She had come all too close to being one of the "totals" herself. "If I'd totaled, would you . . ."

His eyes on the ground speeding past them, Lars reached out to grab her hand. "If you were totaled, Killa, you wouldn't be aware of anything that was happening to you."

"But would you subject me to . . ." She couldn't continue, horrified at the very idea of someone crawling about her mind without permission, at that ultimate loss of privacy. The painful grip of his fingers increased, jolting her out of such considerations.

"I told you I didn't want to be Guild Master. Lanzecki left me with quite a mess to cope with, only when I agreed, I didn't know the half of it. Full disclosure wasn't required of him." Lars's smile was droll. "But I did have some ideas on how to revitalize the Guild, to reorganize it for efficiency and predictability. I can't leave so much to the vagaries of the singers and the weather."

"Vagaries?" she repeated indignantly. "*Vagaries?*" His choice of word infuriated her.

"Yes, singers are permitted far too much leeway—"

"Too much? When we risk our sanity every time we go into the Ranges?"

"That's the most haphazard part of the whole operation," Lars said scornfully. "Most singers—and you are not in that category, Sunny, so relax and listen up—cut just enough to get off-planet. They leave viable sites long before they need to quit because of an approaching storm. They don't remember from one time to the next where they've profitably cut and waste a lot of time trying to locate old sites or find new ones. This paranoia that keeps a singer from noting coordinates of claims is absurd. It's easy enough to use codes."

"If you can remember it later," Killa put in.

"Numbers aren't that hard to remember," he said, "and something has to be done to make such invaluable information available to the individual. It'd cut out the guesswork and make every trip into the Ranges far more profitable. Our friend Terasolli's another example of wasted time. He gets top price to set that octave, and he won't come back to Ballybran until crystal itch drives him back. That'll be a year or so—a year or so of unproductivity. That's got to stop."

"Stop?" She sputtered the word in her amazement at his uncompromising attitude.

"Two, maybe three months, should be respite enough for a singer."

"How the fardles would *you* know?" Killa demanded. "You've never set black crystal. You don't know . . ." She had to stop, she was trembling so badly. "Set this thing down. I'm not going any further with you. I'd rather walk back to the Guild than stay another minute . . ."

Lars did set the vehicle down, but he also shoved in the doorlock and swung his back against it so she couldn't reach it. His face was set and his eyes flashing with anger. He took her by the shoulders.

"You'll stay and you'll listen! If I can persuade a mind as closed as yours against any change in wasteful habits and stupid archaic perks, maybe I have a chance of pulling the Guild out of the hole it's in." He gave her a little shake, his fingers digging into the flesh of her upper arms. He ignored her squirming. "I'm trying my damnedest to save this Guild. Its position in communications is no longer as secure as it used to be because people have got tired of waiting for Ballybran crystals and have developed alternatives. Not as good as our crystal but performing much the same functions and . . . always . . . available . . . for replacement . . ." He spaced the last words for emphasis. "I've got nine orders for black crystal I can*not* fill because my singers can*not* relocate the sites where they've found black. So they go wandering about in the Ranges, looking, trying to remember. I want them to remember. I've been patient long enough—just as Lanzecki was patient—but there's an end to patience and I've reached it. I'll do anything I can to supply black crystal, to build up a backlog of the stuff, to reinstate the Guild to its former prominence. And if it means I have to plumb the depths of crazed minds to find out where black crystal is, I will. But it'd be much easier to have a live singer willing, and able, to cooperate with me."

His bitter gaze held hers, and she could see his deep anxiety, his frustration, his fears in the dark agony of his clouded eyes. His voice was harsh with desperation.

"How could I cooperate any more than I have?" she asked in a low voice, shivering internally with fear of what this compliance might do to her.

"Oh, Sunny . . ." He embraced her tightly, holding her head under his chin with one hand, stroking her body as if contact would express his gratitude and relief. Then he held her slightly away, her face in his hands, stroking her cheeks with gentle thumbs, looking deep into her eyes. "You *know* where you cut blacks. It's there in your memory." One hand cupped her head tenderly. "We just have to access those memories . . . it'll all come back. Donalla says that with the proper clues, you could remember everything . . ."

Killashandra stiffened, regretting her impulse, pulling herself free. "I don't *need* to remember everything, Lars. I don't *want* to remember everything. Get that straight now."

"Honey, all I'm asking is landmarks for the black-crystal sites you've cut. I've remembered only two, and I know there were more. I have *got* to have black crystal!" And he pounded his fist into the plas above the control panel with such force that it left a dent.

She reached for his hand, to prevent him from repeating the blow. Immediately he covered her hand with both of his.

"If we could only"—and his voice was low now, his frustration vented—"get singers to note down landmarks so they can get themselves back to the best sites . . ."

Killa gave a snort, not as derisive as she might have been because she was not going to exacerbate Lars's despair. "Now that's asking a lot, love," she said wryly. "You know how paranoid singers are. Put something down that another singer could find and locate?" She shook her head. "Not to mention roping singers back to Ballybran before they absolutely have to return."

Lars looked deeply into her eyes. "That's why your cooperation is so vital, Sunny. You're senior among the working singers. If *you* can be seen to accede to executive orders," he said with a bitter smile, "the others will accept them. Especially if you start bringing in more crystal, better crystal, because you know *exactly* how to get back to workable sites."

"I've already cut more crystal than any other singer . . ."

"You have that enviable reputation, Sunny," he said with a hint of his customary ebullience.

"So how does this regression process work?"

He straightened up, his eyes losing their grimness. "Under hypnosis. Donalla's become expert. She found the coordinates I needed to access one of our old claims the last time I went out."

"You—by yourself?" The notion that he had risked himself like that made her choke with fear.

"As Guild Master, I had to set the example, despite my partner's illness. I can't ask singers to do what I won't do myself, you know."

"And you talk about capricious singers!"

"Don't shout, Killa. I cut, I got back, and at least filled another order."

"Order? *Order!*" She was indignant.

"An order that's been unfilled for twenty years, Killa! It's no wonder the Guild's reputation has been suffering. I've finally got permission to inaugurate a more active recruitment campaign, but it's experienced singers I need and right now—and out in the Ranges, not carousing on Maxim's or Baliol and spread out across the galaxy."

The bleak expression of a man who was not given to desperation, the flat, despairing edge to a voice that had always been rich with humor and optimism, moved her more deeply than she had been moved at any other moment in a basically egocentric and selfish life. She owed Lars Dahl, and now was the time to repay him in the only coin that mattered.

"So, let's get back to the Cube and let Donalla beguile me, or whatever it is she needs to do."

"Regress your memory."

"I can't, and that's that," Donalla said, swinging her stool around and projecting herself off it. She paced angrily about the room. "You don't trust me, Killa. It's as simple as that. Until you *can* trust me, hypnosis can't happen."

"But I *do* trust you, Donalla," Killa insisted, as she had over the past few days and the increasingly frustrating sessions she had had with the medic.

"Look, ladies," Presnol said, coming out of the corner of the room where he had been as unobtrusive as possible, "there are some folk who are psychologically unable to release control of their minds to anyone, no matter how they trust the operator. Killa's been a singer a very long time now . . ."

"Don't keep reminding me of that." Killa heard the edge on her voice, but she was too keyed up by failure to control the reaction.

"Habits are ingrained . . ."

"I've never been a creature of habit," Killa protested, trying to inject a little humor into the tensions that cracked about them all.

"But," he said, turning to her, "protecting your site locations has played a dominant role in your subconscious. I mean, I've sat in on Donalla's sessions with some of the inactive singers"—Killa approved of his euphemism—"and often it's sounded to me as if they were keeping the information from themselves: the subconscious refusing to permit access of knowledge to the conscious."

"Ha!" Killa folded her arms across her chest. "I go to sleep telling myself to remember. To dredge up the necessary referents. I *dream* of fardling spires and ranges and canyons and ravines. I *dream* of the act of cutting; I *dream* of crystal until I wake myself up thinking I'm asleep on a bed of the nardling shards!"

"Like a mystic?" Donalla tried to cover up the giggle that had slipped out.

Presnol looked shocked, but Killa grinned. "I know the sort you mean—total disregard of the purely physical. Mind over matter! Oh, Muhlah, if I only could . . ." And she groaned, covering her face with her hands.

"Wait a minute," Donalla said, drawing herself erect at a sudden inspiration. "You get thralled, don't you? By crystal?"

"It can happen to any singer," Killa said guardedly.

"Yes, but thrall's a form of hypnosis, isn't it? I mean, the crystal triggers the mesmerism, doesn't it?"

"Indeed it does."

Presnol caught the significance of their exchange. "But that would mean you'd have to go into the Ranges."

"What's wrong with that, Presnol?" Killashandra asked, slapping her hands to her knees. "I'd be doing something constructive at the same time, instead of sitting on my buns here accomplishing *nothing*. Sorry, Donalla. You've tried. I just can't comply! Maybe, in the Ranges, and in thrall, you can get through."

"But—but—" Presnol floundered.

"But you've never been out, have you?"

"Only to rescue singers." A convulsive spasm shook the medic's frame.

"Well, it's about time you saw the Ranges at their best," Killa said, amused.

Presnol gulped.

"No, I'll go," Donalla said, giving her lover a reassuring smile. "I'm—supposedly—the hypnotist. And I'm not afraid of the Ranges."

"I'm not, either," Presnol protested, but the women exchanged know-ing glances. "I'm not, truly."

"Donalla's presence is sufficient, I'd say," Killa said.

"One of us should remain here, Pres," Donalla said, "and you could continue the hypnotics with—" She hesitated, glancing at Killashandra. "—another patient."

"Yes, I could," Presnol said, beginning to relax. He was not as adept at the process as Donalla, but he had been successful with two of the in-active singers. "That would be a much more useful disposition of my time right now. Ah, when will you be going?" he asked, turning back at the door.

Killa and Donalla looked at each other. Killa shrugged. "We'll check with Lars . . ."

But when they explained their plan to Lars Dahl, Killa could see plainly his resistance to the idea of her going out into the Ranges without him. She herself had had to override her own reluctance to go out in the company of a nonsinger, however dispassionately involved with the singing of crystal.

"There's been no tradition of nonsingers—" Lars began.

"Ha! Since you've been demolishing tradition all over the place, why cavil at this one? The results could be exactly what's needed. At least with me," Killa said. "As you point out, I'm one of the oldest still active singers . . ."

"Killa!" His tone held a warning not to try his patience just then.

"Look, we can rig lots of safeguards. Weather's behaving itself right now, so we can cancel that worry. Donalla can wear a combutton direct to your console, so if you have to do a rescue flit, you'll be the first to hear," Killa went on, perversely determined to undermine any argument he might voice. "Donalla's stronger than she looks, if it comes to her having to break thrall." She grinned. "Know any good throws?" she asked Donalla, who dismissed the question. "So, teach her your special techniques, up to and including setting my cutter sour. Muhlah knows that the reward could be worth the price of a cutter."

"Don't let Clarend hear you say that," Lars remarked with a good at-tempt at genuine humor.

"Hmmm, too right." Killa grinned back at him. Over the decades they had both taken plenty of abuse from the cutter.

"You'll lend us the double sled then?" Killa asked. She looked out the broad window, beyond the Hangar. "Hell, it's only midday. We could be deep in the Ranges and cutting in a couple of hours." She leaned across the desk toward him, daring him, silently urging him to agree. "Of course, if you happened to have some black-crystal coordinates handy, I could be productive on several levels."

"Killa, you do *know* what you're doing, don't you?"

"No, but Donalla thinks that thrall will help her get past the barriers I can't seem to lower."

He sighed deeply and threw his hands out in capitulation. "If you could come back with some black . . ." He set his lips firmly, hearing the desperation in his own voice.

He propelled himself out of his chair, and while Killashandra contacted the Hangar and arranged for his sled to be readied and stocked, he demonstrated to Donalla the various ways in which thrall could be broken.

"I didn't realize thrall was that dangerous," Donalla said, her eyes wide with the newly acquired information. "And you *let* Killashandra stay thralled to green . . ."

"That was a most unusual situation. Killa needed the overdose of crystals to counteract deprivation. I would never have permitted her to thrall to black—it's far harder to break out of. And that's why I *don't* like just the pair of you going."

"Well, if you want another singer along to see where we've cut black . . ." Killa teased.

"There isn't another singer *in* or you can believe I'd send someone."

"Who's that dork at Trag's desk then?"

"Certainly not yet a singer," Lars said sarcastically, "but she does have business management experience and she's capable of organizing pencil files and auditing accounts."

Killa smiled, relieved by his disparagement of the very pretty girl's abilities.

"Now, if you can't break thrall by any of the methods I've demonstrated, you club her behind the ear and haul her bodily out of the Ranges. You are checked out on sleds, aren't you?"

"You know we all are, Lars," Donalla said, giving him an almost condescending smile. "I've even driven some of the worksleds when there was extensive storm damage to patch up." Lars nodded acceptance of her competence. "But I'm not charmed by the idea of bludgeoning Killashandra Ree into submission. I'll bring along something soothing."

"You have to be careful, though," Lars held up a warning hand. "A singer in thrall can become violent. Strap her down in the sled if it comes to that."

"Now that you've given her the worst-case scenario, how else can you scare her out of this attempt?" Killa asked in some disgust. She turned to Donalla. "Anyone would think he didn't want this to succeed. I've never slugged him yet. Though I might start . . ." And she lifted her fist in mock anger.

He raised both arms and pretended to cringe from her blow. "Just in case," he added, his manner lighter and a sparkle in his blue eyes, "have you any idea where you're going?"

She grinned at him. "You need black. So, since you have already bared the location of your latest black location to Donalla, I thought you wouldn't mind entrusting it to me, your partner."

His smile deepened. "Here." He thrust a slip of paper at her. "When you're on course, eat it!"

"You are all heart, Lars Dahl," Killa said, and marched Donalla out of the office and to the lift.

In the descending car, Killa was amused by the way Donalla eyed her. "Sorry?"

"Not a bit," Donalla said, scowling sternly; then her expression altered to anxiety. "It's just I hadn't realized the possible complications."

Killa laughed. "You don't, unless you've had to work with 'em. Lars shouldn't have scared you like that."

"He doesn't want to lose you again, Killa," Donalla said, her fine eyes intent. "He idolizes you."

"He has an odd way of showing it at times," Killa replied, trying for a casual acceptance to conceal her surprise at Donalla's appraisal.

"Sometimes that's because it's too important to admit, even to himself."

The intensity of those quiet words rang in Killa's mind. Lars had so often told her he loved her, but usually in a sort of offhand manner, as if he didn't really mean it, or was astonished by blurting out the declaration. Always his hands and eyes had conveyed more than he actually said aloud. Even when she was denying him, she couldn't genuinely deny her love for him, just her dependence on the affection of any other human being.

The lift door opened and, taking a deep breath, she led the way out to the Hangar and the double sled waiting and ready.

As there was no other sled in sight, Killa set the course directly toward the coordinates Lars had given her and, making a little display of it, dutifully chewed and swallowed the note. Donalla gave her a nervous smile. Killa found the fidgeting of the usually self-confident medic amusing. Well, her self-confidence was only to be expected—in an infirmary. But now she was in the singer's bailiwick, and the Ranges were awesome. No question of that.

When Donalla relaxed enough to watch the spectacular scenery streaming by, Killa made something hot to drink and broke out some munchables. They hadn't had any noon meal, and she wanted something in her belly if she was to let herself get thralled.

There was one problem, Killa mused, now that she focused her mind on the actual process. She never remembered a thing from any period in which she had been thralled. It was all a blank from the moment she lifted the crystal free to the moment thrall lifted. Of course, Donalla had carefully explained that one didn't remember the span of a hypnotic incident, either. Well, Killa thought with a shrug, finishing the last of her ration bar, it was worth a try! Lars needed the boost a success would give him.

Between sessions with Donalla, Killa had done some surreptitious poking in general files, from Recruitment to Deliveries, all readily accessible information. There certainly had been a drop in the numbers of applicants to the Guild. There had only been six in the last bunch to be processed, and a mere ninety signing up for Guild membership over the last decade. She checked back over four decades, when the totals had been up to the two hundred mark. More singers were rated "inactive" than active on the roster. No deaths listed in the past twenty years. Killa's thoughts were grim. The cost of caring for singers was higher than the budgets of Research and Development, yet profits were dwindling. Lars had been all too correct in saying that the Guild was in serious trouble. She really should have brought in . . . she frowned, for the name escaped her. She had found someone, hadn't she? With the perfect pitch required. Could that sort of ability be on the wane in the modern world? It was a trick of the ear and the mind.

Gradually as the state of affairs of the Guild became obvious, her initial repugnance over invading singers' damaged minds to find the location of their sites began to subside. At Donalla's suggestion, she sat in on a hypnotic session with a man whose symbiont was visibly failing him. He was gnarled and wrinkled with age, joints thick with calcium deposits, veins engorged on fleshless limbs and digits. He seemed content, though, wrapped in a warm, soft blanket and smelling of a recent bath. There hadn't been much intelligence in the dull, deeply receding eyes, despite the fact that they were following the movement of the random fractals ever-shifting on the large screen in the corner of his room. He was an improvement over some of the living corpses Killa had seen on her way to his small single room.

"I chose Rimbol, because at least he's tracking what's on the screen," Donalla said. "I've had some luck in restimulating one or two of the least damaged singers. I've just turned off the music in here, but we've found he does respond to aural as well as visual stimuli. I think whatever we do to try to reach their brains is better than just letting these poor hulks have nothing to see and hear. Rimbol's more receptive to hypnotism than some of the others."

She held up the prism and turned Rimbol's head slightly so that the crystal was on a level with his eyes. She twisted the chain so that the prism caught the light, and immediately Rimbol's eyes were captured.

"Watch the prism, Rimbol, watch the lovely colors, shifting and changing. Your eyes are getting heavy, you can't hold them open because your lids are so very heavy and you're falling asleep, gently falling asleep . . ." Donalla pitched her pleasant contralto into a slow rhythmic pattern, and Rimbol's eyes did flicker and close, and a sigh escaped his lips.

"You will sleep and you will not resist. You will answer my questions as best you can. You will remember where you were when you have cut black crystal. You will remember what the landscape was like, if there were any prominent landmarks. You will also tell me the coordinates, because you *do* remember them. And you *do* remember this particular site because you cut black crystal there, four fine crystals in the key of E major. You made enough credits to leave Ballybran for over a year. Records show that you went to your homeworld on that occasion. Do you remember that time, Rimbol? Do you remember the landmarks about that site, Rimbol?"

"Ah, the E majors? Best I ever cut. I 'member." The words were slurred, but both medic and singer listened hard. "I 'member. Two peaks, like cones, and then the flat part . . ." The words became more distinct; the voice even sounded younger, more vibrant. "Narrow ravine, winds like an S, had to tip the sled and damned near lost her but I knew there was black around. Fardling steep slope up to the peaks, sharp to climb, slipped often but crystal's there . . . feel it in my knees and hands . . ."

"The coordinates, Rimbol. What are the coordinates? You saw them when you finally set the sled down. You know you did. So put yourself back then, when you're looking down at your console. Now, you can see the figures on the scope, can't you?"

"See 'em . . ."

"What do you see, Rimbol? Look closely. The numbers are very clear, aren't they?"

"Clear . . ."

"What numbers do you see?"

"Ah . . ." And another sigh escaped the old man. "Longitude, one fifty-two degrees twenty-two, latitude sixteen degrees fifteen. Didn't think I'd 'member that. I did!" He smiled contentedly and his closed eyelids trembled.

Killashandra had jotted down the coordinates and then looked at the figures, still uneasy about obtaining such information.

"He'll never make it there again, Killa," Donalla said softly. "He doesn't need them. The Guild which cares for him does."

"Someone else could probably find the claim without scouring it out of his mind," Killashandra said, resisting the intrusion for Rimbol's sake. His name sounded familiar, but he had altered far too much for her to recall what he had looked like as a young and vigorous man.

"There isn't time for random chance." Then Donalla turned back to her patient. "Thanks, Rimbol. You have been marvelously helpful."

"Have?"

Killashandra was astounded to see a smile return to tremble on the wasted lips, a smile that remained even after Donalla ended the hypnotic session. She said nothing when she noted that Killashandra had seen that smile. She turned up the music, a lilting, merry tune, and, as the two women left, Killashandra turned back and saw a distorted finger lift in time to the rhythm.

When they had finished their snack, Killashandra checked their flight path and estimated that they were nearly there. They overflew the black-and-yellow chevrons ten minutes later, and she circled, mentally chanting the choosing rhyme—eeny, meeny—as she looked for the landmarks he had told her marked the exact location of the black crystal.

She had turned 160 degrees before she recognized the configuration of ravines: three, one rising behind the other, in frozen waves of stone. At the base of the third, she should find signs of workings. She did: recent workings because sunlit sparkles caught her eye.

"Here we are," she caroled out to Donalla. "Behold!" She gestured expansively out the front window. "An actual crystal site!"

Donalla's lips parted and then a slight frown marred her high forehead.

"No, it's not much to look at," Killa said, lightly teasing. "A place known only to few and treasured by many." She locked down the controls, noting as she did so, as she always did whether she had realized it before or not, the coordinates on the screen before she shut the engines off. She had to admit that such an automatic scan was as much a part of a landing routine as turning off the engine—so automatic that she wouldn't remember she had done it three seconds after she had. There would be hundreds of such flashes for Donalla to probe . . .

She reached for her cutter and gave the lined carrier for cut crystal to Donalla to tote and opened the sled door. Through the soles of her heavy work boots, she could feel the ripple of the nearby black. She swallowed hard. The call of black was strong. Maybe Lars had been right: she wasn't ready for black yet. But they hadn't much choice, had they?

She led the way to the face, visible because of the regular steps where crystal had been recently cut. Nothing looked familiar. She knew from checking files that he had cut alone for nearly a decade—a decade she hadn't even known had passed while they were estranged. But, and she shook her head in surprise, the claim bore *their* chevron markings. Lars was a bundle of contradictions, wasn't he? He was too sentimental to be a good Guild Master, she thought; then, thinking of recent examples of his ruthlessness, she reversed her opinion.

As she narrowed the distance, she explained once more to Donalla exactly how a singer proceeded on site: finding a clear side of crystal, sounding a tuning note, setting the cutter, and then excising the crystal.

"The dangerous part is when I hold the crystal up. If sun hits it, I'll go into thrall." Wryly she glanced up to check the position of the sun, trying to ignore the hard cold knot developing in her stomach. "Well," she said, exhaling a deep breath, "here goes!" She motioned for Donalla to step back a bit, farther away from the business edge of the cutter.

Killashandra eyed the crystal face. Yes, these were Lars's cuttings. She would know them anywhere. Recent storms had not damaged his distinctive style. She brushed some loose splinters away and felt the crystal resonance just a note away. She pressed her hand flat against the surface and, setting her diaphragm, sang a clear mid-C. The crystal vibrated almost excitedly to the sound. She set the cutter. Putting the blade perpendicular to the face, she rammed it in, disengaged the blade, sliced from the top to her lower cut, then quickly shifted position to make the second downward cut, freeing the shaft. She turned off the cutter, letting it slip down the harness that held it to her shoulder.

"Now, Donalla," she said. She lifted the black crystal high, high enough to catch the sun, and felt the beginnings of thrall paralyze her. She could no more have evaded that than Rimbol had been able to evade Donalla.

Hard grit dug into her face, irregular hard objects poked her the length of her body, and her ears rang with an unpleasant dissonance that would soon split her skull. Abruptly the unendurable noise quit.

"Killa! Killa! Are you all right?"

A hand on her shoulder shook her, tentatively at first, then more urgently. But the voice was female. She had never cut with a woman! She propped herself up, one hand automatically feeling for the cutter. Her cutter? Where was it? She couldn't have lost her cutter! Dazed, she looked about, patting the ground. Her eyes were dry in their sockets and ached.

"Killa?"

Boots scrabbled on the litter and someone's face peered anxiously at her. But the someone held her precious cutter in one hand and a black-crystal shaft in the other.

"I didn't drop it . . ." Killa was weak with relief.

"I was about to shatter it if the cutter noise hadn't worked," the woman said.

Killa peered at the anxious face. It was familiar. She forced a tired mind to put name to face. Ah! "Donalla!"

"Who did you expect?" Relief made Donalla's voice sharp.

Killa eased herself to a sitting position. She couldn't trust her legs yet. Her right shoulder ached, and her arm was riddled with sharp needles of renewed circulation. She massaged her shoulder, gradually becoming aware that darkness was rapidly shadowing the narrow ravine.

"So?" she asked Donalla curtly as memory flooded back. She had cut black to go into thrall, which she had obviously done, and the thrall had lasted much longer than planned.

The look on the medic's face answered her question. "You were more impenetrable than when I tried back at the Infirmary," she said, with a weary sigh. "You just stood there, holding this wretched thing." She gave the black shaft a careless waggle. Killa lunged to save it. Donalla drew it sharply back into her chest.

"I'm all right now, Donalla. It can't thrall me again. Just don't damage the thing."

"After what it did to you? I thought I'd never get it out of your hand." Donalla regarded her burden warily.

"Then put it in the carrier." Killa wrenched her upper body about, looking for the carrier, and jabbed her finger at it. "Just don't drop it," she added as Donalla obeyed. Her voice was strident with anxiety. She cleared her throat and went on, controlling her voice, "For some reason, fresh crystal cracks faster than at any other time. Ah!" She sighed in relief as the medic stowed and covered the shaft.

Killa got to her feet then, brushing off clinging bits and pieces of dirt and crystal. She was tired, but glancing at the sun, she saw there was enough light left to make a couple more cuts to add to this bigger C.

"What are you doing?" Donalla asked, her voice sharp with concern.

"I'm going to cut." She had to use force to get Donalla to release the cutter.

"But I couldn't break through the thrall."

"Shouldn't keep me from cutting. Especially as it's black."

Killa went down a fifth, sang loud and clear, heard the answering note, and set her cutter. Donalla stepped in front of her.

"Out of my way," Killa said, appalled that she had been about to swing the cutter into position—a movement that would have brought the blade slicing right through Donalla's thighs.

"I can't let you."

"Ah, leave off, Donalla!" Killa tried to push her away. "There's no sun. It's the sun that starts thrall. For the love of anything you hold sacred, let us use the light that's left."

"You're sure? It took me hours . . ."

"Well, it won't happen at this time of day." Killa blew out with exasperation. Donalla was worse than any novice she had ever shepherded. "Sun's nearly down. Now, move out of my way!"

Hesitantly and watching Killa very warily indeed, Donalla stepped aside. Killa sang again and tuned the cutter, neatly slicing beyond her first cut. She excised that one, managed two more quick ones in the same level—smallish and stocky but black! She had the cutter poised for a third when the face turned sour. There was an intrusion or a flaw. Cursing under her breath, she stepped back and signaled Donalla to bring the carrier over. She finished packing crystal just as the last of the sunlight faded from the ridges above them.

The two women stumbled back to the sled, the carrier between them. Only when she had seen the carrier secured behind straps and the cutter properly racked did Killashandra allow fatigue to creep up on her.

"How long did you say I was thralled?" she asked, slumping into the pilot's chair.

"I forgot to check the time right away," Donalla admitted, "but from the time I did till I threw you down, it took three and a half hours!"

Killa chuckled weakly. "Don't doubt it." She rubbed at shoulder muscles still twinging from a long inactivity. "And I wouldn't answer?"

"You kept staring at the crystal. I tried every single maneuver Lars showed me and you might as well have been crystal yourself for all the blind good it did me."

She had been scared, Killashandra decided; that's what was making her angry now.

"Don't reproach yourself, Donalla. I got out, and the crystal's okay. I'd've been out of thrall once the sun went down. Or did Lars remember to mention that?" He hadn't, to judge by the expression on Donalla's face.

"Fix me something to drink, will you? I'm too tired to move, and my throat's so dry . . ."

Donalla banged the cup on the counter as she hauled the water out of the cooler, her movements revealing more plainly than any words the state of her feelings.

With food in her stomach, Killashandra took a hand beam and went out to examine the face. If she could cut past the damaged crystal to clear stuff, she ought to. She was damned lucky to find black—then she laughed, recalling that luck hadn't entered into the discovery. *Knowing* that she would have black to cut in this site took some of the elation out of the work. It was the mystery, the challenge of having to *find* the elusive material. But the work was still rewarding—and Donalla had had the chance to acquire firsthand Range experience to augment her clinical knowledge of crystal singers.

Killa hummed softly, listened for an answering resonance, and heard none. Cursing under her breath, she went back to the sled. She would have to wait till morning to see how deep the flaw was. Worse than not finding black was finding it uncuttable.

She woke in the night, aware of the warm body beside her and instantly recognizing it as Donalla's, not Lars's. That was another matter they had neglected to explain to Donalla. As the woman was apparently unremittingly heterosexual, Killa decided she would have to manage on her own—morning song could be rather more of a shock than Donalla was ready to handle.

Moving carefully, Killa rose. She found an extra thermal blanket in the cupboard and let herself out of the sled. This wouldn't be the first time she had slept on the ground. Rolling herself up under the prow of the sled where she would be protected from any heavy dew, she wriggled around until she got comfortable and dropped off to sleep again.

Dawn and crystal woke, singing her awake. She took deep breaths to reduce the effect on her until she heard Donalla crying out. Grinning, but as uncomfortable as Donalla probably was, Killa endured. She waited until the effects had faded before returning to the cabin.

"What was that? Where did you go?" Donalla demanded, her tone almost accusatory.

"That's crystal waking up to sunlight. Fabulous experience, isn't it?" Killa grinned unrepentantly, folding her thermal to stow it away again. "I felt discretion was the better part of retaining our growing friendship."

"Oh!" Donalla flushed beet red and turned away, looking anywhere but at Killashandra. "No one told me about this."

"I know," Killashandra said sympathetically. "It's another case of us knowing it so well we think everyone else knows it."

Donalla took another deep breath and managed a weak smile. "I gather—I mean—well, is that why certain partnerships . . . Oh, I'm not sure what I mean."

Killa laughed, flicking the switch on the hot-water heater as she began preparations for cooking breakfast. "It has a tendency to make minor quarrels disappear in the morning."

By the time she had eaten, Donalla had turned clinical in her examination of the sensual effect of sunwarmed crystal on human libido. Killa answered honestly and fully, amused at Donalla's professional curiosity.

"What's astonishing is that more singers don't sing duet," the medic finally announced, turning inquiringly to Killa, who shrugged.

"I suppose it's like anything else," she said. "Palls after a few score years."

"You and Lars were partners for—" Donalla bit off the rest of her sentence.

Killa regarded her for a long moment. Those of the Guild who did not lose "time" in the Ranges were taught not to make comparisons that could upset singers.

"A long time," Killa said. "A very long time." She paused. "It doesn't seem like a long time. How old am I, Donalla?"

"You certainly don't look your age, Killashandra," Donalla said, temporizing, "and I won't put a figure to it."

Killa grunted and heaved a big sigh. "You're right, you know, and I don't really want a figure."

"You don't look older than four, maybe five decades," Donalla offered as compensation.

"Thanks." Then Killa rose, having finished her meal. "I've got black I might be able to cut out of that face. I've got to try." She waggled a finger at Donalla. "Only today, you make bloody sure you take any cut right out of my hand the moment I've pulled it free. You wrench it from me, if necessary; and carefully, mind you, stow it in the carton."

Donalla stood ready all day to follow those orders, but they were never needed. The black had fractured right down into the base of the site. Killa swore, because she had cut so carefully the day before. She hadn't heard the fracture note as she finished cutting the third shaft. Usually a crack like that was not only audible but sensed even through the thick soles of her boots.

"Damn, damn, and double damn," she said, admitting defeat in midafternoon. She had even tried to find an outcropping somewhere else in the rock but hadn't heard so much as a murmur from crystal.

"What?" Donalla asked, rousing from a state of somnolence. She had been patiently watching Killa's explorations from a perch on the height.

"It's gone. No point in staying here."

"We're going back?" Donalla's expression brightened.

"We shouldn't. We should look around."

"Lars only gave you these coordinates."

"Yes, but somewhere around here," Killa said, waving her hand in a comprehensive sweep that took in the entire ravine, "there'll be more black crystal."

"How long will it take you to find it?"

"Ah . . ." Killa waggled her forefinger. "That's the rub. I don't know where."

"Well, then, let's go back to the Cube and get coordinates to another known black-crystal site," Donalla said, pushing herself off her perch and brushing dust from her trousers.

"It'll take us three hours to get back," Killa heard herself protesting. "Why, I could be—"

"Circling the area unprofitably for hours, days, more likely," Donalla said. "Let's do it the easy way, with another set of coordinates. Huh?"

Killa considered this, sweeping aside all the arguments she was ranging against the common sense Donalla was speaking. She owed it to Lars. He had been right. She had some black to return with. She shouldn't waste time. She should cut where they knew there was more.

"You're right. Absolutely right. We go back. We do it Lars's way."

Chapter 10

Lars was pleased with the four she brought back, disappointed by Donalla's failure, and relieved that they had returned. He had other coordinates for Killa to use.

"I don't really *like* this," she told him. "It still feels like claim jumping."

Lars grinned at her. "You won't say that when you have to share the proceeds, Sunny."

"There's that, too, of course," she said, making a face at him.

She went out by herself within the hour, after getting a severe lecture from Lars about remembering to stow black the instant she cut it.

"If I find it!"

"You will."

She did, but whatever crystal might have been there once was now buried under a mass of rubble and boulders too big to be shifted. She sang at the top of her excellent lungs and didn't hear so much as a squeak from the buried crystal.

So she returned to the Guild, arriving just before dark and, while Lars was willing to give her another set of coordinates, he wasn't willing to let her start until the next morning.

"Take a long bath, have a good meal, sleep in a good bed," he said with a wink and a leer. "Missed you, Sunny," he added in a soft voice, and pulled her to him, to kiss her neck. He pulled a face as he licked his lips. "Yugh! You need the bath."

"Thanks!"

"Look," he said, becoming serious, "I badly need your help, Sunny. Really, more your presence and a nod or two when necessary. If you seem to be going along with my scheme, the others're more apt to."

"Go along with what scheme?" she demanded warily. Lars was wearing his Guild Master's face.

"I've got three other singers who I believe—I hope—are still flexible enough to go along with me in this."

"In what?"

"Easy, Killa!" He grinned down at her, a twinkle returning to his eyes. "Using coordinates from the inactives."

"Oh." She began to see both his problem and his scheme.

"I also want to see how they respond to that alternative Donalla's suggested."

"Which is?" She had slightly eased herself back from his embrace.

He scrubbed his head with his knuckles, a sure sign that he was uncertain and nervous. "If singers didn't spend so much time trying to *find* claims they haven't worked in a while, if they could just go right back to them, they'd save a lot of time."

"So you want them to permit Donalla to hypnotize them and force memory of their coordinates?" Killa asked, cutting to the gist.

He nodded.

"I don't think they'll go for it," she said, shaking her head.

"You took mine and found the black. You took Rimbol's and got to his site."

"I know it can be done, and you might get some singers to use inactives' coordinates, but I don't think you'll get them to submit to hypnotic recall of their own sites. You know how paranoid we all are about claim locations."

"Paranoia doesn't have to enter the picture."

"Ha!"

"Look, Donalla's not a cutter and she's demonstrated her integrity as a medic. She's certainly not going to violate their trust."

"First she has to get it."

"All right, but she's not about to go mouthing off coordinates. Muhlah, but she could implant—in herself—a posthypnotic command to forget what she's just heard."

"She could?" Killashandra was surprised.

"Even better, she wants to give each singer who'll go for this a keyword. She may have to keep track of keywords, knowing the fragile memory of singers"—and Lars gave Killa a wry grin—"but that keyword would allow them to recall their own coordinates without any other further assist.

"I mean," Lars continued, beginning to pace the room in his enthusiasm, "this is the way it'd work, according to Donalla. She gives them a posthypnotic command to remember coordinates whenever they set down the sled. That's locked in their memories. Guild records show what they cut, if not where they cut. When they want to return to a site, they say the password, and that makes the information accessible again. To them, and to them only, so their privacy hasn't been violated."

"It sounds feasible—for those who accept hypnosis."

"You seem to be one of the few who don't," he said, resignation in his voice.

"I've always marched to my own drumbeat," she said in a light tone that masked her own sense of failure. She really did want to help him. "Count on me for support—for however much good it does you."

"Your support'll mean more than you imagine, Sunny," he said, and gave an emphatic nod of his head. "Go on and get cleaned up. I've got a few more things to clear off my screens." And he gestured to a desk littered with pencil files. "I'll meet you in the main dining hall in an hour, all right?"

When she had bathed and dressed with some care, she made her way to the dining hall she had not patronized at all in recent years. There weren't that many diners in the big room, and most of the alcoves were dark. It made her shiver a little. Was it just that all working singers happened to be out in the Ranges right now? That there wasn't a group of novices waiting around to be infected by the symbiont? That the large number of support staff had all decided to eat in their quarters this evening?

She looked around for Lars and then heard his distinctive whistle. He was just loading a tray with beakers of what looked like Yarran beer. Beside him were Donalla and Presnol and three singers, the same three she had recognized at the meeting at which Lars had officially opened inactive claims.

Now he nodded toward a banquet table off to one side of the huge low-ceilinged room, and she turned to meet them there. She managed to drag one singer's name to mind: Borton. Pushing harder, she remembered that he had been in the group she had "graduated" with. He didn't look much older than he had looked back then. But why should he, if his symbiont was doing its job?

"Borton, how nice to see you," she said, smugly pleased that she had placed him. She smiled at the other two, a man and a woman, as if she remembered them, as well. She gave Lars a quick glance.

"Tiagana, Jaygrin," he put in quickly, "do you recall Killashandra?"

"I think we've met either on ships leaving Shankill," Killashandra said, addressing Jaygrin, "or wandering around the moon waiting for a shuttle." She glanced at Tiagana. "Ah, Yarran beer. What would we do without it?"

That seemed to bridge the gap. Everyone reached for a glass from Lars's tray and then helped transfer platters and covered dishes to the round table. Lars acted the genial and diligent host and sent Presnol back for more Yarran beer when the first beakers were empty. Killa saw flashes of amusement in the other singers' faces, as if they were well aware of how Lars was trying to lull them. It had been a long time since she had been in a peer group, or in a dinner party of any kind. If it hadn't been for Presnol and Donalla deftly stimulating conversation, this party might never have come to life. But it did.

"All right, Lars, you've dined us and beered us, so what's this really about?" Borton asked, settling back in his chair as he pushed his empty dinner plate away from him.

"All four of you have been profiting from cutting on inactive singers' claims," Lars began, "and that's exactly what I hoped would happen. But I'd like you four to take this a step further." He went on, using almost the

same explanation he had given Killa an hour before. Had he been rehearsing it on her? she wondered. But since she had heard it already, she could
pay more attention to the way the other three were responding to his
scheme.

Tiagana didn't bother to disguise her reluctance. She leaned away
from Lars, toward Borton, who was sitting beside her. He was not as unre-
ceptive. And as for Jaygrin, Killa could almost see the credits dancing in
his eyes, and his smile was positively greedy.

"How do we know that Donalla can't unhypnotize herself and consciously *know* our claim locations?"

"She can't," Presnol said flatly, his tone brooking no argument.

"I wouldn't want to," Donalla said. "It would be pointless, since I
don't sing crystal, and the cutter is always paid on what he or she brings
in. I couldn't count on you to remember to give me a bribe, now could I?"

Jaygrin laughed, showing narrow, almost feral teeth. "So the deal is,
Lars, that we'll get inactive singer sites plus this hypnotic business to remember where we cut?"

Lars nodded.

"And no share out of the cut?" Borton asked.

"On the first cut of an inactive, you pay the twenty-five percent, but
only the Guild tithe on any subsequent cuttings."

Even Tiagana looked interested now.

"It works," Killa said, deciding to enter the discussion. "I've flown
out and cut as long as the claim was good. Came back in, got another set,
and flew directly to it, ready to cut again. Of course, one claim was buried
too far to be reached, but the coordinates were accurate. Saves a lot of time
and wasted effort."

"You've been doing what Lars described?" Tiagana asked.

"I have," Killa replied, nodding and managing a slightly smug curl to
her smile. "A snap." She snapped her fingers to match her words. "I think
it's a lot easier on a body, too," she added, indolently easing her buttocks
down in her chair. "Muhlah, when I think of the days I've spent trying to
find a site, trying to remember if it was still workable. Sure saves a lot of
stress." She debated putting a word or two about loyalty to the Guild but
knew that wouldn't cut much with singers. Only credit did. And Lars's
new scheme was indeed the key to larger credit balances and fewer dry
runs in the Ranges. "No more dry runs," she reminded the three singers as
they mulled what had been said.

Presnol slipped away from the table and returned with more Yarran
beer. Wisely Lars switched to a discussion of the dinner they had just
eaten, criticizing the preparation of one or two dishes and asking if anyone
else had found them wanting.

Singers could talk food till the galaxy grew cold, and Presnol and
Donalla kept the beer circulating until only Lars and Killa, who had been
more abstemious than was her custom, were able to walk straight.

"Do you think it'll work?" she asked him as they made their way to their quarters.

"We'll know tomorrow. But that Jaygrin's going to try it." Lars chuckled. "Avaricious bastard! But then, he's never come in with any of the darker colors on his own."

Which, in crystal-singer parlance, was the most insulting thing one could say about another cutter.

Chapter 11

As Killa was setting off for the next set of coordinates Donalla had obtained for her, she saw the other three singers readying their sleds in the Hangar. When she came back two days later, she had a full carton of deep amethyst crystals in fifths and thirds. They were not, of course, the black she had been after. But she had remembered that Clodine had said the darker shades were in short supply, so she had stayed to cut rather than return empty-handed.

Before she had lifted from the site, she had jotted down the coordinates and slipped the notation under the sheet of liberated markers taped to her console. In plain sight and yet hidden. Now if she could only remember *that*! She ought to think of some sort of code, something she would twig to the moment she saw it. She began to regret that she wasn't a good subject for hypnosis. She wondered how Tiagana, Borton, and Jaygrin were getting on. She was pleased that she could recall their names so easily. If she wanted to remember something, she really could!

She was in rare good spirits when she brought the cartons in to Clodine.

"Haven't I seen you here a lot lately?" the Sorter asked, grinning because Killa was.

"Sure! I'm enjoying an excellent streak of luck. It was bound to happen," Killashandra said blithely, "given the probabilities. Even if these aren't blacks."

Clodine held up the heaviest of the fifths, adjusting her eyesight to scrutinize the crystal. She put it on the scales and made minute adjustments, nodding all the while.

"Well, you remembered amethyst, and there's a good market for them right now. Two space stations are being constructed, and the big Altairian way station is expanding, so darks are needed for their life-support systems. Lars'll be real pleased to know these have come in."

"I'll tell him myself, hear?" Killa winked at Clodine.

"It's nice to see you like this, Killa," Clodine said, and gave Killa's arm a tentative pat. "And you're not even buzzing."

"No, I'm not. I feel as if I could cut forever these days."

"I'd heard you already had!" Clodine said with rare flippancy.

In great good humor, Killashandra laughed, then chuckled more heartily from her gut when she saw the final figure on two days' work.

Many were the times in her past when she would have killed for such totals. Yes, Lars's idea of getting coordinates out of inactives was brilliant.

Before she went down to her quarters, she stopped in the Hangar office to ask for her sled to be ready for the morning.

"Why don't you just stay out, like you usually do, Killa?" Murr asked. "You're like an overnight homer, in one day and out the next."

"I find what the Guild needs, I cut, I bring it in. Much more efficient that way, isn't it?"

"You're using a lot of fuel," he cautioned.

"I've the credit to pay for it, Murr. Humor me."

She left him there, but his morose attitude had brought her down a bit. The moment she entered her quarters, the communit buzzed.

"Muhlah! Can't I even have a bath first?"

"Killa?" Lars's image came up on the screen. "Glad you're in, C.S. Ree. Would you join me as soon as possible in my office?"

She started to say something snide about his formality, but before she could speak he stepped to one side and she saw that he had visitors in his office: visitors who were wearing the clear plastic suits and breathing masks that meant their errand was urgent enough for them to risk possible contamination by the Ballybran symbiont.

"Permit me time to become presentable, Guild Master Lars Dahl," she said in a similar manner, and waved the communit off.

Curiosity moved her to shower and change quickly. Very few people would take the chance these were. Urgent was almost always interesting. As she strode into the office, there was a new person at Trag's desk who looked up, seemed about to challenge her presence, hesitated, and then looked quickly back to the screen. She palmed the door and entered Lars's office.

"Ah, Crystal Singer Ree, I appreciate your alacrity. These are Klera and Rudney Saplinson-Trill. Klera, Rudney, this is the other member of the original Guild survey team." He gestured for Killashandra to be seated.

She noticed that there were snacks on the table beside her and blessed him for such thoughtfulness. He had even managed drinkers for the suited Saplinson-Trills. But he hadn't managed to indicate why they were braving the dangers of Ballybran.

"I'm not sure if you can recall the planet we visited some years back . . ." Lars began.

"Twenty-four years, five months, and two weeks, to be precise," Rudney Saplinson-Trill said with the quick, humorless smile of someone to whom accuracy is more important than courtesy. The tinny and nasal quality the helmet speakers gave his voice increased the impudence of that unnecessary correction.

"Yes, the one with the opalescence which we investigated for the late Guild Master," Lars continued. "It was posited at the time that Heptite Guild members, protected by their symbiont, would be safe from the infection which had killed the original exploratory team exposed to the opalescence—"

"Fluid metal, Guild Master," Rudney said, "is a more accurate term for the material—FM for short."

"We called it Jewel Junk," Killashandra said, mimicking him. He didn't notice, but Klera did.

"Yes, we did, didn't we?" Lars said, clearing his throat. "For lack of a more accurate designation," he added, nodding toward Rudney. "You will remember that we actually made two trips there, the second one after our visit to Nihal Three. On the second one we fed some trash to several of the Jewel Junk aka FM."

Killashandra wanted to giggle at Lars, but mastered the urge.

"Actually, *nine* of the now twenty FM manifestations," Rudney said.

"Yes. As I was saying . . ." Lars's nostrils flared, a sign of rare impatience in him, and he gave Rudney a quelling glance. "We also tried to establish communications with the, ah, FM opalescence." When the scientist seemed about to correct him yet again he said more firmly, "Or has the opalescence abated?" Lars fixed the scientist with a cold glare, then looked back to Killashandra, rattling his strong fingers on the table in a complex roll.

What appeared to be a nervous habit of his, plus the use of the words "opalescence," "Nihal Three," and "the infection" began to stir memories for Killa.

"We established a form of communication with it," she said. "Have you managed to enlarge on that beginning?" Why else would they be risking their lives visiting Ballybran?

"We are pure research scientists," Rudney said stiffly. "We are attempting to establish the parameters of an extremely complex life-form."

"Then you agree that the Junk is sentient?"

Rudney made a gesture, discounting her assumption. "We are only beginning to analyze its substance."

"Wasn't it impervious to diagnostic instrumentation?" Killa asked Lars.

"Ours is considerably more sensitive," Rudney continued inexorably, "and therefore we have made progress where the usual sort of instrumentation was inadequate to the purpose."

"So," Killa said, crossing her arms over her chest and focusing her entire attention on him. She had found this to disconcert the unwary. "What is it?"

"We have not yet finished our initial survey," Rudney admitted.

"After twenty-four years, five months, and two weeks?"

"With such an unusual material, one does not rush to conclusions," Rudney informed her.

"Did it ever digest the Ballybran crystal we gave it?" Killa was very pleased with herself for that recollection.

"Ah, no," Rudney replied, and cleared his throat, causing an awful rasping sound to be broadcast. The nonabsorption seemed to worry him.

"In fact," Klera said, plunging in, "all nine FM units prominently display the crystal shards in the center of the reservoir. That's what we call the central node. Though 'node' is not exactly accurate either."

"Would blob do?" Killa found scholarly precision tedious.

"Fluid metal is the proper description of its composition and, even, of its function," Klera said, her round face solemn.

"But have you established any level of communication with my Jewel Junk?"

"Yyyeesss, and nn-no," Klera said, momentarily flustered. "Our xenolinguist had hundreds of hours of recording but . . ." She sagged with a weary sigh.

"No mutual lexicon," Killa said, adding her own sigh.

"The individual FMs, however," Klera said, brightening, "*seem* to be communicating on some level. Though whether or not it's through use of the crystal shards, we haven't been able to ascertain." She shot a worried look at Rudney.

"Just the nine, or the other Junks you've discovered?" Killa asked, wondering if that was the problem.

"We can't be positive that they don't have another means of interacting. But we have established that the crystals send bursts of piezoelectric current," Klera said.

"Though we have been unable to determine the exact reason for the activity," Rudney said, smoothly taking over the explanations. "All the twenty FM deposits show irrefutable evidence of a thermoelectric effect, generating a voltage flow which, we have posited, is due to the extremes of temperature through which the planet goes. There is a recognizable tide, as it were, in the fluctuations of the thermoelectric effect that can be timed to the onset of deviations in the planet's rotation around its primary.

"Naturally, we established a control group of three," he went on, settling himself in his chair for a long lecture. "Caves Three, Nine, and Fifteen remain as we found them on our arrival, complete with their central nub of crystal. We've divided the others into three groups according to size, giving each group a special diet: organic wastes, which seem to have little effect on growth; inorganic wastes, which demonstrably increase the size exponentially to the amount offered; and a mixture, half and half, to the third group, which seems to thrive the best."

"We've done hours of recordings," Klera managed to slip in while Rudney took a deep breath, "which I do maintain are not merely thermoelectric statics. Fizal, our linguist, is certain that the various rhythms are conversations of some sort."

"That's not as immediate or as interesting as the history we have postulated about the primary 478-S-2937 and the planet's relationship to it," Rudney went on. "Star 478-S has been through many stages, and our investigations point to the probability that the planet, Opal, was formed from ejecta of the various stages of the star's development."

"Now, Rudney," Klera said firmly, "you know that Sarianus's theory is equally viable." She turned to Lars. "Our astrophysicist is of the opinion that the star was a huge *new* star, formed near the remnants of others."

"That has yet to be proved, Klera. That theory does not explain—"

"The flares, Rudney," Klera said, and the pair ignored the others in the room to continue what was obviously a long-standing argument. "The solar flares affect the planet. We've noted the exceptional activity of the 'static' messages shortly before and after solar flares."

"Klera, you cannot seriously believe that FM is controlling the flares?"

"I do, Rudney, and there is much evidence to support this." She looked at Killa as if requesting her support. "I believe that the FM has developed intelligence—a bizarre form, to be sure." She pointedly ignored Rudney's crackling snort. "Its vision and sensory systems would be electric and magnetic fields, ions and electrons. Its pain would be changes in the strengths of those fields and their threat to its existence when the solar flares are especially violent. Until recently—well, recently in solar terms— it has been the sun which has manipulated the planet's environment, and therefore it tries to control the sun by emanations of its own thermoelectric fields, making sunspots come and go as needed. Our geologist has noted that the planet has had more than its share of magnetic pole charges, many earthquakes, and some major readjustments in consequence of the polarities. You might say that it's attempting to avoid 'pain.' But it follows that the FM is intelligent, because it is attempting to adjust its environment. Only intelligence seeks to do this. I also think," she added, shooting a repressive glance at Rudney, who kept opening his mouth to interrupt, "it is capable of reproducing itself by asexual fission in order to increase its ability to control the sun. We have monitored a steady growth in all FM units . . ."

"How many levels do they go now?" Killashandra asked, suddenly remembering that part of their investigation.

"FMs with crystal nubs receiving the mixed diet have descended nineteen levels," Klera said, as pleased with such growth as a doting mother. "Those without crystal do not make significant progress and . . ." She faltered, glancing nervously at Rudney.

"Food plus crystal means growth?" Killashandra asked.

"*And* intelligence," Klera said emphatically. "The FMs with crystal nubs exhibit more thermoelectric activity than those deprived of crystal. Who knows what progress could be made in measuring FM intelligence if they were all equal in opportunity? Or if they had undamaged crystal!"

That sentence came out in a rush—and the purpose of their visit became clear to Killashandra.

"We've tried," Rudney said, his tone nearly apologetic, "to obtain a modest budget from the Solar Investigative Society to cover the cost of small pieces of undamaged Ballybran crystal . . ." He trailed off lamely and raised his hands in appeal.

She glanced at Lars's bland expression, not sure if she was amused or annoyed with him. When he was trying to put the Guild on a more solid commercial basis, how could he entertain what was clearly an appeal for a *donation* of crystal for these scientific types on a project that had nothing to do with the Guild? It seemed to her that Lars was seriously contemplating this request. Why else had he invited her to the conference?

As the silence lengthened, Rudney turned redder inside his protective suit; Klera just kept running her finger up and down the seam of her sleeve.

"I gather that no more deaths have resulted from contact with the opalescence?" Killa asked.

"Of course not," Saplinson-Trill said, flicking away that consideration with his fingers as he resumed his professional manner. "We follow a strict regimen of decontam and weekly med checks. We are extremely careful not to touch the FM with anything but the instruments kept in the cave for that purpose which have been made of a special alloy that FM does not melt."

"The lapses certainly haven't proved fatal," Klera added candidly.

Rudney smothered an oath as he glared at her.

"What lapses?" Killa asked, covering her delight with a bland, inquiring expression.

"Nothing fatal, or even producing physical discomfort," Klera said quickly.

"What sort of lapse? Memory loss?" Killa remembered that both she and Lars had spent long moments admiring the brilliant, shifting coruscation in the caves. Like a very sophisticated fractal, it had been beautiful to watch, almost mesmeric.

"What Klera refers to," Rudney told them, the rasping edge to his voice communicating clearly his wish that she had not spoken, "are periods when the FM displays the most thermoelectric activity. Several of our team members experienced what, ah, I suppose, *could* be termed time lapses . . ."

"The Jewel Junk's shifting patterns had a certain hypnotic rhythm to them when we were there, didn't they, Guild Master?" Favoring Lars with a quick glance, Killashandra began to perceive another reason why he had wanted her in on this meeting.

"Yes, they did," he agreed amiably. "While the Guild does not make a practice of assisting outside research in crystal applications, it just happens that there are some useful shapes and colors available from apprentice cuttings that could be released to you. They are now unflawed crystal, having been returned, but not of the size, color, or warrantable stability of pitch to be offered for commercial sale."

Utter relief flooded Rudney's face. Klera, after giving a squeak of delighted surprise, covered her mouth as if afraid she might say something wrong and compromise the offer.

"However, the Guild requires that a singer install the crystal," Lars said, "and right now, the Guild needs all experienced singers in the Ranges. We can't spare one for the time it would take to make the trip."

"But, Guild Master, we've the services of a B-and-B ship," Rudney surprised both singers by saying. "That's the only way we, as leaders of the FM Project, could justify our absence."

"A brain-and-brawn ship with a Singularity Drive?" Lars asked, expecting a negative response.

"Yes, indeed, Guild Master," Rudney said. "Archeological and Exploratory are exceedingly interested in the FM project and put a ship at our disposal for this important mission. The BB-1066."

"How very convenient," Killa said, twitching an eyebrow at Lars. "I'd be tempted to take the assignment, if only to see Brendan again."

"You are, C.S. Ree, one of my most experienced singers," Lars began repressively, and Killa wondered why he was glaring at her. Surely he was merely priming the pump to haggle a good fee for her services. As he had the right to do. The Guild had a reputation to maintain—especially right now.

"I am due some relief time away from Ballybran," she said.

To her surprise, Lars frowned. "This really isn't the time for you to be away from the Ranges, C.S. Ree."

He spoke so firmly that she was uncertain of how to proceed. She was also peeved at him, for she really could use some time off-planet. And who else had previous experience with the Jewel Junk? As Guild Master, he really couldn't leave Ballybran, but she could. Muhlah!

"In that case, I shall plan to return to my duties tomorrow," she said stiffly and, bowing courteously to the scientists, marched out of the office.

"Well?" she asked Lars as he entered their quarters much later that evening.

"Well, what?" he said, scrubbing at his hair with irritation and fatigue.

"Did you give them crystal?"

"You heard me. FM, indeed," he muttered. She had ordered Yarran beer and some light snacks, which she served him. "Thanks!" He sighed with gratitude as he tipped the recliner back.

"So, how much did you get?"

"Hummm?" he mumbled over a long pull of the beer.

"How much for a singer to go install the crystals, and whom have you chosen? Because I insist on going."

"Sunny, I need you here . . ." he began.

"You can do without me for the eight or ten days it'll take by way of the B-and-B. And frankly, I could use the break."

"Not when you're cutting crystal every time you go out."

"Aren't Tiagana, Borton, and Jaygrin?"

"Of course, but—"

"And anyone else you can talk into this direct-line approach to cutting, I'm sure," she said. "I thought that was why you had me sit in."

"I had you sit in to see how much you could remember," he said. He gave her a quick grin. "You did better than I expected."

"I did, did I? Well, *thank* you, Guild Master."

"Donalla says a lot of memory is association. The more—"

"And *thank* you for discussing *me* with Donalla!" Killa wasn't certain why that made her so mad, but it did. "I'm not inactive yet, by a long twig, Lars Dahl. *And* I don't need hypnosis to *remember!*"

"You proved that conclusively today," he said in the mild tone he used whenever he wished to defuse her anger.

"Now *stop* manipulating me, will you?"

"I'm not, Sunny." There was a genuine note of surprise in his voice. In one lithe movement, he slipped from the recliner to her chair and embraced her. She kept herself rigid, refusing to relax and let him think he had cajoled her into a better humor.

"I also had to get someone else in the office or I'd've kicked Rudney out," he went on. "Wasn't he the pompous ass!"

Killa did relax a bit then, glowering and still suspicious. "Asshole, you mean. Though she wasn't as bad. Why would she put up with him?"

"Why do you put up with me?" And Lars flashed a smile at her.

"Then *why* did you give them the crystal?"

"Ah, yes." Nudging his hip against her to make her give him some room, he slid his arm about her. "Well, I received an urgent burst requesting assistance from Archeological and Exploratory. Seems our Jewel Junk is exceedingly important."

"Then why do they entrust it to a dork like Saplinson-Trill?"

"Because, despite his manner, he's tops in his field."

"Which is?"

"Planetary mechanics. His is not the first group to try to solve the mystery of our opalescent junk, but he's had far more demonstrable success than any other. And Ballybran crystal is very important to the success of the next phase of their investigations. Or so A and E seems to think."

"Why didn't A and E pay for the crystal?"

"Too many slices out of their budget already."

"Then who's paying for a singer to install 'em?"

Lars cleared his throat. "The Guild was asked to absorb the cost."

She hauled herself about to face him, scowling. He pinched her lips shut.

"Oh don't worry," he said. "The Guild got concessions I've been trying to wangle for the last three years."

"Such as?"

"Permission to publicize the employment opportunities of the Guild . . ."

"What?" That was an exceptional concession.

Lars grinned smugly. "*And* the Guild is being allowed to actively recruit specialists on nineteen human planets."

"That must be a first!"

"In living memory."

"So, they've finally realized how important Ballybran crystal is."

"I'd say that's a fair comment." He stretched languorously beside her, arching his back, before he cocked his free arm to cushion his head. "A good day, all totaled."

"Who's the new dork at the desk?" she asked after a moment.

"Oh." The frown returned. "Him. Well, he's a spare pair of hands, and he'll be more useful when he becomes accustomed to the filing codes."

"I'd hazard the guess," she said after a long pause, "that you also can't afford to annoy the Council and A and E by sending an incompetent singer to set those crystals."

"I'm *not* letting you go, Sunny," he said sternly.

"Who else can you send?" she asked reasonably. "I'm the only one qualified, and you can't afford to have the installation messed up, can you?"

Lars gave her a long searching look and then sighed. "You're right there. Much is at stake."

Just as he gathered her closer, she caught a fleeting expression on his face that might have been satisfaction. She didn't have time, then, to sift the matter through, because he distracted her thoroughly.

Being aboard the Brendan/Boira 1066 was a mixed pleasure, since Killashandra had to share the ship's good company with Rudney and Klera. Fortunately the two scientists had brought reports with them to study, and they spent most of their time in their cabin, or using Brendan's powerful and complex computer banks.

"They did the same thing on the way out," Boira told Killa.

"The tedium was palpable," Brendan added, in the exact affected tone Rudney used.

Killa and Boira smothered laughs. Killa had taken to Boira the moment she had seen the 1066 brawn. Not that Boira could be described as brawny: she was of medium height, and her figure was compact. She was very attractive, smooth-skinned and with the symmetry provided by reconstruction; her eyes were dark, and her dark hair was kept at shoulder length. She moved with an odd grace that Killa suspected was also due to the accident that had left Brendan unpartnered during the singers' first expedition to Opal. Best of all, Boira had the same quick wit and ready humor that had made Brendan such a good travel companion.

"Do be careful, Bren," Boira murmured. "You'll set me off again. Bren had me in kinks," she told Killashandra. "It got to be embarrassing, because every time they ventured out of their cabin, they'd say something that Bren had lampooned and I'd dissolve—in a coughing fit, of course. Wouldn't do to laugh in their faces!"

"Then it isn't just me," Killa said, grinning broadly.

"Oh, no," Boira assured her. "It's them! The only time they acted human at all was during decomposition."

"Then they were *very* human," Bren said caustically. "Had to circulate and clean the air nine times."

"D'you still have the radiant-fluid tub on board?"

"Indeed we do," Boira said, "and back in your cabin."

"What'll you do about them, then?" Killa asked, jerking her finger in the direction of the Saplinson-Trills.

"Oh, them! This time we may let them stew in their own juices, as it were," Brendan said. "I can close off the vents to their cabin so we're spared the stench. At least they cleaned themselves up afterward."

"And what about you?" Killashandra asked Boira. But apart from a mild headache, Boira was not adversely affected by decomposition.

"Repetition dulls the effect," she told Killashandra, "though it'll never be my favorite way to spend five of the longest minutes ever invented by the mind of man."

"So, did you see much of the FMs?" Killa asked, drawling the term sarcastically.

Boira gave a snort. "After a very lengthy briefing and all sorts of dire warnings about keeping my mitts to myself and going through a rather ridiculously involved decontam. It was worth the effort," she said. "The brilliance, the design . . . I really think they ought to pay attention to the complex patterns—what did you call them? Jewel Junk? I suggested," she added, grimacing at her recollection, "that the patterns the Junk displays could be another attempt at communication."

"And?"

"I got told in long chapters how such a theory was ludicrous and had no possible scientific basis." She shrugged. "I am entitled to an opinion."

Killa mulled that over. "Pattern is as good a method of communication as any other. Aren't *words* patterns?"

"Hmmm. Hadn't thought of it in quite that way, but they are, you know." Bren said. "Full marks to you, Killa."

"I gather they didn't test your theory, Boira?"

"Fardles, no! What does a ship's brawn know about esoteric lifeforms?"

"Fifteen minutes until the first Singularity Jump," Brendan announced, and Killa immediately adjourned to her radiant fluid tank.

Awash in fluid, Killa had only the mildest of decomposition willies. When she returned to the main cabin, where Boira and Brendan were running a systems check, she jerked her head in the scientists' direction.

"Oh, them?" Boira grinned. "This time they took the precautions we always recommend. Never have understood why the cerebral types think I don't know as much about my profession as they know about theirs. Hungry?" She smiled slyly.

"Brendan, did you have to tell Boira about that?" Killa asked, halfway between irritation and amusement.

"She insisted that I explain why I spent so much credit on food stores."

"Why? Did she think you'd wined and dined pretty girls all in a row while she was incapacitated? And thank you, Boira, I am hungry, but not starved and certainly nowhere near another Passover gorge."

Boira liked food as much as Killa did, and they compared notes until the next Jump. Both women were spared the company of the Saplinson-Trills, though Boira periodically inquired solicitously after their health and well-being. The two did emerge when the last Jump brought them into the Opal system. Rudney asked Brendan to open a channel for them, so that he and Klera could get caught up on any new developments. There were enough to send Killa and Boira into the galley to get away from the scientific jargon.

"You'd think, from all that gibberish, that they were activating a sorcerous spell or something," Boira said.

"Equations are a form of spell, aren't they?" Killashandra asked.

"Hmmmm, perhaps, if you get the right answer."

They batted the notion about until Brendan quietly informed them that they would be landing in fifteen minutes.

Rudney and Klera were excited about something, the upshot of which was that they wanted Killa to install the crystals as soon as possible. Rudney sputtered, close to being inarticulate in his instructions. Fortunately he had a diagram of where he wanted crystal installed, though to judge by the strikeouts, the list of priorities had altered several times. He wanted the biggest, or strongest, of the crystal pieces to go in Cave Fifteen which Killa shortly learned was the one that she and Lars had named Big Hungry Junk.

"It already has crystal," she began.

"It must have the best of the crystals," Rudney insisted, spittle spattering Killa in the face.

"I really don't believe that FM Fifteen will surrender the one it has when the larger unit is installed," Klera said, her face screwed up with concern. "I really do feel that we have no way of adequately explaining that we need the old shard for one of the smaller FMs."

"Is that what you want to do? Exchange?" Killa asked, surprised.

"Of course, of course. You only supplied us with twelve crystals. We now have thirty FMs to be brought into the comnet we posit."

"Have you ever tried to remove anything from a Junk?"

"A Junk?" For a moment, Rudney was confused. "Oh, please employ the proper nomenclature."

Killa gave him the sort of look that had once been extremely effective in reducing affectations.

"No, we actually haven't," Klera admitted.

"It's always been on the receiving end, though, hasn't it?" Killa said. "Well, I'll try, but I'm not risking a finger or a hand."

"We're most certainly not asking you to take a physical risk," Rudney said.

To prove that, he and Klera were among those in the A&E installation who suited up to watch Killashandra install the crystal. When Rudney pompously introduced her, she got the usual guarded reaction from the staff assembled in the decontamination room, but there were several broad smiles of welcome as well as help when she began suiting up.

There was one black crystal, not a large shaft but tuned to a dominant, and this was the one she felt Big Hungry Junk deserved.

"Surely this one," Rudney said, pointing officiously to the largest, a pale blue, "would be more suitable."

"It's blue, a minor, and considerably less stable than the black," she said in a tone that she hoped would end the matter.

"But—but—"

"Rudney," she said loudly and firmly. "I am the crystal singer, not you!"

Rudney seemed surprised at her vehemence and stood there, blinking in astonishment. She became aware that everyone else was regarding her with similar surprise. Well, Rudney might be a boor to *her*, but he was clearly held in considerable respect by his staff.

"Black," she began in a milder tone, "is the most powerful of the Ballybran crystal range. Even a small one, like this, is three times as useful as the large pale blue. The paler colors are notoriously fragile." She held up the black, though she could feel the tingle of the damned thing right through her heavy vacuum gloves. "The black is also in a dominant key, which increases its potential threefold. Minors are good for small repetitive jobs, but you want some character for Big Hungry Junk to work with. Now, let's go."

She gestured for the two who had been assigned to carry the crystal-packing carton to put on their helmets as she adjusted her own. A few more moments sufficed for the usual pre-exit tests, and then everyone was checked out as ready to go. She activated her private com to Brendan and Boira.

The airlock cycled open to the black bleakness of Opal's surface. Changes had been made: light flooded the cindery surface, illuminating paths from the facility to the various caves, each path neatly signposted for its destinations. Big Hungry, posing as Cave Fifteen, seemed to be the most popular direction—that path was the smoothest in appearance. Killa struck out, leading the way, Rudney having missed the chance to get in front of her.

As she neared the cave, she could see splotches of brilliance penetrating to the surface. "Big Hungry must be really big," she murmured to herself.

"I can pick you up at that level, Killa," said Brendan softly.

"What did you say, Crystal Singer?" Rudney asked, reaching forward to tap her arm.

"I mutter a lot," she said loudly enough for her voice to carry to his comsystem. Then she smiled. Nice to be one up on Rudney! "You re-

ally have improved the place," she added. The approach had been cleared
of all rubble, and the steps down to the entrance of the cave widened.
Lights weren't needed: blue radiance leaked up the first five steps. And
suddenly dimmed as Killa's helmet filter adjusted to the increased exterior
illumination.

Even with that aid, she was nearly blinded by light as she turned
the corner into Big Hungry's cave. Her gasp elicited a concerned request
for explanation from Brendan and a smug chuckle from Rudney, which
turned into a gargle of surprise.

"Great Muhlah on the mountains of Za!" She was transfixed in the
entrance until Rudney brushed past her.

"Can I have a reading on why the pattern has so dramatically altered?" he asked in a sharp tone.

No one could miss the shower of complex interlacing designs that expanded from the center core. They were different from the idle banding
she had first seen as she paused on the threshold. Majestic, they radiated
down the sides of the cave, to disappear below the floor.

"It's most unusual, Doctor. First time this one has been screened,"
one of the technicians told Rudney.

"Maybe it's a welcome for me," Killashandra said facetiously.

Rudney shot her a fierce look of disgust and denial as he brushed
past her and into the cave.

"There is a considerably high level of static," the technician added.
"Now it's dropping to normal output."

Hastily, Killa stepped to one side, watching the last of the fractal-like
design slide out of sight. She shivered. To divert herself, she looked about
the magnificently festooned cave. No one had told her that the fluid metal
completely covered the walls of its site. She had thought it had merely sent
tendrils to the lower levels. How many had Klera said Big Hungry went
down? Nineteen? Incredible and yet . . . All it may have needed in order to
grow was some decent food.

As the plasglas of her helmet darkened sufficiently in the glorious-
ly lighted cave, she finally made out the central hub of the Junk, a now-
infinitesimal sliver of crystal standing upright at the pulsing core. Rudney
probably used a more accurate scientific name for the heart of the Junk.
Odd, though, Killa thought, searching her memory for details of that earlier visit. She could resurrect little beyond knowing that Big Hungry had
grown.

"Bren," she asked softly, "did we ever measure the original center
of Junk?"

"We did, and . . ." He paused briefly. "Circumference is the same, but
I'd say it was denser, thicker. Ask Rudney. The sort of thing he'd know."

She heard Bren, but her attention was somewhat distracted by the
shift and play of color and pattern that radiated from the core down the
sheet of opalescence. It was more colorful, too, than it had been: speeding
up and down the spectrum of visible color even as arcs of shifting hues and

shades rippled across. Try as she would to follow one pattern, it melded or was overrun by others. She remembered Junk doing that before but surely not as rapidly.

"Our instrumentation is picking up considerable excitation but not on a band usually occupied," someone said over the communit.

"Crystal Singer," Rudney said, bouncing over to her and tapping her shoulder, "let's proceed. There's unusual activity recorded . . ."

"I heard," she said repressively. Abruptly the thought of setting black crystal in that throbbing heart of opalescence disturbed her to a degree she had never experienced before. "Having seen this one, I believe it would be wiser to install crystals in the lesser units first."

"I disagree," Rudney said, appalled at the sudden change of plans. "Cave Fifteen is responding to some sort of—"

"Exactly! I'm not risking my wits on black until the last possible moment," she said, and, gesturing imperiously to the two carrying the carton, she started from the cave. "I'll start with Three."

Rudney objected; he even jumped in front of her when they had left Cave Fifteen in his effort to stop her. She bounced away from him, urging the carton carriers to follow her. He tried to get them to follow his orders.

"You want crystal installed. I do it. I do it my way," she roared at him, and saw people recoil. "Now, do I proceed to Three, or back to the 1066? Because if you don't let me handle the installation *my* way, I'll leave. With the crystals, too, by the way, since they're the *gift* of the Guild!"

That threat, combined with pleas from Klera and one of the other senior members of the team, silenced Rudney's objections, and she was allowed to proceed.

Three had been a small, pretty cap of Jewel Junk when she and Lars had first seen it. Sothi, one of the carton carriers, told her that it had insinuated itself down three levels now. Smack dab in the center of its core was the original splinter of pink. Muhlah, if the Junk could do this well with only bloody pink, it would flood with the good green destined for its second crystalline instrusion.

The rest of the observers had filed into the cave by then, and the portable ladder was erected right under the core. Killa hefted the green shaft and peered at it in the radiance to be sure it had not somehow become flawed in transit. She clamped the forceps about the green and, carefully examining the position of the pink splinter, started to insert the new crystal. The moment it touched the opalescence, it was sucked up so rapidly that only her trained reflexes kept her hand from following it into the core. The forceps were gone. In the next instant, the pink splinter fell, and there was a flailing of gloved hands as three people tried to catch it.

"Got it!" Sothi exclaimed, holding up the splinter for all to see.

"More than a mouthful is impolite," Killa said drolly. She hadn't anticipated any success in trying to yank out the old splinter.

"Ooooh!" Klera's exclamation, anxious and fearful, brought everyone's attention back to the core.

"Bloody hell, it swallowed it!" Killa announced, unable to perceive any trace of the green. "Of all the ungrateful . . ."

"Oh, there it is," Klera went on, pointing as the green slowly came into view again, positioned in the exact center of the core, with two-thirds of its length visible.

"We are monitoring increased activity in Three" was the report from the base.

"No quarrel with that," Killa said, delighted with the effect. And yes, she thought, Boira's theory about pattern talk was an avenue that ought to be explored. She found herself tracking a brilliant display of green, blue and yellow herringbones that flashed from the core to the floor and disappeared.

"Crystal Singer . . ." Sothi had her by both hands, gripping tightly. "You were swaying . . ."

Killa accepted his help down from the ladder. He pressed his helmet against hers. "Don't watch the patterns, C.S. You lose time that way," he murmured.

Her lapse had gone unnoticed, save by Sothi, for the other observers were helmet to helmet in deep consultations. Killa wondered how much time she had lost.

"Does it happen often, Sothi?" she asked.

"Often enough to need to be cautious."

"Which cave is next?" she asked him. In that moment of distraction, she had forgotten.

"Two, which is only a step away," he answered, and suddenly she remembered the entire sequence and where each crystal was supposed to go. Time was not the only thing you lost following Junk patterns, she thought.

Then, when Sothi would have signaled to Rudney that they were leaving Three, she caught his hand and waggled her finger at him. "C'mon," she said, touching her helmet to his. "We can get this all done in half the time if we leave these science types to talk."

Sothi seemed hesitant, but his companion whose suit bore the name "Asramantal," pulled him toward the entrance.

Killashandra had done four, with Sothi or Asra neatly catching the discarded slivers, before Rudney and the observers caught up. She ignored Rudney's harangue and continued on her scheduled round. If she kept herself busy, watching her feet on the cindery paths, even doing a bit of pattern watching, with Sothi or Asramantal to pull her out if she dallied too long, she didn't have to think about installing the black in Big Hungry. As they had trudged from one cave to the next, she had confided some of her anxiety to Brendan and Boira.

"Can I count on you two for a bit of help?" she asked.

"What kind?" Boira asked.

"I might have trouble with Big Hungry . . ."

"What sort of trouble?"

"I'm not sure, really. Ah, well, it's mainly that I hate installing blacks anywhere for any reason," she said, trying not to infuse her voice with the anxiety that she could feel building into full-blown stress. Muhlah! This black wasn't being used—not in the normal sense—as a comcrystal. Maybe she was borrowing trouble.

"Feedback?" Brendan asked.

"Like you never felt before," she said.

"What can we do?"

"Stay tuned—and talk me out of the backlash."

"What form does that take?"

"It sings back through me."

"Gives you quite a jolt, huh?"

"That's putting it mildly."

"How do we help?" Boira asked.

"Could you suit up, Boira, and come down to Fifteen for the finale?"

"Sure. Be with you in two strokes of a hand pump. Only what do I do if you do freak out?"

"Get me back to Bren as fast as possible! I think I'll pull out on my own as long as there's distance between me and the black. And, by the way, Boira, your theory about patterns is not so far-fetched. The Junk radiates them in ever-changing displays."

"Hmm. Int—" Boira's voice was cut off.

"Boira?"

"She's in her suit and has not turned on the com," Brendan said in the patient tone of someone who was accustomed to such bungles.

With her confidence shored up by Boira's promise to be present, Killa completed the other installations. On her way to Big Hungry, she took a swallow of the suit's emergency ration—and immediately wished she hadn't. Somehow she had been expecting something considerably more palatable.

"Yecht!" she muttered.

"What's the matter?" Brendan asked.

"The suit's food!"

"Oh? So you do appreciate the lengths to which I went for you the last time?"

"If that's what I thought I was getting, yes." And the memory of more delectable flavors was indeed vivid in her mind.

She had no time for a pleasant review, for she had reached the cave entrance. Boira stood out from the others lining the big cavern: her suit was not only a vivid citron yellow but of a different design. She lifted her gloved hand in a salute to Killashandra. That alerted the other suited figures. Killa guessed that every member of Rudney's team who could be spared from the laboratory was present. There was a jumble of comments that told her there had been a draw to see who got to attend. Killa also heard excited reports from the few technicians still manning the instrumentation. Activity in the Junks had speeded up, pushing the monitors to designer limits to process the incoming data.

"Watch out, you guys and gals," Killashandra said as Sothi and Asra positioned the ladder under the core. "You ain't seen nothin' yet."

"What precisely do you mean by that remark, Crystal Singer?" Rudney demanded, his apprehension reflected in his voice as well as the sudden stiffening of his suited figure.

Killa had been talking to bolster her own confidence and wished Rudney didn't require so many explanations of casual comments. She sighed as she clamped the forceps firmly about the black. If she could avoid touching it at all, its effect on her would be reduced. She had gotten the hang of jamming crystal into cores now, and she didn't plan to bungle this final, and most crucial, insertion.

"Watch and observe, Dr. Saplinson-Trill." She extended her arm, noting that Sothi and Asra stood ready to catch the old splinter. Oh, Muhlah! she swore silently as a new thought struck her. This wasn't the last she had to install. There were all the old slivers to be put into the new Junks.

"Observe what?"

"Wait and see," she said. Taking a deep breath, she touched the black to the Junk, quiveringly ready to drop forceps and all at any sign that the black was going to react.

The black shaft was ingested so swiftly that her reflexes had no time to respond. Forceps, crystal, and her gloved hand were all pulled into the sudden maelstrom of frenzied, turbulent patterns that cascaded down the Junk—and flowed through Killashandra with such devastating force that she felt her death was imminent! Her whole life flashed across her mind, pushing her down into black oblivion.

Chapter 12

Killashandra Ree was vastly surprised to waken once more to the living world.

"She's back," a low voice murmured, and a cool hand rested lightly on her forehead. "Hey, you made it!" The cheery tone rich with relief was Boira's.

"I'm not so sure of that," Killa replied, spacing her words carefully. Her head felt several sizes too large, and while it didn't ache, it might just as well have. A brightness pressed unmercifully against her eyelids, and she squeezed them tighter. "Got any analgesics?"

"What? A crystal singer needing medication?"

"There's always a first time. I certainly wouldn't blame my symbiont for decamping after that. Whatever it was."

"There's considerable debate on that score back at the base," Brendan said, his whisper rippling with mirth. Or maybe her hearing was impaired.

"Are you whispering for my benefit?" she asked.

"Yes," Boira said in a more normal tone. "You kept complaining about noise, and bright lights. Not that I blame you for that. Big Hungry Junk nearly turned nova when you fed it the black. D'you remember anything?"

"I remember dying."

"You didn't," Boira said. "First thing I did was check your suit readings and, mind you, you were rigid . . ."

"I died," Killashandra insisted.

"Not according to your suit readings, friend, and when I got you back here—"

"Against heavy opposition," Brendan added. "You'd have been real proud of Boira. She mowed 'em down."

"Sothi and Asra helped," Boira went on graciously. "What on earth can I give you that might help?" Killa heard a rattling that rumbled like an avalanche inside her head.

"Try one of the homeopathics, Boira," Brendan suggested. "I think that wouldn't interfere with the symbiont."

"Why isn't it working when I need it?" Killa moaned. "How much light do you have on out there?" The brilliance was instantly dimmed. "Thanks, Bren."

"Ah, this says it's a specific for trauma, injury, and systemic malfunction. See, Bren? What d'you think?"

"Try it," Killashandra said urgently.

The spray was cool against her skin, and she could actually feel the preparation diffusing—diffusing and easing the intolerable and unidentifiable malaise that gripped her.

"Oh, Muhlah! It's working . . ." Killa sighed with infinite relief, feeling taut muscles and stressed nerves beginning to relax. The noise level began to drop, and the light beating against her eyelids diminished to a comfortable level.

"I'm thirsty," she said then, suddenly aware of her parched throat and mouth. She didn't quite have the courage to open her eyes.

Very gently, Boira laid an arm under her and raised her head enough to make it easy to drink from the beaker pressed against her lips.

"It's full of electrolytes and the other stuff a convalescent needs," Boira said.

She couldn't taste a definite flavor, but the moisture was very welcome. It, too, was traceable all the way down her gullet and into her stomach. She could feel her body absorbing the wetness. Was her bloody symbiont fast asleep, zapped out of existence, or working overtime? She had been injured often enough to know that the symbiont's work was generally too subtle to be noticeable. What had Big Hungry done to her?

"Our diagnostic unit says you're in perfect physical condition," Boira said, "in case you're worried."

"I wish I could agree." Killa forced her lids open to a slit and, finding that this was not painful, opened them further. She was in her cabin on the 1066, and the digital dateline over the door informed her that she had lost two full days. "So, tell me what happened?" she bravely asked Boira, who was sitting beside her bunk, an open medical chest on a stand next to her.

"First you went rigid . . ."

"I remember that very clearly." And Killa did, with a clarity that astounded her. In the moment she had anticipated her death, every bone had seemed to harden; every artery, vein, and capillary had solidified. Color had coruscated through her eyes into every cell of her body, rippling in an inexorable tide, lapping back and plunging forward again, as if she were being swirled in some liquid element . . . and all the while her life had been fast-forwarding through her mind.

"I got to you before Rudney did, and your two cronies helped me get you off the ladder. Even the suit material felt petrified but, as I said, your life signs registered normal."

"Normal was not what happened to me."

"Agreed, but that's what the monitors told *me*. And I was relieved. Meanwhile, all hell had broken loose. I mean, the Junk was indescribable. Brendan'll show you his recordings . . ."

"Later," Killa suggested weakly. The thought of seeing all that color again was more than she could handle.

"Of course, whenever you wish," Brendan said gently. "Talk about scientific detachment and impartial observation . . ." He chortled maliciously.

"Rudney and his crew were hysterical. Everyone tried to get through the exit at the same time. 'S a wonder suits weren't ripped in the press."

"I don't blame them for being scared," Killa said charitably.

"They weren't scared," Brendan replied in a scathing tone. "They just wanted to get back to the base to see what the instruments were logging. Rudney kept trying to shut 'em up so he could hear the broadcasts."

"Sothi and Asra were marvelous, by the way," Boira went on. "They helped me get you out of the cave, and then you sort of folded, like an empty sheet. Thought we'd nearly lost you, but Bren was monitoring and kept telling us to hurry you to him. Sothi worried that perhaps we were wrong to remove you from Big Junk . . ."

"Big Junk had just done all it could to me and for me," Killa murmured, though she still had no idea of the extent of the alteration. She merely knew there had *been* one.

"D'you know what it's done?" Boira asked tentatively. "Nothing new registers?"

"Sensory overload doesn't always produce measurable output," Brendan said.

"Is that your diagnosis, Bren?" Killa asked.

"Empiric only, Killa, since it's obvious by your comments and the need for supplemental medication that what you're experiencing is not corroborated by the med monitors."

"Well, maybe it's nothing that a good night's sleep won't set right in next to no time, huh?" Killa kept her tone facetious because she could not discuss, even with such staunch friends as Boira and Brendan, what seemed to have happened to her during that sensory overload. "I do feel as if I'd been turned inside out, back to front, and then wrung dry . . ."

The emotional and physical discharge of her first black-crystal installation had now paled to the insignificance of an insect sting. Lars was going to be furious with her, but there was no way she would ever again cut black crystal. Of that, if nothing else at this particular moment in time, she was certain. On the plus side, she would be able to tell him every single location where she had cut black. Indeed, she now remembered every site she had ever cut, and the type, size, number, and tuning note of every cutting she had ever made over the past one hundred and ninety-seven years. She remembered everything, and completely, to the last petty detail, and the weight of such total recall was worse than having it restored to her.

"Hungry?" Boira asked gently.

Killashandra considered this. "Yes, I think I am."

"Then you must be on the road to complete recovery," Boira said, smiling as she rose. "Any special requests?"

"Chicken soup?"

"The very thing," Brendan replied so heartily that Killa winced. "I've an old family recipe that's supposed to cure anything from ingrown toenails to the worst degree of space fug."

Killa closed her eyes. Chicken soup, no matter how efficacious, was not going to cure what really ailed her. Who needed to remember *everything*? Everything except how Big Hungry Junk had done what it had done to her.

Being aboard the BB-1066 had other advantages besides excellent nursing care and incredible food. Rudney could not get to her, though he demanded interviews on an hourly basis, insisting that she finish installing the crystal according to the contract he had made with the Guild Master. He threatened to sue her and the Guild for breach of contract.

"Tell him I installed the crystals as per the contract. Nothing in it said I had to do the old splinters, too. And I won't."

When Rudney exhorted the 1066 to turn the crystal singer over to him, Brendan informed him that he had no such authority over his passengers.

They remained on Opal's surface only long enough to be sure Killa had sufficiently recovered from the physical depletion to withstand the disorientation of a Singularity Jump. Then Brendan lifted his tail from the planet.

After the second of the three Jumps, curiosity got the better of Killashandra. She wanted to know what had happened to Big Hungry after it had gobbled the black crystal. Maybe that would distract her mind from a constant survey of memories she really didn't want to have on replay.

"Rudney's group haven't come to any conclusions," Brendan said, having discreetly continued to monitor all their transmissions and internal conversation. "They're still examining their data. Thermoelectric emissions have gone off the scale of their instrumentation. Significant growth of all the FM units—"

"Jewels, please, Bren, or Junk," Boira interposed.

"They seem to be oozing into every available cave, crack, crevice, cranny. The planet's rotation has shifted erratically, and sunspot activity has also increased. All the crystals glow, and the static they emit is constant."

"Junk is using the crystals for communication, then?" Killa asked.

"It would appear so," Brendan said, "though to what end, Rudney's group doesn't know. Their semanticist is analyzing the frequency and consistency of patterns, and the rhythm at which they flow, which varies."

"Klera was correct?" Killa asked, quite delighted at the thought.

"They won't commit themselves," Brendan said in a mildly snide tone of voice.

"Naturally. They don't deny the sentience of Junk, do they?"

"They can't when it is obviously altering its environment," Boira said, grinning broadly. "Oh, by the way, Rudney sent off a request for another singer to install the splinters."

"For all the good it'll do him," Killa said caustically.

"Fifteen minutes to the last Jump," Brendan said, and Killa scurried to the radiant-fluid tank.

Lars was waiting for her at Shankill, his worried expression clearing when he saw her striding down the corridor toward him. He embraced her hungrily, burying his face in her hair, his fingers biting into her shoulder blades and then her waist. She leaned into him, grasping him as tightly as he did her. He was warm, strong, and just as lean as he had been when they had first met so many years before on Optheria. The essential Lars Dahl hadn't changed . . . she cut off the other memories that threatened to swamp her. She was getting the hang of censoring recall when she had all she needed. Otherwise all that memory could be overwhelming.

"Honest, Sunny, I had no idea what I was I was asking of you!" he murmured.

"You didn't ask anything," she said, surprised. "I volunteered. Remember?"

He held her off, his expression wretched. "Sunny, I maneuvered you into volunteering."

She reviewed the occasion quickly, laughed, and pulled him back to her. "So you did, but I didn't resist much, did I?"

"How could you, crystal-mazed as you were?" He was so miserably repentant that she chuckled.

"At least you have the grace to apologize," she said. "Lanzecki never did."

She felt the change in him, and this time when he held her away, he apprehensively searched her face.

"What happened, Sunny?" His anxiety was palpable; even the grip of his hands on her arms altered as if she had become noticeably fragile.

"It would appear—" She gave a breathless laugh. "—that Big Hungry Junk reconnected all my memory circuits when it zapped me. The brain's electric, you know, and it got recharged, right back to my first conscious memory."

"Muhlah!" Lars stared at her, appalled.

"And I thought placing that Trundimoux king crystal was bad. The merest piffle in comparison. It's all right, love," she reassured him as she saw his eyes blink frantically. "Now let's get back to Ballybran, which, incidentally, I have never been more glad to see. By the way, did you get Rudney off your back?"

"I did, finally! I had to threaten to sue him for placing my best singer in jeopardy. And you got all your memories back?" She knew that he had briefly assumed his Guild Master's role. "Maybe I should send another singer in . . ."

"Lars Dahl!" She stopped dead in her tracks, pulling him off balance. "Don't you dare, Lars Dahl, don't you dare consider for one moment sending any member of the Guild to Opal for any reason!"

"Was it that bad, Sunny?" Lars was instantly solicitous.

"Was, is, and shall be, I suspect, my love, but I can handle it." She anticipated his next question. "And yes, as a bonus, I can give you the coordinates of every single claim I ever cut. I can't wait to get that off my mind." She began to hurry him along to the airlock where his shuttle awaited them.

"*All* your coordinates?"

"That's right."

She would explain the other side of that coin to him later, and as gently as possible. Maybe out sailing in the *Angel II*. Then she had to cope with a flood of memories, all associated with the word "angel": sailing to Angel Island's back, the storm, sheltering in the command post, meeting Nahia and Hauness, meeting his father, Olav, marrying Lars formally by island rites . . . Ruthlessly she cut off the stream; resolutely she closed down those reminiscences.

Lars handed her into the cabin of the shuttle and would have fastened her harness; but, laughing, she slapped at his hands, saying she could do it herself.

"Oddest thing, Lars," she said in a low tone so that Flicken, the pilot, wouldn't hear. She was going to freak a lot of folk out by suddenly remembering their names, she thought, amused. She forced her errant mind back to what she had to tell Lars. "Big Junk recognized me. I remembered that little bit during the last Singularity Jump. I don't mean it said 'hello,' but I think I was aware of its recognition when I got to its cavern the first time. That's why I panicked and did Three first."

"Hmmm. Interesting."

"Yeah." She smiled in a somewhat maudlin fashion. "I'm glad we put its piece back."

"Is that what it remembered?"

She shrugged. "Who knows what passes for memory with Junk? Rudney certainly doesn't and we decided—"

"We who?"

"Brendan, Boira, and me . . . decided that Klera had the right idea about the *patterns* being part of the communication effort."

"Pattern and rhythm?"

"Pattern, rhythm, and color."

"Hmmm. Complex."

"Too much for this back-planet girl."

"You remember everything?" he asked, dismayed for her sake.

She nodded. "But I'm learning to chop 'em off before they overwhelm me. Too much is not a good thing."

"Hmmm."

He laced his fingers in hers, and she let her head roll to rest on his shoulder. She had been exceedingly lucky to have been kidnapped by Lars Dahl. She hadn't really had any guide by which to measure that serendipity or realize how truly Donalla had spoken when she had said that Lars was devoted to her. She could see it now, in the tapestry of their years together—all hundred and twenty-three of them, incredible as that total was—that he had been more than friend, lover, partner, and alter ego. She remembered how devastated, how lost, she had been when he had been falsely disciplined for the Optherian affair . . . She remembered, with great relish, their first sexual encounter on the beach at Angel—and, more importantly, how the mutual attraction had only strengthened and deepened throughout the years. "Everlasting love" took on a new dimension when applied to what she and Lars shared.

And now she could share even more with him: his duties as Guild Master. She would be Trag to his Lanzecki. Muhlah! Had Lanzecki and Trag . . . She stifled a giggle. Lanzecki had been quite willing, but she had never known if Trag had had any liaisons with Guild members. Lack of memory, a fear of displaying the gaps and embarrassing herself, and Lars, had been behind her resistance to his offers. She couldn't be less than the best for Lars, and now she could take on those responsibilities with a clear conscience—and an infallible memory.

Odd how so many things worked out—if one waited long enough. That initial humiliation back on Fuerte when she had been refused solo status by the bombastic little Maestro Valdi had resulted in her meeting Carrik and discovering the covert Heptite Guild. "Silicate spider," "crystal cuckoo"—Valdi's accusations rang in her head. Foolish little man. Singing crystal had been so much more rewarding than being a mere concert singer, who could expect only three or four decades of a "good" voice! She was still "singing" after a hundred and ninety-seven years.

She turned her head and caught her reflection in the porthole. Well, a quadruple thickness of plasglas might blur lines, but she really didn't have many, thanks to the Ballybran symbiont. She certainly didn't look any two hundred and fifteen years. She smiled at her image. She wasn't much changed from the girl who had left Fuerte with a mind-damaged crystal singer. She gripped Lars's fingers tightly.

Now, if she could manage to cushion his shock that she could never again cut black crystal, she was good for another couple of hundred years.

"You won't mind letting Presnol and Donalla give you a good checkup, will you, Sunny?" he asked, his eyes dark and anxious.

"Not at all," she replied blithely. "Though I'm sure Bren and Boira sent a report on ahead, didn't they?"

"That was hardly reassuring," he remarked dryly. "Especially the part where you were sure you were dead. I don't exaggerate when I say that the heart went out of me."

She stroked his hand. "But as it was me saying it, you had no cause to worry."

He gave her a long and trenchant look. "By any chance, among your newly revived memories, do you have the one of our first night together?"

She ducked her head: the recall was instant, and almost embarrassing in its intensity.

"Did I not tell you then," he said, his voice intimately low and rich with emotion, "that you gave me the most incredible love experience of my life?"

"Lars! You don't remember that?"

He smiled at her, his eyes so filled with passion that she could feel the blood rising to suffuse her face.

"It's one of my fondest recollections, Sunny, and it is so wonderful that you remember it now, too."

He kept gazing into her eyes, stroking her hand, so that she felt like a giddy youngling. Which, she remembered, she had never been, for even at that age she had already been dedicated to the notion of herself as a singer.

"Ah, ahem . . ." Flicken, standing by the open shuttle door, was clearing his throat.

"Thanks, Flick," Lars said, suavely recovering. He reached across Killashandra to release her harness and then handed her out as regally as if she were indeed a queen.

"The courier's scheduled for an oh-eight-thirty docking at Bay Forty-three, Guild Master. Shall I be ready at oh-seven-hundred?"

"That'll be fine," Lars said, and hurried Killa out, obviously wishing that Flicken had not spoken.

"Who's going where tomorrow in a courier, Lars?" Killa demanded as he guided her toward the lift. As they entered, he ran his hand through his crisp blond hair.

"I've put it off as long as I could, Killa," he said apologetically. "Presnol said he'd sit in for me. I shouldn't be gone long."

"Where?" She felt a definite sinking feeling.

He scratched the back of his neck. "I've been putting it off because you were away, and I wasn't leaving until you got back after what Big Hungry did to you . . ."

"Out with it!"

"I'm not sure if you'd remember . . ."

She quirked an eyebrow at him, grinning. "Try me."

He jabbed an impatient finger on the control pad, and she didn't take her eyes off his face.

"All right." He grinned, his eyes sparkling with the challenge. "Recruitment . . ."

"You've got permission for overt recruitment," she replied without hesitating, precisely remembering the scene and where they had stood in his office in relation to each other, "and the courier's taking you where there're some live ones."

"My, my, we are vastly improved," he said, slightly mocking, but his fingers wrapped tenderly about her forearm.

The lift stopped, and he tugged her out. She stopped in the foyer.

"This is not the medical level."

"No, it is not. It is our level, and you can spend tomorrow with Presnol and Donalla, but you are spending the next hours with me, your Guild Master, and your ardent lover who is overjoyed to have his Sunny *compos mentis*, hale, whole, and hearty, back again." With a deft twist of his wrist, he pulled her into his arms and demonstrated his overjoy!

Sometime during the loverly reenactment of their first night together, he spoke of his trip to three overpopulated city-planets where he hoped to find recruits. He also had permission to enlist specific technicians to fill the empty positions or to train up in the specialist support skills.

"We desperately need more medical staff," he told her, stroking her hair as they lay entwined on the sleeping platform. "Too many singers are so long in their craft that they get arrogant about their abilities and lose all common sense and any caution they might have once possessed."

"And a one-way trip to the Infirmary." She thought of Rimbol, poignantly remembering the bright gay chap he had been when they had both first come to Ballybran. That was not a comfortable memory when contrasted with his current condition. She shuddered.

"Which will have to be enlarged unless we can somehow stop the stupid mistakes singers are making . . ."

"You know, Lars, it can be stopped," she said, describing idle circles on his chest as she chose her words. "By knowing where exactly to go to cut, cutting, and coming right back out."

"You tell 'em, Sunny," he said wearily. "They're not listening to me. And if you can get them to listen, I'll love you forever."

"You already have, Lars, you already have."

Such a statement demanded ratification. Later he returned to the subject. "A few of them are, because Tiagana, Borton, and Jaygrin have been loudly declaring how much credit they've made in easy straight-out-in runs. But so many singers are running on instinct now, there's no way to get through to them."

"Maybe I was hasty a bit ago, Lars," she said, "saying you mustn't send other singers to Big Hungry. If he could bring my memory back . . ."

"I think we'll leave that as the solution of last resort. I may be prejudiced," he said, kissing her cheek, "but you were always more than *just* a singer, Sunny."

"Being *just* a singer would have been rather limiting," she remarked, but she meant something different than he. "Which reminds me, why on earth saddle Presnol with pro-tem duties? I'm much better qualified than he is."

"Are you volunteering, Killa?"

"I believe so . . ." She grinned up at him in the dim light of their sleeping room. "But only while you're away. You don't want to risk me getting to enjoy the power, you know."

He gave a snort and wiggled his shoulders into the pillows. "Not bloody likely. You *are* the best singer I've got."

She didn't like the way he said that, but by the time she had thought of a suitable response, his breathing had slowed into a sleep rhythm. An infectious one, because she slipped into it, too.

Donalla and Presnol ran Killashandra through a gamut of tests, sampling her bodily juices and wiring her up to all kinds of monitors that provided reams of printout.

"All of which only tells us that you're in great physical shape . . ."

"For a gal my age," Killa added, preening in front of the mirror. She had been allowed to dress again and was hoping they would think of feeding her sometime soon.

"Ah, yes," Donalla responded, needing to clear her throat.

Killashandra laughed. "Whatever zapped me seems to have burned off the outlived dross and stupidities any human collects along the way. I don't mind being two hundred and fifteen years old. In fact, it's fun, in a bizarre fashion. How's my symbiont, by the way? I'm keenly interested in its continued functioning."

"Oh, that." Presnol flicked his fingers dismissively. "It's as vigorous as mine or Donalla's, and we're both much much younger than you."

"I," Killashandra said quellingly, "may make comments, and even jokes, about my antiquity, Presnol, but"—she waggled her finger at them—"no one else can. Read me?"

Presnol looked properly subdued, but Donalla had to cover her mouth to suppress her laughter. Killashandra focused all her attention on the medic.

"And you, you ingrate," she added sternly, "had better watch your step, too! Imagine! Not showing proper respect to a legend of your planet! Who is exceedingly hungry right now. And I don't care if you need to make more tests. I'm eating first."

"We'll join you."

There were as few diners in the big room as there had been on her last appearance there, Killa noted. "How many singers are actually active?" she asked Donalla, vividly remembering the room packed so many years before.

"Four hundred and forty-two," Donalla said sadly.

"Ouch! That's ridiculous." Killashandra was stunned, all too aware that there had been 4,425 singers when she had joined the Guild. "How many are off-planet right now?"

"Three hundred and five."

"How many inactives?"

Presnol made a face. "Three hundred and seventy-five."

Killa could not recall the appropriate total of that category, but then, she hadn't been interested in the figures. In any event the number was depressing.

"Seventy-four," Donalla said with a sigh. "Rimbol passed on this morning. I hadn't had a chance to mention it."

"Rimbol!" Killa's throat closed after she spoke his name. She swallowed and felt tears forming in her eyes. She hadn't cried in—no, that she couldn't bring to mind. She ducked her head and struggled to get control of herself. A beaker of Yarran beer was pushed into her line of sight. She picked it up, nodding her appreciation to Presnol, and held it aloft. "To Rimbol, a gay lad with a kind heart and a fine tenor voice." Then she downed the beer in one draft.

She looked around her then, to see if she could put names to the handful of singers dining. She recognized two: they had been in the batch of twenty that Lars had recalled to cut black crystal. The tall thin fellow with the long jaw was Marichandim. But search as she did, she could not dredge up a name for the blond woman.

"D'you know her name, Donalla?"

Donalla craned her head over her shoulder. "The one with Marichandim? That's Siglinda. They've done quite well cutting from coordinates."

"How many *have* joined in that program?"

"Of the active singers, only twelve." Donalla shook her head, and Presnol looked solemn. "The others won't even listen. They run if you try to approach them. They're too far gone in their sublimations."

"Well," Killashandra said, rising, "I think I want to go over the Orientation program. If it's the same as I had under Tukolom, I think we'd better overhaul the whole thing. That's where the trouble started. Whatever singers Lars brings back are going to learn more than Rules and Regs!"

It was strange to be in this office, Killashandra thought as she entered the Guild Master's quarters. Trag's desk was clear, empty, waiting. Waiting for her, she decided with a wry grin, even if she had done her damnedest to delay the inevitable.

Lars's desk was neat, with pencil files set in four platoons across the broad surface. One group had the notation "Orient. Revis." And she smiled. She should have known he would consider that vitally important. She peered at the other notations: "Coords," and there were nine files in that group; "Recruit" had seven; "R&D" was the sparsest with only three.

There were several scrawled notes that she couldn't decipher stuck to one side, near his communit, and a hologram base. She flicked it on and was gratified to see herself—a shot taken while they were on Nihal III—and then she noticed that the unit, which could hold a hundred 'grams, was full. She flicked the change switch and there she was again, in the orange wet suit he had bought her for Flag, where he had seen the prototype of *Angel II*. She joggled the switch again and again, pausing only long enough to identify where the 'gram had been taken. She turned the holo off and, hauling the chair firmly under her, resolutely turned to the big monitor and called up the Guild Roster. She had a lot of work to do before Lars got back.

As she had discovered once before on her single foray into administrative work for Lanzecki—she must remember to find out what happened to that dorkish Bollam, she reminded herself—she enjoyed rooting among the files and collating information.

The Guild's operating costs, of which the Infirmary was now requiring an increasingly larger share, came from tithing every singer's cut, a bone of contention between singer and Sorter. Other costs, which the singer bore for sled, fuel, equipment, living accommodations, and food, were presented at market rate. That sank her notion that the Guild took a cut from the supplies, jacking the prices up periodically. The files proved that there was no markup whatever, merely a gradual increase in whole-sale costs throughout the inhabited galaxy. There had been an increase of farming on Ballybran and, to give the Guild fair credit, they paid above the average market price for foods produced on Guild lands.

There were, however, far fewer active singers to produce any tithes for the Guild and more inactive ones—some of those in a vegetable state— who had to be supported by an ever-dwindling income. Fewer cutters in the field meant less crystal to offer, and Killashandra came across orders three and four years old that were waiting to be filled. Black crystal figured largely in these back orders, but all the dark crystals were needed.

Before she could be totally depressed by the outlook, she saw a re-markable upswing over the past few months—since Lars had thrown open unused claims. Her cuts were significant in that revival, though both Tia-gana and Jaygrin had brought in more. To comfort herself, she reviewed the total of one hundred and ninety-seven years of cutting and compared it with the records of any other singer. She was tons ahead of the two younger singers.

She then reviewed Lars's comments on Orientation. They showed the continued emphasis on note-taking after every Range trip and on the re-turn from off-planet jaunts: he planned to have an automatic reminder on each singer's console. He had also been listing the ways in which coordi-nates might be inviolably kept on file. There were notes on compulsory hypnotic sessions that would access such memories.

Lars also had notes on how to modernize the various departments of the Guild, what new technology there was to replace worn machines and at what cost; and many notes on how to capitalize on the talents of the sup-port staff with appropriate bonuses. Most of these possibilities would have to wait on a continued upward turn of filled orders.

He had taken the trouble to investigate the alternatives used by peo-ple weary of waiting for the Guild to supply crystal. Advantage one to the Guild: Ballybran crystal had a longer work life and, if damaged, did not need to be jettisoned but could be retuned and used in other installations. Its competitors could not be recycled. Some of the original shafts of Bally-bran crystal, cut by Barry Milekey, for whom the Milekey Range was named, were still in use after eight hundred years.

"What we need is an advertising campaign, too," she murmured, and tried to think—without much success—of interesting slogans. Ballybran crystal hadn't needed hype: it sold itself. So long as supply met demand.

"Well, there is an improvement," she told herself, leaning back in the conformchair and stretching. "We'll build on it."

The lights had come up when the sensors registered a diminution in available illumination. She swiveled the chair and noted that night had fallen—Shanganagh and Shilmore were chasing each other across the sky, but they were soon to be occluded by the clouds billowing in from the west. She turned the chair enough to see the weatherline blinking on its strip across the top of the room. Barometer was dropping, the isobars were tight with gale-force winds. Storm warnings had been broadcast. She altered the monitor to pick up the Hangar scan and saw the blips of forty or so sleds homing in.

Good! She would have a chance to speak to some of the less productive singers. She accessed the program that would identify returning craft and asked for details of each singer as they came in. She would approach them with facts and figures: the production time charts on those working from coordinates, and the credit they raked in. Something that appealed to any singer was how to make enough credit quickly enough to get off-planet for as long as possible. Only "as long as possible" was going to be curtailed to "as long as necessary" until the Guild had returned to its once-prestigious position.

Somewhat to Killashandra's surprise, she was received with a good deal of awe by the first group of singers she approached. She had quickly scanned the details of the forty-seven who had left the storm-bound Ranges, so she knew what and how much they had cut and how long it had taken them, and she was prepared to talk them out of resisting the proposal.

She marked her victims as she sat drinking with them: the ones who didn't have enough credit to go anywhere interesting. She had been to a staggering number of R&R and vacation planets in nearly two centuries, so she was able to spin tales to make them yearn to visit such fabulous places. It didn't take her long to interest this group, eighteen in all, in using a sure-fire way to achieve their ends.

The insistent buzz of the communit roused her from a deep, dreamless sleep. Once she heard it, she also recognized the emergency code and floundered with her blankets to roll to the control panel at the edge of the sleep panel.

"Killashandra!" The caller was Flicken, his face stark with grief. "Oh, how can I tell you?"

"Tell me what?"

"The B-and-B courier—it's sent out a Mayday."

"A B-and-B courier . . ." She stopped, gasping. Lars had been on a courier ship. "Lars?"

Flicken nodded slowly, his chin quivering and his mouth working. "Just came in."

"How? What? Couriers are . . ."

"Singularity trouble!" Flicken gasped out again. "That's all I know. All I can find out. Mayday and a Jump disaster tag."

"Where?"

He shook his head more vigorously, but there were tears falling down his cheeks and he couldn't control the trembling of his mouth.

"Keep me informed," she said, amazed that she could sound so calm, that she wasn't raging at how abruptly her life had been shattered once again. She palmed the lights up and sat there a long, long time, her mind going in tight circles. B&B ships were very sophisticated vessels. Courier ships were the best of the B&Bs. Both brains and brawn could be expected to function under the most adverse conditions and survive against incredible odds. Singularity Jump disasters were few, but they could happen. Brendan had mentioned, in passing, that, while he was equipped to handle thousands of minute calculations during a Jump, he had several back-up, worst-scenario corrective capabilities. Furthermore, and she began to revive from the shocking news, every B&B ship, every naval vessel, every liner, every tanker, freighter, private yacht anywhere in the sector where the courier ship had been lost would be looking for it. If a Singularity disaster had to happen to a ship, then a courier B&B was the most likely one to survive.

She forced her mind to hang on to that thought and found something to wear. She went to the Guild Master's office and palmed up all the lights. She sat down in the conformchair, brought up the comsystem, and accessed Shanganagh Port Authority.

"Deputy Guild Master Ree, here," she said in an even tone. "Keep me informed on any developments of the—"

"Yes, of course, Deputy Ree. We've initiated emergency proceedings and requested all naval, mercantile, and private spaceships to forward all messages."

"By crystal coms, I trust," she said, mildly surprised that she could be droll at a time like this. A time like this was when a bit of drollery kept you sane, she amended.

"Yes, yes, of course, Deputy. The blacks we have here will pick up whispers in the farthest sectors of inhabited space."

"I think we'll have to find crystal that operates in Singularity space."

"Nothing works in decomposition space, Deputy."

She wondered if Jewel Junk would.

"We'll keep you informed, Deputy."

Deputy! Had she the right to use that title? Well, why not? Lars had appointed her, hadn't he? She was a better deputy than Presnol would be. She was a singer, a sometime diplomat, spy . . . she grinned sadly to herself. Then she pulled the multiholo base to her and called up the earliest 'gram it had stored. What appeared was the holo of herself, sun-bleached hair, the garlands Olav had given her the morning they left Angel about her neck, accenting the color of the lovely gown of Teradia's making. When had Lars taken that? But he had—for here it was.

She sat there, looking at the holo, remembering all that had happened before and after it had been taken. She jumped when someone rapped at the door.

"I've only just been informed, Killa," Donalla said. "Is there *anything* I can do?"

"Yes, there is," Killashandra said, adopting a brisk tone. She had idled away enough time in private meditations. "Would you dial me some breakfast? I haven't had time with so much to put in motion."

"Put in motion?" Donalla stared at her.

"Yes, I must implement the plans Lars made." She gestured at the neat piles of pencil files. "It'll take my mind off the waiting."

"Oh! Then you think there's hope that—"

"There's always hope, Donalla, but I think Lars would prefer it if I didn't sit about moping like a fool, don't you?"

She had her breakfast and then arranged appointments with the Hangar-bound singers she had talked to the previous evening. Since everyone was dazed by the news that had swept through the Cube, she obtained more agreement than argument and sent seventeen of the eighteen off with three sets of coordinates each and a mission to cut where possible—for some claims were likely to be unworkable—and return as soon as they had collected at least a carton of back-ordered colors. She didn't want to see a single shaft of pink or any of the pale blues and greens. Darks, and blacks, whenever possible.

She managed to bury herself so deeply in revitalizing the Orientation program that she was astonished to hear multiple sleds leaving the Hangar: she had worked through the night! She allowed herself four hours' sleep and then was back at the desk, going back over Guild affairs of the past decade.

By the fifth day, she had digested every current file and reviewed older ones on merchandising and research and development so that she was fully up-to-date on Guild business. She had talked four more singers into foraging by coordinates and seen eight of the original seventeen back in with viable crystal cuts, all dark. She encouraged the happy singers to stay overnight, have a good meal, relax with their peers, and talk about how easy it was to work known coordinates.

Each day she allowed herself a glimpse of a new hologram from Lars's incredible collection. With each new 'gram, she accessed the memories of that excursion, as fresh in her mind now as when she and Lars had lived those lovely moments. She could never be grateful enough to Big Hungry Junk for restoring the memories that allowed her to continue living. When she was dead, too, there would be no one to remember Lars Dahl as vividly as she could now. And that would be a real pity.

The restoration of memory brought with it a desire not to lose it again. She would eventually have to go out into the Ranges and cut crystal, but she did not want to jeopardize the reinstatement of so much valuable information. She had a long chat one day with the meteorologists and then asked Presnol and Donalla to have dinner with her.

"It's like this," she began when they were on their cheese and beer. "The Met guys tell me that Ballybran storms are apt to produce more electricity in the air than storms on other planets. Is it possible that an overload of such electrical discharges could affect singers' minds? I mean, most of us *wait* until the last possible moment before leaving the Ranges. Is that why we tend to forget between trips? The electricity has somehow affected our circuits?"

"It *is* a possibility, isn't it?" Donalla said, looking to Presnol.

He mulled it over. "I think we could profitably check memory retention on, say, those singers who are working coordinates regularly, and those who prospect right up until a storm drives them out of the Ranges. See if we can get any relevant data. We could also check just how much electricity is discharged into the atmosphere—sort of a continuous measurement. I'm sure we could find instrumentation to register that sort of emission. Hmm, rather interesting. But what good would it do?"

"If we can prove any correlation between the intensity of a particular storm and memory loss, all the more reason for us to teach the next candidates to come in at the first warning," Killa said. "Or, if we can manage it, keep them all on coordinate mining."

"That would be quite a departure from tradition," Presnol said, clearing his throat. He had been on Ballybran a lot longer than Donalla.

"That's exactly the attitude that needs changing, Presnol," Killa said. "The Guild needs to alter a lot of its thinking and its 'traditions' "—and she imbued that word with disgust—"if it wants to improve. And keep singers active and productive."

"Let's see what we can discover, Pres," Donalla said, smiling winningly at her lover. She gave Killa a wink that suggested the matter could be left safely in the medics' hands now.

The fourth week brought the first of the recruits from Lars's ill-fated journey. Forty-four young, eager persons trained in a variety of skills, and fifteen others with the perfect pitch required for crystal singers. That was more than had applied to the Guild in several years. There were two more groups scheduled to arrive over the next weeks, but once the first group had been processed, Killashandra ordered them right down to Ballybran. She would take the first Orientation sessions herself. She would show them the way to go, to be successful singers. They, and others like them, would revitalize the Guild—in Lars's memory.

The Council, composed of the heads of departments of the Heptite Guild on Ballybran, were becoming more insistent that she formally accept the position of Guild Master, but she resisted. Acceptance meant, in her lexicon, that she had accepted Lars's death, and she couldn't. She still didn't *want* to be Guild Master, no matter how many people told her she had taken command as if she had trained all her life to assume the rank. What she *could* do was implement Lars's plans and have the Guild operating efficiently again.

When Donalla insisted she take a break from the console before her eyes turned square, she would go down to the *Angel II* in its big shed. She felt close to Lars there and could dwell on the memories of their many sea voyages together. Oh, how she longed to sail with him just one more time!

She grieved over her acrimonious griping about his love for the sea, her perverse opposition to his choice of water planets for their holidays. She had been unkind, and ungrateful, to insist on her turn at choosing a vacation place, when she knew how much the sea and sailing meant to him.

She had just returned from another maudlin review of her shortcomings, foibles, and limitations and listlessly entered the office that now felt more hers than Lars's. She was wondering which chore she could use to occupy her mind until fatigue pushed her into sleep when the communit beeped.

"Now what?"she demanded, irritated to have duties press in on her so quickly.

"Patching through" was the excited comment, and then there was an intolerable rasping, squeaking, high-pitched blast.

"Sunny?"

"*Lars!*" His name came out of her mouth in a scream. There was no one else in the Galaxy who called her "Sunny" and no voice with quite the same timbre as his. "You're alive?"

"Kicking, too."

"Turn on the vision, Lars. I've got to *see* you!" Tears streamed down her face, and she had to grip the edge of the desk to keep on her feet. But the voice, the words: it had to be Lars.

His chuckle reassured her again. "Not on your life, Sunny, or mine. Overimmersion in radiant fluid produces curious effects on skin and muscle, but it saved the lives of me and the ship's brawn. They say that we'll look human again soon, but I've my doubts. Brendan and Boira found us. That pair refused to give up. Praise be to Muhlah! We're all safe, though the courier ship'll need a new shell—no, that's wrong way round—the shell person will need a new ship; hers got Singularly twisted."

She didn't care *what* he looked like: he sounded like himself and that was what counted. "But you're alive!"

"I repeat, I am alive! I even survived the Singularity Jump we just made." His voice quavered briefly. "Had to, according to Boira. And I suppose I'll have to again, but not soon! Not soon!" He sighed gustily.

"Where *are* you?"

He chuckled again, teasing her. "Estimated time of arrival at Shankill Base is four hours!"

"Four *hours!*" She was shrieking again. How could she wait that long to set eyes on him! To hold him to her, to feel his arms about her. "Oh, Lars love . . ."

"What did you call me, Sunny?" His voice was tender with surprise.

She swallowed. "I called you 'Lars love,' " she said almost defiantly.

"D'you know," he said, and his laugh was tentative, "you've never called me 'love' before."

"I'll remember to call you that every other breath—Lars love. I've had a lot of time to remember things, while you've been—away." Her voice broke slightly, and she hastily cleared her throat. "I remember all the love you've given me," she went on, determined to say what had become so imperative he know. "I've remembered so much, Lars love, especially that I have always been in love with you, in spite of the way I treated you!"

"It's almost worth nearly dying to hear you say that, Killashandra Ree." He sounded stronger now, almost exultant!

"I'll remember that, love. I'll remember that, too."

The moment she disengaged the channel, Killashandra Ree left the office to meet Lars Dahl at Shankill Moon Base. Exit, triumphant, stage center.

ABOUT THE AUTHOR

Anne McCaffrey shuttles between her home in Ireland and the United States, where she picks up awards and honors and greets her myriad fans. She is one of the field's most popular authors.

═══ DEL REY® ONLINE! ═══

THE DEL REY INTERNET NEWSLETTER (DRIN)
The DRIN is a monthly electronic publication posted on the Internet, America Online, GEnie, CompuServe, BIX, various BBSs, our Web site, and the Panix gopher. It features:
- hype-free descriptions of new books
- a list of our upcoming books
- special announcements
- a signing/reading/convention-attendance schedule for Del Rey authors
- in-depth essays by sf professionals (authors, artists, designers, salespeople, and others)
- a question-and-answer section
- behind-the-scenes looks at sf publishing
- and much more!

INTERNET INFORMATION SOURCE
Del Rey information is now available on our Web site (http://www.randomhouse.com/delrey/) and on a gopher server—gopher.panix.com—including:
- the current and all back issues of the Del Rey Internet Newsletter
- a description of the DRIN and content summaries of all issues
- sample chapters of current and upcoming books— readable and downloadable for free
- submission requirements
- mail-order information

New DRINs, sample chapters, and other items are added regularly.

ONLINE EDITORIAL PRESENCE
Many of the Del Rey editors are online—on the Internet, GEnie, CompuServe, America Online, and Delphi. There is a Del Rey topic on GEnie and a Del Rey Folder on America Online.

WHY?
We at Del Rey realize that the networks are the medium of the future. That's where you'll find us promoting our books, socializing with others in the sf field, and—most important—making contact and sharing information with sf readers.

FOR MORE INFORMATION
The official e-mail address for Del Rey Books is
delrey@randomhouse.com